HOW THE GOOD TAILOR GOT TO HEAVEN

—⚏—

The authorized history of one angel's sojourn through King Jamesburg and the Empyrean.

HOW THE GOOD TAILOR GOT TO HEAVEN

The authorized history of one angel's sojourn through King Jamesburg and the Empyrean.

HOMERE A. DANSEREAU

Rutledge Books, Inc.  Danbury, CT

Cover illustrations by R.A. Whitters
Cover design, colour and photos by Pete Bjerkelund
Interior design by Al Robinson

Copyright © 2001 by Homere A. Dansereau

ALL RIGHTS RESERVED
Rutledge Books, Inc.
107 Mill Plain Road, Danbury, CT 06811
1-800-278-8533
www.rutledgebooks.com

Manufactured in the United States of America

Cataloging in Publication Data
Dansereau, Homere A.

  How the Good Tailor Got to Heaven

  ISBN: 1-58244-173-1

  1. Fiction

Library of Congress Card Number: 2001088294

The Introduction

ALL LENGTHY COMPOSITIONS BEGIN WITH THE AUTHOR'S preface and if they are properly composed, the burdensome chore of perusing the balance of the effort should be rendered unnecessary. After reading it, one might return to other more rewarding activities: washing the car, jogging, watching TV, or pursuing one or more of the seven deadly sins. A proper preface should disclose to students ample information for a credible book report. Literary dilettantes should be able to read the preface, and still be able to impress friends by intelligently discussing the purposes and aims of the writer as well as if they had read the entire dreary thing.

Most authors realize this so they compose their prefaces with obscurely tangential eloquence producing a hybrid as light and exciting as Wagner's *Gotterdammerung* bred with Kant's *Prologomena*, thus forcing scholars, and seekers after truth, to read some of the ensuing pages. With this problem foremost in my mind, I promise it will be necessary for the reader to continue only a few more sentences to have unraveled the Gordian Knot and lay bare this guileless pedestrian plot performed by stereotypical characters.

HOMERE A. DANSEREAU

This work is an idle fantasy except for the parts that are true, and all the action, persons, and places are imagined with the exception of the actual, and well known personalities who have given me permission to use their names: God, Jesus, the Holy Ghost, the angels and archangels; also their sinister counterparts: Satan and his demons and devils. All the rest is pure fiction.

The protagonist of the historical events herein recorded came to me as the voice of God came to the prophets of old: by the divine afflatus. The angel, Lemuel, (Hebrew meaning: Devoted to God) appeared in a miraculous visitation and relayed his life's story to me, much as Mohammed received the divine words from the archangel Gabriel, or as Joseph Smith received the sacred addendum to the Scriptures from the angel Moroni.

The keenest, most fecund mind, despite all proclamations to the contrary, must rely on accredited well recognized authority, hence long bibliographies accompany any book claiming to be a serious work. My bid for a place among the classics of historiography came from two widely accepted sources: a dictionary, given to me by my mother who was tired of deciphering my mail; and a Bible that I stole from my son.

However, the crime of stealing my son's Bible has plagued my conscience for many years, and what has made this crime all the more despicable was that it was his most prized possession; an award Bible that was presented to him for perfect Sunday school attendance. I realize most readers will want to see justice done. I cannot expect complete absolution, but I offer as mitigating circumstances the fact that I believe these two weighty tomes belong in every household, and that all other books are superfluous. But some penance for this horrible crime must be paid, and nowhere in either book can I find an appropriate punishment recommended, so I've had to devise my own atonement. With the Lord's help, and bearing his dictum in mind that: "A man is made filthy, not by the dirt that is upon him, or that enters inside, but by that which pursueth from him,"[1] I promise that everything that proceeds past this point will be of the highest moral fervor.

HOW THE GOOD TAILOR GOT TO HEAVEN

During my guilt ridden search for atonement I came upon the book of Jonah. The Ninevites had also sinned, not half so grave a sin as my own, but inspired by their example, the following prose is my spiritual sackcloth[2]. Arriving at the topic of sackcloth brings us to the propellant of this absolutely inerrant history. Lemuel's sorrowful tale goes beyond the appeasement properties of burlap to the metamorphosis imparted by any garment.

Note: All Bible references are from the King James authorized edition.

Chapter 1

WE ARE INFORMED BY THE BOOK OF JONAH THAT THE LORD'S WRATH WAS appeased because the citizens of Nineveh, from the greatest to the least, including the beasts, clothed themselves in sackcloth[3]. The importance of this meaningful Biblical event is rarely addressed from the pulpit; overlooked is the plain fact that most ministers find it necessary to don special garb to practice their craft and the reasons are never fully explored or explained. Devotees of ancient history should easily recall that in ancient Rome the term, "investiture of the purple" meant that a new Caesar was created by putting a purple robe on an ordinary fellow. If another fellow ever put on a purple robe he'd be courting execution, because that meant he was challenging the coronation and claiming the title for himself. In today's world we can observe how businessmen, wise in persuasion, know the worth of fine tailoring. Or, take the same fellow, either Caesar or tycoon, put him in a sleeveless denim jacket, paint a dragon on his back, and we can create one of the motorcycle bunch. We salute not the man, but the officer's uniform. A "spoiled priest" or disgraced clergyman is ceremonially "unfrocked." Even the nudist, in perverse cognition of fact by heretically shedding his clothes, thereby admits that, "The clothes make the man."

This strange ability to enchant both mortal and deity, and project an image that affects even the fate of our souls; this manifestation of fact which has been heeded for thousands of years by all societies from the most savage to the most cultured, are both historically, and Biblically documented, and yet, we never consider how those powerful forces affect the men who make the clothes.

This gift, the magical ability to create a king or a clown from basic flesh, is unwittingly paid for by the tailors. They lose the power of self-determination over their extra-somatic beings—their souls. A curious force, like some diabolic philosopher's stone that changes gold into lead, transfers sin from the soul of the customer to the soul of his tailor. The Welch, a metaphysically astute race, understand the mystical forces when they pay sin-eaters to dine from the lid of the departed's coffin. It is a noble effort, but unnecessary, because the sins have already been assumed by the deceased tailor.

Our indifference to the scapegoat[4] services of tailors can only be explained as ignorance. Assuredly, no one could ever be so heartless as to damn an innocent soul to Azazel with premeditation, not even to save their own. But the crime of ignorant indifference continues, and worst of all is the effect this has up above. Good tailors by the very nature of their excellence become eternally damned. The reason is simple. Those who can afford the best tailoring are the most worldly and they can afford the most worldly sins. On the other hand, the garment workers with slipshod stitching are usually saved. Their clientele are God-fearing, good people who recognize simple truth so plain for all to see, that a garment is, after all, only to conceal their shame[5]. This strange fact is reflected, sadly, in the garb of the angels, both here and in Heaven.

The results are truly perverse. Down here where first impressions are so important, the angels are often treated as common folk with lowly status. But those evil minions of Satan, the demons, dress in the height of fashion and finery and are usually accorded high regard by the very mortals that they are bent on corrupting. Alas, this is just one more manifestation of the epithet—worldliness.

* * *

One summer evening a mysterious event occurred that would be as portentous as the renting of the veil[6]. Was it a trick, a quirk, a fluke, or was it predestined? After all, "Hath not the potter power over the clay,"[7] and the mortal mind calls coincidence what it doesn't understand. But this seemingly ordinary event was to have celestial ramifications.

Two tailors passed over to the other life. One soul was as black as pitch. His clientele were sordid, worldly individuals, frequently lauded for their sartorial splendors, such as the race track crowd, prize fight enthusiasts, used car salesmen, Keynsian economists, and newspaper reporters. This tailor was the sort who hung a picture of the Warren court on his office wall, read magazines written by liberals, and other un-American types. He told ribald stories to his customers and raucous laughter was often heard issuing from his shop.

The other man's soul was as luminous as an angel's wing, for he made deacon's frock coats, clothing for the county orphanage and Salvation Army uniforms. On the ledge of his battered old desk was a double picture frame. On one side was his mother and opposite her was a picture of Dwight D. Eisenhower. He faithfully read George Will's column to his grandchildren at bedtime. His business brought him meager reward in worldly terms, but the value he received for his inner nature was immeasurable.

Both men died simultaneously, or in the interests of accuracy, since nothing is precise, within the same atto-second. That is a quintillionth of a second, and is incalculable both here and where time is figured in eternities. Within that span of time, roughly equal to a seventeen minute gap in the tape of infinity, or the length of time that a president needs to ponder a pardon for his resigning predecessor, the most important (well, at least within the top ten) event of the universe was given its impetus. Since earth-shattering events have a way of occurring in out of the way places like Concord Bridge, or Chappaquiddic Island, or in this case the small hamlet of…

No! I positively refuse to name it, or even give the date. Having been forced at a still tender age, by harsh pedagogy, to memorize long lists of names, dates, and places, and recalling the shame and utter dejection that I felt when I couldn't answer those questions in class, and remembering the contempt of my classmates and teachers (even myself for myself, as I stood before the world as a beacon of abjection), I vowed never to add to that list lest another child is forced to face similar torment by anything I might do.

But the village is important to this history and I feel that the reader will benefit from a brief description. King James I granted the land from sea to shining sea to several of his most pious subjects in the seventeenth century. A provision in the charter established that the inhabitants, shall be industrious, shall remit their tithes to the church, shall rear godfearing children, and shall faithfully adhere to God's holy word as set forth in King James's inerrant revelation for perpetuity—or until the seventh and final seal is opened and the worthy are taken up in the divine rapture. Let us call the village King Jamesburg, although that's not its real name, but for the sake of scholars who need an actual name to mark down in their term papers, we will use it.

The subsequent centuries since the founding of King Jamesburg have changed the aspect from primitive to prosperous. What was once a rutted trail through the forest has become a broad, billboard-lined dual lane roadway leading from the cloverleaf at the interstate toward the village. It is a journey of several miles made more colorful than the forest's autumn foliage by gasoline escutcheons atop towering masts and graceful orange neon arches. There are fluttering pennants and soaring balloons gracing the used car lots, and in case anyone was doubtful about which nation they were traveling through, there are many flagpoles where "Old Glory" flutters in the breeze. Friendly roadhouses accommodate the travel weary and sociable Dulcineas soothe the enervated.

The observant traveler will take note of the wonderful habitations of the villagers behind this bustling corridor of enterprise. There are neat rows of twelve-hundred square-foot dwellings with colorful asbestos shingles or vinyl siding, and white-asphalt shingled roofs of a five-twelve pitch, and set on ten thousand square-foot lots. Many have extra vehicles, motorcycles, ATVs, and bass boats, parked in their driveways. Toward the village center the houses become older, taller, closer together, and where they once housed but a single family, they have been wisely and tastefully refurbished to accommodate three or four. It is a rather insular community and contact with the outside world rarely occurs, usually, only when some lost traveler from the interstate stumbles in. In this village the stranger is not plied with nosey questions about the world outside, rather, they are greeted with furtive glances and near silence. But do not think these simple villeins unknowing, for several church steeples are evident, and their hamlet lies within easy commuting distance of a major employment center. They are all well-fed, both spiritually and bodily.

A source of civic pride, and a monument to imaginative architecture and intellectual attainment, is the combined primary and middle school of this hamlet. It is a one-story, flat-roofed structure with walls of alternating brick panels and plate glass windows. A foot-wide cornice of sheet metal painted pearl gray caps this edifice, and the school has a large gymnasium which is the school's most prominent structure.

The classrooms are equipped with neat rows of desks, and the American flag stands in the corner of each classroom as a reminder to those students who might momentarily forget where they are. In this room the teacher has lettered on the masonite chalkboard an uplifting slogan, "A MIND IS TERRIBLE THING TO WASTE." Also, neatly printed with moistened chalk down one side of the board, she has lettered the win/lose chart for the school's football team, the Shrikes, the drill schedule for the cheerleaders and the junior cadets, and the number of days remaining until the prom.

This community has a pizza parlor and a movie theater. And lest you think they lead only austere Spartan lives, take note of the fine bowling alley and pool room that is provided for their lighter moments. Also, at the very core of this hamlet, showing an outburst of civic pride, the local historical society urged the town fathers to build a municipal park to preserve the heritage. The park's four-acre expanse was all that remained undeveloped of the common pasture where the original settlers grazed their livestock. This park is central to the fate of the souls of the two tailors, so if the reader will bear with a bit more description, we can get on with this extraordinary historiography.

Within the park boundary is a small swimming pool painted lime green with two tar-filled cracks running diagonally across the shallow end. The neighborhood mothers take turns at lifeguard duty in the summertime. There are four acres of close-cropped lawn, sidewalks that ignore the travel destinations of the people, lampposts, a regulation horseshoe pitching court, teeter-totters, sliding boards, and swings where children's tennis shoes make dusty oval basins underneath.

It is claimed that the sidewalks, which divide the park into equal acre plots, radiate to the four mystical directions. They converge on a circular walk which rings a mound and surmounting the mound stands a huge, mossy-barked American walnut tree of indeterminate age. At twilight, or in the gray of dawn, it darkly overpowers the surrounding landscape with a brooding visage. Long before the ken of the hamlet's eldest citizen, the tree was dubbed with a thunderbolt that left a dead and naked, bone gray, limb reaching up. A raven perches there each day at four o'clock. There is a bit of mistletoe mingled into the foliage, sapping the tree's life and symbolizing Druidic rites perhaps. The villagers are close-mouthed about such things.

The local inhabitants believe that the entire nation is in balance around this point and that if one sits beneath this tree, faces in one of the four mystical directions, concentrates very hard, shuts his eyes very tight, and then leans forward, one can cause the rim of the nation to sink toward the abyss. But they are simple people.

This legend may or may not be true, but it is the national port of entry for ethereal messengers and demons from the pit of despairing souls.

HOW THE GOOD TAILOR GOT TO HEAVEN

They come to shepherd or drag (whichever applies) the souls released from the mortals, such as our tailors, to their place of final reward.

During slack periods the bridge from the utmost star is uncrowded and the angels often arrive early. You may see them seated on the park benches playing checkers or reading, usually the Bible or religious pamphlets, while awaiting their appointments. The other group comes here also. They're the ones you'll see in the shadows pitching horseshoes for money; or leering through the chain link fence at the slender youths in their bikinis cavorting in the pool while thinking God knows what thoughts. They've been known to urge young lads to play marbles. "That sounds innocent enough," you say, but they urge them to play for keepsies! Fortunately, most of the boys do not succumb to the temptations of gambling, but alas, some do go on to pitching pennies to the line, or by using the name of the city that is stamped into the bottom of Coke bottles they, "go for distance" and use American cities' names for gambling. And there is a worse problem. The demons are responsible for those youngsters uttering ungrammatical phrases and colloquialisms. Some never get over it!

Moreover, they're often not satisfied with directing their perfidies at the mortals. Sometimes the demons brazenly confront the angels. They make snide remarks to them, often about the way the angels are dressed, or they'll make obscene gestures or grimacing faces at them. The angels, honorably respecting the cease-fire agreement, ignore the offenders, or they might glare at them and say, "Just wait until Armageddon," or some other witty retort.

Because of these obscene confrontations, it would be absurd to have the higher orders of angels descend on lowly errand duties. It is, quite properly, the lower orders who are subjected to the taunts and blasphemies of the wicked demons. Those rare exceptions, such as the archangel Gabriel's visit to Daniel to give him skill and understanding[8] are very special cases. A more normal occurrence would be the way his guardian angel held the lion's mouth shut;[9] or opened the jail house door and freed Peter out of the hand of Herod[10].

So it is the lowest orders of angels with whom we are ever likely to meet. The lowest rank being the ones required to spend the most substantial amount of time in this world. At the bottom are the guardian angels, as already mentioned in Daniel's case, and as with Cyrus, King of Persia, who incidentally worshiped Bel and Ahura Mazda but was found worthy of the Lord's protection[11]. And we mortals below the rank of sovereign providing we are true believers[12].

Next in rank are the lying angels,[13] and then the evil angels.[14] These are approximately of equal rank, similar to that of corporal. The avenging angels[15] are the next rank, somewhat comparable to buck sergeants. Depending on the job to be performed, these angels may work separately. For example, lying angels put untruths into the mouths of the false prophets;[16] or they can work in cooperation as a team on more extensive jobs. One familiar occurrence that comes to mind is where the guardian angels led Lot and family to safety before the avenging angels rained their destruction on Sodom and Gomorrah. Then an evil angel whistled at Lot's wife from behind her, and a lying angel told her to look back.

For some reason the clergy have been remiss about including these straightforward facts in their sermons and most Sunday schools ignore them, so the full panoply of God's grandeur is often not realized. It's almost as though they were trying to place limits on God's powers. Saint Augustine reminds us: "For he who denies that all things, which either angels or man can give us is in the hand of the one Almighty, is a madman." And as there is nothing too great for God to accomplish, there is also nothing too trivial for his attention. For example, where the Holy Book says, "and thou shalt have great sickness by disease of thy bowels,"[17] is hardly ever referred to from the pulpit. At least I've never heard it mentioned. It is by the designs of evil or avenging angels that these things are brought to pass.

The clergy allow standing without comment, the work of the avenging angel who smote the Philistines with emerods[18]. Because of their inattention to these important details, we ignore the non-surgical method for their removal which is prescribed in the next chapter.[19]

Because of this omission, the medical students are not taught this alternative treatment. Well, maybe placing golden images of your emerods in an ox cart and sending it across the border into the next state may not be practical in this modern age, there being few oxen and even fewer ox carts. I suppose that it might cause economic hardship for the suppository industry. And also in this connected world, one of the more elegant renditions of the advertising industry would be gone. But I think the evangelists are missing an important message: To avoid the swelling, inflammation, and itching of emeroidal tissue: Jesus has the answer. Or, "Get right with God!" for a comfortable seat while you wait.

Since these angels actually control our lives, unless we become possessed by demons, one must wonder why the clergy so diminish their importance. And not only are false prophets attended by lying angels, national leaders are too. If the lying angels are proficient at their tasks, they can cause kings and rulers to make wrong and disastrous decisions, thereby bringing a whole nation down in defeat.[20] The lying angels are the ones who put notions into the politicians' heads that they can get away with lying to grand juries or tell us that they'll cut our taxes, when they know deep down they will raise them. And they convince them that they can build an impenetrable defensive shield when they can't even control marijuana smuggling. As the Bible tells us, "The Lord searcheth all hearts and understandeth all the imaginations of the thoughts."[21] He directs these thoughts to fulfill His grand design by the use of these angels. Of course all fiction writers are suffused by lying angels, and even some historians and newspaper reporters, although most would deny it.

The Lord sends evil angels to handle the small-scale nastiness, such as fights between individuals and small slaughters of less than a hundred people. One example is the time David turned seven of Saul's sons over to the Gibeonites so they could hang them up before the Lord. That caused the Lord to end the famine[22] and insured a good barley harvest.[23] One has to wonder if the Russian harvests wouldn't be improved by applying scriptural advice. One successful evil angel caused anathema between Abimelech and Sechem because of the seventy sons of Jerubbaal that they had slain.[24] Most family feuds, such as the Hatfields and the McCoys, are the result of the evil angels.

Avenging angels are the ones who do the wholesale killing, such as the fifty thousand men of Bethshemesh who were slaughtered for looking into the "Ark of the Lord."[25] Another success for an avenging angel was the pestilence that took seventy thousand Israelites. A minor dispatching that was handled with great finesse was when the avenger caused the earth to open, and swallow up the two hundred and fifty "men that appertained unto Korah," who had, "offered incense."[26] There are so many instances that we haven't the time to go into them here, but faithful daily Bible reading will, I'm sure, enlighten those uninformed. It is important that we learn about the angels to prevent a commission of blasphemy, or to inadvertently give offense to an angel. One flagrant incident of misunderstanding God's grand design was when Voltaire penned his scathing ode about the Lisbon earthquake, questioning the axiom that, "Whatever is—is right!" His soul would be with the demons right now if it were not for the scapegoat services provided by his tailor.

One rank higher than avenging angel is deliverance angel. At this grade we are beginning to add rockers beneath the sergeant stripes. The deliverance angels have nearly attained full angel rank. They are the ones who visit the minor prophets and cause miraculous visitations whereby we canonize the lesser saints. But the bulk of their time is spent ushering souls that have earned their place behind the pearly gates, the alabaster walls, and in the eternal light beyond the ninth celestial orb. The deliverance angels are the ones most frequently seen in the village park at the national port of entry.

Mediaeval theologians specializing in angelology left tomes of research concerning the nine higher orders of angels. In descending order they are: seraphim, cherubim, thrones, dominions, virtues, powers, principalities, archangels, and the lowest rank, angels. These higher orders are similar to the military commissioned grades or the executive

HOW THE GOOD TAILOR GOT TO HEAVEN — 11

ranks of industry, and are, of course, on a far more magnificent scale than any of our banalities. But those ancient sages, because of the limitations of their state of the arts (single sheet hand presses, primitive methods of communications and travel, etc.), omitted the lower grades from their writings. Billy Graham has added to their scholarly work with his own book *Angels, Angels, Angels; God's Secret Agents*. This author's work is intended to supplement those studies.

At the last convention of angelologists, held each July in Secaucus, New Jersey, it was pointed out that the clergy have been remiss. Not only do they seldom mention the higher orders, but they seem to have ignored the lower orders, guardian, evil, lying, avenging, and deliverance angels, altogether. Moreover, many have failed to inform their parishioners about the promotion procedures. These lower orders of angels are novitiate, or probationary, angels. They rise through the ranks by the success of their ministrations, their attitude toward their superiors, and the degree of enthusiasm they exhibit for their vocation. They have to be company men, or women, through and through. Should they botch a job, display willfulness in the slightest degree, or be flippant or extrinsic, they can expect a reprimand, and if warranted, a demotion. They may even be reduced to the lowest rank and have to start all over again. Naturally, all of these probationers strive to do their best at every assignment; not merely for high achievement ratings, there is also a sense of personal accomplishment and they all have inherently obedient natures. Also, when they are promoted to angel they have tenure, so to speak, and cannot be further reduced in rank.

Before these angels of subordination attain tenure there is one final test that they must all undertake. About two thousand years ago it was decided that the system should provide full services and equal opportunity. So as their final task the deliverance angels must descend as mortals and, using only human resources, add ten thousand new souls' names to the book of life.[27] This is a prodigious feat, as any minister will attest, and the task usually spans one adult lifetime. It's only a brief flicker in eternity, but they, lacking their magical powers and enfeebled by their mortal guise, must face Satan, or his demons, or the results of their corruptions. Consider how the fiends are free to walk "to and fro, and up and down,"[28] unmolested, anywhere on Earth; for the angels that brief flicker is like an eternity.

The fiends and demons, on the other hand, are a completely unruly lot and care nothing for tradition, propriety, regulation, discipline, or hierarchical progression. But what else would one expect from demons? We're about to meet one of the loathsome creatures in the next chapter of this historical biography. It's the demon that has come to drag off the bad tailor. Well, he's a good tailor, but a bad man, oops, "judgement is mine, sayeth the Lord."[29] But I am confident that this scapegoat tailor deserves all the torment that the foul demon will dish out, because the sins of his clients were great and, "Thorns and snares are in the way of the froward: he that doth keep his soul shall be far from them,"[30] and he trafficked all his life with those whose "feet run to evil"[31] and, "Who rejoice to do evil, and in the frowardness of the wicked."[32]

Chapter 2

ON THE EVENING OF THE TWO TAILORS TRANSFERENCE FROM the quick to the eternal, Deliverance Angel Lemuel arrived at the port of entry. This was to be his last run as a deliverance angel. He'd sped anxiously over the bridge from the utmost star and his haste made him arrive early. He paced nervously, paused for a moment, consulted his appointment timetable and the moon's declination, replaced the timetable in his breast pocket, and continued to pace. It was a warm, quiet, uneventful evening (appertaining to messenger activity) and there was no one in the park for him to chat with, not even mortals. He noticed a newspaper on one of the park benches and picked it up intending to put it into a trash can, but, since he had plenty of time, he decided to sit down and read about the mortal's current events. The ambient glow from the mercury vapor lamp concealed his own faint radiance.

His angelic features were exactly what you might expect: a complexion like fair-skinned mortals with a perfect tan and a rather long face with a straight nose of honest breadth. His ears conformed with his face, and had slightly pendant, pointed lobes. His hair was of a light chestnut color, full and wavy, and silvered at his temples. His brow was intelligently high, lightly and properly lined above clear blue eyes. It was a nice, trustworthy face, both craggy and gentle at the same time. His hands were slender, but manly, with a light covering of soft amber hairs. He was rather tall with a slim, tough, vigorous body like that of a runner. There was one minor flaw in his appearance: it was the way he was dressed.

The pale gray flannel suit that he wore was ill-fitting and poorly made. Actually his suit looked more like the saggy unpressed garb of an Irani seaman on shore leave in Baltimore. The sort that made spectacles of themselves with the B-girls up on the "block," or sat bleary-eyed in Thompson's all night café clutching thick mugs in the predawn hours waiting to go back aboard their rusty ships. Of course no one but a Bible thief would ever notice a thing like that, and I am mortified that it was ever mentioned.

Lemuel's upcoming mortality assignment made him increasingly apprehensive as the day approached. He'd had problems right from the beginning when as a guardian angel he'd picked one of the offspring of Adam and Lilith. He guessed that Eve was a temporary fling and that Adam would return to his first wife. Then he picked Esau. He figured he couldn't miss with Isaac's eldest and favorite son, and lost there to a bowl of red pottage.[33] Throughout the ages he had problems. At the Colosseum it was a sweet young girl who at the last minute decided to burn incense instead of facing the lions. Of course later an evil angel smote her with emerods. Then under the reign of Constantine I, the emperor who made Christianity the state religion, he selected a young priest who celebrated the Mass with all the zeal accompanying new converts. He maintained his piety right up until the apostate Julian seized power, and then with equal zeal sacrificed to Mithras.

He had bad luck, both as an evil and as an avenging angel. Saladin cut his forces to shreds in the Crusades; the Albigensians turned out to be fundamentalists and not heretics at all; and his Black Death encouraged Boccaccio to write his Decameron, which brought about the Renaissance when the men of God were ridiculed.

HOW THE GOOD TAILOR GOT TO HEAVEN

He fared even worse as a lying angel. He went about whispering to Columbus that the world was round. He told that Slavic heretic, Copernicus, that the planets revolve around the sun, thereby creating the first Polish joke. Then he tried to restore ecclesiastic orthodoxy by getting Galileo to invent the telescope. He even went to the extreme, compounding the mess, by causing Galileo to mutter, "but it moves," after it had been found not to do so by the Inquisition.[34] If it were not for his faith, and the fact that "The potter hath power over the clay," Lemuel might doubt his importance in God's grand design. In the six thousand years since he had been created, he had been up and down through the probationary ranks so many times that he was beginning to feel as though he were the Lord's stepchild. Understandably, it was with trepidation that he faced his final trial.

As Lemuel read the newspaper, a twinkling hint of a smile often lit his face. Suddenly, sensing another un-earthly presence materializing in the park with him, he riffled the newspaper pages to the church section; the printed cross above the daily inspirational message seemed to glow, as if to ward off evil.

This move brought a nasty chuckle from the fiend, now manifestly solid, only a few feet away. It was obvious the demon and Lemuel had crossed paths before by its insolent familiarity as it spoke to the angel. It said, "S'a matter Lem? D'ya think I was your O.D. checking up on ya?"

Lemuel turned, faced the demon and recognized it as one of the most impious imps. He shook his paper, and said disdainfully, "Oh! It's you." Then he turned haughtily and proceeded to find the page he had been reading before. He noisily crumpled the pages as he turned them and as if to emphasize a point said, "We're allowed to read the comics. It's just that I prefer the sermon for the day."

"If you say so, Lem," it said with a sarcastic sneer.

"It's rude boisterous laughter and giggling that's sinful. You must be an awfully dumb demon. You have free run of the world, and you didn't even know that our O.D. [Oversight Directory] is in Amsterdam.

There have been some rumors about fraternization with the mortals." He grunted in disgust, and added, "Your doing, no doubt!"

"Hum! Fraternization, eh? Like those bad old days before the flood?" The demon concatenated a chain of mirthful, nasty sounds and then commented between chuckles, "Still 'coming in unto the daughters of men,'[35] old boy?" It leaned against the lamppost and waggled an index finger at Lemuel and through pouty lips chided, "Naughty, naughty."

This was a small, skinny type of demon, weighing about a hundred pounds, and slightly more than five feet tall. It was wearing sandals and an aquamarine sheath. Her dress was devoid of ornamentation except for the press of her ectoplasm at the thigh, buttock, and hip region, and a slight cupping of the underside of her small breasts. The loose material around her mid-region seemed to accentuate, rather than conceal, her slender firm waist, and as she breathed, her naval was adumbrated by the linen fabric. Her legs were lean and strong, slightly bowed, and her ankles were small enough that Lemuel could have easily touched his middle fingers and thumb tips around them. She had well-formed arms with a slight shading of fine dark hairs between her wrists and elbows. Her long hair, the color of dark chocolate, was parted in the center and then hung, shimmering with highlights, almost to her shoulder blades. She had a wide smile and impossibly white teeth, made even more startling by her dusky complexion which was several shades darker than Lemuel's tan. Her nose turned down slightly, hinting Semitic origins or a suggestion of Babylon. Her eyes were the color of a deep-woods fern and even without make-up, her long dark lashes and nearly black eyebrows attracted attention. She might be considered pretty if one didn't know she was a demon.

Lemuel glared at her and hotly defended his celestial companions. "They were only sampling mortality. They had to give up their angel status and all their angel powers when they took on human form, and some of them were never seen in Heaven again."

The demon clasped her hands and said with false concern, "Oh my,

HOW THE GOOD TAILOR GOT TO HEAVEN

isn't that a shame?" While wearing a sardonic leer she nodded her gleeful confirmation about their fates. Then she rubbed her palms together and suggested, "You're not tenured yet. There's still time, Lem. Why don't you defect, too? Our side has more fun."

Lemuel was barely able to control his outrage. "Fun? It's not supposed to be fun! Doing the Lord's work is serious business." And as to her insulting proposition, he said in high dudgeon, "Defect to your side? Hah! Never! I'd rather spend eternity as the lowest rank probationer. And why do you, a demon, think you have the right to accuse angels of sinful conduct?"

"We're the experts, remember?" she explained and smiled.

"Besides, that all happened thousands of years ago. There were no laws handed down yet, and we fixed up the mess it caused with the flood."

"Oh, you admit that it caused a mess?" she mocked.

"Well, no. I misspoke. Angels are good and don't make messes. Besides, the mortals have only themselves to blame, going about like the daughters of Zion, 'haughtily, and walking with stretched forth necks and wanton eyes, walking and mincing as they go, and making a tinkling with their feet.' 36"

Wearing a wanton smile, and with a stretched-forth neck, the demon crossed in front of him with mincing steps, and her hips swayed slightly as she sashayed before him. Lemuel raised his arm and pointed a cautionary finger at her. His arm followed her awkwardly. "Keep your distance Abigail! You fiend!" Then she sat on the bench beside him like an overly-friendly, stray kitten, and smiled up at him coyly.

"Well," she purred, "you remembered my name. Does that mean you're finally ready to loosen up a bit?"

"Oh my God! You're impossible!"

"Is that why you're still on probation, Lem? Did you spend too much time going in unto the daughters of man?"

"Don't be ridiculous! I wouldn't...I'd never do anything like that! Boy! You demons degrade everything and everyone. For a peccadillo that happened before there were any rules about right and wrong, you try to smear us angels. You're just plain wicked. You're so infested with sin that you can only think sinful thoughts. You're filled with sin, right up to your eyebrows." He raked his index finger across his forehead and hissed, "Whatever you see, it's through the slime of sin. Goodness, faith, and devotion to God are loathsome to your kind. Now that the humans have received the Ten Commandments, you can't stand the competition. It must really irritate you to see the gloriously pure human souls laying up credits toward their final reward by doing good works now that they have a moral guide. When Moses received the Ten Commandments on Mount Horeb, I'll bet it made you demons shudder."

"Oh pish posh! It didn't make any difference at all." She waved a dismissive hand in his direction.

His arm snapped out toward her and she thought he was going to strike her. She flinched, but he swung it woodenly upward with his index finger pointing into the sky, and declared, "They're made in His image. He breathed His goodness into them. He never dreamed that laws would have to be handed down. He thought it would all come naturally." Then his arm flashed in her direction as he shook his finger at her and exclaimed, "It's all your fault! You demons! You corrupted God's creation. You befouled their natural goodness with sin! You caused them to be cast out of paradise!"

Abigail gave him a patronizing smile. "Oh come now. Me? I didn't do it." Then she taunted, "Old Moses sure found out what came naturally to them when he came down from that mountain top."

Lemuel scowled. The demon leaned back against the arm on her side of the bench, rested her legs along the seat, crossed them at the ankles, and extended them toward him. He pressed harder against the arm on his side of the bench and clasped his hands together in his lap. She grinned while remembering the orgy[37]. Then she clapped her hands with glee and denied any fault or responsibility. She laughed, and through her wicked smirks said, "He came down that steep mountain trail wearing that long hot robe and carrying those heavy stone tablets. I

HOW THE GOOD TAILOR GOT TO HEAVEN

didn't have a thing to do with it. His own brother was the ringleader!"[38] Then sniggering her evil demon snigger, she said insolently, "Then the silly nit had a temper tantrum." Another snigger. "And he smashed the tablets.[39] And then...and then...he had to climb all the way back up that mountain and fast for another forty days, and do them all over again."[40] Then stammering with glee she sputtered, "And you know what? I'll bet Moses forgot how the first batch went and got the second batch wrong."

"That's about what I'd expect from a demon." He said with disgust in his voice.

"Oh! Okay! You're an angel and I'll bet you can't recite all ten, and in order."

"You wouldn't know whether I was right or not, smarty. Why don't you go back and stir your slime and shovel your brimstone."

"I thought so . You don't know."

"I do so."

"Okay, let's hear them then."

"Which version do you want?" He glared at her, and counted on his fingers, "Protestant...Hebrew...Lutheran... Episcopalian... or Catholic. So there!"

That silenced her. She blinked and then her eyes widened in astonishment. After a long thoughtful pause, she asked, "But... but... how can there be different versions of the Ten Commandments? I thought they were chiseled in stone." She cocked her head and her brow knit quizzically as she gnawed on a fingernail.

Lemuel mulled over an answer. His lips moved while he recited silently and counted them up on his fingers. Finally he explained, "If you take what each sect claims to be the Commandments, you come up with twelve, but in a slightly different order."

Never one to miss the opportunity to make angels feel uncomfortable, the demon said, "That proves what I was saying about the commandments. What if He made the first ten different from the second ten? Maybe your people should call them the Dozen Commandments, or the Twenty Commandments. Wow! I'll bet that if you permuted the possibilities you'd come out with a hundred different combinations." A playful smile deepened little crescents on either side of her mouth and her eyes shone with merry green lights.

Lemuel, lost in calculations, and looking even more perplexed, was still counting on his fingers. He said, lowly to himself, "And Jesus added two more[41]... hum ... ?"

With that, Abigail burst into unrestrained laughter while trying to hold her sides and cover her mouth at the same time.

Then, with one of his better evil angel glares, he sneered at her and said, "Wouldn't you feel more at home sitting in a boiling cauldron of pitch? What difference does it make if there's ten, twelve, or fourteen commandments? They've given the mortals a dependable moral code. They've laid down the law for attaining grace. They're the foundation for the entire Judeo-Christian civilization." He folded his arms across his chest, and said smugly, "I'd hate to see the corrupt laws that you demons would enact. What would the poor mortals do if they were left to Satan's laws?"

"We terrestrial angels don't care what they do as long as they leave us alone."

"Terrestrial angel? Isn't that a euphemism for cast out, traitorous, rebellious, disobedient, spawn from the pit of torture and despair?"

She prodded his thigh with her sandaled foot and said, "Lay off the slurs. Do I look as though I torture souls? And I'd never have anything to do with boiling oil, or pitch, or...yucky old slime."

"Oh, you may not look like that now, but I know what you're really like. We've all been pretty well briefed regarding that. We've studied Dante's *Inferno*, and I know what you're up to right now." He shuddered and added, "You're here to pick up some poor lost soul and drag it off to your foul pit to torment it."

"Deliver it from your sanctimonious clutches, you mean. Sure, I'm here on business, the same as you. I'm supposed to pick up the soul of another fortunate mortal, another tailor I think."

"Fortunate, huh?" he interjected, and grimaced.

HOW THE GOOD TAILOR GOT TO HEAVEN

Abigail added, "Yes, lucky to be out of your pious serfdom. I wish you'd lay off that popish poppycock and all that scare propaganda that you use to get the mortals to support your churches and their ordained agents. It's all lies, you know. I get sick and tired of listening to all that nonsense about my home. Of course it's not as posh as your Vatican, but it has lovely grounds and the buildings are very nice, even extravagant. Mammon was the architect, you know. It's something like the campus at Berkeley. Of course there are no deans or rules of any kind."

"How vile! It's just like Milton said, 'Hell is chaos and pandemonium.'" And he slid closer to the arm on his side of the bench they shared, and shifted his leg so her foot no longer touched. Then he looked at her out of the corner of his eye. There was a cold glint in the blue and he spoke softly, to evoke a sense of confidentiality. "Be honest Abigail. Tell me some of the terrible things that you do to those poor damned souls when you get them."

She smiled, fluttered her long lashes and winked lasciviously at him. "Just imagine the opposite of what your side does with them."

He smiled, uncertainly, not sure what she implied with her wicked leer. Then he recalled a few lines that Jesus said would be preferable to the torments of Hell. Jesus said that it would be preferable to cut off one's hand or any other offensive body member, or plucking out one's eye if it offended. He said that would be preferable to, "being cast into hell fire: where their worm dieth not, and the fire is not quenched."[42] He thought to himself, what could He have meant by that? A worm that dieth not? Hum? Then the thought struck him, a permanent erection in the fires of Hell, and their desire is never quenched! Lemuel looked away quickly, to hide his blushes. Heaven was sinless and all the moral certitudes were fulfilled, so Hell must be the opposite: riddled with sloth, disorder, hedonism, and worldliness. Then, after a few moments, he recovered his composure and asked, "Are their cries for mercy very loud?"

"What cries? A few peals of laughter maybe, but no cries. I told you what it was like, except there are no papers to write, or tests, or rules of any kind. They get nice rooms with daily maid service. We provide them with nice restaurants where we have great chefs and pretty waitresses. There are lounges with live entertainment and skillful bartenders. They have heated swimming pools, riding stables, a golf course, and there's a large game room with pool tables and darts. If they want, they can go on one of our day trips to the beach. We have a nice library where they can read anything. There is cable TV in all the rooms, and all the latest VCR cassettes."

"Ugh!" he grunted. "Uncensored, too, I suppose."

He didn't believe a word of it, and turned away, but he was especially disgusted by her diabolic implication that they used the souls in their licentious perversions. At the same time he wondered how it was possible. The demons are the same as angels, physically, and the celestial angels can't have sex. Mortals have coitus so they can procreate, but the flesh must be quickened, and the immortal soul, being spirit, cannot conjoin. There's no procreating after death: "For when they rise from the dead, they neither marry, nor are given in marriage; but are as the angels which are in heaven."[43] And coitus outside of marriage is a forbidden mortal sin. Angels do not marry, and, of course, there is no sin in Heaven. Those angels that went down in the early days had to drink the waters of life, become mortal, and then they could go in unto the daughters of men. He knew there were no sexual enticements in Heaven, but he reasoned, Hell is probably well stocked with that commodity.

He said, "That would be real torment all right! The most diabolic punishment of all. Think of it: complete emersion in sin; no thoughts of goodness or decency; and no reward for character improvement. That alone would crush the spirit out of them. Oh yes, that would be torture…pure psychological torture!"

"Well you needn't look so apprehensive, they sort of enjoy it."

Her soft mocking words pounded like spikes into his brain and then he thought, she's lying, that must be it. "Tell me the truth Abigail. That's not the way it is. That's too monstrous. No punishment is the worst punishment of all! Their poor souls are tormented by their burdens of sin.

HOW THE GOOD TAILOR GOT TO HEAVEN   23

Their sins weigh so heavily, trampling the innate goodness that God breathed into them. They expect the release that only punishment can bring, a soul cleansing with fiery brimstone for having offended their Creator. Do you mean that you do nothing? That's horrible!"

"They do seem terrified when they find out where they are," she said thoughtfully, tapping her lips with a forefinger. Then she added brightly, "But they soon get over it."

He got angry, pointed an accusing finger at her, and said, "You're lying! Tell me the truth. Tell me about the ten concentric rings of Hell, each stage deeper, more terrifying, and more painful. What about the rivers of boiling pitch that you throw the souls into? Oh how you must enjoy your real nature. It is not as you appear now, but like you really are: a foul, black, bat-winged devil riding in your scow on that boiling river, gliding through the acrid fumes, and prodding any soul that tries to surface with your staff, pushing them under again and again like frying donuts in hot oil. Tell me about the trident lances, the red hot pincers, the thumb screws, and the foul stink of the air. Do you have mechanical torture machines like the rack? Have you seen Satan locked in the icy bowels of Hell with all of the most blasphemous souls? What about their eternal wails and screams? And the deep soul wrenching groans? How about the pain and horror they show on their faces when they realize that they must remain there forever? What kind of whips do you use? Cat-O-Nines? And do you load the tips? Do you make them crawl over broken glass and hot coals? Do you poke red hot needles beneath their nails? How about…"

"Stop it Lem!" Exasperated by his sadistic delight, she cut him short. "Just stop and think for a minute. We demons like our comfort. We weren't cast down, that's another one of the lies they tell you. We just got a bad rap and left of our own accord. We wouldn't follow orders then, so just who do you think is going to make us do that now? And another thing… do you have any idea how much work it would be, wielding the lash, lifting those heavy spears and hot pokers, prodding souls, and sweltering over hot fires? That's work! Hard work at that. Our souls don't work, and I'm sure not going to do any work!"

"Work too hard? Don't tell me you have something against work. Oh! You are vile!"

He turned from her in utter disgust. He checked the angle of the moon once again; there was still time before his appointment, so he decided to catch this sly demon in one of her lies and make her admit that she was a liar. He had noticed that most demons dressed well and he grudgingly admitted even this foul one seated beside him did as well. Although her dress was simple, it fit her flawlessly and was impeccable. There were no charred spots that he could see and there wasn't a trace of oil or ash on it anywhere. Then his imagination raced, Sure, that's it! That's what they do to the souls. His other vision of Hell was archaic, and not a subtle enough torture. He imagined that their methods had to be truly evil. They must force the souls to work under intolerable conditions, poor lighting, clouds of poisonous chemicals, dust-laden air choking their lungs, cold drafty concrete floors, sweltering heat in the summertime, inadequate and dangerous machinery, and with deafening noise levels just under the point where it would drive them insane. Yeah, that's it! That's what they do. The demons must force their souls to work at the most demeaning jobs, What could be worse than being a slave to demons? And then they deny them their daily bread which they prayed the Lord to give them and their families. Maybe they intensify the eternal tedium by making them stand for hours in long lines just to get to work and then after work, more hours of long lines. Lemuel grew more serious, and thought to himself, And they probably don't even get Sunday off, to praise the Lord. Then he sprang his trap and he asked casually, "Where do you demons get the nice clothes you wear, if your souls don't sew them for you and keep them clean for you?"

His question startled her. "What? What do you mean? We buy them in the stores from the living mortals of course. They do all the work for us. I bought this dress right off the rack at Lord & Taylor, and I bought the sandals at Gucci on Rodeo Drive. When my clothes get soiled, I drop them off at the cleaners or buy new ones." Now her mind

HOW THE GOOD TAILOR GOT TO HEAVEN — 25

raced. This was something she had never thought about before, and she asked uncertainly, "Do you mean that your souls must...work when they get to Heaven?" As she uttered the word "work," she swallowed hard.

"Of course they work! They want to work! Working is one of the cardinal virtues! What would you have them do...become fat, slothful, and riddled with indolence? Say! Just what is it that you're insinuating? There's no sin in Heaven! You know what they say about idle hands being the Devil's workshop. It's the surest road to Hell!" His hand raised and his index finger pointed skyward as he evoked the Holy truth. Then he spat out angrily, "You do know the Lord's prayer, don't you?"

She shrank back, shook her head and said, "Our kind don't do much Bible reading you know."

"Thy will be done, as is in heaven, so in earth!"[44] His loud voice washed over her and vibrated throughout the park, and she cowered. "Everyone up there works, except God of course. He's still resting, but we all work and we're glad to do it. And there's promotion for accomplishment, just as it is here on Earth." It was with some uncertainty that he mentioned promotion and he hoped that she wouldn't bring up his own promotion record. He silently vowed that when his mortality detail arrived there would be no slip-ups. He'd have flocks of mortals kneeling before his altar and basking in the revealed truth.

He was so intent on throwing her evil charges back in her teeth that he almost missed a statement she'd made. She had said that she bought her clothes from the mortals. She said the demons buy things. Buy things? His eyes narrowed shrewdly. He'd caught her! "You said that you bought that dress from the mortals? *Bought*, you said! You *bought* it? Just where did you get the money to pay for that dress that you say you bought from the mortals? Did you steal it?"

It is a fact that demons and angels have identical powers. Those powers are also restricted. They can all part small bodies of water,[45] (only God can do seas,[46] or cause the earth to turn backward on its axis by ten degrees[47]), but they can raise up whirlwinds, cause great clouds to appear, and swirl up fiery pillars,[48] cause sticks to turn into serpents,[49] they can cure lepers,[50] and raise the dead,[51] or cause axe heads to float,[52] but any really useful miracles are impossible for them. They can't conjure up an automobile, even a cheap one, or a house. They can neither get rid of dirty dishes without soap and water, nor grow a weed-free lawn that never needs mowing. In the past, the demons, being earthbound, and also very lazy, tended to earn their subsistence by the easiest way possible. They worked as fortune tellers, chiromancers, spirit mediums, gamblers, hurdy-gurdy players, trained animal exhibitors, fakers and sellers of counterfeit Stradivarius violins and old masters' paintings, horse copers, water dowsers, magicians, ventriloquists, and sellers of magic charms, and that is why some of these professions still retain an unsavory notoriety. But what became essential to modern economics was a bonanza for the demons. The time came when people would actually give things of value, even of great value, and toil at the most demeaning kind of work, only to accept bits of paper in return. While it is impossible for either a demon, or an angel, to conjure gold or silver,[53] since they belong to the Lord. However, they can easily make bits of paper and printed in any pattern. So the answer to Lemuel's question was quite simple.

Abigail replied, "Why here, with a little practice, you can do this too," and as she spoke, she held out her hand, and a two-inch stack of fifty dollar bills appeared. Then she offered, "Here, these are already made. Why don't you take some and buy yourself a new suit?" Then she thrust the stack forward toward Lemuel.

He shrank back in horror. "That's forbidden!" After recovering his composure, he scowled and remonstrated her, "What are you thinking about Abigail? Don't you know what that would do to the world's economy? If enough of that sort of thing were to occur, it could cause currency imbalances, people would lose faith in their banks and their

HOW THE GOOD TAILOR GOT TO HEAVEN

governments, and there'd be manias, booms, panics, and crashes in the financial world"

"Oh, don't be silly. What's a few hundred for a new suit? Get a good one. Take a thousand." She smiled innocently and fluttered her long lashes above her fern green eyes as she and pushed her hand forward even more insistently. "Go ahead. Take some." her voice urged like a Jewish mother with a tray full of blintzes. She sensed his resolve softening and she chided, "I know what you're thinking. It's because I'm a demon. You're afraid you'll be caught trafficking with the enemy. Okay, it's your choice."

As she made the stack of bills dissolve, he gulped. She saw his wistful expression, and added to his torment. "I don't see what your problem is. That's how we survive, and it's how we maintain our souls. It'll be even easier when everything gets computerized, but it's really great living down here now. One advantage to having Hell on earth is that we can hire living mortals to do anything for these bits of paper." Then with twisted demon logic, she rationalized that Lemuel's inflexible adherence to the rules was retarding his advancement.

"Pride and vanity, that's what your problem is Lem. And aren't those sins? You'll never make it to full angel that way. And about the money…it helps the mortals and it creates employment." She clucked her tongue disparagingly and chided, "Just look at the suit you're wearing. It's a disgrace to our profession. I've watched you angels go off from here and it looks like the boat unloading the Irish immigrants during the potato famine."

Lemuel winced; that remark stung. He wasn't the only probationer who had felt the cool response of the mortals to the angels in their shabby mufti. He'd heard some of them muttering their complaints when they were out of earshot of the higher orders. He got up and smoothed his suit with his hands, then he hitched his flabby coat to make it hang more presentably. It was an unsuccessful attempt. He asked hesitantly, "It doesn't look so bad. What do you think?"

Abigail shook her head and made a wry face.

"We're not allowed to wear our robes down here, unless it's a miraculous visitation or some special event. We have to appear as ordinary mortals otherwise."

"Oh sure…robes. Anybody can make robes. Cut a hole in a sheet and you've got a robe, but a three-piece suit…that's impressive!"

"Why should the mortals object to our appearance? The truly saved are only concerned with spiritual purity. What we wear shouldn't matter to any of them," he said petulantly.

Abigail shrugged her shoulders and raised both hands, palms up, and said, "Gee! I don't know. But I do know that the successful preachers dress just as well as we terrestrial angels. And your poor but proud attitude is liable to cost you your promotion again. If you won't take my money, you better take my advice. You shouldn't expect a mortal to heed a message from a slob."

"These clothes were made in Heaven," he asserted.

The shameless nasty sniggering that came from the demon showed what foul disrespect they were capable of committing.

Lemuel narrowed his eyes angrily, but her taunts had started him thinking. He envisioned all the past eons, mentally scrolling backward to the dawn of man's creation, and contemplated the entire stock of tailors they had in Heaven. Even the ones who sewed their robes weren't first-rate. He looked suspiciously at Abigail. She was ignoring him, looking up to the stars, and softly whistling Offenbach's *Can Can*. He began to feel that something was wrong. An embryonic but persistent idea began to form and he sensed a plot. Why didn't they have good tailors? Was it some sort of demonic plot against Heaven's angels? The fiends were wholly capable of it, and worse. Some of the angels let the demons' taunts about their clothes annoy them, and the demons had free run of the world, so they had motive and opportunity. They could easily mislead a small group of guileless tradesmen into damnation just to harass the angels. It was a scheme well within the ability of their crafty minds. He glanced sideways at her. She was still whistling and looking off into the dark. Then he remembered her comment about being there to pick up some "lucky guy, a tailor," she thought. He pulled the appointment card from his breast pocket and muttered, "Hum, tailors? I'm supposed to pick up a tailor in a few minutes."

Instantly, she became attentive. "What a coincidence. I'm supposed to pick up a tailor too. Show me your appointment card." Demons don't carry appointment cards. They're very careless about their souls. They've been known to let souls wander about the world for centuries, where they become poltergeists or socialists. Abigail swung her legs around, and sat beside him studying his card. Finally she said, "That sure is odd, my date is for the exact same time as yours is."

"What do you mean, exact? We're precise in our calculations, unlike some I could mention, and the time of death and occupation are the twin admitting keys. Your side has probably made another mistake."

"Nope, no mistake. Their shop addresses are different and their clients are very different. But it sure is odd, the time is the same, right down to the atto-second." Then she enumerated, as well as she could remember, a brief rundown on the character of the soul that she was to pick up.

A phrase from the scriptures flashed across Lemuel's mind. "Hath not the potter power over the clay?" It seemed to be written large across the card in his hand, in the sky when he looked up, and on the sidewalk when he looked down. Deep in thought, he tapped his pursed lips with the edge of his card. Was it because he wanted a good suit for his upcoming evangelical detail that he had these thoughts? The demon's tailor was sure to be excellent; he could tell by the natty dressers that he had for customers and he knew that the orphans at the county home were not fashionably dressed. Or, was this a test where failure could send him spinning back down the ranks once more? He reread the list of merits of the soul that he was to deliver. What's this? A picture of Eisenhower! Wasn't there something about his chief of staff and a vicuna coat? And didn't Ike himself admit lying about a U2 plane, and Gary Powers?

It is true that God knows the thoughts of men, and angels,[54] but neither ethereal nor fallen angels have any special talent for reading the minds of each other, or of mortals. But some have an intuitive sixth sense, as with some mortals. Abigail had such powers. She had feminine intuition. Finally she interjected, "Wasn't he supposed to have had an affair with his female driver during the war, and didn't his wife have to go to an unboozery?"

Demons always think of the sordid.

Lemuel ignored her slander, but he was considering a more profound sin: those Salvation Army uniforms. Wasn't this tailor flaunting the ability of his craft to control the powers of right and wrong? God ordained sackcloth for the penitential! Then, wouldn't this tailor be committing some form of idolatry? A horrible abomination... worthy of damnation!

With one lithe motion, Abigail swung off the bench and stretched catlike before him. Of course he paid no attention to her slender waist, or to the soft furrow her callipygous shape adumbrated in her sheath, or to her shapely calves, or to the graceful arch of her foot, not to the soft way that her hair curled under gracefully, and not even to how cute she looked with her head cocked to one side. And if one didn't notice the mischievous glint in her eye, one could easily forget she was a demon. Of course Lemuel noticed none of those things.

Reluctantly she said, "I'd love to stay and chat, but I have to go now. My date is farther away than yours is. But it's a pity things are the way they are. My tailor's customers are those sportsmen and Keynesian economists who only have fairytale like dreams, really childlike hopes, and certainly nothing evil. And the reporters are the pariahs of the world. Really, they are your sort of people. They're martyrs. They make too much money to be accepted by workers, are not accepted by the intellectuals, and don't earn enough to be accepted by the wealthy. Their best efforts become puppy training paper."

He thought, Demon or not, there's a lot of truth to what she said. If only he had more time to think this through. She was getting ready to leave right now. And if there were a demonic plot, and she was just tantalizing him, mocking him with what he couldn't have, he couldn't talk her out of her soul anyway. Oh, she might look innocent, but what she's doing now is being a tease, he thought. She was shamelessly flaunting fine clothing, and taunting him with false concern over his shabby suit. She needled him with psychological barbs that demons, especially the female sort, can throw so well. He thought how he would like to put one over on her, and his jaw set hard.

Just then she turned and giggled impishly. She quickly covered her snicker with her hand and propositioned, "Wouldn't it be a big joke if we swapped souls?"

Lemuel's palms began to sweat. Had she sensed what he wanted most of all? He wanted a decent suit to impress the mortals on his mortality detail. What if she was lying? She had no proof to show. She might not even have a soul to pick up and was trying to steal his soul. He said, "I couldn't do anything like that." And he also thought, I wonder why her dress has that slit halfway up her thigh.

"That's one way you could get a decent suit."

"How do I know I can trust you? You may not even have a soul to collect." She looked deeply hurt by his accusation. "Well, I suppose it could happen, a mistake in the record section. I don't see where my soul's merits are so great. It's just that two tailors have never died at the same moment before. I guess it could happen, though."

"Well you'd better make up your mind quickly! I have to go."

What to do…what to do? His face reflected the strain of indecision. He raised his arm and scratched his head. The material of his jacket strained, the seam at his armpit ripped and the lining protruded. Was this a sign or some trick? He didn't know what to do. Then he gritted his teeth, and, throwing all caution aside, and risking career and all, he said, "Okay! Here!" He handed her his appointment card.

She gave him an address and said, "Maybe you can get this tailor to fix that tear while you're waiting at those pearly gates."

As he sped off to keep the appointment, he thought he heard her say, "See you in Berkeley."

Chapter 3

IN THAT REALM OF PUREST LIGHT BEYOND THE UTMOST STAR lies the precincts of the ninth celestial orb. It is the crystalline sphere beyond which no sin has ever penetrated, and no sinner can be admitted. There lies Heaven.

Lemuel's return to Heaven was unusual. One might say it was extraordinarily unusual. He'd never been met at the pearly gates by an archangel before. At first, while he was still uncertain about swapping tailors with Abigail, he felt a shudder of cold fear chill his spine when he saw Uriel approaching. He was sure he was doomed. He had visions of Abigail sneering triumphantly over his downfall, but the archangel was pleasant to them. It was an unusual attitude for archangels confronting novitiates and ordinary souls. Uriel rushed them to the head of the line and after a perfunctory admittance (Saint Peter was exceptionally polite, bordering on servility) the archangel took charge of the tailor's soul and led him off to Thelassar[55] where the Trinity and the higher orders of angels dwell. Lemuel stared after them in amazement as they walked off together, with Uriel taking the tailor's arm. Lemuel hadn't even had a chance to have the tailor mend the sleeve of his jacket.

As he strode along the main thoroughfare, the Glory Road, a detachment of United States Marines, the guardians of the streets of Heaven[56], raced past him to break up a fight between an Arab soul and a Jewish soul. The other souls, who had been on street cleaning detail with them, took sides. There was a lot of pushing and shoving, waving of street cleaning tools, and loud jeering by the other sanitation souls. It seemed like it might turn into an ugly brawl. The marines charged in with their riot sticks and soon put an end to the fight.

The marines were a fairly recent addition to the streets of Heaven. The Ethereal Establishment tried very hard to comply with the people's prayers, so in response to their wishes, the United States Marines became the peace keepers on the streets of Heaven. Lemuel considered them to be a big improvement. The mortal souls didn't leave their animosities behind when they arrived in the empyrean, and because of the population explosion since the gentile admission policy, keeping the peace between the clash of cultures became a problem. Joshua's enforcers could no longer keep order; the addition of Swiss guards was eventually overcome; and even the combined constabulary could no longer handle the policing duties. When the Marines arrived, a century ago, Joshua's police force was inducted into the corps and the Swiss guards' duties became mostly ceremonial within the walls of Thelassar.

Lemuel was to receive his instructions about soul saving in the fabulous gardens of Thelassar for his mortality detail. Probationers all received their final briefing beside the fountain where the waters of life flowed. His step was light and his pace brisk. His robe of unbleached muslin flapped about his ankles and his rope sandals creaked a merry song along with his cadence. He wore a smug smile because of his coup. He had really out foxed that sly blasphemous demon, Abigail. He'd really put one over on her when they switched souls. That message he envisioned in the park in King Jamesburg, 'Hath not the Potter power over the clay,' was all the sign that he needed to know that he should make the switch. It must have been planned all along; all part of the Lord's grand design.

HOW THE GOOD TAILOR GOT TO HEAVEN

Lemuel had a cheery smile for everyone today, both angel and ordinary soul received a grin, and an acknowledging nod, as they passed one another on the sidewalk. His destination was the garden of Thelassar where he was to receive his final course of instruction, his Bible, and a flask of the waters of life[57]. This was to be his final briefing before embarking on his mortality mission. Just this one final trial remained, a mere one lifetime, and he would have tenure. As an angel he'd be able to move from the common bunk room and into his own private monk's cell. He would wear white linen robes, sandals of leather, and most importantly, only for very exceptional circumstances would he be required to descend to the wicked world. There would be no more obscene confrontations with demons until the final battle between good and evil.

For once Lemuel did not feel as though he had botched the job. He did wonder if the good tailor would be able to make the suit for his mortality mission. He began to have doubts about that, the way the archangel snatched the tailor away from him, but he reminded himself: God knows best. 'Hath not the potter power over the clay?'

And now that he too was going to be a full angel, the sting of resentment that he'd felt toward all the others who had been promoted ahead of him lessened. His own utility in the grand design had been unconventional; it's just that the Lord moves in mysterious ways.

Lemuel's eyes had readjusted themselves to the eternal light. The brilliant rays glinting from the miles of white marble buildings and rows of Heavenly golden spires no longer caused him to squint. One could always tell a recent returnee by the way they shielded their eyes. He supposed that after a long mortal life in the changing world of light and darkness, the readjustment period would be longer.

There was time before his appointment so he decided to visit a very close friend: the angel Esther. Esther's mortality detail had been many, many, years ago, nearly twenty-five hundred years ago, but Lemuel thought she might be able to tell him honestly what it was like to be mortal. Esther taught the second grade in one of the Heavenly schools.

Homere A. Dansereau

The schools are provided by the Ethereal Establishment to train the souls of the mortal children who have been called to their reward. As far as possible, where they do not conflict with Scriptures, all of the moral certitudes are observed in Heaven. The seven principals of morality, as laid down by the moral majority/Christian Coalition, are: one, the sanctity of life, (naturally this one no longer applies, for obvious reasons); two, monogamy (another custom not observed in Heaven since they are not married nor given in marriage.) three, common decency; four, the work ethic; five, the Abrahamic covenant; six, a Christian centered education, (those bereaved parents should be delighted to learn that just because their children have been taken to their final reward, does not mean that their education will be neglected.) and seven, acknowledging as divine the institutions of: the home, the state, and the church. All of Heaven is now home for the souls, and there is no need for churches in Heaven since the function they performed (guiding the soul to their final reward) has been brought to fruition. So basically what remains of the moral ethic is common decency, the work ethic, the school, and the state. The state functions are all performed by the angels who are there to serve the ordinary souls, just like their own public servants do on earth. Lemuel thought this would be an excellent opportunity to familiarize himself with teaching methods since the children's salvation is always an important function of the clergy.

In the schoolyard the first graders were performing a tableau under the watchful eyes of a teaching angel serving the class. Lemuel sat down on a chalcedony bench to watch and learn what impresses children of that age so he could be more effective in saving their souls.

The tableau was about dawn in the garden. The children had erected a greenhouse of gossamer that served as a backdrop for the performance. The children were dressed as flowers and their costumes were made of crepe paper as they would have been on earth. Each child wore a broad and colorful collar imitating the petals of petunias and daisies. On their heads they wore crinkled crepe paper caps representing the yellow buttons of daisies, the eyes of Brown-eyed Susans, or pistils, crowns of flowers more boldly sexual. Their arms were sleeved in green and they held broad, fan-like leaves in each hand, which they fluttered as though moved by gentle breezes. Their bodies were swathed with green wrappings simulating flower stems, and their feet were covered with brown crepe paper concealing the fact of mobility, so as to appear planted.

They were singing, as they arose from a crouch, *Another day is dawning/ Dear Master let it be/ In working or in waiting/ Another day with Thee.* One of the students wore coveralls and a straw hat. He led the chorus using a hoe for a baton. A little girl dressed in a dotted Swiss pinafore and a sunbonnet pretended to be watering the flowers. The teaching angel clasped her hands in swooning delight over their performance.

Lemuel noticed that one of the boys did not appear to be all that delighted with his role in the garden of the Lord. He was costumed as a pansy with fuchsia petals and a yellow crown. He was a chubby lad with round cheeks and curly golden hair, and Lemuel got the distinct impression that the boy would have rather been off surveying the aspect from a tall cherry tree or trying to discover what makes those squiggly lines in the moist bottoms of partially dried-up mud puddles. He realized that his flash of intuition must be wrong, because this was how the children were taught group cooperation. They were shown how to take direction and how to channel their thoughts toward common goals on earth, to the delight of their parents, teachers and school boards, and they always know best. As they grew older, the students would learn to refine these skills with team sports. This Heavenly school had a prize winning football team called the Shrikes.

Lemuel soon became bored with the performance, arose from the milky white alabaster bench, which glittered in the eternal light, and proceeded toward the school building. It was a low structure. It had one story with a flat roof and a magnificent gymnasium. The walls were large masonry squares alternating with plate glass window panels. Of course this building was not the same as the elementary and middle school in the hamlet of King Jamesburg. In Heaven everything is done to perfection. The masonry panels were large panels of grained red rhodochrosite, that only resembled brick from a distance. The glass was glass, but set in golden frames with silver operating levers. The coping around the roof was real mother of pearl, instead of twenty gauge sheet metal painted gray. This building was altogether different.

A sign on the corridor wall, inside the school, indicated the way to the classrooms, the administrative office, and the gymnasium. The clerical soul behind the counter in the office was a tall, thin soul who wore pince nez glasses and had a pencil stuck into the tight bun of hair at the back of her head. She asked Lemuel to wait a moment while she called the principal. Lemuel was permitted to remain for a brief visit after gaining permission from the principal angel, who granted it only after coming to the threshold of her office door and coldly studying his appearance.

Esther had taken her class on a field trip, so the clerk soul suggested that he might like to audit teaching angel Bradamante's class in room six. They were seventh graders, about twelve or thirteen years old, and Bradamante's lesson plan showed that she would be teaching them about the Creation. Then she confided softly, "Some of the little beasts learned it all wrong when they were in the world."

Lemuel found the room and approached the teacher lecturing the class. She was an angel about as tall as himself, but he guessed that she had at least twenty-five pounds over him. She had sparse red hair and he guessed that her forearms were of a diameter that equaled his thighs. The muscles of her fore arms rippled rhythmically where they protruded from her robe as she leaned forward and placed two freckled meaty hands on the desk before her. She asked what he wanted. Her blue eyes were small and mean looking, and she had a jaw that reminded him of Benito Mussolini. Her teeth resembled the tombstones in Arlington cemetery, and nearly as widely spaced. He meekly requested permission to watch her teaching methods for a few minutes.

She said, "Providing you sit in the back of the classroom and be quiet." Lemuel quietly followed her instructions.

HOW THE GOOD TAILOR GOT TO HEAVEN — 39

She was finishing her lecture on the second law of thermodynamics and the infallible proof it provided that both science and the Bible agreed about the creation. The blackboard behind her was filled with equations and she asked, "Any questions?"

Lemuel glanced around the room at the students. All of them shook their heads and some uttered a muted "no." Then several students shot surreptitious bewildered looks around the class to see if they were the only ones to not understand the correlation. Lemuel nearly spoke up. He was about to say that he didn't understand it, but he noticed smug looks on the faces of two or three children and decided to remain silent. He knew, "Even a fool when he holdeth his peace, is counted wise: and he that shutteth his lips is esteemed a man of understanding."[58] So he agreed to agree with those children who were uncertain, and such an impressive scrawl of chalk surely must be correct.

Then Bradamante instructed them to open their Bibles and read the first two chapters. When they got to the end of the second chapter they were to sit quietly with their hands folded in their laps and contemplate what they had read.

The children's heads bent over their books. Some read with silently moving lips and a few used their index fingers to rapidly move from word to word. They were all dressed alike in robes of the same muslin material as Lemuel's robe, but with starched Peter Pan collars. The girls' collars were lace and their hair was tied back with ribbons. The boys wore their hair in Dutch boy cuts, like Buster Brown. Bradamante, whose robe was the white linen of a tenured angel, sat behind her desk with her small eyes constantly roving the room looking for infractions. Her right hand groped in her desk and brought out a palm load of manna, which she pushed into her mouth and chewed silently.

Lemuel's muslin robe was not the result of any unworthiness on his part. All probationary angels wore the simpler garb of the ordinary souls. The decision to have all probationers wear muslin came about through a well-studied, cost benefit analysis by a panel of virtues.

A little over four hundred years ago a select commission of virtues was impaneled to determine the proper way to obtain grace. Prior to that time, nearly everyone agreed that grace was acquired by receiving the sacraments. Several disputed this. They felt that it was also necessary to have faith, to pray, to study the scriptures, and to do good works. Another group of virtues felt that grace was a predestined gift of God and that one either had it, or one didn't. This dispute between the virtues continues to this day, and since the panel could not come to an agreement on this subject, they decided to see if there were any subjects on which they could agree. Cost benefit analysis became their forte. They reasoned that it would be far more economical to have the probationers dress as ordinary souls since they spent much of their time in the world on assignment and wearing expensive mortal garb. The report of the "Grace Commission" was sent on to the Office of Managing the Benefices (OMB), and it was quickly put into effect.

Lemuel used this silent time in the classroom to look around to see what a well-equipped, model classroom should be like. The children's desks were of birds-eye maple with slanted tops, and inkwells were in the upper right hand corners. Two or three quill pens rested in shallow grooves at the top of each desk, and a sand shaker for drying the India ink was on the left. The wooden floors were teak and the blackboards were large slabs of real slate, not some composition board. The chalk ledges and frames were of walnut and given the sheen of a French rub finish. In one corner was an American flag. Lemuel was about to ask the teaching angel about it, but her glare demanded silence, so he averted his eyes from her back to the flag.

Then, glancing above the blackboard, he noticed that there were inspiring words from the Holy Book in Gothic script all around the room in the space between the blackboards and the ceiling. The legend above the flag partly answered the question he wanted to ask Bradamante. It proclaimed, "The wicked shall be turned into Hell, and all the nations that forget God."[59] He decided that the flag was there as a sort of honor, and that it would be replaced by another nation's flag if they ever surpassed the Americans in Godliness. He recalled that America had the highest percentage of believers in God of any of the modern industrial nations. It was above ninety-five percent of their population. Also, their high officials all swore their loyalty to God and truth, when upon taking office, they took their oaths with their hand on the Bible. Their elected representatives began each day's session of law making with prayer, and their currency proclaimed their trust in God. On consideration, Lemuel realized that the flag truly deserved its place in this Heavenly classroom.

The students were still at their assignment and he had time to read some of the other verses. Above Bradamante's head was lettered: "For the Lord searcheth all hearts, and understandeth all the imaginations of the thoughts." Lemuel was very familiar with that cautioning advice that David had given to his son Solomon, since it was also printed on signs, carved on the walls, and placed on posters in the workplaces, and at other places of gathering. The next helpful thought inscribed onto the classroom wall was: "They separated themselves from all strangers, and stood, and confessed their sins, and the iniquities of their fathers."[60] That's a very wise thing, Lemuel thought. It's like having God's little informers in every household. Beneath that, and in capital letters, was "FOR THERE IS NO MAN WHICH SINNETH NOT."[61] Fortunately God forgives the repentant sinners, or Heaven would be empty, Lemuel reasoned. And beside that was the familiar verse of the Psalmist: "The wicked are estranged from the womb: they go astray as soon as they be born, speaking lies."[62]

Along the side wall Lemuel read a verse explaining how God demonstrates his love: "For whom the Lord loveth he correcteth; even as a father the son in whom he delighteth."[63] I suppose that explains my promotion problems, Lemuel thought, and he read the next verse. "He that spareth the rod hateth his son: but he that loveth him chasteneth him betimes."[64] The next scriptural quotation read: "Withhold not correction from the child: for if thou beatest him with the rod, he shall not die. Thou shalt beat him with the rod and shalt deliver his soul from Hell."[65] Lemuel knew how important that message was after his encounter with Abigail. Just imagine...exposing the lost souls of these children to all that sin. Lemuel gazed to the back corner of the room and read: "The blueness of a wound cleanseth away evil: so do stripes the inward parts of the belly."[66] Beneath this informative verse, on a diamond-studded golden hook, hung a bamboo rod about an inch thick and five feet long, with a dark brown leather wrist thong. The handle was shiny, as though it had a lot of use.

Lemuel started to read the verse about stoning the disobedient son to death,[67] when Bradamante barked, "Okay, that's enough time. All eyes front!" All heads instantly turned toward her, even those who were still struggling with the words, and so did Lemuel's. The schools of Heaven were the ideal of every pedagogue; there were virtually no disciplinary problems, and they used good old-fashioned, results oriented, teaching methods. While the power to eat a scroll of words, and to then recite them, may have been given to Ezekiel,[68] no such reliance could be placed on these children. Bradamante was about to interrogate her charges about what they had just read, and to answer any questions they might have. She asked, "Any questions?"

One hand shot up and after Bradamante nodded in her direction, a young girl asked, in a tremulous voice, "What is, B...B...Bdellium?"

"Fragrant gum resin. Any more?"

Another hand edged uncertainly upward. This student wanted to know what was meant by the plural reference to God. His voice quavered as he read the verse that puzzled him: "Let us make man in our image."[69]

"I am glad to see that you are alert, Ira. That is a very good question. But I'm sure that if you give it some thought you can arrive at the answer yourself."

Ira's thinking mechanism strained; his face frowned with the effort.

"Come Boy! Put on your thinking cap."

Lemuel wondered, Did he really read that from the Bible?

Ira expelled the breath that he had been holding and shook his head.

Bradamante turned from the boy in disgust, and asked, "Does anyone want to enlighten this oaf?"

HOW THE GOOD TAILOR GOT TO HEAVEN — 43

Lemuel slouched slightly and hid behind the student in front of him.

One student waved an eager hand. Lemuel noted that it was one those students who had understood the second law of thermodynamics. When Bradamante nodded in the boy's direction, he said triumphantly, "The Holy Trinity."

"Yes, of course that's the answer. It's the first Biblical reference to the Trinity, because the next verse clearly states, 'So God created man in HIS own image.' Any more questions?"

Another student, a thin attractive girl whose good looks would have caused her much trouble, and who had obviously been corrupted in some worldly, sex education class, asked, "Did Adam and Eve have belly buttons?"

"Yes they had navels, Dulcinea. They were the pattern for all who came afterward." Bradamante replied, and sounded as though her patience was being stretched.

Boy! Where do these kids get these questions? Lemuel thought.

Dulcinea persisted. "Well…does God have a belly button?"

Oh! What insolence! This is certainly Abigail's doing, or some demon even more brazen. Except for the paleness of her skin, she resembled Abigail too. He was keenly interested in how the teaching angel handled this young upstart.

Bradamante's jaw set hard, the muscles twitched in her cheeks, and in even controlled tones she answered, "In his mortal form he had a navel. And let me warn you Dulcinea, you young snippet, any more of that and you may be needing condign correction." And she nodded in the direction of the corner where the bamboo rod hung.

Dulcinea blanched and looked meekly downward. Then the same oafish boy, who didn't know that The Trinity was the explanation for the plural 'our image' reference, hesitantly raised his hand and pulled it back quickly. Then he tentatively pushed it back up again.

"Ira? What is it?"

Ira gulped and winced, and then finally asked his question. "In the first chapter, after God created the earth and the waters, and the land,

and he brought forth the grass and the trees, it says: 'He brought forth abundantly the moving creature that hath life and every winged fowl from the waters.'"[70]

"Yes, that's right Ira," Bradamante replied.

"Then over here in the second chapter it says: 'God formed every beast of the field and every fowl of the air out of the ground.'[71] How come? Did God create the birds and the animals from the ground, or from the water?"

Bradamante's face looked as though she had been scalded. She stood, placed both of her powerful hands on the desk, leaned forward, and glared at Ira. Her lips parted in a fearsome smile that bared her headstone-like teeth. She said in a deep husky voice, "You've brought this on yourself Ira. I see that I must try to save your soul from Hell once more. Go fetch the rod, then get up here before the class and bend over the whipping horse."

Lemuel decided not to stay for the oral exam. He wanted to find out if Esther had returned yet. As he left the room the oafish boy was bent over the horse before the American flag, and Bradamante was flailing away with steady strokes. To watch her, one might imagine the broadsword of a crusader meting out truth to the infidels as the boy howled with each cut of the cane. Lemuel called out, "Goodbye…and thanks," but she didn't hear.

Lemuel hoped he might meet Esther outside. That would be better. Then she could speak more candidly about her mortality detail when they were out of earshot of other angels. Once in a while unguarded comments had a way of making their way to the ears of the higher authorities. He thought Esther would tell him honestly how it felt to have life coursing through your veins. He wanted to know some of the details about simple things like: did it hurt to digest food? Or to expel the waste? He doubted those subjects would be discussed in his briefing.

Chapter 4

LEMUEL LEFT THE SCHOOL MUTTERING TO HIMSELF, "IT'S ALL the fault of the demons with their lies about the truth and our organization. If they were to have their way there would be chaos everywhere. Abigail wouldn't have bothered to correct that misguided young soul. She'd have let him intimate that there were contradictions in the Holy Book. She'd have thought it was too much trouble to respond to Ira's doubts. Thank God there are angels like Bradamante to answer these youngsters with the only thing they seem to understand. As they say, 'spare the rod.'"

"Some of the other deluded young souls needed a touch of the cane too. Humph! 'Does God have a navel?' What impertinence! Nearly obscene! Positively shameful. It's the sort of thing Abigail would have thought was very funny." Lemuel rubbed his chin and mused, I wonder if the Holy Ghost has... "Oh this is crazy! Now they've got me doing it."

Lemuel could not shake his thoughts of the demon and he wondered if it was possible that she might have possessed his soul. Mortals can be possessed, but angels? He seemed to envision her in flashes, like in the eyes of the young girl who asked if Adam and Eve had belly buttons. Bits and pieces of her appeared in his mind at random times without conscious effort on his part. What made it even more maddening was that he couldn't seem to connect her parts: her smiling eyes, her sandaled foot, the contour of her thigh through the slit of her skirt, the shape of her ear, the way she combed her hair, and frequently her laughing mouth would appear, but he couldn't make himself recall her image wholly. Then she'd suddenly appear unbidden and then disappear. It was maddening. It must be a possession of some kind, he thought, but I better not say anything about it that might jeopardize my promotion.

He left the school by the rear door, cut across a pasture where the white war horses[72] were kept, and through the stables where the souls of the sons of Canaan[73] were busily cleaning the stalls. The loud speakers in this building played Negro spirituals as they did in their separate quarters and gathering places. Lemuel joked with one of the grooms, "Hey boy, you gotta shoes?" The man responded with a wide white grin "Oh yassuh boss, I'ze gotta shoes." Then he did a graceful, soft shoe shuffle in his rope sandals. "An cum Sunday, Ah gonna put on mah shoes an I'ze gonna walk all ovah God's Hebben."

It's strange what mortals pray for, Lemuel thought, but he had to admit the marines that they prayed for were a good idea. Heaven was becoming overcrowded with souls, and they needed strict guidance occasionally.

The percentage of conversions and salvations had remained constant throughout the centuries, but two thousand years ago the standards were relaxed to accept gentiles. That caused the population of human souls entering Heaven to soar, and adding to the problem was the population explosion on Earth. Now there was an even greater number of human souls to be saved, and served. It necessitated a larger official infrastructure. Heaven was expanding exponentially. Vast areas that were once open space were being covered with urban sprawl. More office space was needed, more roadways to connect the offices, more factories to build the desks to go into the offices, and more book

HOW THE GOOD TAILOR GOT TO HEAVEN   47

binderies to bind the record books. More and more of everything was needed. It was a logistical nightmare. Retraining was a big problem. Newly arriving souls rarely knew traditional hand tool construction methods, or how to use pen and ink anymore. To avoid the Babel problem, all of them had to learn the language of God: Hebrew. Adult education was a big problem all by itself. Fortunately, minds far more acute than our feeble mortal wits directed these operations.

Whenever troubled, Lemuel soothed his nerves by watching the bustling construction workers. He liked their self-confidence as they grappled with things of sober reality, creating things of solidity. Since he was frequently troubled, he was a veteran sidewalk superintendent. He regarded the carpenters as the princes of the tradesmen. Not only did a master carpenter have to know his own trade, but he had to have a wide knowledge of all the other trades. Their judgment was often heeded by the superintendent angels.

Construction sites also have a magnetic attraction for young boys. Anything under construction works a magic spell on them and they want to scale the staging, run along the tops of the walls like balance beam acrobats (the higher and more dangerous the better) or sit astride the ridge pole of a roof and pound in nails. All young boys like pounding nails into boards. They want to do all the fun things they've seen the workers doing. But they also have a tendency to be destructive and so they are chased off when they come around.

Lemuel walked around to the back of the building to watch the masons placing a heavy section of the architrave atop fluted columns when he heard a few weak sobs coming from a small grove of Rose of Sharon trees.

Silently he crept into the grove and saw two young boys sitting on rocks with their heads buried in their hands and they were sobbing. As soon as they saw Lemuel they darted away, but he was too quick for them and grabbed each by the backs of their robes. "What's this now? Truants? Both of you are big enough to know that truancy is a very serious offense." They were about seven years old.

He said severely, "This will have to go down in your permanent record."

Permanent records are the principal reason for there being so much office space in Heaven, and so many office workers keeping the records. There were miles and miles of library shelves with thick books containing permanent records.

"We didn't run away. We had the teacher's permission."

"Oh?" This was a serious charge, if true. Teachers were forbidden to allow their pupils to wander about without supervision. This teacher should be reported. "Who is your teacher?" Lemuel asked.

The boys looked at each other and by their expressions it was plain that they were in a dilemma. They didn't want to betray their teacher. After much childish evasion, Lemuel finally dragged the story, and the teacher's name, from them. The lesson that day had been about Levitical proscriptions of women, and their clean and unclean cycles. The boys were bored by the whole subject and to keep them from distracting the class with their fidgeting, she had let them leave.

Their teacher was Esther, and she was the "pertiest, most beautiful, an the best lady since our moms. Esther allus give us nice hugs when we got to blubbering."

Lemuel knew Esther quite well and what the boys said of her true. She was a statuesque beauty with long, raven black hair, dark, royal blue eyes, and a soft compliant manner. She was one of the few angels that did not wield their superior rank over probationers, and they frequently passed time together. She was very interested in his impending mortality detail and recently expressed the fanciful wish to help him with the ordeal. Lemuel thought that she was generous to a fault. Esther was everything that Abigail was not, and if she occasionally uttered a coarse expression it, was only her way of being sociable. He could always recall Esther's full image and certainly would not report her for this minor infraction.

Lemuel assured the boys that he would not tell a soul about their adventure, but he wanted to know why they were crying. "This is Heaven. There shouldn't be any sobbing children in paradise."

HOW THE GOOD TAILOR GOT TO HEAVEN —⚬— 49

This reminder of their sorrow brought another spate of tears rolling down their cheeks and they wailed in unison, "We want to go home to our moms. We've been here long enough and we don't like it."

"Boys, boys. You can't go home from here, and you shouldn't want to. This is Heaven. This is your eternal home. It's your reward for having been good boys and believing in God."

The boy with straight, ash blond hair and big blue eyes, said; "Well, I believed in Sandy Claws too, and I'd rather go to the North Pole and live with him and the elves, but mostly, I want to go home."

Having never been a child Lemuel, could not quite understand the degree of fantasy necessary to equate Santa Claus with the Almighty, but the sad little boy's distress made him realize that he had to say something. This situation was enigmatic. Here were two little children before him, they obviously believed, and this was the kingdom of Heaven, and Jesus said "Except ye be converted, and become as little children, ye shall not enter into the kingdom of heaven."[74] How could they not be happy? All of the moral certitudes were being fulfilled. These children were getting their God-centered education. What was wrong?

Esther could be frivolous at times. Perhaps she had not stressed the glorious future that was laid before them. Their unblemished spirits would learn useful trades and spend all eternity doing goodly works. Or, if they had been sinners, the torments of Hell that was the fate of wicked boys would await them.

Lemuel decided to sooth their distress with words of uplifting piquancy, and that should stop their crying. "Some things cannot be undone and this is one of them, but our loving God must have needed you for special merit or he would not have called you. I'm sure that you have heard that God's ways are mysterious (they both nodded) but you should also know that He has a grand design for the world, and though we may not understand His plan, you must believe that everything He does is for the eventual good of all."

"Well for what He done to us kids I think that Sandy Claws should put lumps of coal and switches in his stockings."

Exasperated, Lemuel blurted out, "There isn't any Santa Claus! Whoever told you that is a liar. That's a fairy tale that parents tell their children to get them to obey so they'll be good, and then they reward them with presents at Christmas. The whole concept of Christmas is a remnant of paganism, and celebrating Christmas results in a sinful waste of valuable time." Regretting his impatience, Lemuel sank to his knees. This made his head on a level with theirs and he placed an arm over each boy's shoulder. "I'm sorry that I snapped at you." Then with a stern inflection, he lectured them. "You must never say anything like that again. It is being disrespectful to God and He is the creator of everything. If there were a Santa Claus, he would have been created by God, and we know that there isn't, so such stories are just fairy tales. Do you see?"

"Is there an Easter bunny?"

"No, that's just another fairy tale."

"Well...how about the tooth fairy? When my tooth came out I got money from the tooth fairy." The brown haired boy with green eyes showed Lemuel the gap as proof. "Under my pillow in the morning."

Lemuel shook his head and became very sad. What sort of parents did these children have to fill their heads with stories about false gods? Abominations. They had been raising them in heathen practices; thinly disguised images of Bacchus with a red suit, animal worship, letting them believe in pixie-like creatures. It was sacrilege. It was a clear violation of the first commandment, unless you were Jewish, and then it would be the second commandment, but if you were a Baptist, then the Jewish first commandment would be considered a preface...unless you were Episcopalian...and then... The green eyed boy stared at him curiously and his fern green eyes gave Lemuel a start. He imagined he saw Abigail in them and she was clucking her tongue and wagging her finger disapprovingly. He decided that explaining the Commandments to the boys would only confuse them, and he said, "Just trust me. It's wrong to believe those things. Get Esther to explain it to you."

Over the centuries he had actually spent very little time getting to know the mortals he dealt with. As with most of the angels, all of his contact with them was business. This was standard angel conduct because of the nature of the angel's duties: spreading plagues, causing fires to rain down, or the earth to open up swallowing wholesale lots of them, and so forth. If familiarity and fraternization were to occur they might loose their objectivity. To put the situation in earthly terms, it would be as though an IRS auditor was too familiar with the taxpayers. Familiarity can breed contempt on the part of the audited, or more dangerously, compassion on the part of the angel. So the angels maintain a professional distance.

With his mortality detail eminent, Lemuel wanted to learn more about mortals, and children were a reflection of their parents' customs, burlesqued perhaps, but on the whole, accurate. He hoped that he wouldn't be sent to the nation that these children were from. It was a land where idolatry and worshiping false gods was rampant. Demons were the only rational explanation: the whole nation must be overrun with demons. These boys may have been taken up in their youth to protect them from demonic possession. From their own lips he'd heard them admit to worshiping false gods.

Lemuel sat down on one of the boulders with the two boys facing him, and asked, "How did you come to be here?" He half expected to hear that they had been sacrifices in a Satanic ritual.

The question brought terrified wails and screams from the two young souls and after getting them calmed down enough to talk, they told him what had happened.

The green eyed boy spoke. "Oh God, it was horrible. It was the worst thing that had ever happened in our county. There was blood and guts everywhere. Some of the kid's innards were spilled out all around on the ground with them still trying to crawl away from those grizzlies. And those bears just drug 'em back and tore off their arms or their legs. And the blood was spattered everywhere."

Both boys were sobbing into their hands and Lemuel looked horrified. "Grizzlies? You mean bears did this to you? And you say there were other children killed? That is terrible!"

"There was forty-two of us killed that day. The other kids are all up here in this place som'mers. An I don't think they like it any better'n we do."

"Were you boys tormenting the bears? Is that why they attacked you? Bears defend their cubs. You boys weren't…"

"There warn't no cubs. We never seen those bears before. All of a sudden they dashed out and bit and chewed and slashed us."

The tow-headed boy, his large blue eyes teary pools, told the rest of the story: "A whole bunch of us kids was out hiking up near the spring that supplies water to the town. All us kids was from Bethel. It's a little ole town up in the high desert country, west of the Pecos. Water was scarce as furry toads and we had to get our water out'en an ole alky spring over to Jericho. T'warn't too bad. You got us'ta the salty tang it had. So while we was up there some of us was fishing. It was real good for fishing. This old coot with a long beard and a shiny dome, wearing a long robe, and carrying a big heavy stick an a big burlap sack full of sumpin over his shoulder was there. He come up to our spring and dumped the whole sack into it. Some of the bigger boys tried to warn him away; tole him it was the water supply for the whole town. But it didn't make no difference to him. He musta been loco. Crazy ole coot! Then he strode off muttering sumpin about the Lord."

"That sounds like he was spiteful about something. Did he have a grudge against the town?"

"We dunno. We never seen him afore. So we kids follied along behind him, saying sumpin like: 'Go up old bald head. Go up old bald head.' An he stopped dead in his tracks, an he raised that big heavy stick. We thought he was gonna hit us with it, the way he waved it around, but he shook it up at the sky and yelled sumpin about the Lord again. That's when those two bears came out of the woods and slashed and bit and chewed forty two of us to death."[75]

Feeling embarrassed, Lemuel's only comment was, "The Lord works in mysterious ways, but I'm sure you will understand eventually." But he thought, It must be because of that demon that I don't.

HOW THE GOOD TAILOR GOT TO HEAVEN

The green eyed boy said angrily, "We didn' do nothin bad, an we want to go home. This is a terrible place. Hit don't even get dark at bedtime." He made a disagreeable face and added in disgust, "An all we get to eat around here is this ole manna...yuck!" He pulled a handful from the pocket of his robe and threw it on the ground.

The tow-headed boy agreed. "Back home we ate freely from the garden. We had cucumbers and melons."

The other boy drew his tongue across his upper lip greedily, and added, "An we cud get fish from the brook. Boy they was good."

"I'd even like to see some leeks and onions," said the blond lad.

"Even garlic would be better than this stuff."[76] The green eyed boy said flatly, and pulled another handful of manna from his pocket and put it in Lemuel's hand for his decision.

Lemuel chewed on a big mouthful of manna and said, "It tastes the same as it always does. There's nothing wrong with it." But to be fair to the boys, Lemuel had no point of reference. He had never eaten anything else, nor had any of the other angels until they went on their mortality details.

Both boys were at an emotional nadir and Lemuel thought that a tour of some of the Heavenly mechanisms might raise their spirits. "Boys, I know something that I'll bet you're both eager to see. How would you like it if we flew over to the nature works? Wouldn't you like to see the proof that reveals the truth, the succession of works for which nature never smelted iron nor beat an anvil? Wouldn't that be fun?"

"Do we hafta?" they chorused wearily. "Esther already showed us that stuff."

"Oh. Well I know of another marvelous work and wonder that is even more fascinating. How would you like to see that very star which from the Earth seems the smallest, but from here would seem to be a moon." They both shook their heads.

"How about the mechanism that causes the motion that circles the cosmos fastest?"

"Esther already showed us those things a couple of times."

"Well, what would you like to see?"

The green eyed boy scratched his neck thoughtfully, and then peered out through the Rose of Sharon trees toward the building that was being constructed. It was the same one that Lemuel was inspecting when he discovered the boys. "We wanted to watch those workmen over there, but the overseer angel kept chasing us."

Lemuel took each boy by the hand and led them up onto the hill of dirt that was excavated for the foundation, and the three of them watched the workmen putting up the new office building.

Chapter 5

LEMUEL AND THE BOYS WATCHED THE CONSTRUCTION WORKers for nearly an hour. The carpenters were finishing another tier of staging for the masons and the laborers had shifted the gin pole into position so the heavy stone pieces could be hoisted into place. Lemuel accepted the boys' promises that they would return to their school and asked them to tell their teacher that he would like to see her when he completed his briefing session. He left and resumed his little walk.

A squad of souls on policing detail marched up Glory Road singing encomiums to the Lord: "Sound off/ Praise the Lord/ Sound off/ Praise the Lord/ One, Two, Three, Four/ Praise the Lord."

Lemuel stood at the polished jadestone curb and watched them pass. Their badger hair brooms with ebony wood handles, or silver shovels with teak handles, were all held at a precise forty-five degrees over their right shoulders. All but one that is. The last soul in the line was impudently tossing his manna into the air and catching it in his mouth like popcorn. A hard glance and a curt word from the angel shepherding this flock soon brought that soul back to proper form.

Their voices trailed off and Lemuel wondered what his job might be when he returned from his mortality detail. He hoped it would include some of the souls that he had led to salvation and then he could continue to be their pastor throughout eternity, or at least until he got promoted to archangel.

Across the golden cobblestone street was the office of the heavenly Income Recording Secretary (IRS). This bureau kept track of every mortal's worldly income and recorded whether the proper tithes[77] on that income had been given to the church. One needn't be too concerned about having a deficit when they enter the eternal, because they'll have ample opportunity to work off their debt once they arrive by putting in a little overtime.

Naturally there is no consumerism in Heaven. There are no hucksters or garish shops or malls to prey on those afflicted with self-indulgent greed. And there are no restaurants or quick food stands because the souls are fed on the food of the angels: manna. In Heaven all needs are freely provided so there is no, what we would think of as, a commercial district. But there is a "downtown" area and Lemuel was presently strolling through this neighborhood. It would approximate the Federal Triangle area in Washington, D.C., on a far grander scale, you understand. For example, the IRS building, across from Lemuel, was not a five-story, dingy, featureless building begrimed with gritty road dirt and pitted with acid rain and air pollution. It was a soaring fifty-story structure with gleaming alabaster walls and a cornice of English fluorite dentil with graceful plumes carved on their face, and inset with pearls of enormous price that created an egg and dart frieze all around the building. The fenestration are ogive arches inset with iridium cames, and quartz quarrels. Here and there, panes of topaz or ruby cast delightful colors onto the souls working at their desks inside. They are cognizant of ergonomics in Heaven, and the height of the desks were adjustable so that the soul working there could stand all day with minimal back strain. The souls working on the ledgers worked with traditional implements, quill pens, and permanent India ink, and they all soon learned to reproduce the meticulous script of Heaven and the language of God: Hebrew.

In Heaven one does not find those dehumanizing instruments of worldly technology like video display terminals or computers, but those devices are not needed when one has an eternity of six-day work weeks to accomplish their tasks. And with the eternal light there is no need for vision-destroying flourescent lights. The only near nod to modernity is the piped-in singing of the angel chorus. Speakers are placed all over Heaven so that one is never out of earshot of those glorious sounds.

There is a pair of huge bronze doors on the IRS building that are worth noting. They are easily thirty cubits high and seven cubits wide. This pair of doors are set into frames of Madagascar agate and swing effortlessly on jeweled hinges. They are embossed with figures that express some of the finest examples of the metal worker's craft. The images are in bas-relief and are relevant to the function of the office. The depiction on the right-hand door shows Joseph predicting what would happen to Egypt if the Pharaoh did not take the necessary preventive measures. Joseph's hand is upraised and he is talking into the Pharaoh's ear. He is showing the people starving in a terrible famine. All the granaries are shown as empty and all the horrors that would follow from that disaster. We know from the Bible that Joseph advised the Pharaoh to raise the people's taxes by 20 percent[78] (since the Egyptians did not use money; taxes were paid in kind, or with labor). Joseph advised Pharaoh to store their grain against that terrible time.

The Pharaoh was so impressed by Joseph's advice that he gave him the highest position in his administration[79]. As the Pharaoh's favorite, Joseph had immense power: the power of eminent domain over the people's property[80]; and he was given the daughter of the high priest of On (known as Heliopolis to the Greeks), for a wife[81]. We know that one Pharaoh was the monotheistic Pharaoh, and that he forced his belief onto the people. Wouldn't it be surprising to find out that Joseph had influenced the Pharaoh? Heliopolis was the center for that worship. It was like a Vatican City for the Sun god, Ra, so the husband of the daughter of the high priest would have had powerful spiritual influence as well. And then Joseph proceeded to collect the taxes.

On the other door there is another depiction of Joseph that shows the result of his tax policy. The people of Egypt all looked to be the same as on the other door, just as Joseph had predicted they would look. But now all the granaries are full, and the people are lined up and coming to Joseph on their bended knees. They seem to be signing something away. There's an inscription, written small: "There is not aught left in the sight of my lord but our bodies and our lands: wherefore shall we die before thine eyes, both we and our land? Buy us and our land for bread, and we and our lands will be servants unto Pharaoh; and give us seed that we may live and not die, that our land be not desolate."[82] There is another inscription. It is Joseph responding: "Behold I have bought you this day and your land for Pharaoh: lo, here is seed for you, and ye shall sow the land."[83]

Not all of the people living in Pharaoh's Egypt seem to be in misery and willing to sell themselves into slavery. One section of the panel shows some very prosperous people off in the land of Goshen. They are fatted with cattle and kine, and they all have men servants and women servants. They seem to be well off indeed.[84] They are Joseph's relatives: Jacob, a.k.a. Israel, and all of Joseph's brethren, and they multiplied exceedingly according to the will of the Lord.

All of this is well-known to those who regularly read their Bibles, and when they get to Heaven they should make a special effort to examine closely the fine workmanship. It is thrilling to see this pictorial of scripture so marvelously reproduced in bronze. The detail that the workers have been able to craft is breathtaking: the Pharaoh has his arm around Joseph's waist as he slips his ring of authority on Joseph's finger.[85] (He must have really thought a lot of Joseph. It's almost like a marriage ceremony.) The image of the Pharaoh shows a shortish, paunchy man with effeminately wide hips, and a long face with hollow cheeks and thick lips. He has a look of dissipation. Oddly enough he bears a strong resemblance to the tomb depiction of Akhenaton (the monotheistic pharaoh, born 1375 B.C.) who was reputed to have been very fond of his son-in-law, one Smenkhkare, whom the Egyptologists claimed had unknown antecedents. It's almost as though he appeared

HOW THE GOOD TAILOR GOT TO HEAVEN   59

from out of the desert. He was so fond of Smenkhkare that his beautiful wife, Nefertiti, got jealous, and taking her son with her, left him. But her departure did not seem to overly annoy Akhenaton who merely changed his in-law's name to Neferneferaton, showing that he thought Smekhkare was twice as beautiful as Nefertiti anyway. Nefer means beautiful in ancient Egyptian.

Obviously this sort of historical speculation is yellow journalism at its worst and should be left to those sordid weeklies sold at check-out counters, and the author must apologize to any serious Bible scholars.

However, the Bible does record that Joseph did not remain in this high position. And neither did his relatives. A new Pharaoh ascended the throne. (Probably Nefertiti's son: Tutankhamon. Note the different name endings: Tutankh-amon, and the father Akhen- aton, and Nefernefer- aton. Those were rival religious sects, Amon being the more ancient and traditional which included the whole pantheon of Egyptian gods; and Aton worshipers worshiped only the sun god, Ra. It was a monotheistic religion that excluded all the others.) The new Pharaoh restored the old gods. Also, the Bible uses an interesting choice of words regarding the incident. It was a pharaoh who, "knew not Joseph."[86] Tutankhamon was only nine years old at the time, and his mother was probably harboring a lot of scornful resentment over her rejection and she may have poisoned the boy's mind against Joseph.

Also, the Bible uses the term, "knew not Joseph," as in, "to know," in the Biblical sense. It makes one wonder if Potiphar's wife[87] was very homely, or if Joseph didn't care all that much for women. Perhaps the slaves that Joseph's brothers sold him to[88] taught him the gay way. He was a young virgin, as was shown by his coat of many colors,[89] and he brought a very high price: twenty pieces of silver. And where the Bible says that, "his bowels did yearn upon his brother"[90] seems to describe his tendencies quite graphically. We should remember that all this occurred before the law was handed down to Moses, which forbid this common practice. Otherwise, Joseph might not have been so gloriously enshrined.

But with the coronation of the new Pharaoh the children of Israel lost all their perquisites and were made slaves. It is one of God's little ironies. Since Joseph had enslaved the Egyptians, all that King Tut had to do was to make everyone in Egypt equal. "But God meant it unto good,"[91] as the last chapter of Genesis whimsically tells us.

Lemuel did not ponder any of these things and he barely looked in the direction of the IRS building. He had seen it many times before and he was accustomed to Heaven's grandeur, but the doors are great works of art, as is everything beyond the ninth celestial orb.

There was little chariot traffic on the road and few pedestrians. Lemuel did pass another probationer on his way to his mortality detail. He was dressed in a cheap, badly-tailored blue suit, and he carried a small suitcase and a cheap hardbound Bible. Lemuel wished him good luck, and asked him about the latest scuttlebutt. There was a rumor circulating through the ranks of angels that the higher orders had made an angel of a human soul, and Lemuel asked him if he knew anything about the rumor. Moreover, he'd heard that this phony angel was to be the catechist who instructed the real angels for their detail. "Positively shocking," Lemuel said.

The other angel looked surprised and assured Lemuel that someone was playing a sick joke on him. "Mortals don't have the intellects to be angels; they're definitely at the lower end of the bell curve. They are brighter than chimps, but very childish." He assured Lemuel that his instructor had been Tomas, all by himself, and the same angel who had been the instructor for centuries. He confided to Lemuel that the whole thing was a snap. Tomas just gave him a few friendly tips, his Bible, and a flask of the waters of life. He showed Lemuel the Bible. It was printed in Tibetan because the angel's post was Katmandu. He was eager to get there and start making converts. As he hurried away, Lemuel thought, Maybe they won't laugh at his cheap suit in Tibet.

The next building that Lemuel passed was a twin in size and construction to the IRS building, but it was named simply: Numbers. It would be comparable to our census bureau and it is where the names

HOW THE GOOD TAILOR GOT TO HEAVEN — 61

that are entered into the book of life are recorded. The great bronze doors on this building are of the same dimensions as on the IRS building, but the bas-relief images are different. The scene on one door shows a wrathful Lord moving David to number Israel.[92] The Lord and David are in the foreground at the base of the door, and with excellent perspective up the height of the panel are all the tribes of Israel. Their faces all have sorrowful expressions since to be numbered was to acknowledge subservience to authority. It was thought to be taking a particle of their free spirit from them, but they were a stiff-necked people.

Lemuel paused to watch two Muslim souls, one Shiite and one Sunni, as they went about their work oiling the great jeweled hinges on the doors. These Arabs happened to have been in the oil business when in the world and this was the only work available for souls with their MOS (Mortal Occupational Specialty). Many of the Muslims were soldiers in life and went directly into the armies of the Lord. But if Lemuel had not noticed them he would have never noticed a difference in the images on the two doors. It is odd how one may pass something a thousand times, and not notice something that is quite plainly there, and has been all along. He noticed that the image on the left-hand door did not show a wrathful Lord moving David to number Israel. Instead of the Lord it was Satan[93] who stood where the Lord stood on the other door and moved David to take the census. There he was, cloven hooves, arrowhead tail, horns, Van Dyke beard, and he was twisting his mustache and he had an evil leer on his face.

Lemuel rubbed his eyes in disbelief. He examined the images carefully. "That's wrong!" he muttered to himself, as he looked from one door to the other. This must be more doing of that demon Abigail. She must have bewitched me; cursed me with a spell that causes me to see contradictory visions. He turned from the doors and walked away hastily, as though he were being pursued.

Lemuel realized that he was wringing his hands and he forced himself to stop. He covered the distress that showed on his face with a false smile. He was only a few hours away from starting on his mission and he would need all the self-confidence that he could muster. Somehow that demon had managed to infuse contradiction into his mind. There was no counselor he could turn to. First loyalty of every angel is to the establishment, and they'd probably turn him in. If his catechist ever got wind of his dilemma, he'd probably report him and there would go his promotion. He'd have to remain in the BOQ (Before Ordination Quarters) for eternity. No monk's cell. No linen robes. No leather sandals. No bright nimbus to wear on his head. And no chance for promotion to a higher managerial position: archangel.

And what was it she said, no organization? Ha! She said that the demons weren't organized, and that they didn't care what the angels did to the mortals. She said they were indifferent to the whole religious thing. Well if that was true, why did she go to the trouble to befuddle my mind with these confusing and contradictory visions? I can imagine the grade she got on her performance rating chart for this bit of demonic treachery. It was probably an "excellent," with an "exceeds all standards" notation, and three stars. No, they wouldn't award stars; pitchforks probably. The expression on Lemuel's face changed from a plastic smile to sober thoughtfulness, and then he thought, I won't let her win. This is just temporary, like a head cold. It has to be. Whenever these perverse visions enter my head I'll just ignore them. I'll pretend that I don't see them.

Lemuel knew that the incident with the demon in King Jamesburg was a clear violation of the rules of disengagement. The treaty that gave the demons free run of the world had clearly stated that the demons were to allow the angels free passage to collect their souls; work miraculous visitations; and all the rest of their duties without fear of obstruction, possession, or witchcraft, until Armageddon. But he could not report the incident without risk of revealing his own collusion with Abigail in switching the tailors.

He squared his shoulders, determined to fight her and her whole evil empire alone if need be. He'd carry out his mission without denominational assistance if necessary. He'd show her his mettle.

HOW THE GOOD TAILOR GOT TO HEAVEN — 63

Lemuel was lost in these thoughts when a thundering roar intruded in his consciousness and startled him. He looked around and saw that he had walked all the way to the promontory that overlooks the valley where the Lord's legions were going on with their daily war games.

The higher powers spared no amount of effort to reproduce this battlefield to the exact dimensions of the earthly plains of Megeddo. Megeddo is the etymological root for the word Armageddon. The plains of Megeddo is where the final battle between good and evil will take place, and as we all know, the demons have free run of the world, they have access to the real battlefield, and they can carry out their maneuvers under actual conditions. Heaven's preplanning division decided that this might give them some slight edge on that day of battle, so they reproduced the whole battlefield in Heaven where the Lord's armies practice for the final battle. The area is exact to the last piece of rock and blade of grass.

In the vast valley spread out below, ten thousand chariots wheeled in battle formation. Great sinewy war horses, some red, some white, some speckled, and some, covered in bright armor with spikes affixed to their foreheads, were pulling the battle wagons. The hubs of the ivory-wheeled chariots had blades fixed to revolve and slice, and rip the limbs from the enemy, and these blades are serrated and razor sharp. The charioteers were expert Roman or Anatolian drivers, and their battle mates in the chariots with them were all muscular, seasoned, expert archers and swordsmen, and all were alert and battle ready. Another hundred thousand cavalry warriors mounted on swift Arabians charged the imaginary foe swishing burnished scimitars or leveling lances through the swirling dust. Here the Assyrian and the Crusader fought shoulder to shoulder against the common evil. Be they called demon or jinn, they would perish. The sons of Israel went in advance as spies and raiders, according to their own expertise. Behind the horses came ten hundred thousand of infantry, the captains and their fifties. The Roman squares and Greek phalanxes advanced afoot, urged on by screaming sergeants, and scores of shrill, clear clarion trumpets. The brilliant eternal light gleamed from polished armor, glittered on a wheatfield of waving pike staffs, and somberly illumed the thickly, spiked iron maces.

On a propitious ridge with an enfilading command of the scene stood the campaign tents of the seraphim. Their tents were of red and saffron brocaded silk with silver poles and golden tie lines that were tasseled and fringed. The entryways of the tents were covered with a diaphanous silk edged with lace, now drawn up and tied with purple sashes. Seated on campaign chairs in front of the tents, with their attendant angels standing at parade rest behind them, were some of the seraphim in their finely embroidered robes and bejeweled miters. They were sketching battle plans in the dirt for the day's maneuvers with their crosiers. Their nimbuses shone spectacularly. In an arc behind the command center stood a row of platinum flag poles with fluttering pennons of blue, green, and maroon, and bearing the crests of the battle groups of the souls that were in the field that day.

On another ridge at the other end of the valley stood the encampment of the enemy. Not really, no demons or sinners are ever permitted beyond the ninth celestial orb, but it was erected as a grim reminder of the evil empire's forces that these holy warriors would face in the battle of Armageddon. The enemy in the evil camp had slouching black leathern tents with tarnished brass center poles and with cressets of burning brimstone, and the whole ridge was bleak in brume shrouded ominousness.

Lemuel knew that this was only a small portion of the Lord's army, but it was impressive even with these reduced numbers. He assumed that the rest were practicing close order drill or attending to some of the many important duties that occupy a large standing army. There was a rotation system so all the forces were ready for battle.

A few skeptics might question the wisdom of Saracen, and Christian; Greek and Turk; Croat and Serb; Pole and Russian; Jew and Arab; Baptist and Catholic; being comrades in arms, but in Heaven all these minor differences disappear once they understand that they all worship the same God and that they are all united in the defeat of their common enemy—Satan and his evil empire. Logically, there are no insurmountable problems in getting the lion to lie down with the lamb, given enough training and the constant oversight by the marines.

For those who have chosen the path of Islam to Allah, or God, there is one small deviation from their vision of paradise. It is a slight delay and it will be complied with right after the final battle between good and evil. Originally Allah, or God, created the houris to minister to the faithful who had sacrificed all for Allah.

When the angel Mohammed was on his mortality detail, his conversion work among the idolatrous Ishmaelites was so astounding that he was instantly promoted to cherub. Shortly after his return, the houris of the Moslem section of Paradise came to him complaining that the souls of the faithful, to whom they had been assigned, had worked so hard every day that they were exhausted and they just wanted to sleep when their shifts ended. The houris were being ignored and they wanted Mohammed to do something for them. When he explained the problem to the authorities, they decided that to silence their clamor it would be best to bring them into Thelassar and have them attend to the higher orders. The houri population was so large there would have been an enormous surplus, so they were allotted according to the angel's rank. Mohammed was assigned twenty-two and one half times the promised number. He pointed out that Solomon, who was a mere mortal, had nine hundred wives when he was in the world and he thought that he should have an equal number of houris. As there was a lot of the sloe-eyed, doe-eyed beauties to go around. All the cherubim were given nine hundred houris, the seraphim were given nine hundred and ninety-nine each, and the lower ranks were assigned lesser quantities down to the principalities who, in keeping with their basically austere natures, took the number that was to be allotted to ordinary souls: forty. On occasion, if an archangel has done something exceptional, they are given the use of an houri, from the houri pool, for a brief period of time. The Archangel Gabriel, because of his essential role in bringing down the holy word to Mohammed, was assigned ten permanent houris. However, he has not been promoted because he forgot to number the pages, and so, there is some question about the proper sequential order of the verses in the Koran.

* * *

At that moment, the hierarchical chain of command and their problems were far from Lemuel's mind. His immediate concern was how to get out of his probation. The raw power of the armies that he saw spread out across the plain beneath him caused a trill of pride. It was reassuring to know that he was part of the mightiest organization in this cosmos. There's no way the forces of evil can defeat our mighty forces of good. We will win and those crafty, sly demons will have to surrender their evil grip on the mortals. We'll get all the souls. Not one soul will be left to the evil empire. If Abigail could see all this power she'd fall on her knees before me and beg me to save her. She'll beg to join our side.' He indulged in a brief mental vision of that scene when a momentary image of her smile destroyed the savor of his envisioned gloating. He angrily shook his fists alongside of his head and with growling anguish he cried, "Arrgh! Can't she let me alone inside of my own visions?"

He looked around hastily to see if he'd been observed in his guilty temper tantrum. There were only two ordinary souls. One soul was busily sweeping the roadway, and coming from the other direction, another soul was dusting the chalcedony benches. Lemuel restored the plastic smile to his face and looked carefully at the two souls to see if he could recognize them. It was hard to distinguish species now that the probationary angels dressed like ordinary souls. He knew that the angels never performed menial labor, but was afraid that they might have been a couple of novitiates spying on him. Although he hated the expression, he thought it apt. Some of his fellow novices were known to "suck up" to the angels by informing on their peers. Lemuel had always wondered how the front office had gotten wind of that clandestine meeting about the seniority issue. He had suspected Winfred, one of his bunk mates, of being an agent provocateur.

Some novitiate had complained aloud that seniority in grade should

HOW THE GOOD TAILOR GOT TO HEAVEN — 67

count toward promotion. Some of the others agreed and there was a lot of dissension. Incendiary trigger words like "fair play," "earned advancement through service," and "loyalty is a two-way street" were uttered. A detachment of marines besieged the barracks and rounded up the rebels. Although he took no part with the complainers, Lemuel was also taken into custody. The whole probationary platoon was made to stand at attention on the parade ground for three days while the parable about the laborers in the vineyard was read to them. The owner of the vineyard had paid each laborer a penny no matter how long they had worked.[94] It's the parable that ends with the words "Is thine eye evil, because I am good? Is it not lawful for me to do what I will with mine own? So the last shall be first, and the first last: for many are called but few are chosen." It was read to them until they could recite it by heart. So, ever since that episode, Lemuel was always cautious of his behavior, even around ordinary mortal souls, because now that they all wore the same muslin robes one could not easily distinguish them from probationer angels at a distance.

As the two came closer Lemuel judged by their vapid faces that they were just ordinary souls. The two souls drew abreast of each other, paused in their work, and exchanged greeting smiles. Although he had not intended to snoop, he overheard their brief conversation.

The male soul had been sweeping the dust of the road into piles along the jade guttering where it would be picked up by a follow-up crew and replaced back onto the battlefield below. He leaned on the teak handle of his push broom and said, "They're sure kicking up a lot of dust today." This soul was Isaac, the son of Abraham.

The other soul, a female, stood with her feather duster held at her hip. It was a wonderful feather duster; a feather duster anyone would be proud to use, made of ostrich plumes with a golden handle. She looked in the direction of the Lord's army and she spat. She followed that filthy demonstration with a bitter comment. "Those morons down there; that's all they're good for—creating a cloud of dust." She cleared a larger gobbet of mucus from her throat and spat toward the battlefield again. "I'll bet my father is down there in the middle of that bedlam having a great old time. When I called them morons, I was upgrading his intellect. He wouldn't make a moron's apprentice."

"Here, here! Just what do you mean by that disrespectful outburst," Lemuel sputtered.

"I thought it was obvious what I meant!"

"That's insubordination! Showing disrespect to your male parent breaks one of the commandments. (He wasn't sure which one, but that wasn't the point.) And making disparaging remarks about the Lord's mighty army is conduct unbecoming a saved soul. That sort of behavior borders on treason! Unless you apologize, and get down on your knees this very minute and beg the Lord's forgiveness, I'll have to report to your superiors, and make a formal report to the head office. It will go down on your permanent record."

She waved the duster in figure eights at Lemuel, and sneered, "Well, la, de, da, to you too buddy."

Isaac dropped his broom and held her arms down to her side as he pleaded with Lemuel, "Please don't report her. She didn't know your rank, sir. Honest, she thought you were just another ordinary soul. She didn't notice your halo with all this dust around."

Lemuel stiffened at the personal insult, mistaking him for an ordinary soul, though he realized the mistake was unintentional. He decided to let the slur pass, but not without straightening out this female soul's attitude. He said very sternly, "Those warriors are training for your protection. The higher powers have spared no effort to assure your safety. They've built this training field so our troops cannot be ambushed somewhere on the real battlefield and if they raise up a little dust, it's to keep us all secure. The price of freedom is eternal vigilance. We must be prepared for that final battle against the evil empire which is the focus of all evil."

"My, my, my! Did the higher powers get many callouses building it?" Her dark brown eyes flashed insolently.

"The least you can do is to clean up after our freedom fighters, and

HOW THE GOOD TAILOR GOT TO HEAVEN —⚘— 69

do it without complaining about things that you don't understand," Lemuel snapped back, and he continued ominously, "Would you have the evil empire win? Would you want the demons to conquer Heaven? They'd cast your body onto their fiery altar and you'd be a burnt offering to Satan. They'd enslave you. They'd force you to live out eternity in a hell of their design."

She gave Lemuel a fearsome glare. She took his elbow, led him near the edge of the drop off, and peered intently at the army below. After a few minutes search, she pointed to a soul off in the distance. "Do you see that slope browed, poor excuse for a pea brained ape, that miserable son of a whore[95], wearing a general's suit? He's over there, leading that band of raiders."

Lemuel looked in the direction she pointed and after a few moments saw who she meant, and said, "Why yes, that's Jephthah. I know him well. Surely you can't be directing your invective at him. It was because of his excellent leadership, and faith in our Lord, that we prevailed over the Ammonites. The Ammonites refused to proffer the proper hospitality to the Lord's chosen people when they entered the land that the Lord had given them. Oh yes, I remember."

Lemuel tugged at his ear, and recollected, "I was an evil angel[96] in those days, and I went in with the troops. That's where the Bible says the spirit of the Lord came upon Jephthah[97]. That was me. I was that spirit. Whomsoever the Lord our God shall drive out before us, them will we possess.[98] Things were going well for the Israelites. We'd passed over Gilead and Manassah, and over Mizpeh of Gilead already, and then we got to the borders of Ammon and Jephthah vowed to take them too. They had rudely ignored his messenger and refused to surrender to him. When Jephthah saw how rude they were, he drew off to the side and communed once more with the Lord. He told the men that he had spoken to the Lord and had made a deal with him. It was something about a fitting sacrifice and that the men should renew their efforts and the Lord would not let them down. So more avenging angels were dispatched to the scene. Jephthah led the charge just as you see him doing now."

Lemuel swung his arm in an upper cut motion. "Boy! We gave 'em the old what's for. From Aroer to Minnith with very great slaughter, and the cities of the plain were delivered into the hands of the children of Israel."

Her face distorted with rage and anguish. With tears rolling down her cheeks, the soul attacked Lemuel with both of her fists pommeling his chest. Isaac pulled her away and guided her tear-stained face to his shoulder. "She blames you for it you know. I'm sorry, but she does. Both you and the Lord."

Lemuel was shocked. "Blames me for what? It was a great victory." It was Lemuel's smoothest running job. Almost too easy.

She turned away from Isaac's shoulder and spat at Lemuel. Hissing like an angry cat, she said, "Yeah, at my expense."

An outburst like that can't happen in Heaven, this sort of thing is unheard of, Lemuel thought. Everything seems to be going wrong for me today. What is the matter? It must be that blasted demon. This poor soul is so distressed that only demons can be responsible. He searched his memory of those glorious conquests with Jephthah. Hum, she hates her father and blames me and the Lord. Strange. Then he started to remember some of the less important details, like the deal Jephthah made with the Lord.

He said to her, "Oh come on now. I know that it was a rash thing to promise, but didn't they send word to your father later on to release him from the deal?"

"Oh, you mean at the last minute. Like when I was all trussed up on the altar for sacrifices and my father, Abraham, was about to take my life like the Lord commanded? And at the last moment the Lord accepted the ram to be sacrificed, instead of sacrificing me?"[99] Isaac asked. His eyes flashed with hatred and he continued, "No, there was no substitute sheep for her."

Lemuel stuttered and sputtered. He snorted with a self-effacing cough and then waved his hand as though waving off a disagreeable odor, and said, "That can't be. No way is that possible. If that were the case, then you're accusing the Lord of allowing a human sacrifice, a young maiden, like some barbaric savage god. That is no better than Baal, or Molech, or Chemosh?"

There was no reply except their eyes briefly looked into Lemuel's face, and then down at the ground.

"Well I don't believe it. Jephthah must have acted too hastily. The Lord probably didn't have enough time to stay your father's hand. Agamemnon sacrificed his daughter, Iphigenia, to his pagan god so his armies could prevail over Troy, but our God would never allow His altar to be stained with human blood."

"Well, God had plenty of time if he wanted to prevent it. My friends and I went up into the mountain and cried together for two months."[100]

Lemuel was perplexed. "Two months? That was more time than it took Him to write the law of the Ten Commandments on the stone tablets. He created the world and all therein in six days. I don't believe it."

"He didn't need any time if he wanted to prevent it. He's the Almighty, isn't he? And He knew what would happen. He's all knowing, isn't He? No, He knew what would happen. He wanted it to happen, and I was sacrificed at the hand of my father, my life snuffed out in a searing fire, my young virgin body was spread out and tied to the horns of the altar like a sacrificial lamb. My young virgin flesh must have made a savory aroma to please the Lord." She was beginning to become hysterical. "Did the priests come and eat my charred flesh with their dirty greasy fingers? Did they tear my virgin flesh from my bones with their ritually clean and kosher flesh hooks? Isn't that what they do with sacrificial lambs?" She was sobbing uncontrollably and Isaac pulled her head down onto his shoulder again to muffle her crying and to comfort her.

Lemuel let his hands drop helplessly to his side and he shook his head. He muttered, "Virgin, virgin, virgin. She mentioned that at least three or four times. Is sexual intercourse all these humans ever think about?"

He walked away shaking his head. "And she blames me. How was it my fault? When I put that idea into Jephthah's head I didn't expect him to actually sacrifice his own daughter. It wasn't my fault. Where was her guardian angel? It was his fault. Hadn't he read the oath board? It must have been posted on the oath bulletin board. Oaths are always posted until they're fulfilled. Her guardian angel should have sent a goat or a chicken out ahead of her. When I was a guardian I always read every one of those notices, all the recent ones anyway. He should have taken her case up before the appeals board.

"Furthermore, can't these mortals ever learn that God's ways are mysterious? The fight against the forces of evil is not an easy one to be fought without sacrifice." Lemuel's thoughts continued in this vein until he heard the carillon chiming the hour.

"Gosh, I'm nearly late. I'll have to dash." As he loped toward shining spires of Thelassar, he thought, At least the rumor about making an ordinary soul an angel wasn't true. I'll have a real angel as my instructor, and what was his name? Oh yeah, Tomas.

Chapter 6

LEMUEL HEADED TOWARD THE CITY WHERE THE SONS OF Eden dwelt long before. As he neared the environs of the palace wherein was the apogee of all goodness; the glorious citadel upon the hill; the measure of all true worthiness; the veritable pinnacle of perfection, Lemuel quit his ungainly galloping and proceeded at a stately pace as befits an angel. He was too near promotion to risk any more demerits on his permanent record.

All Heaven is hallowed, but the area surrounding Thelassar is even more so. It is a restricted zone. All conversation must be held in softly modulated tones. Genteel laughter is permitted, but to be on the safe side, smiles that show no molars are preferred. The glorious tones from the loudspeakers broadcasting the Heavenly angel chorus have been muted. No chariot traffic or flying is permitted within three miles of the high walls which enclose the compound, and over flights are strictly prohibited. That infraction would bring any angel severe and immediate punishment.

Lemuel stepped as carefully as he could, but his rope sandals creaked embarrassingly with each step and he squeezed his lips in a firm thin line. His hands were clasped over his stomach with his fingers interlaced and his index fingers steepled. He combed his fingers through his hair to straighten it, if it had been mussed during his jog, and then continued as before with his head bent forward submissively.

His course took him past the wall surrounding the sacred compound. It was twelve cubits high and the top was decorated with sharp spikes made of diamonds, emeralds, and rubies, which glinted wonderfully in the eternal light. The sidewalk, over which he passed, was made of large onyx and alabaster squares laid in a checkerboard pattern between the base of the wall and the jade curbing. The wall itself, where one might expect to see brick or ashlar stone if this were on earth, was carved with high relief images of cunning design and craftsmanship. The scenes were reminders of why the wall was placed there. They were of the entire period before the flood.

In those early days, "the sons of God saw the daughters of men that they were fair; and they took them wives of all which they chose, and they came in unto the daughters of men, and they bare children to them." And God saw that His sons were drinking from the fountain of the waters of life, and committing evils with the daughters of men: "And God saw that the wickedness of man was great in the earth, and that every imagination of the thoughts of his heart was only evil continually."[101] He built the wall around the sacred garden with its miraculous fountain to prevent unauthorized angelic access to the waters of life and to prevent any further corruption of the angels. The world was left to the demons and the mortals. The carvings on the wall were of the evil acts that men, and their daughters, were doing with the angels before God exterminated all mankind, except Noah and his family, with the flood.

They were graphic reminders for the angels of the worldly pitfalls that awaited them on their details to the mortal earth. Lemuel was shocked by some of the antics his brother angels had committed. The pornographic carvings in Khajuraho, India, adorning the walls of the temple of the Kaula sect, both inside and outside of the temple, and which show the apsarases and devadassis engaged in every sort of sinful sexual act possible, would be a crude, but representative, example of the carvings that Lemuel was passing. He stared at only a few, and thought, And that is the sort of disgusting thing that Jephthah's daughter was bewailing having missed? The final panel of the wall showed the flood washing out all the evil, with everyone drowning, and Noah riding triumphantly atop the waves.

At the gateway to the glorious garden, with the mystical waters, cherubim guarded the entrance with flaming swords[102]. They checked his stenciled orders and they asked him to say the word, "Shibboleth."[103] Disoriented by the strange request, he paused, and one cherub seemed to be gauging the distance to Lemuel's neck for a swing with his flaming sword, but he pronounced the word correctly and they let him enter. Inside the garden walls was a paradise breathtakingly luxuriant: the flowers were profuse; the trees bore golden fruit; babbling brooks flowed through verdant meadows; and all was meticulously tended. This garden celebrated the Lord's greatest creation (after the immortal soul)—life itself. Although the eternal light was undiminished, it seemed gentler here, absorbed by the lush greenery. The very air seemed fresher. The walkways were not hard paving such as in the rest of Heaven, but seemed slightly resilient, and Lemuel noticed that it was made of pea-sized golden nuggets. As seen through a mortal's eyes, if a superlative beyond paradise were possible to express, it would be this garden.

This Eden impressed even Lemuel, whose mind was usually focused on the higher truths. He took a deep satisfied breath, and thought, So this is what God intended for man on earth? How could they have been so foolish as to lose all this? And for what? Knowledge![104] Of what use is knowledge compared to obedience to the loving God who made them, and the chance to pass their lives in this lovely idyll.

Lemuel noticed that paradise was not lost for all time for all mortal souls. There were many souls that, having led exemplary obedient lives, or performed outstanding services for God, had regained this Eden. They were there by the hundreds doing their chores as God had intended for them: "And the Lord God took the man, and put him into the garden of Eden to dress it and to keep it."[105] Lemuel could see them going about their chores of dressing and keeping it. Some of the souls had managed to work up quite a sweat working with their platinum spading forks and hand cultivators.

To Lemuel's right was a large standing billboard with an exquisite mosaic made of sardonyx, jasper, peridot, opal, emerald, tourmaline, jade, and other precious gems that showed a map of the garden. An arrow made of ruby pointed to one of the winding paths on the map, and seed pearls spelled out: "You are here." He studied the map of the garden. All the points of interest were labeled, and he saw that his way was up toward Lenox Avenue, where the higher orders of angels reside. While he stood there a wizened and bent old soul, carrying a silver rake with an ebony handle, approached and smoothed the few golden nuggets on the walkway that Lemuel had disturbed as he walked.

He could see that Lemuel was trying to memorize the turnings toward his destination, and offered, "You're going to meet with your catechist, right? I'll guide you."

"Oh, as Virgil guided Dante?"

"No. Like a yardman who has been assigned to straighten up this path after you walk over it. But I'll be glad to show you the points of interest when we pass them."

As they proceeded, Lemuel learned the soul's name was John d'Arc, and that he was the great philanthropist who, when in the world, had given a shiny dime to every needy person that he met. God blessed his generosity and awarded him his place in Eden where he rakes the golden nuggets of the walkway into their proper place. John d'Arc named and pointed out some of the other souls who had been blessed with similar rewards. Out in the middle of a vast expanse of American beauty roses was Joseph Armack who spent his time weeding out the tares, and over in a vast bed of poppies was Saint John the Divider who spent his time separating the good flowers from the bad on either side of the seventeenth parallel. Lemuel paused to examine the flowers, but to his untrained eye they looked alike. However, Saint John knew the good

HOW THE GOOD TAILOR GOT TO HEAVEN

from the bad. One recent arrival was William Kay See, who carried water in a golden water bucket for the holiest of holies behind the veil; and there were some old timers such as Old Hickory whose multifarious deeds ranged from winning battles after the war was over, to preserving the sacred unseen hand of the money lenders, to ousting the almost heathen red savages from the eastern territories they had always occupied. So diverse was this truly renaissance soul that he was kept busy everywhere. The roll call of goodness was too long to list here, but there was a rare instance of two Mathers, of the Boston Mathers, being rewarded. However, Cotton Mather, of Salem fame, was not, since he had been an angel on mortality detail. John d'Are implied that influence had been used to get Richard and Increase into Eden, but Lemuel doubted that.

Celebrities of Biblical status, after the flood, were accorded higher honors than merely being permitted to "dress and to keep" this Eden. Statues that recreated, and commemorated for all time, these heros' likenesses in their most heroic moments were raised in their honor. The renowned mortal was reproduced in gold, or rare pure white onyx, or quartz. Those participants assisting the deed, if any, were of silver, common marble or other less valuable material; the villains and blasphemers were cast of base metals such as iron, bronze or antimony, or they were sculpted of common black granite or ebony wood. All of the statues were life-sized and crafted with meticulous attention to detail. Fingernails were made of nacre, teeth of ivory, and eyes of ivory inlaid with irises of precious stones that matched the hero's color perfectly. The detail was finely done and their clothes were so perfect one could see the stitching and the weave of the fabric. It was as though real live people were frozen there.

Lemuel paused at one of the first tableaus. It was of Judith and Holofernes, and Lemuel thought it was very artistic the way the artisan had placed a few ruby droplets of blood to glisten on the bag that Judith was stuffing Holofernes' severed head into. John d'Are snorted, "She don't belong here. Tain't part of the real Bible: 'ts pocraphal!"

Lemuel let the comment pass as the opinion of a compulsive grouch who saw schemes everywhere. Lemuel studied the group carefully. He seemed to be looking for something, and then he asked, "Where's her guardian angel? She wouldn't have been able to cut his head off if her guardian angel hadn't gotten Holofernes to drink too much."

John d'Are cackled, "Heh heh heh! There ain't no angels honored here. This garden is a memorial to humans, an' none of you is counted as being human." He stared up at Lemuel through his bushy eyebrows, and on his face was the kind of half-concealed smirk that a groom would have for an earl who had just been unhorsed into a hog wallow.

Lemuel was startled by John's impertinence, and he shot back, "I'll be alive in a few hours and when I come back from my detail, I'll be made a full angel." Then he added with smug superiority, "And that's something you'll never be." He added as a threatening joke, "Maybe I'll request you for my personal servant when I come back."

John d'Are nodded slowly, and wearing a sly smile that means secret knowledge, he cackled, "You got a surprise coming, mister almost an angel."

His knowing leer puzzled Lemuel and he strode away passing more memorial statues. He barely looked at the memorial tableau of Joshua standing atop a grassy knoll in the midst of his warriors slaughtering the inhabitants of Jericho, or was it Ai, or Hebron, or perhaps it was Judah. The floral lettering of lavender phlox at the base of the exhibit did not say which people were being slaughtered, only that: "Joshua destroyed all that breathed as the Lord commanded."[106] Next was Sampson slaying a thousand Philistines with the jawbone of an ass[107]; and then the commemorative statue to Adino who slew eight hundred with his spear[108]. At the statue of Shamgar who killed six hundred with an ox goad[109] he paused, put his hands on his hips and muttered, "Where would any of them be without the assistance of us angels?"

At the statue of Moses, dressed in his royal finery, slaying an Egyptian for smiting a Jew[110]; he stopped and asked rhetorically, "What's so great about that? Just one more ordinary murder as far as I can tell, and his own people turned on him and he ran off like a coward. Why didn't they show him receiving the Commandments? This isn't heroic…Bah!" He waved his hand at the exhibit in disgust.

At the scene where Jael had lured Sisera into her tent, lulled the fugitive to sleep with soft words and milk and honey, then drove a tent nail through his head with a hammer and pinned his skull to the floor of her tent[111], he turned to John d'Are, held his hand toward the display, and asked, "Do you think that's the sort of thing that ought to be glorified?"

"Why yes. That's proper scripture, so it is not like Judith. That there's real inerrant King James version. From Judges I believe."

These ordinary souls are hopeless. And they all stick up for one another. Let one of them do something very ordinary and they praise it to the heavens. I guess it's like the pig that played checkers. It wasn't that he played well, but it was amazing that he did it at all. With these thoughts churning in his mind, Lemuel indicated a group of statues that raised the bile to his throat. It was a memorial glorifying Rahab. "A common whore," he muttered in disapproving undertones.

This group of statues showed Rahab of Jericho peering around the partially open door of her apartment telling the king's men that she had entertained two men earlier, "There came men unto me, but I wist not whence they were."[112] The door opened through a wall and from the side where Lemuel stood, all that was visible were the king's men and Rahab. Only her head, an arm, and one bare shoulder was exposed. She seemed to have caught her breath in surprise. The king's men were trying to see beyond her into her room, but she would not let them. Lemuel looked around the wall into Rahab's room and there were Joshua's men, completely naked, as was Rahab. Behind her, one man crouched by the wall and was partially covered with reeds. He had reached up with his fingers and poked into the crease of her buttocks, giving her what is commonly called a goose, which explained the surprise on her face. The other was lying under her bed stifling a laugh with his hand. At a table off to the side were Rahab's father and mother, and her brethren, all of whom appeared to be delighted by her deception.

Lemuel spun about, and stamping away, exclaimed, "What a lovely maid! Just wonderful! Um! Some heroine! Some family!"

"Hey there! Stop scattering the pebbles! I got to straighten 'em up," John d'Are shouted after him.

Lemuel turned, and between clenched teeth said, "It was an angel that brought down the walls of Jericho, a high ranking angel who appeared as a captain of the Lord's hosts.[113] The angel told Joshua how to bring the walls down. He told him to have seven priests walk around the walls seven times blowing on seven ram's horns; that's what he told him; and the walls will come tumbling down! That's what Joshua did, and that's how the walls came down.[114] That whore, and the so-called spies, had nothing to do with it, absolutely nothing. It was the angels that did it! You human souls will stretch any incident for a little fame and glory."

John d'Are shrugged. "The Bible says she provided an important service, she hid the spies."

"Spies? What did they spy on? More likely they were a couple of soldiers who decided to go AWOL and sneaked into town to visit a whorehouse. Then they made up that story about being spies so Joshua wouldn't punish them."

"You don't have a very high opinion of us human souls, do you, mister almost an angel? Yep, you got a real surprise coming."

Lemuel walked by the rest of the tableaus and barely gave them a glance. He thought that most of their acts weren't any different from what was shown outside the walls, the pornographic abominations that occurred before the flood. There was Lot having intercourse with his daughters;[115] Tamar playing the harlot with her father-in-law;[116] The adulteress whom Jesus had defended,[117] and her paramour. The woman of the well with her sequence of five husbands;[118] Joab slipped his knife beneath the fifth rib of several people,[119] and slaughtered the inhabitants of several cities, as the captain of all David's hosts.

David himself led the Jews against Rabbah, and he took their king's crown and placed it on his own head, and they spoiled the city; and then:

"They brought forth the people and put them under saws, and under harrows of iron, and under axes of iron, and made them pass through the brickkiln: and thus did he unto all the cities of the children of Ammon."[120] Lemuel pointed to the brickkiln and asked, "Are those gas chambers?"

John d'Are quickly assured him, "Oh no, there wasn't any gas then. That's a brick kiln."

"Sex and violence. Sex and violence. Assassination and genocide; don't you humans want to immortalize the refined arts and the humbler joys of life? Where's your compassion and your love for others? Where is your service to the Lord?"

"Shall man be above his master? Don't the Bible tell us that: 'It is enough for the disciple to be as his master, and the servant as his lord.'[121] And as you said youself, 'You angels of the Lord deserve a lot of the credit.' Now here's an example of man's humility right over here. A little humility that the Lord has promised. This is the yet to come section."

John d'Are led Lemuel to another grouping. The group of statues showed dozens of mortals lying in fawning prostration before several upstanding and pride-filled people. At first Lemuel thought they were ordinary souls and angels, but the golden lettering inlaid into a black onyx tablet proclaimed, "It shall come to pass that men of all nations shall take hold of the skirt of a Jew, saying, 'We will go with you: for we have heard that God is with you.'[122] John d'Are said sarcastically, "It's from Zechariah. Now ain't those gentiles being humble enough for you? An over here, ain't this service enough for you?"

This tableau was of several well-fed, richly clothed people lying on downy cushions beneath an arbor. They were dining on rare fruits and drinking from goblets brimming with nectar. The scene looked like a sumptuous feast out of the Arabian nights. They were being attended by meekly bowing servants, and beyond the arbor other servants attended flocks, pushed plows and dressed vineyards. The engraved placard read: "Ye shall eat the riches of the gentiles, and in their glory shall ye boast yourselves. And ye shall have double because the gentiles shamed you."[123]

A concerned tremor crept into Lemuel's voice. "When's this supposed to happen, this prophesy; this promise of things yet to be?"

"Worried about your mortality detail, ain't you? What if it happens before you saved your ten thousand souls?" John d'Are said sadistically, and shrugged. "I dunno when…the millennium mehbe? I think that tailor you brought in might have…"

"How did you know about that?"

"Was he Jewish?"

"How should I know? And how did you know about the tailor? You're just a low ordinary soul—a yard man!"

John d'Are tapped his finger alongside of his eye and said, "Tain't only the Lord is got eyes every place. All us low ordinary souls got eyes too, an there's lots of us, an we see things. Heh Heh. Yep, you got a surprise coming, mister almost an angel."

Beads of perspiration began to break out on Lemuel's forehead and under his arms he could feel rivulets run down his rib cage. He bent to wipe his forehead with his robe and thought, Don't let him see you sweat. That's what he wants. He's just a jealous, spiteful, old, ordinary soul. He doesn't know anything. He raised his head imperiously and strode away; but his mind started calculating. The World was created four thousand and four years before Christ was born, and then there was the first millennium, and another year would make the second millennium…Oh God! Nineteen ninety-nine! And I'll be on my mortality detail!'

Chapter 7

"AT LAST," LEMUEL SIGHED. HE HAD ARRIVED AT HIS DESTINAtion, the fountain in the foreyard of the palace; the fountain where the living waters flow. This fountainhead of the river of life where the waters streamed off into the four mystical directions: down jewel lined beds to form the sacred streams named Pison, Gihon, Hiddekel, and Euphrates[124]. The magical water, silvery and slippery with life, coursed from four outlets carved into a low basin a hundred cubits in breadth, and nearly three hundred fifteen cubits in circumference, made of highly polished, iridescent azurite. The cerulean stone basin was shot through with flecks of gold, forming star clusters, galaxies and comets. The low rim of the basin was wide and seemed to extend an invitation to sit, but when Lemuel neared a Swiss guard with a pike staff warned him away with a fierce look. "Get back! You must be on solid soil to partake of life." Then he lowered his weapon threateningly. Lemuel remained standing. John d'Are raked the golden nuggets back in place and hissed, "Stop being so nervous. You're mussing up my walkway."

Lemuel ignored him. This is it. The big moment. The other angel said it would be a snap. He said Tomas gave you few words of encouragement, your Bible, and a flask of living water. I'll soon be alive.

Long heavy minutes passed. Each moment seemed to be laden more heavily with dread than the last. The carillon chimed; the catechist was late. Lemuel had been on time, several minutes early in fact. He began to think something was wrong. John d'Are's insubordinate needling, and those monuments of Biblical heroes, made him uncomfortable. "Why doesn't he come? What's the matter?" he muttered.

"It's an old management trick. Don't you know anything?" John d'Are said in a hoarse whisper. "When I was alive, I pulled it all the time. I was a big boss then."

Lemuel looked at him quizzically, and John d'Are explained. "The boss makes you wait long enough to test your trepidation. It is never so long as to bring on truculence which might cause retaliatory feelings of hostility, but sufficiently long to make you aware of your humble position within the order of things. Understand?"

Lemuel was surprised. Had he heard that speech from this yard man, who was a mere mortal soul? d'Are said, "Close your mouth and don't look up. They're watching us from one the windows in the palace. If you ever do get to be an angel, you'll be in a minor leadership role. In order to be a good leader you have to be a good follower and never question your bosses' actions. They're testing your nerve. Don't look like it bothers you. Look around and act like you're interested in these marvels. They're intended to impress, so be impressed."

Lemuel didn't believe John d'Are, but he didn't want to be seen having a conversation with an ordinary soul, and he replied while seeming to study the fountain in the basin, "They wouldn't be that childish."

* * *

A fountain stood at the very center of the reservoir of life. It was a huge hemisphere of green malachite, quarried in the heart of darkest Africa. It had been compounded with diamond dust and it was as flawless as the finest telescope mirror. This dark green basin was ten cubits across and five cubits in depth, and thirty cubits in circumference[125] and it had the thickness of a hand breadth. The brim was unbroken by any imperfection, and it was so perfectly level that the waters cascaded in a single thin sheet all around its perimeter. It was as though clearest glass had come alive and turned into foam in the larger body of water into which it flowed.

This basin, with its thirty cubit circumference, balanced on the backs of twelve golden oxen yoked in spans of three, each team faced in one of the four mystical directions, and the basin contained a volume of three thousand baths. Although Lemuel had never seen it before, the design looked familiar. Lemuel's self-appointed cicerone told him that, "Solomon had the great artisan, Huram, cast an exact duplicate of the fountain in bronze. And when Huram complained that he didn't think that he could make the basin in those exact dimensions because they conflicted with the laws of geometric mensuration, Solomon, who was noted for his wisdom, replied, 'Listen Huram, I ain't no gynecologist, but I got nine hundred wives. Do you think I don't know about menstruation? Cast it like I said. There are higher truths.'"

Then he made a proprietary sweeping gesture with his arm to indicate the flowers that circled the fountain. "These flower urns at the edge of the walk are the models for the ten lavers that Solomon put into his house of the Lord, and there's the hundred basins of gold, and the columns. Ain't they nice?"

Lemuel nodded absently. His mind was on his mortality detail. If Solomon had nine hundred wives, what would be expected of him? Where would he find the time to lead the ten thousand souls to salvation? That was one of the questions that he supposed Tomas would explain to him. This lesson was to be a snap. A few encouraging words of advice, a Bible, and a flask of the waters of life. He looked doubtfully at the reservoir; the promise of life now seemed fraught with ominousness. At the far side of the pool was a statue of Jesus being laid back into the waters of life and being baptized by John the Baptist. Lemuel wondered, Did he...?

His question hung incomplete, and forgotten. A startling clatter of chains broke the silence, and for the first time, Lemuel turned and looked fully at the fabulous city that towered above everything. A drawbridge descended slowly from the wall and spanned the moat. The fly edge landed with a slight thump fifty cubits from where he and John d'Are stood. There was the sound of more chains running through blocks, and the portcullis arose smoothly within its casing. From where he stood he could see deeply into the splendors of Thelassar. A squad of Swiss guards ran out of the guard room set within the cheeks of the entry in the thick walls, and positioned themselves along the sides of the bridge with their halberds held smartly at their sides.

The interior courtyard appeared to be cobbled with rubies, and Lemuel saw a strange broad ladder like stairway. It must have been made of sapphires and blue diamonds, because its deep blue was so brilliant. Descending the steps were three angels wearing white linen robes and with flaming glories about their heads. "No wonder Jacob was amazed.[126] This must be the ladder that he saw leading up to Heaven. Awesome! You said I'd be surprised," he muttered to John d'Are.

John d'Are cackled evilly, "Heh, heh, heh."

Lemuel got the distinct impression that the astounding scene before him was not the surprise John deAre meant. The small procession of angels crossed the drawbridge and Lemuel's spine stiffened. He became a bit more erect; his knees straightened; his arms hung naturally at his side with his hands slightly cupped; index fingers touching thumbs; thumbs along robe seams; head erect; chin well in; heels touching; and feet at a forty-five degree angle...and God! Oh how he wished that he were back at the barracks with the other probationers.

He glanced at John d'Are out of the side of his eye and saw that he was highly amused at a private joke of his own. From what he'd heard about all the other briefing sessions, this briefing by three angels was irregular. The thought struck him that he was being singled out for a mortality detail of an unusual and extreme nature. Oh God! Maybe it is the millennium. Or what if my mission is among headhunters and cannibals? They've always let the human missionaries work those areas.

HOW THE GOOD TAILOR GOT TO HEAVEN

The foremost angel had the burly shape of a stevedore, or a lumberjack, and with a coarse ruddy visage to match. His nose appeared to have been broken. His auburn red hair swirled upward in a majestic wave, and a short grizzled beard circled beneath his chin. He carried a thick, leather-bound volume beneath his arm, and he wore a golden chain around his neck with a large key on it. As he walked, he planted a tall richly ornamented crosier before him at every second step as though he were claiming that amount of territory. His bearing was that of one leading the multitudes to the promised land, instead of merely two other angels to a tutoring session.

The next angel was small and slender with sallow, pock-marked cheeks, a big nose, slicked back black hair, and large bulbous, slightly squinty eyes. He carried a clipboard that had a legal pad filled with notes. He held his crosier awkwardly close to his body. Instead of its appearing as a staff of authority, he seemed to regard it as just one more thing that he had to carry around. Obviously, he was unused to the power it signified. The third angel appeared to be rather frail, and very old. He was balding in the way of very ancient mortals. His eyes seemed to have no irises nor pupils, and they were shiny gray and gummy like oysters. He shuffled along behind like an antique scarecrow leaning on a plain blackthorn crosier.

Lemuel glanced at John deAre who was trying to suppress a smile, and then he looked around at the many other ordinary souls who had suddenly found work to do near the lesson area. They were all keeping extra busy polishing the statues and urns, weeding and mulching the flower beds, and even the normally somber-faced Swiss guards had merry twinkles in their eyes. Suddenly it dawned on Lemuel. The rumor had been true: one of these angels had been promoted from ordinary soul. He was Lemuel's superior. *God! Why me? But at least it wasn't the millennium or cannibals.*

The tall, robust angel with the key stepped forward and smiled at Lemuel, and then he said, "I presume that you have noticed something different about this briefing session." He raised his hand to halt any comment. "Oh, I know that word leaks down to the lower ranks. I was once a probationer myself, so don't try to deny it." A laugh, and he continued, "We want you to know probationary angel…ah…"

The sallow-faced angel pulled a pair of tortoise shell-rimmed glasses from his robe pocket. "His name is Lemuel, your Eminence," he replied after consulting his clipboard. Lemuel never saw an angel who needed glasses. This must be the human soul.

"Ah yes, Lemuel. We want you to know that you have been carefully selected for the honor of being the first probationer to have the benefit of our modernized intensive training course. It has come to our attention that some of the probationers have been sent off on mortality details with very sketchy information about their mission, and how best to achieve satisfactory soul saving.

"In order to give our novitiates the finest tutoring we held a Bible quiz with a sample group of angels and found, much to our dismay, that many of our angels were not as knowledgeable about the Bible as we thought necessary. We were amazed to discover that this ordinary soul knew more about the Bible than any of the angels. When we checked his record, we found that, as a mortal, he had spent his lifetime studying and translating the Holy Word. And he continued to study in his spare time all the while that he has been with us.

"Oh you may believe that it took some doing, there seems to be some subconscious racial prejudice against the human souls that we serve, but we finally convinced the promotion board to promote this ordinary soul to angel. You are very fortunate to have the new angel, Myles Coverdale, as one of your instructors."

Lemuel thought, *Why me? Why do I have to be the experiment for these new educational theories? Why not Winfred, or one of the other probationers?* and he noticed that the thin angel with the oystery eyes was facing away with a detached expression. Lemuel felt that he disapproved also.

"It was only because of your outstanding performance in the…ah…"

The angel with the clip board ran his finger down Lemuel's rating

HOW THE GOOD TAILOR GOT TO HEAVEN

sheet and muttered to himself, "No, not that. Nope. No. It couldn't be that." And then he proffered, "The Galileo thing?"

"Ah yes, the Galileo affair. The Holy Office of the Inquisition has reversed its original findings, and so with the ascension of his immortal soul from purgatory, we have found you worthy of this honor. In my position as the seneschal of Thelassar, it had come to my attention that the curriculum was too complex for the catechismal efforts of our principle instructor." He nodded toward the frail oyster-eyed angel. "Tomas stands head and shoulders above the usual angel when it comes to understanding theological theory, but he seems to be too entrenched in the time worn liturgies of the past to provide the well rounded formulas that are needed in today's modern world." Tomas cleared his throat and drew a Papal Cross in the gold nuggets with the tip of his crosier.

The seneschal addressed him directly. "You know it's true. Not many mortals in the world want to acknowledge papal infallibility anymore, and in the country where we are sending Lemuel…" He smiled at Lemuel and sounded pleased with himself. "See I remembered your name." Then continuing to chide, Tomas added, "Would you deny salvation to those souls? Handicap Lemuel's chance for promotion? Lord knows his task will be difficult enough, and he has to be mentally ready for the whole American culture."

"The Americas?" Tomas queried vociferously. "What do you need this artificial angel for? That's a Latin continent, and they're mostly Catholic!"

"Tomas, Tomas, Tomas! You are sadly behind the times. Your outburst demonstrates just how old-fashioned and behind the times you are. This is the Bible that they use in the America that he is going to. It is an English Bible."

"English? You mean like British, English? Not even Spanish?"

"They speak English in America."

"Since when? They speak either Spanish, which is my forte, or else they speak French or Portuguese, which are both good, Catholic countries," Tomas said indignantly.

The seneschal heaved a big sigh and looked to Lemuel for an indication of sympathetic understanding. Then he looked to Tomas, as though dealing with a senile old man for the hundredth time, and said, "Ever since the Mexican War, during my mortality detail, way back in 1848, English has been the dominant language in the whole North American continent. Now almost everyone there speaks English."

"Or a form of it," The angel with the clip board added, and smiled slyly.

The seneschal turned to Lemuel, and said, "See what I mean? Tomas has not kept up to date with world history. He still uses defunct names for countries, pays no attention to sovereignty, or new borders, or forms of government, but he is still the finest theologian among the angels. Now, where were we? Oh yes. In order to make certain that you probationers have the finest, most up-to-date instructions, we held a little impromptu quiz on the Bible, and we must sadly admit that there wasn't an angel who knew this Bible as well as Myles does. He will take you through the liturgical part of your course so you can decide which best suits your own temperament and the culture of the nation you have been assigned to. Tomas will brush you up on the psychology of theology, but I'm sure that the entire course will merely be a refresher course for you." Then he suggested, "Let's regard this as an informal little seminar." Then to John d'Are, he said, "Please hang our glories over there, on an urn or something."

Lemuel handed his own pale nimbus to John d'Are and noticed how insignificant it looked beside the other flaming glories. Now they appeared to be four friends taking a break from their duties. Myles seemed to relax. Tomas tottered forward on spindly legs and proposed that they take seats beside the pond. This brought a cautious look to the faces of the Swiss guards. A sharp stare and a shooing motion of his bony hand by the old angel directed them, and they quickly moved away from their posts.

The seneschal offered the thick book to Tomas who looked at it blankly and made no effort to accept it. Looking slightly disoriented by this obvious slight, he placed the Bible on the wall between Lemuel and Myles, moved away, and smelled the blossoms of the tree with the golden apples. But, he remained near enough to listen to the lesson. Lemuel looked down at the Bible. It was a fine, brand new, richly-bound in Morocco leather, King James Bible. The letters were embossed in genuine twenty-four carat gold. The pages were edged in gold and it had several different colored satin ribbons for page markers.

Tomas steadied himself with his crosier, looked at the ground, and began without ceremony. His tone was without emotion as though from rote, and much practice. "You have satisfactorily acquitted the tasks that you have been assigned. Nothing notable, but it's not for me to judge." He glanced toward the seneschal, and continued. "The shepherding of parturient souls from worldly mortality to the eternal has been handled acceptably."

Lemuel swallowed. He thought of how he had swapped souls with the demon. Abigail's grin crossed his mind and he quickly blinked to erase it.

"Now you are about to embark on one final mission. An important mission, and one where you will be exposed to the evils of worldliness for a lifetime."

He droned on with his high, soft voice, inflectionless, as though he did not genuinely care. "I'm aware of the talk that goes on among some angels. The boasting of ribald and unsavory antics is indicative of sophomoric mentalities, and we know that some of it trickles down to you probationers." Then there was a change in tone. He fixed his oystery eyes upon Lemuel and two hard-piercing black dots appeared. His voice had the businesslike sound of a sawmill slicing off pine planks. "Do not allow this barracks' talk to sway your purpose...or to cause your downfall!" His hand swung downward with surprising vigor, and his index finger pointed at the ground and quivered with intensity, and a promise of stern punishment.

Lemuel glimpsed in Tomas' face the look that had intimidated the Swiss guards, and a chill flowed over his flesh.

Now his voice sounded hard, like steel wheels rolling on concrete. "Try to imagine the abode of the damned: strait, dark, and foul-smelling; the abode of demons and lost souls; filled with flames that give heat and smoke, but no light. For in that sinkhole of corruption is eternal darkness. In Hell the nostrils of the damned flow with great streams and gobs of mucus, all slimy and black, and their eyes tear perpetually, washing rivulets down their sooty faces. Their throats are perpetually raw and they cough up bits of soot with rasping pain and aching chests. Their flesh chars and blisters in the volcanic hot vapors, and they are there eternally imprisoned, all heaped together like cast away garbage in the blinding darkness. They moan in pain as they slither over one another in perpetual torment."

Ah ha! I thought so. Abigail was lying to me. I'm getting the truth about Hell now, Lemuel thought. *Yeah, that's more like it. She was trying to convince me that it was like a country club or a college campus. The little liar.*

Tomas was finishing his horrifying dirge. "…it is the sinkhole for all the filth and offal of the world." He spat out the word "World." "And who will you find in this eternal misery? The self-willed, the disobedient, those that turn their backs on the teaching of the true church…"

The seneschal cleared his throat.

Tomas resumed in a more softened tone, "But we offer them the love and the light …the glorious eternal light." His pupils returned once more to indistinguishable dots. "And that is why we must save as many souls as possible from the eternal torments."

Tomas resumed his monotonous toneless dissertation. "As you are already aware, the final task of your probation is to secure ten thousand new souls' names for the book of life. However, there is one condition that you may not be aware of because it is not usually stressed. They must be obtained with the full consent of the donor, or their parents or guardians, as the case may be. Those souls we receive at christenings and infant baptisms are temporary dedications and commit their souls only up to the age of awareness. At which time they must, with fully mature understanding of what they do, volunteer to be confirmed.

HOW THE GOOD TAILOR GOT TO HEAVEN

"The heathenish idolaters who worship false gods, gods which are no gods, usually parody our sacred rites with a burlesqued imitation. The learned usually see them for what they really are: puberty rites. Their rituals are nothing more than obscene rites of passage; celebrations of their children having arrived at an age when they are old enough to procreate. What they celebrate is having reared another generation of infidels who will mimic their parents' blasphemous behavior. At these superstitious rituals they have one or more shamans officiate at this mumbo-jumbo in absurd get ups, and chanting meaningless incantations. And all their souls will burn in Hell's fires!"

"This is one of the principle objectives of our school system. We take every effort to educate those youngsters about the horror that awaits them if they refuse to accept salvation. However, never let it be said that we have stolen any souls."

As though he'd been hit with a sharp right cross, guilt swivelled Lemuel's head toward the catechist. *Was that an implication, given with their own consent? He didn't object, and I didn't exactly steal that tailor's soul. It was an even swap.* But Tomas's face was expressionless. There wasn't a trace of accusation and Lemuel was puzzled. *Stolen souls? What else could he have meant by that?*

Tomas didn't notice Lemuel's guilt pangs, and droned on. "Once their commitment has been made, we have them for eternity. The confirmation itself is a simple ritual where they partake of their first communion, bar or bat mitzvah. They may have holy water poured over their heads, or flicked into their faces from the minister's fingers, or be sprinkled on from an aspergillum, or you can really get carried away and dip them bodily into a tank or pond or river." Tomas allowed himself a small smile, and asked, "Can you swim? You'd better learn how to swim if you go in for that one."

Myles interrupted. "Tomas, I think you are straying into my subject. I'm supposed to be teaching about rituals and ceremonies."

"The fields overlap."

"They do, but not as far as you went Tomas," the seneschal spoke out. "And I think you should temper your Romanish inclinations with a bit more objectivity."

Myles's smile was triumphant and Tomas matched it with a grotesque leer of his own. "You Bible translator," he muttered as though it were a curse.

"Let's see, where was I? Oh yes, confirmation, perpetuity, sin. I hadn't gotten up to sin yet." He resumed his monotone. "Once the soul is tilted toward Godliness, they are able to recognize sin. They are able to do this because our ministers, priests, rabbis, imams, etceteras, etceteras, tell them what sin is."

"I see. Of course. How would they know if we didn't tell them?" Lemuel mused aloud.

As though picking up on Lemuel's revelation, Tomas droned on. "Once they become knowledgeable about sin, they will become your unwitting missionaries and they spread the knowledge of sin among their family and friends. And their friends will tell their friends about sin and soon you have the knowledge of sin being discussed everywhere."

"That's marvelous. And then pretty soon, when everyone knows about sin, they stop sinning." Lemuel was pleased with how simple it was, and modestly gave himself an imaginary star for having grasped the principle so quickly.

"No! And stop interrupting." Tomas said impatiently. "That is not why you tell them about sin. You tell them about sin so that they will want to be forgiven for their sins. You must make them believe that they are all sinners, and then you will be able to grant them the blessings of forgiveness. If they don't know they have sinned, how do you expect them to know that they need to be forgiven?"

"Oh sure, that makes sense," Lemuel said hesitantly, without understanding at all. He'd have sworn the reason to eliminate sin was to deliver them from evil, like in the Lord's Prayer, and out of the clutches of Satan and the demons. That way the souls would be as free of sin as in Heaven. He decided that he had better pay close attention to this teacher. *I wonder how I got it wrong?* he thought.

HOW THE GOOD TAILOR GOT TO HEAVEN

Tomas had a few strands of pale, graying blond hair that adhered to the oils of his shiny bald pate. His right hand plastered them down more firmly with absent-minded strokes, and he asked, "Why did God create sin?"

The question caught Lemuel off guard. He knew they had taught that at the academy, but that was centuries ago and he couldn't remember. *Let's see, it was Augustine…or was it Aquinas…oh what was it?* Then he blurted out, "To make goodness all the more glorious to behold. It's the contrast…"

"No! *Stupido!* Dummy! And I didn't expect you to answer. That was a rhetorical question. We have sin because it is the primum mobile for the liturgies. Without sin the humans would accept God, thank Him very much for His creations, and go off about their business, and never be heard from again. And where do you think that would leave the churches and Empyreal establishment? Sins are what keep the churches in business."

Tomas resumed his monotonal lecture. " The granting of forgiveness is an art form which you will learn by practice. You must never give them the impression that they have been completely absolved of their sins. Make it perfectly clear that you are only an intercessor and that absolutions are the purview of the higher powers. Once you have firmly established your position as an intercessor between their worthless, sin-infested beings and God, like magic, they will bring their children to you, even unto the third and fourth generation, as the scriptures say."

His skepticism was not well-concealed and Tomas noticed the look of disbelief that crossed Lemuel's face. "Oh…you doubt. You doubt they'll bring their children to you. You doubt the Ten Commandments, do you? Do you even know the ten commandments?"

"No! I mean yes! Of course I do. It's just that I can't see where the Commandments…" The accusation seemed to have taken a familiar turn and then, to his horror, he imagined a pair of impish green eyes laughing at him. Eyes that delighted as they accused him of not knowing the Commandments, and when he tried to prove that he did, eyes that merrily mocked his stumbling efforts. She was the reason for all of his perverse thoughts…Abigail. She was the reason he saw the Devil on that door and she was the reason that he let those children get away with truancy. She was reason he didn't report Jephthah's daughter, and she was the one who made him see only sex and violence in the statues of Eden. She was the one who had caused him to question and forget the greatest tenet of all: whatever is, is right. These things are all according to God's plan.

"Of course I know the Commandments. It's only that…I can't seem to recall…at this moment anyway…which one tells about bringing the children…"

"Dolt! Where did you finish in your class at the angel academy, anchor man? It doesn't say it that way. Why do you think I've been stressing sin? The second clause of the First Commandment states: 'I, the Lord thy God, am a jealous God, visiting the iniquity of the fathers upon the children unto the third and fourth generation.'[127] Are you so simple as to suppose that the parents would only seek forgiveness for their own sins? They will naturally want their children's sins forgiven also."

Lemuel strove to blot out those green-eyed thoughts of perversion from his mind. "Oh yes, of course. It has been ages since the academy and I must have gotten the precept twisted around in my mind." To show that he wasn't completely stupid, he said, "I thought that was the Second Commandment." The thoughts that were flashing around through his mind, however, as though written on coruscant banners, were, *The children did not sin! That's unfair! They didn't need to be forgiven sins that they haven't committed!* He reached into the pocket of his robe and pulled out a few bits of manna, and asked, "Do you mind? I'm feeling a bit dyspeptic."

Tomas waved permission, and continued. "Twixt twelve and twenty are the optimal ages for your salvation efforts. During these fertile years they all go through a crisis stage when they are most receptive to innovation, and their ardent natures can be directed into the most impassioned faith.

HOW THE GOOD TAILOR GOT TO HEAVEN ~ 97

"By then they have seen rents in the veil of their parent's superegos. They are also becoming aware of the world's multiple schizoid priorities—the confusion at Babel seems like sanity by comparison. Their childhood was a time of inquisitiveness, and experimentation, and a time of make-believe. They tested their bounds, and learned by persuasion or force, that there were limits, but, twixt twelve and twenty, they notice that these limits, the guidelines of decency, were often ignored by the limit makers themselves. Their parents and other adults in their lives were ignoring the guidelines, sometimes occasionally, sometimes often, but frequently enough. Then their childlike ability to pretend to not see through the tattered veil and observe that their natal idols have feet of clay has vanished. They will be seeking certitudes.

"The parents themselves, having long since abdicated responsibility to experts of every stripe, authorities, and councilors of every field, the multiplied layers of overseers above them, and driven by their basic instinct to survive for just one more day, are eager to relinquish these disoriented children onto the church."

Lemuel raised an incredulous eyebrow.

"Oh, they most assuredly will. They have long since escaped the drudgery of decision making. They have learned that citing authority is easier than thoughtful reason. They have been broken to harness. 'Behold, we put bits in the horses' mouths, that they may obey us; and we turn about their whole body.'[128] They will bring you their children, even as Abraham brought Isaac."

"Then when you have those children before you, corrupted with the sins of their fathers, corrupted with sins of their own doing, and corrupted with the sins of the worldly, you must be fearless." The frail and delicate old angel that Lemuel had seen in Tomas was becoming transformed. He no longer appeared enervated and dry as a willow leaf in autumn, but merciless and hard like the eagle that furiously tore away the flesh of Prometheus. Tomas extended his hands. and his slender fingers tore at the air like talons. He sibilated, "Seize those sins; tear the sin from their viscera; reach in and grapple with the demons inhabiting their entrails." He raced about like a frenzied spider and his arms were grasping at imaginary demons as he splashed the golden nuggets of the walk in all directions.

John d'Are tried to rake them back into place and Tomas bumped into him. He spat out, "Get out of the way, you imbecile." Tomas pushed him and sent him reeling. "Your lily white, gringo, Baptist soul ought to be burning! You heretic! All of you weak mewling…"

"Tomas! Tomas. Please stop this tirade. They are all God's children. Stop dwelling in the past." The seneschal's eyes squinted shrewdly and he asked, "How did you know that he was a Baptist? You're not authorized to look into the personnel files."

"He smells like river bottom," Tomas replied caustically. "He has silt clinging to his toes."

The seneschal admonished him. "Don't be absurd Tomas." And then in an oily, solicitous voice asked, "Perhaps you have been overworked. Would you like to be relieved of your instructorship for a while? Teaching all these probationers, year after year, can be very tiring. I'm sure that Myles would be willing to stand in for you, and of course, you can be assigned to something less arduous."

"Oh, you'd like that, wouldn't you? You'd let that ersatz angel mislead the novices? That imitation Catholic with his lying secularly derived and royally authorized verses? Not in a million years! You may have jumped over me for now, but that doesn't mean that I'm out of the running for the next archangel slot."

Lemuel felt embarrassed to witness this heated exchange between his superiors. Moreover, this quarrel was being overheard by all the ordinary souls within an earshot. It would be common gossip all over Heaven tomorrow. He managed an humble effacing grin and looked over at Myles. Myles was grinning too, but smugly, not humbly, and Lemuel quickly turned away. *Why me? Haven't I had enough trouble? Why, when it's time for my mortality, do they have to change the system?*

The seneschal spit back at Tomas, "If you had taken the trouble to

HOW THE GOOD TAILOR GOT TO HEAVEN

read that Bible, maybe we wouldn't have needed an expert. You're out of step Tomas! Times change—get with it!"

An artery pulsed in Tomas's temple, and the spider veins in his cheeks and nose stood out and became plum-colored. He breathed hard for a few moments, turned abruptly from the seneschal and regaining his poise asked, "Where was I?"

"Sin and the adolescent, I think." Lemuel replied.

"Humph, yes. This is a vulnerable age for them. Their emotions range beyond their heads. The idolaters, the infidels, and the accursed blaspheming heretics who commit whoredom with unappropriated gods will also be competing with you for their souls. All that you have to know about their rituals and foolish beliefs are that they are obscene. The Bible does note, albeit superficially and with much derision, these abominations, so I must make mention of them in this course. Fortunately, you will have little of that to contend with in the Americas. The church has cleared away the idols and dealt with the abominators centuries ago, almost eliminating the false gods from that hemisphere."

A question arose, but fortunately Lemuel stopped himself just short of asking it. It was obviously another demon induced perversion. *What did Tomas mean by "unappropriated gods?"* He'd foiled those smiling green eyes just in time.

"You must be the first to answer their soul's inquirendo. Make sure that they are enrolled in the book of life before the idolaters can lure them into their evil ways. Remember, get them young. Keeping the faith is always easier than winning it over. And when you have established the Lord's suzerainty over their souls you can depend on their own self-love, it's a form of self-preservation, to keep them committed."

"It is not difficult to understand the reason for this. The mind of mankind is more complex than that of the lower beasts, although the function is similar. Man can envision very abstract ideas. This, the lower beasts cannot do, but, like the lower beasts, the mind is wedded to their flesh. The mind, and its animal core of instinct, is fed by the same blood and nerves of the body as any other organ. For them to admit a flaw in what their mind has embraced would be tantamount to admitting to having a sick mind. And once this mind has accepted a belief, the belief seems as part of their body. Dislodging their beliefs has, for them, all the attraction of an amputation, or, considering the importance they give to sex, castration. That is why you must establish belief early in their young minds. Do not allow conflicting notions to gain a firm foothold.

"You notice that I say a firm foothold. Intimating doubt. Yes doubt! As they grow older, they all doubt. The Popes doubt! Holy men have been known to gird up their loins with sack cloth and wear hair shirts under their vestments for their entire lives because of their doubts. They know it is sinful for them to doubt, but they doubt anyway. And that doubt is one more sin, their personal sin, to be added to the sins inherited from their fathers. They reject the doubt, deny its existence, and then it arises unbidden and stronger. Then you must bring your most potent tool into play, the liturgies. Without the liturgies their souls might be lost."

Myles instantly defended his territory. "I'm supposed to teach him about that, Tomas. You're getting into my field."

"Judas Priest! I can mention the word, can't I? Or would you rather that I use the word "sacraments," "the Eucharist," or how about "the Holy Mass?" I'm trying to be as nondenominational as possible for Christ's sake." He hissed in a stage whisper, "I'd like to translate your internal organs for you, you Bible scholar!" And he made an obscene motion with his blackthorn crosier.

"What was that, Tomas?" the seneschal inquired.

"Nothing, your Eminence. I was merely explaining that Lemuel needn't wear a Roman collar. I was telling Myles that I'll leave the Bible to him, since he is obviously so much better founded in the subject. I'm still on the psychology of salvation."

"I know these distractions are making this briefing difficult for you Lemuel." Tomas apologized. "Please excuse these little disagreements. When this intellectual's turn comes, I promise you that there won't be any rude interruptions from me.

"Now then, back to the subject at hand. The reason for the liturgy, in which this scholar (he pronounced 'scholar' as though it was a curse, and he glared at Myles) will instruct you is to overcome doubt." Tomas's voice resumed his tutorial monotone. "As you well know, the subjugation of the will to God is the essence of our bliss. It is the supreme state of true holiness. But when doubt arises, it is an irritant. It disturbs their tranquility. And if it is allowed to grow and fester, it becomes as vermin. Vermin that are infested with fleas and ticks and lice, there in bed with them between the sheets of the divine marriage. Unattended, doubt will grow, and eventually their faith will disappear like a bursting soap bubble. These vermin of doubt gnaw at the faith, so we try to keep these thoughts out of their consciousness. Most mortals have a very short attention span. The time frame between faith and its dissolution as a bursting soap bubble is usually slightly over a week. And that is why we say that the Sabbath was invented for man."[129]

"This is a highly refined balancing act. Consider this: doubt like other concomitant sins is like the grain of irritant upon which an oyster creates a pearl. That pearl is the liturgy. We overlay the irritant with the balm of ritual. With ritual the painful doubt eases for a time, but after several days the balm we have applied has hardened. Sinful doubt once more begins to fester in the mind, and so we must apply another reassuring balm of ritual." While he spoke, Tomas's hands moved in a rotating motion, as though working a daub of putty into a ball. "It becomes an ongoing cycle: the doubt, the sought after reassurance, and we apply the balm of ritual. Then again, the disbelief, the request for forgiveness, and again the ritual. The prayer, the liturgy, the cycle of sin and regeneration; the soul being constantly reborn, and recommitted, through the skillful ministrations of the clergy."

During the discourse about building the pearl of faith, his molding hands moved farther and farther apart as though building up the layers of a pearl. Finally Tomas held out his hand as though presenting a product. He pointed to what would be its irritant core and said, "But the irritant is essential to create this pearl, so it is an important part of the concept. Do you see?" As he asked, the index finger of his other hand shuttled rapidly toward his open palm.

Lemuel nearly said that he couldn't see either the pearl or the irritant in that empty outstretched palm. Abigail's entire form and face sprang into his imagination. She was wearing that sheath with the slit up the side and she gave her hips a wiggle. He crammed his eyelids together forcibly, and prayed silently. *Oh Lord, free me from that imp and I promise that I'll never traffic with demons again. Please help me to see the truth.* And when he reopened his eyes he saw a pearl in Tomas's hand: a perfect pink orb about the size of a volleyball. He said to the catechist, "Why of course I see it, and it is very beautiful too."

The reply momentarily astounded Tomas, and when he realized what Lemuel meant, he said sharply, "The concept, Imbecile! Do you see the essentiality of sin in order to grant sacramental forgiveness?"

Now utterly confused, Lemuel saw the pearl incandesce briefly and then like a light bulb, it burnt out and disappeared. Lemuel sought comfort in the face of the teacher, and saw oyster-gray eyes in a face of vulpine shrewdness. Myles also looked at him questioningly, as did the seneschal. He gulped down a handful of manna without asking permission and he sputtered out a reply. "I understood what you meant. I meant that the cycle of faith was beautiful. Your pedagogic talents make everything so lucid that for a moment I could almost imagine a pearl in your hand. Oh yes, everything is straightforward and simple the way you explain it."

Tomas snorted at Lemuel's explanation, but he had been having a hard time lately, and this mild flattery pleased him. He joked, "It's one thing for a mortal to hallucinate, but angels are supposed to be above that sort of thing." As though it were a fencing foil, he thrust the tip of his crosier into the waters of life and slashed little wakes with the tip. "You haven't been sampling the brew, have you?" he joked.

"It only takes a gill or so and you're one of them. Yup, this water, and a handful of cheap chemicals, is all that any of them are worth. You'll keep that in mind, won't you? It helps you to maintain perspective."

HOW THE GOOD TAILOR GOT TO HEAVEN

Tomas ignored the glowering looks Myles gave him. "But they all have souls and minds," Myles interjected.

"Yes, and that is what we are after. Their souls are very valuable to us here in the Empyrean." Tomas indicated the multitude of souls working in Eden with an encompassing wave, and then he gripped the fabric of his robe and observed, "How else would we get our laundry done?"

"Essentially the trick is a lawyer's device. You cause them to see, just as you saw the pearl, that their spiritual essence, their souls, their egos, or their minds if you prefer, and their bodies are separate entities, similar to a legal contract. Their body is merely the paper the legal contract is written on, the important essences are the meaning of the words written on the paper."

Myles interrupted, "That's not a good example, Tomas. Jesus said: 'Woe to ye lawyers! for ye have taken away the key of wisdom.'[130] Lawyers dissect one clear simple thought into meaningless segments and then proceed to argue about the meaning of the scraps."

Tomas replied, "And the gospel according to Saint John says, 'In the beginning was the Word, and the Word was God.' You cannot have knowledge without the Word. The Word is the Spirit. If the contract is burned, would that destroy the knowledge of the words written on the paper? And that is the essence of faith, of belief, of the spirit."

"As you know, no sane person cuts off a hand, or plucks out an eye willingly. But…if they believe that their hand or their eye has offended them,[131] then through the power of that belief…Ah ha! Do you see the love of self, which they identify as being the same as their minds, or their souls, is able to override their normal urge to preserve their bodies? Since they know that their souls are immortal, they will even shed their life as dross, as worthless as a tinker's dams. This is why they will often make the most glorious sacrifices in the name of their abstract rationalizations, and then we have them in our power. Then, they'll charge into cannon fire, or immolate themselves or their neighbors." Tomas was cooing with pleasure, and his leer bared pink gums and one yellowed and blackened rooted tooth.

"In the extreme this self-love is vanity, and is of course sinful. They may even be possessed by demons. They have become voluptuaries reveling in their bodily torments. While you're burning heretics at the stake, if you find one that embraces the flames too eagerly, or takes too readily to torture, they are probably possessed by demons."

"But no more about belief and sin for now. We'll get into possession later. You'll find a mimeographed handout on the subject in your Bible. It explains how to diagnose the affliction and some practical remedies. Just make sure that you have an adequate supply of branding irons, pliers, thumb screws, and sharp knives at hand." Tomas started to salivate and he wiped the spittle from his lips with the back of his prehensile claw. His eyes became distant, as though envisioning a fond memory. He continued absently, "Your church should have some of the bulkier appliances in its dungeon: charcoal braziers, racks, wall chains, a sturdy chair with arm and leg clamps; you know, the usual devices for getting the possessed to confess the truth."

The seneschal looked apologetically at Lemuel and then corrected the tutor. "Tomas! The secular authorities in America won't let you..."

"Won't let you what?"

"They won't let you test for demonic possession that way."

"Oh? Have all the demons been cleared out of the Americas?"

"No, some of the worst are there. One of them has immense powers of possession," Lemuel interjected.

Tomas's choler began to rise. "And their king obstructs justice? He must be possessed himself. Have him answer to the ecclesiastical court. If necessary, burn him at the stake and install a new king."

"They don't have a king," the seneschal said wearily.

Tomas waved off the semantic nicety. "Their emperor then, or caesar, or tsar, or whatever..."

"They have a democracy," the seneschal explained.

Both Myles and Tomas were astonished, and said in unison, "A democracy?"

Myles added, "You mean like the Greeks? They were all pagans!"

HOW THE GOOD TAILOR GOT TO HEAVEN

The seneschal, better informed than the others, and quicker, said, "Well that shouldn't present any problem. I've dealt with democracies before. Quite successfully I might add. They're not a nation of infidels, and if you can get enough faithful to lobby for the practice, I'm sure that a vote by the majority will give the church the authority to reinstitute the inquisition, and that should take care of the demons and witches."

"Yes, and have the archbishop withhold the church's sanction from their acts until they do," Myles offered.

Tomas glared at him and said, "The pope you mean. And threaten them all with excommunication. That'll wake them up."

Lemuel's confidence in the competence of his instructors teetered as they bickered. His own knowledge of America was limited to brief forays to shepherd the parturient souls, but he knew that the popes didn't wield much influence over their legislators, and the Archbishop of Canterbury had even less. He humbly and apologetically told them what he had observed. "They have something called a Supreme Court."

"Well, what is the dominant sect in America? Are they Jewish, or Muslim, or what?" Tomas asked.

John d'Are's lips made sounds like escaping flatulence as he squelched his laughter, and his body shook with the restraint. Lemuel said, "Baptists appear to be the dominant sect, your Eminence."

"You mean Dippers? Those ignorant rustics with their salacious appetites for young girls? Those lechers who use religion to satisfy their lustful urges to fondle the pubescent flesh in their baptismal pools?" Tomas moaned, "Oh Father, what has become of your people?" He made the sign of the cross, "Oh God, what is to become of the church?" He crossed himself again and began to pray in Latin, "I have exalted thee with great power, and thou hast hanged me on the gibbet of the Cross."

The seneschal commanded, "Tomas! Stop being so melodramatic. The soul of the lowest true believer is worth as much as the soul of a pope. Remember what Jesus said about the widow's farthing?"

"Don't bring Jesus into it. It's the fault of this imitation Catholic and his poking into things that are none of his business." He brought the crook of his heavy black crosier down onto the Bible with a sharp smack. The report echoed throughout Eden like a rifle shot. Lemuel and Myles both jumped, and Myles clasped at his chest.

And Tomas sneered, "It is your turn scholar. Let us hear these pearls of erudition that you have gleaned from your years of study." He flipped open the Bible with his staff, as though its touch would soil him. "Ah, I see, the King James version. Autographed by him too. How wonderful." Then to Lemuel, "Pay attention, novice. In the land of the Dippers it's the manual for their apostasy."

Chapter 8

"APOSTASY IS A SUBJECTIVE TERM, LEMUEL," THE SENESCHAL said as he sat along side Lemuel and placed his hand on Lemuel's forearm. "And angels should be above petty parochialism."

Tomas worked his lips in agitation and muttered softly, but Lemuel heard the word, "liberals," clearly.

With his other hand the seneschal made a sweeping gesture with his crosier, and said, "Heaven is a large and glorious place. Within these vast bounds we accept Christians, Jews, and Moslems...there is room for all who worship the true God. Here you will find Sunnite, and Shiite Moslems; Hasidic, Orthodox, and Reform, Jews; the Pharisees, and Sadducees; you will find Roman, Greek, and Russian Orthodox worshipers; as well as Copts, Baptists, Mormons, Disciples of Christ, Jehovah Witnesses, Lutherans, Presbyterians, Hutterites, Methodists, Mennonites, and Episcopalians: all of the facets of the same jewel, and all working joyfully together here in Heaven. And it is the duty of the Empyreal Establishment to provide for their happiness. They're all our responsibility, not just one denomination; we angels serve them all without favoritism. Their prayers while they are mortal tell us what they want and we respond to their wishes."

"'Ask and ye shall receive, that your joy may be full,' John 16:24," The angel with the clip board confirmed.

With a rapidity that was barely perceptible, the seneschal's eyes flicked toward Tomas and then returned to Lemuel's face. "Most angels remember their mortality details with fond nostalgia and I am sure that this will be true in your case, but there are a few angels that become obsessed with that brief period of their existence. Keep it in the proper perspective. After all it is only one lifetime. As the apostle James has said, 'For what is your life? It is even a vapor, that appeareth for a little time, and then vanisheth away.'[132] Keep sight of the higher goals." And in a barely perceptible whisper he added, "Like the promotion board."

The seneschal picked up the Bible and caressed its fine leather binding, and then handed it to Lemuel. "This fine Moroccan, leather-bound Bible has been especially produced for these English-speaking nations. Feel the texture of that binding, and that gold embossing is genuine twenty-four carat gold. We have even had King James sign your copy for you. Look inside on the flyleaf."

Lemuel checked and saw written with a quill pen, *"Sette forth by His majesty's most gracious license: James, King of England. 1611, Anno Domini ."*

"Tomas is not as case hardened as he sounds. This Bible is his gift to you. Tomas, why don't you come over here and sign your gift to Lemuel." Lemuel saw the elder's sadistic smile as he addressed Tomas.

Tomas's face darkened and white blotches appeared on his bony cheeks. Then he checked his temper and smiled evilly. "Why certainly, your Eminence. That is only proper." He strode forward and taking a quill pen and the inkwell from Myles, wrote, *"Para mi amigo Lemuel...Peligro, este libros contiene heces...Tomas de Torquemada."* Then he picked up some gold dust from the walkway and sprinkled it onto the wet ink.

* * *

HOW THE GOOD TAILOR GOT TO HEAVEN

The seneschal praised the qualifications of Lemuel's next tutor with superlatives generally reserved for an agent's press releases. With each "wonderful," and "marvelous," and "highly erudite," and "unparalleled excellence" Tomas jerked and moaned as though hit with a lash. Lemuel reasoned that since he had no choice in the matter, this hype was finding its intended mark. He also suspected that the seneschal was trying to convince himself, and also pressure Myles to come up to these expectations. *The seneschal must have a personal stake in this*, he thought.

The seneschal introduced Myles Coverdale.

Myles was not an impressive looking angel. He was small in stature, and thin, with straight black hair pomaded and brushed close to his skull. Large eyes with bulging eyeballs were made more bulbous by his thick glasses, and he had a rather large nose. As he was being exhorted, he smiled modestly and looked away. "It is really William Tyndale or Thomas Cranmer who should have had this honor," he said shyly.

"Tyndale and Cranmer were both burned at the stake for their heresy! Is that your idea of angel material? Angels obey their superiors!" Tomas spat out. Then he sneered, "And you would have been roasted too, if you hadn't run off and hid."

The seneschal rapped on the ledge of the pond with his crosier, and cautioned, "Tomas! Behave. The fact that Myles wasn't burned at the stake had nothing to do with this appointment. He was appointed because he was the first mortal to translate and publish the entire Bible, including the Apocrypha, in English. It was an immensely difficult and very brave undertaking against the powerful opposition of the pope, and the entire Catholic church. Because of his work, the English-speaking world can read the Holy Bible without knowing Latin. By Myles's efforts, ordinary men have access to the Holy word."

"And you think that's an improvement, do you? Undermining the authority of the priests and the Holy Father in the Vatican? Look at the division it has caused."

"Jesus promised to bring division. It wasn't my doing." Myles protested. "I was merely the instrument of his will." He picked up the

Bible and looked for the relevant passage. "It's in Luke, I think." He searched through the pages rapidly, and after a few moments exclaimed; "Here it is! 'Suppose ye that I am come to bring peace on Earth? Nay; but rather division.' Luke 12:51. And as you must admit, Tomas, we have a burgeoning population of believers of every persuasion."

* * *

The scholar had a tutorial air about him as he rose to begin his instruction. Lemuel decided this pedagogue's mortal experiences would give him practical knowledge which should be extremely valuable. Myles had spent much of his life on the run from the papist inquisition and hiding among the theological intellectuals of Amsterdam and Geneva. Myles lived among the Calvinists where he learned that the Holy Scriptures are the sole source of Christian truth, not the edicts issued by the corrupt Vatican. He held the Bible beneath his arm and began to read from the lesson plan written on the legal pad on his clip board. "You understand it would be practically impossible to perform all the forms of ritual and to reproduce every altar described herein." He removed the Bible from beneath his arm and waved it awkwardly in Lemuel's general direction. "Nor could you enact all the pivotal melodramas, but that is not necessary for the salvation of mortal souls. We, therefore, consider the missionary's individual judgement, and the mortal soul's personal predisposition to worship, to obtain grace, to receive revealed knowledge, and to cleanse sin from the spirit."

"Your mode of operation may be either stabile and kinetic from a church building, or peripatetic and dynamic. It is anyplace that you happen to be where the spirit moves you to preach. As we know, Jesus used both methods to spread the gospel. He worked in taverns among wine bibbers, and publicans, and harlots, and in the temples, and in the treasuries of the temples. He preached to the multitudes from altars no more elaborate than a hummock. He spoke from river banks, and as he passed among the people in the streets. The important thing to remember is that wherever you are is a sanctified place. Also, from the same passages we can see the bifurcating nature of the sacerdotal rituals. John the Baptist

HOW THE GOOD TAILOR GOT TO HEAVEN — 111

scorned all forms of human pleasures, and Jesus clearly accepted them[133]. But first things first; we'll get to feast or fast later."

"Like Jesus, it is not necessary for you to preach in a mighty cathedral, nor some ornate palace like Solomon's temple, nor reverence one location such as Mecca, or the Vatican. The only essential is that you maintain an atmosphere of sanctity. The ambiance you should try to maintain should be like unto the first altar."

Myles decided that a comradely chat would be as effective as the formal lector to pupil method that Tomas used. He leaned his crosier against the coping of the fountain, sat beside Lemuel, and placed the Bible on his lap. That way he could show the relevant passages to his student. He riffled through the pages to a passage in Genesis. "Here's what I was looking for.

"'How dreadful is this place! This is none other than the house of God.' Do you see? That is the ambience you should strive for: your worshipers should feel dread. You are not putting on a circus. As Jacob set up the stone that he had used for a pillow, he said, 'And this stone which I have set for a pillar shall be God's house; and all that thou shalt give me I will surely give the tenth unto thee.'[134] There you have the basics; your parishioners should feel a sense of solemnity at your services, and they must show this by tithing."

Lemuel frowned, and asked uncertainly, "I'm afraid that I don't understand the tithing part. That sounds like an odd thing to promise, unless you mean that one God is giving him things and that he is going to give a tenth part to some other God."

That interpretation of the passage had never occurred to Myles and he had never heard of it occurring to anyone else. He was dumb struck and sputtering. The seneschal moved off a few paces and occupied himself by pointing out a bird of peace dropping on one of golden statues to an attendant soul.

Breathing heavily, Tomas stepped over and spat out, "That's not it at all, Nincompoop!"

Lemuel observed defensively, "Wouldn't it be sacrilegious to return a gift that God had given you? Even to return a portion of it? It would be awfully rude anyway."

Tomas took a few deep breaths and said icily to Myles, "Well scholar! Explain it to him!" Then he turned and pointed the tip of his crosier at the seneschal, and said, "See, I told you this would never work. I said, just give them the book and let them figure it out for themselves. But, oh no! You wanted to complicate things, just so you could add a few more angels to your section."

The seneschal said calmly, "Now, now, Tomas. That's why Myles is here, to explain these small details. Go ahead Myles. Explain it to him."

Myles flipped nervously through the Bible. In bewilderment he looked from Lemuel, to the seneschal, to Tomas, and turned pages with shaking hands. As he scanned the words, he rapidly ran his index finger down each page. At last he brightened, and said hopefully, "Here it is! 'He that sacrificeth unto any god, save unto the Lord only, he shall be utterly destroyed.'[135] Does that clear it up for you?"

Lemuel's brow knit in consternation. He thought the statement proved his contention. It sounded as though there were more than one god. That was obviously not what they wanted to hear, so he said, "Oh yes, that clears everything up for me. Please continue with the lesson. I promise not to interrupt again."

"You do know the Ten Commandments, don't you?" Myles asked.

Lemuel peered at him suspiciously, wondering if Myles were serious or taunting him the way Abigail had. That's what was wrong. This was all Abigail's fault. She had infected him with these perverse ideas.

Myles turned to the Commandments and read, "Thou shalt have no other gods before Me."[136]

Lemuel pressed hard against his forehead with the palm of his hand. He was getting something the mortals call a headache. He said, "Yes, yes! I'm sorry I brought it up. Please..." and he motioned for Myles to continue.

Myles assured him that he could find a score or more like references in the Scriptures if he needed any more authority. "Like the revelations

HOW THE GOOD TAILOR GOT TO HEAVEN

of Jethro, who said, 'Now I know the Lord is greater than all the gods.'[137] There's absolutely no reason for confusion on that point. Now then, about the ambience that you use to instill dread in your parishioners. By God's instructions to Moses, the first altar was a mound of dirt[138]. The next was a rock, and God instructed Moses that no cutting tools were to be used as they would pollute God's natural formation.[139] But you are not forced to confine your place of worship to a rock or a mound of earth. The scriptures allow wide latitude. For example, study the chapter which describes Solomon's temple. Saint Peter's, in the Vatican, does not surpass its splendor: he built of fine cut stone; timbers from the cedars of Lebanon; and he overlaid the walls with sheets of gold."[140] Myles continued to exalt the splendors of Solomon's temple, reading from the Scriptures.

Lemuel had logged many hours over the centuries as a sidewalk superintendent. He had watched buildings being erected both in Heaven and on earth, and there seemed to be a contradiction between what he knew of construction methods, and God's prohibition against using tools to fashion his temple, and the elaborate structure that the Bible said Solomon erected. Lemuel had always been a stickler for carrying out orders to the letter, but there seemed to be a contradiction that he felt compelled to ask about. Driven by some perverse impulse he blurted out, "How could the stones for the temple be cut without polluting them?" Then he bit his tongue, but it was too late. He realized this was one more demonic induced perversity.

"That is one of the better Biblical examples of the way in which Solomon used the wisdom the Lord had given him.[141] He, 'had the stone made ready before it was brought thither· so that there was neither hammer nor axe nor tool of iron heard in the house while it was in building.'"[142]

"Oh, I see. I'm glad you explained it to me. I must have misunderstood God's commandment to Moses. I thought that the tools would pollute the altar. It's the noise pollution that is offensive, not the work itself." He added thoughtfully, "That Solomon certainly was wise." He wondered silently how they fastened the boards together without using hammers, and he conceded that Solomon was surely smarter than himself to have figured that one out. Hadn't he also figured out the dimensions for the basin with the thirty cubit circumference and the ten cubit diameter?

Tomas shook his head slowly and muttered to himself, "I told them: don't go into detail, just hand them a Bible and pray they never read it. Let them figure it out for themselves."

Myles turned from Solomon's tabernacle and directed Lemuel's attention to the chapter in Exodus which described the mobile tabernacle tent that the Lord commanded Moses to construct. The Lord gave detailed specifications for constructing the place of worship for the Israelites to use while they wandered in the desert for forty years. Very exact details, including even the garments the priests were to wear. Lemuel was attracted to the mobility concept.

"A movable mission would be able to reach out to more people and greatly improve my chances to bring the ten thousand souls to salvation," he observed.

He was also impressed by the luxury of the movable tabernacle and thought the roving life could be quite comfortable. Tomas butted in and suggested that Myles pass over these superficial tools of the trade and get down to the meatier issues: ritual and hermeneutics. He summarized, "A priest can do his job with a small case of altar implements."

From Lemuel's point of view, these details were not superficial. He knew that mortals were impressed and drawn toward artfully contrived constructions: just as they were by well tailored clothes. But Myles had launched into the hermeneutic portion of his dissertation.

"Tomas used a noxious comparison between the words of a legal brief and the Word as God, as set forth in the opening words of the book of John. Perhaps he had been too busy reading all those papal bulls and edicts to have read how Jesus felt about lawyers. He knew them for the evil sophists they are.

"John begins his gospel, 'In the beginning was the Word, and the

Word was with God, and the Word was God;' thus one can see that the Word was the matrix for all that followed. Only man can utter words, or God of course, and the angels of God, speaking through prophets or the Scriptures." He placed his hand on the Bible and said, "And herein the Word is made manifest for all of mankind. The Greek term for this is, *logos*, meaning "the divine word." As wisdom made incarnate in Christ, the Word made flesh in the son."

"The word without understanding is gibberish, and your vocation is to instill and inspire this revealed knowledge. This understanding is of the spirit and not of the intellect. It is a mystical understanding we call, *gnosis*. Unlike most knowledge which is gained only after much contemplation and study, and leaves those who pursue knowledge empty and realizing that they can never know it all, this understanding is arrived at first, and then all further study of the subject layers the understanding and reinforces the mystical wisdom."

"That principle is very similar to the way Tomas explained how the layers of ritual created the pearl that hid the sin," Lemuel said thoughtfully.

Myles sat quietly for a few moments, then turned and examined Lemuel's face; his own reflected suspicion. "You seem to have a perverse turn of mind, Lemuel. I didn't say that this special understanding was an overlay on sin. I said that knowledge reinforced the primary understanding. It is good on top of more good. How can you confuse anything I ever said with some analogy of Tomas's? Did you and he get together before this lecture? And that bit about the other gods, who put you up to that?"

"I don't know what you mean. I've never seen Tomas before we met here, together, just now." Lemuel had guilt written all over his face as he denied Myles's accusation. There was no way that he could reveal the actual truth: that his perverseness had demonic origins. The icy grip of fear began to grip his heart. If they found, out he'd have to go before the trial board. "My only excuse is my own ignorance," he pleaded.

Myles thought of the story of Parsifal and the Holy Grail. Only a perfect innocent could be trusted to go on the quest. A true innocent would also be a guileless fool who shot down swans without remorse. And if that were the case, Myles decided, Lemuel would be the perfect choice to bring back the Grail. Myles forgave him and related a better parable. Tomas, however, was not wholly innocent. It seems that Lemuel had been slated to go to Katmandu, and Tomas had peeked at Lemuel's record and switched assignments with the angel who told Lemuel the instruction was a snap, nothing to it.

"Let us say, for example, that the first bit of knowledge is like the first daub of paint that an artist puts on his canvas, and as he adds more brush strokes of paint to it." As he spoke, Myles flipped through the pages of the Bible. "Here, I know this is mixing metaphors, but consider Jesus' description of Heaven. 'It is like a grain of mustard seed, which a man took, and cast into his garden, and it grew, and waxed a great tree, and the fowls of the air lodged in the branches of it.'[143] Do you see? First comes the seed, or the first daub of the artist's brush, and the magnificence builds from that. Like the leaven hid in the meal, the fullness of faith grows to become like a painting, but pointing to the first brush stroke is impossible. In contemplating the tree, one often forgets the seed, but it had to come first."

This murky logic left Lemuel as confused as he had been all along. Nothing was making sense, beginning with Bradamante's explanation about the creation and the second law of thermodynamics. Now, when it was more important than ever that he understand so he could bring understanding to the mortals, his reason seemed to have deserted him. Perhaps he was what Tomas had called him: a dolt, an idiot, an imbecile; and Abigail was only partially to blame. Fearing that he would expose his inadequacies, he affected a solemn pose, touched his fingertips together on his lap, and nodded sagely.

Myles suspected that he was instructing an angel with a diminished mental capacity, if not actually obtuse. "Instilling the gnosis is not a matter of the intellect, Lemuel," he said and pointed with his index finger at the center of his own forehead, "it is of the heart." He pressed his clenched fist against his chest. Sometimes the unschooled lout is the most capable of understanding, while the degreed and lettered soul may be incapable because of intellectual barriers. They have heaped up in their hearts profane and vain babblings, oppositions of their so called false science;[144] they have spoiled their souls with philosophy and vain deceit, after the conceits of the world.[145] Both Peter and John were considered unlearned and ignorant men;[146] but the wisest of the erudite took gnosis from them who had been with Jesus."

"Consider the profundity that his Eminence, the seneschal, has made lucid, 'Life is a vapor that vanisheth away,' but the fate of one's immortal soul is at God's disposal. You should get that across to them in your sermons if you never make another point. You might even say something of the fires of Hell that Tomas described to increase their receptivity. You should point out the wickedness of the world; there is a perpetual market for that sermon. Tell them that sin is rampant on Earth, but in the Empyrean all is in order in the eternal presence of the Lord. Use the words of John: 'Love not the World, neither the things that are in the World. If any man love the World, the love of the Father is not in him.'[147] Then emphasize the point with James: 'Whosoever will be a friend of the World is the enemy of God.'[148] And then tell them how fortunate they are that Jesus has redeemed them from the corruption that is round about them."

Myles sought the approval of his superior angels. "How was that? Have I got it right so far?"

The seneschal virtually glowed with pride over his selection of Myles as tutor. The stars on his rating sheet would dazzle the eyes of the promotion board. He beamed a smile at Myles and nodded his approval.

Tomas granted him nothing by way of approval and scanned the group of ordinary souls at work in Eden. He idly observed, "It might be prudent to soft peddle the glory that awaits, and the eternal light and all. Don't get too specific. Use that mustard seed parable Myles used, you know, about the phantasmagorical tree with the bird's nests and such. Use metaphor and parable as much as you can." Then he motioned for Myles to continue.

Myles checked through the papers on his clipboard. "Here's a memo from the CIA (Central Intelligence Angels), and it says that there is currently a 'back to basics' movement in America. That might be a wonderful overall theme for your mission. It is simple, easily understood, and if this memo is correct, it should attract the mortals like a county fair. Those early Christians really had love for one another, and true fellowship. They thought of themselves as brothers and sisters of their Father who art in Heaven. They recognized the futility of laying up wealth in the temporal world. The true believers scorned things of the world. They believed that the primary manifestation of evil and worldliness is the ownership of private property, and they cast off their personal wealth and laid up true wealth of the spirit with God. The true believer should scorn all possessions, for in reality, these things end by owning their souls, and are like unto demonic possession. The mortal that has been infused with the true spirit has no use for possessions of any kind. The apostles, who Jesus had trusted to spread his gospel, had all their followers sell all of their property, withholding nothing, and put their wealth into a common fund. The purest Christian community was one where they lived out their ephemeral existence in common and where wealth was taken from each according to his ability, and sustenance given to each according to his need."[149]

"Harumph!" Tomas cleared his throat and prodded the golden nuggets of the path with his crosier. "Doesn't that contradict the teaching of Proverbs? I seem to recall something about sinners enticing the unwary by saying, 'Cast in thy lot among us; let us all have one purse.' The Proverbs warn, 'Walk not in the way with them, for their feet run to do evil.'"[150]

Myles rejected Tomas's comments with a wave of his hand. "That's Old Testament, Tomas. The inspired words of the blessed and sainted Paul lucidly explain the meaning of the New Testament when he said: 'And the law is not of faith: but the man that doeth them shall live in them.'[151] Christianity is about faith, Tomas, not the law! For 'Christ hath redeemed us from the curse of the law.' That's the real truth of Christianity. What had been before became erased and was found reprehensible. Ownership is worldliness, and the law which allows ownership is worldliness, and it is an evil. A sin in the sight of God! And if I could go with him, I'd like to help Lemuel establish a truly Christian church in America."

"You lecherous, ersatz angel. I know why you'd like to help his mission, but that's not the point. I can't see him preaching that in the Americas. The whole idea is to successfully evangelize among the mortals, and I suspect that acquiring private property is just as important in the Americas today as it was to the fifteenth century Europeans who brought the true faith to those shores. I understand that the Aborigines had some peculiar notions about land ownership, but we can't turn back time, can we? His mission should have popular appeal."

Doggedly, Myles contended his premiss, "That is outrageous. Are you so steeped in cynicism that you would place man's laws, above God's? It is clear from the Scriptures that the communal life is how God intended for man to live until the rapture comes. If not, then why did God dispatch that evil angel to strike down dead Ananias and his wife Sapphira for holding back from the common fund.[152] Explain that! Does that sound as though God intended for Christians to possess anything beyond their daily bread?"

Myles spoke softly to Lemuel. "I don't understand it. He won't touch the Bible and now he seems to have forgotten the Lord's Prayer. He should have been replaced ages ago. It's shocking that he's still allowed to teach." Then he spoke louder for Tomas's benefit. "The central idea behind being freed from 'the curse of the law' is because worldly secular humanists will try to codify their middle class morality and raise their sins of mortal ordination above God's New Testament. Their laws, ownership of property, civil rights, marriage, and so forth, are treasonous evils in the Kingdom of God. Their worldly laws are contrived to circumvent faith. They're against the Holy Spirit. Their laws are worldliness."

Tomas had a strange look on his face. It was a smile, but a smile so filled with evil that it was hard to remember that Tomas was an angel. Tomas looked at the ground and drew another small Papal Cross with the tip of his crosier.

Myles proceeded happily with his lecture. "That ideal is the most blessed way your parishioners can live since it is also nearest to the way the souls here in Heaven spend eternity. It's best to give all to God, and that avoids any later problems with the people at the IRS." He noticed Lemuel fretting and obviously wrestling with a problem, and he continued cautiously. Lemuel's disturbing questions had a way of throwing off his train of thought. "They wholly deny worldly flesh, and seek purification of the soul." He proceeded hesitantly as Lemuel's frown grew. "That is how the early Christians lived before they were corrupted three hundred years later at the first council of Nicaea." Finally, he asked, "All right, what's the problem now?"

"Oh, no problem. I was merely wondering about the tithing part. If they give everything they own to the apostle, and then in turn the apostle gives them everything that they need, are they supposed to return ten percent of what they were given to God? Or would the ten percent be given to God only after they had used up the value of the goods they had given to the Apostle? Or could it be that if they gave everything to the apostle, that they should expect to receive an amount nine times greater than the amount they had given? I know that it sounds a bit confusing, but as I said, it's just a minor little question and I'm sure that you can clear it up for me."

Myles fumed. He saw Tomas turn his back toward them, but not far enough to hide his mirth. Tomas's shoulders were jerking with cackling laughter. Myles glowered at Tomas, and he thought, *This Lemuel was no Parsifal, he was an agent of the papists sicked on him by Tomas.*

The seneschal said, "He has an interesting point there, Myles. Why don't you explain it to him?"

After several moments of thought, and some gritting of his teeth, Myles said solemnly, "How does one explain faith? Faith is the substance of things hoped for; the evidence of things not seen.[153] And have ye not read this Scripture, 'The stone which the builders rejected is become the head of the corner: this was the Lord's doing and it is marvelous in our eyes.'"[154]

HOW THE GOOD TAILOR GOT TO HEAVEN

Then after several more quotes of similar pith, he leveled a glare at Lemuel and said, "Thou fool, this night thy soul shall be called of thee: Then whose shall those things be which thou hast possessed?[155] That is your answer." He waved the Bible at him and said, "Everything that you want to know, or that is worth knowing, is between these covers. But please, with all the ground that we have yet to cover, I beg of you, do not interrupt with such idle ruminations."

"But you handled the question masterfully, Myles. I fear that I would have had trouble fielding that one." And the seneschal asked for them to sympathize with the problems of a harried executive. "With a staff of sixty-four angels, and a workforce of hundreds of souls to oversee, and keep well disciplined, those golden hours for meditation and Bible study are very rare. If you become the bishop of a large stake, Lemuel, and are responsible for the young missionaries bringing in the souls of converts, and of so many details, you will understand. Oh! I didn't mean to try to influence your selection of denomination, but should you choose the LDS church there is an advantage to having those mortal missionaries. You send them out, two by two, and they create more missionaries, who create more missionaries, the salvations expand exponentially, and all of the salvations are credited to your tally."

This blatant recruitment ploy by the seneschal shook Myles momentarily, but he owed his advancement to the seneschal. He flattered the seneschal for his management abilities. "A lesser angel would be overwhelmed by the deluge of responsibilities that you must face each day, your Eminence." But he ignored his obvious ploy to induct Lemuel into the Mormon church. Then, he turned to Lemuel and said, loud enough for Tomas to hear, "He's a wonderful boss. When you return from your detail I hope you are fortunate enough to get one as good."

He shifted closer to Lemuel and spoke softly, and confided: "I know what the angels think of us ordinary souls, but we naturally born souls see a lot from the bottom that is often hidden from you created angels. This is just a friendly word, be careful about picking mentors. Tomas is an old, hide-bound Guelf. Get in with the Ghibelline faction if you decide to go with the Roman church, or the reformed LDS church, if you go that route, and want to get anywhere in this company. But the best is High Church Episcopalian. That's where the money is. 'The poor is hated even of his own neighbor: but the rich hath many friends.'[156]" He gave Lemuel a sly wink.

Tomas walked over and stood threateningly close, and Myles got busy searching for a passage in the Bible. Tomas glared accusingly. "What's he whispering? More slander against the church? I caught that snide comment about the Council of Nicaea. Let me tell you, without the discipline they instilled into the Christians there, there would be no Christian religion today."

Myles jeered, "Hah! That's some example: Discipline imposed by a Pagan!"

"Constantine was a Christian!" Tomas sputtered.

"Yeah! Ten years later, on his death bed he became a Christian. But when he forced the church to do his bidding, he was still a pagan!"

Tomas sat next to Lemuel and placed his gnarled old hand on Lemuel's arm, and patted it. "Don't you see what he is after? You are going on your mortality detail and he's trying to poison your mind against the Catholics. He wants you to bring your saved souls into the Protestant church. He's trying to close off half of your options. Now tell me, what was he whispering?"

For Lemuel, Odesseus' passage between the Scylla and the Charybdis was like a cruise through the tunnel of love, compared to the forces which churned through this dilemma. He was no oily talking politician, but he tried. "Be fair Tomas. Would you betray the confidences of the confessional? And as for my choice, I'm sure that God will direct my footsteps onto the proper path."

"Well said, Lemuel!" the seneschal acceded. "You'll make a fine saint."

"For your information Tomas, I was telling him of the dual aspect of worship available to his ministry. I was just looking for the right passages." He found what he was looking for and said, "Here, God is speak-

HOW THE GOOD TAILOR GOT TO HEAVEN — 123

ing through Isaiah: 'I form the light and create the darkness: I make the peace and create the evil.'[157] It is as I said about Jesus and John the Baptist. One led a life of austerity and self denial, and the other luxuriated on a couch while, 'a woman of the city which was a sinner,' massaged his body with precious unguents.[158] Which would you say was the proper path to the Empyrean? The answer is both."

"Similarly, there were two opposing schools of worship among the early Christians. One school practiced austerity, or fasting, and fleshly denial, like the Carthusian monks, and the Albigensians; and the others demonstrated their scorn for the flesh, and the parsimonious customs of the World, by the indulgent consumption of everything, like the Nicolaitans[159]. Although Saint John the Divine hated them, their practices were as divinely inspired as the other. This was the feast."

Lemuel, as ever, unable to hide what he thought, again looked puzzled, and Myles expanded. "The mortal who is fixated on the world, and Worldliness, wants to conserve the things of the World. He stores up things of the World for his, and his heirs', future in the World. He passes on these sinful things of the World to his children.[160] He is a conservative, a worldly, faithless, person, 'that layeth up treasure for himself.'"

Myles continued. "First let us see what would be the practices of the school of the fast. This fast may be abstinence for long periods of time. It will, if endured long enough, bring the corporal more in tune with the spiritual. And if the fasting person persists, for as long as forty days, and forty nights, the body will grow weak, the vitals quiver, and then divine illusions will form."

"Consider Saint Francis of Assisi. He is a wonderful example of piety and self-denial. He gave away everything that he had; wore a hair shirt, or went naked; preached to the birds; and grazed on grass. Another example of devotion is Origen…"

Tomas snorted, "Harumph! Another heretic and Bible translator. Ignore him Lemuel. Like Myles, Origen was another rebel against ordained authority."

"He was a great scholar, writer, and teacher, and a believer in the literal interpretation of the Scriptures. Where Matthew says, 'and there be eunuchs which have made themselves eunuchs for the kingdom of heaven's sake. He that is able to receive it, let him receive it.'[161] And so, as an expression of self denial, Origen castrated himself."

Now the seneschal was shocked by his protégé's advice. "That's a bit extreme, Myles. My nineteen wives and fifty-seven children are all glorious additions to the Empyrean. Heaven is more wonderfully endowed because of my attentions. But if I had followed that advice…"

Tomas added, "Matthew didn't mean for that to be taken literally. Every priest of the church is a figurative eunuch, ever since the Middle ages. And most practiced celibacy even when they were permitted to marry."

Myles snorted, "And that's why you never hear about any Roman Catholic priests fornicating? Hah!" Then he turned to the seneschal, and explained, "This is about the symbolism of fasting and self-denial. I'll get to the feasting part in a moment."

Tomas glared at Myles and his mouth worked like a goat chewing on brambles. "Does not the book of Leviticus say, 'Whosoever hath a blemish, let him not approach to offer the bread of his God?'[162] And then there is a long list of blemishes unacceptable to God: the lame, flat-nosed, broken-footed or broken-handed, crook-backed, or dwarfed, or that hath a blemish in his eye, or be scurvy or scabbed, or that hath his stones broken.' In other words, no castration!"

"That's Old Testament stuff, Tomas. Remember, 'He hath freed us from the curse of the law'[163] When Jesus died on the cross, 'the veil was rent'[164] Do you understand what that means?"

"I have a feeling you're about to tell me," Tomas said wearily.

"Only a few privileged priests were admitted behind the veil into the Holy of Holies. But when the veil was rent, everyone could see God sitting on the mercy seat. The sacred mysteries were opened to all."

For the first time the seneschal looked askance at his pet protégé. The mention of allowing the unclean to enter the Holy of Holies was like

HOW THE GOOD TAILOR GOT TO HEAVEN

fostering abominations. But Myles, flush with victory over Tomas, did not notice, and he continued, "However, it is not necessary to go as far as Origen. Denial of the flesh can be a simple matter of self flagellation. Try to organize groups of pilgrims to go through the streets of the villages scourging and beating themselves with chains. A more startling effect can be produced by welding nails and bits of sharp metal, etceteras, into the chains. Also, if they wear anything, they should wear sack cloth, the rougher the better, or hair shirts, and pour ashes over their heads and bodies. They should let their hair and beards grow long, and be as unkempt and dirty as possible—the riper the better. Going barefoot in midwinter adds a nice touch, and a few should have crowns of thorns sunk into their scalps; those two-inch thorns of Barbary work wonderfully, and they should be carrying rough heavy crosses. Have them make a point of accosting everyone they see by grabbing at their clothing and crying. Repent! Repent!

"It is a well-known fact that these pilgrims often have the God-given gift to sense the presence of heretics, and witches, and they can point them out for you. When Tomas was on his mortality detail, many a heretic or witch would have gone undetected except for these believers with their extrasensory perceptions."

The seneschal agreed that some people have these powers. "When the angel, Mather, was on his mortality detail in Salem, Massachusetts, he was fortunate enough to have the assistance of several young girls that were likewise gifted." He added thoughtfully, "But I don't recall him mentioning that they were any more pietistic than the rest of the Puritans."

Myles consulted his clipboard, speaking softly to himself, "Hum, Massachusetts? That's in America, isn't it? Yes, there is something. The CIA memo reports that witch hunts are conducted with regularity in America, and although the Biblical proscriptions are no longer carried out, the evil doers are ferreted out and condemned."

"But, as I recall," the seneschal continued to reminisce, "the Puritans as a group strongly practiced denial of fleshly desires. We did also, and were persecuted for it. They hounded us from town to town because of our no nonsense approach to the Scriptures. We were forced to move farther and farther into the wilderness and finally we settled in a vast wasteland by a great salt lake. The land was so poorly that the Indians didn't even want it. Eventually President Fillmore saw that we were blessed, and he made me the governor of the territory."

While the seneschal was lost in these reveries of his own mortality detail, Myles proceeded. "Above all, Lemuel, do not let yourself be drawn into the sin of worldliness. Middle class morality with its sins of mortal ordination is a yawning trap. It is too easy to be drawn into their soft slovenly ways. They'll tell you to go along, to get along, but they mean go along to get along in the world." He leafed through the Bible to the last book, and read, "I would thou wert cold or hot. So then because thou art lukewarm, and neither cold nor hot, so I will spew thee out of my mouth.'[165] Those who choose the easy lukewarm path will be spewed out! Be careful, shun the harlot at the gate of middle class morality."

Tomas gripped his black thorn stick for support and placed his forehead against the shaft, and slowly rocked back and forth while slowly shaking his head, and moaning: "No...no...no...no." A few long wisps of blond gray hair swayed on his creased old neck.

During Lemuel's recent forays as a deliverance angel he had the opportunity to observe many bits and snatches of modern human practice. With the exception of a few zealous believers living in the Middle East, he saw practically no intentional mortification of the flesh being practiced as a devotional ritual, although there was some body piercing and painful tattooing among fad obsessed cliques. He told Myles of these observations.

"That is because they have chosen the alternative to fasting," Myles said without hesitating. "Remember, the other school of worship, the feast. Your parishioners may prefer that path to glory. You may also alternate between the two: fasting and mortification of the flesh on some days; and feasting with no regard for the morrow on other days. And

HOW THE GOOD TAILOR GOT TO HEAVEN — 127

with that body piercing and such, it sounds like they're already mortifying their flesh and they just need spiritual guidance to turn it into a devotional.

"In my days in the world there was an echo of that among the Indians of the West Coast." The seneschal became very solemn. "It is how they lost the way, but they kept the ritual Potlatch. You knew that the Indians were the descendants of the lost tribe of Israel, didn't you? And that Jesus visited with them before he ascended."

Tomas looked up and said softly, "Lord give me strength."

"Let us examine the feast as the alternate way to salvation," Myles continued. "As Paul, with divine inspiration, states, 'All things are lawful for me.'[166] So, you and your flock may feel more devout with the feast. The divine feast is not merely fuel for the workaday world, it is anything but, and the more opulent and voluptuous the better. It should be indulged to the complete exhaustion of mortal flesh and worldly possessions. At this divine sacramental, thanksgiving indulgence, and love for all is ever present; love for God, his wondrous bounty, and for all of God's children. It's another way of fulfilling Jesus' commandment that they love one another."

"From the Scriptures it is clear that all manners of pleasures are to be indulged. 'He cannot sin because he is born of God,' 1st John 3:9. Bear in mind that for those imbrued with the Holy Ghost all things are lawful: as they were for Paul. Also, note Peter's vision of the things which were forbidden by Old Testament law: pork, finless and scaleless sea creatures, certain fowls, etc. were followed by the divine invitation to feast. Nay, not merely an invitation, but the command, 'What God hath cleansed, that call thou not common!'[167] See, all of God's creations are wonderful and man should not presume to scorn any of them."

He showed Lemuel another passage. "In the Revelations of Saint John, he enlightens us further. 'Thou art worthy, O Lord, to receive glory and honor and power: For thou hast created all things, and for thy pleasure they are and were created.'[168] That means that all of God's gifts are to be celebrated as the Lord's bounty, and for mortals to shun these wondrous gifts would provoke his displeasure."

Tomas had closed his eyes and was lightly tapping his bowed head against his crosier. The seneschal cleared his throat and asked, "How far do you intend to pursue this tack, Myles?"

"All the way to salvation, your Eminence."

"Some people like horseradish on their roast beef, and some like a rich brown gravy; do you mean that they must eat horseradish if they don't like it, just because the Lord created it?" the seneschal asked.

"Oh no! Paul says, 'I know, and am persuaded by the Lord Jesus, that there is nothing unclean of itself: but to him that esteemeth it to be unclean, to him it is unclean.'[169] So if you don't want to put horseradish on your meat, you don't have to. The key to the feast school of worship is enjoyment. You see, harsh custom and the laws were discarded when the veil was rent. Understand?"

The seneschal nodded sagely. "That's good. Lots of people don't like horseradish. Wouldn't want to lose any souls over something like that.

"I do not like to belabor a point, but one cannot stress too much that God created all things. And naturally this includes the flutters and stirring of sensuality. In this King James Bible, John says, 'Beloved, let us love one another: for love is of God; and everyone that loveth is born of God, and knoweth God…for God is love.'[170] Those lukewarm middle class moralists, whose tongues run to call a divine creation common, will try to confound the full meaning of love. They will say, this is proper and that is wicked and sinful, but who are they to judge the presence of love in another's heart or how God has chosen to move that person to express that love. They prove that they have no love in their own hearts or they would rejoice over this evidence of God in another.

"Paul's letter to the Colossians warns us about these sins of mortal ordination. The ordinances of men which will make you dead in Christ: touch not; taste not; handle not; are the commandments and doctrines of men.[171] When the veil was rent, the Levitical prohibitions regarding

HOW THE GOOD TAILOR GOT TO HEAVEN — 129

clean and unclean were abolished in the flesh of Christ. He has freed us from the curse of the law. Just as these prohibitions no longer apply, neither do the laws regarding sexual relations. Women no longer have clean and unclean days, and since we know that women can not conceive during their menstrual cycle, and that intercourse is now to be allowed at this time, sexual intercourse is a proper expression of God's love. And in the book of Revelations, this verse about the twelve manners of fruits of the tree of life which yielded her fruit every month[172], clearly refers to the woman's menstrual cycle..."

Tomas interrupted and quietly pointed out that that verse referred to a woman's fertile periods, not to the infertile ones. "Sex is for procreation," he stated firmly.

"Fruit is to be eaten, and enjoyed, Tomas," the seneschal said with a sly smile. "If one has a large orchard, like wise Solomon, one need never have one's sensual hungers go unsated, and also may comply with your contention." He looked off dreamily and said wistfully, "One might occasionally dine on a luscious, mixed fruit salad."

"But if Lemuel's mission is to take the form of the early church, the ownership of the orchard would be of the whole congregation of believers," Myles pointed out, and referred to the Scripture which said, "'And the multitude of them that believed were of one heart and one soul: neither said any of them that aught of the things which he possessed was his own; but they had all things in common.'[173] Heaven forbid that they should be so selfish as to claim exclusive possession of a wife, or children. The wives and children would be shared among the congregation as the need to express the God-given love arose."

In spite of the frown growing on the seneschal's face, and Tomas's black glares, Myles plunged ahead. "This expression of love is the single most important tenet of the church: love of God, and love for each other. If you recall, I made the qualifying statement that we are using the King James version, and this is not the Bible that Tyndale, Cranmer, and myself translated. In fact we were all dead when this was published in 1611 but the King did use much of our work. However, take this very familiar passage about faith, hope, and charity, and you can see that the translation was not rendered faithfully. Ah, here it is: 1st Corinthians, ch. 13: 'Though I speak with the tongues of men and angels and have not charity, I am become as sounding brass, or a tinkling cymbal.' That word charity, should be love. It is the only way this passage makes any sense. Here where it says: 'And though I bestow all my goods to feed the poor, and have not charity it profiteth me nothing.' That makes no sense, bestowing all one's goods to feed the poor is charity. But if you change that word to love, and you bestow all one's goods without love; then it profiteth nothing…see? That is how we translated the verse, and we worked from the old Hebrew, Aramaic, and Greek writings. Some papist changed it. Now read that same chapter and each time you read charity, substitute the word love."

Tomas snapped, "That love you're talking about is agape, not copulation, you dimwit!"

"Yes, it includes that, but it does not exclude the other. Leave it to the Curia Romana to split legalistic hairs over the interpretation of Scripture. Oh, woe to ye lawyers! And if your contention is to be believed, then why does Paul take such pains to elevate, even glorify, the genitalia in the foregoing chapter. 'And those members of the body, which we think less honorable, upon these we bestow more abundant honor; and our uncomely parts have more abundant comeliness.'[174] And the meaning of 'we bestow more abundant honor,' how would you propose that to be interpreted? Certainly not by a life of celibacy."

Tomas stalked off muttering violent oaths. The seneschal was greatly perplexed and Lemuel was very confused. He shook his head as he read the indicated passages. "I didn't think that religion was so involved in sexuality. You might think it allowed sin and lechery, but it says, 'all the members rejoice with it.'"

"Yes, it's a pity that so much of the Scriptures have been bowdlerized. Although the Acts of John were cast out, there remains some of his God-inspired message." Myles closed his eyes and patted his forehead with his right palm, as though to jolt his memory, and then recited,

HOW THE GOOD TAILOR GOT TO HEAVEN 131

"Glory be to thee Father! And we all going round in a ring answered—Amen.' You see, Lemuel, they weren't satisfied when the first Nicene Council butchered the Holy Words, so they had to have another little conclave called the second Nicene Council in the eighth century. They consigned some of the best Scripture to the flames.

"We scholars, working outside of the corrupt church, restored most of it for The Great Bible we dedicated to King Henry the Eighth. He was a fine man, played the recorder beautifully, and even composed some music for the instrument.

"I'll try to remember a few verses. This is John's recollection of the way Jesus sang, and what all the faithful did just before Jesus went to his death. His song goes like this: 'Let us praise the Father in a hymn of praise, and so go forth to meet what is to come.' Then he bade us make a ring, holding each other's hands. And he said, 'Answer me with amen.' After which he began to sing a hymn of praise:

And we all responded: 'Glory be to thee Word! Amen.'
'And wherefore we give thanks, that I will tell,
'I will be saved, and I will save,'
and we all going round in a ring answered,
'Amen!'
'I will be begotten, and I will beget!'
'Amen!'
'I will be washed, and I will wash!'
'Amen!'
'I will be freed, and I will free!'
'Amen!'
'Grace paces the round. I will blow the pipe, dance the round around!'
'Amen!'"

Myles was silent for a few seconds to let the words sink in, and then said, "All that remains of that joyful occasion in this Bible is this pale reflection in Revelations: 'Four and twenty elders fell down before the lamb, having everyone of them harps and vials full of odors, which are the prayers of saints. And they sung a new song.'[175] Do you see? It's a joyous celebration with the Lord, and bestowing the kiss of peace. Your rites don't have to be fraught with nagging sermonizing which add up to: touch not, taste not, eat not; which are the doctrines of men. Sing, dance, caress, love one another, be free. And this other little passage over here, the wedding supper of the lamb. 'And his wife hath made herself ready; and to her was granted that she should be arrayed in fine linen, clean and white: for the fine linen is the righteousness of saints.'[176] Obviously the linen is cast aside, and everyone is as naked as Adam and Eve for the washing and begetting part of the ceremony where the fruits of the tree of life are indulged, and the bestowal of more honor on the less comely members take place."

Lemuel was thoroughly bewildered, but had the wit to respond, "Oh yes that would be prudent."

Myles continued, "The ancient rites by some Gnostic sects were given to fasting and fleshly denials. But others practiced mortification of the flesh with ceremonies that seemed to be, by the papists, voluptuous celebrations of fleshly delights, but in reality both rituals elevated the soul above worthless flesh and middle class worldliness."

The seneschal rubbed the auburn whiskers on his chin and looked at Myles. His mortality detail had been more recent than the tutor's, and he asked, "Would some form of birth control be practiced in these orgies? I mean, what if some of the women got pregnant? The children wouldn't know who their fathers were."

One could almost see black scowl rings emanating around Tomas's lips. He swished his black thorn crosier viciously and nearly hit John d'Are with it. John d'Are had been hovering nearby listening with stunned interest to this interpretation of the Scriptures. He side-stepped Tomas's crosier, and then he offered meekly: "I've heard that they have a pill now." Tomas drew his crosier back for a swing at John d'Are's head and the seneschal yelled for the yard man to duck. It was just in time, and Tomas's follow through spun him around and off balance, and he sat down hard in the middle of the walk.

HOW THE GOOD TAILOR GOT TO HEAVEN

Myles was flustered by this show of vehemence, but he responded to the seneschal, "No, I think that it would defeat the purpose. The semen, as well as the menstrual flows, were reveled in as a delight of the loving God. In order to bear fruit, the tree of life must be fertilized with the semen. But as for paternity, Jesus said, 'And call no man father upon the earth: for one is your father, which is in heaven.'[177] But God does not impregnate women. His offices are fulfilled by the aroused libido of the worshipers. Any children would then be the offspring of God although sired by the honored comely male members. These children of love belong to the whole community of believers. Remember, aught of the things which he possessed was his own, but they had all things in common. Of course, that would include the children."

Tomas scrambled to his feet with surprising agility and brushed the flecks of gold dust off his robe. Then, after regaining a modicum of poise, he asserted, "Lemuel's mission is difficult enough without you filling his head with your radical interpretations."

Myles replied smugly, "Radical means pertaining to roots or origins; fundamental. It's the truly fundamentalist early Christian way, Tomas."

With his ire raising, Tomas responded, "No matter how basic and fundamentalist you imagine the Americans to be, that sort of ministry will be looked on with extreme disfavor. His objective is to make converts, not to experiment with some absurd theological theory you've cooked up. I doubt whether that form of ministry would appeal to ten thousand Americans."

"But think of the worship services if ten thousand did," Myles said dreamily.

John d'Are interjected, "From what I've heard from some of the newer arrivals, far more than ten thousand are already performing those rituals, but without the clergy. It seems that there was something called Woodstock."

Tomas gray face turned black. He shook his staff above his head and then leveled it threateningly at Myles while sputtering violent threats, then he strutted away angrily. He swung the crosier like a ball player warming up for a turn at bat, and it made swishing sounds that hissed and echoed back from the walls of Thelassar. He whimpered, "Passed over for promotion...twice! They send me out here in this miserable park to instruct all these dim-witted probationers...give me all the weirdos and wackos to work with...I'll never understand how they get up here."

Suddenly the gilded bole of a tree was before him, and he gave it a heavy thwack with his blackthorn and caused a golden apple to fall; it barely missed his head. He picked it up angrily and spat out, "That damned Newton! You'd think that up here they'd drift down softly." He looked at it sorrowfully. He brought it near his lips, and his mouth worked with a reflexive recollection, and then the hand holding the apple dropped to his side. He sighed, reached into the pocket of his robe, brought out a handful of manna, and munched on a few grains. Then he spat it out in disgust. "Bah! Coriander seed![178] Just because they don't want to put in crappers, we have to eat this tiresome swill."

Ignoring Tomas' tantrum Myles continued, "You should make every effort to invite the unsaved into your worship services, ostensibly as observers, but by seeing the joyful passions of the devoted there will be many who will end up being saved. And although it is advisable to scorn all worldly conventions there will be times that an unbeliever will be married to one of the faithful and, according to Paul, you will be able to approve that sort of mixed marriage.[179] But you should make every effort to bring the unbeliever to salvation. Your ceremonies may relax their misguided faith in worldly custom and they may become attracted to the singing and dancing, and what other forms of ritual you use to lure them into the church. And even if they remain adamant, if they have children, you're sure to get them. As Paul says, 'some might be saved.'[180]"

Chapter 9

IT IS COMMON KNOWLEDGE AMONG ANGELOLOGISTS THAT angels never need to bathe, except while on mortality detail, so the thought of parishioners washing each other's bodies as a liturgical act had never occurred to Lemuel. However, the ring dance ceremony that Myles prescribed included washing. "I will be washed, and I will wash—Amen!" Lemuel glanced over his shoulder toward the statues of John the Baptist baptizing Jesus and saw himself performing the ritual washing. But Lemuel's uncontrollable imagination had raised the shocking vision of a nude Abigail, and he was washing her. It quickly was replaced by a more modest image of her in her aqua sheath standing beneath the lamp post in King Jamesburg Park. As she had before, she waggled her finger at him, and said, "Naughty, naughty."

Without realizing that he spoke aloud, he blurted out unconsciously, "I am not."

Myles looked at him strangely. "What?" he asked.

Very flustered Lemuel answered. "I am not...ah, sure that you meant that you would want to invite all the nonbelievers." He groped for the right phrase. "Er... Ah... well... suppose a demon was to show up. I know you wouldn't allow..."

The seneschal laughed at Lemuel's misunderstanding of demonic mentality. "You can't classify demons as nonbelievers, Lemuel. The Scriptures tell us, 'the devils also believe, and tremble.'[181] The demons fear the Holy Spirits of consecrated ground, Lemuel. They'd never set foot on sacred property. Anyway, they're a pack of disobedient wretches who'd rather suffer the torments of Hell then to bend their wills to serve God. You'll never get any of them to your worship services."

The seneschal added, "It would be quite a coup if you could get one of them to return to the fold. Remember, all Heaven rejoices more over one sinner that repents, than over ninety-nine just persons which need no repentance.[182] It has never happened, but the salvation of one demon might be worth a thousand mortal souls." He smiled benevolently as he spoke and opened his arms wide, as though welcoming the multitudes.

Lemuel stared, transfixed by the seneschal, and he imagined Abigail in the begetting part of the ritual, along with several lusting worshipers. He said, "Well, there's one demon whose salvation I wouldn't rejoice over."

Myles chided him for his lack of Christian charity. "Now, now. We mustn't let our personal animosities toward the enemy become so hardened as to deny them repentance. Remember, we are supposed to love our enemies."

"Another much maligned group that the bourgeois lukewarm moralists often treat as shabbily as though they were unbelieving sinners, are homosexuals. There are, of course, no longer any proscriptions against them expressing the love God has instilled in their breasts. We are freed from the curse of the law. There were never any restrictions about lesbian lovers, and with the advent of the New Testament, men have been given equal rights. And all of those absurd incest rules have been removed. You may run into a few vestiges of the old, pagan Roman

HOW THE GOOD TAILOR GOT TO HEAVEN — 137

civil law, but remember, it is worldly law, forced onto the church by the Pagan Constantine, and therefore sinful.

"After all, why should the mortal's affections between brothers and sisters, or their mothers, be thwarted by some silly pagan taboo? Those rules magnified male dominance over their wives and according to the book of Leviticus, their daughters. This is another case where the New Testament has led to more enlightenment. Roman law forbid fathers to have sexual relations with their daughters, but if one assumes that what the Scriptures does not forbid is to be permitted, there were never any Levitical restrictions against fathers and daughters expressing their love for each sexually.[183] Although Paul seems to have mentioned a slight caveat: 'But if any man think that he behaveth himself uncomely toward his virgin, if she pass the flower of her age, and need so require, let him do what he will, he sinneth not.'[184] So she must have begun to menstruate, and now mothers may equally love their sons."

Tomas' agitation heightened. He set his jaw in a fearsome rage. His fingers gripped the solid gold apple so hard that his fingers whitened. As though he was pounding with a jack hammer, he pounded the end of his blackthorn crosier hard into the gold nuggets of the walkway, and he kept glancing at the seneschal with black looks and waiting for him to utter a word of dissent. He looked toward the gates of Thelassar, and expected the anti-perversion police to appear at any moment and grab this lunatic.

Oblivious to Tomas' mounting rage, Myles plunged ahead. "Who are our mothers or brothers, or sisters? We believers are all brothers and sisters of the love of our Father which art in Heaven. 'For whom shall do the will of God, the same is my brother, and my sister, and mother.'[185] So if we are all brothers and sisters to each other, then obviously none of these incestuous restrictions apply to the Lord's family. If you trace Jesus' heritage back through the Scriptures, you find that his familial antecedents began with Lot's relations with his daughter. Then through Ruth and Boaz, to Obed, and to Jesse, and so, the house of David had Moabite ancestors, Lot's seed."

"Are you going to let him get away with that?" Tomas roared at the seneschal.

The seneschal responded, "Tomas, Tomas. He is a Bible expert and he is citing the Scriptures. 'All Scripture is given by inspiration of God, and is profitable for doctrine, for reproof, for correction, for instruction in righteousness: that the man of God may be perfect, thoroughly furnished unto all good works."[186]

"Good works? Do you call voiding every moral precept, good works?"

"Our hardy band of faithful were likewise accused of immorality, Tomas." The seneschal said, while nursing a vision of his own persecution at the hands of bigoted moralists in Eastern America.

John d'Are had been listening quietly. He also prided himself on knowing some Scripture. He asked, "Do you mean that you can even do it with animals?"[187]

The question was met with all of the enthusiasm of the proverbial fart in a crowded elevator and after the initial blast, it hung in aromatic silence. The way Lemuel and the others looked at Myles he knew that he was expected to respond. So, after several seconds passed, he replied, "Of course that prohibition has been abolished too, John, but I think bestiality is generally caused by carnal lusts and that would be fornication; it would not be an expression of love. It is only indulged in by some because they have been unable to find a normal outlet for their repressed emotions. But with all of the women of the congregation, as well as the men, being eager to satisfy these repressed expressions of God's love, I wouldn't think that anyone would want to do it with animals. Myles shrugged his shoulders and admitted, "I don't really know the answer to your question John. Perhaps another catechist with more experience..."

"You might want to explain to John how the Satanists use a goat in their Black Masses." Tomas interjected, seething with rage.

Myles ignored him, and continued, "As Paul says, 'The body is not for fornication; it is the temple of the Holy Ghost.' He is very determined

HOW THE GOOD TAILOR GOT TO HEAVEN —⚘— 139

on this point, and he says: 'Shall I then take the members of Christ, and make them the members of a harlot? He that is joined to a harlot is one body, is one flesh, and he joined unto the Lord is one spirit.'[188] So I suppose the same reasoning would apply to copulation with animals.

"To make this more understandable, let me stress that Paul was instructing the Corinthians. Corinth was a city in Greece where temples to Aphrodite were numerous. It was a seaport, and with many horny sailors, as you may well imagine. The harlots worked in these temples doing their offices as priestesses of their goddess. But for a Christian to join as one flesh his temple of the Holy Ghost with the temple of Aphrodite, would indeed be a sin. 'If any man say unto you this is offered in sacrifice unto idols, eat not for his sake... but, the earth is the Lord's, and the fullness thereof... , and these harlots are part of the Lord's fullness... so Paul said, 'why is my liberty judged of another man's conscience? For if I by grace be a partaker, why am I evil spoken of for that which I give thanks? Whatsoever ye do, do all to the glory of God.'[189] So if one copulates with goats 'to the glory of God' then that would be an acceptable act of devotion.

"And what's more, Paul does say, 'God hath chosen the foolish things of the world to confound the wise; and the base things of the world, and things which are despised, hath God chosen, and things which are not, to bring to nought things which are: That no flesh should glory in his presence. The world by *wisdom* knew not God, it pleased God by the foolishness of preaching to save them that believe.'"[190]

He had turned to look at Tomas just in time. Nearly blind with rage Tomas let out a blood-curdling roar and flung the golden apple at Myles with the force of a catapult. Myles ducked, and it splashed, skipped twice across the waters of life, struck the statue of Jesus and John, bounced off, and plopped into the water at the feet of the oxen under the basin with the thirty cubit circumference and the ten cubit diameter.

Having missed with this heavy missile he gripped his crosier like a lance and charged at Myles. He would have run him through, too, if it were not for the quick action of the seneschal who thrust his own crosier between Tomas's legs, tripped him, and sent him sprawling. He laid there flailing at the ground with both arms and legs gyrating wildly, and he emitted loud piercing shrieks like a trumpeting elephant.

"Shut up Tomas!" the seneschal ordered. "Do you think that's any way for a senior angel to behave? Show some dignity for your office, even if you have none for yourself."

Tomas rolled over, but remained seated on the ground and breathing hard. He looked off toward the spires of Thelassar, and calmly said, "Haven't you been listening to the lessons that this vomit-brained cretin, no, not lessons, festering malignant obscenities that this artificial angel, this so-called Bible expert, has been teaching to this simple probationer?"

"They came from the Holy Book, did they not? And all Scripture is given by inspiration of God, and is profitable for..."

"Yeah, yeah! I heard you before," Tomas interrupted him.

"This little outburst of yours is sure to attract attention," the seneschal warned.

Tomas got to his feet, brushed the gold dust from his robe and looked up toward the spired holy city. He caught a glimpse of several heads retreating inside from a dozen windows, and he smiled his sinister smile. "You are right as ever, your Eminence. I'll try to be more flexible regarding Bible interpretations in the future. Forgive the momentary truculence. Please continue."

Lemuel placed his hand on Myles's arm, and said, "I think I have the general idea, the main thrust of fundamentalism, so to speak, but Tomas may be right about this type of ceremony having limited appeal in America. Are there any other ways that I could structure my mission, besides orgiastic feasts, or starving the faithful and mortifying the flesh?"

"You could be sensible about the mission and go with a nice, normal, main line religion, and forget everything this artificial angel has told you," Tomas suggested. Then he pointed to the Bible and said, "You could also use that book for a door stop, and never open it again. I heartily recommend that you do that."

HOW THE GOOD TAILOR GOT TO HEAVEN — 141

With mild disappointment, Myles slowly turned the pages of the Bible. "I think you are rejecting a really zestful possibility. You know that we angels do get worldly assignments from time to time, and I would be willing to stop in once in a while to see how your mission is progressing."

"That's very thoughtful of you to show such personal interest in a novice, and I'm not rejecting those methods of worship, I just wanted to know if there were any other liturgies that might be scripturally authorized." Although he thought Tomas was cynical about the mortal's souls, Lemuel believed that he was basically a devout angel and dedicated to the Empyreal Establishment. His violent outbursts had a cautioning effect, and Lemuel assumed that Tomas was trying to protect the company, and at the same time insure the success of Lemuel's mission. Lemuel added, "Like Tomas, I think it would be a good idea to be flexible."

Myles mumbled, "Most churches take care of the flexibility by having alternate feast days and fast days." He continued to search through the pages. "It's the lukewarm casually committed that you should avoid." Then, brightening with renewed enthusiasm, he asked, "How about serpents? Do you like serpents? They can be used very effectively."

At the word "serpent," the seneschal cocked his head toward Myles, and Tomas inhaled sharply. Tomas warned, "You are stepping over a dangerous line, Myles. I think you'd better avoid that." And for once the seneschal nodded his head in agreement with Tomas.

Without heed Myles plunged ahead enthusiastically, "The serpent signifies the powers of regeneration and life everlasting, just like a Crucifix does."

Both Tomas and the seneschal stood before the tutor and his pupil with glowering faces.

Myles continued, absorbed in teaching his lesson and without a hint of caution, "Medical doctors use a caduceus, which, as you know, resembles the cross, and to signify the healing powers of their arts. The entwined serpents copulating on Hermes' winged staff signify the given life passed on, as in the book of Genesis which states, 'go forth and multiply.'"

Lemuel observed, "Sexuality seems to be much more important in religious dogma than I'd ever realized." And he wondered if, as a mortal, such activities would be required of him. At the same time another conundrum arose: what business did a symbol in pagan mythology have to do with the true faith? Tomas had used the expression, 'unappropriated gods.' Of course there was only one true God, but perhaps incorporating the symbol of a false god might be helpful in acquiring salvations.

"Sex is only foremost in the minds of those preachers whose brains are located south of their navels. It's a common mortal affliction," Tomas explained caustically. Then he advised Myles, "Perhaps it's not necessary to delve into the deeper mysteries."

"I resent your aspersions against my former mortal condition. Although Luther, Cranmer, and Tyndale may have taken wives, I was as celibate as yourself. Since Lemuel has indicated an interest in the deeper hermeneutics, I thought that a discussion of the role of the serpent would be informative." Myles looked into the solemn faces of the seneschal and Tomas, and furthering his case pointed out, "The seneschal admitted that his administrative duties didn't leave much time for Bible studies, and you, Tomas, have made no secret of your aversion to the Scriptures. You wouldn't want to send Lemuel out into the world to make converts with an imperfect understanding of the mysteries, would you?"

The seneschal nodded reluctantly, Tomas strode off angrily, and Myles proceeded to tutor his bewildered pupil in more depth. "The anguine trail through the scriptures is as fascinating as the scaley multi-patterned creatures themselves. They seem to have a fascinating effect on mortals, an ambivalent power to attract and to incur revulsion, at one and the same time. A more apt symbol of both natures of God cannot be found in nature; hot or cold, the power to make the peace or create the

HOW THE GOOD TAILOR GOT TO HEAVEN —⚭— 143

evil, the fast or feast. The serpent has a powerful psychological effect, I'm surprised Tomas didn't mention it.

"The serpent on a pole is symbolic of the theme that is central to our faith. Here in John, his Gospel tells us, 'As Moses lifted up the serpent in the wilderness, even so must the Son of Man be lifted up. He that believeth in him should not perish, but have eternal life.'[191] What John referred to is this passage in Numbers: 'The Lord said unto Moses, make thee a fiery serpent and set it upon a pole: and it shall come to pass, that everyone that is bitten, when they looketh upon it, shall live.'[192] It is the clearest Old Testament reference to the crucifixion and the resurrection of our Lord, and the eternal life offered to the faithful. This knowledge, or gnosis, our belief in the resurrection, is what defines us as Christians."

Before Myles could say anymore, Lemuel put his hand on the tutor's arm, and asked haltingly, "Surely you do not mean to draw a connection between Jesus and the serpent who corrupted Adam and Eve with the fruit of the tree of knowledge?"[193]

"Oh, but I certainly do. You have a swift mind to have figured that out."

"What you ought to get is a swift kick for opening that can of worms, scholar." Tomas intoned menacingly.

The seneschal's eyes opened widely in amazement. He said, "I was always under the impression that the serpent was Satan in the guise of a serpent."

"That's not what the Bible says, your Eminence. It just says serpent. I know that a much harried executive such as yourself wouldn't have the time to go into these small details. Isn't that why you advocated my promotion? So I could work out these minor misunderstandings for you?" Myles smiled sweetly, and the seneschal nervously motioned for him to continue.

"If you will recall when Moses saw the burning bush in the wilderness and God spoke to him, God told Moses to tell the people; 'I, AM, hath sent me unto you.'[194] To those of us of modern times that seems enigmatic, but to Moses, who was raised as a prince in the house of the

Pharaoh, and where Ra was their principal deity, Am was another god. Which god? The Egyptians had many, and not only that, each god had many names.

"His identification is clear when one reads the Bible. (Tomas paced and kicked up some pebbles.) We know from the words of Solomon, 'The Lord said that he would dwell in the thick darkness.' And this phrase is reiterated in Chronicles.[195] And in the synagogue the Mercy Seat behind the veil in the Holy of Holies is a place of thick darkness. And in the Egyptian pantheon, the god who dwelt in thick darkness was Apep. They thought him most fierce of all their gods. He was their arch fiend.

"He was the huge fierce serpent that Ra must fight with and overcome each night in the darkest depths of the Tuat in order to arise each morning to ride in his ark of the sun on its journey through the firmament. So the Egyptians believed that in order to assist Ra, they must make waxen images of Apep, burn him, crush him under their left heel, and curse Apep in all of his many guises and names. One of his many names was AM: therefore, Moses, being raised by an Egyptian princess, would instantly know who it was that spoke to him from the burning bush."

"So it only makes sense that if we worship God who prefers to dwell in the thick darkness, it follows that for us, our evil god must be the god of the light. That is why Satan is referred to as the angel of light;[196] and Lucifer as the son of the morning.'[197]" Myles smiled beatifically at Lemuel, and said, "See how simple it all really is? It's angels like Tomas who complicate matters. And that explains why God told Moses to raise the fiery serpent upon the pole. Do you understand?"

The seneschal cast worried glances up toward the Holy spires of Thelassar and walked heavily over to the rim of the pool and settled uncomfortably on the coping. Tomas, as ever, sneered disagreeably. Lemuel was completely bewildered, and the mocking green eyes of the demon Abigail leapt into his imagination. He confessed, "No, not quite. How did Moses know it was the Lord, and not Satan?"

HOW THE GOOD TAILOR GOT TO HEAVEN — 145

"Because he was told, 'I am the Lord thy God!'" Tomas spat out quickly, and the seneschal nodded a vigorous agreement.

"Oh sure, I guess Satan wouldn't have said that," Lemuel said hurriedly, and blinked his eyes and massaged his temples to rid himself of the image of Abigail doubled over with laughter.

Myles hoped that Lemuel had gotten over his Parsifal-like simple-mindedness, but he was relieved to see that he wasn't doing Tomas's bidding either. He was just a run of the mill simpleton who didn't understand anything. Myles had presented the truth as clearly as he knew how, and said wearily, "I think I can clear this up."

"You better!" Tomas and the seneschal ordered in unison.

Myles was beginning to see the advantages of having only one instructor in the classroom, and behind a closed door. "Once and for all, you must get this straight in your mind. Do you recall all those Biblical references about threshing floors?" Then fearing what this naive simpleton might try to respond, he held up a cautionary finger. "Wait, don't answer. I'll tell you what they mean."

"Israel's son, Joseph, was much favored by Pharaoh."

"Oh yes, I've seen the carvings on the doors of the IRS many times," Lemuel replied.

"Well, Joseph was married to Asenath, who was the daughter of Potipherah, and he was the high priest at On. The Pharaoh was convinced that there should only be one god and he decided that Aten, or Ra, should be supreme, and as it happened, Joseph's father-in-law was his high priest. Joseph, for appearances sake, seemed to have gone along with this monotheistic king and his high priest, but he secretly continued to worship the same God that his family had always worshiped. How do we know this?"

Myles once more held up his hand to silence Lemuel before he could say anything, but Lemuel was so mystified now that he could not utter a word, and so was the seneschal. But for some reason Tomas wore a sinister smile.

Myles continued, "We know this because when his father Jacob, or

Israel, died, they had him mummified and entombed as any good Egyptian would do for his father. But then Joseph and his family did something else: they worshiped and mourned for seven days on the threshing floor at Atad.[198] The god of the threshing floor was the serpent who kept out the rats who would eat the grain. So even then the Jews must have known how God represented himself to them. Also it is highly likely that Joseph, being given charge of the Pharaoh's granaries, used the power of his God, the serpent, to enslave the Egyptians.

"That is why the threshing floor turns up so frequently in the Bible. Ruth the Moabitess, descendant of Lot and his daughter, and a distant ancestor to Joseph the husband of Mary through the house of David, met with Boas on the threshing floor in Bethlehem[199]. And where did Mary place the baby Jesus? It was in a manger, and while a manger isn't a threshing floor, it is a place for grain."

Lemuel was so confused now that he wondered if Myles hadn't been tutored by Abigail... or Satan himself. So far Myles had taught that his parishioners either torment their flesh with whips and chains, and fast to the extreme, or else expend their wealth with prodigality. But serpents? What could he do with serpents? "How do I use serpents in my mission?"

"Let the Bible guide you, Lemuel," Myles said, waving the Bible at him. "Here, look at this passage. 'And these signs shall follow them that believe; In my name shall they cast out devils; they shall speak with new tongues; they shall take up serpents; and if they drink any deadly thing, it shall not hurt them; they shall lay hands on the sick, and they shall recover.'[200] And then Luke, the beloved physician, says, 'Behold, I give you power to tread on serpents and scorpions, and over all the power of the enemy, and nothing shall by any means hurt you.'[201] There's the whole liturgy spelled out for you: gather as many poisonous snakes and scorpions as you can find and pass them out among the parishioners, and up on the altar you have the fiery serpent on a pole. And there is no need for you to bore them with vain sermonizing, let them speak in tongues, and you can pass cups full of poison around among the faithful."

HOW THE GOOD TAILOR GOT TO HEAVEN — 147

"And if any of them are possessed by demons, you can cast out devils; and if any are sick, they can be healed by the laying on of hands. Now wouldn't be that a far more lively worship service than the bleak, washed-out, Catholic services, with their pompous processions, Holy water, censers, and chants that Tomas would like you to do."

"In fact, I don't see any reason why you shouldn't also include washing and begetting as part of your service. Bid the faithful to fall down among the serpents and beget until they're exhausted, and on the other side of the temple, other worshipers could be scourging themselves and wailing: Repent! Repent! And have the believers who speak in tongues wander about through the worshipers..." Myles raised his hands, and exclaimed joyfully, "Oh! What a glorious testimonial of faith that would be!"

The seneschal held his head with both hands, his eyes were shut tight, and he moaned miserably as he rocked back and forth. Tomas, with heavy sarcasm, opined, "Yes, that would certainly drive out the demons."

John d'Are, a fount of ethereal gossip, observed, "I'd go easy with the poison cup; heard that nine hundred souls who practiced that service arrived all at once from a place called Jonestown." He poked thoughtfully at the nuggets with his rake. "Guess their faith wasn't strong enough."

* * *

Lemuel's instruction by Myles progressed along the same lines for some time. Myles felt that his first pupil should have a thorough understanding of all aspects of the Holy Scriptures. And more than once, Lemuel discovered that he had misunderstood Biblical doctrine. It was when Myles got into genealogy that the lesson was abruptly terminated. It completely mystified Lemuel how such a dry subject could have caused the trouble.

Myles got into the subject by showing Lemuel the infallible proof that God created the earth in 4004 B.C.E. He showed Lemuel the family trees that he had worked out from the Scriptures, and that he had previously diagrammed on the yellow legal pad to aid this tutoring session. It was the same sort of thing that when he was mortal he had started, but it was very tedious work, and he'd left it unfinished. His effort was taken up and completed by Bishop Usher after Myles's death.

The excitement did not happen when Myles once more launched into the history of Sodom and Gomorrah, and the events leading up to Lot's relationships with his daughters. Tomas carried on with his usual bombastic flow of denunciation, but he did that about everything in the Bible anyway. The seneschal had excused the incident of incest as an act by three frightened survivors who believed that they were the last three people in the world.

Myles had corrected this common misconception by pointing out that the family of Lot had spent the entire time that God rained down the fire and brimstone onto the cities of the plain, safely housed in the city of Zoar[202] where their guardian angels had assured them they would be safe,[203] and which God did not destroy. It was in Zoar that Lot's wife was turned into a pillar of salt. But the girls knew that they could have taken husbands in Zoar, and Lot could have taken another wife there. "So, it is certain that they wanted very much to preserve the seed of their father within their own wombs."[204] Myles concluded.

"And it's a good thing they did, or else there would have been no house of David." Myles went on to show the connection and the intricate maze of lines and names he had drawn on his genealogy chart. Lemuel was getting weary of all the Biblical begotting and the begetting, and he knew he couldn't keep it all in his head.

While Myles enthusiastically tracked all the genealogical lines for Lemuel, Eden returned to the usual humdrum; the seneschal felt more at ease and yawned; the souls went about their chores; the bells chimed another hour; and Lemuel was having a hard time keeping his eyes open and feigning to pay attention. Then Myles got to the first page of the New Testament. There was a bit of static over the loudspeakers broadcasting the angel chorus, and then silence. It was as though a switch had been opened.

HOW THE GOOD TAILOR GOT TO HEAVEN — 149

Myles did not notice the sudden silence, and droned on: ". . . see how nicely Matthew works out the rule of the fourteen generations. And this conformed with all the prophesies regarding the coming of the Messiah. And Matthew makes out the lineage from Abraham, to Isaac, to Boaz, to David, and on down the family tree right to Joseph.

"However I have one small problem with that," Myles admitted, and held his thumb and forefinger about a millimeter apart to show how small. "Mary was with child by the Holy Ghost and not Joseph; and she and her cousin Elisabeth descended from Aaron[205] from the house of Levi, not Judah! And so if the prophets are to be believed, and Matthew's genealogy is correct... "

There came a sudden blast of a shofar over the loudspeakers, and an extremely authoritative voice said calmly: "Attention! Swiss Guards! This is the Archangel Gabriel speaking. Would you please escort Angel Myles to the guard room, immediately!"

Two very large Swiss guards from the detail guarding the waters of life strode over. Each grabbed one of Myles's arms and pulled him from the rim of the fountain. A squad of halberdiers raced from their positions along the drawbridge, their boots clumped hollowly as they ran across the bridge, and the guards holding Myles's arms dragged him toward them with his toes making furrows in the golden nuggets.

Still adamantly pedagogic, as the guards prodded Myles along with their halberds, he turned and finished his lesson. He shouted to Lemuel: ". . . so that would make his brother, Judas,[206] the Messiah, and not Jesus."

Then the angel chorus resumed singing in the middle of the hymn, *Nearer My God to Thee*. Several awkward minutes passed while the two remaining angels and the probationer looked at each other without saying a word. Tomas wore a sinister smile and the seneschal looked worried. Then, ominously, the angel chorus stopped once more and the voice of a female soul, obviously a secretary, announced, "It would be convenient at this time for the Seneschal Brigham to meet with the Board of Principalities for an interview." Then the singing resumed.

As though in a daze, Brigham trod heavily toward the drawbridge dragging his crosier after him. Tomas called after him, "Don't forget your glory, your Eminence. You'll want to be in full uniform for your appointment."

He chuckled gleefully as he came over and sat down beside Lemuel on the rim of the pool. Still chuckling, he bent down and picked up the Bible from where it had fallen, and said, "Give them enough rope, Eh! Now for the real stuff, Lemuel…"

Chapter 10

"*ASI ES! EL PUERCO , SATANIST!*" TOMAS SAID, SLAPPING HIS hands together like a gardener ridding them of manure, and added with an amused chuckle, "That ersatz angel would have had your parishioners fornicating on the altar. A few more minutes and he'd have been advising you to turn the cross upside down and worship goats."

The foregoing events left Lemuel baffled, but Tomas' indifference, even slightly bemused acceptance of a devil worshiper entering Heaven, and even being promoted to angel, added to his confusion. His eyes were wide with astonishment and disbelief, and he asked as though his ears had deceived him, "A Satanist?"

"Why sure. You didn't know?" Tomas' wispy hairs wafted back and forth against the collar of his robe as he shook his head at Lemuel's naivete. "Myles is a Satanist."

"Will he be cast down?" Lemuel's Adam's apple bobbled, "into Hell?" He tried to imagine Abigail tormenting Myles in the foul sinkhole of perpetual torment, the reward of all who worship evil that Tomas had described. He tried, but couldn't. True to her demonic perversity, she refused to appear when bidden. At least not in her earthly disguise. *Her true nature must be horrible. What evil is she really capable of? Her pretty face and figure are a meretricious cover for her real nature.* He imagined flashing green eyes behind a black leathern face covered with scales and warts, and shuddered.

"What for? Oh, you mean about the devil worship? Of course not. He just needs a bit of reeducation regarding his genealogical ideas. He was pretty stupid, but they'll soon wise him up." Tomas saw that Lemuel was still puzzled, and he thought, *God! Some of these probationers are dense.*

He admitted candidly, "Every sect accuses the others of being the spawn of the anti-Christ. The Empyreal Establishment can't be bothered with their trifling accusations, besides, God forgives all sins. That is why we get the Satanists. They recognize the higher powers and as any service industry, we can't turn away paying customers."

"What did you think this organization was? Some little pushcart outfit? Did you think that this was a store front mission in a village street? We are bigger than the biggest conglomerate on Earth. All power is God's to give or withhold. We control the worldly powers from the mightiest superpowers and global corporations, down to the local school boards and town councils. Brigham only named a handful of the members of our corporation." He opened his arms wide and exclaimed, "We welcome everyone, no matter what sect they belong to: Methodist, Catholic, Mormon, Moslem, Jew,or Satanist. Even the Rastafarians and the Baptists! They're all part of the same system of belief, All have endorsed the Abrahamic covenant and that's all that matters. Of course we get the souls of Satanists. They're just the other side of the same coin." Tomas imparted a fundamental truth with a sly wink. "What difference does it make in which store they shop when you have a monopoly on the product they want to buy?"

Still unable to accept such a diametrically opposed proposition, the absolute foundation of his belief, the belief he had held for his entire existence, he asserted: "Surely, those souls go to Hell. They are cast down with Satan and his evil empire? You know, the focus of all evil!"

HOW THE GOOD TAILOR GOT TO HEAVEN — 153

"No. Most of them aren't evil, they're merely sinners, and we forgive them their sins.[207]" Lemuel couldn't hide his incredulity and it disturbed Tomas. It was a policy with which he didn't agree, and he cursed silently. *Damned Liberals!* But he had to sell the program to this guileless probationer, apparently even less guile than his permanent record showed. *Better crank up some of the usual propaganda.*

He said, "But every soul that Satan gets is devoted to conquering us. Satan and his army of demons and their brutal hordes, each one schooled in the arts of evil, would invade our wonderful Heaven. They would cast out all goodness and cast out those whom we revere. They would enslave us all if we didn't keep our forces on constant alert. They would come here and loot, and burn, and commit rapine against the good, clean, honest souls of Heaven. They would destroy all this grandeur that we have worked so hard to build and because of our expanding army, we've had to accept a few less desirable recruits."

"Remember this," he said as he pointed upward, "we must always be ready to protect Heaven from those tyrants! Be ever on guard! The price of freedom is eternal vigilance! Extremism in defense of liberty is no vice!"

Lemuel continued to mull over the riddle: how could a soul dedicated to Satan enter Heaven among God's faithful? Still reeling with shock, Lemuel formed the question simply. "Well... who are the damned then?"

"Those evil doers who worship the world, just as the Bible tells us," Tomas replied. Lemuel's perverse inquisitiveness, which Tomas had used against Myles, was becoming troublesome to himself. *Damn! Now I have to invent something.* "The damned, eh? Those are the idolaters and witches who worship false gods, and the animists, and the worst are mortals who recognize no power higher than themselves. Those who deny that their talents are God given and think that their accomplishments are by their own efforts. Those who want to improve the world, eliminate the evil in the world, and presumptuously think that the power to do so is within themselves.

"Also, the demons get those mortals who think that they have no one to blame but themselves for their own failures in the world. They're denying our powers; the Lord giveth, and the Lord taketh away. But all a mortal has to do is to have a moment of weakness, and ask, 'Why, Lord?' or utter one, 'Thank God!' and we have them. To these people we readily and mercifully extend our helping hand. We of the Empyreal Establishment give them the comfort of being able to blame some higher power. We tell them that they can lay their troubles in Jesus' hands."

He saw how crestfallen John d'Are was. Tears moistened the gray eyelashes of the old soul, and he snuffled and wiped his nose on the sleeve of his robe. He had put so much of himself into the elevation of one of his own kind to angel that with Myles's disgrace, he felt that it was a reflection on himself and all the other ordinary souls. But Tomas was pitiless, and he walked over and prodded John in the ribs with the tip of his crosier and ordered him to, "Get to work! Clean up this mess!" He pointed with his blackthorn crosier to the furrows that had been raised by Myles's feet. And as the old soul bent to his task, Tomas planted a hard kick against his bottom and sent him sprawling. He laughed evilly and then hissed, " *Estupido ser! Puerco Bautista* !"

Lemuel was not particularly disturbed at this open display of abuse. There were many among the race of angels who discriminated against the mortal souls and it was a common occurrence. And while he would never do anything like that himself, unless it were an order from his superiors, he was inured to Tomas's attitude. Tomas returned and sat beside him once more, wearing his evil leer, apparently the only form of a smile that he could muster. The action served to bring them both back to reality, and Lemuel asked, "Well, if they won't cast Myles down among the demons will they demote him to his former ordinary soul condition?"

"You know they can't do that. Once you're an angel, you're an angel." His smile grew even more villainous, and he said, "Of course he won't be instructing novices for a long time. They'll just give him tough assignments when they're finished with his reeducation." He rubbed his talon-like hands together, and added, "Like assistant to Abaddon[208], heh, heh, heh."

Lemuel shuddered, and John let loose a heart-rending sob. Abaddon was the angel who tended the pit full of locusts with men's faces and woman-like hair, and teeth of lions, who wore breastplates of iron, and whose wings had the sound of running battle horses, and their tails like unto scorpions whose stings have the power to hurt men for five months. It was just about the worst job in Heaven, and he often wondered what the angel had done to deserve such an assignment. The rumor among the probationers was that he had failed to save his quota of ten thousand souls, but Lemuel didn't believe it. He thought it was just one of those things they tell you to frighten you.

Tomas continued to rail. "If I told them once, I told them a hundred times. You can't make an angel out of a mortal." He gestured at John d'Are who was bent over his rake as he worked, and said, "Just look at that. Do you think you could imagine that as an angel? And the scholars, especially the scholars, haven't an ounce of common sense. Those lily-livered liberals, like Habakkuk, want to sit above the ordinary in their towers of ivory, high above the fray 'and watch to see what He will say unto me, and what I shall answer when I am reproved.'[209] They are fools, challenging the powers..."

To Lemuel's surprise Tomas picked up the Bible and flipped the book open to the exact page, and, without even looking, pointed to the exact verse with his cracked yellow fingernail.

"Fornicators, not they, it is beneath them; Idlers, not they! They have their studies. Idolaters? What? Them, and how down to idols? Never! They have this silly book to worship. They're Bibliolaters. They want the word; utter nonsense! Actions speak louder than words.

"They presume they can speak for God: 'Thou art of purer eyes than to behold evil, and canst not look on iniquity.'[210] How do they know that? Have they ever seen God's eyes?"

Involuntarily Lemuel looked into Tomas's oystery gray, lifeless eyes and shuddered. Then there came a scream from the open gateway of Thelassar. It was hard to tell whether it was a man, woman or beast that screamed, or it could have been the screech of tearing canvas. Then a man's voice, distorted with pain, echoed out across Eden from the walls of the spired city. "No! OH GOD, NO! NO! NOOO!" There were faint sizzling sounds, like raw meat dropped into a hot pan.

Tomas smiled his grotesque leer. He said, "Sounds like Myles's reformation lesson is coming along nicely."

Lemuel looked through the open gateway and saw several angels wearing hooded black robes bending over some prostrate form on the ruby paving stones. They were prodding the form with long iron rods that glowed white hot at their tips. He raised his eyes and scanned the palace walls. The heads in the windows were plentiful. Some windows held three or four heads, and it was obvious that some of the owners had pulled up chairs and stood on them to see over the head in front of them. All attention was concentrated on what was happening in the courtyard. Most of the faces expressed mirth. Here and there arms were thrust out and pointed downward at whatever was going on. Some even waved gaily to friends in other windows. Even the souls tending the garden had found something to occupy them near the open gate and strained to look inside.

Lemuel had heard rumors that wayward angels were subjected to correction, just as the human souls were. His hands trembled and he vowed even more assiduous efforts in his assignments. The form on the ground ceased to jerk when prodded with the hot irons and the black robed angels walked off to the side and stood in a huddle.

Tomas redirected Lemuel's attention to the immediate agenda: his mortality detail, and this training session. "I know that you are bright enough to ignore nearly everything Myles was trying to teach. It wasn't that he was wrong, nothing is wrong, but it would have extremely limited appeal. Do not make the mistake of trying to twist the Bible around to fit your own prejudices; twist it around to reflect the prejudices of your parishioners." He nodded toward the open gateway, and added, "Otherwise, you could get into a lot of trouble.

HOW THE GOOD TAILOR GOT TO HEAVEN — 157

"When he quit his carpentry job, and put all of His time into his work, the greatest evangelist was Jesus. Within three years he had converted many more than the requisite number of souls. I mention this just so you know what is possible if you try. Another major success was Mahomet; the sword can be used very effectively. Since the Americas are mostly Protestant Christian, we give you a King James Bible instead of a Douay Bible, or the Koran, or the Torah. Your superiors send you into the world to be successful on your mission and they don't want to place obstacles in your way. Remember, when you drink the waters of life you will be on your own and free to pick your own mode of winning souls.

"Paul was nearly as good an evangelist as Jesus. Jesus tended to be too confrontational. Most try to emulate Paul, and perhaps you should use him as your model. Saint Paul traveled far and through many lands and cultures to do the Lord's bidding. Notice how subtly he changed his message to match the regional temperament. When in Rome, I believe is the obvious expression, so let us turn to the book of Romans." Tomas's fingernail probed the book and he flipped it open to the exact section.

This was the second time that Lemuel watched Tomas open the Bible that way. *How could anyone do that without having an extremely thorough knowledge of the book?* And his next thought was, *Tomas professed ignorance of that Bible, even hostility to it. Why?*

Tomas' oystery eyes once again looked lifeless, and Lemuel wondered how many probationers had he given this same lesson to. Speaking in a bored tone, and without reference material, Tomas continued, "First you should assess the cultural mean of the society where you are working. The Romans loved bureaucracy, adored military authority, and the social strata from slave to patrician were scrupulously maintained. Did Paul go into Rome preaching some form of equality and down with tyranny? Absolutely not! 'The powers that be are ordained of God,'[211] was his message." And Tomas traced along the lines with a cruel fingernail.

Tomas probed the book once again, and his experienced finger probed the pages to another section. "When Paul went into Athens, a city whose citizens had a reverence for logic, who were accustomed to centuries of sophisticated learning and abstract thought, note how he changes his tactics. Did he go to the city of intellect and march up Mars Hill with a big wooden cross and perform a few magic tricks? Of course he didn't. Look at his speech on Mars Hill. 'Ye men of Athens, I perceive that in all things ye are too superstitious.' And here, 'God that made the world dwelleth not in temples! ... to be worshiped as though he needed anything.'[212] You see, it's a marvel of sophistry. He appeals to something their intellects tell them anyway and then he signs them up for the book of life... and without ever mentioning the hereafter.

"When he went into Corinth, the city renown the world over for beautiful hetaerae... had a thousand temple prostitutes dedicated to Aphrodite... "

Once again Tomas skillfully turned to the section without even bothering to look. Lemuel wondered, *Was it possible that Tomas had feigned ignorance to trap Myles, get him to show off about how much he knew, hoping he'd go too far?*

"... Did Paul go into Corinth preaching chastity, celibacy, or scold them for their licentious behavior? Did he scold the saved about consorting with pagans? Of course not! Paul even bade them to intermarry[213]. He said, 'But meat commendeth us not to God: for if we eat are we the better? neither if we eat not, are we the worse?'[214] Note his attitude, 'For me all things are lawful.'[215] So when he joined the pagans in their feasts of love it was not as a devotee of Aphrodite; it was as a man who freely used his God-given member as God intended. But he does take care not to do it while any other Christians are around, in case they might misunderstand."[216]

Paul was the epitome of mortal evangelists, and all his salvations were made without resorting to miracles. Look how he preached to the Jews, 'I became as a Jew, that I might gain the Jews.'[217] And although he was free of the law, he became as one under the law. 'To the weak,

HOW THE GOOD TAILOR GOT TO HEAVEN — 159

became I as weak, I am made all things to all men, that I by all means save some.'[218] Now do you understand? When you get to the Americas, size up the mean, find the cultural low water level of the people, and preach to that."

Lemuel's eyes darted evasively from his interlocutor off to one side, and then down to the ground.

"Something seems to be troubling you. What is it?"

"It seems a bit insincere," he replied.

"Nonsense! You sincerely want to enlist those souls into the army of God, don't you?"

Lemuel's demon once again brought her lips close to his ear and whispered, "Why don't you ask him what you need such a big army for anyway? Satan couldn't have much of an army if even the souls of the Satanists get into Heaven? Go on, ask him."

Lemuel scrubbed at his temples, and blurted out, "NO!"

"What do you mean, no? Don't you want to make your quota? Do you want to be a probationer forever?"

Lemuel wanted to confess to clear his conscience of the sinfulness that was perverting his judgement. He wanted to admit that he had been possessed; admit that he had trafficked with the enemy, and traded souls; admit that he had abetted those boys in their crime of truancy; admit that he hadn't reported Jephthah's daughter; and even admit that he suspected Tomas of manipulating Myles through him so as to get the seneschal in trouble. Just as he was about to confess, the knot of black robed angels once again surrounded the form on the ground and began to lash at it with long black snake whips as pitiful howls and moans came from the courtyard.

Lemuel changed his mind and explained, "I didn't mean it that way, but I did wonder why we go to so much effort to save them?"

"What do you mean? With the forces of the evil empire right on our borders? We need every soul we can get. We've had several border incidents already… "

"Borders? What borders? This is Heaven!"

Tomas's cheeks drained of color and his eyes darted up toward the city spires, and he said hastily, "Why the godless communists of course. That's what I meant... down in the world."

Lemuel wondered if any of the poses that Tomas affected were genuine, or if he could believe anything Tomas said. He certainly wasn't senile, and he seemed to know the Bible as well as Myles did, and he had kept up with current events in the world. Then Tomas shut the book with a snap and handed it to Lemuel. "We've already spent too much time reading in this book. You'll be on your own down there and you'll be free to pick your own mode of operation.

"According to that book," he tapped the Bible in Lemuel's hand, "if you want to pass around serpents and scorpions, that's alright; or if you want to have a sex orgy, you may; if you decide to wash one another's feet[219], that's an acceptable ritual; mutter gibberish, that's all right too; scourge your own flesh; burn heretics at the stake; fast yourself into slow starvation; eat poison; or castrate yourself; all of those things can be accepted as devotion to God and the path to salvation. You can even convince your parishioners that some dry, wheat paste wafer is the flesh of Christ, and that fermented grape juice is his blood. There is something in that book for every taste... no matter how bizarre.

"You can even put up a brazen serpent on a pole and say that it is God, but I'd go easy on that one. Hezekiah had to break up the brazen serpent that Moses made, because the children of Israel did burn incense to it, and called it Nehushtan.[220] It's very easy for mortals to backslide into idolatry. They'll even make believe that that book is God's inerrant word, if you let them."

"But if you want your mission to be successful, observe your marks for a time. Seek their cultural water level, something they are already doing, want to do, and think is right to do, and like Paul, twist it around and say that it is what God wants them to do. And then sign them up for the book of life."

"You make it sound simple. When you were on your mortality detail, how did you bring ten thousand souls to salvation?"

HOW THE GOOD TAILOR GOT TO HEAVEN

"I signed your Bible for you. Didn't my name mean anything to you?" Tomas was surprised that Lemuel didn't know who he was, and drew up indignantly. "And I brought many more than ten thousand to salvation. I brought more souls to the faith than any angel has before or since. More than Paul, Mahomet, and even Jesus himself!"

Lemuel glanced hurriedly at the name Tomas had inscribed... Tomas Torquamada. It was merely an obscure Spanish name as far as he knew. It was odd of it self. Most angels took ordinary names like Smith or Jones on their mortality details. Or if in Spain, something like Gonzales. "I'm sorry, but I didn't know you were famous."

"Did you never hear of the Spanish Inquisition?"

Lemuel shifted position, suddenly feeling uncomfortable. "That was one of the subjects they generally glossed over at the academy," he explained.

Tomas could hardly believe it. "The most successful mass salvation ever accomplished... and they glossed over it?" The rage in Tomas' gorge was as hot as a fire in cellulose nitrate, and he glared at the spires of Thelassar. "Oh! I get it. The liberals have adulterated the history books too. They weren't satisfied when we were a highly principled group of God's elect; they kept lowering the standards and now we've become like an old whore with her legs spread wide, and accept any insult to our integrity.

"Those milk soft liberals insinuate their corrupt blasphemies and heresies into any niche or weakness. On the surface they appear soft, maybe a bit naive, even eccentrically lovable, and that is when they are the most dangerous. Nothing is sacred to them. They spread their cancerous message throughout the institutions of faith. Human rights! The most evil notion ever conceived of. Humans have no rights! Their philosophy is the kind of insidious message that undermines the God-fearing and the earthly institutions of government, the Fourth Estate, colleges and universities, and even the classrooms of children, and their textbooks. They lure unwary souls with utopian dreams of worldly Edens, and preach egalitarian claptrap to innocent young children.

"And we have to compensate for their indiscriminate eagerness to please every crackpot notion, pseudoscientific theory… E -VO - LU - SHUN! What nonsense!"

Tomas strutted about like a challenged fighting cock and muttered oaths under his breath. "The pendulum swings back novice; our side is resurgent; my time will come!" He spun suddenly and pointed his crosier at Lemuel. "The nation they're sending you to, in the Americas… well, without us they'd still be heathens! They'd still be sacrificing virgins in cenots; still be offering up living humans to their pagan idols, Tlaloc and their Quetzacoatl, on their bloody altars. They'd still be bowing down before their heathen priests on their religious holy days like obedient sheep; the misbegotten being led by the unscrupulous!"

"Oh, didn't we put the fear of God into those Indians." He grimaced his evil leer. "The good old-fashioned way. We tortured, and burned, and intimidated, and terrorized them until the true faith drove out every trace of heresy. As instruments of God's will we spread pestilence and plague, and made their cities desolate, and they ate the flesh of their sons, and the flesh of their daughters, and the flesh of their friends in the siege and straitness we straitened them[221]. We taught them to fear God, and to cease worshiping Baal and their whorish idols of fertility. We purified their souls with whips, mounted lancers, armor, and pious cruelty. Once again Dagon fell down before the Ark of God[222]. I put real meaning into the term, 'God-fearing.'"

Tomas could see confusion in Lemuel's face and he raged inwardly about how the liberals had cloaked the true history with falsity and palliatives. His own contribution to the discovery of the Americas, and consequently, their subjugation to the Catholic church and Spain, had been buried in their lies. "I was appointed Inquisitor General by their most Catholic majesties, Ferdinand and Isabella, in 1483. One year later an Italian came to court with some crazy idea that the world was round and that he could reach the Indies by sailing westward. He wanted the King to finance the expedition. Well, such ideas were heresy, and it was my job to root out and prosecute heretics. We caught them by the thousands… "

HOW THE GOOD TAILOR GOT TO HEAVEN — 163

"I heard that over ten thousand heretics were dispatched," Lemuel observed.

"Oh, no! Before we were done, it was at least triple that, and those were just European heretics. In the Americas there must have been hundreds of thousands of Indian heretics. But when Columbus first came to court, I didn't have him burned at the stake; instead, I filed away his idea for later. At the time all of southern Spain was under control of the Moors. In nine short years we pushed out the black infidels who had occupied Christian territory for two centuries. The year was 1492, and when the hostilities ended, there were a great many unemployed soldiers roving the countryside. Hardened fighting men, without a war to fight, and with time on their hands, are sure to be troublesome."

"We had a surfeit of battle-tough Christians, and as Ferdinand put it, what did it matter if they sailed to the edge of the World and dropped off? At least they wouldn't cause him problems. So we heard Columbus' petition, but we were lacking money for the adventure. Driving out the Moors had nearly bankrupted Spain's treasury, so we petitioned Pope Sixtus to finance 'furthering Christianity,' and he agreed to our noble cause. The discovery of America was financed by the Catholic church."

It dawned on Lemuel that Torquemada must have been on his mortality detail at the same time that he was on lying angel duty. He remembered clearly that he had planted the idea of a round world in Columbus' head. He had been assigned to bring a lie to the World, and he wanted to do his best and think up a real whopper. But the big lie turned out to be true. Then Lemuel saw vividly the master plan of the great Architect of the Universe. His part fitted into God's grand design. It was no accident that his lie turned out to be true. He became excited and exclaimed, "Tomas! You won't believe this, but I was the one who put that idea into Columbus' head. I told him the world was round. Don't you see how neatly this all fits? There is a grand design and we're all part of it... it's awesome. Don't you see? This proves that there is a sensible destiny directing our every step. And now with Galileo's manumission from Purgatory, and his grant of absolution coming at just this time, I'm certain that my mortality detail is destined for greatness." The glow of revelation shone on Lemuel's face and he clutched the Bible to his chest. "Perhaps my mortality will be as great as yours was, Tomas."

Tomas knew that the proper time to end a briefing session was on a rising tide of self-confidence. He agreed with Lemuel and assured him that he, too, felt that Lemuel was destined for greatness; and that he would surpass even himself.

Chapter 11

LEMUEL WAS DISAPPOINTED BY THE UNCEREMONIOUS WAY that Tomas presented the flask of the precious waters of life. He was about to embark on mortality. His entire being would be changed when he took on human form, and he would be susceptible to every human frailty. He had expected a ceremony of some kind. Tomas had merely reached into the pocket of his robe, pulled out what looked like a half-pint liquor bottle, filled it in the fountain, and screwed the cap back on. As he handed it to Lemuel, he cautioned, "Be sure you don't drink any of this while you're in Heaven. You'd fly off into outer space and mortal flesh would never survive the trip to earth; have both feet firmly planted on solid ground, and then drink it all down." Then he seemed to step out of his formidable persona for a brief moment, and asked, "Do you want to hear a good joke? This one will kill you."

Lemuel thought joking was out of character for Tomas, but he said, "Yes."

Tomas said, "That was it." And he walked away chuckling.

Lemuel sighed, tucked his Bible under his arm, pocketed his flask, and proceeded with his guide back to the gates. John d'Are selected a different route through the garden so Lemuel could see more of the fabulous monuments to the Biblical heros during their moments of glory:

A golden David was shown celebrating the return of the Ark by dancing with all his might before the Lord[223], and Michal, Saul's daughter, made of rusted iron, was saying: 'How glorious was the king today who uncovered himself in the eyes of the handmaidens, as one of the vain fellows shamelessly uncovereth himself!'

"In the next scene David was saying, 'The Lord chose me over thy father, therefore I will play before the Lord.' And the tableau showed how he played.

"All the statues were nudes, except for Michal. There were a dozen polished white marble maidservants. Eight were bent forward with their bottoms up and hips together, and with their fingertips touching the ground lined up in an arc. Two were assisting by guiding David's erect penis for coitus, while another digitally stimulated his prostate. Still another was spreading the vulval lips of the girl that was next to receive the king's honor. David was saying, 'And I will yet be more vile than thus, and of the maidservants which thou has spoken of, of them shall I be had in honor.[224] Therefore, Michal, the daughter of Saul, had no child unto the day of her death.' Thus did the Lord punish Michal because of her obstinate attitude by refusing to join in the celebration of the return of the Ark.

Lemuel shook his head and walked on. The next tableau showed Moses and his chief priest, Eleazar, surveying the spoils of their war with the Midianites. As he looked over the battlefield, Moses noticed the Israelites had committed a mischief, and he asked angrily, 'Have ye saved all the women alive?' Then he ordered them to, 'Kill every male among the little ones, and Kill every woman that hath known man; But all the women children that have not known a man by lying with him, keep alive for yourselves.'[225] And the Israelites found thirty two-thousand virgins among the captives, and slew all the rest.'[226] The tableau showed many of the Israelite warriors checking virginity and claiming their maidenheads right on the battlefield. The artistry of the tableau

HOW THE GOOD TAILOR GOT TO HEAVEN

was so realistic that the ground actually looked wet from the blood of the slaughter.

"Sex and violence, sex and violence. Is that all you mortals can think to glorify? I hope none of these Biblical scenes are shown on television for little children to see. Do you have to portray all this sex and violence so graphically?" Lemuel asked his guide.

And John d'Are replied, "These scenes are right out of the Bible. It's inerrant Holy Scripture. It's God's power made manifest. You'll see when you spend a lifetime on earth that nothing much has changed."

Lemuel would never admit it to another, but he was having trouble seeing a rationale to God's grand design. Still, he told himself these things must be taken on faith. *What ever is, is right. Hath not the potter power over the clay?*

When Lemuel arrived at the entry gate to the fabulous garden, the cherubim with the flaming swords stopped him for a routine search to make sure he was taking nothing from the garden except the Bible which was issued to him, and one flask of living water. One of the cherubs told him that sometimes they discovered contraband waters of life flasks that other probies had stolen for a friend, or some golden fruit that might be converted into cash for their mortality details. The gold would have given them an unfair advantage over the probationers who played the game honestly and started out with the regulation issue.

Lemuel passed the inspection and retraced his steps back toward his BOQ (Before Ordination Quarters). The warriors were still at maneuvers for the final battle between good and evil on the plains of Migido. At the precipice overlooking the battlefield he recognized Esther seated on one of the observation benches. She was gorgeous! She had long, thick, black hair which was iridescent in the eternal light. Her eyes were deep dark blue with long lashes and her skin was the unblemished color of thick rich cream. This beautiful angel was tall and friendly like a complaisant amazon. She sat in a relaxed position with her arms outstretched along the back of the bench and her feet propped up on the fence rail in front of her. This position snugged her white linen robe against her voluptuous figure, which Lemuel was sure she was not conscious of presenting so freely. After all, she taught impressionable young children.

She noticed his approach, gave him a beaming smile, and patted the seat beside her, and invited him to sit. She said, "The boys told me you wanted to see me before you left. I see you've been given your Bible, had the official indoctrination course, and you probably think you're ready to face the mortal world." She winked at him and fluttered her long black eyelashes, and added, "Come sit. I'll give you some lessons that those theologians don't mention."

"Oh please, no more instruction. I don't think they missed anything, and if they did that stroll through the garden, with those obscene statues, filled in any points they might have overlooked. I've been so filled to the brim with instructions that I doubt my brain could hold another fact."

"Don't be silly. My lessons are about fun." She patted the bench again and he sat warily, expecting more lessons. She fluttered her lashes again, and said, "That theology stuff is all nonsense. You got your bottle of life water didn't you?" He showed her the small flask and she involuntarily licked her dark red lips with her pink tongue. A momentary longing dimmed her smile, which she quickly willed back in place. Finally she said, "That's the good stuff. After you drink that you'll be able to do it."

"Well I hope so, but saving all those souls is a difficult job. I hope I can do it."

"Oh yeah! That too. But the 'it' I was referring to was what the mortals can do that you can't do now. That little bottle of water will wake up your hormones and send real passion flowing through your veins. You'll love doing it. It feels like every particle of your ecstacy was being drawn down your spine and sending little fiery charges through every nerve. It goes up to your brain, pounding at your temples to escape. When it's really good you can feel your bone marrow quiver, the blood rushes to your cheeks, and inflames your face… even your toes will flex."

"Awgh! That sounds awful!"

HOW THE GOOD TAILOR GOT TO HEAVEN 169

"Don't knock it 'til you've tried it. Like they say, it's the most fun you can have without laughing." She smiled widely, showing her perfect, porcelain-white teeth back to her molars. She looked coyly away and then back into his eyes. "You're a handsome fella, by mortal standards. I'll bet they didn't explain the uses of that to you, with their theology and liturgics. Good looks are an asset in the salvation game. I saved more souls than that old buzzard Tomas just by laying on my back and enjoying myself."

Lemuel was still contemplating what she had rhapsodized about. Her assertive exuberance over the delights of the flesh caused trepidation regarding his unused member. The awkward flaccid appendage seemed so inadequate for its purpose. Esther took coitus out of the theological abstract and made clear that he was expected to be a physical participant in the grotesque conjoining, and he said thoughtfully, "I had supposed there would be some torment, with blasphemy and sin rampant. I know I have the ignorance and lies of idolaters to overcome." He thought of Abigail, and added, "And there's the proximity of all those demons to contend with too." He compared his mental image of the dark little demon to the fair sweet angel seated beside him. Esther would never taunt him about his suit, nor laugh at the Holy word. But he wondered if there might not be something wrong with her too, maybe all females, if she thought he'd enjoy having his nerves jangled. He sounded resigned to his fate as he said, "I suppose I can withstand unpleasant physical sensations as well." Then he asked Esther, "How did you save your souls?"

"Passed over that, did they? That bunch of male chauvinists. They never want to give the women any credit."

"They talked about Ruth and Lot's daughters, and about the begetting rituals..."

"Sure! Keep 'em barefoot and pregnant!"

"Oh no. At one point, Myles seemed to be saying there was more to it than that."

"Hum... Myles sounds fairly progressive. I've never heard of him."

And then she said, "Wait, is he the mortal soul they promoted to angel?"

"Yes, but Tomas said he was a Satanist."

"Well, Tomas thinks that everyone that hasn't kissed the pope's ring is a devil worshiper. But as for my methods, there's a whole book in your Bible about it. Since they ignored it, I'll tell you the short version. It's lucky you ran into me." She patted his thigh and went on with her tale.

"There was this king called Ahasuerus in the Bible, and Xerxes by the Greeks. He ruled all the land from the Indus River to the Red Sea; all of ancient Persia. And as royalty often does, he loved to party. With such a large kingdom he had many princes to oversee his many provinces and most of them liked to party too. So one time he was having this really big bash with all his princes and everyone. They'd all been drinking for about one week solid[227]; and just when things were getting good and merry, the serving girls were getting worn out and bowlegged. So the king said, 'This will never do,' and he called the queen to come out and entertain his guests.

"Well, Queen Vashti, like some prissy, little, finishing school semi-virgin, yelled back from the women's quarters: 'If you think I'm coming out there and expose myself to all your drunken friends, and put up with their lewd advances and insinuations—and Lord knows what else you'll want me to do—you've got another think coming, Buster!'

"Oh my! Didn't that make the King mad? He booted her out of the palace. But when he sobered up he realized he needed a replacement, and decided to hold a beauty contest.[228]

"Coincidentally, I had just arrived for my mortality detail and had taken lodgings with an old geezer named Mordecai." She smiled and continued, "Old Uncle Mordecai used to bring some of his friends home for me to meet. Since one of the best places for him to meet these friends was near the palace he often heard about some of the goings on among the hoity-toity. When he heard about Vashti, he came running home as fast as his bandy little legs would carry him. All excited he said, 'Get yourself all dolled up, we're going to meet the King.' Then he told me about the beauty contest."

HOW THE GOOD TAILOR GOT TO HEAVEN — 171

Esther sat up straight, crossed her ankles, arched her back, and thrust her voluptuous breasts forward. They pressed hard against the thin linen fabric of her robe where her nipples made tiny hillocks atop the luscious mounds. She gave Lemuel a slow wink, pushed her moist lips out as though forming a wet kiss, and said, "Well! I figured I could handle anything the king and his friends could hand out, and the palace guards too, if need be. I was very eager to take Vashti's place, and when the King saw my attributes, that ended the talent show.[229]

"But after I got inside the palace I found out there was a problem: the king's chief lieutenant, Haman, was anti-Semitic. He hated Jews, and he hated Uncle Mordecai worst of all[230]. At the same time I was trying to get old Uncle Mordecai a cushy job inside the palace. You can see the problem, can't you? Of course Haman didn't hate all Jews, he used to eyeball me up and down pretty good. So Uncle and I put our heads together and figured out a plan.

"One day I put on my most revealing royal attire, the gold jewelry was about all that you couldn't see through. I shaved my legs, painted my toenails, kohled my eyes, and went strolling past the king, who was holding his... ah... royal scepter. His eyes lit up and he bid me to approach, and then he held out his royal scepter to me. So I took ahold of it and gave it a couple of strokes, whereupon his majesty moaned with delight, and said, 'What have I got in this entire kingdom that you want most of all? Oh! Speak up child.[231]

"Our plans were working. I knew the king loved to party, so I said, 'Let's have a banquet, something small, just you and me, and Haman.' He went for it like a pike after a minnow.

"Well! We drank steadily for about two days[232]. The king was getting a bit woozy. Meanwhile, on the sly, I was showing a bit of thigh to Haman, who was getting hotter all the time. The wine was making him careless too. That's when I told the king that there was a plot against the Jews, and I whispered, 'It's your royal lieutenant, Haman, that's causing all the trouble.'

"The king got up in a rage and went outside to clear his head. At that moment Haman jumped onto my couch with me saying, 'Come on you little tease.' Just then the king walked back inside.[233]

"To make a long story short, Haman was hanged, and Uncle Mordecai got his job.[234] Then Uncle's friends slew about five hundred of Haman's family and friends there around the palace;[235] and throughout the kingdom the Jews rose up and killed about another seventy-five thousand idolaters. And in one very short period of time, all of the Jews that had committed whoredom with false gods came back into the fold.

"You see, dear, if you work it right, getting your quota is no trouble, and the rest of the time I had a ball."

Lemuel contemplated the Bible on his lap and wondered how many Americans it would be necessary to slaughter in order to make them disavow idolatry and bring them back onto the paths of righteousness. Then he remembered the flag in Bradamante's classroom, and considered that the Americans were probably more righteous than the Persians. He said to Esther, "You make it sound easy, but we're not all blessed with your charm and piety."

"Neither was old Uncle Mordecai, 'til I came along. What you need is a shill," Esther said as she slid closer to Lemuel. While her left hand toyed idly in the hair at the nape of Lemuel's neck, her right hand caressed her abdomen somewhat south central of McByrny's point. She cooed into his ear, "Just for you, I wouldn't mind going back for a while and I could teach you things." Her appealing blue eyes sought his, and she asked in a hushed tone, "You could sneak me out, couldn't you? There's always a big crowd at the pearly gates and they wouldn't notice." She took his hand and confided softly, "I sure would like to help you on your mission."

"I appreciate the sacrifice you're willing to make, Esther, but even if I could take you with me, the thought of you giving up this most glorious and perfect paradise for just the brief span of one lifetime would be too much for my conscience." He thought about the Amsterdam incident. "Besides, even if the O.D. didn't bring you back, I might get hit by a truck or something. I'd have to start my probation all over again, but you'd be left alone, and with only your own resources." He shuddered as he contemplated Esther being in the hands of the evil forces without male protection.

"Oh sure!" she said and stood before him haughtily, and in spite of her shapeless robe, she was a majestic blandishment of female impulsion. She swung her shimmering black mane with a sudden movement of her head, and said throatily, "I must get back to my little darlings." She strode off like a proud queen toward the flat-roofed school building.

Lemuel called to her, "If you do get sent down on a miraculous visitation or something, please stop in for a visit." He watched her stately sweep along the walkway, sighed, put his Bible under his arm, and headed toward his unit's barracks.

Passing one of the posters showing the face of God, they're ubiquitous in Heaven, Lemuel thought he saw mockery in God's face. These posters are placed on nearly every vertical wall or post, and sometimes even on ceilings in bedrooms. They all bear that popular inscription from Proverbs—"The eyes of the Lord are in every place, beholding the evil and the good."[236] And the artistry of the painter managed to create a trompe l'oeil effect so that the Lord's eyes, no matter where one stands, seem to be looking at you. These posters were placed all around Heaven a couple of thousand years ago to fulfill a statement by Jesus. He promised that in Heaven the angels do always behold the face of my Father which is in heaven.[237] Well, it would have been impossible to crowd all the angels into Thelassar, so the authorities did the next best thing and had posters with the Lord's face placed everywhere. However, the face that Lemuel saw looking back at him from the poster was not the usual stern face of the Lord; God's face seemed to be mocking him. Surely that little demon has caused these confusing thoughts. Hadn't she caused him to see the Devil on the census bureau's door, and imagine a pearl in Tomas's hand, and to think evil thoughts of the tableaus in the fabulous garden?

Lemuel's barracks was one of a long line of like buildings that fronted on the street running along the drill field. His building was of dark gray granite with pure silver grapevine mortar joints and crenelated parapet walls with rounded turrets on each corner. The stairs to the second floor squad room had the whitest possible birch risers and highly polished ebony treads. The squad room itself was plain with only enough furnishings to be functional. No curtains or shades dimmed the eternal light; the floors were lustrous and polished highly enough to mirror features; and the rows of bunks were aligned as precisely as though a theodolite had been used, as were the sandals beneath each bunk, and the footlockers at each simple iron bedstead. The blankets were pulled drumhead tight over each thin mattress and tucked in with hospital corners. Five of the thirty bunks had thin striped ticking mattresses stripped and rolled up into closed horseshoe shapes. Their occupants were off on a lengthy detail in the world. This had been Lemuel's home for the last six thousand years and he knew he would miss it.

All the other angels were out on their various duties except for one, a heavy set angel who was lolling on his bunk reading a copy of the A.R.s (Angel Regulations) and absent-mindedly munching on manna. Some grains had fallen down his chin and crumbs were scattered down his robe and onto the olive, drab, camel hair blanket. He greeted Lemuel and said, "Off to see the big world and get in some daring do, eh?"

Lemuel returned the greeting, and commented, "I heard that the review board had demoted you to lying angel, Winfred."

"They tried, but I went sick."

That was the trouble with lying angels, you never knew if they were malingering. Lemuel doubted that Winfred was sick at all. He'd never heard of angels getting sick.

"I think I got a good case for an appeal," Winfred said. "Here under AR 1261: Accused not advised of right to plead. They never advised me of nothing. A squad of marines hauled me before the board, the prosecutor said some mumbo jumbo, and the judges ruled me guilty and decided that I should be demoted to liar second class, so I went on sick call." He became more serious and said, "Here, listen to this, Lemuel. '*Held*, that such a plea would have been a complete defense to the charge, the

HOW THE GOOD TAILOR GOT TO HEAVEN — 175

failure to inform the accused of his right to enter such a plea, injuriously affected his rights within the meaning of A.R.37. C.M.111329.' The statute of limitations had run out before they brought me to trial and they never told me about it. That's a complete defense to the charge, ain't it? Besides that, I wasn't AWOL anyway. I was doing some important research work in Amsterdam for my mortality detail when the O.D. showed up."

Lemuel smiled and rolled his eyes up toward the ceiling.

And Winfred said, "Where's this Washing Tub Dee Cee, anyway? It seems like they have shortage of liars there. The civil authorities could only find one liar in the whole place, and they really made a big to do about it. The head office wants to send in a platoon of us lying angels to rectify the situation. We're to be called the truth squad!"

Lemuel stripped his bed and took an armload of robes from his wall locker, and the extra sandals, and put them all in a pile on top of a blanket to make a bundle. Then he said to Winfred, "I wouldn't appeal that sentence if I were you. I heard that it was the Appeals Board that gave Abaddon his assignment."

Winfred shuddered, and then said, "Aw! G'wan. That's just a story they tell you so's you won't make waves."

"I don't know. I just work here, same as you. How about helping me carry my stuff down to the supply room." Lemuel took his shepherd's crook from the rack, checked the serial number, and slid it through the bundle to make a hobo bundle.

Winfred picked up Lemuel's footlocker and asked, "Where are they sending you?"

"America."

"That's nice but I hope they send me to someplace exotic, like Bali. That would be the greatest. Those sweet, little temple dancers, nude to the waist, and they say they have the best shaped tits in the world. With lotus blossoms behind their ears, and those young nymphet bodies swaying to the seductive music... "

"You're supposed to be saving their souls, Winfred." Lemuel reminded him impatiently.

"I know that, but there's nothing says I can't enjoy myself, and besides there's not much competition. You get special dispensation for hazardous duty. There's cannibals nearby."

"If you want to get there anytime soon, I think you should learn to grovel at the assignments department, just like the rest of us do, and forget the appeals court."

* * *

Lemuel waited at the supply room counter. Above the wicket in the golden wire mesh separating the supply room the goldsmith had woven into the diamond mesh screen the proverb: 'But if a thief be found, he shall restore sevenfold.'[238] The green jade counter had a smooth hollow worn, as ancient limestone steps become worn, in front of the wicket by the countless issuances made through that port.

Orson, the supply angel, was seated at his littered desk behind the counter. He leaned back in his battered, old rosewood swivel chair, legs crossed and elevated with both feet resting in an open file cabinet drawer. His body filled his robe like a spinnaker in a gale. He held a crockery mug of nectar, obviously purloined in some deal with a commissary angel (nectar was only allowed for the higher orders), and a large brown rubber band hung loosely on his thickly-haired wrist. His head was bald and shiny, but with a half-wreath fringe of coarse and kinky black hair that descended in front of his ears in long heavy sideburns.

Beyond him in the dim light loomed shelves full of wings, glories, halos, stacks of robes, piles of sandals, and an assortment of censers, chasubles, chalices, scepters, and wands. Further into the gloom of the supply room, Lemuel could see stacks of psalteries, hymnals, and cheap hard-bound Bibles. There were unopened bundles of religious handbills alongside the books, and the stacks had the appearance of a city skyline in miniature, with a few leaning towers. Several sandal trod, religious tracts, requisition forms, and inventory cards lay helter skelter on the gray marble floor.

Orson swivelled to face Lemuel, and he growled, "Wha'da ya want, Willy?" The light from his goose-necked lamp made his sallow com-

HOW THE GOOD TAILOR GOT TO HEAVEN

plexion look orange. The eternal light was dimmed in the deep windowless recesses of the supply room.

"I am a probationary angel, sixth class, and my name is Lemuel, not Willy. And I want to turn in my gear and check out the essentials for my mortality detail."

"Yer all Willys to me, so you are," Orson said and gave Lemuel a friendly smile. Then he told Lemuel, "Slide yer stuff through the window and I'll get Rosy to put it back in stock." He yelled, "Rosy!!!"

"Shouldn't we go over the list of items that I'm charged with?"

Orson looked puzzled, and then brightened, "Oh! You mean that sign up over your head. Naw... you look honest to me. I trust ya. Besides, didn't you know they just put those signs around to keep you on your toes? Anyway, wings and wands, and that other stuff don't work when yer a mortal... so they don't." Then he yelled back over his shoulder, "Rosy!!! Rosy!!! Getyerass in here and check in this Willy's stuff."

He placed his mug on a cleared space on the desk where there were already many shiny sticky rings the size of his mug base. He clapped his meaty hands together and rubbed them together in a washing motion, and said conspiratorially, "Ya might lose those powers Willy, but you get others in return." He winked, adding, "It ain't a bad trade off either... so it ain't." He leered, and asked, "Didn't ole Esther hit on ya, coming back from the orientation with yer life juice?"

"She made a very generous offer to help with my mission, if that's what you mean." Then he added, "We've been friends for a long time."

"Oh! I'll just bet you are close friends." His coarse laughter echoed throughout the storeroom, and his body shook like molded aspic. He sputtered, "Special sacrifice... huh? Just for you... huh?" Between mirthful sputters he informed Lemuel, "She's very friendly with all the probationers, and she's been hittin' on every mortality-bound Willy for the last two thousand years just hopein to meet one ats dumb enough to help her sneak out. Even me, if ya kin imagin. They say Abaddon did sumpin like that."

Lemuel was starting to take a dislike to Orson because of his crude intimations regarding Esther, and he said in her defense, "You just have a dirty mind, and besides that, it wouldn't be possible anyway. There's no coitus without marriage, and so the Lord closed up all the wombs in Heaven,[239] so she couldn't do it, even if she were on earth."

"Look, all the Lord did was regrow their hymens, an it's true we're all limp as wet noodles up here, but the ladies still got clits, an two other holes, an two hands, and Esther has that nice cleavage between her tits. Come on, she's cock crazy... so she is."

Lemuel was stunned, then he remembered the lewd wink Abigail made when he asked her what they did with their souls, and he shook his head. That would have made Esther as bad as that little demon and he didn't believe it possible.

Orson could see that Lemuel was upset, and he said, "After you've been mortal for a while you'll see things a little differently."

Lemuel thought that might explain those orgiastic rituals that Myles suggested. Myles probably resented his impotence.

Orson said, "Lemme tell you about Esther's mortality detail. They say that when she was down there she put more horns on ole Xerxes head than Christ had thorns in his crown." With a salacious wink, he repeated the lurid gossip of the back rooms:

"Xerxes was doing pretty good; his papa had left him an empire. A'course he had to squelch a passel of rebellious Egyptians, so it warn't all fun an games. An he had ambition, so he did, and he wanted to expand Persia so's to include Europe. There was just that little stretch of water, called the Helspont twixt him and his goal, an on ta other side was only a bunch of Greeks who were too busy squabbling among themselves to resist a well disciplined army. Well, you know how it is when you're bent on world conquest; ya need lotsa money. Down in the world, armies have to be paid. But he learned that right there within his own empire, in Babylon, the satrap had let them build this huge idol of Marduk. Imagine this if you can: solid gold, eighty feet high, an twenty feet accrost; we don't even have anythin like it up here... so we don't.

HOW THE GOOD TAILOR GOT TO HEAVEN —⚭— 179

Anyhow, Xerxes went inta Babylon an pulled that idol down an melted it for the gold he needed for his bigger army... and then he met Esther.

"Ya see, she was in the nature of an experiment. As you know the waters of life were walled in and guarded after the miscegenation incidents that created all those half breeds that God decided to wipe out with the flood. Then for thousands of years us angels went about our normal angel duties and since we couldn't get to the living waters, we couldn't mix the race of man with the race of angels. But the race of man started worshiping other gods and boy, didn't that make Yahweh mad! He was called Yahweh back then, or Elohim. Anyway, God's chosen had backslided and started worshiping these other gods. And it wasn't only Baal, and Molech, and Marduk, there was Isis, and Ishtar, and Astarte, and all those fertility goddesses they was worshiping with their circumcised peckers. So God decided to send Esther down in mortal form. Ya get it? Ishtar... Astarte ... Esther? They all mean star, like the star Venus, another love goddess. And there's more to it. You know old Uncle Mordecai? Mordecai wasn't no sheeny name back then. That was Assyrian for Marduk. So you had Yahweh's champeen love goddess down there in mortal form. Esther went to work on Xerxes with her looks and special talents, and with Mordecai as enforcer, between the two of them they brought those Jews right back to worshiping Yahweh.

"Well, Xerxes got Esther, and he was happy as a bear with a honey pot, but he had already raised his army and had made all the necessary alliances to conquer Europe. And so far as the Greeks being a threat, he figured he could whip that bunch of puny pederasts on any Monday morning. He planned to whip their asses real quick and then shoot on back to Esther and her bag of tricks.

"He had the Phoenicians build a pontoon bridge clean acrosst the Helspont. Then he moved his whole army acrosst in a week and he quickly had that pack of fairies racing for the hills.

"So far so good, ya say? Well that's when he heard about Esther's voracious appetite for cock. She'd have made Messalina and Theodora look like a pair of spinsters from the watch and ward society. Yeah, what's it say there in the book? 'Vashti the queen hath not done wrong to the king only, but to all the princes, and to all the people that are in the provinces,'240 an seen from that point Esther didn't do no wrong to nobody, except she did it without the king telling her to. And of course she couldn't get to all the people that are in the provinces, but she did pretty good with the entire palace guard and much of the army. So what did Othello say? She could have had em all, down to the lowest foot soldiers detailed to fix the roads, if only he hadn't heard about it. Well, it's pretty hard to keep secret the long line of horny men lined up at the queen's bedroom door and naturally Xerxes heard about it—you know how army scuttle butt is. Well, it's pretty hard to be a leader of men when you believe half of them have screwed your wife. As you know leadership is all puffery anyway, and Xerxes had lost the ability to command. While he watched from a hillside, that disorganized Greek rabble beat his army at Thermoplae and sunk his fleet at Salamis.

"He warn't much good after that. He went back to Persepolis and built a bunch of buildings. They say the hall of ten thousand columns he built was dedicated to Esther's boyfriends, one column each. He tried to patch things up with her, but her current boyfriend, the captain of his own palace guard, stabbed him to death."

Orson winked and made clicking sound with his tongue, and said, "I'll bet he wished he had old Vashti back after Yahweh's love goddess got through with him. You weren't thinking of taking her up on her offer, were you Willy?" Orson came close to the counter and whispered, "Ya heard about the time she tried to sneak past the cherubim? She strapped a couple of crosiers together and tried to pole-vault over the wall, and she'd a made it too except the strap slipped and her robe got caught on some of those diamond spikes. That broad would go down and join the demons if she thought she could get away with it, except she knows the waters of life are up here."

"Don't they know about her problem at the front office?"

"Sure, and that's why it took five hundred years before they tried that mortality experiment again. It was when they decided to accept

HOW THE GOOD TAILOR GOT TO HEAVEN — 181

gentiles. Only the next time they used a male, and started him from infancy."

He hollered for Rosy again and complained to Lemuel, "Ya know those MOS (Mortal Occupational Specialty) records that they keep are a waste of time." And indicating with his thumb the frail wan soul who had just appeared shuffling out from behind the stacks he complained, "Julius, here, is supposed to know something about stores and warehousing. He ran one of the largest retail outfits on earth, an just look at this place!" Then the supply angel pulled Lemuel's bundle through the wicket and dropped it on the floor behind him, and the heavy footlocker beside it, and shoved them both toward Rosy with his foot. As Rosy struggled with the burden, Orson asked, "Have you made up your mind which of the divisions you'll join: Anabaptist or Roman? Them's the only realistic choices you'll get in America. There's a few fringe groups ya should avoid, Scientologists and such, and you should avoid the secular humanists with their utopian dreams of an earthly paradise. We want to get those souls up here in this paradise."

"At this point I'm tempted to try it on my own, you know, travel about like Paul."

"Naw! Take the easy route. Go with one of the big established churches and you got a sure thing... no sweat."

"I don't want to sound selfish, but if I ally myself with one of the establishment churches I'd have to divide my salvation points with all the other angels in the same organization. Some of them might be tempted to shirk and it would make the duration of my worldly torments that much longer."

"Or you might be the one goofing off, Willy! Naw, it's fair that way. You divy up the pot, even steven, and you get to cadge a bunch of souls from the mortal ministers." Orson pointed a stubby finger at him, and opined, "I don't think you got the necessary charismatic appeal, you know that show biz personality, that you need to make it on your own. Go with one of the big outfits. Ya got what they call cultural conditioning going for ya, and that's all thanks to the big organizations. Ya owe em, Willy."

Then a leer slid onto Orson's face, and he said, "I know what you're after, you sly dog. You think you'll get a lot of strange poontang out there on the road. Well, let me enlighten ya, Willy. I was with the Roman church an' did just as good there in Altoona Pee Ay as any of those tent show Lotharios, and without getting callouses from driving tent stakes."

"Why… that's a terrible thing to accuse me of. I'd never bring any discredit to the cloth!" And remembering Tomas's reference to the celibate priesthood, asked, "What about your vow of celibacy? Wouldn't that lead to your loss of grace? And also the mortal's state of grace? And were you not afraid that sexual overtures by their priest might cause their corruption and damnation."

"Naw! Look Willy, lemme clue you into the system. First of all I didn't make no passes, they did. If there's anything that'll make those broads hotter than advertizing that yer celibate, I don't know what it is. They can't stand to think you're rejecting them and have denied yourself what it is that they have to offer. They throw themselves all over you, so they do. And as for the state of grace, ya both make an act of contrition. A few Hail Marys and a couple of Our Fathers, an that's all there is to it. Acourse there is one thing ya hafta watch out for. Ya can't get too interested in any particular one. That'd make your screwing premeditated. The church understands a momentary slip, a weakness, but if ya get serious, then it becomes a willful mortal sin. But a piece of tail, for which you are most heartily sorry, two or three times a week, is okay." Orson became serious and advised sagely, "Yeh, go with one of the big outfits and that way you can regard the whole experience as a bit of R and R. Say! You could go with the Anabaptists down in the Bible belt. You know what they say about them southern preachers. Their two favorite things are fried chicken and pussy."

"I don't have to make any quick decisions. I'll think over your advice, but my main vocation is bringing salvation to the humans, and not licentious behavior or gluttony. I don't even know whether I'll ever develop a taste for mortal food." Then Lemuel peered cautiously about and asked Orson in low confidential tones, "Must I be issued the standard kit, or is

HOW THE GOOD TAILOR GOT TO HEAVEN   183

there any possibility of getting a suit made by that tailor I recently delivered. Sometime I'll have to tell you of the trouble I had getting him from the clutches of a foul demon, a really horrible creature, dark and hairy, and with talons out to here." He grossly exaggerated the length of Abigail's fingernails.

"Naw! Forget that notion. That tailor has shot up through the ranks faster'n anythin I ever seen. I think he's the human soul they're gonna promote to angel. I know you've heard the rumors that they was gonna do it."

"They already did, and I had him for a catechist. And boy, did he get in trouble! His name is Myles. I didn't understand half of what he was teaching. Those scholarly theologians get very involved in religious esoterica. But somebody must have understood, the way they came out, dragged him back inside, and then they called for the seneschal to come inside for a conference. Apparently the seneschal was his mentor and had something to do with getting him promoted. Then Tomas had to finish my lessons. You don't suppose he said something blasphemous do you?"

"When they worked him over, did they use the whips and give him the hot iron treatment? How 'bout the rack? Did they put him on the rack?"

"I couldn't see anything, but I heard a lot of slapping sounds and then I smelled what could have been burning flesh, and someone was doing a lot of moaning. Then I heard what sounded like the pawls of a ratchet, and someone was doing a lot of screaming. When Tomas went inside I heard him remark on making Myles taller and smarter."

"Oh Ho! He did blasphemy arright. Wa'd he tell ya?"

"I didn't understand it, but they came and got him while he was saying something about Didymus Judas being the Messiah if the prophesy foretelling his coming from the house of David was correct, and if his genealogical charts were accurate. Joseph, who came from the house of David, was Judas's father, but not Jesus'. He said it was because Mary was a Levite."

"Heh! Heh! Heh! That's blasphemy, so it is."

"It seemed no more profane than the rest of his lesson. He said that middle class morality was worldliness, and therefore sinful. And then he became involved in threshing floors and serpents. And I don't understand if Jesus wasn't the Messiah, then who was he anyway?"

"Yeah, yer better off avoidin' that stuff, Willy. Just do like I tole ya. Go with one of the big outfits an' put all that stuff out of yer mind. They ain't no sense in strainin yer gray matter. They already done all the thinkin for ya, an' all you gotta do is rake in the rewards."

Then, Orson mused thoughtfully, "Strange things are going on, but nothin's leaking down the grapevine. I don't know what HQ has in mind, but the battle maneuvers in Migeddo are more highly pitched, and there's talk of doubling the draft."

"Tomas did say something mysterious. He couldn't divulge the particulars, but he hinted it was to happen soon, maybe even during my worldly detail."

Orson gave a nasty laugh, and said, "Maybe you'll have to double your quota." And then he countered his jest by saying, "You can't pay any attention to that old buzzard. That's his 'the world is coming to the end' baloney. He does that to every probationer. But there has been some trouble on the southern border. Ya knew about that, din't ya? One of the ordinary souls cleaning out the throne's boardroom overheard one of them say, 'we could call it an incursion,'and then they sent him out of the room. Strange Huh?" Orson shrugged and raised both hands palms up, and said, "Well! That's higher ups doins. Let me see your shopping list, Willy." He reached through the opening for Lemuel's requisition form.

He called Rosy once again and stood examining the form. "I see it's all the usual stuff: Kit, M3 toilet article; shirts, sport, three; shirts, dress, three; shirts, under, six; pants, under, six…ah, did you want boxer M1 or jockey M2, shorts? You didn't indicate… "

"I don't know, either one, or three of each. But what did you mean about trouble on our southern border? I didn't know about any border problems. I didn't know we had any borders in Heaven."

HOW THE GOOD TAILOR GOT TO HEAVEN —⚬⚬— 185

Orson became flustered, and said, "I dunno, just some rumor I heard." Then he returned his attention to Lemuel's requisition. "M7 tie, neck. You can substitute an M27 for this M7 if you want. It's one of the newer styles, and on these shoes, leather. You can have the M2 plain blucher, or the M3 moc. blucher, or the M4 wingtip bow with the Goodyear welt. You might think the M4's too fancy for ministerial work, so you'd better stick with the M2's. Socks, assorted, six pair. You better stick to all black, an' then you don't have to fuss with pairing. Slacks, civilian, two; suit, civilian, one. Rosy will find you something nice. Handkerchiefs, three plain, and three striped borders. I see you've been issued your Bible already, and you get a nice soft-sided valise, and three hunert in U.S. currency. That covers it. You'll soon get the hang of buying whatever else you need in the stores on earth, but be careful, that three hunert won't go far. And you'll have to get used to paying for your room and board."

They heard the sound of heavy metal wheels rolling across the stone floor and then the stock soul appeared pushing a flat warehouse truck. Atop the splintered truck bed was a small pile of clothing, a shaving kit, and a soft-sided vinyl suitcase. Julius picked up the bundle of clothes and flopped it onto the counter, then the kit, and finally the valise. He reached into the pocket of his robe and withdrew a length of sash cord, and explained, "Sometimes the hasps on these newer model suitcases don't work," and he tossed it onto the pile.

"Ya can change over there," Orson said and indicated a rosewood misericord against the wall. The brace that held the seat was of a carved monk's head and shoulders peering up from between the legs of a naked woman, and obviously administering cunnilingus. Although startled by the imagery, Lemuel decided that it was just another demon-induced hallucination.

While he changed clothes he listened to Orson berating Rosy. "Ya left the sandals all in a heap on the floor, so you did; and the crosiers are a jumbled mess, so they are; an none of the halos are in their right bins. How'd ya expect to find the right size? Just look at this place! It's a mess, so it is. You better shape up. How'd ya like to spend a couple of hunnert years keeping house for Abaddon?"

Lemuel dressed rapidly. The suit that Rosy had selected for him was a double-breasted blue, a shade lighter and brighter than a royal blue, and flecked with maroon threads. One sleeve was slightly shorter than the other, as were the trouser legs, and the button was slightly askew of its mating hole. However, only the most critical eye would have detected that one shoulder pad was slightly misplaced toward the rear causing one shoulder to be higher than the other.

Since the spirit cannot be reflected by mirrors, and they only appeal to one's vanity anyway, there were none around for Lemuel to discover these slight tailoring flaws. He packed his suitcase, putting the flask with the living waters inside, blessed Rosy's forethought for the sash cord since the hasp wouldn't stay closed, picked up his Bible, and as he left, he called out to Orson, "So long, Willy."

The marines at their sentry boxes were not required to salute anyone in civilian clothes and none saluted as he passed. It was a lonely walk down Glory Road. All the souls and the angels were busy at their work. He braced up his shoulders as he strode along Hallelujah Avenue, where Isaac was busily sweeping the street. He set his jaw with a determined thrust as he turned onto the Boulevard of a Thousand Hosannas and he steeled himself to meet the demonic competition. He looked back at the shining structures in the eternal light of the empyrean where all the souls have their fondest wishes granted...to be gainfully employed...forever! As he passed through the pearly gates he looked back at the iron arch above the gates; the arch bore a legend in German, *ARBEIT MACHT FREI*. Translated, it means: work makes you free.

At the admittance office the stream of souls was heavy that day, and Lemuel could see them backed up for miles. It was a usual weekend crowd. The souls expected to be greeted by Saint Peter and each was, but it slowed the registration process. The souls' occupation and time of death were checked, and they were assigned their MOS (Mortal Occupational Specialty) number, which was tattooed onto their wrist.

HOW THE GOOD TAILOR GOT TO HEAVEN

There were several signs along the entrance road which read "Deliverance Angels—Curb Your Souls."

He showed his pass to the cherub at the turnstile and noted that Esther couldn't have made it past the well-guarded gate without a pass. The guards on the walls, to keep out sinners, would have seen her if she tried to soar across. And so, Lemuel left Heaven for his mortality detail.

Chapter 12

THE SPEED OF LEMUEL'S DESCENT FROM THE EMPYREAN through the revolving concentric rings of the Ptolemaic universe to the Nature Principium Corporis would contradict those scientific notions about the physical laws regarding the properties of matter, the speed of light and gainsay all quantum mechanics. Or put another way, Lemuel's descent from the utmost crystalline orb upon which the stars rotate at the edge of the universe to the central most planet, about which all revolves, and which is the habitat of mortals and demons, was fully consistent with the inerrant Holy Bible. The reader must be generous regarding modern academe's astrophysical groping and remember that only a few short centuries ago they were equally convinced the earth was flat. And so his flight was consistent with the insight of rational man, genus Homo infused with the true logos and gnosis, and proved with methodical precision, experiment by experiment, by Hermetic lore in the alchemists' crucibles.

Lemuel raced over the tenuous links from the Spera Octava to the Spera Stelata, to Spera Saturni, and gained speed past Jupiter, Mars, Sol, Venus, Mercuris, and Luna. He reached the four mundane elements: Aer,

Aqua, Terra, and Ignis where he entered at the U.S. port of entry for other world beings near the walnut tree in the small park in King Jamesburg.

After manifesting full ectoplasmic display, the first sight inflicted on him was someone's behind aimed approximately in his direction. The lower half of this torso was covered in a pair of faded blue jeans and the other part, which was head down in a wire mesh trash container, was covered by a lime yellow bulky sweatshirt that had "U. of C. Berkeley," printed across the chest. Some young woman was rooting through the litter in the bottom of the trash container.

Somehow, the practice of gleaning the fields[241] *has reached an undignified low,* Lemuel thought. He went over to offer her the gift of faith and encouragement. *Perhaps the poor girl would kneel in prayer with him and he could read a few uplifting verses to her from his new Bible. I'll show her how the Lord's distant maternal ancestor once gleaned the fields for her sustenance.*

As he approached, flipping through the book looking for something appropriate, the girl righted herself. and yelled to a group of kids in the play area. "Hey kids, we're lucky. I found some," and she waved several pieces of paper over her head for them to see.

Lemuel stopped suddenly, as though frozen, and he thought, *Oh no! It couldn't be.* But it was Abigail.

Anger furrowed Lemuel's brow, and he ran up to her and commanded, "Stop! You fiend! I can't let you do this!"

"Darned if it isn't Lem! Hi!" She greeted him cheerfully, and then asked, "What can't you let me do? What's shaking your tree now? Honestly, I've never seen such a bunch of prigs."

He snatched the papers from her and held them aloft while looking at her with withering disgust. He said, "You're obviously up to something evil with those children." He held the papers high above her jumping reach, and snarled, "Some kind of smut, no doubt, to poison their minds with filth." And he prayed, "Forgive me Lord, but I cannot help questioning the wisdom of allowing Satan's fellow travelers to rove

HOW THE GOOD TAILOR GOT TO HEAVEN — 191

freely among the innocent children of the world." Then he started to throw the papers into the trash can.

"Come on Lem," Abigail pleaded. "Have you got any idea how hard it is to find real wax paper in this plastic wrap world? Give them back... pu-leeeze. They're just sandwich wrappers," she pouted.

Slightly shaken, but still unrelenting in his vocation to stamp out wickedness, he sneered, "I don't know what kind of Satanic ritual you're intending to perpetrate, but you won't do it while I'm around."

He lowered the papers and saw that they were, just as she had said, pieces of waxed paper. She snatched them from his hand, and said, "Don't you angels know anything? It rained last night and that makes the sliding board too slow, so the kids sit on the wax paper and slide down to wax the sliding board, then it gets really slick and fast."

Then she noticed his suit. "What happened to the tailor I gave you? I know he didn't make that suit." She laughed and walked off toward the children at the sliding board without waiting for his reply.

With mixed feelings Lemuel watched the children playing. Just as Abigail had said, the children were sliding faster. He suspected that they were doing something wicked, but he didn't know exactly what it was they were doing that was wrong. Their overly happy expressions and their elated cries were too gleeful for them not to be doing something bad. Abigail moved from the small cluster of children at the slide over to the swings. A mother had been trying to keep two tots' swings going at the same time and Abigail went over to push one of the children. She was laughing and joking with the mother. Lemuel was incensed over the free and easy way the mortals accepted demons in their midst. Then it dawned on him, *This is blatant worldliness. That's how she does it. She tempts them with worldly pleasures; and they, poor deluded things, forget to be dutifully pious.* He turned page after page of his Bible to find an appropriate verse. Some of the mothers took notice of him rapidly scanning the pages of the Bible and exchanged glances. Then he found a suitable verse. His lips moved as he read softly: "'And these words which I command thee this day, shalt be in thy heart: And thou shalt teach them diligently unto thy children, and thou shalt talk of them when thou sittest in thy house, and when thou walkest by the way, and when thou liest down, and when thou risest up. And thou shalt bind them for a sign upon thy hand, and they will be frontlets between thine eyes, and thou shalt write them upon the posts of thy house, and on thy gates.'242" Then he realized exactly where the wickedness lay; the women and children were acting without piety. It wasn't so much what they were doing, but the things they were doing were not being done as an act of devotion to God. They were using their own self will, and being abetted in this worldliness by the demon Abigail.

He stood and shook his Bible in the air, and he shouted, "This worldliness must cease! All of you are being led astray by demons." Several of the mothers and the older children looked cautiously in his direction, but Lemuel paid no heed, and he thought, *Why not start my ministry right here at the portal, right here in front of the eyes of that demon?* Tomas had instructed him to pay particular attention to the children. "We'll have an altar call, right here, this very morning, under the Lord's clear blue sky." He was determined to show that demon a thing or two and save those souls right now, in this bright beautiful dawn.

He took the small flask from his suitcase. His hand was unsure as he unscrewed the cap. He was aware of the irony. The magic waters that Ponce deLeon sought to give him eternal life would start his aging process, and end in certain death. Lemuel wondered how many mortals would have the courage to enter if they knew their fates beforehand but it was all part of his trial. He swallowed it down in one gulp and tensed with anticipation. He was surprised that there seemed to be no effect whatsoever. He flexed his arm and felt his biceps. No difference at all. In fact he felt excellent. He tossed the flask into the trash container and walked toward the children.

The happy cacophony of children's voices while they played stirred his heart as he approached. *All those dear little souls, and very likely not one has received the blessings of revealed knowledge.* There must have been thirty children there and none seemed to show the slightest pietistic attitude

HOW THE GOOD TAILOR GOT TO HEAVEN 193

in their activities. *What a way to begin. There were only 9,970 more souls to go.* He approached a group climbing on the Jungle Jim and cooed, "I have come to teach you of God's eternal love."

When he made his move, several mothers started toward their children, and as he neared them, they led their children away. One lady, heavy set and breathing hard, ordered him out of the park. Another, short and broad, said to a thin frizzy haired freckled one, "I'm going to call a cop, Lois."

To which Lois answered, "I see my husband coming. He'll take care of this pervert!"

Abigail tried, and barely succeeded, to hide her delight as she ran to his rescue. She announced to the ladies, "This is my brother, Lemuel. He's home on leave from the state hospital. He's a little peculiar, but he's harmless."

Lois's eyes darted from Abigail to Lemuel, and then she said to Abigail, "Listen, sweety, those religious nuts are the ones you've got to watch out for. They get messages from the Lord telling them to do weird things, and they can be really dangerous. His kind are a real menace. I hope you got someone at home to protect you in case he goes berserk."

Abigail took the hand of the startled angel and led him away as though he were a child. She reassured one mother that he only had water in his little bottle. "Of course he wouldn't drink anything that was forbidden by the park rules. Just what do you think I am?"

The heavy set woman planted her fists on her ample hips, and sneered, "Well, he looks like a wino, or a doper to me. I think you better let me get the police for your own protection, Hon."

Lois's husband was quickly bearing down on the scene, and he was either a wrestler or a weight lifter, judging by his size and musclebound gait. Unfortunately, by drinking the waters of life, Lemuel was human now, in all ways, and it was impossible for him to disappear, to cloud their minds, freeze their motion, to darken the skies, or to cause the earth to open and swallow them, and he couldn't even fly away. He tried them all, but nothing worked. Fortunately Abigail knew Lois's husband. He'd made several propositions to her while they were sharing cocktails down at Leary's Social Circle, but she always modestly declined. She whispered into his ear, "I'll tell Lois what you've been trying if you lay one hairy paw on my brother, the poor sick boy."

It must have been a world record. If the *Guinness Book of World Records* has a category for "Depths of Ignominy," surely an angel being saved by a demon from the very souls he was trying to lead to salvation would win the prize. This roughly describes how Lemuel felt as he sulked from the scene accompanied by Abigail.

Conversely, if any awards are given for nasty sniggering and unbounded glee over a rival's obloquy, Abigail would have captured that title. But demons are notoriously outrageous in their attitudes concerning the discomfiture of their betters. Lemuel picked up his suitcase and trudged from the park, and Abigail practically skipped along beside him.

There may be some validity to the local folk tale about the walnut tree being the pivot of everything, because Lemuel thought he felt the ground shudder. The more distance he gained from the irate mothers and that big bruiser in the park, the better he felt, and his step became firmer. With Abigail at his side, he walked up to the town's main street. "Get thee behind me Satan!"[243] he hissed at her.

"I can't. The nice people released you in my custody Brother dear! You wouldn't want me to let Goliath get you, would you?"

"Just fly off on your broom," he growled.

"Oh soaring's pleasing, but so is teasing." And her tinkling peals of merriment echoed from the walls of the line of shops across the street.

* * *

Lemuel had no idea where to go or how to start his mission, but he was determined to lead a few souls to salvation right under the nose of the demon. *That would show her!* Myles told him to remember that everywhere he stood was sanctified, and Tomas pointed out that Jesus spread the gospel in the streets.

At the corner was a gasoline station. He thought that might be a good place to start. There was an open area big enough for a small multitude to gather to hear his message and he could stand on the raised concrete island at the gas pumps. He no sooner started to summon the multitude when a wiry little man in greasy clothing, brandishing a tire iron, ordered him off of the property. Abigail watched from across the street and hid her laughter behind her hand.

Back on the sidewalk he noticed the spires of a church on the next corner. He decided that perhaps Orson had given him the best advice. Maybe he should join an established organization, at least until he got the hang of things. His first attempts at soul saving made him realize that evangelizing to unreceptive mortals was going to be difficult, and his confidence was shaken. As he walked toward the beautiful, little stone church, he began to envision life among brother clerics within cloistered walls. He hoped he would be fortunate enough to meet with a fellow angel on mortality detail; a sagacious companion to mentor him around humanity's little eccentricities, and a fellow spiritual guide. He looked across the street at Abigail, and thought, *She wouldn't dare invade consecrated ground.* At least the church would be a good place to start. The good brethren of the cloth would welcome him with open arms, give him shelter for the night, and he also had an unfamiliar clutching feeling in his mid-section. Then he realized that mortals do not have an unending supply of manna, and the annoyance he felt must be hunger, but he was sure the good men of God would take care of that too.

He strode along the gradually rising grade of the sidewalk past the line of shop windows. There were shoes on display in one; nurses uniforms, and paraphernalia in another; a realtor exhibited some of the ugliest examples of house photography to be seen in two counties; the black window of a pool hall reflected his negative image between posters of menacing pugilists; a pharmacy exhibited dolls, board games, trash cans, plastic and aluminum lawn furniture; and opposite the church was a small department store with fashionably clad mannequins in its windows. Abigail trailed fifty feet behind him, and as he crossed toward the spires of the church, she paused to examine the merchandise in the department store window.

He approached the sacred grounds feeling as buoyant as if it were a homecoming, and he glanced over his shoulder to see if the fiend would dare follow him onto holy soil. Abigail remained on the other side of the street studying some frilly lingerie. He climbed the concrete steps and made a mental note to inform the minister that in heaven, the steps would be pure jasper, unless the minister was like himself, an angel on mortality detail. If he were, then he too would be aware of heaven's grandeur. He reached the church door, and gripped the heavy, hammered iron, door handle (in Heaven door pulls are solid gold), and there would have been no locks. Slightly frustrated, he glanced about and noticed a glass enclosed sign board on the front lawn. The movable plastic letters on the black felt background indicated the hours the church would be open to hear confessions and the schedule of Masses for the week. The subject for next Sunday's sermon was: "Has the Lord Touched Your Life Today?" At the top of the sign was the name of the church, in gold leaf: "Our Lady of Miracles." At the bottom, also in gold leaf, was the word: "Rectory," and an arrow pointed to a stone dwelling beside the church.

Lemuel noted how similar the stonework was to his barracks, except in heaven, mortar joints of rubble work are pure silver to imitate veins of ore. The doorbell was answered by a heavy-set priest with a plum colored nose and liver-spotted jowls. He wore a black suit and a Roman collar. He invited Lemuel into the large oak-paneled foyer and they stood together on the large black and white squares of the rubber tiled floor. The priest introduced himself as Father Angus and asked how he might be of service.

Lemuel shook the priest's hand vigorously. Although the priest's face was unfamiliar to him, that would be expected in an organization as large as all the heavenly hosts, so Lemuel decided that the direct approach was best, and he asked, "Are you an angel too?"

The priest's warm smile gelled to a frozen grimace. He withdrew his

HOW THE GOOD TAILOR GOT TO HEAVEN 197

hand from Lemuel's, and clasped both of his hands over his ample belly. Lemuel continued, "I thought you might be because you seem to have copied the sidewalk pattern of heaven so well here in your foyer, and the stonework of your house is nearly the same as our barracks. Of course there, these squares," he indicated the floor, "are onyx and alabaster, and the mortar holding the stones is polished silver, but you seem to have captured the ambiance. He took Father Angus's elbow and led him away from the door, and explained in confidential tones that he was being pursued by a demon.

Father Angus was a very devout man, perhaps no more so than other clergymen, but certainly not less, and he had a fine humanitarian nature. However, he was nearing retirement age. Over the years he had eased many tormented souls. Although he had never been called to perform any exorcisms, he was quite prepared to face a fire-breathing, venom-spitting demon of the most heinous nature. However, his long years of dealing with human beings had also inculcated a certain degree of incredulity. He had learned that occasionally humans behaved irrationally. So, after examining this stranger in an ill-fitting blue suit and tan wingtip oxfords, carrying a large Bible under one arm and a cheap suitcase lashed together with a piece of sash cord in hand, and claiming to be an angel, he decided on a course of action. He knew the Scriptures said to entertain strangers because they may be angels,[244] but he doubted that Lemuel was an authentic angel. He invited Lemuel to step into his study with him.

With a graceful gesture, he bade Lemuel to be seated in the chair by his desk while he dialed a number on his telephone. While he waited for an answer to his phone call, he asked Lemuel if it would be possible for him to see the demon that was pursuing him.

"There she is! See her? Over there, lurking in front of that store window," and Lemuel pointed out Abigail.

The priest peered out through his window in the direction that Lemuel pointed and saw an attractive young woman in blue jeans and a sweatshirt tilting her head from side to side as she examined the store window display. He said into the mouthpiece of the phone, "This is Father Angus at our Lady of Miracles. Would you mind coming over as soon as you can? There's someone here that I think you should meet." Then enunciating carefully, as to a child, he asked loud enough for the party at the other end to hear, "Did I understand you to say that you are an angel?"

He held the mouthpiece of the phone toward Lemuel as he answered, "I sure am, and I've just arrived for my mortality detail."

And Father Angus said into the phone, "Oh good! Then you'll be right over. Be seeing you. Good-bye."

For all of his six thousand years of dealing with mortals, Lemuel never considered what it would be like dealing with them as equals. All angels are guileless at first, and most take a few days to become accustomed to mortal life before they drink their life waters and relinquish their magic powers. It's not that he was especially obtuse, but the demon had caused him to act hastily. Orson, the crafty supply angel's first contact with a mortal as an equal, was a used car salesman who promptly sold him an Edsel for all the currency that he had been issued. God, in his infinite wisdom, has arranged it that way so only a guileless angel could ever be sent for the grail, and to insure that the sacred goblet would never fall into the hands of demons who are all worldly and sinful, and would abuse the divine goblet if they ever got their hands on it. Except in the rarest cases, only angels would qualify.

So Lemuel had no notion as to what Father Angus had planned. He proceeded to show, with much pride, the Bible that Tomas had presented him to use on his mission. Of course he omitted the part concerning Myles's blasphemy. Parsifal would have been brighter than to do that.

Father Angus checked his watch and looked out the window, then became very interested in Lemuel's Bible. "Presented to you by Torquamada, you say? And personally autographed by King James? Oh yes! I can tell. Those are their signatures all right." He checked his watch again, and commented, "It's strange that a good Catholic, like Torquemada, the Grand Inquisitor of the Spanish Inquisition, would have presented you with a Protestant Bible."

HOW THE GOOD TAILOR GOT TO HEAVEN   199

Lemuel explained that Heaven was non-sectarian and accepted many more souls than the worldly ecumenical councils were prepared to admit. "All who worship the God of Abraham are accepted there." Then he told the priest that he hoped it wouldn't be too much trouble for the good Father if he boarded and lodged in the rectory with him. "Just until I'm settled into my own parish, you understand."

After consulting his watch once more, Father Angus explained that he regretted that there was no more room at the rectory, "Because of the heavy influx of angels taking up all the spare rooms, you understand. But," he continued, "there is a special monastery provided by society for the overflow of angels. You will meet others there, and maybe even Jesus himself."

Their conversation was interrupted by the wail and whoop of sirens. An ambulance and a police car screeched to a halt at the curb in front of the rectory. Two attendants and two police officers walked rapidly toward the door. Father Angus said, "Oh good! Your chauffeurs have arrived."

Abigail saw the canvas coat with the leather straps in the ambulance driver's hand and considered the situation. She had a wicked smile on her face as she imagined Lemuel being dragged, kicking and screaming, off to the asylum. Then she reasoned, *Things have been dull lately, and he wasn't a bad sort—for an ethereal angel.* Obstructing mortal authorities was almost as much fun as teasing angels, so she decided to go to his rescue. There was also the possibility that if she worked it right she could cause his damnation.

She entered the rectory and headed for the room where she heard the commotion. Lemuel was backed up against a bookcase that held missals, theological tomes, papal bulls, catechisms, notes on historical synods, lists of forbidden writings, a doctrinal thesis on the rhythm method of birth control, and several pro-life books. Lemuel had already thrown several of the weightier tomes by Aquinas, and Augustine, and a small paperback titled *The Church and The Homosexual*, and many copies of *The Catholic Digest* at his would be captors. Now he stood clutching the Bible to his chest with his left arm and his right hand was preparing to catapult the *Short Guide to a Sacristan's Duties.*

The four uniformed men stood in a semicircle in front of Lemuel with their arms spread wide like infielders waiting for a grounder that might take a bad hop. Father Angus had retreated to the opposite corner. He stooped in a half crouch, warily prepared to duck, and he urged hoarsely, "That's it boys. Don't let him get past you."

Abigail brushed past the policemen and stood before Lemuel with her arms akimbo, and scolded, "You're a naughty boy. You promised me that you were only going to say ten Our Fathers and ten Holy Marys, and you promised that you wouldn't be bothering the fathers." She turned and faced the uniformed men, and explained, "I'm awfully sorry for this mess. He's my brother and has just been released into my custody as part of the new home rehabilitation program." Then returning her attention to Lemuel, she said sweetly, "You promised the doctors that you would only go to church once a day."

"Did you know he thinks you're a demon?" Father Angus asked.

"Sounds like he might be dangerous," one of the policemen said, adding, "we just had a report of a pervert over in the playground. He matches the description. You better let us put him away for your own protection, lady."

Lemuel had lowered the sacristan's manual and glanced from the twinkling green eyes of the demon to the grim faces of the officials. He asked hesitantly, "What do you mean pervert? And put me away where?"

"You know, back to the nice safe room with the rubber walls and the nice doctors." The ambulance driver held the canvas coat toward him and said with feigned compassion, "Here, let's put on your nice jacket. It'll help to keep you warm." The group moved closer.

One other angel had managed ignominy in such a brief span of time, when he metamorphosed in Austin, Texas amid a convention of atheists. He still resides at the state hospital. And Lemuel, equally innocent, had no idea why this hostility was directed at him instead of this demon in their midst. His inadequate understanding of mortals was beginning to dawn on him. Without his celestial powers, he was at their mercy. He wished that he had waited to drink the living water. He could have conjured a torrent of frogs to rain down from the ceiling; or impressed the priest by changing his wine into water; or turned the policemen's billy clubs into serpents; or simply disappeared. No such options existed for him now, and although he didn't completely understand his predicament, he suspected that Abigail did. And while it would be harsh to say that he harbored a grain of racial prejudice, still, Abigail, with all her faults, was closer to his own kind than they were.

Abigail too, was feeling tense. She could have done all of the things Lemuel had contemplated, but that would have been unsporting of her. She thought that it might be fun to drop by the asylum and torment this angel, but he had to be free if she were to cause his downfall. Locked away, he'd probably consider it martyrdom and it might strengthen his resolve, so her tension was more in the spirit of an angler working a big one up to the surface and not having a landing net.

Lemuel decided to trust Abigail. He thought, *I'll escape from her later*, and the poor fish gave one mighty leap, and landed himself right into her boat. He said, "I'm sorry Abigail, dear sister Abigail. I'll behave myself. I promise. Let's go home now."

The senior policeman said, "I'm sorry, lady, but he'll have to come along with us. We've had a report and it has to be followed up. You may ride along in the ambulance if you like."

"Are you arresting him? I didn't hear you read him his rights."

The officer reddened and his eyes narrowed as he sized up the little hippy type in front of him, and he said, "We're just doing our job, Mizz. Unless you got something to prove what you say, we're going to have to hold him. Do you have his furlough papers with you?"

Abigail's merriment was well-concealed. She could have easily produced furlough papers, presidential pardon documents, or any of the miracles that Lemuel had thought of, but demons are obstinate players as well as perverse. They like tormenting human authorities almost as much as they like tormenting angels, so she said, "Of course not. They're back at the house."

The policemen exchanged skeptical glances and the senior one, eager to catch her in a lie, asked, "What's your address Mizz? We'll go along with you. It's regulations, you understand. We're required to check."

Abigail sounded as though she were pleading, "Couldn't you, please, carry this as a needless response?"

By evoking the constabulary's *bete noir*, a citizen's Miranda rights, she had disinclined the officers to be generous. She also raised the policeman's suspicions further by using an official term, 'needless response,' which made the officer believe she was very likely experienced in matters of law enforcement, and he doubted she was on his side of the "thin blue line." He thought this would be a good opportunity to make an unwarranted search of a suspicious household. With his pencil poised over his notebook, he asked, "What's your name, and address, Mizz?"

"Abigail Jones, 1016 Grove Place. I'm sure you must have seen me around there, Officer Flaharety. It's right next door to your friends, the Monahans. You know, Tim and Kathleen. And feigning a thick brogue, she continued, "Sure, and I think it's a foin thing you're a doing there, Officer Pat, keepin the lonely woman company while Tim's at work. It must be a load off his mind to know he has such a foin friend as yourself, a sharin the lonely luncheon hours with his wife. And I don't blame you one bit for parking your lovely new automobile behind the house when you visit, what with all the vandalism in the neighborhood." The innocence of her fern green eyes would have melted a bishop as she asked again, "Don't you think you could be carrying this as a needless response?"

Flaharety's jaw sagged and his face looked pasty. His partner stifled a laugh.

Abigail turned her attention to him. "And you, Officer Nero. It certainly was generous of you to collect the Christmas whiskey for your fellow officers from Mr. Pearson at the Economy Beverage Shoppe.

Remember how full of the Christmas spirit he was. He must have loaded twenty cases into that Dodge van of yours."

Flaharety's face darkened as he muttered, "You said it was ten."

"She's lying!"

Abigail continued like a bad opera. "And how sweet of you two to let the girls continue working Fourteenth Street, and for the modest sum of only a hundred dollars a week. Why, I'll bet the extra protection they need is worth a lot more than that, even with all the valuable information you get from them."

Then she said that she knew they were kidding about locking the girls up, and after that she pointed at the two ambulance attendants, and smiled. She told them that she thought it was quite proper for them to keep the twelve hundred dollars they found in Charlie Slade's pocket the night he froze to death in the alley behind Nelson's Machine Shop. After all, the old drunk had just murdered that junkie, Ralph Waldo, who had stolen the money from the Tewksbury house. Then to the cops, she said, "You know, the Tewksburys. They run the dice game in their family room every weekend. Of course you do, I see you slip by there every Saturday." But she said this to their backs, since they were leaving just as fast as they'd rushed into the rectory. The ambulance attendants were pushing the policemen through the door.

Father Angus was bewildered by what had just happened, and he slogged over to his desk and sat heavily in his chair. His face turned red when she told him what his handsome new curate was doing with the altar boys and girls in the sacristy, and then turned ashen when she said, "How silly of me to tell you. You watch them through that peep hole in the storeroom." Then she said to Lemuel, "Pick up your things, dear. We must be off now." She paused at the door as they were leaving and waved her hand, and all of the litter that Lemuel had caused returned to the bookcase.

Father Angus placed his jowls into both his hands and rested his elbows on his desk. He recalled that he'd read of such things: mental telepathy, psychokinesis, and the faint aroma of Tanis that lingered. It must be one of those new after-shave lotions.

Lemuel was determined to escape from Abigail as soon as they reached the public walk. However, outside, a group of interested citizens had gathered, and stood in small clusters on the church's lawn, and on the sidewalk, and across the street. Abigail could see trouble brewing. There were hostile sounding murmurs and threats coming from the mob, but Lemuel paused at the head of the stairway, and said, "Oh good, here's a multitude." Then he opened his Bible and reading from the Scriptures he began to preach to the mob. "And seeing the multitude He opened his mouth and taught them, saying, Blessed are the poor in spirit: for theirs is...[245]"

Officer Flaharety ordered the mob to disperse, and to go on about their business. He yelled to them, "He's out on pass from the nut house!" Then, leaving Lemuel, and Abigail to their own devices, he got into the squad car, and slammed the door. One of the mothers ran over to the squad car to report; "My little Tamar says he fondled her in her special place." She shook her fist at the receding squad car, and yelled, "I'm coming down to the station and make a complaint."

Lois's burly husband had been in the crowd and Abigail saw him run into the pool room. Then he, and some of his more robust companions, emerged from the pool room and advanced with angry determination up the hill toward them. They waved fists and pool cues, and a couple of them had black leather saps that they pounded weightily and meaningfully into their open left palms.

With the rectory door closed behind him, and the angry mob in front of him—it was a multitude, but they weren't behaving as though they would listen to a sermon—so Lemuel decided to stay with Abigail for a few more minutes. Abigail raised her hand and swirled it around once, and immediately a black cloud formed overhead and hail started to fall. Large stones ranging from grape size to golf balls. The less determined citizens ran for cover. Although the unofficial *posse comitatus* still quested justice, their advance was deterred as they slipped, skidded, and fell on what seemed like ball bearings under their feet.

Abigail grabbed Lemuel's Bible and held it over her head, and he protected his own head with his suitcase, as they raced across the street and up the block. In a supermarket parking lot she indicated a shiny, new, blue and cream pickup truck with a matching fiberglass cap over the truck bed. Lemuel noted that the truck had California tags. They slammed the doors and she took the ignition keys from beneath the seat. Then they sped out of town and onto a two-lane highway.

Chapter 13

LEMUEL'S HASTY DEPARTURE FROM KING JAMESBURG, ONLY steps ahead of the mob that would have treated him coarsely, was, he decided upon reflection, all Abigail's fault. He sat silently stewing over her treachery as they sped down the highway. He took the Bible from the hump between the bucket seats, where she had carelessly tossed it, and while glowering at her, muttered, "Sacrilegious use of the Holy Book."

He carefully wiped the water drops from the binding with his handkerchief. He opened the book to dry any wet pages and accidentally came upon a verse that read, "A man that is a heretic, after the first and second admonition, reject.[246]"

She was afraid he would lead them onto the paths of righteousness, and that was why she rushed him out of town before he'd had the chance to admonish the townfolk even the first time. Now she was speeding off with him to Lord knows where. He said, "Now that you've captured me, I suppose you are taking me off to hell. I saw those California plates. That's where Berkeley is, isn't it?"

Abigail concentrated on driving the twisting highway and diverted her eyes from the road to her oversized, rear view mirrors every few seconds to make sure they weren't being followed. She pointed out, "You know better than that. You're a living mortal now and I can't take your soul until after you're dead. And I'm sure not waiting around for you to die just to get your soul ...you're not worth the trouble." This, of course, was a lie. Capturing an angel's soul would have made her famous among the demons, but demons, just as God's angels, can only take souls that are freely given and have seriously contemplated the metaphysical mysteries.

Still inwardly seething about their hasty getaway before he had the chance to communicate with the multitude, and admonish them for their misguided notions about his purpose, he said, "I was reading from the Holy Book, the Sermon on the Mount, the Beatitudes, and that would have calmed them. Then we could have prayed together. But you convinced them I was mentally disturbed and rushed me away before I had a chance to have them commit to the Lord and save their souls."

"You really are nuts! That mob had blood in their eyes. They'd have crucified you!" She shook her finger at him, and said, "And now neither one of us can go back there and some other demon will have to do my work for me. You've really made a mess of things!"

"Well! I don't want to be near you either. Just let me out at the next crossroads."

She let the truck drift to a stop and he looked apprehensively at the wall of dense foliage paralleling the road. "You can get out right here if you want, but you'd better think again. Tamar's mother is reporting you to the desk sergeant this very minute and everyone is talking about the pervert in the park. Those cops will have your description on the wire by now. But don't worry about it, you can save all the souls in the penitentiary."

Lemuel hesitated uncertainly, and Abagail said sternly, "Go ahead! Get out! There's an old moonshiner's trail over there. Follow it along a few miles to the interstate and hitch a ride."

He slowly put his hand on the door handle and opened the door slightly. She inquired solicitously, "I suppose they issued you identification cards of some kind?"

HOW THE GOOD TAILOR GOT TO HEAVEN

He held up his Bible.

She shook her head and frowned. "No, that's not what I mean. You know, a driver's license? A Social Security card?"

Lemuel shook his head.

"A birth certificate? A bank book? A letter of credit? Rent receipts, utility bills, a phone bill? Any proof of citizenship?"

Lemuel shook his head to each query.

"A green card? A work permit?"

To Lemuel's comment about a free country, she clucked her tongue against the roof of her mouth. "Tisk, tisk. I guess you should have taken care of that before you changed. That makes you an illegal immigrant." Then, wearing a bright optimistic smile, she said, "I'm sure you'll be okay. Just keep a low profile for about six months or so. You'll get the hang of the underground economy in no time."

"We don't concern ourselves with worldliness in Heaven. How would I know about such things?" But he closed the door and, as though he were doing her a favor, said, "I suppose I can tolerate a demon's presence for a little while longer."

"Well!" Her indignation turned to amusement as she said, "Excuse me. I don't want to cause you any discomfort."

"Ah...I don't suppose you'd have any manna to eat, would you?"

She chuckled and said, "I heard that manna doesn't stay with you for very long. Yes, I think I can find something for you, a couple of scrambled eggs, or something. And you can use the front bunk in my trailer for a couple of nights. Just a few days, mind you. After all, we terrestrial angels have our pride." Then she said sternly, "And just because I'm female, and you're mortal now, I don't want you getting any funny ideas ...you understand?"

The dwellings along the highway had long since thinned. Now there was only an occasional clearing with a poor hovel or a battered old house trailer sitting in a muddy yard. Most had battered and muddy vehicles parked nearby and everything was placed in just the right position to exhibit the maximum degree of squalor. *She said she lived in a trail-*

er, he recalled. *This is how a demon would live.* At the crest of the next hill he could see ahead for miles and there were no more visible habitations, just mile after mile of forest. His fear returned. *She's going to use me in some obscene rite. That's why she's dragging me out here in the middle of nowhere. She can have her way with me and no one will witness the horror of it. And what kind of funny ideas was she referring to?* Then he remembered the conjoining Esther had described. He imagined electric pulses shaking his nervous system and distorting his toes, and he shouted, "I'd have fared better with the humans. Let me out!"

"Oh, don't be silly. We're almost there, and I'm getting hungry myself."

The demon's pickup seemed to gain speed the deeper, and more foreboding the forest. Trees and underbrush became a green black blur at the periphery of his vision and he had to look far ahead of the truck to see distinct features. Prior to his mortality, speed was accepted casually, but now, he was aware of the fragility of life and he wished she'd drive slower. He didn't want to die in the arms of a demon and without having saved one mortal soul.

The storm Abigail raised in town had turned into a soft morning shower in the countryside, and it gave the foliage the appearance of dark green patent leather. Lemuel imagined that the hard green shine reflected something of the demon's eyes as she gripped the steering wheel and they hurtled down the highway. Finally she slowed, and they turned off the highway onto a side road.

This road, unlike the coarse macadam of the main road, was a smooth blacktop lane and the wheels of the pickup hushed to a low lullaby. *Soft and easy is the way to damnation,* he thought. Their slower speed allowed him to gaze more deeply into the forest. The road made lazy turns between flowering laurels and rhododendrons, and towering oaks and maples formed half arches above the lane with a cerulean and cirrus sky making the keystone. Dogwood blossoms seemed to float against the dark woods and red buds cast carelessly tossed strings of tiny fusca flowers, which seemed suspended in the morning damp. The dark cool shade accentuated the clusters of blossoms and the glossy leaves had droplets sparkling in the mottled sunlight.

He stole a few surreptitious glances at her profile and realized she was fairly attractive. He had to admit that despite her evil nature, her darker complexion and modest proportions, she was nearly as pretty as Esther, but in a sordid earthy way. Then the thought occurred, *Why am I thinking about her that way? And worse! Comparing her to an angel like Esther? I'll be damned for sure.* He clutched the Bible more closely to his chest. Then he amused himself by imagining what she would look like if she were a mortal and subject to aging, just as any other mortal. When she was old and toothless those cute pouty lips would be withered and sunken, and her cheeks would lose their fullness. Her nose would become sharper and more prominent, and with her teeth gone, her pointy chin would turn upward toward her sharp nose. Her smooth complexion would wrinkle and get darker, her smooth graceful neck would be furrowed with creases, and the skin on those graceful hands would be dry, liver-spotted, gnarled, and more like claws. She'd look just like what she is …a witch.

Abigail leaned over and pushed a tape into the radio causing Lemuel's grotesque imaginings to disappear. He was instantly faced with her attractive reality. She had selected Gounod's *Faust*, and as the opera filled the cab of the truck she sang softly, in contralto harmony with the baritone singing Mephistopheles's part. Lemuel thought that her voice was good, not as good as the heavenly chorus, but very pleasant. Then realizing he was being charmed by the demon, he thought, *I'm damned for certain. She and her familiars will use my mortal flesh in some obscene ritual, and capture my soul when I die, and luke it off to hell.* He knew that she'd lie, but he asked anyway, "Why are you helping me, Abigail?"

"You're welcome, Lemuel, or was I mistaken. I thought I heard you say something like, thank you, Abigail, for helping me out of that jam."

"Thank you, Abigail, for helping me out of that jam. Why did you do it?"

"I don't know …professional courtesy? Maybe it's because we're the same age, or siblings, in a manner of speaking. Maybe I'm just curious about things back in the old empyrean. They were pretty bad when I left, with all that rigidity and regulation. Her voice mocked shrilly, "Do this! Do that! No, you can't do that! No! No! No! It was everywhere. Do they still have those encouraging little signs all over the place? 'God's eyes are everywhere beholding the good and the evil.' Humph! When I was up there, He was still called Yahweh, and he was a pain in the patoot then. He was the most egotistical god I ever saw. Boy! Talk about delusions of grandeur."

"Every well-run organization has to have rules and strong leadership. It's imperative for maximum productivity, and when the mind is freed from having to make decisions, it results in inner peace and tranquility. When every thought and effort is directed to the common quest for all pervading virtue, the result is heaven, and without it, the result would be chaos! I don't know why you demons consistently turn truth and virtue upside down. 'Woe unto them that call evil, good; and good, evil; that put darkness for light; and them that are wise in their own eyes, and prudent in their own sight[247].' The good people of King Jamesburg, who threatened us, were probably corrupted by demonic influences. Your sort passes through their town all the time."

"Demonic influences, huh? You're one of the faithful. Why didn't you cast the devils out of them?"

"Because everything happened too quickly, and you spirited me away before I could recover my senses." He gave an exasperated sigh, elevated his eyes, and prayed, "I know you've sent this trial to test my strength Lord. I know thy ways are mysterious, Lord, but why have you let me fall into the clutches of this merciless demon?"

The second act of *Faust* was being sung and Abigail sang along with Marguerite, "Once there was a king of Thule, who was faithful even until death…" Lemuel stared glumly ahead.

Lemuel looked deeply into the forest expecting to see fauns and satyrs leering at him from the shadows. A great horned owl blinked at him and he was sure it was a dreadful cockatrice; the horrid monster born of a rooster's egg and hatched by a serpent. Fortunately it was not a basilisk, or he'd have been turned to stone. A fallen log seemed to be the dreaded Lamia; the upturned roots looked like the head and body of a monstrous woman, and the trunk formed the rest of her serpentine tail. Abigail's comment about being hungry took on an ominous interpretation. He clutched his Bible tightly and schemed to escape. Maybe the dreaded man-eating Lamia and Abigail would fight over him, and he could escape during the battle.

Suddenly Abigail slowed the truck to a crawl and then stopped. She pointed out his window, and said excitedly, "Look, do you have anything that pretty in Heaven?"

Lemuel bobbled his head about. His eyes were wild and fearful as he sought some horrible monstrosity: a gorgon with serpents for hair, a scaly dragon breathing fire, at the very least, the woodland dryads in some shameless bacchanalia, or Pomona coming for him with her pruning knife.

"Right there! That spider web with the water droplets. See how they shine against the black loam. Look at the pretty colors." Then he saw the delicate, evenly woven strands which were covered with droplets shimmering their ephemeral display against the matte black, velvety soil. She said, "See, we have pretty things down here, but you have to know how to look. Part of the charm is the constant change. A few minutes earlier and that shaft of sunlight wouldn't have caught the web and in a few more minutes it will have evaporated the moisture."

"How can you find anything pleasant in such chaos. Where is the satisfying constancy? The comfort of knowing that each time you look it will always be the same. Besides we don't have spiders in heaven, but if we wanted to reproduce that, we could, and even..." Abigail threw the shift lever into gear and trod heavily on the accelerator. The tires gave a small squeak and Lemuel's head was jerked backward, and he finished "...make the filaments of platinum, and the water droplets of opal and diamond." Abigail sighed with disgust.

After several hundred more yards she turned onto a road surfaced with pea gravel. Lemuel told her, "There is a similar pathway in heaven through the loveliest of gardens, except there, instead of yellow stones, the gravel are nuggets of pure gold." Abigail merely shut her mouth tighter.

He didn't mention the graphic tableaus of the heavenly Eden, and fully expected that in this abode of imps and fiends, he'd be forced to witness many iniquitous examples of demonic salaciousness. He guessed that this was where the demons had attempted, in their imperfect fashion, to create an Eden. In spite of his fears, he snickered smugly over the rude log structure they had erected for the gate guardians. At least he didn't have to face Cerberus; the guards appeared to be ordinary mortals. Abigail stopped at the gate house, and Lemuel presumed she had to show them her special orders. "I suppose you can tell them that my occupation is minister, and my mortal metamorphosis occurred at seven o'clock this morning." Then he asked, "Is this where they'll tattoo my wrist?"

"This is a state park, Lem. I registered several days ago and I'm going inside to tell them that we're leaving today so they can give my campsite to someone else."

Continuing along slowly, they turned at a fork in the road where a sign made of halved logs indicated: Campsites 1-30. They came to a clearing where a group of jabbering imps, dressed in blue uniforms with gold piping, were drinking orange soda pop and eating moon pies, and they passed several shiny aluminum trailers. Although he couldn't see anyone outside, he thought he saw demons moving about behind the windows. At one site he saw a couple of demons sipping something from plastic mugs, and they raised their mugs as a salute to their sister demon as they drove past. Abigail waved back. At one site a pair of fiends were hunched over a smoking, black, metal altar of some type while three small imps sat exchanging jibes at one of the crude cross buck tables. He saw long motor homes and pop top, wheel-mounted tents. It was just the sort of chaotic mish mash he expected of demons.

Abigail's trailer was at the very last site. It was quite different from the others. It looked like a huge chromed loaf of bread. There was a broad blue band stretching from just behind the curved front windows all the way down the side with the word "excella" toward the front. In script above the front window was the word "Airstream." The inside had eggshell white walls that curved to match the outside contours, and the cabinet furniture looked to be dark teak with brass trim. There was an upholstered club chair beside the door, and a small, single-legged table under the windows on the opposite wall. Beneath the curved, wraparound front window was a sofa upholstered in wool damask with a woodland pattern of leaves and vines. Lemuel assumed that was where Abigail intended him to sleep.

Underfoot was an olive green, loop twist rug that felt cloud soft and extended the length of the vehicle, about thirty feet, to a creamy bathroom at the rear. To the left of the door was a small, but complete, kitchen, and opposite were pantry doors and a refrigerator. The area between the kitchen and the bath was Abigail's bedroom. All of the curtains were drawn over the windows. Abigail motioned for them to open and they magically drew back. Lemuel was surprised at the plush luxury. It was really more spacious and comfortable than an archangel's quarters.

She asked him to be seated, indicating the sofa, and switched on the television set. She wondered if there were any news about the morning's incident. The local station was featuring the event and there hadn't been anything this sensational in King Jamesburg since a school teacher had left her husband and run off with one of her eighth grade students. But that was two weeks ago and was already old news. Abigail asked Lemuel if he wanted juice to go with his eggs. "Orange or tomato?" Lemuel was intent on the TV and just shrugged.

Officer Flaharety was saying, "No comment until we capture those fugitives." And he pushed a meaty palm up to the camera.

Abigail handed Lemuel a large glass of orange juice and turned to beating eggs in a bowl. Father Angus made a direct plea requesting them to turn themselves in and assured them that no matter how grievous their crimes, the Lord would forgive them, and that the good citizens of King Jamesburg would treat them fairly in court. Abigail poured the whipped egg and milk mixture into a frying pan greased with sweet cream butter and stirred it with a fork. Next she put a couple of pieces of bread into a toaster as Tamar's mother was allowing herself to be interviewed on camera.

It was contrary to the station's policy of keeping juvenile sex victims names and faces confidential, but in the interest of, "...making the public aware of the growing number of pedophiles that are terrifying mothers and fathers everywhere, and preying on our innocent children..." Abigail served his breakfast with a jar of marmalade and coffee, and said, "I see Tamar's mother has put on a fresh frock. Doesn't she look nice? I wonder if those are real or silicone?" Then she said, "You better eat. We've got to get out of here."

Lemuel's hands began to tremble and he watched Abigail eat without a trace of concern.

Abigail realized he'd never eaten real food or used knives or forks before, so she had to demonstrate their proper use. He began to understand how inadequate his mortality briefing had been. He heard himself being described as a raving mad sexual deviant, and he bristled, "She's bearing false witness. They swear on the Bible, vow it is their moral guide, and then ignore its teaching. Do they ever read it?"

"A whole lot more than I do," Abigail replied, as she calmly spread marmalade on her toast.

"After this incident, I'm beginning to wonder if Amnon really did rape his sister. He may have been innocent. I'll bet she lied, just like this Tamar is doing about me."

"You mean David's daughter? Boy, they think they have dysfunctional families today. Of course Amnon raped her. That's why Absalom killed him, wasn't it?"

After a thoughtful pause, Lemuel said, "Tamar enticed him[248]."

"You men always use that excuse."

Abigail realized their situation was getting out of hand. It must have

HOW THE GOOD TAILOR GOT TO HEAVEN 217

been a slow news day: the morning show was filling in air time. The station's always available, all purpose, authoritative psychologist was being interviewed on the nature of sex criminals. The psychologist explained that sexually abused children often carry on these perversions themselves when they reach adulthood. The interviewer also touched on the subject of incest, and the psychologist cited some statistics and deplored the ruined young lives such perversion causes. Abigail said, "We can't stay here. Someone is liable to recognize us. We'll have to really hide out for a while. You better stay with me for a few days until this thing blows over. Come on, finish up. You do the dishes and I'll get us hooked up to the truck."

Abigail waved a hand and the table cleared itself, the breakfast dishes flew to the sink, and all the loose objects inside the trailer flew into their assigned cupboards. She pushed a button to lower the TV antenna, but outside, where her psychokinetic powers might startle the other campers, she had to do everything manually. She hefted the heavy ball hitch into its socket under the rear bumper. Next she backed the truck, and skillfully positioned the ball under the tongue. She had electric powered stabilizers and an electric jack post to raise and lower the heavy trailer, so those took no exertion. Next she connected the electric cable that controls the trailer's running lights and brakes, attached the safety chains and emergency cable, and levered the sway bars into position. She threw the wheel chocks into the back of the pickup, coiled the water hose and stowed it away, and disconnected the light plastic sewage line, rinsed it out, and slid it into place in the boot. The electric cable was coiled in on top of it. It took her about three minutes, and they were ready to travel.

Once they were away from the park, and out on the highway, Abigail said, "I doubt they'll be looking for a trailer, but you sure made a bad beginning. And stop telling people you're an angel. You'll give the race of angels a bad name."

He ignored the slur and thanked her for the breakfast, and he admitted it was tastier than manna. Then he asked, "How long before they'll forget?"

"Not long. Mortals have an attention span of about two minutes and a learned recall rate of two weeks, maximum. So, unless it's dinned into their minds every day, they soon forget. They'll be in a dither about something else pretty soon."

"I suppose you're right. That's fairly close to what Tomas said about the need for liturgical layering." He decided to not give her the satisfaction of knowing how her spell had caused him to hallucinate a pearl in Tomas's hand.

"So you can figure that about two weeks after you are no longer news, you can travel openly."

They drove along at a steady speed, about two miles an hour below the speed limit. Abigail did not want to be stopped by some policeman who might recognize them. The traffic was heavy and most cars passed them. Lemuel was absorbed by the unfurling pageant of America's highways. He decided that because of the totality of confusion he witnessed, salvation was definitely needed in America. No two cars were alike and they all seemed to travel at different speeds, passing each other every few miles. Interspersed in the melee of automobiles there was a confusion of trucks, varying in size from Abigail's pickup, to monstrous behemoths towing two enormous box-like trailers. Most of the trucks had garish advertizing painted on their sides. An enormous bus, loaded with mortals, passed them at a high rate of speed causing Abigail to compensate for the airwash that the bus pushed before it. He saw the nation as the mother of all chaos. He was eager to start his ministry and tell them of the divine order that awaits.

There were other campers on the road varying in design from simple boxes mounted in pickup truck beds, to a mixture of trailer designs and sizes, to some that looked like trailers but towed a car behind, and some as large as the interstate bus that had passed. There were a few that appeared identical to Abigail's. Then he noticed something strange happen. As the trailers that looked like Abigail's approached in the oncoming lane, they flashed their headlights and Abigail flashed her's in

HOW THE GOOD TAILOR GOT TO HEAVEN   219

response. None of the other trailers flashed their headlights. After five or six such occurrences he was certain he'd observed demons signaling to each other. Now he was sure this country was overrun with thousands of demons. *They may profess to like chaos, but they all have the same kind of trailers.* He began to gauge the enormity of his task. *Demons are rampant. He'd fallen into their clutches.* If that were true, Abigail could have staged the whole incident with the assistance of a few other demons to act as agents provocateurs. He realized it would be pointless to openly denounce their calumny. She'd lie and twist the facts. He decided to approach the problem obliquely. He said he was especially disappointed by the way Father Angus had received him. "The laity could be excused, but a clergyman should know better."

"Don't worry about it. They'll soon forget, and you can go out and save souls to your heart's content."

How clever. She pretends indifference, but she wants their souls herself, and mine as well. Then he said, "I wonder if he really was a priest. A priest would know the Scriptures, say to entertain strangers 'for thereby some have entertained angels unawares.'"

"Of course he was a priest. What did you think he was? But doesn't that bit of Scripture you quoted imply that you're not supposed to tell them you're an angel. You're supposed to be incognito, the same as us terrestrial angels."

I knew she'd twist things just like that. And imagine, calling herself a terrestrial angel. And he disparaged the euphemism. "Terrestrial angel, humph! A fallen angel, to say the least; a devil to be more accurate, or a fiend, demon, witch, tempter, betrayer …"

Abigail stuck her tongue out at him, and sneered, "Name caller."

"Your name is legion for you are many[249]." Then he asserted, "I saw you signaling to those other demons with your headlights."

"What?"

"Those other demons with trailers like yours."

Abigail stifled a laugh. He had mistaken Airstream owners' customary courtesy greetings to other Airstream owners for demon signals. She thought, *Let him stew*, and said, "Yeah, I guess you caught us. You're too smart for me, Lem."

This confirmation of the demons' intrigues made him realize that he would have to be extra wary, but, at the same time, there was a self-satisfied glint in his eye, like that of a truant officer who'd caught a liar feigning illness.

She decided to tweak his conscience a bit, and said sternly, "I hope you're happy about what you've done to me. You've made me a fugitive too. Like they say, no good deed ever goes unpunished."

This notion had the opposite effect and he scarcely hid his delight over her problem. "Will you get in trouble with your supervisors?" He barely hid his schadenfreude.

"Huh?"

"You know, your bosses, your chiefs, the management? The archfiends? The chief demon, Beelzebub! Satan!"

"Are you kidding? Didn't you know, we all do our own thing. I haven't had to take an order since I left the ninth celestial orb. Taking orders is your thing. We terrestrial angels do as we please. But now that you've made me a fugitive, my freedom is restricted."

"The humans can't do anything to you. You have magical powers and you can force them to obey you or suffer the consequences."

"Oh sure, and call attention to myself. Have them all cringing with fear and pointing me out. Or worse, sucking up to me, and asking for favors. If they ever found out I had angel powers there'd be a zillion of them lined up to swap their souls for favors. You didn't think that the story of Faust was real, did you? Do you really believe that Mephistopheles would waste all that time and trouble just to gain one soul? Some of these humans would sell their souls to win a ball game or to get a promotion. They'd want me to divert streams, change the weather, make them more attractive, cure their ailments, or buy them a Mercedes Benz. I'd never have another peaceful moment. Haven't you seen those mobs at Lourdes? And they're just the ones that want to get healed or cured or something. Add to that mob those asking to be made rich, or powerful, or want to be movie stars. That's what they'd be pestering me for. We terrestrial angels have to keep very low profiles. It's the only way we can keep our freedom." Then, pragmatically accepting their predicament, she shrugged, and said, "Since I'm on the lam too, let's make the best of a bad situation. We can pretend we're on vacation. We'll head up to the mountains. It's nice there this time of year, and there will be a lot of tourists. We'll blend in."

She turned the rig off the interstate at the next cloverleaf, and the narrow secondary road undulated over and around the Piedmont hills. Ahead on the horizon he saw an irregular blue line of mountains. He turned to her and asked, "How long will we have to be in hiding up on the mountain?"

"I don't know. I've never done this sort of thing before, but considering the number of bombings, plane crashes, rapes and murders, fires, political chicanery, corporate conniving and stock swindling, banking failures, terrorism, and warfare they have going on, I guess they'll have forgotten about us in about forty days."

"Forty days …and forty nights? And will I be expected to fast for the entire forty days and forty nights?"

She looked puzzled and said, "Of course not. We'll eat. I wouldn't expect you to go without eating for forty days. That would give any mortal hallucinations and all sorts of weird ideas. You'd probably try to eat stones if you starved that long. Where did you ever get a notion like that?"

"Under the circumstances, I thought it was the conventional procedure, and length of time.[250]"

"I'm glad you reminded me. We'll have to pick up supplies in one of these little stores." And looking critically at his blue suit, and wing-tip oxfords, added, "You'll need to get something else to wear. You look out of place dressed like that."

Abigail stopped in a small, picturesque village that had a line of shops that sold wares ranging from handmade candles to autographed limited edition prints, to pictorial maps of the locally fought Civil War battles, and genuine Daguerreotype photographs. One shop sold nothing but hand-knitted sweaters and real estate. While Abigail shopped in a quaint grocery where sugar cured hams and bacon hung in the window, Lemuel entered the "Western & Saddlery Shoppe." A snooty salesman condescended to sell him the proper "togs" for camping. He assured Lemuel that his wares were every bit as good as any outfitter in the country. This was Lemuel's first experience in the world of commerce, and it didn't take him long to figure out that the three hundred dollars he had been issued would not go very far. When he left the shop he had two pair of blue jeans of unassuming manufactory, a couple of chambray work shirts, a blanket-lined denim jacket, a pair of engineers' boots, and thirty-seven dollars and forty-two cents. He was certain though that when he hit the salvation trail the collection plate would soon restore his fortune.

Leaving the small village they rolled onward through the pastoral peace of the Piedmont hunt country. Cattle and horses grazed behind painted board fences. At one farm a pack of wildly yelping foxhounds wriggled under, or crawled through, the rails of a zigzagged split rail fence, and mounted horsemen and horsewomen wearing pinks and jodhpurs leapt over. In many places there were ancient stone fences that were built before the founding fathers were born. Here and there were small flocks of sheep, and nearly every farm had hunters bred for the steeple chase, grazing, or frolicking in the pastures. Tree shaded lanes lead to grove ensconced dwellings. There were slender columned Georgians with two-story high porches; or solid brick colonials, often painted white; and traditional style farmhouses with porches and porch swings; or an occasional long, low modern rambler with wide sheltering soffits. The foundations were cloaked with carefully trimmed English Boxwood or Japanese Yews; and flowering Azaleas with white, pink, or deep red blossoms softened the bases of the houses to merge the homes with the manicured lawns. A profusion of Dogwoods and Judas trees, flowered as though by fairy painters, were intermingled with giant oaks. There were huge, gambrel-roofed barns with vertical board and batten

HOW THE GOOD TAILOR GOT TO HEAVEN   223

siding painted the traditional barn red with white trim, or occasionally left to weather to a silver gray patina, or whitewashed to a snowy white. Once in a while, Lemuel saw black caretakers tending to maintenance chores, as they would do in Heaven: sweeping, mowing, painting, pruning, or in one paddock, leading an auburn hunter toward the barn while his mistress, dressed in pinks, jodhpurs, and riding hat, walked toward the main house.

"Picturesque," Abigail commented.

"If you mean uncivilized and unkempt, I agree. There are tares in the pastures, weeds along the roadsides, the only statue I saw was a cast iron jockey, and it was crudely made, the fences are rough-sawn boards, and some were just split logs stacked like jackstraws. Was someone too lazy to dig a post hole? And those stone walls look as though no one ever came near them with a dressing chisel; they're just piled up rocks. No two houses are alike and they don't have enough souls tending the grounds to do a proper job. Why do they let them dress in such shabby clothes. In heaven the souls' robes are alike and kept sparkling white."

"My! My! The faithful really have something to look forward to, don't they."

"If these are the conditions under which the faithful are forced to live in the world, I can imagine the squalor that you demons provide for your souls. If, as you say, you let them do anything they please and you don't make them work, and you demons are too lazy to work, then how does hell get cleaned up?"

"I told you before. Didn't you believe me? The live mortals do it for us, of course! One advantage to having hell on earth is they'll do almost anything for money. We hire landscapers to care for the grounds, janitors and maintenance people to clean and repair the buildings and caterers supply their meals."

"You mean they eat mortal food instead of manna?" he asked incredulously.

"Of course. They can order anything they want and it's served to them by pretty waitresses. We have a tobacco shop, a well-stocked liquor closet and wine cellar, a bar that looks like an English pub, and a very posh night club with live entertainment. There's a very nice golf course, and swimming pools, tennis courts, riding stables, and if they want to, they can take our chartered bus to the sea shore."

"Sloth! Gluttony! Drunkenness! Indolence! Debauchery! And disporting diversions! Have you no sense of shame? No compassion at all? They're all sinful already. They've been damned because of their sins. They need condign correction. They need to be punished measure for measure for their sins and you steep them in interminable corruption? Where is your sense of justice?"

"Well …" She said thoughtfully, "we found out it was easier to keep them entertained and happy, and then we didn't have to worry about them wandering off and getting into trouble. This way we terrestrial angels are free to do whatever we want and we don't have to worry about them trying to escape."

Lemuel was dismayed and sunk back heavily into the leather upholstery. He was confused by the weight of her simple logic. It was a proposition he had never considered, his mind refused to acknowledge it, and he stared morosely ahead.

The rig nosed more and more upward, the big engine throbbed deeply, and then as the transmission shifted to a lower range, it sped up to its normal purr. Abigail whistled accompaniment to the gay, frivolous sounds of Offenbach coming from the radio. "*Orphee aux enfers,*" she replied to his question.

"I might have known."

"Lively, isn't it? You can almost see the chorus girls showing their flounces as they do their high kicks." And she drummed her thumbs on the steering wheel in time to the music. At the very top of the grade they turned onto another smooth blacktop road, similar to the one at the campground they had left. They came to a small toll booth, Abigail paid the girl ranger an entry fee, and they drove on.

Up here the road twisted sinuously along the mountain ridge and Abigail deftly maneuvered her sixty feet of coupled vehicles. The

HOW THE GOOD TAILOR GOT TO HEAVEN —�— 225

scenery below them was marvelous, and along the road in small roadside clearings they saw an occasional doe with her fawns, which seemed tame enough to pet. At one trash barrel a black bear was upended, as Lemuel remembered Abigail doing only a couple of hours before. A tourist recorded the bear with his camera. So far the events of this day had been so filled with tumult that to Lemuel, it seemed an age had passed since he emerged in the King Jamesburg Park. It was the eleventh hour of the first day of his mortality.

At a scenic overlook, Abigail rolled slowly into the parking area, stopped and switched the engine off. She got out and led Lemuel over to a low stone wall, where she bounded lightly up and stood atop the broad flagstone coping. This made her nearly a head taller than Lemuel, and she put a hand on his shoulder and made a sweeping gesture with her other arm. "Isn't it beautiful?" she said, indicating the valley below. It was a clear day and the panorama was spectacular: lush green rolling meadows were transected into irregular-sized pastures by white board, or split rail fences, or verdant lines of brush formed hedgerows between the fields. Off to the west, a field was being plowed, and tiny, speck-sized, white gulls fluttered behind a tiny tractor looking for worms in the rich brown loam the tractor turned up with its plow. A few fluffs of clouds, slightly beneath the level of their feet, drifted by and made racing dark shadows across the multi-patterned, varicolored, softly rumpled counterpane of the landscape. A willow and oak-lined river, the Shenandoah, meandered a scalloped border between the deep green cobbling of the forest at the foot of the range, and the productive Eden below. As Lemuel studied the individual details of man's created artistry, Abigail got a pair of binoculars from the glove compartment and handed them to him.

He watched a straw-hatted, overall-clad farmer plow his field, and the occasional car which seemed to crawl along the black ribbon of road. He studied the neat white farmhouses and watched a couple of men exchanging banter at the gas pump in front of a country store. He visually traced the serpentine coils of the gentle, lazy river and found two small boys fishing along the bank. They reminded him of the two boys that he had found crying and tried to console up in Heaven. Even with his multiplied vision he could not see the boy's faces, but Lemuel knew by the tilt of their heads and the expectant hunch of their shoulders that they were intently absorbed in serious fishing.

"It'd be nice if they caught a couple of nice ones to take home to their moms. Wouldn't they be proud of themselves?" Abigail said, smiling broadly.

"Oh yes. Lord, let it happen."

Immediately both of the boys' poles arced, they reeled wildly, and landed a couple of nice catfish. As the fish writhed, and the boys excitedly unhooked their catches, Lemuel raised his eyes and said, "Thank you, Lord."

Abigail turned her head aside so Lemuel couldn't see her amusement.

Lemuel handed the binoculars back to her and with his unaided eyes panned the valley from the horizon to the laurels flowering just beneath his feet. Then he asked, caustically, "Is this where you offer me the world? Tempt me to leap from this pinnacle? Or do I have to wait the full forty days?[251]"

"Sure! How would you like it wrapped? We'd better use a plain brown wrapper …parts of it are X-rated. Is your room, back in the empyrean, big enough to hold it? It would need a pretty good-sized stand if you intend to put it into the corner of your den."

"You don't have to get angry."

"What makes you think the world's mine to give?" she asked hotly, and then stamped off—noiselessly, because of her sneakers. She flipped her long dark hair with an angry toss of her head and added, "If you want to jump, go ahead!"

Lemuel stuttered, "Well I thought …well, from something you said…it must have been something I read." Then he implored, "So much has happened to me today. Aw…please …come on now…you don't have to cry about it."

Her nose twitched tearfully, and she whimpered, "I've done my very best to try to help you. I've showed you all the dear things that I thought were pretty, and you've done nothing but belittle me and make fun of the things I like." Her sniffles became sobs as she bawled, "I'm going back home."

He hung his head sheepishly, walked over to her, and said, "I'm sorry, Abigail." He cradled her weeping face against his shoulder and held her small body as it heaved with expansive gasping emotion. Then he lifted her tear-stained face, dabbed the lachrymal fluid from her cheeks with his handkerchief, and kissed each moistened eye. Then he lifted her chin with his hand, looked deeply into her dark green eyes, and said, "Please forgive me." He bent down and kissed her trembling lips, and he felt her tongue brush lightly over his lips. Finally, the whimpering ceased. Hand-in-hand they walked back to the truck, and as she started the engine, he leaned over and kissed her cheek. She patted his hand and smiled at him.

And it was just noon on the first day of Lemuel's mortality.

Chapter 14

LEMUEL COULD NOT UNDERSTAND THIS STRANGE NEW emotion he felt. It made him happy as a child with a delightful new toy, and he saw Abigail in a new light. But at the same time it terrified him, because he felt it competed with his soul. An extra claim had been staked against the territory comprising his duties, wants, and ambitions, and he feared that it had the capacity to expand itself and consume all of him. But he also felt that he could not give it up. Now they drove on in silence, except for the radio. Both of them exchanged shy glances from time to time and he wondered if Abigail felt the same. Her first response after the incident dashed his hopes.

"What happened back there was just an impulse, a momentary mortal weakness, and I think we should both forget it ever happened," Abigail said.

"Yeah sure. I suppose you're right," Lemuel replied, and then spent a long time staring out of his window without seeing anything.

Abigail said, "I know a secluded hideaway on a backwoods road where hardly anyone comes, but we don't have time to get there before dark so we better spend the night in the park campground. We'll go there first thing tomorrow."

"Whatever you say," he responded dully.

When they pulled into the campground at Big Meadow, the ranger at the registration office told them that all the campsites were filled. No sooner were the words out of his mouth when two trailer rigs pulled up from the other direction to check out. They said the federal park facilities were inadequate: "No swimming pool! No rides for the kids! No liquor at the commissary! And no hookups! Just what do you people do with all our tax money? We're going to a commercial park where they know how to treat the public!" So Abigail and Lemuel were admitted.

At their assigned site Abigail jackknifed the trailer and backed it into a woodsy cove. She said, "Let's get something to eat. I'm sure you're famished, with nothing to eat since breakfast." She jumped out lightly, reached upward and stretched her back muscles, and Lemuel looked at her wistfully. She said, "We have to do a few things first. Don't stand there mooning, come on and help me set up for the night. We won't have to disconnect from the truck, but we will have to level the trailer."

She adjusted the ground jacks while he chocked the wheels. Lemuel's morose condition was obvious to anyone with a modicum of sensitivity. Abigail, having spent six thousand years among humans, was well aware of the psychological affliction that had seized him. In fact it was all part of her plan to capture his soul, but her shrewdly calculated inducements to get him to defect had overshot their mark. All this intense emotion was directed to herself, and herself only. She wanted a defector, not a love-smitten adolescent. He was sitting at the picnic table with his back against the top and his legs spread out in front of him. She sat beside him and took his hand, kissed his cheek, and said, " Lem, we have to talk about something."

"What you are feeling is a common mortal condition. And there's no end to the trouble it causes. You and I are above that sort of thing. Even though you're an ethereal angel, and I am a terrestrial angel, we're both of the same substances, are both the same age, come from the same place, and if it were not for your mortality, have the same powers. Most of the angels coming down on mortality detail have a ball screwing every human being they can. As you know, I won't satisfy you that way, no more than one of your ethereal angels would. If that's what you want, you'll have to find some nice mortal girl …or girls, if that's your inclination."

She looked into his eyes, and added, "But we both have a real problem. Both of us made a mistake in King Jamesburg and we're fugitives from the law. Unless you want to start your mortality in prison, or an insane asylum, the hiding out part of this adventure is real. We have to do it. I owe you that much for the tricks I played on you."

She was still holding his hand and her clear explanation made Lemuel feel a bit better. He put his arm across her shoulder and gave her a hug. "I know you're right, Abby. This mortality stuff is new to me. I'll have to learn to control my emotions." At the same time his feelings were soaring. *She doesn't hate me*, he thought happily.

"Let's go inside and I'll fix supper."

With his emotions settling into normal midrange, he sat on the sofa and watched the television news. Here, more than a hundred miles away, they were mentioned. Their description was broadcast and an artist had drawn their images from eyewitness accounts. The pictures were generic and could have been of nearly any adult male and female. They depicted Abigail darker than she really was, and Lemuel was fairer. *There are plenty of darker angels than she is*, he thought. And then he had a really wild idea. *Suppose I could get her to return to Heaven*. He cast aside Tomas's warning and fantasized about saving this demon, a feat never before performed. He imagined the warm reception he'd receive with his tally of mortal souls, if on that list he also brought home a demon. He remembered that the seneschal said that one demon's soul led back on the paths of righteousness might be worth one thousand mortal souls.

While he was lost in this revery, Abigail prepared two small drinks that she called martinis. "Just some dry vermouth, it's a white wine, and some neutral spirits they call gin, an olive, and well chilled with ice," she explained. Then she surprised him by offering to do something he could never imagine a demon doing. She actually offered to help with his ministry. "After things cool down I'd like to help you get started down the salvation trail. I could help you with lots of things like healing and stuff, and turning water into wine. I do a really neat fiery pillar. Just so long as they think you or the Lord are doing the miracles and not me." Then she set the cocktail in front of him, raised her stemmed glass, and said, "*Aukko tu pios.*"

"What?"

"To your health."

"That was the Romany tongue." Her dark complexion and the trailer began to make sense. "My God! I've been kidnaped by Gypsies! And a Gypsy demon at that. I don't know what you're planning, but the organization will never pay ransom."

"Don't be childish. Drink your martini."

He raised his martini and swallowed a large gulp, followed by a gasp.

"You're supposed to sip it," she said, and then she raised her glass, and said, "*Nostrovia.* Does that make me Russian?"

"You could be both. There are Russian Gypsies. They're the ones who traveled with the Mongol hordes keeping their swords and knives sharp. And the Russian royalty kept them as entertainers. But Romany is a thief's argot, secretive, and intended to conceal intentions from the Gorgios."

"Oh, like the Latin mass."

"They don't use Latin anymore, smarty."

"I think the potatoes are nearly done. It's time to put on the steaks and make the salad. Do you know how to set the table?" He shook his head. "Watch and learn." As she set the table she explained that in civilized society, dining was more than eating and was as ritualized as the liturgics. She laid out a sparkling, white linen tablecloth, fine bone china with gold pinstripe edging, and properly placed the delicately worked silverware and crystal goblets for their wine, linen napkins, and long

HOW THE GOOD TAILOR GOT TO HEAVEN   233

white tapers in cut glass holders. It was growing dark outside and she lit the candles, "to save the batteries."

Lemuel remembered how the eggs tasted that morning and wondered if this evening's meal would be as delicious. She served a sirloin that had been brushed with soy sauce, broiled to a rich cordovan and pecan brown, and sliced diagonally into tender, thick, juicy slices with pats of butter melting on top. The potato skins crinkled as she opened his, dabbed a spoonful of butter into the steaming white cleft, and decorated it with a sprig of parsley. The salad was halved, ripe, cherry tomatoes and tender, cubed carrots, and small, pimento-stuffed olives cradled in endive lettuce. It was gleaming with an oil and vinegar dressing and garnished with spices and minced onion. Small, oddly shaped rolls with hard crusts and soft insides were served in a napkin-lined basket and covered to keep them hot.

Fortunately, Abigail didn't eat very much since Lemuel ate about three quarters of the steak. He discovered he liked to dredge the bites of steak in the rich brown gravy. He gobbled down the salad and finished off the potato, skin and all. He thickly buttered one of the rolls and dipped it in the steak juices to sop up the remainder. Then he helped himself to the remaining slice of steak and scraped the juices from the serving platter with another roll.

Abigail said, "Now that you're a mortal, you'll have to watch your cholesterol."

"I'll watch it tomorrow," he said, and washed his meal down with the dark purple wine. He patted his full stomach, and said, "Timothy recommends a little wine for thy stomach's sake, and thine often infirmities."[252]

"If you keep eating like that you'll get an infirmity called the gout," she said, pulling one leg up beneath her. She settled back in her large overstuffed chair and sipped her wine. "Do you have any room left for desert?" she asked as a jest, certain that he was stuffed.

Lemuel thought it over for a few seconds, and asked, "What do you have?"

"Blueberry pie and vanilla ice cream," she replied.

Not wanting to appear egregious, he recovered his angel's decorum, and said, "Well, just a very small piece and a tiny dab of ice cream, thank you."

Abigail watched in mute disbelief as he devoured a third of her pie and nearly a pint of ice cream. "Don't they feed you angels?" she asked.

"Oh yes, and very well. We can have all the manna we want, but this mortal food is ...different. I think I could develop a liking for it."

She served coffee with a dollop of Irish whisky, all the while contemplating, *Tenure huh? I'm surprised they get any of them back after their mortality detail. I wonder how many of them have defected? We ought to keep records.* Her eyes narrowed as she assessed her prey's commitment to his organization; it seemed slight at the moment. She decided to try a small test. "You forgot to say grace before supper," she said, wearing a sly smile.

He had been so hungry that he hadn't even considered it, and he sought a plausible explanation. "As your guest, I didn't know if it would offend you. You provided the supper. You're a demon and I wasn't sure where to direct my gratitude."

"*Sore simensar si men by Dovvel's kerrimus,*" she said, and added, "all related by God's doing. I wouldn't have been offended, but remember, I prefer to be called a terrestrial angel."

Once again Lemuel was forced to wrestle with her twisted logic. *All God's children? I suppose it's true in the broadest sense. And Abigail wasn't at all demonic, in the traditional sense of the definition. She wasn't foul-mouthed, surly, covered with warts and coarse hair, and smelly.* With a full stomach, and another Irish coffee he grew expansive and generous. He considered her to be fairly pleasant company and quite pretty in the candle light. "All right, if it won't offend you. I would like to say my prayers on every appropriate occasion."

"And I can just put my fingers in my ears," she joked. "But there is one thing. Since we are forced to share the next few weeks together, it's only fair that we share some of the work. Now that you've had a taste of

HOW THE GOOD TAILOR GOT TO HEAVEN

mortal fare, there's a job that's not as pleasant as eating. It called doing the dishes. I cooked, so now it's your turn."

"Yes, my little Gypsy girl. Or should I say—*Ava, mi Romany chi.*"

"Where did you learn Romany?"

"Remember that very busy time we had back a half century ago. You remember, don't you? There were millions and millions of souls …the lineup at the pearly gates stretched for miles. We were so busy that they had to send down tenured angels to help the deliverance angels. Saint Peter's receiving line was like a foot race. The souls barely got a nod from him."

"Oh yeah, war time is always busy. It was when some of God's avenging angels went berserk over the Russian problem. The Russians were calling themselves Atheists and the lying angels invested spiritual powers into the Germans to squelch their heresy."

"Yes, that's right. Anyway, I was working a place called Auschwitz and picked up a few Gypsies there. I learned a few words from them."

Abigail's face drained of all softness, and her eyes instead of reflecting the candle light, looked dull and clouded. She said, "Oh yes! I remember. 'Praise the Lord, and pass the ammunition, and we'll all stay free.'"

"You shouldn't look gift horses in the mouth, Abigail. Your side must have done quite well. More than thirty thousand Gypsies were killed, and most of them worshiped false gods."

"No, we only got a handful of their souls and none of the Atheists."

"You silly girl. We get all the Atheists."

"Huh?"

"Well, of course. As Tomas explained it to me, it all depends on which god they don't believe in. It isn't any trick for a Russian to not believe in some Australian aboriginal demiurge but for them to deny the God of Abraham's existence, with the evidence of His faithful surrounding them, takes thoughtful concentration. And as soon as they concentrate on the matter, we have them. It's like the Satanists; we get them too. But the Gypsies actually believed in some other god." He watched her suspiciously and wondered why she would lie about the number of souls they got. He assumed she would be proud of their coup.

Abigail covered her surprise by taking another sip from her coffee cup. She also wondered why Lemuel would lie about something she expected him to boast about. "It's odd, isn't it." They both said in unison.

She said, "This shop talk is depressing, so let's just drop the matter. I think we should leave early in the morning. It's not far, but there are no facilities at all and it will take a lot of work to set up our camp. And we may have to do some clearing on that old logging road too. I'm sure you'll like the place. It's quite pretty. There's a stream and a small pond where we can go swimming."

Lemuel thought, *swimming*? Once again, he began to consider his limitations. He had lost all of his angel powers. He couldn't make himself invisible anymore; he couldn't soar; and he wouldn't be able to walk on water. Moreover, he had virtually no mortal skills at all. "That sounds nice, Abigail, but I don't know how to swim. I never had to learn."

"Don't worry about it. I'll teach you. And I think you'll have to learn how to drive too. That's essential today. I can soar and travel at the speed of thought, but you can't go anywhere without driving. I'll give you your first driving lesson tomorrow."

It was getting late and she said, "That sofa makes up into a bed and I'll get your sheets." She brought him bed linen, blankets, and a pillow. Folded the table against the wall and opened out the sofa bed. "I guess you know how to make your own bed, don't you?" He nodded. "I feel like an old school marm, giving all this instruction. Oh, another thing. Down here most people take showers every day. Come on, I want to show you how the shower works. We have to be careful with the water." Then, calmly, and with no more sense of shame than removing her gloves, she pulled off her sweatshirt, slipped out of her jeans, and stood naked before him.

Lemuel fully understood her casualness. All angels, whether celestial or terrestrial, are essentially asexual. Furthermore, since the demons and Satan were cast down before Adam and Eve were created, they never did have access to the waters of life. They never experienced mortality the same way the ethereal angels have, and as Lemuel was now experiencing. Therefore, he understood that Abigail, by preceding all the mortals, and having never been mortal, was, in that respect anyway, a vestal.

But Lemuel, just that very morning, became a mortal, human as any other, and the sight of that small, brown sylph ambling down the narrow aisle ahead of him and into the ivory-tone bathroom aroused some strange sensations. Emotions he had never felt before. He stood and watched, wide-eyed, slack-jawed, and dumb, while she showed him how to use the hand held telephone type shower head. "First you get yourself wet all over, like this"; she said, as she swirled the spray quickly over her body and made it glisten. "And then you cut off the water with this little button." Then taking up a bar of soap, she said, "Next you get yourself all soapy."

Lemuel felt a sudden urge to help her with the soaping and rinsing. Then at that moment, a thought struck. He suddenly remembered part of the lesson Myles had taught him from the Acts of John; it was part of the ritual prayer circle: 'I will be washed, and I will wash.' *Terrestrial angel, huh*? Abigail was a full-fledged demon, and she was trying to cause him to commit a sacrilege by washing a demon. *Ah huh! I'm too smart to be trapped by this Gypsy demon. She lured me here with a lie about having to save the water.* Finally, he said, "When I had my powers as an angel, I could have kept the water tank full for us with a wave of my hand."

She squinted out through the suds coursing down her face from her lathered hair, and replied, "So can I. It's the tank at the other end of the plumbing to hold the waste water, that's the problem. Neither one of us was given the power to wish that away. Back then the environment wasn't considered." She rinsed and dried herself roughly with a towel bringing a rosy glow to her tawny skin, and after drying her hair, tugged a large white comb through the tangles. She said, "What are you waiting for? The shower is all yours. Be careful with the water though. If the holding tank overflows, we'll hear about it. When you're a fugitive, you have to be extra careful about the rules. We don't want to call attention to ourselves."

It was not until Lemuel was hesitant about undressing in front of her that she realized what he had been thinking. Now that he was a mortal, she was as much woman as sprite to him, and that made the color of her reddened flesh deepen.

By the time he'd finished his shower she was asleep, and he eased past her bed to get to his own in the front of the trailer. He looked down at her while she slept peacefully in the moonlight. Soft, subtle shadows played across her dark features making shades of burnt sienna and umber flit over her as the bower of leaves closing over the trailer moved in the gentle night breeze. Her hair cascading over the pillow looked black with shifting colors of port wine, and one dark bare arm lay on the white sheet, while the other bent upward with her hand lying on the pillow beside her head. Her carotid throbbed slowly beneath her ear, and he felt that he would like to nuzzle her gracefully sculpted neck, and run the tip of his tongue over the rim of her delicate ear. The small form of her body was dimly outlined by shadows in the sensually-molded linen and soft, pastel yellow blanket. As she breathed the bed covers rose and fell softly, evenly, and gently. He couldn't imagine why she was having this effect on him. When he lived in the barracks none of the other angels aroused the slightest emotion in him, and he barely noticed them unless they snored. Even that most beautiful of all angels, Esther, never caused the internal tremors that he now felt.

He put on the pajamas that he brought from Heaven. They were sky blue with large white wings printed on the back. He made his bed, knelt along aside it, and prayed. He asked the Lord to help him resist temptation, and thanked Him for the courage he summoned when Abigail tried to get him to test his faith by jumping off the mountain.

Chapter 15

IN THE MORNING HE AWOKE TO THE AROMA OF COFFEE PERcolating, bacon and eggs frying, and biscuits baking. Abigail urged, "Rise and shine! Come on, sleepyhead, grab your socks, we've got a lot to do today."

Lemuel scratched his head, rubbed his eyes, and stared sleepily at her. It took him a few moments to realize where he was. No joy was found in that recollection. The mess he'd gotten himself into was no cause for joy, and he thought that if there was one plus mark on his first day of mortality, she was preparing their breakfast. Things had to be pretty bad when the high point of your day was meeting a demon.

Abigail wore a pair of cutoff chino shorts, a blue tank top, and an oversized navy chamois shirt for a smock. Her hair was pulled back into a ponytail and tied with a ribbon the color of her undershirt. The air that lingered from the night was cool and she had her feet thrust into fuchsia angora fur slippers. Lemuel had not been issued slippers (The economist angels of the G.A.O. [God's Accounting Office] thought it would be thrifty to dispel with that frivolous practice, and the savings would be immense over the period of eternity.), so he pulled on his new boots.

Abigail started to snigger when she saw the huge white wings printed on the back of his pajamas, and laughed aloud when she saw the blue sateen robe he pulled on was printed with the same pattern.

He brushed past her with cold aloofness, and muttered, "What did you expect an angel's pajamas to look like?" He went into the bathroom and slammed the sliding door behind him.

She called to him, "You remember how to use the toilet, don't you? First you step on both pedals to flush and then the one on the right to form a water seal." Then she heckled, "Do you want me to come back there and help you?"

Lemuel ate his breakfast in silence, while Abigail chattered blithely about some of her experiences on the road: discouraging amorous truck drivers at overnight rest areas; forgetting to fill her gas tank, and having to propel the whole rig with her psychokinetic powers for twenty miles; "That was exhausting"; and about the time she was driving down the Pacific Coast Highway on a rainy foggy night and had a flat on her trailer, and the road was so twisting and narrow that she had to run with that flat tire for five miles before she could find a place wide enough to pull off and change it. "But," she assured him, "we won't start your driving lessons on any road as tricky as that one is. You can start on one of the back roads where you're not likely to scare some poor mortal to death."

After breakfast they decamped and returned to the parkway. While they drove Abigail explained some of the operation of a motor vehicle to him. "It's simple. You'll get the hang of it in no time. You push down on this long thin pedal here when you want to make it go, and if you want to make it stop, you push on this other wide pedal. If you want to make it go backward, you just jiggle this lever until the arrow (see that little indicator there), is pointing at the R. But first you should come to a complete stop and push on the wide pedal before you jiggle the lever into reverse. When you want to go forward again you jiggle the arrow back to the D, that stands for drive."

"What are those numbers, one and two, for? Are they important?"

"Oh, it'll be easier to show you when we get off the parkway. Just watch what I do. You'll pick it up."

They drove along the ridge for an hour or so, and Lemuel could see that it really was simple. When she could see a rising grade ahead, she pushed down on the long thin pedal so they would speed up, and when she got to the crest of the hill she'd ease off of the pedal. If they started to go too fast down a grade, she took her foot off of the long pedal and pushed on the wide one, and that slowed them down. Once or twice the engine sounded different, and she explained, "That's because it's automatic. It shifts gears all by itself."

Lemuel, from his sidewalk superintending, knew a little about gears from watching the souls using hoists and pulleys. Big gears made little gears turn very fast and little gears turned big gears slowly. He noticed two other letters on the little window where you moved the pointer arrow to make the truck go. They were P and N. "How about the P and N letters? Are they important?"

"The best way to learn is by doing," she said.

At a saddle in the mountain range Abigail turned off onto a gravel road and he noticed that she stopped by pushing down on the pedal for stopping. That was easy, just as she said. Then they exchanged seats. Because of the dense foliage he could only see down the road to the first bend, but it looked straight and only slightly on a down grade. While he sat behind the wheel, she expanded on his lesson. "There's a few things I didn't mentioned before. Altogether, we weigh about ten thousand pounds, but the heaviest part of it is the trailer. It's a little over three tons, so don't jam on the brakes suddenly. The truck has power booster brakes and the trailer's are electric. If the truck brakes grab before the trailer's, the trailer is liable to want to keep going, and jackknife. You want to keep the trailer straight behind you at all times. Now then, both sets of brakes work from the foot pedal. That's fine for normal highway and city street driving, but up here in the mountains, remember the trailer is a lot heavier than the truck, and it has a tendency to push you ahead on a down grade, so, if you start going too fast, slow yourself with the trailer brakes first. That's the little lever over there sticking out from that little black box under the dashboard. You work that with your left hand, and gently pump the foot brake. Don't cram down on the brakes because it would cause the drums to expand from the heat and the linings to glaze over, and then you won't have any brakes at all. Do you understand?"

Lemuel hadn't noticed her doing any of those things while they were on the parkway, but he would never admit that a demon was more capable than an angel, and he nodded. "Okay, you have to keep the transmission in low range. That's the one and two numbers you asked me about. Start off in two, and if you have to, step on the brake, slow down, and shift it down to one. That way the engine helps to slow you down."

Lemuel mentally imaged the big gears and the little gears, and nodded again. "But whatever you do, don't let that trailer do any tail waving. If it gets away from you, it could flip us right off of this mountain."

They started down the grade. At the first turn Lemuel raised his foot to touch the brake pedal, and Abigail warned him to use his left hand first. From that switchback the grade slanted sharply downward. The road ahead twisted wildly into valleys, and around knolls, and at places it was hidden, but always inexorably down. Soon he was swinging the steering wheel frantically back and forth, and he began to get confused about which to use, hand or foot. *First hand, then foot,* he reminded himself. The instruction signals transmitted over his nervous system were traveling like alternating current, and he became confused as to which was his hand or his foot. His palms began to sweat and the steering wheel became slippery. He felt that he was going too fast to control the rig, and then he remembered that he could shift down another gear. He grabbed the lever and moved the little arrow, but he moved it too far. It pointed at the N, and the rig shot forward even faster. He pumped the brake pedal and the hand lever, but his brakes failed. There was no awareness of trees or scenic views then, only the road and the sharp drop off at the side, or the cruel outcropping of ledge rock ahead at the next turn. The din of gravel thrown up against the fenders sounded like the ear-splitting staccato of a machine gun. Beads of sweat began to form on his brow and drip off his nose, and his arm pits and back were sopping with acrid sweat. Fortunately, the road started to level off before they were hurtled off a precipice, or smashed against the rocks, and he was able to slow, and down shift into low gear. The grade leveled off, he slowed, and finally stopped. His whole body trembled, and he leaned forwards and placed his wet forehead on the steering wheel.

Abigail chirped. "That was fun. Want to go back up and do it again?"

He said weakly, "If that was my first driving lesson, I can hardly wait for my first swimming lesson."

"I wouldn't let anything happen to my new truck. Have a little faith," she said, and smiled. "You did very well. You only made one mistake that would have killed you. You've got pretty good reflexes, but this next road, where we turn off, is a bit tricky. I'd better drive."

The forest was thickly wooded with young trees each trying to survive among the other's need for space, but suddenly Abigail turned into the dense woods at an angle, and onto a weed and brush-choked road that would have been invisible to the average passerby. The space between the trees was barely wide enough for the trailer, and in places limbs scraped along their sides. After fifty yards or so, the path widened and became a small field. At the far edge of the field was a dilapidated shanty with a tin roof, and whose weathered boards had never been painted. Next to it was a kitchen garden plot protected by several strands of barbed wire. Dense clumps of honeysuckle covered several of the fence posts, and ran tendrils with fragrant blossoms along the wires. A tethered Holstein cow grazed in the field. The cabin had a porch that ran down the length of the front wall with peeled cedar logs for corner posts, and hanging at each corner were galvanized buckets with petunias growing in them. There was a small stack of split stove wood on the porch, and the brick chimney had a faint wisp of smoke curling up, but it was evident that no one was home; the padlock hasp on the door was fastened with a whittled stick.

They drove past the cabin and plunged once more into dense woods. There was a road of sorts; deeply rutted with writhing rain-washed channels. Abigail merely shifted into a lower gear and revved up the engine. The trailer wobbled crazily along behind them. They climbed diagonally across the face of the mountain over a trail that seemed no more than a footpath in many places. After a mile of re-growth thicket they came to an area of ancient trees with huge trunks, and the forest floor was nearly clean of underbrush. Abigail deftly maneuvered through the trees and they came upon an opening where the ground leveled into a natural meadow with a small lake fed by a brook. The clearing and the pond were the result of generations of beavers, and here and there sharpened, tulip poplar stumps showed evidence of their logging operations. They joggled along at the edge of the trees toward the stream.

Abigail placed the trailer on a level area beneath giant white oaks with boles so large Lemuel could reach only halfway around them. Their front window faced the wildflower bespeckled meadow, and pointed lengthwise down the little pond. She had parked near the brook that fed the pond, and this gave them a side window view from their table of a small waterfall splashing down its channel over the ledge rock and into a deep natural pool. Here, where this natural clearing allowed sunlight to penetrate the thickly leaved canopy above them, low thickets of mountain shrubbery grew along the opposite shore of the pond and into the forest for several yards.

She handed Lemuel a pick and shovel, and assigned him the task of digging a pit, three feet across and four feet deep. "Our own sewerage system," she explained. While he dug, she set up the rest of the camp. She pulled her essentials from the back of the truck: folding canvas yacht chairs; an aluminum table with folding legs; and a collapsible coffee table japanned black, decorated with gold leaf scaley dragons spitting fire, and framed with chrysanthemums. She unloaded a rolled up

HOW THE GOOD TAILOR GOT TO HEAVEN — 245

Oriental rug, several cushions of assorted size and color, and a charcoal grill. After placing the rug and the furniture around, she unrolled a large awning from the side of the trailer and hung a half-dozen Japanese lanterns from the awning's frame completing her patio. She'd nearly doubled their living space.

When Lemuel finished digging she handed him a hatchet and a small bucksaw and told him to bring enough limbs to make a cover over the hole. The sticks were laid crisscross over the pit; their sewer line was laid to it, and they covered the entire thing with a plastic sheet, and piled the dirt back on top to make a tight seal. Lemuel had frequently watched the souls at work, so he understood the principals of pick swinging, dirt shoveling, and buck sawing, but he'd never actually done it, and he quickly raised some very sore blisters. Abigail could have healed them, but she felt that he should experience one of the less enjoyable facts of mortality and merely offered him a soothing ointment.

They accomplished quite a bit by lunchtime, and Lemuel was hungry. Abigail made ham sandwiches, thin slices of ham piled high on rye bread with Swiss cheese and mustard, ice cold beer, and crisp spears of kosher dill pickles. While they ate their conversation turned to shop talk again. They both wondered what had happened to the missing Gypsy souls who'd gone to their reward in the Nazi concentration camps. He looked around to make sure no one was nearby and he said softly, just above a whisper, "Tomas said something strange during my catechism lesson; something about unappropriated gods. Do you think that has any significance?"

"How would I know. I don't pay any attention to theocratic politics."

"All right, but consider this, because I think it may mean something. Before the Conquistadores, we didn't get any Indians, and we naturally assumed you got them all. Have you got very many Indians?"

"Hardly any."

"Do you see what I mean? If we didn't get them, and you didn't get them—where are they? We didn't start to get any Indians until they started identifying their Great Spirit with the Lord. Maybe it's the same with the Gypsies?"

"I see, you think that they didn't have souls. Yeah, that's probably it." Then she quickly changed the subject. "When you've finished eating, let's go exploring. This is a beautiful spot and hardly anyone knows about it."

He thanked her for the nice lunch, and she taunted that once again he'd forgotten to say grace. "The Lord is always uppermost in my thoughts," he replied. Then he said, "This is a very nice little table. These chrysanthemums …Shinto symbols, aren't they?"

She smiled enigmatically, and asked, "How do you like my rug? It's a Turkoman that I picked up a couple of centuries ago." The central design of the carpet was an image of a female with six arms sitting cross legged in a lotus blossom. "That's Kali," she said. "And that beer that we had, an Egyptian invention. They were making beer thousands of years before Christ."

He replied, "I noticed you like to collect icons of the infidels. For instance, I saw four ancient pieces of Egyptian pottery decorated with images of their gods, on that shelf over the refrigerator."

"Those are Ramses' canopic jars. I cleaned them out and use them for a canister set." She took his hand, and urged, "Come on, enough about mortal's souls. Let's take a hike."

They walked around the pond, and the simple things he'd paid no attention to in his former state now drew his interest. The diversity of life awed him. Devil's darning needles hovered above the cattails in a marshy spot at the edge of the pond; monarch butterflies flitted about the wild flowers in the meadow; they startled a covey of quail; and he saw a small brown snake about thirty inches long, and quite pretty with tan mottled circles on its hide. It had a triangular head and a dark brown pate the same color and shininess as Abigail's hair. He reached for it saying, "There's always a serpent, isn't there?" Then he quoted the Scripture, "In my name they shall take up serpents."

She grabbed his arm, and said, "I don't think you should take

HOW THE GOOD TAILOR GOT TO HEAVEN   247

up that serpent. That's a copperhead ...they're poisonous."

"That's alright. Myles, the Bible translator, was one of my catechists, and he taught me that they can be used in the worship services. Are there any rattlers, cottonmouth moccasins, or coral snakes around here?"

"There may be some rattlers and they're more dangerous than the copperheads. If you want to keep on living, you better stay away from them."

He dismissed her warning with a casual wave of his hand and told her what the Bible had to say on the subject.

"It sounds like getting bitten by the Bible is a lot more dangerous than getting bitten by a rattler."

"If the Bible says that those poisons are ineffective against the faithful, it must be true, 'For God hath not given us the spirit of fear; but of power, and of love, and of a sound mind[253].'"

Abigail smiled indulgently, and said, "That's not what I'd call a sound mind, but if you want to test your faith, go ahead. When the deliverance angel comes to take your mortal soul, I'll be here to tell you the four most beautiful words in the English language: I ...told ...you ...so!"

They walked on and Abigail showed him other things to be wary of: ticks, black widow spiders, a nest of hornets, poison ivy and poison oak, deadly berries, and mushrooms. She also showed him some of the things that were good to eat and medically useful. Her Gypsy nature made her more of a forest creature than a city girl. Then, in the stillness of the forest, they heard a sound like paper rustling. She put her index finger to her lips and pointed with her other hand up into an ancient oak. "*Ruko mengro,*" she whispered. Lemuel looked to where she pointed just in time to glimpse a gray squirrel scramble around the loose bark and hide on the far side of the tree. "They'll soon become braver and even brazen. When the animals get used to us, they'll all come out and you'll be able to see the menagerie all around us."

"You act as though I don't know about these things. Of course we never concerned ourselves with which were harmful and which were useful, but it's nice to be able to watch the birds and the animals and the flowers and such without having to do anything about them. They've always been such a pesky chore."

"What are you talking about?"

"I guess you don't know. It happened after you were cast down. We become invisible when we're on that detail. We call it sparrow duty."

"Huh???"

"You know, marking the fall of each sparrow; clothing the lilies; feeding the fowls of the air.[254] We have to do all that stuff. It's just one of the jobs we probationers have to do in our spare time."

"You don't seriously expect me to believe you, do you?" She put her hands on her hips and asked incredulously. "You expect me to believe that angels are detailed to care for all of this?" She swept her arm in a wide arc to indicate the forest and the fields.

"Well, certainly not all of this." He made a sweeping gesture, mimicking hers. "After the creation, most things were left on their own, but Jesus mentioned certain things, and they put it in the Bible. It's Gods inerrant word, so ever since some things get special attention."

"Very funny, Lem. Come on, you can show me how to dress a lily."

They continued their stroll and she could see that he wasn't impressed by the natural beauty that she found so enchanting. Then he commented, "It's not very well tended, is it?"

"It doesn't have to be tended. This is an unspoiled, completely natural eco-system. We're the intruders."

"Umm!" he said wryly and swatted at a mosquito. "The ground is uneven, those clusters of bluettes are sort of pretty, in a dainty way, the buttercups have crooked stems, and the daisies grow in disorderly clumps. They're really just weeds. We wouldn't tolerate them in Heaven. And this pond…some of the shore is marshy, and no real gardener would have planted those blue flags among the cattails. If I had a squad of souls for a couple of weeks, we'd get this place neat and orderly. This is chaos." Then he put his hand on her arm and pointed across the pond. "What caused those slick wet chutes over there along the bank? Does

HOW THE GOOD TAILOR GOT TO HEAVEN — 249

some sort of man-eating serpent or dragon live in this pond, Abigail? You expect me to swim in it?"

"Those are beaver runs, and this pond wouldn't be here if it weren't for them." She pointed to a mud and stick mound rising above the water, and said, "That's their house. You can only get into it from underwater. Aren't they clever? Come on, I'll show you the dam they built."

At the dam Lemuel looked at the jumble of sticks, logs, mud, and twigs, and said, "They sure are messy, aren't they? If this were Heaven, the bank would be evenly graded, or bulk-headed with marble, and there would be a wide marble or alabaster walk for us all around it." He opened his arms wide, waved his hands about, and exclaimed, "Where is the order that mankind was created to impose on this wild chaos that you call nature?"

"We have that too. You know, like the park in King Jamesburg. The wealthy humans can live nearly as lavishly as the highest orders of angels do in Heaven. I think they're both nice, but I really prefer this place. Opulence makes life too complicated. Here we have it all to ourselves. It's like we're the only two beings on earth."

"Like Adam and Eve?"

"Sure, if that's how you want to imagine us, but remember, I'm no Eve."

* * *

Their evening meal was sumptuous: a standing rib roast, asparagus spears, cooked carrots sweetened with sugar and butter and seasoned with rosemary, parsleyed potatoes, a tossed salad, a nice rose wine, and another big chunk of blueberry pie with vanilla ice cream. After their dinner, Abigail settled back into her easy chair and over their coffees, strong and hot that only demons know how to brew, she said, "I've never tasted manna. What's it like?"

He looked down bleakly at the remains of their meal, and said, "Manna? Oh yes, it's very good. There's no food on earth that can compare to it."

"Before we left the ninth celestial orb, we used to go over to the other god's sectors to eat once in a while. Do you still do that? Of course the variety wasn't as good as we get down here, but we'd get ambrosia, roast ox, cracked crab, roast pork. That'd really make him mad. You know, some of those harvest gods ate pretty well." She smacked her lips and said, "That wine Bacchus served was the best vintage I've ever tasted."

"Are you deranged, Abigail? There are no other gods!"

"Yeah, that's what Yahweh kept telling us, but we used to sneak out anyway. Oh, by the way, take those table scraps over to the edge of the woods. The animals will appreciate them. How about animals up there? Do you have animals?

"Of course, and they're magnificent. We have red, white, black, and pale horses; doves of peace; and there's the lion that lies down with the lamb; the calf; a beast with a face like a man; a flying eagle. Let's see now, we have lambs with seven horns and seven eyes; a red dragon with seven heads, and ten horns; a leopard with bear's feet, and a lion's mouth..."[255]

"You must have some beef cattle, and sheep. Even if they won't feed you meat and veggies, your shoes are made of leather, and that disgraceful looking blue suit they gave you to wear had some wool in it, so the calves must grow up to be cattle, and the lambs grow to be sheep."

Lemuel had heard rumors that the higher orders of angels ate different food than the ordinary souls and the lower orders of angels. And where did Orson get that cup of nectar? Abigail had a smirk on her face. She was reverting to her demonic nature; she was trapping him and taunting him. He asserted, "Manna is very good. It's a complete wholesome food, and there's no waste to dispose of."

"Unless your horses eat manna, and all those other animals you mentioned, I imagine you've got quit a bit of waste to dispose of."

He remembered the rumor he'd heard, that the pectoral crosses that the archangels wore were really keys to the executive wash room. Then he noticed the smug expression on Abigail's face and realized that this was just the sort of insidious mind game that demons always used to

HOW THE GOOD TAILOR GOT TO HEAVEN — 251

tease the angels. He wanted to show her proof. *Yes, here in the Bible. She can't dispute that.* He opened his Bible and read, "'And I have led you forty years in the wilderness: your clothes are not waxen old upon you, and thy shoe is not waxen old upon thy foot. Ye have not eaten bread, neither have ye drunk wine or strong drink: that ye might know that I am the Lord your God.[256'] So there! With God, all things are possible. If it was important for us to get mortal style food, we'd have it."

"Including a standing rib roast? Naw, He's a cheapskate, a penny pincher. And do you expect me to believe that the clothes you brought down with you would last for forty years?"

"No, at least I don't think so...the subject never came up. Why do you have to be such a nit picker?"

"Me? A nit picker?" She opened her mouth with mock surprise, and placed her hand on her chest.

"Well, you expect me to explain a lot of insignificant details. There are some things you have to take on faith."

"I'll try to remember that. Should I write it down? Now be an angel, and take the food scraps out for the animals."

He left with a platter full of scraps and she waved her hand in the direction of the sink. *I may have to use soap and water, but I don't have to get my hands in the dishpan.* The dishes became animated and piled themselves into the sudsy water. The sponge swirled inside the glasses, danced over the plates, wiped itself on the silver, and a scouring pad polished the greasy pans. The rinsing hose rose up and undulated like a cobra, and as they were being rinsed, Lemuel came back inside. He laughed and said, "You shouldn't have bothered. I'd have done them."

As evening approached, Abigail said, "If you want to watch the TV we should start the generator. My set will work on the battery, but it's better if you use regular household current. It's gasoline powered, so would you be a dear and get one of the gasoline cans out of the truck?"

There were four five-gallon Jerry cans in the truck. Lemuel got one and Abigail showed him where to fill the generator's fuel tank, and how to check the oil.

"Why did you bring so much gasoline?"

"If we're very careful, that's about enough gasoline to last us a month. I can turn water into wine, but not into gasoline."

Their second night together was a repeat of the first night, except Abigail didn't need to give Lemuel any more shower instructions. As she slipped naked from her bedroom into the shower, Lemuel wished there were some small detail on which he needed further instruction so he could get close to her again. At his prayers that evening he prayed, not for strength, but for much less strength in that region of his body that had never shown so much strength before.

*　*　*

The next day promised to be hot. By ten o'clock, the thermometer on the control panel that measured the outside temperature was nudging ninety, and that was in the shade. They decided that this would be a good day for Lemuel to learn how to swim. "I have no swim trunks. Do we wear our underwear?"

"Don't be silly. Who are you going to shock...the beavers?" She pulled her tank top over her head, slipped out of her shorts, and ran over to the pond near the waterfall. She took off her sandals and dove in.

Although Abigail's strip had been quickly done and her dive into the pond almost immediately afterward, the same sensations that gripped him last night as he watched her go into the shower returned. He chided himself. *What's the matter with me? She's a demon.* Then he reasoned, *If we don't wash each other, there's no sacrilege.* He removed his shirt and pants, and sat down on the rock to remove his shoes. *And the begetting ceremony is an impossibility, so where's the harm?* He stripped off the rest of his clothes, crossed his legs, and watched her frolic in the pool. She turned somersaults, swam like a frog, and floated on her back with her arms going like the paddles of a side wheeler. She called to him, "Come on in," and dove under water. She swam like a joyful otter.

When her head reappeared, he shouted at her, "I can't swim, remember?"

"It's not that deep," she replied, and stood on the bottom holding her arms straight up. The water barely covered the crown of her head.

He sighed, "Why not?" and jumped in.

The water was as cold as deepest hell where Satan resides, but he was grateful that it caused the obvious betrayer of his concupiscent inclinations to shrivel. He bounded about on the balls of his feet, and Abigail praised him saying, "That's it. Can you feel a buoyancy? Your body is slightly lighter than water."

She put him through the standard drill for novice swimmers, and soon he was doing a fairly respectable doggy paddle. He was pleased with his new skill, and became accustomed to the frigid water. Soon he was doggy paddling all over the pond. He was still swimming about when Abigail climbed out of the pool and lay drying in the sun on the warm rocks by the side of the pool. He'd also discovered another skill, that of cupping his hands and shooting great rooster tails of water ahead of him. Abigail's eyes were closed as she luxuriated in the warm sun. Lemuel dog paddled toward her, and was about to put this second skill to mischievous use, when suddenly he rose completely out of the water and stood with the surface ripples lapping at his feet. Abigail's eyes seemed to shoot green fire and he felt his body tilt forward. He was forced to put one foot ahead, and then the other. He was walked right over to the rock, and made to step off of the water. "You weren't thinking of splashing me were you?" she asked sternly.

He looked down sheepishly and dug at the rock with his great toe. She laughed and patted the rock beside her, inviting him to sit. Although he didn't get to splash her, he did have the small satisfaction of dripping some cold water onto her warm bare back, causing her to make the appropriate squeals.

* * *

I do not want to leave the reader with the impression that Abigail was an immodest creature. If she and Lemuel had been at a public beach, she'd have worn a swim suit. In fact, her swimsuits concealed far more than is currently the fashion on beaches today. This is because she had been endowed with a glorious bush, which she was quite fond of, and except for some minor trimming of a few stray hairs, she positively refused to alter what nature had given her. She felt that her pubic hairs were as honorable as the hairs on her head, but when they peeked out from below some skimpy strip of cloth, they looked slatternly. It was far more decent to wear nothing at all, and she was not the sort to wear anything to call attention to herself. She always wore understated but stylish things to suit the occasion. But here in this idyllic glade, where flora and fauna were the only life for miles, she wore only what God created for her to wear. She felt that she would have been immodestly striking an unnatural, unharmonious note had she done otherwise. That is how she explained her nudity to Lemuel. Besides, she didn't want pale areas indecorously subdividing her darkening flesh.

Abigail's figure was such that if seen on the average beach any crowded weekend, the eye would note with interest and pass on to other more pulchritudinous forms exhibiting grander proportions. But the aesthete, given their discriminating viewpoint, would easily envision her atop a marble plinth. She could have been Pygmalion's Galatea, or had Apelles seen her, her form would be on his oil of Aphrodite rising from the sea, and Praxiteles would have sculpted her figure in polished marble, instead of the beauteous courtesan, Phryne—the model for both. Abigail's small, firm, upswept conical breasts would never have held up a pencil beneath them, and her callipygous behind had two small dimples in her lower lumbar region where even the most stone-hearted would feel impelled to bestow a kiss. Extending beneath those luscious fleshy melons, if a golden mean could be said to apply to legs, they adorned this exquisite body. They were neither too long nor too short, nor wiry with muscular definition, and yet firm with graceful feminine curves; not exactly straight, but slightly bowed, as though offering a sacred communion with the mysterious cleft above. Her flesh was satiny smooth and resilient to the touch, and although they were not visible, Lemuel could feel a feline-like musculature rippling in her back as he spread sun screening lotion over it. He condescended to do that, at her request, and he hoped that it wouldn't be mistaken for a washing ritual.

Besides Bible reading, prayer, swimming, and dining on fine fare, Lemuel went on long walks with Abigail. She was an excellent forest guide and knew the names of all the plants and animals, but he was surprised to find out how frail female demons are, and their hand had to be taken so as to help them over roots and rocks. Occasionally, they had to be carried bodily over streams, but Abigail was light, so he did not object. What began as making the best of an intolerable circumstance was becoming the most tranquil and absorbing time of his entire existence. He had almost forgotten about his mission when an accidental encounter with the outside world restored his purpose.

Chapter 16

THE MOON HAD NOT YET CLEARED THE MOUNTAIN RIDGE and it was a good evening for stargazing. The stars and the milky way filled the open sky above their meadow. Esther was but one bright blue sparkle among the many. Orion dominated the black above them, and Ursa major, or Orson, was off to their right. Abigail pointed out the constellations of the Babylonian zodiac. Crickets and katydids accompanied a bullfrog, and the seldom seen, but often heard, whippoorwill called from across the pond. An owl hooted, and then the symphony of night was shattered by the sound of leaves rustling, twigs snapping, and a heavy body rushing through the underbrush and down the embankment toward them.

"A bear?" Lemuel asked with tension in his voice, as he considered what two of them had done to forty-two children.

Nearby came the sound of cloth tearing and saplings lashing something, and a human voice spoke the words, "Muv-folk!"

Abigail answered Lemuel in Romany, *"Kaulo guero."* She turned the trailer's outside lights on, and into their illuminating ring stumbled a small black figure. The boy's eyes were wide with terror, his clothing was torn, and his face and hands had welts and long bleeding scratches caused by the tree limbs and briars.

The boy said, "Ah sho am glad ta see y'all. Ah thought dat ole cortswhup had me fo sho." Terror as written all over his face.

His dark form was barely visible against the blacker woods. Abigail went over to the boy, put an arm over his shoulder, and led him under the trailer awning while gently wiping his tears away with her fingertips. He was nearly as tall as she was and about ten or twelve years old. In the light, where she could see better, she noticed the scratches. She took him into the trailer, washed the welts and drying blood with a soapy washcloth, and sprayed on a soothing antiseptic. Then she got a plate of brownies from the cupboard and poured a large glass of milk for him. The boy calmed down enough to give her a wide, white-toothed smile, and then his dark eyes roved about the trailer. He had never seen more plush surroundings. Enormously awed, and intensely curious, he asked, "Wot yo'all doin up heah?"

"Camping," she explained. "My name is Abigail, and this is Lemuel. We're sort of on our honeymoon. What's your name?"

"Zotis," he replied, adding, "Ain't ya'all skeered O da corts-whup?"

Lemuel said, "You said something was pursuing you. I'm very familiar with fearsome beasts, but I've never heard of a beast called a, what did you call it, a kotsup?"

"Y'all white folks ud say court's whip," Zotis said, enunciating carefully.

Lemuel shook his head with a puzzled expression. "No, I've never heard of that. I know about dragons, and cockatrices, and basilisks, and unicorns, and sphinxes, and griffins, and leviathan, and even the dreaded ouroboros, the serpent that swallows its tail." He turned to Abigail, and said, "You didn't mention there might be any court's whips in this forest." Then he asked Zotis, "What are they? What do they do? Do they roar and belch fire?"

"Dey don mak no sounds at all. Yo neva hears dem comin. He be

HOW THE GOOD TAILOR GOT TO HEAVEN —⚜— 259

kinda like a big snake 'bout as long as y'all's trailer. An if'en yo's out afta dahk, he come afta yo, an he grab yo, and wrap 'round yo, an knock yo on de groun. Den he commense ta whup yo, an whup yo, an whup yo wif his big hard tail. He try to whup you t' deaf. Den if'n yo tries to fool him, an play lak yo's dead, he got dis sharp pointy tail, an he take it an tickle inside of yo's nose, (Zotis demonstrated with his little finger) an if'n yo stirs one mite, an if he thinks yo's still alive, he whups yo, an whups yo, an whups yo some moah."

"Your court's whip reminds me of the dreaded ouroboros," Lemuel said. "They hold their tail in their mouth and roll like a hoop after their prey. When one finds a likely target, it flings itself like a javelin, tail first, and he has a powerful magical stinger in that tail. Their poison turns the victim into another ouroboros, and it too rolls about the countryside looking for another innocent victim."

"Lem, stop making up tall tales. You know the ouroboros is just an old alchemic symbol. There's no such thing Zotis. They don't exist and neither does your court's whip."

"Yes dey do, Miz Abigail, 'cept'n heah 'bouts, we calls 'em hoop snakes. An Pearl, das ma momma, tole me 'bout dat ole cort's whup, an what he be doin ta me if I stayed pas dahk."

"I see," Abigail said, while trying to keep a straight face. "And just what were you doing up here after dark; and after your mamma warned you what would happen to you?"

"Ah didn' know what time it was, an it got dahk all uv a sudden."

Abigail realized Zotis had probably been watching them for days. All he had to do was to follow their tire tracks, and she suspected the boy knew these woods better than the rangers who made their living there. That swimming hole was too powerful an attraction for it not to be discovered by a young boy exploring the woods. "You weren't up here spying on us were you?"

"Oh! No mum." Zotis said bashfully, and his dark cheeks got darker as he reached for another brownie. Then he redirected their attention by noticing the Bible that Lemuel had left on the table. "Dat sho is a nice

Bible. Ah dun think ah evvah seen such a bodacious Bible. Duz ya'all read it a lot?"

"Well …he does. He's a preacher, and I'm a Gypsy princess."

Nothing on earth could have impressed Zotis more than that, not even the truth about their real identities. "Is yo really a princess? A real Gypsy princess? Wow!"

"Yes, that's right. We gypsies have mysterious powers and I can tell that right now your mama is worried sick about you. Let's put the rest of these brownies in a napkin and you can take it with you. We'll drive you home."

"Duz ya'll know where ah be stayin?"

"Of course. Gypsies know everything."

The unencumbered pickup drove easily down the mountain and when they reached the dooryard of the shanty, a woman carrying a kerosene lantern rushed out of the door. As they walked toward her, Abigail said, "We're sorry Pearl. Zotis stopped by for a visit and we didn't realize how late it was getting. My name is Abigail and this is Lemuel. We've been camping up at the beaver dam."

"I know'd somebody was up there. I seen yo'alls tire tracks. An I told him to leave you alone. Get yo's skinny ass in hea Zotis!"

Zotis said, "She's a real Gypsy princess, Momma," as though that would explain everything.

Lemuel said, "I'm just starting my ministry," as though that could explain anything. "And you needn't have worried. He was in good hands."

Abigail said, "I don't blame you one bit, Pearl. He should have obeyed to you. There are a lot of strange people about: perverts, drug addicts, and just plain mean bastards."

Pearl invited them to have coffee with her. She hung the kerosene lantern from a nail in a beam above a battered, old, round table. Pearl's cabin had two rooms: a large room which served as living, dining, kitchen, and everything room; and a tiny bedroom; and a loft under the rafters. There was no electricity or plumbing, and their water came from

HOW THE GOOD TAILOR GOT TO HEAVEN   261

the well and hand pump beside the house. The only heat was an old, cast iron wood stove. It was like going back a hundred years in time. She placed cups of diverse manufacture, and saucers that didn't match the cups, in front of them, and poured the coffee from an old, porcelain enamel coffee pot. Pearl was an attractive woman, somewhat darker than Abigail, and they looked to be about thirtyish, but Pearl was thin and worn down by her life. She said, "I don't have anything stronger to offer…" then quickly covering her mouth, she apologized, "I'ze sorry. I forgot. What with you being a preacher…"

"I'm not temperance. There's nothing in the Bible that requires abstinence, in fact Timothy recommends 'a little wine for thy stomach's sake.'"

Abigail said, "This coffee is fine Pearl, and if we had remembered our manners we'd have brought a bottle of wine with us. Next time we'll remember."

"Is you really a Gypsy?" Pearl asked, nearly as awed as Zotis.

"Sure, and I notice that like the Gypsies, you dabble a bit in the mystic arts as well." Abigail motioned with her head toward the wood stove where a voodoo doll was hanging by a wire from the metal smoke pipe.

Pearl sobbed, "Ah don' know wa else to do. Ah prayed, an prayed, an mah prayers don work. Mah potions don work, but now ah's mad, an ah's gwine ta hex somebody. Mebbe ah cain't win, but ah's sho gwine ta get even."

Abigail went over to the doll and examined it. She touched it with her index finger and it jumped about wildly. "Did you get all the necessary ingredients?" she asked.

"Oh yassum. Fust ah plugged his toilet, an afta he come out, ah gos an get some of his shit, an a bit of his piss. Dey's a mite diluted. Duz ya spose it be okay?"

"Oh yes, that's fine. You don't need much. How about his hair and nail parings?"

Lemuel bounded up from his seat as though it had suddenly become electrified. He sputtered, "This is sacrilege Abigail! How dare you abet this profaneness right in front of me?"

"Oh sit down Lem. We're doing something important here. Besides, you show me where, in the Bible, it says that it's wrong to make voodoo dolls. You've always told me that the Bible is the inerrant word of God. If He didn't want people to make voodoo dolls, He'd have said so. He handed down instructions about everything else."

Then, as though they were discussing a cooking recipe, she said, "Good! what other ingredients did you manage to get?"

"Well, ah did find a couple of strands of his hair in his comb, but ah couldn' fine no hairs from round his pecker."

"Oh, what a shame," Abigail said consolingly.

"But he lef his 'lectric razah on de wash stand, an ah got some of his wiskahs ...."

"Oh, that's nearly as good."

"An ah got a ceegar stub he be chewin on."

"That's very good. I've never tried it myself, but they say the saliva from a cigar stub is wonderfully wicked on their teeth and gums. The doctors blame the cigar, but it's really the voodoo." Abigail touched the doll and again made it jump. "I guess it would be too much to expect, but did you get some dead skin from between his toes, or toenail clippings?"

"No'um, but dey was a few flakes of dan'ruff on his comb."

"Well, that's almost as powerful. That'll give him the mange. It seems like you've taken care of everything for now. I think you may want to jab a pin in one eye on a dark moonless night and he should feel the results in a few days."

Lemuel sat in silence and fuming with rage. He suspected they were doing some kind of witchcraft, but Abigail was right: he could not think of any text that specifically forbade what they were doing. He planned to study his Bible very carefully when they got back to the trailer. He recalled the Bible story about the woman of Endor who had familiar spirits, but she used her powers to call up spirits of the dead, and Pearl wasn't doing that. The witch of Endor had summoned the spirit of Samuel to meet with Saul. This took Samuel away from his more important duties in heaven, and Samuel even scolded them for bothering him.[257]

Lemuel began to see Pearl and Zotis as pagans, and very much in need of salvation. Perhaps this was fortuitous and he was sent to save both souls. He needed his Bible.

Another thing that annoyed him was Pearl's obsequious behavior toward the demon and her casual indifference to himself. Like now, Pearl was asking Abigail if she should address her as "Your Highness" because of her being a Gypsy princess.

"Just call me Abby. You're not a Gypsy, so we can dispense with the formalities." Then she asked, "Who is this that grinds the faces of the poor,[258] that you're putting the hex on?"

"He de big cheese down at de welfare office. He say ah cain't get my check no mo. He say I got ta get a job. I duz a little housework once in a while, if dey come pick me up. But I ain't got no car, an ah coudn' 'ford ta run it if you was ta give me one, an dey ain't no public transportation 'bout heah. How'm I sposed to get to work? My man lef ovah six years ago, an ah got dis boy ta raise. An he's a good boy; he do his chores; an he go ta school ever day. But dey won't let me ride de school bus ta go ta work." She sighed, "Well da big cheese say I can move ta where de jobs is. Dis place ain't much, but it's mine, an ah own all de lan you see cleared 'round dis shack, an a bit of de woods, where ah gets mah firewood. An ah kin grow mos uv my own food. We got a milch cow, an some chickens. An I'm sposed ta go ta some town, an rent someplace from some thievin landlord jus so's ah can get a job? Well da big cheese say iffen ah don't, dey kin put Zotis out ta foster." She poked at the doll with a well-sharpened boning knife. "How dat feel?"

Lemuel knew many stories more heart-rending than Pearl's from the Bible, but he believed that things usually worked out through faith. Look at Job. He decided that the proper course was to bring them closer and let them hear God's glorious words directly from the Holy Book. He said, "Tomorrow is Sunday. If Abigail and I came to get you, do you think you and Zotis could come up to visit our camp? We'll have a picnic and spend the day just having fun."

Zotis was delighted. "Yeah Momma, please. You jus got ta see their trailer."

Abigail was surprised by Lemuel's offer and ascribed his softening to her own influence. She said, "That's a wonderful idea Lem," and to Pearl, "Sure, we'll have a great time. How would you like it if we barbequed. We'll have flank steak and ribs. There's plenty of cold wine and we'll make sangria. Please say you will."

Pearl accepted the invitation, and offered to contribute a cockerel to the feast.

* * *

The next day, about mid-morning, the four of them were seated around Abigail's coffee table and Pearl told them of the miracle that had happened after they left. Last night she poured a glass of water from her water pitcher and it had turned into wine. Abigail was delighted and explained that it was a favorable sign from the good fairies.

Lemuel said wryly, with a sharp look at Abigail, "Praise the Lord."

Abigail said, "You know Gypsies are excellent fortunetellers. Would you like to know the future? Then you can avoid any pitfalls and improve your opportunities. We can alter futures if we know what to look for. Think, Pearl. How many misdirected steps would you have taken if you knew the outcome?"

Lemuel stamped into the trailer and re-emerged with his Bible. "See what it says here? 'Saul put away those that had familiar spirits, and the wizards, out of the land.'"

Abigail replied calmly, "Didn't King Saul lose favor with God long before that, and wasn't that why he went to the woman of Endor, and then God replaced him with David? Personally, I thought it was a bad move. David was a dirty little sneak, an adulterer and murderer, and no better than a gangster." She continued, "Knowledge is the power the gods fear most. Their power weakens in the presence of knowledge and they tremble."

HOW THE GOOD TAILOR GOT TO HEAVEN 265

"Rot!" Lemuel exclaimed angrily. Abigail was twisting the Scriptures again. The Bible says the demons tremble. He was even angrier because Abigail never noticeably trembled. He asserted, "We're all in Gods hands. Surrender your will to the Lord, and…" His words turned into croaking sounds and it enraged him further. 'How dare she turn his voice into the voices of frogs, the unclean spirits that issued out of the dragon, and the beast, and the false prophets?' [259]

"Don't get so excited Lem. You'll give yourself hiccups. Here drink this," and she handed him a glass of water. "Didn't God kick Adam and Eve out of Eden because they had gotten knowledge? It's plain to me that God fears it." Lemuel's face was crimson, and Abigail leaned over and kissed him on the forehead, and said, "I'll get my tarot cards. Be back in a minute."

While she was gone, Lemuel asked Pearl and Zotis to overlook his momentary distemper, and he explained that it was not unusual for couples to have slightly different interpretations of the Bible. He regarded Abigail's misunderstanding of the Scriptures as positive input that keeps himself cognizant of the misdirected thinking that seemed to be so prevalent today. He was just asking them, "Have you committed yourselves to the…" When Abigail reappeared.

She was completely transformed into a Gypsy princess. Abigail delighted in dressing to suit the occasion. Her simple peasant blouse was finely embroidered with delicate handiwork. She wore a colorful, ankle-length skirt that was full with many gathers, and it was worn over several others for petticoats. Her feet were bare and she wore a delicate gold chain around one ankle. There were golden bangles on her wrists, a double chain necklace of gold sovereigns lay against her chest, and a pair of golden hoop earrings dangled from her ears. She wore a saffron shawl over her shoulders and she'd teased her hair to look fuller and more feral. She did not wear the shawl on her head since her virginity entitled her to go bareheaded. At the outer edges of each eye she had placed three small dots with an eyebrow pencil, to ward off the evil eye. She carried herself with a stately bearing like a savage empress, and for a scepter she carried a long silver cane that was ornately tooled with stars and quarter moons.

Abigail dispelled their astonishment with a cheerful smile and she held up a thick deck of cards, riffled them with her thumbnail, and said, "Yup, all here. Are you ready?"

She cleared the clutter from her coffee table and spread a cloth that was decorated with the same symbols as the ones on her cane. She seated herself opposite Pearl. Next she passed her hand over the table in an invisible triangle around the tarot cards. "This triangle represents the past, the present, and the future. All is known to the cards and knowledge is power. Are you afraid of the power Pearl?" Pearl shook her head. "We can ask the cards to disclose their secrets, if you do not quail. We can acquire some of the power of the fates and they will tell us what is causing your problems, and what we must do to alter your run of bad luck." She leveled her eyes at Pearl, and her green fires sought the depths of Pearl's gleaming black eyes. Then Abigail closed her eyes and held her palm out above the center of the table, and above the center of the invisible triangle.

Pearl knew what was required, and said, "Ah ain't got no silvah to cross yo's palm wif, kin ah use papah money?"

Abigail said, "It's these modern times, Pearl. Silver coins are from another era, aren't they?" She told Zotis to bring her cane over to his mother and explained to them that the mystic power of the silver would be gone if she handed the cane to Pearl herself, and that the transfer had to be through a third person.

"The toe of this cane has walked through many lands and in many ages. It has magical powers." She asked Pearl to make the cross on her palm with it. It was done and Abigail judged that the necessary precondition had been satisfied. "I sense that the ancient Etteilla pattern will be the most beneficial to you Pearl." She instructed Pearl to count down to the eighth card and remove it, and Pearl obeyed silently. Then Abigail picked up the cards and began placing them onto the table counterclockwise: eleven on the left, eleven on the right, eleven across the top,

HOW THE GOOD TAILOR GOT TO HEAVEN

and eleven across the bottom. Next, a circle of cards were placed around the invisible triangle, and Pearl was told to place her card in the center.

Abigail looked at the card and exclaimed happily, "Your fortunes will improve wonderfully." Then as she authenticated the cards' omniscience by reading Pearl's past, her face became serious. She placed both hands on either side of her face, rocked her head from side to side, and moaned, "Oh! *Tungis amande, tungis amande.* Such a lifetime of trial." Of course all of her revelations would be plain to anyone, whether they were auguries or not.

"The vision isn't clear, but I see by this card that you must pray to Mautia. She's the queen of the fairies, and the protectress of the disinherited and the poor. The cards show that you qualify for her intercession, but over there, that card shows an evil spirit. Some malevolent force is confusing the emanations. It comes from your purse. You didn't bring something from the evil man at the welfare office with you did you; something you used to make the voodoo?" Pearl shook her head. "You mentioned paper money; let me see it."

She quickly opened her purse, took out a worn wallet, and removed fourteen dollars. "Das ever cent ah got," she said.

"Oh yes. There's evil emanating from those bills, Pearl. The person who gave that money to you did so begrudgingly, and is an evil, mean-spirited person. With that money you have carried his curses with you. We must purify the money with fire and drive out the evil *O Bengh*. Then the fog of confusion will clear away from the cards." As though mesmerized, Pearl dumbly offered the bills to Abigail. Abigail shrank back quickly, and said, "Oh no! I can't touch it. It is *vassavo!* Put them in a pile on the table."

Pearl had brought a freshly-killed chicken as her contribution to their picnic, and Abigail said to Zotis, "The roasting pan that you brought the chicken in, bring it here and put it on the table."

Pearl's dealings with Gypsies were slight to nil, like most of us, and like most of us she was unfamiliar with the crooked art of *Boojo*. Zotis brought the pot, put it on the table, and Pearl piled her money beside it.

Old habits die hard, and Abigail's hand reached toward the money, and her little finger known as the magpie among Gypsies, and signals what one is about to steal, barely touched the pile of bills. At that point a deft switch would be made, but Abigail quickly withdrew her hand and announced solemnly, "Yes, it's filled with corruption. I dare not touch it. Quickly, put all of it into the pot."

Pearl did as she was ordered and Abigail took the charcoal lighter fluid and soaked the bills. Her shadow briefly darkened the table, and then she snapped her fingers, and instantly flames shot up from the pot. There was a look of horror on Pearl's face, and she said, "Dat was ever cent ah had in dis world."

"But that money was corrupt. It was causing your misfortune," Abigail said. Then she ordered Zotis to take her cane and to stir the ashes in the pot with it. And to Pearl, she said, "While he stirs, I want you to think of the benevolent fairy, Queen Mautia. Keep saying her name over and over to yourself and pray for her intercession. Abigail held the rim of the pot as Zotis stirred, and there welled up, seemingly from the ashes, fresh crisp new twenties, and fifties, and hundreds. When Zotis stopped stirring, the money stopped coming, but there were several thousand dollars in the pot. Abigail said, "That money was not given begrudgingly, Pearl. There is no taint on it because it came from a fairy queen who has warm and tender feelings toward you."

Pearl was astonished by the money. When Abigail told her that she could keep all of it, she held it up to her face and wept tears of joy . Then she said, "Fust thing ah's gonna do is to go down ta tha 'lectric co-op an have them put 'lectric inta mah house. Zotis need a 'lectric light to study by, stead o dat ole lantern."

"That sounds like a very good way to use that money. Don't forget to thank the queen of the fairies."

"This is the Lord's doing Pearl, and not some mythological fairy," Lemuel said, and made a steeple with his hands in prayer. "It has blessed origins. You should thank the Lord." Abigail wondered by what sort of upside down logic Lemuel used to reach that conclusion, and so he opened his Bible and read: "The Lord maketh poor, and maketh rich: he bringeth low and lifteth up. He raiseth up the poor out of the dust."[260]

"Well, ah prayed to de Lawd all my life, an de Lawd, sho 'nuff made me poah; an ah never heerd O Queen Mautia till ten minutes ago, an look what she done."

Zotis asked, "Cud we get a phone too, Momma? With 'lectric, an a phone, I cud get one of those computers dey's giving out at school."

"Dey's givin away computers?" Pearl asked incredulously. "Ah did'n know that. You sho?"

"Yeah! But ah couldn' take one cause we didn' have no way ta use it heah."

Lemuel knew Abigail had beaten him again, but the lad's schooling might open a way to bring them to salvation, and forswear their idolatry. He knew nothing about computers. They didn't use computers in Heaven, but he recently sat in Bradamante's class while she was instructing children just about Zotis's age. He was curious to know how Zotis's class compared. "What do you learn in school, Zotis? What's your favorite subject?"

"Ah likes science; right now we's learning bout the universe and the beginnings of life."

Lemuel rubbed his hands with delight. This was made to order. Zotis was getting the same lessons here on earth that Bradamante was teaching her students in heaven. He had the Bible right there on his lap, and he opened it. "So you're learning that God created the earth in six days? That's marvelous! And about Adam and Eve?" He read from the first chapter of Genesis, "And God said, 'Let the waters bring forth abundantly the moving creature that hath life, and fowl that may fly above the earth...'" He didn't want to confuse the boy with the ground, or water, controversy so he disregarded the second chapter's version and he thought he should ignore the part about the second law of thermodynamics, since he had trouble understanding it himself.

Abigail and Pearl busied themselves getting the grill ready and setting the picnic table. Zotis was left to his own resources, and since he was an honest lad, not given to dissembling or the sycophantic arts, said, "Owa teacha, Miz Gould, said it was like some kinda big 'splosion. She say everthin was scrunched down inta one bitty ball, an then it blew up, and all de parts flew apart, an deys still flying apart, an goin into all kinda ways, an bumpin inta each othah." He gestured wildly with his arms to demonstrate the soaring and crashing of the big bang theory. "An she say dat life started as little bitty cells, sumpin like germs. She say dat life might'a come from one of the things that was flying around an bumpin inta things. An it all took billions and billions of years."

"Your teacher is a daughter of Belial to fill your head with such profaneness." Lemuel shook the Bible at Zotis, and said, "This is the inerrant word of God, and it says God created it all in six days." He started to read, "In the beginning God created the heaven and…"

Zotis was only six feet from Lemuel, and Lemuel was declaiming with the intensity of a sermon delivered in a large church that would have reached the back pews, and startled into wakefulness any dozing parishioners. Zotis drew back fearfully as Lemuel continued reading down through the six days of creation.

Abigail was startled by Lemuel's outburst, came over to put a hand on Zotis's shoulder, and said, "Lem, cut it out! You're scaring the boy." But Lemuel continued reading and Abigail rotated her index finger near her temple, pointed it a Lemuel, and said softly, *"Dinnelo."*

"I am not possessed! This is truth!"

She sat in one of the yacht chairs and winked at Zotis, and said, "Oh sure, that's what it says there, but it doesn't give you any of the details. Actually, God created the world in the same way that we say the pharaohs built the pyramids, or Louis XIV built Versailles, or Pericles the Acropolis. It all happened a long, long time ago, and I'll tell you what really happened. Way back then God was called Yahweh. He was just an unimportant little god and all the other gods paid about as much attention to him as grownups pay to little boys. Well…he wanted them to think that he was just as important as they were. The Titan, Cronus, used

HOW THE GOOD TAILOR GOT TO HEAVEN — 271

to say, 'Get away kid, you bother me,' and the Olympians would chime in, 'N'ya, N'ya, N'ya'; and Apollo made dirty finger signs at him. So Yahweh stamped off to another part of heaven where Quetzacoatl waggled his plumes and skinny forked tongue at him. Yahweh wanted to take Tlazolteotl out on a date, but she wouldn't go out with him, and Xolotl whirled up a big dust storm and drove him away. Everywhere he went in heaven it was the same thing. In Valhalla, Odin and Thor ignored him, and Loki pulled his beard and snipped off one of his dreadlocks. He went over to see if he couldn't get Geb, and Nut's youngsters, Osiris and Isis to come out and play, but the brother and sister were having more fun up in their bedroom and didn't want to come out. Then he went over to see …"

Pearl joined them with a look of bemusement on her face, but Lemuel was livid. "Abigail! Stop this! You're poisoning their minds with blasphemy. Pay no attention to her. There are no other gods!"

"I think your Bible says there are, Lem. You could get pretty good tacos at Tonacatecuhtli's stand." Then she continued with her story.

"Yahweh went over to see the gods in the Vedic section and they didn't want him around. Shiva scared him near to death waving all those arms of his with mean-looking weapons and tools, so Yahweh stopped off nearby at Ekur, the house of Enlil. Ereshkigal, the queen of that part of heaven, told him that Inanna and all the others were just sitting down to supper, and slammed the door in his face. So Yahweh got very angry. You know … like wrathful. He was always wroth about something and he was also a jealous god, and he said, 'They don't like me just because I'm Jewish.'"

Both Pearl and Zotis were so rapt by the Gypsy's story that they paid no attention to Lemuel as he flipped through the Bible looking up all the references to blasphemy. He'd find a verse, punch at it with a stiffened index finger, and say in a clipped, and strained voice, "See what it says here Abigail … stoning! …And over here …hanging and stoning …and then there's burning…"

They ignored Lemuel's outrage, and Abigail continued, "So little

Yahweh changed his name to Elohim, but it didn't do any good; they all knew he was still Jewish. Boy, was he ever angry. He kicked at the clouds and went back to his own section of heaven with all the rest of the Jewish angels: the Erelim, the BeneElohim, the Malachim, the Hashalim, the Tarshilim, the Shishanim, the Cherubim, the Ophannim, and the Seraphim. And even they snickered at him for wanting to associate with the goys. He called them all a stiff-necked bunch, stamped down into the basement, and sat in the darkness. That's when he got this big idea: 'I'll build a world—that ought to impress them!'

"So, just like Shah Jhan, who we say built the Taj Mahal, or how Mister Blandings built his dream house, he went out to hire a contractor.

"There was this one angel who had a great big assembly plant. His name was Lucifer. He was the lowest bidder on the job, and he promised to have it done in one work week …five days. So Lucifer got the job, and put his whole crew to work, and even hired extra help. The bids were tight, but Lucifer figured that he could stand twenty-seven percent of the workforce doing overtime, pay the night differential, and still make a profit, as long as he didn't have to pay double overtime for the weekend. Yahweh said, 'Five days, huh?' and he got another brainstorm. 'That's perfect,' he said, and signed the contract."

"Yahweh was anxious about what he had planned and he'd come into the front office every few hours to see if it was going to be done on time. The girl angel at the desk would reassure him that everything was going to be all right. 'Don't worry about it.' But in a few more hours he'd be back. He was making a real pest of himself. Lucifer finally came to the counter and told him how they got the light separated from the darkness and Yahweh said, 'That's good.' Then Lucifer offered, 'Why don't you go down to the Burning Tree Country Club as my guest? You know, sit by the pool, sip a little Manaschewitz, play a few rounds of golf, and I'll call you when it's finished.' But Yahweh was too excited, and didn't want to go too far away from his project, and Burning Tree Country Club was way out in Bethesda, Maryland.

"Well, they got the waters and the firmament done by the third day,

HOW THE GOOD TAILOR GOT TO HEAVEN — 273

and Yahweh said, 'That was good.' But the next time he came back, the girl behind the desk—who was filing her nails and snapping her chewing gum—blew the filings away from her fingertips, and said, 'Mister Lucifer wants to see you. Something about trouble with the specs, and one of the subs had a problem with the bonding company.'

"So Yahweh stormed into the office, and Lucifer said, 'Now calm down Yahweh. I want to talk to you about this faulty design. My shop foreman tells me that your architect hasn't designed enough shear strength in these pins that hold the plates together.'

"'Architect! Shmarchatect! What's this trouble with a subcontractor all about?'

"'Oh, that's all been taken care of; we had to get another outfit for the landscaping. Beautiful Gardens by Lotis Ink had some personnel problems. Lotis had some sort of row with Dryope, so we hired Thammuz of the Purple River Corporation to handle the vegetation.'

"'The girl at the desk said something about insurance?'

"Lucifer was taken aback, and said indignantly, 'What do you take this company for? We deal with no suede shoe outfits; we have our reputation to protect.' Then he asked Yahweh to come with him over to the drafting table. 'I want you to see these blueprints.' You understand that was before they had Ozilid prints."

At this point Abigail had three spellbound listeners. Lemuel had ceased to fume and grumble, and threaten. He put down his Bible on the coffee table, poured himself a tumbler of sangria, and munched on one of Abigail's brownies. The same fascination for morbidity and horror that grips most mortals had evidentially been quaffed down along with his waters of life. He knew that she was mixing things up in such a grotesque way that if these two poor innocents believed one word of her lying abominable tale, their souls would be lost forever. He hoped that he hadn't lost these souls to the demon, with her corrupting money and her phony Gypsy performance. He was like a spectator in the street watching as mangled, bleeding bodies were removed from a tragic wreck.

Abigail continued, "Lucifer explained to Yahweh, 'Do you see these dotted lines here on the drawing? They represent where the pins go. You'll either have to put in more pins or else use heavier material.'

"And Yahweh asked, 'Do they show?'

"And Lucifer said, 'No they don't show, but they'll cause you trouble later on. I can't guarantee the product if you don't make some design changes. Another thing: your man skimped on the cee-o-two in the atmosphere. You're not going to be able to maintain even temperatures on the surface if you don't use more cee-o-two, and it helps the vegetation. Look, why don't you check back with your architect, and...'

"Yahweh shouted at him, 'I see what you're up to, you schmuck! You're trying to worm out of your contract and raise the price. What do you take me for, some kind of schlemiel?' When he got excited, he'd forget that high-toned Hebrew and revert to speaking Yiddish.

"So Lucifer shrugged, and said, 'It's your world,' and he punched a button on the intercom. You could hear the drills and grinders and hammering, and the roar of a forge in the background, and he said, 'Mister Mulciber, put it together just like it is on the plans.'

"A voice, shouting above the background din, came back over the intercom, 'Did you tell him his tectonic plates are going to slip?' And Lucifer replied, 'Yes I did. Do it anyway.' And Mulciber's voice returned, 'There's gonna be lots of wasteland; some places too cold for anything, and others will be too hot, and most of it will be underwater. He's not planning to put anything important on it is he? It's too cold, or too hot, or too rocky, or too wet...'

"'Just do it Mulciber!' Lucifer ordered, and shut off the intercom.

"Then Yahweh went to the door, and as he was leaving said, 'I like your chutzpah, Lucifer. You just tried to finagle the wrong god. I'm too smart for you. And another thing, don't try to weasel out of the time clause. I've got big plans, and if you mess it up, I'll slap you with all the penalties the law allows.'"

Lemuel saw a glaring flaw in Abigail's fictitious account. "Why do you keep insisting it took five days? The Bible says it took six."

HOW THE GOOD TAILOR GOT TO HEAVEN — 275

"Because that's what the time clause in the contract read, but you're right, it did take six days. Well, five and a half to be exact, and it caused Yahweh all kinds of trouble, not to mention what it did to the Lucifer Corporation."

"Oh, I suppose that you're going to tell us that, that was why Lucifer was cast down."

"No, that's not why. At least not the direct reason."

Zotis asked, "How come Yahweh wanted it done in five days, anyway?"

"As I said, Yahweh wanted to impress all the other gods. He had a notion that if he did something spectacular they'd think he was just as important as they were, but he didn't want to take chances. You see there was a football game on Saturday afternoon, a really important game. Something like the Super Bowl, the Rose Bowl, and all the other bowl games rolled up into one. It was the final game of the series which was to decide the cosmic champions. The Asgard Vikings had won their division title after a terrific long uphill battle from the cellar. They were the sentimental favorites. They were matched against the Vedic Bull Brahmans. The Bulls had a lock on their division, in fact they had won so many pennants and cosmic championships that there was talk of breaking up the team. And besides that, the Vikings had a flashy new quarterback named Balder, who was the favorite of all the gods. All the tickets were sold way ahead of time and the scalpers were cleaning up, and the betting was running pretty high too.

"So Yaweh thought he would have the grand opening of the world on Friday night. Not only would the gods be impressed with his world, but he invented something entirely new called the pre-game pep rally. That would certainly get them to come, and they'd all see what a magnificent god he was. He had his sons blowing up balloons, and the girls cutting out plastic pennants and making those crepe paper streamers. He even rented some of those big war surplus anti-aircraft searchlights, and bought several cases of ballpoint pens, made up with the slogan, 'Yahweh is the Greatest,' printed on the side. The next time he saw

Lucifer, he asked him to include a bonfire, but Lucifer told him it wasn't in the contract and would cost extra. So Yahweh thought he'd do that himself."

"That's the most absurd story I ever heard, Abigail. They didn't have searchlights or ballpoint pens then." He warned Zotis, "Don't believe a word she says. It's all a pack of lies."

Abigail turned her nose up with stagey indignation, and said, "I didn't tell him your story was a lie. In fact I'm agreeing with you. I'm only filling in some of the details that you omitted."

Zotis reached over and tugged at her skirt, and said, "Go on Miz Abigail. What happen next?"

She sniffed dramatically, as if to say, "There!" She continued, "This is exactly what happened, and, just like it says there in the Bible, it took more than five days. Even working three shifts, and with all the extra hired hands, Lucifer just couldn't get it done. Most of the workers had lots of overtime too. Lucifer felt bad about it, but there was nothing he could do. He suggested to Yahweh, 'Have your gala opening on Sunday, and that big blast you have planned; make it some sort of after the game celebration. You can call it a victory party.' He even offered to throw in the bonfire for nothing, and he pointed to the calender on the wall and told him that the first day of the week would be a good time for a grand opening.

"Yahweh wouldn't do it. He was stubborn. As he himself said, the Jews are a stiff-necked people. So he opened the world, and nobody came. They all went to the ball game. He grumbled and groused and swore that if he ever had anything to do with it, he'd outlaw football from sundown Friday and all day Saturday, and make them play their games on Sunday. So Yahweh wanted someone to come to his grand opening, and decided to make a man. Well, no one had ever seen a man before, and Lucifer asked him, 'What's this *man* supposed to look like?' Yahweh answered, 'I'm not sure, but he should have a strong back, because I want him to take care of my world for me.' And Lucifer suggested, 'Why don't you make him in our image?' And Yahweh said, 'Ya

HOW THE GOOD TAILOR GOT TO HEAVEN — 277

dumb shmuck, then he might start thinking he's one of us.' So he made a whole bunch of experiments. He tried four-legged ones, and thousand-legged ones, and some that flew in the air, and others crept, or crawled, or slithered. Many had backs strong enough to do the kind of arduous labor he wanted, but none of them showed the slightest interest in doing the work. So finally he took Lucifer's advice and made man in their image."

Lemuel heaved a big sigh, and muttered, "You really take delight in twisting the Scriptures, Abigail. Just because it says man was put there to tend it and keep it ...what's this, the Gypsy version?"

"Yeah, that's the way they tell it, but the Gypsies were excused from the hard work. Much later, when a Gypsy stole one of the spikes that was intended to nail Christ to the cross—that's why they used only three spikes—ever since, the Gypsies have been allowed to steal without breaking The Commandments."

Then she continued with her yarn. "But let me tell you what happened after the cosmic ball game when the other gods were coming home from the stadium; this it the most interesting part. Some of them were very high-spirited and up to mischief. All of them had imbibed too much of Bacchus' favorite beverage. The Great Spirit looked down at the world, took some of Yahweh's trial attempts, and made the Indians. That's why they make totem poles with their animal ancestors on top. The Titans did something original: they made human beings round, like balls, but with four arms and four legs, and they were very strong. In fact they were so strong that Zeus thought they would rival the gods, so he cut them in half and made two people out of them, one male and one female, and now they go around looking for their other half so they can regain their former strength. Over in another part of the world, which we call China, the goddess T'ai Yuan made something like the Titan's round balls. She divided hers to look like two tadpoles, but they were really a male and a female. And down under the world, in a place called Australia, the Great Bandicoot, also named Kaora, apparently had way too much to drink and laid down on the ground to sleep it off. His sweat dripped down onto the ground, and people sprang up from the soil and his sacred sweat. Then over in the Indus valley, Purusha was in mad pursuit of one of the Bull's cheerleaders and when he nearly caught her, he shouted, 'All is won.' But he ran into a tree and immolated himself. Out of his head came the Brahmans, from his arms sprang the Rajanya, the Vaisya came out of his thighs, and the Sudra crawled out of his feet. They decided to glorify their creator by crying out his final words, 'All is one!' They shouted, but they got it wrong.

"Then over in Mesopotamia, Gilgamish and Ishtar, she was a temple *lubbeny*, and Enki, and Nammu, she was Enki's wife and mother, were touring the Tigris and Euphrates Valley when Gilgamish dared Ishtar to copulate with Enkidu, a bull who was grazing in a pasture. It was one of Yahweh's failures. Well she did it, and conceived twins who were two-thirds gods, and one-third Man. Then Nammu got the idea that she'd like to have something like them for herself. 'They'd make excellent servants and slaves,' she said. 'Just think of the offerings and sacrifices they could bring us, and they could help with the dishes too.' Enki pointed out that Ishtar's children were nearly gods themselves, and he suggested, 'Why don't you form the heart and body from the mud of the river bottom, and when I cut them loose from the earth you can have them for servants.'

"Meanwhile, over in the Nile Valley, a god named Tem was peeping in the window watching Osiris, and his sister Isis, celebrating in their own fashion. Tem got very aroused from watching them. He ejaculated on the ground, and Shu and Tefnut were born from his seed. They were the ancestors of all the pharaohs of Egypt and of all the people."

"Abigail, stop it!" Lemuel ordered. "You're being obscene! Obscene as well as blasphemous, and in front of this innocent young lad. You're corrupting his morals as well as his soul."

"Oh no she ain't, Mista Lem. Dey teaches us 'bout sex, and where babies comes from in school."

Lemuel slapped his forehead with an open palm, looked upward, and said, "Oh! My God."

HOW THE GOOD TAILOR GOT TO HEAVEN — 279

Zotis tugged at Abigail's skirt again, and said, "Gawan Miz Abby. Tell me about how my people got birthed."

Abigail looked briefly at his head, traced his ear with a fingertip, and finally determined, "I can see that you come from many gods. That is most auspicious." She reverted to her powers as a Gypsy fortuneteller. "I see that your ancestors are mostly Ibo; offspring of the great Earth Mother, Ala, and there's a bit of Amma, Chukwu, and Soko, as well as a smidgen of Yahweh's creation."

"Pay no attention to her, Zotis. She's just telling you a lot of superstitious nonsense. There is only one God—Jehovah! Anything else is a myth. Just look at her face. You can tell she's lying. The very idea! Gods going to a stadium, and playing football, running taco stands, and chasing cheerleaders…"

"Oh yeah, I almost forgot about the ball game. The Vikings lost. There was no joy in Asgard on that dreary afternoon. All the Aesir gods were peeved with Balder, their quarterback. He went from being their favorite, to being their favorite target of abuse. They began to pelt him with rocks and shoot darts or throw spears at him. They all knew they couldn't really hurt him because he was a god, but Loki got a sinister idea. He'd bet heavily and lost a lot, and he was especially mad. He knew that mistletoe had supernatural properties and he got Hoder to throw that at Balder, and it killed him. Well, his mother Frigga, Woden's wife, grieved over him for about a quarter of an hour and decided that what they really needed was expendable ball players; big stupid lummoxes that wouldn't know any better than to bash their brains out over a number on a scoreboard. If anything happened to them there would always be plenty more. So Frigga went down to Yahweh's world, scraped up some dirt, and made men of that."

Lemuel's foot swung agitatedly. He crossed his arms tightly over his chest, and said, "You're just doing this to peeve me. You can't get me upset, but it's a shame that you're deluding this poor lad about creation."

"You're the one who brought it up, talking about the Creator. I thought he should know the truth and let him make up his own mind."

"Truth?" And he sputtered, "Why you ...you ...you ...lying little imp! Here's the truth! The truth! Do you hear me?" And he waved the Bible at her. "The first man was Adam, and his wife's name was Eve, and God created them both."

She put her hands on her hips, and insisted, "It's the truth, what I said. You know it, and I'll prove it to you."

Their eyes locked. Lemuel's angry blue was equally matched by Abigail's green, and she said, "So, with all of these other people around, Adam took himself a wife." And smiling smugly she continued, "And her name was Lilith!"

Lemuel slumped back into his chair, beaten. *Oh me, oh my. She knows about that.* His first job as guardian angel had been their kid. It was his first mistake. *Boy demons can be vicious,* he thought, and clamped his mouth shut.

Abigail was triumphant; her voice and mein reflected it, as she continued: "When Yahweh saw what was going on between Adam and Lilith, he clapped his hand to his forehead, and shouted, 'Oy vey!' He had completely forgotten about something. So he built this big fenced-in yard, and took a rib from Adam's side and made a 'help meet' for him. And Yahweh warned Adam sternly, 'From now on you leave the goyim alone.' He shook his finger at him and ordered, 'And you don't have anything to do with the shiksa women. See, I made this nice Jewish girl for you.' And he pushed them into his fenced yard, and said, 'Now play nice ...go forth and multiply.'"

"That's the most grotesque distortion of the truth I've ever heard. Why don't you use your blaspheming tongue and tell them what happened to Lucifer and the rest of that foul crew? Go on, let them know what disobedience to the Almighty means."

"Okay, but you were the one who was worrying about corrupting the boy. As I said, there was an awful lot of betting on the game and Yahweh had put a bundle down on the Bulls, and they had won. Yahweh was really kicking up his heels with delight. At the same time, Lucifer tendered his bill for the world. Lucifer was fed up with the job and wanted to be

HOW THE GOOD TAILOR GOT TO HEAVEN — 281

rid of it altogether. He was certainly in no mood to go to court to collect, so he went easy on the charges for the extras. He just wanted his money and to forget about the whole affair. And Yahweh had this bundle coming to him from his bookie. They didn't have legal off-track betting yet, and as he saw it, Lucifer's cost overrun was only a tithe of his winnings. So Yahweh slapped him on the back, gave him a big cigar, promised him a bonus, called him his son of the morning.[261] He even called Lucifer, 'a real mensch.'

"Then he went around to the tailor shop to collect his winnings. The tailor was also a bookie. The door was locked and there was a big closed sign in the window. He went around back and pounded on the door. Across the alley, Cassandra poked her head out of her window and yelled at him to pipe down. She said, 'He skipped, ya dumb sheeny! He took all the money, went down to your world, and opened up shop there.' Yahweh boiled. He didn't like Cassandra, but he knew you could always believe her.

"He was enraged. He blamed Lucifer for abetting the tailor's flight by providing a hideout, and he stormed back to Lucifer's factory, threw the bill on the receptionist's desk, and announced that any further contact with him would have to be through his attorney. Not only was he refusing to pay the bill, but he was instituting a lawsuit for nonperformance, to wit: overrunning the time clause; building an unguarded, to use the legal term, an attractive nuisance; allowing trespassers on the job site; switching subcontractors without written authorization; failure to display proper building permits; and anything else his attorney could think up.' If he wants to settle out of court I'll pay him ten cents on the dollar.' And he slammed out of the office.

"So Yahweh hired this slick-talking shyster angel named Aaron. He was more slippery than most lawyers. Aaron could have hidden behind a corkscrew. Just to show you where his ethics were while his brother Moses was up on the mountain getting the Ten Commandments from Yahweh, he was down below making the golden calf and leading all the Jews to worship it. Then he denied having any part of it and helped slaughter the ones who had worshiped it. But that all happened much later. He knew Yahweh's case would be heard in Maat's District Court. She was the Egyptian goddess who weighs the souls of the dead, and is the overseer of moral law, right, and truth. Well, her court was the last place that Aaron wanted to have the trial and Yahweh agreed with him, so they applied for a change of venue. They charged prejudice, and Maat pointed out that both litigants were from the same sect, so she was not likely to favor one over the other. However, her docket was full so she allowed them to move their case to another court.

"They shopped around for just the right judge and they found a minor goddess up on Olympus whose name was Themis. Being a minor goddess, she was blind with ambition. That's why they show her blindfolded. Aaron got her aside, in chambers, and made a deal with her. He'd see to it that the mortals would put up statues and pictures of her in their courts, and Yahweh would have judges instead of priests decide the mortal cases, if she would decide in their favor."

Pearl had been quiet all this time, but she broke in, "You is sho tellin it right Abby! They was a time when black folks was honest, an did honest work, but now dey's takin to lawyerin, an bein judges, an dey's jus as crooked as de white folk. Dare was a time when dat nigga on de West Coast would'a been strung up, but he got dis slick-talkin black lawya, an got off." And she apologized, adding, "Ah didn' mean ta innerupt, but yo's sho'a tellin de truth."

"Well, here's the part Lem was waiting to hear: how some of the angels were cast down. Lucifer faced a rigged trial right from the start and Themis declared that he was guilty of nonperformance according to the time clause; shoddy workmanship; weak and unreliable materials; and erecting a dangerous structure, so he and the chief stockholder of the corporation, Satan, and the entire workforce, was sentenced to live eternally on earth. Lucifer objected and pointed out that if it was shoddy it was because he was following the plans that Yahweh had submitted. He said that he warned him, but that Yahweh had insisted. And Themis told him that he should have had enough professional integrity to refuse to build the hazzard in the first place, and then she added: 'It ought to be razed.'"

Then Abigail snorted, "Huh! Can you imagine? She actually used the word integrity, like she had some notion of what it meant. And that's when Yahweh showed his true colors too. He said, 'No, No, let's not be hasty your Honor. Don't tear it down. I think it can be fixed up. A little bit of paint and putty, and it'll be just fine. And I promise that I won't let the tenants throw trash down the air shafts, or clutter up the entry with bicycles, and I'll see to it that there's adequate fire protection.' Well! You know Themis wasn't about to order the world razed. She liked the idea of being edified by the mortals, And Yahweh figured he could get his ten percent out of their earnings, like rent. And what other grandiose schemes he has planned, we've yet to find out."

Lemuel was far beyond his earlier rages and like most of us when we're faced with no other alternative, he started to think. His experiences with mortals had always been touch and go: keeping his assigned soul steadfast in their belief; telling a lie here; bringing a plague there; causing the earth to open up over there; and bringing about slaughters, great and small. These things never really let him understand the human psyche. Even his long stint as a deliverance angel didn't help; that was just dash down, pick up the soul, dash back, deliver it, and go back for another one. Abigail had lived among them for six thousand years. She had the home court advantage. He knew that nearly everything she told them was a lie. She'd have made a superb lying angel; a master of the craft. *But there is one thing she can't weasel out of: original sin, and man's corruption by woman.* He said, "So far, Abigail, you've had a great time entertaining everyone, but don't you think it's time to tell them of the evil perpetrated against mankind by the serpent in the Garden of Eden?"

"Do you really want me to?"

"Why yes. You've made him out to be a sympathetic character in your little concoction. Now tell them what the serpent did to all mankind; that supreme perfidy by the consummate master of villainy. Tell them how he beguiled the sweet naive Eve and through her, Adam, and through the two of them—everyone—including Pearl and Zotis. And doomed them all to suffer the fires of hell until they become saved, and commit their souls to Christ. Tell them."

Abigail shrugged, and said, "Okay, but remember that this is by your request. It all started when Prometheus brought the mortals fire; then Mimir dug a well of knowledge under the Yggdrasil tree for the Norsemen; and Brigit was giving her mortals the benefit of her wisdom. But Baylor cast an evil eye on her, at least that's what Queen Mab said it was. It was a good thing or else we'd all be a speaking with an Irish brogue now.

"Over in the Nile Valley, the goddess Maat gave knowledge to the result of Horus's seed; and in India, Krishna did the same for Purusha's offspring. In China, the great Yu gave the Shu Ching to the mortals made by T'ai Yuan. In fact, in each and every place that the gods created mortals, one of their associate deities took pity on the frail and ignorant beings, and gave them knowledge. Most of the humans were thankful for this wonderful gift. In Persia where Ahura Mazda created his mortals, he also gave them wisdom and light. He didn't think they should be like the ignorant beasts, and doing things only by instinct, and without the ability to reason. Mazda, like Lucifer, was the lord of light, and Mazda's wicked enemy was Angra Mainyu, the lord of darkness. He dwelt in the thick darkness, and he wanted to keep all the humans in darkness and ignorance. He wanted them about as self-willed as a flock of sheep. Hum…do you suppose that is why they call ministers, pastor; and we refer to his congregation as his flock?" And she continued without pausing.

"Yahweh, exactly like Angra Mainyu, didn't want humans to be able to think, so he forbade them to eat from the tree that bore the fruit of knowledge. Yahweh was afraid that if they ever wised up, he wouldn't be collecting his ten percent."

Lemuel slapped the arm of his chair, and said, "That's enough Abigail! Let that be a lesson to you Zotis: never trust a woman. They'll twist the truth or tell whole lies, and try to make you think up is down

HOW THE GOOD TAILOR GOT TO HEAVEN 285

or evil is good." Pearl and Abigail both chuckled as Lemuel continued, "This is exactly why the Bible says men are to rule over women[262]; and command them to be obedient to their husbands. Every word out of her mouth has been a lie. There are no other gods, but there is evil and a prince of evil. The fruit on the tree of knowledge was the knowledge of good and evil. The prince of evil came as a serpent, a serpent far more evil than a court's whip, and beguiled Eve into tasting the forbidden fruit. And Eve, who now understood what evil was because she had tasted the fruit first and so she knew good from evil, chose to do the evil, and corrupted the noble, and still pure, Adam. The prince of evil caused them to disobey their creator and make a place in their hearts for evil, in other words, for himself. And all mankind suffers because they disobeyed God. God made them leave Eden and now, all mankind must earn their bread by the sweat of their brow."

"I suppose that you'll accuse me of twisting things again, but I always thought Eve had chosen the good. And maybe you can explain this: What reason does your Bible give for the Lord putting Adam in Eden in the first place? You just mentioned it a little while ago."

"To dress it and to keep it," Lemuel said in muted tones, thinking of the souls dressing and keeping the Eden above.

"Uh huh! Do you suppose man could have worked in that garden without their brows sweating?"

And Zotis asked, "If'n de Lawd didn' want them to eat de fruit, why'd he plant dat tree in de fust place?"

Pearl defused that bomb by telling Zotis to "hush up," and reminded them that today was the luckiest day in her life and they were there to have a good time, and that Abigail and Lemuel ought to quit bickering over things they couldn't do anything about. She pointed out how lucky they both were to have each other, to have such a nice trailer and a pickup, and so many nice things. They ought to kiss and make up, and their barbeque was ready.

Chapter 17

AS THEY DROVE AWAY FROM PEARL'S CABIN THAT NIGHT, Lemuel lost no time in severely criticizing Abigail's impieties and blasphemies. She had made the whole outing a corruption of the Sabbath; encouraged worldliness by belittling God, telling lies about the creation, and by telling Pearl and Zotis that there was more then one god. "Outrageous Abigail! Having that poor benighted woman pray to some pagan fairy queen, ("Mautia" Abigail interjected.) who doesn't exist. And worse, abetting her in some savage ritual mysticism that wasn't forbade by the Scriptures because it was probably too base to mention … voodoo. Humph!" Then he said, "And you did fortunetelling, Abigail. That's soothsaying, and that's forbidden by the Bible…."

"I didn't tell her fortune. I can't see into the future. The whole thing was a game and they enjoyed it. All I did was create a little paper money for them. Where's the harm in that? We spent a lot of time talking about God. You should be happy."

"People are supposed to work for their money; earn their bread by the sweat of their faces. It's God's will. Work is good for the soul. You and your kind will wreck the economy. The Lord is supposed to raise them up, or bring them low, and not some blasphemous Gypsy demon perverting God's will. Isn't it bad enough that the mortals try to subvert what God hath ordained with their government welfare offices? That's atheistic secular humanism! You know perfectly well that she should have gone to her church first and if she were truly deserving, the board of deacons, or the church wardens, would have determined her needs."

She reached over, patted his knee, and chided, "There's no free lunch! Is that what you mean?"

Oblivious to the irony that he was eating free lunches provided by a demon, her satire escaped him, and he said, "Those dedicated men and women understand the needs of the poor. It's a noble calling, doing God's work."

"Yes, dear, I know. I suppose rice Christians are better than nothing. And when they pass over to the other life you can decide then whether they were sincere or not."

"You fiends take sadistic delight in twisting things around. You tried to make it look perfectly acceptable to worship false gods or indulge in a lot of superstitious tommyrot, and don't your ears just perk up when you hear that someone is worshiping the serpent. Well, I've got news for you, miss smarty, if you spent less time traipsing around naked, and sunning yourself, and more time reading the Bible, (he vividly recalled Myles explaining the serpent on the pole, and Christ on the cross analogy) you'd know that they might not be worshiping Satan's corruption of mankind, but our Lord and Savior's powers of regeneration."

He stole a glance at her and noted with satisfaction that she was uncharacteristically startled, but she quickly regained her composure. Then her eyes narrowed as she appraised this intricate new puzzle.

They left the scrub brush and when they got to the ancient oaks, Abigail turned off her headlights and drove using only her amber parking lights. "We don't want to disturb the creatures any more than necessary," she said.

"We don't want to run into these trees," Lemuel replied, suddenly purblind by the absent bright lights. Gradually his eyes became accus-

HOW THE GOOD TAILOR GOT TO HEAVEN — 289

tomed, and he could make out tree trunks, and catch a glimpse of the moon and stars through the foliage. As they reached the edge of the meadow, the moonlight reflected on the little lake and shimmered liquidly from the waterfall that in places looked frothy white, like whipped cream on a chocolate pie. The arc of light from the trailer lit the carpeted side yard they had made, and then out onto the natural carpet of leaves and pine needles of the forest floor. He felt compelled toward the soft glowing lights and the moonlight reflecting dimly from the aluminum shell. An unusual feeling of tenderness and security seemed to draw his soul toward the warm glow. Recollections of Abigail and himself exploring the wild game trails, swimming and sunning by the pool, playing games, and their bantering disputes tumbled in out-of-sequence jumbles across his thoughts. It was the eighth day of his mortality.

"Almost home," Abigail announced.

Only then did he realize how close he had come to apostasy. Home is in Heaven, where there is eternal light and everything is perfection, and where there are no dark gloomy places, except for the darker corners of Orson's storeroom. Inside the trailer he reproached himself as he settled into Abigail's soft easy chair. He thought about bringing in one of her canvas yacht chairs, but even those were softer than the hard stone benches of heaven. He made a silent vow not to be corrupted by her soft easy ways as he accepted an Old Fashioned from her.

She changed out of her gypsy costume and now wore something frilly, diaphanous, pink, and short. His sour mood moderated as he studied the ingenuous gamin-like creature with her legs curled up sitting at the far end of the sofa. She was sipping her drink and twisting her head sideways as she read from Lemuel's …his heart leapt. *She is actually reading the Bible!* A warmth glowed in his stomach, a warmth that seemed to radiate from his center out through his limbs and a few more sips of the Old Fashioned improved the glowing feeling, as well as his disposition.

Abigail turned the pages and idly passed her hand down each page, not actually reading more than a phrase here and there, and after several silent minutes, she asked, "What did you mean tonight when you said the serpent could represent Christ's powers of regeneration? Over the years I've heard millions of preachers and I never heard any of them say anything like that, but I don't pay much attention to their sermons. It doesn't take them long before they're ranting and raving about demons and Satan, and telling lies about us causing the mortals to sin. The humans don't need us for that; they can think it up all by themselves. But what about the serpent? What did you mean?"

Lemuel wished he hadn't said anything. No matter what he said, she was sure to twist its meaning into something blasphemous. Then he thought that by introducing Abigail into the deeper mysteries she might realize the truth. He said, "Look in Saint John. That's in the New Testament, Abigail, toward the back of the Bible."

After much searching she found John, and he said, "It's in the third chapter: 'And as Moses lifted up the serpent in the wilderness, even so must the Son of Man be lifted up.[263]' That refers to the section in Numbers where the children of Israel complained about being led into the desert and to punish them the Lord sent poisonous serpents among them, and then the Lord commanded Moses to make a fiery serpent and put it on a pole. You see, the pole is symbolic of the cross that Jesus was crucified on and the fiery serpent represents Jesus and all who look upon it, meaning to recognize it, shall live." Abigail was turning pages and Lemuel said, "Numbers is in the Old Testament, Abigail." He continued, "So the meaning here is clear. The serpent upon the pole saved the people and prevented the poison, meaning sin, from killing them."

"Oh! You're telling me that Jesus was a poisonous serpent?"

"No! That's not it at all! I knew you'd twist things around. Jesus saved them and gave them life."

She smiled brightly and said, "And the serpent in the Garden of Eden gave them knowledge, and Yahweh considered knowledge poisonous. Yeah! I see."

He gave an exasperated sigh, but she made the same observation that he had uttered to Myles. Myles hadn't cleared up the exposed dichotomy between the Creator and the Christ with his dissertation about Apep/Am of the Egyptians. He had only confused Lemuel further with his lengthy explanation about serpents guarding threshing floors and mangers and such, and Lemuel doubted his tutorial skill was equal to Myles's. Abigail was sure to misinterpret. Tomas had simply asserted that there was no such division, but something Abigail had said about Ahura Mazda and Angra Mainyu now confused him. Why had the Magi, the priests of Zarathustra, come to Christ with gifts when their false religion taught the exact opposite, as that of the Jews? Their religion placed the good for evil, and the evil for good.

He finished his drink, ate the cherry, and munched on his orange slice garnish. Then he asked Abigail for another. Suddenly, the question exploded in his mind, *Was he becoming a Satanist?*

Abigail counted out the drops of bitters onto the sugar in his glass and stirred in a splash of water, and discoursed idly, "The serpent seems to crop up in most of the religions that I know of. From the headhunting Druids of the Britons, where the serpent was said to have mystical powers, to," she drew an arc in the air with her spoon, "the headhunters of Borneo, all the way round the globe, where they believe the Great Serpent mated with the celestial Mother and produced their original ancestors. They believe that the first boy went into the belly of the serpent and brought out fire to cook their meals. Then they were no longer beasts, because they no longer had to eat their food raw." She poured out a couple of ounces of good bourbon, added the garnish and a few ice cubes, and handed him his drink, and said, "See, in almost every religion the serpent is the good god that gives the mortals nice things, like wisdom and freedom." She curled up once more at the end of the sofa and added, "And isn't that what Satan, as the serpent, was supposed to have done for Adam and Eve?"

Fortunately, Lemuel remembered Myles's response to the seneschal Brigham and Tomas on that point. "The Bible doesn't say it was Satan, it just says the serpent."

"Oh, I didn't know that. I was just going by what I've heard the preachers say down here. But who was the mysterious serpent? Aren't you admitting there's more than one god?"

Lemuel sipped his second drink. He was beginning to see the common sense behind Tomas' position. *Just give them the Bible, and hope they never read it, better yet keep it in some language nobody can read.* "No Abigail, there's only one God, but it might have been some angel on lying angel detail who got his assignment fouled up. I have made a couple of mistakes myself." This discussion was upsetting him and he recalled the mistake Myles made and the lashing he had undergone, and he winced, and exploded, "Holy Mary, Mother of God! Haven't you any instinct for truth?"

"Yeah, that's another thing. Why do women play such a minor role in your Empyreal system? That's about the only time I've heard you come close to the truth."

"What truth? Are you telling me that you think Mary was God? She was just a woman."

"You just said it yourself: 'Holy Mary, Mother of God.' Unless Jesus was an apotheosis, she'd have to be. And I think Eve should be given credit for her part in giving mankind intelligence. It seems to me that your people have done nothing but try to keep women down."

He muttered angrily, "It's bad enough to be kidnaped by a Gypsy demon, but does she have to be a feminist too?" And more loudly, "Maybe I should call you Mizz Demon."

"I thought we agreed it was to be a terrestrial angel. You know that other word is discriminatory; but you should admit you're trying to peddle a flawed product. Half of the human species is female, but does Yahweh pay any attention to the female gender? Nooo! All the other religions do. Their mortals worship the ladies. They have fertility goddesses, and love goddesses, and earth mothers, but does Yahweh have any goddesses? Nooo!"

"There's Esther, and I've always thought highly of her."

"Oh yeah, estrual Esther. What does he have her doing now? Working as a receptionist? I mean something with real dignity."

"She teaches the second grade."

"That sounds just like him. Absolutely no regard for women, except for women he can intimidate. I can see him now. He used to come sneaking through that swinging gate in the counter with that long, unkempt beard, wearing that black hat ...did you know he never took his hat off in the office? And his shoes always seemed two sizes too large, and he always kept his long black coat on too. His finger nails were cracked and dirty and he'd come sneaking in wearing an evil leer, and the dirty old thing was always, 'going to discover our secret parts:[264] Heh! Heh! Heh!'" She mocked him nastily. "He'd say, 'Uncover thy locks, make bare the leg, uncover the thigh. Thy nakedness shall be uncovered, yea, thy shame shall be seen. Heh! Heh! Heh!'—No wonder he couldn't get a date. There were lots of goddesses who would have gone out with him; all he had to do was to clean himself up a bit, get a decent suit of clothes and shave. So what does he do instead? He takes out his frustrations on the poor human women."

Perhaps it was the effect of the two double Old Fashions, but Lemuel could see crude, albeit childish, logic in Abigail's fabrications. As a creature created on the second day, rebellious and perverse by nature, and with her diminished capacity to understand the metaphysical mysteries; she may even believe her absurd yarn. Charitably, he conceded that if she told herself those lies often enough, she could conceivably come to believe any sort of myth. And yet ...he had to admit that a feminine touch might improve the organization. Abigail yawned and stretched, curving her back like a cat reaching out, and he thought, *I wish she'd wear more clothes.*

* * *

That night, visions of pure metaphysics danced through Lemuel's dreams as sugar plums. He was just on the verge of discovering the untarnished first cause of everything, and had nearly solved the coterminous junctures of all bounds, when he felt his shoulder being jostled. His disappointment at being awakened before he had solved the esoteric calculus was mollified by the vision of that small brown body, with the dark chocolate, hair kneeling across his legs. He was glad she didn't wear clothes, nude was her proper condition, and he reached for her playfully. She put her finger to her lips, as a silencing gesture, and then pointed to something outside the window. "*Stannyi*, and *stannyo*," she whispered.

Instead of Mautia, and the fairies and hobgoblins, or Queen Myrta and the Wilis cavorting with a black drake, he expected to see, because of the delight showing on her face, he saw two deer grazing not ten yards from the trailer. They seemed to take turns, alternately grazing and watching. Lemuel shifted his position, the trailer moved on its ground jacks, and both deer bounded away showing white furry pyramids above their rumps. "Aw, you scared them," she said, and sat back on her heels, and added, "but I told you they'd become less afraid. Weren't they pretty?"

He wanted to say, *Not nearly as pretty as you*, but asked instead, "Do you think they'll come back?"

* * *

Although Lemuel and Abigail had special attributes, he an angel, and she a demon, their domestic arrangement was spent as any two unmarried mortals would under similar circumstances. Lemuel spent much of his time reading the Bible and since he still hoped to save her from the horrors of Armageddon, he often read passages aloud to her that he thought might convince her. She watched the soaps on TV or crocheted a few rosettes for the antimacassar she was making for the sofa. They spent a lot of time bird-watching or feeding the *ruko mengros* who were becoming tame enough to come under the awning and eat on the table. A pair of red foxes, that Abigail called, *welshen juggals*, allowed themselves to be seen occasionally as they gathered up the scraps that Lemuel put out for them. And they went on nature walks where they saw, *kaulo sappors,* and *chaw sappors*, but no more copperheads. A colorful wood duck and his mate nested in the reeds by their pond.

They both swam every day and Abigail spent hours sunbathing on the ledge rock. She was becoming nearly as dark-skinned as Pearl and at their next weekend visit, Pearl joked about it. "Is yo tryin' ta pass, Abby.

HOW THE GOOD TAILOR GOT TO HEAVEN — 295

Yo cain't. Dey ain't no green-eyed blacks, an yo'all don' have the right kinda hair?"

Lemuel's ability to swim improved greatly. He usually spent the entire time Abigail sunned herself thrashing about in the icy pond. And the food Abigail served would have added inches to his waist if he hadn't used up the calories by swimming. One afternoon, when Abigail had made club sandwiches served with potato chips and pickles, Lemuel picked up one of the sandwich quarters, examined it, and asked suspiciously, "Where's all this food coming from?"

"Well ...you see ...there's this huge cauldron ...once used to make witches' brews ...and it's laden with an unending bounty of good things. Late at night, after you've gone to sleep, and when the moon is full, I sneak out to get whatever we need."

He gingerly placed the sandwich back on the platter and Abigail laughed at him, and chided, "You know perfectly well that we can only do that with wine, or olive oil, maybe a bit of porridge, fishes and loaves, that sort of thing. And you're right, I have almost run out of food. We'll have to go down to the store and get groceries. And while we're there, maybe we can find out if you're still a wanted man."

The whole disagreeable episode came back to him and how it was that he came to be up on this mountain with a demon. At first he blamed himself for neglecting his mission, but then he soon saw that it was all Abigail's fault. "Now I know what you're up to. You're purposely diverting my attention away from my mission. The longer you delay me, the less chance I have of completing my assignment."

She gave him a disgusted look, waved his indictment away with a hand, and said, "Bosh! Don't blame me. Have I done anything to make you go strolling through the woods? You liked that, and the sunning, and the swimming ...I didn't force you."

"But you interfered when I tried to bring Pearl and Zotis to salvation, and made them worse pagans and secular humanists than they already were."

"I think you did that all by yourself." she interjected.

"Well, I need to learn my craft. I should be using this time writing sermons, practicing my delivery, deciding what form of ritual to use, and instead, you've got me cavorting about like an undisciplined child."

"All right, from now on you can sit here under the awning all by yourself and you can study to your heart's content. I'll do my swimming and sunbathing over on the other side of the trailer where you won't see me. I understand that you need your own space once in a while."

He frowned and cleared his throat. "I suppose this hasn't been a total waste. I did learn how to swim, and that's very important for an angel in my position." Abigail looked puzzled. "Suppose I was to accidentally drown while baptizing my converts. If I hadn't saved my ten thousand souls, I'd be in big trouble. They would demote me at the very least, but they might even make me stay as an ordinary human soul."

Abigail gave him an incredulous stare and then started to laugh.

"It's not funny! There have been cases …right here in this nation's capitol. A preacher led his flock into the river to be baptized, stepped back to offer prayers, and accidently stepped into a deep hole and drowned with his whole flock looking on. It's dangerous work!"

Abigail tried to hide her amusement while she said, "I had no idea that the ministry could be so dangerous. In fact preachers should get some kind of medal …yes, even a presidential award for heroism. Perhaps a day should be set aside for the people to gather at the water's edge and float Roman collars upon the waters to commemorate all those poor lost preachers."

"That's the wrong church Abigail. Those ministers don't take any chances. They just sprinkle holy water from a font."

Abigail was trying to keep a straight face and she covered her mouth. Then seeing how sincere and injured he was, she said, "All right, I'm sorry. I'll tell you what. I'll help you practice for your ministry. What do you want me to do?"

Lemuel thought, that this was an opportunity too good to be passed up. After all, she had been trying to trick him into committing blasphemy. *Why not?* He studied her cautiously and tried to sound indifferent.

HOW THE GOOD TAILOR GOT TO HEAVEN 297

"I suppose you might be able to help—if you really want to. How about letting me practice baptizing you?" He imagined himself laying her back in the water and baptizing her in the name of the Father, and the Son, and the Holy Ghost, and snatching her soul. And once she's relinquished her soul, then he'd be free to do the washing ritual with her.

"Any excuse to put your hands all over me, huh? Okay. I said I'd help, and I will, but I'm not going to let you do any yucky stuff like the mortals do."

He protested. "Why, the very idea! What are you accusing me of?" But he knew she had hit the mark and that his thoughts would not have been about the Holy Trinity. "You're right. There's not much to a baptism ceremony anyway. Would you mind auditing sermons. I shouldn't stumble around in the text as I read the passages."

"Why sure. I'll be glad to do it. Do you think I should wear a hat?"

"Now that you mention it, you might put on a housedress."

"Oh, I've got the very thing. Wait, I'll go put it on."

Lemuel decided to make his ministerial image complete and changed into his blue suit. He was standing at the edge of the carpet reading his Bible when she reappeared. She was wearing a filmy nebulous concoction made up of seven translucent, different colored veils. "How do you like this outfit? It's very biblical." She whirled in front of him while making chinging sounds with the timbrels she held in each hand.[265]

"Salome was not one of the nobler women of the Bible."

"This has nothing to do with that tart," she said sharply, and raised her nose in the air. "All proper young ladies wear something pretty on special occasions. See the pretty little bells I put on my toes?" and she tinkled them for him. Then she sat, put her feet on the coffee table, crossed her arms over her chest, tinkled her little bells again, and said, "Okay, preacher, convince me."

"This is my first attempt, you understand."

"Just pretend that I'm a whole congregation, and do as you've seen the other preachers do."

"Except for the TV, I've never actually seen preachers preach." Abigail looked incredulous. "Well, it's true. I was a deliverance angel for the last few centuries and the only time I was ever in a church was when I was shepherding one of the parturient souls from there. Normally the minister stopped giving his sermon if someone in the assembly dropped dead."

"That's understandable. So why don't you just give me one of the services that they perform in Heaven?"

Lemuel shook his head. "I can't," he said.

"Oh go ahead. I won't tell any of your secrets."

"There aren't any churches or church services," he admitted.

She laughed and clapped her hands. "Do you mean to tell me there aren't any churches in Heaven? Don't your souls have to attend worship services?"

"Why should they? The souls have earned their final reward and that's the only reason the humans have churches. They'd be redundant in heaven."

"What about your precious Sabbath? Surely you don't profane the Sabbath by having them work on that day."

"Of course not! That's their day of rest, and they spend the day kneeling on the prie-dieu beside their cots in the ordinary soul barracks. It's a beautiful sight: row upon row of souls kneeling, reverently praying, and there is organ music piped into each bunk room."

"Do they spend all day Sunday, like that?" she gulped.

"Why, of course. That is all except for the marine guards. They remain at their posts, but they can pray while they stand there."

"Oh my! All that and manna too. I think it might be wise to be evasive when you are describing the bliss that awaits the faithful." She gave a nasty chuckle. "Okay, let's hear your sermon."

Lemuel stood stiffly erect with the soft-bound Bible in his left hand. It was open to approximately four-fifths of the volume, and a couple of the page-marking ribbons fluttered in the breeze. He started in a moderate tone. "Brothers and sisters, I have come as God's servant to bring the inerrant truth into your lives today."

HOW THE GOOD TAILOR GOT TO HEAVEN

Abigail nodded, and silently mouthed the words, "Very good opening."

"The Bible is our moral guide, as well as our spiritual guide, and it is our truth. Its message is why we are here this glorious day and I know that all of you are eagerly awaiting the holy word." Then he started reading at Matthew, chapter twenty-seven. "When the morning was come all the chief priests and elders took council against Jesus to put him to death ...." And he continued reading until he came to the end of verse forty-six: "My God, My God, why hast thou forsaken me?"

Then, using one of the marker ribbons, he flipped the pages to near the center of the book, and continued reading at the first verse of the twenty-second Psalm. "My God, My God, why hast thou forsaken me?"...and he continued reading the entire thirty-one verses of malediction and lament. When he got to the final line, "That He hath done *this*," he solemnly closed the book, looked about, as though scanning an audience, and asked: "Are there any among you who want to dedicate your eternal soul to God this day? Make that commitment now, tomorrow may be too late. Please come forward and kneel before me at the rail." Then he looked hopefully at Abigail, and asked, "Well!"

"Maybe I shouldn't judge your sermon, Lem."

"Why, what do you mean? Didn't you like the way I tied Jesus' last words on the cross with the Psalms of David."

"Well ...to be honest, I thought it was a put off. I doubt that you'd make many converts with that sermon."

"It's the core of the whole Christian religion. That, and the resurrection. God gave his only begotten son to free the mortals from their sins," he protested.

"It's dismal, depressing, and assuredly does not inspire faith. At the end, Jesus lost his faith and David blamed God for all his troubles. First of all, you read entirely too much from the Bible and you hardly put any of yourself into the message."

"This is the word of God! I'm asking them to commit their souls to God, not to me."

"I don't know what idiot would commit to that religion, if that was what they were told about it. None of the ministers that I've seen have ever read that much from the Bible. Of course we earth angels try to keep our distance from them and that's getting harder to do everyday, what with radio, and TV. It has gotten so bad that the politicians and businessmen are starting to preach about being born again. But from what I've observed, the preachers will only read a verse or two, never more than four, and then they explain what it means for about forty minutes. And they skip around a lot. They'll combine a verse here with another over there and use a lot of slippery rhetoric and high sounding words in between."

"Your characterization of the men of God is crude, Abigail."

"Crude? You should hear what some of them say about us terrestrial angels. Oh! And some of the threats!"

Lemuel persisted to defend his delivery. "If a few verses have the power to inspire the multitude, it is only logical that a whole sermon from the Holy Scriptures would compound the effect. And I did just what you said they do: I skipped from New Testament to Old Testament, and tied in the focus of the whole Christian religion."

"No, what you did is read a lot of dreary stuff about some poor sad sack who was betrayed by one of his flunkies, was abandoned by all the rest of them, shunned by all the people who heard his words of wisdom, and even abandoned by the God he was trying to get them to worship. It's hardly inspiring. Then, instead of magnanimity and ennobling promises of glory, you read the worst litany of small-minded reproach ever heard from the pulpit. The worst, that is, except for the constant stream of vituperation the preachers aim at us earth angels and the human sinners. Certainly they are not very elevated thoughts that a Lord and Savior would be expected to utter."

"But he was resurrected...."

"Yeah, that's what you sell ...the promise, not the fact."

"Do you mean that I shouldn't use God's Holy word?"

"All I know is that the preachers use that book as little as possible.

HOW THE GOOD TAILOR GOT TO HEAVEN —⚜— 301

Come over here and sit down." As he sat, she continued, "This is going to come as a surprise, but here on earth they have miles of book shelves weighted down with religious writings. Almost every town has at least one book store where they sell nothing but religious gobbledegook, stacks and stacks of anecdotes, row after row of testimonials, and ream upon ream of pamphlets that validate everything from the discovery of Noah's ark to the location of Gog and Magog. There are whole libraries filled with volume after volume of big, important-sounding words on the subject—and they also sell Bibles. Every single home has one, sometimes one for each family member. They use the Bible to swear in judges, politicians, and witnesses in court, but nobody ever reads it. They read all the other books, and the preachers read the thick books with the big words, but they never stand up before an audience, and read whole passages from the Bible like you did."

"I see your point. If they all own a Bible, I guess they can read it for themselves."

She sighed, and muttered, "Close enough." Then she sprang up from her chair and pirouetted gracefully before him. She said, "Watch …it's like this." She glanced coyly downward, pulled a veil across the lower half of her face, fluttered her long eyelashes, and beckoned with a sideways movement of her head. The timbrels rang: ching …ching …ching …in perfect time to his heartbeat, and the tiny bells on her toes seemed to tinkle with a promise of gaiety and freedom. Her swirling veils emphasized the flesh they were purported to conceal, she emitted a couple of sighs, and repeated the beckoning motion with her head. Lemuel watched her dance with rapt attention for about ten minutes and then startled out of his trance, he said, "You can't do that in church!"

"I don't see why not?"

"It's …ah …it's obsce …." Then the image of David dancing before the Lord and the whole David tableau in the garden surrounding Thelassar came to his mind. The dancing David was far more salacious than anything Abigail had done, exposing himself to the maid servants, and then having a begetting ceremony with them. He altered his tack.

"It's entertaining, but not something I could do. I've a more stolid nature."

"It is supposed to be entertaining; it's show business. Churches have choirs and music, and all you'd need would be to get a few dancers from one of the local clubs and have the congregation join in the singing. Get some of those spirituals that have some life to them. I'll bet Pearl could help you there. You'd hardly have to preach at all."

"What about the Scriptures; God's holy word? Am I supposed to forget about the Bible?"

"Of course not. Wave it around a lot. They gave you a good book for that, that gold-edged paper will really impress them." She sat on the edge of the coffee table, picked up the Bible in one hand, and demonstrated how to present it before him, as though offering a salver filled with rare and delicious condiments. "And just as any other form of show business, don't forget the gate receipts."

"People won't believe it's a real church if you don't constantly hound them for money. You should spend about five minutes telling of the fine work of the missions in Africa and Russia who need something more substantial than faith, and how the Christian school is turning out such fine examples of American boys and girls, and that it would be dreadful to deny any student access merely because of the school's limited capacity, and they should give a bit extra for the school's building fund. Remember to allude to the condition of the church's roof, and while your choir sings something soft and soothing, you pass the plate."

"That's terrible! You make it all sound mercenary. I'm here for their souls, not their money. Jesus never passed a collection plate."

"Yeah, and look what happened to him. The mortals have a saying: 'Put your money where your mouth is.' They don't think it shows conviction unless they're willing to put out their hard-earned cash."

Lemuel thought for a few minutes, and said, "Jesus advised a rich man to sell everything he had and give the money to the poor[266]. Do you think Jesus would have been better off if he had told the rich man to give all his money to him." Then Lemuel brightened, and said, "Of course! That's exactly what the apostles had the believers do when they came together after the crucifixion. The believers sold everything they had and laid the money at the apostles' feet, and distribution was made to every man according as he had need. And all that believed were together, and had all things common.[267]"

"But my catechist, Tomas deTorquamada, seemed to think that would be too harsh a requirement, and it would discourage converts. What do you think?"

"I think they'd call you a communist and, since you don't have any proof of citizenship, you'd be deported. How do you like Cuban food?" And she added, "Even with papers, I can make those for you, they'd find some way to toss you into the pokey."

"I'm assigned to this country, America."

"In that case you'd better do as the Americans do."

"That's wonderful, Abigail. I'm very pleased. You must have been reading the Apostle Paul. To the Romans he became as a Roman; to the Jews he became as a Jew; to the Greeks he became as a Greek; to the Corinthians, as a man from Corinth; and so here in America, I guess I should become as an American."

Abigail had never realized how Machiavellian these men of God could be to gain souls and she shook her head sadly. But then, with an impish smile, she said, "I've an idea. You want some way for them to demonstrate their submission and to raise money for the church without taking every cent they have. You need to keep them working so they can earn more money and give you a share of it. What you should do is something that excites their little mortal minds; something they'll be willing to spend money for, but where you won't have too much outlay."

"Their salvation is free," he remonstrated sternly.

"That's not what I meant. It should be something they're willing to pay for and at the same time express their dedication and their submission. They'll all feel united in a single cause."

"Bingo? Do you seriously think I should run a bingo game?"

"No, but it should be a social activity that appeals to a basic mortal instinct."

"Bingo does that. It's called gambling and it's also sinful."

"No, that's not what I had in mind. You'd have these stalls along the side of the church…"

"You want me to rent space in the church to money changers and merchants?"

"No, no! This activity would be of a purely spiritual nature, a sort of catharsis, a kind of blessed release. You convince the mortals that since their mortal flesh was created by Yahweh, as well as their souls, that the sacraments must be indulged in bodily, as well as spiritually. They owe their souls and their bodies, and should be willing to show their gratitude unselfishly."

"What would that have to do with stalls?" He scratched his chin, and mused half aloud: "The Roman church has little stalls along their walls where the priests hear confessions. A confession is a kind of catharsis, a communing, but where does the bodily aspect come in? Let's see. They go in to confess; to commune with. (Abigail grinned, and urged him on as though playing charades) to talk with; to have a dialogue with; to have intercourse with …Intercourse with! Is that what you mean?"

She nodded, snapped her fingers, and winked, and said, "You got it."

"You think I should be having sex with my parishioners? You little demon!"

"No, no! Of course not! Not you …how would you raise any money that way? What you should do is have all the women loiter in the church yard wearing their Sunday finery, like I'm wearing, and that would attract the men. And, as they would naturally pair off—the church is a great place for people to meet, much better than a saloon—they would both go into one of the stalls and redeem the flesh they owe their creator. He, by parting with a small amount of his wages, and she by…"

"That's temple prostitution, Abigail!"

HOW THE GOOD TAILOR GOT TO HEAVEN — 305

"You could collect the money the same as if it were Bingo, and you wouldn't have all the expense of cards, or tokens, or numbered ping-pong balls. You should require a quota: it would give them a goal to aim for, and they'd feel fulfilled when they paid off their debt to their Lord for having created them."

"Evil blasphemy, and sacrilege! I was warned...there's no hope for demons."

"Are you sure? About the sacrilege, I mean. Does the Bible say that temple prostitution for the Lord would be evil or sacrilegious?"

Lemuel sputtered indignantly, "Of course it does! It must. There's lots in here about lust, and fornication, and adultery, and about the harlot lying in wait at every corner[268]. Her house is the way to hell, going down to the chambers of death."

"Oh, you are so right. Street corners lead to nothing but trouble, but I thought I made it clear that they'd meet at the church."

Lemuel fingered his Bible and thought about the New Testament, and he couldn't recall any specific prohibitions there. Then he resorted to the Mosaic laws. He mentally ran through all the thou shalts, and the thou shalt nots: Exodus; Leviticus; Deuteronomy. He looked for something to refute her absurd proposition. There's something about the tokens of virginity, and amercing of a hundred shekels.[269] *I can't use that, she'd just give it one of her little demon twists.* "Ah Ha! Here: 'Thou shalt not bring the hire of a whore, nor the price of a dog, into the house of the Lord.[270] As his finger descended to point to the very words, a sudden gust of wind flipped the pages to the book of Luke, and his finger came down on the verses that told how Mary Magdalene; and Joanna; and Susanna; and many others ministered to him of their substance.[271] His well-tanned complexion turned ruddy, and he declared, "That doesn't mean what you think it means, you treacherous little trickster."

Abigail said with surprised innocence, "I haven't any idea what it means since you haven't read it to me yet."

Then a throaty female voice, that Lemuel recognized, said in musical sing-song tones, "Oh, yes it does Lem. Their only substance was their bodies, everything else belonged to the men." The faint odor of ectoplasm wafted through the air as Esther materialized sitting cross-legged on the hood of the pickup. When fully fleshed out, she added, "I think the little darky has a pretty good idea there, Lem." Esther was wearing her miraculous visitation robes, (She'd been scheduled to make an appearance over a winding sheet in Turin, Italy.) and a very nice halo, with a stylish glory that gave golden fires to her glossy black hair. She gestured with her hand, and said, "Of course, if you want to be stuffy about the letter of the law, about bringing the hire of a whore into the church, all you'd have to do is collect before they went inside. And I think a nice added touch would be a bulletin board with a list of the girls at services and any special devotionals they're willing to perform. Then she winked lewdly at Lemuel, and asked, "Trying to change your luck, old boy?" and indicated Abigail with a thumbing gesture.

Although Esther's allusion to mixed race coupling was lost on Lemuel, Abigail was not amused. Although smiling, she commented sarcastically, "My, my, I thought it was only Hindus who sanctified cows."

Lemuel interrupted Esther's observation about a "smart-mouthed little nigger bitch," to admit that he had indeed had a run of bad luck. He explained apologetically that although it must look peculiar, his being there with a demon, that she was actually helping him out of a jam. Then he told her that, although he held the usual low opinion of demons, that as demons go, Abigail was a very nice one. He implored Abigail to not think of Esther as a "holier-than-thou type," and added, "Esther is a regular sport."

Abigail responded, "Oh, I can see she's a real sportin gal, all right."

And Esther shot back, "What is it you're selling, honey, with those veils?"

Abigail's eyes sparkled green fire as she looked Esther up and down. "Wouldn't a polka-dot ensemble be more apropos of your agglomerate collations, dear?"

HOW THE GOOD TAILOR GOT TO HEAVEN — 307

As sister angels, Esther and Abigail were getting along about as well as Leah and Rachel.[272] They exchanged smiles about as warm as mortuary slabs. Esther slid from the hood of the truck and asked, "Been gathering any May apples dear?"

Abigail replied, "Oh, I don't think I'd need the mandrakes if I wanted to tilt. That would be more your style."

Lemuel said, "While you two discuss fashion and gardening, suppose I mix up a batch of those vermouth cocktails. It will relax you, Esther, after your long trip down. It's made with just a smidgeon of wine, diluted with a lot of a liquid they call gin. I know I'd sure like some."

Lemuel returned with a pitcher full of martinis and poured a round. Esther took a couple of sips and complemented Lemuel on the concoction by aiming a long tight wink at him, which lifted the corner of her mouth. "Wow! If we had anything that potent, it wouldn't have taken me two days to maneuver Haman out of favor with Xerxes. Not only could old Uncle Mordecai and I have taken Persia, we could have had Babylon and the Scythians, too."

"Gosh, that was a long time ago. Didn't he have some problem with the Greeks?" Abigail snickered impishly, and added, "That's right, I remember, you replaced Vashti as his queen. After his armies got beaten, he turned his attention to construction work. I understand that you were the inspiration for the Hall of Many Columns in Persepolis. Didn't he dedicate that great big hall to you?"

"Most have considered it a temple of worship, not a hall, dear," Esther replied sweetly.

"I imagine it's greatness must have awed many a worshiper," Abigail said waspishly.

Sometimes Lemuel had a way of making a statement which sounded innocent, but one could never be sure if he was innocent, or actually quite clever. He said, "How nice. You two seem to have a mutual interest in ancient Persian architecture. Good architecture is a delight to behold, but it's a shame that mankind doesn't devote as much effort in elevating his soul as he does in the erection of his columns."

Somehow that seemed uproariously funny to both Esther and Abigail. They found that in spite of their polemic orientations, they did share commonality with the universal sisterhood that sways powerfully over the source of man's ignominy. They both understood that, no matter how apt the simile, it's not by his nose that man is led. The tension eased and Esther told Lemuel that she thought Abigail had been generous when she described his sermon as boring; she thought it positively repulsive. "That's why I stopped in. I heard your voice delivering that awful sermon."

"Oh, then you caught my little cooch dance?"

"It was very nice, but you should have put more umph into it. I'll show you." She gulped down the remainder of her drink, hung her halo and glory on the pickup's rear view mirror, and made a few sinuous bumps and grinds. The full effect of the erotic way her belly muscles gyrated were somewhat concealed by her miraculous visitation robes, but enough raw sexual allurement was emitted to cause Lemuel to turn beet red. Esther sat back down, and said, "It's best when all I wear is a waist chain and a few bangles."

They had another round of drinks, chatted for a while, and Abigail said, "I don't mean to criticize you, Esther, but that lipstick you're wearing is the wrong shade for your coloring." It was a reddish-orange. "I think a shade of raspberry would be more becoming. I have a tube in my makeup case." She invited Esther inside to try it on.

In the bathroom, Esther expressed her thanks, saying, "I'd have felt like a bitch, squatting behind a bush. Those drinks seem to go right through." Abigail found the lipstick, and Esther was delighted. "I wish they'd consider the ladies more when they requisition supplies. Would you believe it? Everybody gets the same shade."

Abigail told her to keep it since she could always buy more at the drug store. Esther rolled her eyes upward, and sighed. "Oh, the store! Do you realize it's been over twenty-five hundred years since I've been shopping? Do you know how lucky you are?"

"Why don't you stay? We'd be glad to put you up for a while." Only later did Abigail's use of the nominative plural pronoun register.

HOW THE GOOD TAILOR GOT TO HEAVEN   309

Esther shuddered and replied, "I'd love to. You don't know how much, but I'm not even supposed to be here now. Boy! If they ever found out."

Back outside, they had another round of drinks. Esther picked up Lemuel's Bible and said, "Watch, I'll show you how to deliver the Lord's word." Then to Abigail she asked, "Will you assist me, sister?"

"Yeah, sure," Abigail replied.

Esther walked with stately grace, erect and proud as Juno. There was just a slight sway as she turned and faced the couple. The gin had given her cheeks a slight flush. Esther's head was bowed, her eyes closed, and her thick black mane hung heavily and glossy like a sable mantle about her shoulders, and darkly framed her porcelain countenance. Abigail began to sing softly something she remembered hearing from the Broadman Hymnal. "Sowing in the morning/ Sowing at the noontide/ Sowing in the evening/ Sowing the precious seed by the way..." Esther held the Bible clasped on a diagonal between her breasts, drawing the material of her white robe as snugly as a wet t-shirt over her large twin mounds. Her areolas and button-hard nipples looked like dusty roses beneath the fabric. She stood calm and silent for several minutes, and Abigail's singing lowered to a barely audible humming. Esther shook her magnificent, thick, black hair, then slowly raised her head; her eyes remained closed. Then she started to speak in a full, throaty contralto, still keeping her eyes closed. "I have had a vision . The pure flame of the Holy Spirit is surrounding the tabernacle...

Abigail gasped softly, "Oh, Hallelujah, sister."

"We are in the presence of the divine power."

Abigail's humming grew louder.

"DO YOU FEEL IT?" She opened her eyes, and deep blue pools mesmerized Lemuel drawing him magnetically.

Abigail intoned, "Oh glory be, sister. Yes, I feel his divine presence.

Esther's voice cajoled and implored, "Oh Glory be! Feel that power! The pure sacred flame of the Holy Spirit has the power!" Her body quivered, and her breasts jiggled. "Come wash your souls clean in the Holy flame.

"There! DID YOU FEEL THAT TREMOR IN YOUR HEART?

"Oh...yea...ah, sister!"

Then Esther swung her arms wide, and shouted, "OPEN YOUR HEART TO JAY ...SUS! Then she slammed the Bible back closely to her breast, and clasped it tightly with both hands.

"Forget those worldly evil cravings."

"Oh AMEN! Sister."

"Open your heart to Jay...sus. Cast off those bonds of shame... COME! Come forward! Unburden your soul! Be washed in the blood of the Lamb. Accept the love of Jay...sus! And so on and so forth." Esther walked unsteadily, sat down, crossed her legs, and picked up her martini once more. She winked at Abigail, and said, "Thanks for the help, Sister." And after taking a healthy gulp of Gin, she asked, "Don't you think tha'sh more like it? Didn't you feel urged to come for'rard?"

"Not me, but I'm sure Lem felt something," Abigail said with a lop-sided grin.

Esther blushed and covered her embarrassed laugh. "You can be the demon in my amen corner anytime, honey. You're good."

Lemuel said, "I'll admit you had magnetism, and I was on the verge of reaffirming the commitment of my soul, but you didn't use the Bible one time."

Abigail objected, "Of course she did! Didn't you see it there pushing up her breasts. That's what I was trying to tell you before. You never actually read the Bible ...you use it as a prop."

"Gee, you're a brick, Abigail. Ish nish of you to splane it so clearly." Then Esther hiccuped.

Abigail said with alarm, "Oh, oh! She's supposed to make a miraculous visitation. We better got some black coffee and some food into her quick."

While Esther sang off key, a ditty about someone's "Navvy boots," Lemuel brewed a pot of coffee and Abigail prepared a large steak and some eggs and made Esther down a large glass of tomato juice. After eating like a trencherman, Esther nodded and dozed, and they decided to let her sleep it off. After thinking for a little while Lemuel said, petulantly, "My sermon would have sounded much better if I'd have had a demon in the amen corner."

* * *

Esther left, still slightly tipsy, and later that evening the anchorman on the six o'clock news reported that there had been a miraculous visitation over one of the flags raised at the U.S. Capitol building. It was taken as a propitious omen, since the flag was being raised for the senator from North Carolina, and was to be presented, by him, to a popular TV evangelist whose program was broadcast daily from Charlotte. And there was another miraculous visitation reported by a lone sailor who was soloing across the Atlantic. He said the angel had appeared above his jib sail, but the tale was regarded as an obvious prevarication. The indecency she supposedly performed with him was considered to be a hallucination by a lonely sailor, since no angel would ever do anything like that. Also, a guard at the Louvre in Paris reported a miraculous visitation by an *"Angel, tres fou"* with a crooked halo who did the can-can above the Gobelins tapestry of the Baptism of the Dauphin. And at Turin, the gathering of bishops and cardinals examining the admissibility of the shroud as a sacred icon, decided that the miraculous visitation that they witnessed had best go unreported.

Footnotes

1 Matthew 15:11

2 Jonah 3:5 So the people of Ninevah believed in God, and proclaimed a fast, and put on sackcloth the greatest of them even to the least of them.

[3]Jonah 3:8 But let man and beast be covered with sackcloth, and cry mightily unto God.

[4]Leviticus 16:21-22 "And the goat shall bear all their iniquities."

[5]Revelations 16:15 "lest he walk naked and they see his shame."

[6]Luke 23:45

[7]Romans 9:22

[8]Daniel 9:22

[9]Daniel 6:22, and Acts 12:11

[10]Acts 12:7-11

[11]Ezra 1:1

[12]Psalm 91:11, among others

[13]2nd Thessalonians 2:11; 1st Kings 22:19&23; 2nd Kings 19:6-7; 2nd Chronicles 18:21-22; also Lord deceives, Jeremiah 20:7; False Prophets Micah 3:5, among many other references

[14] Psalm 78:49; 1st Samuel 18:10, also 16:15; and 19:9
[15] 2nd Samuel 24:15&16, etc.
[16] 2nd Chronicles 18:22
[17] 2nd Chronicles 21:15
[18] 1st Samuel 5:9
[19] 1st Samuel 6:11&17
[20] 2nd Kings. 19:7; Psalms 22:28
[21] 1st Chronicles. 28:9
[22] 2nd Samuel 21:1
[23] 2nd Samuel 21:9
[24] Judges 9:23
[25] 1st Samuel 6:19
[26] Numbers 16:33-35
[27] Revelations 20:12
[28] Job 1:9
[29] Matthew 7:1&2
[30] Proverbs 22:5
[31] Proverbs 1:16
[32] Proverbs 2:14
[33] Genesis 25:29-34; and Malachi 1:2-3, "Yet I loved Jacob, And I hated Esau."
[34] Galatians 1:8 "But though we, or an angel from Heaven, preach any other gospel unto you than that which we have preached unto you, let him be accursed."
[35] Genesis 6:4
[36] Isaiah 3:16
[37] Exodus 32:19-25
[38] Exodus 32:25
[39] Exodus 32:19
[40] Exodus 34:27-28
[41] Matthew 22:36-39, (Commandments Ex. 20:1-17)
[42] Mark 9:44, 46, &48
[43] Mark 12:25

[44] Luke 11:2. Author's note: The more familiar version is Matthew's; Ch. 6: 10 "Thy will be done in earth, as it is in heaven."
[45] 2nd Kings 2:28
[46] Exodus 14:21
[47] Isaiah 38:8
[48] Ezekiel 1:4
[49] Exodus 7:10-12
[50] 2nd Kings 5:10&14
[51] 2nd Kings 4:32-35
[52] 2nd Kings 6:5-6
[53] Haggai 2:8 "The silver is mine, and the gold is mine, sayeth the Lord of hosts."
[54] 1st Chronicles 28:9
[55] 2nd Kings.19:12 "The children of Eden which were in Thelasar?"
[56] From the last stanza of the Marine Corps' Anthem. "If the army, and the navy/ever glanced on Heaven's scenes/ they would find the streets are guarded/ by the United States Marines."
[57] Jeremiah 2:13 "The people committed two evils; they have forsaken me the fountain of living waters, and have hewed them out cisterns that can hold no water."
[58] Proverbs 17:28, as quoted
[59] Psalm 9:17
[60] Nehemiah 9:2
[61] 2nd Chron. 6:36
[62] Psalm 58:3
[63] Proverbs 3:12
[64] Proverbs 13:24
[65] Proverbs 23:13-14
[66] Proverbs 20:30
[67] Deuteronomy 21:18-21 "If a man have a stubborn and rebellious son, which will not obey the voice of his father, or the voice of his mother…then shall his father and his mother bring him unto the elders of his city; This our son is stubborn and rebellious, he is a glutton

and a drunkard: And all the men of his city shall stone him with stones, that he die."

[68] Ezekiel 3:1-4 "Son of man...eat this roll, and go speak unto the house of Israel."; and Jeremiah 15:16

[69] Genesis 1:26
[70] Genesis 1:20
[71] Genesis 2:19
[72] Revelations 19:14
[73] Genesis 9:25
[74] Matthew 18:3
[75] 2nd Kings 2:21-24
[76] Numbers 11:5-7
[77] Genesis 28:22
[78] Genesis 41:34
[79] Genesis 41:40-41
[80] Genesis 41:41
[81] Genesis 41:45
[82] Genesis 47:18-19
[83] Genesis 47:23
[84] Genesis 47:1-12
[85] Genesis 41: 42
[86] Exodus 1:8
[87] Genesis 39:12
[88] Genesis 37:28
[89] Genesis 37:3
[90] Genesis 43:30
[91] Genesis 50:20
[92] 2nd Samuel 24:1
[93] 1st Chronicles 21:1
[94] Matthew 20:1-16
[95] Judges 11:1
[96] Judges 9:23
[97] Judges 11:29

HOW THE GOOD TAILOR GOT TO HEAVEN 317

[98] Judges 11:24
[99] Genesis 22:9-13
[100] Judges 11:30-40
[101] Genesis.6:2&4
[102] Genesis 3:24
[103] Judges 12:6
[104] Genesis.3:24
[105] Genesis 2:15
[106] Joshua 10:40
[107] Judges 15:15
[108] 2nd Samuel 23:8
[109] Judges 3:31
[110] Exodus 2:11-12
[111] Judges 4:21
[112] Joshua 2:3-4 and Joshua 2:12-13
[113] Joshua 5:14
[114] Joshua 6: 13 - 20
[115] Genesis 19: 36
[116] Genesis 38:15 - 26
[117] John 8: 4
[118] John 4:17-18
[119] 2nd Samuel 3:27 and 4:27
[120] 2nd Samuel 12:29-31
[121] Matthew 10:24
[122] Zechariah 8:23
[123] Isaiah 61:5-7
[124] Genesis 2:10-14
[125] 2nd Chronicles 4:2
[126] Genesis 28:12
[127] Exodus 20:5
[128] James 3:3
[129] Mark 2:27
[130] Luke 11:52

[131] Matthew 18:8-9
[132] James 4:14
[133] Luke 7:33-34
[134] Genesis 28:17 and 22
[135] Exodus 22:20
[136] Exodus 20:3
[137] Exodus 18:11
[138] Exodus 20:24
[139] Exodus 20:25
[140] 1st Kings 6:2-35
[141] 1st Kings 4:29
[142] 1st Kings 6:7
[143] Luke 19-21
[144] 1st Timothy 6:20
[145] Colossians 2:8
[146] Acts 4:13
[147] 1st John 2:15
[148] James 4:14
[149] Acts 2: 44-45 and 4:32-34
[150] Proverbs 1:10-16
[151] Galatians 3:12-13
[152] Acts 5:1-10
[153] Hebrews 11:1
[154] Mark 12:10-11
[155] Luke 12:20
[156] Proverbs 14:20
[157] Isaiah 45:7
[158] Luke 7:33-34 and 37-39
[159] Revelations 2:15
[160] Luke 12:15-21
[161] Matthew 19:12
[162] Leviticus 21:16-24
[163] Galatians 3:13 and Eph. 2:15

[164] Matthew.27:51, Mark 15:38 and Luke 23:45
[165] Revelations 3:15-16
[166] 1st Corinthians 10:23
[167] Acts 10:9-16
[168] Revelations 4:11
[169] Romans 14:14
[170] 1st John 4:8
[171] Colossians 2:20-21
[172] Revelations 22:2
[173] Acts 4:32
[174] 1st Corinthians 12:22-27
[175] Revelations 5:8-9
[176] Revelations 19:7-9
[177] Matthew 23:9
[178] Exodus 16:31
[179] 1st Corinthians 7:14
[180] 1st Corinthians 9:22
[181] James 2:19
[182] Luke 15:7
[183] Leviticus 18:6-18
[184] 1st Corinthians 7:36
[185] Mark3:35 and Matt. 12:48-49
[186] 2nd Timothy 3:16-17
[187] Leviticus 18:23
[188] 1st Corinthians 6:15-20
[189] 1st Corinthians 10:28-31
[190] 1st Corinthians 1:21 and 27-29
[191] John 3:14-15
[192] Numbers 21:9
[193] Genesis 3:1-6
[194] Exodus.3:14
[195] 1st Kings.8:12, 2nd Chronicles.6:11
[196] 2nd Chronicles.11:14

[197] Isaiah 14:12
[198] Genesis 50:10
[199] Ruth 3:2-6
[200] Mark 16:17-18
[201] Luke 10:19
[202] Genesis 19:23-24
[203] Genesis 19:22
[204] Genesis 19:32
[205] Luke 1:5
[206] Matthew 13:55
[207] Romans 11:32 and Hebrews 8:12
[208] Revelations 9:6-11
[209] Habakkuk 2:1
[210] Habakkuk 1:13
[211] Romans 13:1
[212] Acts 17:22
[213] 1st Corinthians 7:12-14
[214] 1st Corinthians 8:8
[215] 1st Corinthians 6:12
[216] 1st Corinthians 8:9-10
[217] 1st Corinthians 9:19-22
[218] 1st Corinthians 9:19-22
[219] St. John 13:14-15
[220] 2nd Kings 18:4
[221] Jeremiah 19:8-9
[222] 1st Samuel 5:4
[223] 2nd Samuel 6:14
[224] 2nd Samuel 6:20-23
[225] Numbers 31:14-18
[226] Numbers 31:35
[227] Esther 1:10-12
[228] Esther 2:2
[229] Esther 2:17

HOW THE GOOD TAILOR GOT TO HEAVEN

[230] Esther 3:6
[231] Esther 5:2-4
[232] Esther 7:2
[233] Esther 7:7-8
[234] Esther 7:10 and 8:2
[235] Esther 9:12 and 9:16
[236] Proverbs 15:3
[237] Matthew 18:10
[238] Proverbs 6:31
[239] Genesis 20:18
[240] Esther 1:16
[241] Ruth 2:3-4
[242] Deuteronomy 6:6-9
[243] Luke 4:8
[244] Hebrews 13:2 "Be not forgetful to entertain strangers: for thereby some have entertained angels unawares."
[245] Matthew 5:1. The sermon on the mount.
[246] Titus 3:10
[247] Isaiah 5:20
[248] 2nd Samuel 13:13 "Ask the king; he will not withhold me from thee."
[249] Mark 5:9
[250] Matthew 4:1-4. "Then was Jesus led up into the wilderness to be tempted of the Devil, and when he had fasted forty days and forty nights, he was afterward a hungered. And the tempter said, if thou be the son of God command these stones to become bread." and Exodus 24:18 and 34:28. Moses goes up on the mountaintop and fasts for forty days and forty nights, and receives the Ten Commandments.
[251] Matthew 4:9 "All these things will I give thee, if thou wilt fall down and worship me."
[252] 1st Timothy 5: 23
[253] 2nd Timothy 1:7

[254] Matthew 6:26-30 and Luke 12:6
[255] Revelations 6:2, 4, 5, 8; Rev. 4:3, 7; Rev.5:4, 6; Rev. 12: 3, 5; and Rev. 13:2
[256] Deuteronomy 29:5-6
[257] 1st Samuel Ch. 28
[258] Isaiah 3:15
[259] Revelations 16:13
[260] 1st Samuel 2:7
[261] Isaiah 14:12
[262] Genesis 3:16
[263] John 3:14-15, Numbers 21:8-9, 2nd Kings 18:4
[264] Isaiah 3:17 & 47:3
[265] Matthew 14:6
[266] Mark 10:21
[267] Acts 2:44-45, & 4:32-35
[268] Proverbs 7:12 & 7:27
[269] Deuteronomy 22:19
[270] Deuteronomy 23:18
[271] Luke 8:2-3
[272] Genesis Ch. 30

Chapter 18

A DEMON IN THE AMEN CORNER

Spera Venus resumed her steady rotation around the mundane, central-most point of everything, and she promised the Cherubic Review Board to not disconcert mortal stargazers by straying from her assignments forevermore, so she was moved up to teaching the third grade. *Spera Sol's* sphere revolved forty times causing the sun to rise and set an equal number of times above the very center of the universe. There had been twelve hundred and ninety-seven robberies in King Jamesburg, also sixty-seven rapes; four hundred and eighty-nine aggravated assaults; seven hundred and twelve major fires, two hundred suspected arson; automobile thefts were at an all time high; and Tim Monahan had shot Officer Flaharety with his own service revolver, which he found hanging on his bedroom doorknob one afternoon. Tamar's list of molesters grew to include her school counselor; the hook-nosed, wiry, gas station attendant; the druggist; and three of her elder brother's male friends. These last three went unreported. The president assured the nation that the efficacies of his policies were the reason for the decline in the crime rate: "I can see the light around the bend in the tunnel," he said. Then he RIFed a further sixty-seven clerks who compile such data. The Sacred Roman Rota confirmed the papal encyclical, which stated that fellatio was not a sexual act so long as it was heterosexual.

One of the heated controversies on the national scene was whether the Pentagon building should be placed on wheels and moved about on a racetrack with appropriate concealment to foil any enemy's "smart missiles." Some of the un-American doves in Congress were willing to sell out to the patriotic hawks in return for the hawks support of their bill. The doves wanted a publisher of pornography, who had become a born-again Christian, to be authorized to write the school prayer for the nation. It became political because the president's sister had led the publisher to Christ. The price of stock seesawed wildly led by advances and declines in the cement industry, and a certain pornographic magazine.

One of the more reliable weekly newspapers headlined the fact that a famous movie actress had given birth to five, even more startling was that they were all Doberman Pinschers. So all in all, Abigail was right. The world soon forgot Lemuel, and his wanted poster became a shabby discard at the bottom of a high stack of others. The world had gone on to better things.

After his dismal sermonizing performance, Abigail thought Lemuel could learn something of the craft by watching some of the electronic evangelists. She also wanted to prove to him that although they often waved it about, they seldom dared to read more than two or three lines from the Bible to make their point. He soon developed an addiction for the temples of the airwaves, and Abigail soon wished she'd never opened that channel of pious adulation. She heard her kind being blamed for all of mankind's woes with hateful acidic rhetoric several times a day, and she'd stick out her tongue at the TV set or toss down a couple of ounces of ninety proof bourbon. Even worse than the hell, fire, and damnation preachers, who saw sin and demonic possession everywhere, were the syrupy sweet ones with their plastic smiles and optimistic messages; they'd cause her to eat a pickle or bite a lemon to get rid of the treacly aftertaste.

HOW THE GOOD TAILOR GOT TO HEAVEN — 325

Eventually, Lemuel began to notice omissions in their sermons. These preachers all seemed to be terribly misinformed. They hardly ever gave any credit to the angels of the Empyreal Establishment. He began to take the slight personally; moreover, they frequently credited demons with causing some mortal political policy. Their messages diminished the Lord's power, and the ministrations of the guardian, lying, evil, and avenging angels. Were these preachers all conspiring in some massive disinformation campaign? When bad things happen to good people, it's certainly not because the Lord is powerless or indifferent, it's all part of His grand design: the potter hath power over the clay. The demons were indifferent to the fate of mankind; none of them even bothered voting.

Venting his outrage, he said, "Haven't any of them read their Bibles, Abigail? It states quite clearly: 'Being predestined according to the purpose of Him who worketh all things after the council of His own will.[1'] The Bible says *all things*! How many times have they said; 'If the Lord wills it, or by God's will.'[2] Do they think those are meaningless expressions? They have no power over God's will. Their politicians tell lies, and the Bible explains, 'And for this cause God shall send them strong delusion, that they should believe a lie:'[3] It's the Lord's way."

Lemuel's ecclesiastical ratiocination caused Abigail to pour herself another big drink of Beam's Black Label, and say, "You can straighten them all out from your pulpit, Lem." If she was less committed to her cause, Lemuel's damnation, she would have chucked the whole project, but Abigail could be stubborn.

So could the TV preacher who, at the moment, was railing about the execrable fate that was awaiting those who used strong drink and tobacco. "Demon rum! And the Devil's weed."

Abigail decided to light up a cigarette to go with her drink. She had been trapped by her own stubbornness into drinking whisky, smoking cigarettes, and sucking on lemons. She finally got Lem to reduce his listening and viewing time by pointing out that he was neglecting his Bible studies.

During one particularly scathing attack by an electronic evangelist, she snapped off the set, and said, "They're all a pack of hypocrites! If their message is: 'The way to salvation is to love everyone, including your enemies,' how come you never hear them say a kind word for demons?"

"They rarely mention the angels either, Abigail, but I love you."

"What if the demons were really suffering the torments they describe? You'd think they'd show some compassion, but all you hear from them are vituperation and criticism. It's only good manners, you know. If you can't say something nice about someone, you shouldn't say anything at all."

Lemuel agreed that he would bear that point in mind during his sermons.

He also questioned the unscrupulous methods some of the preachers used to collect souls. Some used a very questionable method indeed. They bade the mortals to commit to the Lord by kneeling before their TV screens and said they could be saved by placing their hand against the picture tube. One charlatan even claimed to be able to heal them by this method, and the Bible clearly says: "They shall lay hands on the sick, and they shall recover."[4] Another thing that disturbed him was the opulent auditoriums available to these ministers, and he could see how large their congregations were as the cameras panned the multitudes. He started to fear that there might not be ten thousand unregenerate souls left in America.

"Oh sure there are," she replied encouragingly. "You'll see. But you'll have to come up with an appealing act." She tapped her teeth with a fingernail, and mused, "Something they'll really want to get involved in…"

"Temple prostitution is out, Abigail."

"Esther thought it might be a good idea, and you're not going to attract them with the power of your oratory."

He stared bleakly into his palms. Maybe Tomas and Orson had been right when they advised him to go with one of the big organizations…still, there was that disagreeableness with Father Angus. Lemuel was a brown study in despair, and all attempts by Abigail to cheer him up with sweet morsels and soft words had failed. Even when smoothing sunscreen on her posterior, he seemed distracted and uninterested in her satiny flesh.

His moodiness affronted Abigail's feminine pride, and she finally said, "How do you know you'll fail? You haven't tried yet. I'll help, if you want me to. We'll leave here and visit a few churches, and you can decide what you want to do then. There's plenty of time. You don't have to decide right away."

Her encouraging words didn't help; he didn't have plenty of time. Abigail was ageless, but he was aging. He thought he should have started from a more youthful age. It was a mistake to think that a few gray hairs at his temples would command consideration and respect. America was currently enamored by youth. "How old would you say I am, Abigail?"

"I know how old you are. You are the same as me, created on the second day. We're six thousand years old."

"No, I mean as a mortal. How many years do I have left?"

"Oh, I'd say you're fortyish, so you've got plenty of time. Thirty years or so."

He did the mental arithmetic. "That means that I have to save over three hundred souls a year for the rest of my life." Then he moaned, "Oh why, oh why, didn't I start from a younger age? Come on let's get started. I'll do what you say. We'll visit a few churches. Maybe I'll stumble onto something useful."

* * *

They cleaned up their campsite, stowed their gear, hooked up the trailer, and started to leave. Something compelled them to stop after they'd driven fifty yards, and hand-in-hand they walked back and stood silently regarding the peaceful glade where they had spent the last forty days and nights. They both felt a sense of regret as they walked slowly back to the truck. At Pearl's cabin the good-byes were awkwardly tearful, but there was happiness too. The electric co-op was bringing in the power lines.

At the road Abigail thought it was time for Lemuel to resume his driving lessons and turned the wheel over to him. He discovered it was easier driving up the twisting mountain road than it had been coming down. When they reached the parkway they decided to head south, by the flip of a coin. At Waynesboro they came to an interstate and flipped the coin once more, and headed west. Then at the next interstate they turned southwest, as the coin decided. It was near Bristol where they set up camp, and Lemuel began auditing live church services.

Abigail told him that, taken as a whole, the Baptists were the largest denomination in America. He was aware of the sect, and corrected her by prompting, "You mean Anabaptists." She shrugged indifferently, and went on to explain that there were several schisms under the general heading, but that the Southern Baptist Convention claimed the largest membership. So they decided to attend a small, nearby, rural church that belonged to that group.

If the reader has a mental image of the little brown church in the wildwood; the little brown church in the dell; this church was its model. The parking lot in the side yard was full of pickup trucks, dusty sedans, and three shiny motorcycles laden with chromium tubes, cooling fins, caps, and long, black leather seats.

The services had already started, and voices of the singing congregation greeted them. There was a group of teenagers standing on the lawn sharing a couple of cigarettes. They stopped talking and stared at Abigail and Lemuel as they went up the steps to the front door. One of the boys said something too low for Lemuel to hear, and the girls giggled. Abigail nudged Lemuel with her elbow and whispered, "You ought to reconsider my idea about temple prostitution. What'd I tell you?" He gave her a stern disapproving glare.

Abigail wore a simple, white linen suit with a green silk neckerchief that matched her eyes; a leghorn hat set at a rakish angle; brown and white spectator pumps; and carried a matching handbag. The white suit accentuated her dark skin, and she was easily the darkest person in the congregation. Lemuel wore his blue suit, but it was not out of place. The menfolk, who wore suits, looked as though their suits had come from the same tailor. Several of the parishioners exchanged glances as they took seats in a pew near the back of the church. The low buzzing sound of whispers permeated the fourth stanza of, "We Would See Jesus," and Abigail distinctly heard the words, "High yella." in the low buzzing. Lemuel heard nothing but the music from the electric organ and the elevated voices.

The minister was a man in his late twenties or early thirties who wore a smile as sincere as naugahyde, a dove gray suit with maroon pinstriping, black shoes, a white shirt, and a striped yellow tie. He had dark blond hair that was brushed to a patent leather smoothness. His voice projected above all others during the singing.

Abigail noticed a shellacked plywood plaque, shaped like an ogee arch, on the right front wall. She surmised that the numbers affixed to the plaque denoted the songs to be sung, so she took a hymnal from the rack on the back of the pew in front of them, and found the page: A hymn titled "Others." She nudged Lemuel, and held the book so he could follow the lyrics. He whispered that he knew the words of all the hymns, having heard them so much over the centuries. During the next singing Lemuel's tenor overpowered the minister's baritone, and with a momentary tremolo, the minister elevated his volume. Not to be outdone in piety, Lemuel raised his voice a couple of decibels, and the minister did also. By the time they got to the third stanza, Lemuel and the minister were belting out about the needs of others at the top of their lungs. The rest of the congregation's decibelic piety was a pallid thing compared to the lusty voices of the two men.

The preacher decided to skip the next hymn and get right to the sermon. He started off in modulated tones about their good fortune to be born in this blessed land, and commended the wisdom of their forefathers for having brought God's seed to these shores. Next he evoked the Lord's highest blessings on the sainted entrepreneurs who provided employment in the nearby furniture factory, and asked the Lord to forgive the misguided labor union organizers, "outsiders," who had come to their peaceful town to make trouble, and restrict a worker's right to work. He was soon pacing like a caged panther as he inveighed against: "drugs, the devil's weed, and demon rum." Abigail slouched slightly. Then he drew a parallel between the "Communist conspiracy" to enslave us, and "drugs, the devil's weed, and demon rum," and Abigail slouched a bit further. She wondered how such a pleasant-looking young man could manage to twist his features into such a horrible mask. He ranted and paced, and he smote the palm of his left hand with the back of his right hand several times. He came back to the rostrum and gripped the top with his hands on either side of the large open Bible. He proclaimed, "Satan's brew, alcohol, has corrupted the entire Russian nation." It was the main reason for them turning from God. By their own government's statistics they admit that ninety-seven percent of their population is besotted. "Drunkenness, atheistic Satanism, and Communism are all entwined like serpents in that evil empire, and focus of evil."

Abigail decided it would not be polite to freeze the preacher's face at the point of its most grotesque expression, or to rain down a torrent of frogs on the congregation since this was a training session for Lemuel, but she did whisper to him, " Isn't 'atheistic Satanism' a contradiction in terms?"

Finally, the crescendo of bile receded, and in the waning volume they heard the preacher praise the work of their missions in Asia and the need to give encouragement to the fine work of the Christian schools, and that a special collection was being taken up for the new baptismal pool to be installed behind the altar. Although she was not normally given to spite, when the collection plate was passed to her, she clanked a quarter against its rim and changed all the currency inside of the pledge envelopes to one dollar denominations.

They lingered behind since Lemuel wanted to have a few words with the minister. As the parishioners filed past, most stared inquisitively at the two strangers and many wore forced smiles. Others looked disapprovingly from Lemuel to Abigail. Some of the men glared harshly at them, and Lemuel overheard one of them mutter to his wife, "Never thought I'd ever see any miscegenation here on Walker mountain." Lemuel wondered how the man knew that Abigail was a demon, and was about to inform him that there wasn't any genating going on between himself and Abigail, but Abigail put her hand on his wrist and warned him to keep quiet.

As Lemuel and the preacher stood together on the porch of the church, he mentioned that he noticed that the only time the minister read from the Bible was when he was comparing the owner of the vineyard[5] who paid equal wages for unequal work, with the worker's rights in the furniture factory to independently negotiate their wages. He complemented the minister about the way he had drawn a neat parallel between the complainers in the vineyard, who thought they should have received higher wages, and the radical labor organizers. He congratulated the preacher for having the insight to inform the parishioners about the Lord's position on labor unrest, "As in heaven, so on earth." Then he informed the preacher that he was also a man of the cloth, and that he was wondering if the preacher knew of any churches that needed a minister.

The preacher complimented Lemuel on his fine singing voice, and informed him that he had heard of a church that was looking for a minister. It was two counties over, and into the next state, but he couldn't recall the name of the church. However, he was certain that if Lemuel went over to the next state, and asked around, he would find it.

A conclave of deacons stood on the lawn, holding their Bibles and engaging in an intense discussion in very low voices. As it happened, they were in the process of hiring a new preacher, and this preacher was trying out for the job. But to judge by the expressions on some of their faces, it wasn't likely they would be interested in Lemuel and his dark wife.

When they arrived back at the trailer, Abigail kicked off her shoes, sank into the club chair, and asked Lemuel to hand her the bourbon and a glass. She downed two double shots.

Chapter 19

BRISTOL STRADDLES THE BORDER BETWEEN TWO STATES. Geologists and naturalists studying the terrain, flora, or fauna of the area can discern no appreciable distinctions on either side of the line. However, the more profound thinkers in the legislatures of Nashville and Richmond can see the difference. Also, entrepreneurs, whose selfless quest to provide the consumer with those commodities for which they have "effective demand," can see the difference. So those purveyors of "goods and services" that are frowned on in one state capitol, but regarded as beneficent in the other, agglomerate here. And while merchants on both sides of the dividing street vie with each other in tawdriness, one side, because of legalisms, has an advantage, and the other is handicapped. Lemuel declared that the Tennessee side of the town was the worst sink of degenerate humanity he'd seen since Babylon and maintained that opinion right up until he saw Texarkana.

Before that revelation, Abigail and Lemuel meandered over and around the mountains and hills of the region looking for the parish that Lemuel had heard was looking for a preacher. Abigail, although knowing virtually nothing of church affairs or politics, manufactured a doctor of divinity diploma from a highly-regarded heartland seminary, as well as an excellent transcript, *cum laude*, and she inserted his name in the circuitry register, as well as several letters of recommendation. But the sought-for, shepherdless flock always seemed to be two counties away, or so the preachers, deacons, and elders informed them. In the all-white churches, Abigail was thought to be a mulatto or an Indian. In the all-black churches, Lemuel's complexion was only half the problem; Abigail was thought to be Hispanic, Sicilian, or Jewish. Lemuel found many religious denominations headquartered in the region, but the divinity schools were matriculating theological scholars in record numbers and the registries of clergy seeking positions were lengthy. Despite his excellent credentials, he received no referrals. Although Abigail was losing some of her tan, she was still dark enough to cause deacons to sneak questioning glances in her direction.

They also audited any church service that was in progress. In the rural regions the services, and the congregation's attitude, were much the same as the wildwood church. In the metropolitan churches, where the congregations were occasionally of mixed races, a mixed race couple still drew attention. Their quest took them to churches of many denominations, as well as mosques, synagogues, tabernacles, chapels, and cathedrals. Abigail felt that she was erroneously maligned in every one of them.

Satan, the demons, and their fellow travelers (the Communist sympathizing socialistic liberals) were blamed for: drunkenness, herpes, AIDS, abortion, promiscuity, the loss of family farms, bureaucrats, the drug problem, prostitution, homosexuality, the national debt, unionism, divorces, corrupting children, OSHA, rock and roll music with Satanic messages when played backward, pornography, the EPA, the ERA, the Arab conspiracy, the Jewish conspiracy, the UN, the feminists, and the Tri-lateral commission and its pinko religious liberal organization, The World Council of Churches. They were also responsible for removing prayer from the classrooms, the fifty-five mile per hour speed limit, the American Civil Liberties Union, welfare going to the undeserving poor, the anti-gun lobby, the anti-defense lobby, the crime rate, constipation, and back pain. And in one church, the preacher went into detail about how the second law of thermodynamics proved that the Creationists were right. Lemuel still didn't understand, and Abigail didn't care. During this period her breath wore a constant aroma of bourbon.

Another thing Lemuel noticed was there was no mortification of the flesh and no hint of ritual fasting, nor did he see any signs of the alternative worship—the voluptuous feast and celebration. These people were obviously the lukewarm moralists Myles warned that he should avoid. Some young people were moved by the Holy Ghost to confess their sins and the sins of their fathers. With tears streaming down their faces, they fell on their knees before the congregation and were forgiven with resounding "Hallelujah"s and "Praise the Lord"s.

Only in one service did Lemuel find a congregation approaching a high degree of ecstacy. The preacher was a crude and grizzled rustic, wearing a broad-brimmed felt hat, a chalk-striped, blue serge suit, and a pair of yellow cowboy boots. His worship service was near to one Myles had taught. It was held in a woodland glade and the parishioners groveled on the ground and spoke in tongues. Serpents were handed around and they drank poison from mason jars. Everyone became dusty and covered with crushed leaves and seed pods as they quivered their spastic ecstasies of fusion with the Holy Ghost amid several terrified rattlers. Abigail swore the only ecstasy that minister felt was when he put his hand on her thigh. "The laying on of hands, sister; here try it," he had whispered.

Only one service pleased her. It was in a medium-sized cathedral. There was a caparisoned priest at the altar; the singing of the choir was beautiful; the organ music majestic; the parishioners intently prayerful; all the motions of the priest and his assistants solemn and graceful—and then Lemuel explained what the Mass celebrated. They were there to witness the priest drink the blood and eat the body of Christ, and all those people lined up were going to eat His body also. She had never known that before and nearly vomited.

After one especially churchified weekend, Abigail and her fellow demons had been the brunt of much acrimony and false indictment. The whole messy affair at Calvary was laid to demonic possession. Whereas the electronic church caused her to down a couple of shots, the real, in-the-flesh, hell, fire, and damnation variety caused her to down three quarts of ninety-proof bourbon over that weekend. On Monday morning, Abigail awoke with something that seldom affects demons: a hangover. It was a stomach-churning, head-pounding, eyeball-burning beaut. She staggered to the refrigerator, got a can of tomato juice, a bottle of Tabasco sauce, and fixed herself a Snappy Tom with a shot of vodka. This slapped her to her knees once again, this time in front of the toilet, where she tried to vomit out all that hatred. Between nauseous gasps, and retching dry heaves, she vowed she'd never go near another church again. If any of her souls got loose inside of a church, they'd have to find their own way out. The retching caused her belly muscles to ache, adding to the intestinal distress. Her head ached, but worse was the impression that she was becoming hydrocephalic. She looked into the mirror, expecting to see the bulbous evidence, but there was only an ashen-faced, hollow-eyed, stringy-haired wretch staring back at her.

Lemuel nursed her for two days, and tiptoed about. The slightest wobble of the trailer caused her to moan. Faith healing had no effect; Lemuel tried that. Finally, after drinking a gallon of Alka Seltzer, she could hold down a soupy mix of milk and ice cream, commonly known as drunkard's delight, and a few vanilla cookies. And so what the Lord could not, or refused to cure, time at last healed, and she could hold down some dry toast. Then she had a couple of soft scrambled eggs, and some tomato juice—neat. Alas, like so many of those Monday morning vows, with the color back in her cheeks, and a spring once more back in her step, she allowed herself to backslide and started discussing Lemuel's churchly vocation once more.

The experience did teach them both something. Lemuel vowed there would be no spewing of hatred from his rostrum. An even hand, a kind word, and simple faith within the bounds of the Holy Bible would be his message. She made an overly-stagy facial expression with her tongue in her cheek to demonstrate her skepticism that it was possible. He tried to reassure her. He said he could depend on the assistance of the other ethereal angels working behind the scenes to assist. "The potter hath power over the clay," he reminded her. He explained that Tomas advised him to lower the content his services to the low water mark of the cultural mean, like the apostle Paul did: To be, all things, to all people. But Lemuel assured her that he would focus on Jesus' commandment that they love their neighbors.[6] "Sometimes the way people want to be led are of a coarse and brutal nature and provoke intense feelings of animus toward others. We've just experienced that. There's no good reason for sermons to be so filled with hatred. My message will be of love and togetherness and forgiveness, and everyone can come and feel wanted, even terrestrial angels."

During this period of pastoral foraging for a flock, they wended their way on a zigzag course on either side of the Mississippi River, and then along the north Gulf coast: the redneck Rivera. They found much loudly-asserted piety, but little actually practiced. Hedonism of the coarsest variety was the norm. What little remained of the former Southern gentility, was pushed aside to make room for the floating casinos, saloons, and the usual collection of strip-mall sleaziness of tourist meccas. These were supported by the pay checks of the mortals from the military bases, ship yards, weapons manufacturers, chemical plants, oil refineries, commercial docks, steel fabrication plants, and oil tank farms. Above ground pipelines snaked from one industrial complex to another, or down to the barges on the river. It all made a mockery of the state's slogan, "Sportsman's Paradise." A perpetual haze floated in the air.

Abigail said, "This is what causes their meanness. They see this ugliness, breathe the fetid air, work here, and live here, but their preachers and politicians applaud their industry. They bury the obvious squalor in their subconscious and it surfaces in their conscious thoughts as blaming someone else; the blacks, whitey, the Vietnamese, demons, and so on, for their problems."

Lemuel could see why the Empyreal Establishment imposed such strict regulations on the mortals' souls, and resisted mechanization, if this was the result of worldliness. He said, "Surely this is the result of demonic influence. We have industry without squalor in heaven."

"No, we terrestrial angels stay out of their affairs as much as possible. They did this on their own, or else Yahweh made them do it to annoy us terrestrial angels. There are still a few places left that are natural, like the glade where we stayed in the mountains. The government holds back the commercial interests, but the government is starting to be overwhelmed by the greed and population pressures."

* * *

Their travels had taken them as far south as they could go and remain in the United States. The next country was Mexico. They turned eastward and crossed the high bridge to South Padre Island. At its southern tip the island was undergoing massive development and the gleaming white apartment towers reminded Lemuel of the gleaming structures in Heaven, but there was every sort of sordid commerce at street level. They decided to head north on the narrow spit of sand, and set up camp on the beach by the intensely green Gulf waters. They drove several miles along the shore, slightly beyond the bathers and surf fishermen, to where they had the beach mostly to themselves. Lemuel was depressed by the months of rejection, and decided that if he could not go to the people, he'd stay in one place for a while and let the people come to him.

Lemuel was still addicted to the electric ministry and Abigail usually went for a walk while he watched the television preachers. Her hangover was still fresh in her mind and she didn't want to be driven to drink. He was also interested in the other programs, and the subliminal messages about the American way of life registered clearly on his mind. Obviously the southern quadrant of the nation that he had just seen must have been different from the rest of the nation, because all the dramas clearly showed a different America where the real beneficiaries of the American system were the black race. Pearl and Zotis must have been the exceptions. For the most part, these dramas showed the black race as clearly in the upper stratum of society. They held supervisory positions in police departments or were high government officials, and they seemed to excel in the professions and the performing arts. Their prowess at sports won fortune and celebrity for them, and scholarships to the finest schools in the country. When they chose menial, lower level, types of employment, they were always far more sagacious and more honest than the whites who employed them. They often saved their white employers from their own misguided stupidities. Occasionally the news programs tried to portray a somewhat different viewpoint, but he dismissed these as being badly cast performances, as they had a tendency to overact for the scenes where they were shown in squalid surroundings.

By far, the mortals who received the least benefit from the "democracy" system were the white American farmers. Their plight was so harsh and miserable there on Walton's Mountain, or out on the Western prairies, that Lemuel wondered why God had chosen to make their lives so miserable. He commented to Abigail that perhaps if they prayed more often, God might let them become happy employees behind the counters of the fast food outlets he saw in the commercials.

Lemuel was not surprised by the sex and violence which was a staple fare of much of the programing. The tableaus in the Garden of Thelassar that glorified the acts of Biblical heros were actually much bloodier, and sexually perverse, than anything he saw on television. He grumbled that, once again, like those tableaus in the heavenly Eden, the mortals ignored the involvement of angels in their lives with the exception of one or two programs. And then they were misrepresented. If Abigail was any example, they misrepresented the demons too. But for Lemuel, the television set was the "nonpareil information disseminator that welded the diverse elements of the American mortals into a coordinating nation."

Abigail saw it somewhat differently. She described it as "an intellectual cornucopia that worked in reverse. It sucked up any diverse elements of wisdom, like a vacuum cleaner, and spit out a bland pablum like mush from a very narrow mouthpiece." But despite her low opinion of television programing, she was not above using it to cause Lemuel to descend a further notch toward apostasy.

They had been together for nearly four months, and so far Lemuel hadn't been able to gather a flock or to save even one soul. Abigail hadn't been able to cause his defection either. He was madly devoted to her, but that was not the same thing. He was also dependent on her for his food and lodging, and since he had never had to fend for himself, he didn't think of food and travel expenses being supplied *gratis* as a debt to be repaid. Abigail didn't mind, since creating a few extra dollars was no trouble, but she thought he might be forced to come over if he was made to face the real world. Lemuel still had the same thirty-seven dollars change from his original three hundred heavenly-issued currency, and he adamantly refused to touch any of Abigail's demonically created money. Tennessee Ernie Ford's ballad about the plight of the coal miner who owed his soul to the company store gave her the idea. If she could get Lemuel to want something bad enough to borrow money from her, then she'd have him. The slave chains of debt are not easily cast off. She'd get him to borrow some money from her, make him sign a note, in blood of course, using his only valuable collateral—his soul.

Her chance came during a regular Sunday morning broadcast of America's foremost purveyor of electronic salvation, and Abigail was about to go for a stroll along the beach instead of seeking the fallacious subreption of bourbon. Lemuel made an offhand comment that while the preacher was Biblically correct, he displayed considerable self-indulgent sanctimony. He idly wondered if the preacher was actually an angel like himself. His eschatological knowledge seemed inordinately extensive for him to not have first-hand knowledge, obviously well above simple mortal faith. "But I don't think that the Lord himself could exhibit that much arrogance. Look closely, Abigail. He's just coming to the part about the shortage of schoolroom space in the Christian schools. Do you think he could be one of yours?"

HOW THE GOOD TAILOR GOT TO HEAVEN

"That's absurd!" she replied indignantly, but looked closely just to make sure. As she studied the image, she muttered, "He is a pompous ass. No terrestrial angel would ever make such a ridiculous exhibition of themselves." Then she whistled low, and said, "Look at the suit he's wearing. That's very expensive tailoring."

"Maybe it's a terrestrial angel doing it for the money?" he suggested, using her preferred appellative. He now used the term demon only when he was angry with her.

"You know we conjure our money and we certainly don't have to stoop that low. Maybe back in the old days before paper money, but not now."

"Maybe he gets a thrill from the power he holds over his parishioners. See how they hang onto his every word."

"No, that kind of attention would restrict our freedom. He's just another ambitious mortal." *But he could be a useful one*, she thought. His expensively-tailored suit might provide the leverage she needed to get Lemuel to sign over his soul. She said, "But you could learn a lesson from him. Just imagine yourself up there before that huge audience and broadcasting your image into millions of homes. Then imagine yourself wearing that shabby suit that you brought down from heaven. Who do you think you would impress? Nobody, that's who! They didn't even issue you a vest. See, he has one. See how important and knowledgeable his suit makes him look? Now that's the sort of man humans will place confidence in."

"Gee! I don't know…ah…how much do you think…"

She was way ahead of him. "Oh, I'd guess about a thousand dollars. You'd also need shoes, shirts, neckties…yeah. Let's say about twelve-hundred for each outfit. And you ought to have two or three."

"I've only got thirty-seven dollars."

"And you look it, too. That's probably why those churches wouldn't hire you."

Lemuel thought for a few moments. His moral rectitude would not allow him to ask her for the money. *She may be right about the suit, though.*

He said, "I know what. I'll get a regular job, and I can earn the money that way. When we came through the town I saw a sign at one of the construction sites. They wanted carpenters and helpers."

"Do you have any experience at carpentry?" she snickered skeptically.

"Well...not exactly what you'd call experience, but I've watched the souls at work up in heaven, and it didn't look all that hard."

"Uh huh. Well, your camping clothes should be all right, but you'll need tools. Those guys have to supply their own tools. If you get a helper's job you'll need a hammer, a hatchet, a tri-square, a folding ruler and tape, a carpenter's pencil, and a nail apron. They'll cost you about fifty dollars, and of course I'll be happy to fix your lunches until you get your first pay."

"All that?"

"Sure, and that's not much. A regular carpenter has to spend over a thousand dollars for his tools. He has to have handsaws, chisels, drills, drill bits, levels, a framing square, measuring tapes, a folding rule, chalk line, screw drivers, planes, power tools..."

* * *

Abigail dropped Lemuel off at the job site at a quarter past seven in the morning. Since he wouldn't accept money from her, he did without the hatchet and used the free nail apron the lumberyard gave away. The project was a large, two-story motel, and Lemuel was put to work with a short, stocky Chicano laying the plywood roof sheathing. The Mexican complemented Lemuel on the wisdom of choosing a Mexican *esposa*, and then they began the business of pounding in nails. They had not been working for ten minutes when the Mexican asked him if he had ever used a hammer before. "What is it with this, tap, tap, tap? Drive them suckers in! You ain't playing patty cake, you know."

Lemuel watched as the Mexican set the eight-penny nail a third of its length, and the second blow drove the nail up to the head. Gradually he learned to drive the nails home with three blows. He hit his thumb with the hammer and howled with pain. The sun rose higher and the day got hotter. His back and underarms were wet with sweat, his shirt clung to his dripping wet torso, and his pants were drenched down to his thighs. The Mexican continued like a machine: whup, wham, whup, wham, whup, wham. His hammer beat out its two-note rhythm, and he only paused to lay in another sheet of plywood.

Lemuel skinned his arm on the rough edge of the material, drove several long slivers into his palm, and the hammer handle raised large watery blisters on the palm of his right hand. The blisters soon broke and became raw, and both hands raged with pain. The thumb on his left hand throbbed from the hammer blow, the punctures in his palms ached, and the raw meat under his broken blisters burned with hellfire. At lunchtime they scrambled down the ladder and ate in the shade cast on the north side of the building. It seemed as though every muscle in his body ached. The Mexican calmly ate a couple of burritos from the lunch wagon, and drank a Modelo. He offered Lemuel a beer from his cooler, which was greatly appreciated, and Lemuel noticed the girth of the little Mexican's arms, like a weight lifter's, and his hands were gnarled and horn hard.

He had no sooner finished swallowing the last bite of his sandwich when a whistle blew, and he and the carpenter scrambled back up the ladder. The noise of construction resumed: the siren loud whine of skill saws, the thumps and poundings of hammers, the grating of handsaws, the rattle and clatter of a load of pipe being dumped somewhere, and the deep powerful guttural voice of a bulldozer raised and lowered as the operator graded around the building.

Abigail came at four o'clock to pick him up. He was sitting on the ground with his back resting against a stack of lumber. The rest of the workmen were joking and laughing with each other while they climbed into their pickups and cars and headed home, or to a nearby beer joint. Lemuel stumbled over to Abigail's truck, got in gingerly, and sat silently as they drove back to the trailer. He had drawn his pay for the day: twenty-nine dollars and fifty cents. N*ot even enough to pay for the instruments of my torture,* he thought wryly, and prodded the tools lying at his feet with a boot.

He did a bit of quick calculation in his head and determined that it would take him nearly two months to earn enough to buy one suit like the one the TV preacher wore. He doubted that he could last a week if today was a typical workday. Then he began to rationalize. *My calling is the ministry. What am I doing out there pounding nails? I can't save any souls that way.* And so, like another famous carpenter, he decided to give up the trade and to devote his full time to other people's salvation.

Back at the trailer Lemuel soaked his aching body in a tub full of hot water liberally softened with Abigail's scented bath salts. While he lay in the soothing, silky, warm bath he was planning his next step. For an angel who had only been exposed to orthodox Ricardo-Smithian-Malthusian heavenly economics, his mind was toying with some decidedly Keynesian theory. *She could conjure the money and let me use it, and then as soon as I get established and the congregation puts their money in the collection plate, I'd pay her back. She could make the money disappear as the loan was repaid, and that way it wouldn't upset the mortal's economy. After all, if we take back exactly what we put in it should all come out even, and think of all the souls we would save.*

Lemuel came out of his tub a new man. He picked Abigail up and twirled her about, and told her that he had figured out a solution to the problem. She was flustered, but pleased to see him so elated, and returned to the lamb roast she was preparing. He told her the general outline of his plan. She congratulated him for finally coming to his senses and agreed that it was a marvelous idea, and immediately conjured a thousand for his new suit. "Since this will be a legal contract, I'm sure you want everything done properly. We'll have to draw up some paperwork. Nothing too complicated, or legalistic, you understand," she said while wearing her most disarming smile.

"No! no! We'll need much more than that. Let's build a church!" he said enthusiastically, and picked up the small pile of bills, folded the packet double, and put it in his robe pocket. Abigail smiled at his *bitti fakement* (small theft), understanding that he had quickly learned to value money.

During supper Abigail playfully asked him if he thought that he had learned enough about construction after only one day on the job to build a church. Lemuel replied that he wasn't going to do the actual construction himself. "You know, that's only a figure of speech. Naturally we'll hire a contractor." Abigail chuckled, but was much too ladylike to point out the obvious parallel between his comment and her own story of how the world was created.

The next morning Lemuel was stiff and sore, but happy that the Lord had shown him the way. He and Abigail walked along the beach, hand-in-hand, discussing the project. The Gulf waters were pale green, and calm, lazy waves curled at an angle to the hard, white sand, turning it brown and washing warm, white foam up and over their bare feet. The weekend beach crowd flowed up the beach populating their sanctuary with families, couples, and solitary fishermen. Small children splashed about in the shallows, and farther out older children and teens swam and hand paddled surfboards. The sea was calm, but there was enough breeze to propel several brightly-colored sailboards, which skimmed along at a modest speed. Abigail conformed to convention and wore a modest canary yellow swim suit, and Lemuel wore blue jeans and was bare chested.

Abigail described a cute little church which she had seen in New England: white clapboard with a soaring steeple, with snow white pews and walnut trim. "Everything looked so chaste, and clean looking." But Lemuel thought that because they were situated in a region that was very much like the Holy Land: the seashore, the desert, and irrigated farmland, (Abigail added silently, *'border problems and fundamentalist*) that the design should reflect the locale.

Then she described a "dear little adobe church" that she had seen in Ranchos De Taos, New Mexico. Lemuel thought that might be a good idea, but since they decided that Texas was so very much like the Holy Land, that their church should be authentically Biblical. Abigail reminded him of his promise that the services couldn't be offensive to her: "No hell, fire, and damnation preaching. And absolutely no more lies about the terrestrial angels."

He swore on his word of honor as an angel that his services would conform to her requirements, and to the Scriptures. That would be the right thing to do, since she was the one who was putting up the money. They also decided that since Lemuel was only concerned with the more elevated matters, such as the soul and heaven, that it would be best if the terrestrial angel managed the earthly matters, such as the money. Abigail would be the church's treasurer.

They walked back to the trailer to study the Bible and see what the Bible advised. Lemuel was secretly tickled that he was finally going to get her to read the holy word. They sat outside under the sheltering awning with the book on her lap. Lemuel showed her the passage where Jacob set up the stone he had used for a pillow as "God's house."[7] Abigail scanned the passage and a puzzled expression grew on her face, and she asked, "Why would he want to give back part of what Yahweh had given him? And why would that cheapskate, Yahweh, take it back? Wouldn't that make him an Indian giver? That is unless some other god was giving Jacob stuff, and he was sharing it with Yahweh."

Lemuel gulped. It was the same question he had asked Myles, and Myles' explanation only added to his own confusion. He decided that Abigail would really twist his words, so he ignored her observation, and said, "A small rock would hardly be suitable for a church to attract the multitude, don't you think?" Then he rapidly turned to Exodus, and said, "Here's what the Lord told Moses: 'an altar of earth thou shalt make unto me,' and he also gives him the option of using uncut stone instead of earth."

He noticed that she was not reading where he was pointing. She was running her finger down the column at the far side of the other page, and she said, "I thought you said the Lord didn't allow prostitution. Look at what it says here about the maid who was enticed: 'if the father refuses to let them marry; the guy has to pay the father.'[8] That sounds just like prostitution to me, except I thought the money should go to the church instead of a pimping father. Doesn't the Lord's Prayer begin with 'Our Father who art in heaven?' That justifies giving the money to the church, doesn't it?" She laughed, and nudged him. "See, I do know some of the words."

He sneered at her. "Go ahead. Have fun with your little demon twists and then we can get back to the more serious business of figuring out what kind of church to build."

"Okay, I'll be good. I promise, no more jokes about temple prostitution." Then she said, "A congregation of Texans won't feel inspired by a holy rock or a mound of dirt." They both agreed that in this age of soaring glass obelisks, where people can look down from their penthouses upon low-flying cumulus clouds, something more impressive had to be contrived. "Are there any other church designs in there?" she asked.

"Threshing floors are spiritually significant. Ruth met Boaz on the threshing floor[9] near Bethlehem, and when Jacob died, his family mourned for him on the threshing floor near Atad. When David was bringing the Ark of the Covenant into Chidon, the Lord smote Uzza for laying his hand on the Ark.[10] It was just as the Ark passed the threshing floor. It must mean something, because the Bible mentions it. The Lord commanded David to set up an altar in the threshing floor of Ornan, the Jubsite. David paid six hundred gold shekels to Ornan, and set up the Lord's altar there.[11] Maybe we should buy a threshing floor to set up our mission. Or even better, we could have threshing floors all over the state."

Abigail shook her head. "You can't. They don't have threshing floors anymore. They have these huge combines that harvest the crop and thresh the grain, all at the same time. They chute the grain right from the harvester into big trucks that go right out into the field, and then it's taken to the silos and dumped on a conveyer belt. Hands never touch it. You won't find any threshing floors today." She was also calculating, *Hum, six hundred gold shekels, that would be about ninety thousand today.* It would take her a little time to create that much, now that the largest denomination was a hundred dollar bill, but if she could get him to sign over his soul, it would be worth the effort.

He insisted on the idea. "We could build a symbolic threshing floor, or better yet, we can build threshing floors all over the state. You wouldn't find threshing floor services offensive, would you?"

To the contrary, far from offensive, she thought the idea was intriguing. "That sure doesn't sound like the Yahweh I knew and detested. It has an earthy pagan quality about it, like the old Roman lares who watched over the household. It's delightfully heathen, you know, like fertility rites and asking the gods to be generous." After a few moments of thoughtful silence she asked, "Didn't they give you instructions about what sort of chapel they wanted you to use?"

Her intimation that such worship was nearly pagan jolted him. He felt himself being pushed into another corner with the serpent coiled to strike. He didn't want to get into another confusing dissertation about the role of the serpent, and Adam and Eve; and about the Egyptian god Am; and the serpent being the protector of the grain of the threshing floor; and Moses's fiery serpent on a pole; and Jesus being laid in a manger which was a place for grain. He avoided that bottomless abyss, and said, "If they use those big combines and trucks now, the spiritual meaning of the threshing floor would be hard for the mortals to identify with God." Then he said, "Let's see what else is here.

"This looks interesting, Abigail. I'll bet people would come for miles just to see this." He handed the Bible to her and pointed out the words of description. "Maybe we should erect a tabernacle like this."[12]

She studied the dimensions of the most sacred temple of Hebrew lore: a building about one hundred feet, by thirty feet, and forty-five feet tall. "Pretty small by today's standards." Then she smirked salaciously. "But all those small chambers along the side walls could be useful," and she laughed.

"Alright, stop teasing, Abigail."

"At least with such a small building it shouldn't cost too much, and you'll have your debt repaid in no time. Your flock should be happy." She continued to read while mentally calculating the cost of cedar from Lebanon. "We'll have to make a substitution here. We can use fir, that's no problem," and she mumbled an appreciative, "um hum" or "ah hah"

HOW THE GOOD TAILOR GOT TO HEAVEN   349

over the carved decorations. "Knops and open flowers, very pretty." Then she turned the page where her finger stopped at the word: gold. She read faster, tracing down the printed page with her finger and pausing each time she came to the word "gold." Without saying a word, she got up and went inside for her small hand-held calculator, a scratch pad and pencil. As she punched in the numbers, she commented, "We could use gilt paint here, couldn't we?"

"We want to be authentic. This is the temple Solomon built to the glory of the Lord, because of the wisdom God gave to Solomon.[13]"

She sighed, and said in a tone that meant he should be sensible, "Assuming a twelve-twelve pitch on your roof; you've got at least seventy-two hundred square feet of gold-plated walls and ceiling. Then there's those two gold-plated cherubim. It's hard to tell how much gold for them because of the irregular surfaces, but they're thirty feet high and ten feet wide. What was he trying to do, outspend the Babylonians with their idol of Marduk? And not only that...look at those big gold plated doors." She snorted. "Humph! And you were afraid to take a few hundred for a new suit, because of what it might do to the mortal's economic system? What do you think will happen if I create that much money?"

"I've already explained it to you. It's very simple. First we put it in and then we take it out, and you make it disappear. It all comes out even."

"But what if the mortals don't want to replace it? You may be a real flop as a preacher, and you'll have to have armed guards around this place twenty-four hours a day. That's very expensive."

"Nonsense! They wouldn't rob God's house. Remember this is for the disposition of their eternal souls. It's for their salvation. You don't think I want this out of personal vanity, do you?"

Abigail muttered, "Mammon was a piker compared to this Solomon. Look at this part of the building called the oracle. There's another three thousand feet of gold-plated walls, and then there's this gold-plated altar, and the gold chains...why didn't he cover the floors with gold while he was about it?" She slapped her forehead with the palm of her hand, and cried, "Oh no! He did!" She sobered and began to consider her own well-being. "Lem, be serious. Even if you use gold leaf, the gold will cost more than a million dollars, and then there's the cost of the rest of the materials, the land, and the labor—this chapel would cost several million dollars. When you're done, you would have a little chapel that would cramp a hundred people if they all stood.

"And think of me, will you? Terrestrial angels survive very comfortably by our anonymity. If you and I started to spend this kind of money, we'd have to explain where we got it, and we made an agreement, remember? No lies. If the story ever got out about where the money came from, I'd have to leave you and you wouldn't like that."

"Naturally I'd protect you. I wouldn't tell them where I got the money. I wouldn't lie, I just wouldn't say anything."

She was amazed at his innocence. He didn't know how prosecutors could twist the laws to suit a desired outcome. Demons were amateurs when it came to twisting the truth. She considered how the same law that granted immunity and freedom to confessed murderers in return for their testimony, was applied to a young woman who was involved in a real estate scam, and was chained and imprisoned for years for refusing to accept the judge's arbitrary dictates. Lemuel actually believed that people couldn't be made to betray their friends. He didn't understand how the corrupt Themis blinded judges to the truth.

She continued reading about Solomon. "That's a pretty extravagant palace. Where did he get the money to build it?"

"Solomon was renowned for his wisdom and wealth," he replied.

"So I've heard, but where did his wealth come from?"

"His judgement was nonpareil; the people marveled."

"Uh huh! But the money…where did he get the money?"

"From God, of course. God raises high, or brings down low."

"Did all right by him in the wife department, too. Seven hundred of them." She continued reading, and then chortled, "God, huh? That's not the way I read this: 'Thy father made our yoke grievous.' This is where his people are talking to Rehoboam, Solomon's son, and they say: 'Make thou the grievous service of thy father, and his heavy yoke which he put on us, lighter, and we will serve thee.'[14] That sounds like a tax revolt to me, unless you're saying that God regulates the taxes. I thought taxes were the civil government's business."

"God's power is in all things. He is the master potter who creates the design of mortal clay. He is omnipotent and omniscient, and no detail is too insignificant, too trivial, or of too great a magnitude for his attention."

She was sure he was joking, and in the spirit of humorous incredulity, she observed, "So that would make the IRS an instrument of God's will?"

"Of course it is. It is so important that it takes the full attention of two principalities, a squad of archangels, twelve companies of full angels, and several million ordinary souls in the record department. Everything is weighed and judged, collated and balanced, and all in ancient Hebrew." He took the Bible from her and found the book of Romans. "See what it says here: 'The powers that be are ordained of God.' Naturally, the IRS, being one of the most powerful of the powers, receives a lot of attention."

"Do you mean that people who cheat on their tax returns are actually cheating God?" She was delighted by that notion.

"No! Of course not. Those people are all under the influence of lying angels. It's all part of the plan. Oh, never mind. I doubt that you'd understand." He was amazed by her incomprehension of the simple concept of omnipotence. He patted her hand, and tried not to sound patronizing. "I suppose it's natural for terrestrial angels to be ignorant in matters of theology."

Abigail wondered if he was deluding himself into thinking that if she funded his project that it would somehow be God's will. She decided that he probably would, in the same way that he tried to give God the credit for the money she created for Pearl.

Lemuel confided that he had applied for an appointment to the tax section when he returned from his mortality detail. "I don't know how well I did on the exam though. They ask so many trick questions. You know, like, 'if a corporation has surplus deductions and can sell their surplus deductions to another corporation, should a taxpayer who has a great many dependents be able to sell his surplus deductions to another taxpayer?' I know how to do the math, but it's those blamed judgement questions concerning logic and intent that have me worried."

"Perhaps you'll understand after you've spent your whole mortality here," she said. "But you have cleared up something that has been nagging me for a long time. I've always wondered why the churches didn't have to pay any taxes. If God is the head of the IRS that explains why. You see, I didn't know that."

"You mean that we won't have to pay taxes on the money that comes into the collection plate?"

"Of course not. You won't have to pay any property taxes on your church or your rectory, or any other property that's used for religious purposes." She didn't want to upset him by pointing out that she didn't pay those taxes either, but her methods were a bit simpler than filling out long forms, and justifying deductions. She merely conjured enough money to pay cash for whatever she wanted and never asked any questions about the taxes. She thought haggling over taxes with government functionaries was so bourgeois.

The day was getting warm so Abigail caused the offshore breeze to swing about and come off the ocean, and went inside and fixed a pitcher full of ice cold Gin Bucks, using fresh limes and a lot of ice. When she returned she said, "If you build that temple, you'll be stuck in one place. I don't know how long I could stand that. I like to move around, seeing different things. That's why I live in a trailer. If I want to pick up and move my house, there's nothing to it. I liked your threshing floor idea. We'd be moving from place to place, preaching to different people all the time. It sounded interesting. I guess it's just the gypsy in me."

There was also the problem of conjuring millions of dollars. She didn't figure it out exactly, but if it took her ten minutes to conjure a hundred thousand, it would take her an hour and a half to conjure a million, and the gold for the temple was several millions. Then there was the problem of accounting for all that cash. They might be accused of being drug traffickers. They both had warrants out for them in King Jamesburg. She didn't say this to Lemuel, but she thought it.

Lemuel was also doing some thinking. Abigail was like a deer, wild and free, apt to rove and find more succulent browse, or sate her natural curiosity elsewhere when the grave and constant became boring. He was afraid he'd lose her if he tried to tame her. There was no real reason to establish a permanent church building; the apostle Paul traveled all over; the tabernacle tent Moses erected held attractive possibilities. The revivalist tradition was strong in America—*why not use a tent?* he thought.

"Abigail, I've got another idea. It occurred to me that the Jews wandered in the desert for forty years and they took their tabernacle with them. It was a portable place of worship."

Abigail was enthusiastic about that idea and flashed a wide smile and clapped her hands. "Like a circus, you mean? I've seen those revivalist preachers set up their tents, and that does sound like fun." Also, she liked the idea of not having to finesse so much currency into the system. She thought, *after all, how much could a tent cost?* She didn't know what happened after the slaughtering began at Horeb, and Moses destroyed the golden calf. Bloodshed always distressed her and she left. So she hadn't considered that the Jews would need a place to worship their Lord even though they were now wanderers, like the nomadic Ishmaelites.

Lemuel explained, "In addition to the Commandments, the Lord also instructed Moses about his tabernacle, and gave him some very specific details. The dimensions, the materials, and the whole layout is described in Exodus." He indicated the section. "This is the tabernacle that the Lord told Moses to have the people make. As you can see, it's all portable."

After reading for a few moments, Abigail gave a low whistle.

"Whew! That's some tent...curtains of fine twined linen, blue, purple, and scarlet; looped through fifty taches of gold; with covering curtains of red died goat skins. Poles of acacia wood with silver ends to fit into silver sockets. Badger skins over the goat skins. Wow! Look at the ark. More rare wood, and that covered with gold, and the mercy seat...gold...and golden cherubim, and look at the size of those candlesticks, also gold. Did you know that almost every tenth word in this description is something of gold? Oh, here's something: the horns of the altar for the burnt offerings, and some of the utensils are brass. And then on out into the courtyard. That's not too bad, a lot of that stuff is silver. Hum, here's the bill." Her eyes widened, and she gave a double whistle. "Twenty-nine gold talents, and seven hundred and thirty...sanctuary weight, they're double the commercial value...gold shekels; and for the silver...one hundred silver talents, and seventeen hundred and seventy-five... sanctuary weight, naturally...silver shekels—and that's not counting the hides, the drapery material, and the rare woods."[15] She lofted the Bible in a high arc onto the coffee table, it thudded heavily. Her stomach muscles worked hard and she asked, "Do you have any idea how much that is in today's dollars?"

"I have no idea, but I think it would attract attention."

"That's an understatement. You'll need an army to keep the thieves away. Capturing that much gold would be a temptation for a small country." She picked up her calculator. "Let's see how much it comes to." Her pretty features became hard and deep furrows formed between her eyebrows as she held the calculator. "It's been a long time since I've figured in sanctuary shekels. They're double the weight of the royal shekel, and a talent is equal to three thousand of them." She sat quietly for several minutes entering numbers, and marking figures down on the scratch pad. Finally, without raising her head, she announced, "That comes to thirteen million, six hundred and two thousand dollars... give or take a few thousand one way of the other. And that doesn't count the labor, or any of the other materials—fine-twined linen, badger skins over goat skins..." She sighed, got up, and

HOW THE GOOD TAILOR GOT TO HEAVEN

poured another Gin Buck. She said, "You'll want to substitute some less costly material, won't you?"

"We want it to be authentic, don't we? These are the Lord's instructions. I don't think we should use base metals or synthetic materials."

"Uh huh! The price of admission to worship Yahweh sure went up. That's a far cry from a mound of dirt or an uncut rock." She swallowed deeply from her glass and asked, "Are you sure you wouldn't rather have your own Notre Dame cathedral."

Lemuel didn't understand sarcasm and seriously considered her proposition for several moments. Then he rejected it for the same reason he had rejected the Solomon Temple replica. "No, I don't think so Abigail. You'd get bored, even if it was like Paris."

She assumed he was joking, but she realized he was serious about the tabernacle tent. The utter magnitude of that much money began to sink in. About fifteen million for the tent and another million for trucks and equipment to haul it around. *God! What if he wants to use camels and asses?* She started working with her calculator while he was sketching the plan for the tabernacle on a sheet of paper, and she coughed to get his attention. "I hope you realize that this much money will take me quite some time to conjure. If I make a stack of hundreds, fifty to a stack, every fifteen minutes, it will take me over a month to conjure that much. And that's if I work at it night and day."

"Can't you make larger bills?"

"They don't make larger denominations, and that much currency would fill all the trailer's storage space. There are T-bills, but I've never tried them before." She did some more figuring, and said, "If I make those, fifty at a time, and ten thousand is the usual denomination, it will still take me over seven hours. And then there's the problem of laundering that much money. The banks have rules about reporting. Contractors and suppliers will want currency or checks, and I don't even have a checking account. Even if I juggle the Treasury's books, there's still the IRS, and they'll want their share. They'll want to know where we got the money, and there'll be forms to fill out. Then I'll have to do some more juggling just to pay the taxes. That'll be another four or five million."

She could see by the glazed-over look on his face that she still wasn't getting through to him. He said, "I thought you said churches didn't have to pay taxes?"

"We're not a recognized church yet." Then she conceded that she could also fix that, but getting Lemuel's soul was becoming pretty expensive, and very complicated. This was getting to be several cosmic magnitudes greater an investment than she had ever planned. It was a far cry from the price of a couple of suits.

He said compassionately, "I don't want you to overexert yourself. Just make a few stacks of money every now and then, whenever you're in the mood."

She sighed, sipped her drink, and tried again. "Look at it this way: if you were a well known evangelist, explaining away a few million would be no problem. If you were a drug peddler, you'd have connections to get the money laundered. But no one has ever heard of you or me, and we're not connected. We can't say we inherited it or won it, because that all gets reported. So if we started spreading that much money around, questions would be asked." Lemuel's blank smile confirmed his understanding was disconnected, and she said impatiently: "It's one hell of a lot of money!"

"Oh yes, I know that." He held his glass for her to pour him another drink, and as she poured he said, "You've got two of the cutest dimples, Abby…"

"Try to understand it this way. Your mission is to bring ten thousand souls to salvation and the tabernacle will cost about fifteen million dollars. That means that the price for each one of those souls is fifteen hundred dollars."

"Oh no! Salvation is free."

She ignored him and continued. "And you are going to try to get that money back in the collection plate? (He nodded.) Okay, do you remember yesterday when you worked as a carpenter? (He frowned and nodded.) Good! How much money did you earn?"

His frown developed into a scowl. "Twenty-nine dollars and fifty cents." He looked at her suspiciously. "What are you doing? Are you trying to back out?"

"Oh no! I thought we should consider the economic facts of salvation, that's all. You're supposed to save ten thousand souls, right? A bit of simple arithmetic shows that at your daily wage you would earn about three hundred thousand dollars in forty years—one entire lifetime of work. Your expected take from that amount would be a tenth, right? That would be thirty thousand dollars per soul. But you've agreed to repay your debt to me, so five hundred of those souls belong to me."

In somber speculation Lemuel envisioned his army of souls passing in review before him, battalion after battalion marched by in square formation, and led by standard bearers carrying pennants with their regimental colors. He could see them passing in review; solid phalanxes of white-robed souls, all in step and singing lustily, *Onward Christian Soldiers*. But, there beside him on the reviewing stand, was Abigail. She was wearing a scarlet red uniform with gold piping, black Cossack boots, a black Persian lamb Cossack hat tipped at a rakish angle, and she was pointing with her Gypsy cane, saying, "I'll take that one, and that one, and that one…"

Naturally he didn't want to lose even one soul, but he had to consider the ends. The thousands brought to truth and light; the thousands brought to God. Then he rationalized that in the battle between good and evil there will be some losses on both sides. Oh how he empathized with those generals having to make the hard, lonely decisions.

He reread the description of the tabernacle. He doodled a perspective drawing of it, and filled in the valances and hangings of fine twined linen with the golden taches; and the incense altar; the gold mercy seat, and the gold cherubim; and he could envision the unredeemed coming in droves to stand in awe and become saved. From time to time he glanced over at her and then he came to a decision. Her terms were too harsh. His conscience wouldn't let him commit five hundred souls to eternal damnation. The most he would concede was five hundred souls sent to Purgatory, with the hope of eventual salvation; that would be a just price. Neither could he allow her to pick the souls. She'd pick the most purely spotless souls: nuns, ministers, youth fellowship councilors, the entire membership of the Moral Majority, and two-thirds of the Republican Party would be at risk. He was not accustomed to bargaining, but he made a counteroffer. Five hundred souls' lifetimes in Purgatory was all she could extort.

Her eyes narrowed shrewdly. "Would that be productive working lifetimes, or do you mean average life expectancy lifetimes?"

"What's the difference?"

"About a million and a half years. Five hundred life expectancy lifetimes would be three million, five hundred thousand years, and five hundred productive lifetimes would be two million years." Abigail didn't like to haggle, but she had committed herself and was not going to back down now. "If you sign up for five hundred life expectancy lifetimes we'll allow you to amortize the annuity with an easy payment plan, but if you select a productive life policy we'd want a single cash payment on your death. If you are able to pay off your note early, we want an early release penalty of ten percent. That's fifty more souls."

He swallowed his Gin Buck and said, "Okay Abigail, it's a deal. I'll let you have your five hundred souls, but not for eternal damnation. They're to go to Purgatory, and will be released as soon as their time is served."

Smiling sweetly, she said, "I don't want to force you into anything, but this should be handled in a business-like manner. It's nothing personal, you understand. And, of course, as soon as you've repaid the debt we'll burn all the mortgages." Then trying as hard as she could to sound casual, she said, "Since we're both dealing in the value of souls, how much would you say an angel's soul would be worth? Would you say that five hundred mortal souls would be worth the equivalent of fifty angels' souls?"

Lemuel instantly understood what she was after, and he thought, *Oh the cunning little imp…she's after my soul.* "The Bible says that all heaven rejoices more over one repentant sinner, than over ninety-nine which need no repentance. I'd say the exchange rate should be at least a hundred to one."

"We don't think virtue is worth that much. We'd allow a ten to one exchange rate."

"It's a moot point. I'd never ask forty-nine other angels to obligate themselves to my contract."

"We can work around that. All you have to do is to agree to serve all fifty contracts." She poured them each another drink, and said, "Take your time. Think it over—after all you've got the rest of your life to consider the answer, but I'll have to have some sort of commitment in writing. I'd never be able to face my fellow terrestrial angels if I didn't get you to sign a contract."

There it was—the Faustian bargain. He had to concede that she was clever, the way she had worked him into that box.

Actually Lemuel was better equipped to negotiate than Abigail because of his years of experience dealing with Heaven's bureaucracy, and he knew that the lump sum payment at the end of this lifetime was the better deal because he would have the full use of the entire amount for his life. And there was always the chance the seventh and final seal would be opened and the final battle would begin, and with God's forces victorious, he'd be liberated from his obligation to the forces of evil. He accepted the two-thousand-year obligation.

Abigail smiled, and then forced herself to appear very solemn. "This is just a formality, but you know this sort of contract has to be sealed with blood, don't you?"

He nodded. She took a clean sheet of paper, and wrote, "I.O.U. fifty lifetimes of my productive labor years to be served in Purgatory, or fifteen million dollars on my death bed." She pushed it toward him and said, "Sign it, and make your mark."

He was a bit tipsy, but sharp enough to say, "Not until I get my tabernacle, you crafty little demon."

"That's easily fixed." And she took the paper on which he had sketched the tabernacle, and wrote, "I.O.U. one tabernacle, as depicted above, built to the exact specifications in the book of Exodus. If the tabernacle is not delivered, Lemuel's commitment is voided." Then she signed it and handed it to him.

He grimaced as he stuck a pin into his thumb and made his bloody thumb print over his signature with a shaking hand. He pushed the paper toward her, and she picked it up and waved it in the air to dry the mark. The contracts were signed just as the sun was at high noon over Corpus Christi.

Abigail grinned mischievously and asked him if he would like to have the sun momentarily darkened to honor the occasion.

"Positively not!" was his reply.

"How about a clap of thunder, and a bolt of lightning?"

"No!"

"A pillar of fire? I do a good pillar of fire...all green, and purple, and orange...with little silver sparklies scattered..."

"No! No! No!"

"Speaking of pillars of fire, here's something that puzzles me. I didn't think about it at the time, but remember when the Lord raised up the pillar of fire to stop the Pharaoh's army, and all the Jews crossed over the sea, and then they had that really big bash. When I was younger I used to go to a lot of big affairs...and they worshiped the golden calf..."

"They were a stiff-necked people, as the Lord said, and that's why they worshiped the golden calf."

"No, that's not what I was thinking about. They had all this gold. Where'd it come from? They were supposed to be a bunch of runaway slaves, downtrodden and forced to make bricks without straw...if you believe what they tell you. Anyway, I never thought about it before, but where did they get all the gold and silver? The golden calf was pretty big, but this big tent with all its gold and silver, and the hides and fine fabrics...you know how much it was worth? Fifteen million dollars. Where did a bunch of impoverished slaves get that kind of money?"

"It's all here in the Bible. You really should study it now that you're in the church business yourself." Lemuel opened the Bible and placed it on her lap. Pointing to the passage, he read aloud, "And the children of Israel did according to the word of Moses; and they borrowed of the Egyptians jewels of silver, and jewels of gold, and raiment: And the Lord gave the people favor in the sight of the Egyptians, so they lent unto them such things as they required; and they spoiled the Egyptians."[16]

"Oh, that answers my question..."

"You'll find that the Bible answers all questions."

"Now I see. God told Moses to have the Jews borrow all that stuff." She tapped her lips with her forefinger, deep in thought, and then she asked, "Did they ever pay the Egyptians back?"

"I don't think so. That's what spoiled means, and there's no other mention of it in the Bible."

"Do you think that seeing the Jews making off with over fifteen million dollars worth of spoils might have been the reason that the Egyptian army chased them into the Red Sea?"

"That's not why! Everyone knows how mean the Egyptians were to the Jews."

"They don't sound mean to me. They were nice enough to lend them jewels and raiment, and it says they also took with them, 'Flocks, and herds, even very much cattle.' And that certainly might explain why the Egyptians and the Jews have so much trouble getting along now. If they borrowed all that stuff and never paid it back, can you imagine how much that would come to with the interest, compounded daily...ever since Moses?" She picked up her little calculator, and was murmuring to herself, "Let's see, that's fifteen million, and money at six percent doubles every fifteen years, and that would be about three thousand years since Moses, and that means the fifteen million would double itself two hundred times...Lem, there isn't that much money in the entire world."

Chapter 20

THE HOLY/UNHOLY ALLIANCE BOUND EACH TO THE other. It committed each to suffer restraints on their diametrically opposed, diversely acculturated, ethos driven, personalities. Abigail's *id* was dominant, and any restrictions to her personal freedom were to be avoided, as might be expected of demons. Lemuel's *ego ideal*, his notion of personal excellence, was to rise within the Empyreal Establishment and get right up there close to God. Which one made the worst bargain is best judged by those gifted with hermeneutic skills. Lemuel had ceded fifty lifetimes of existence within the strict organizational structure, where achievement or failure brought reward or punishment, in exchange for a two-thousand year sojourn in an unstructured chaos, where normal constraints were unknown, and every soul was free to do his or her own thing without regard to character improvement, personal advancement, shame, or demotion. Abigail's commitment was immediate. She had bound herself to the strait sanctimony of a cleric bound by personal ambition and Biblical canon. Although Lemuel's sentence could only begin with his death, hers was to commence immediately and last until Lemuel died, or until he recovered the money in the collection plate. She did not judge this possibility as very promising.

Resigned to this fate, she decided to move farther up the beach; far from the confining ethos of the mortals, where, for a few more days, she could breathe free. At least until they started off on their mission. They drove north along the beach to put more space between themselves and the high rise condos, beach shops, restaurants, bait and tackle shops, modestly and immodestly clad tourists, and the dusty vehicles cruising at gondola speed whose drivers were seeking any diversion from the grave and constant of their reality. Their quest took on a grave and constant reality of its own as they conformed to the unvariable rules of the quest.

She drove beyond the paved road and they had to lower the air pressure in their tires so as to spread more rubber over the softer sand. They continued past the Star of Texas, a sea-going tug that had been washed ashore during a violent hurricane and was now a rotting home to transient beach enthusiasts. The dunes became less trampled, and the sea oats performed their useful function of keeping the sandy strand from washing into Mexico. They came to a lonely, hard-packed washout in the dunes, and set up camp on a safely-elevated level space in the lee of a high dune. Their site was ten miles north of the last bait shop in civilization.

Abigail was satisfied with the site, and she climbed the high dune to spectate the green and white serenity. The high-rise condos to the south were pale misty specters in the distance, and to the north was nothing but clean white sand and gently curling green surf. Toward the sunrise, the Gulf lay like a dappled green proscenium before the turquoise backdrop which began at the horizon.

Then she heard the most piteous wailing and sobbing to ever come from male vocal chords. Up the beach, on the next dune, she spotted a man kneeling in the tall dune grass. There was no one else on the beach, only herself and the sobbing man, so without bothering to disappear, she flew up beside him. He cringed back in terror, and begged, "I don't want to go back; please don't make me." He was slender, even slight, and his face was pitted as from acne or small pox. His nose was large, his hair was dark and slicked smooth to his head, and he held a pair of heavy, tortoise-shell glasses with thick lenses in his hands at his chest. He was wearing a white linen suit, and he had a writer's inkhorn at his side. He wore white buck oxfords, and white stockings, which, as Abigail silently noted, were spattered with blood. There were spots of blood on his white suit, a caking of blood on his hands and in his hair, and a red smear on his cheek. He cried incessantly, and begged and prayed to Abigail to not take him back there. Then his eyes widened in some recalled horror, and he sputtered through saliva frothed lips, "I should have marked the babies anyway!" Then he stared at her with dead, lifeless eyes and said, "Did you know that when those bullets enter their soft little bodies their insides explode?" He bowed low and pressed his forehead against the top of her tennis shoes and cried, "Oh no! I didn't mean that. I know they didn't qualify for exemption. It was right that they should die too."

She withdrew her foot from his clutching hand, and backed off a pace. She asked in a voice filled with disgust, but calm, "What did you do? And who are you?"

"I'm the angel, Myles. I was carrying out the Lord's will."

She prodded him with a forefinger, and said, "You don't feel like an angel."

"I was mortal. I died in 1569, but they made me into an angel...and then I blasphemed. They reduced me in rank, and this is my first worldly assignment. I've been in the condign correction course ever since I sinfully and wickedly gave an angel probationer erroneous doctrinal instruction." His eyes cleared and he studied Abigail closely, and with a very puzzled look asked, "Aren't you an angel? I thought that when you flew over here you were sent to make sure I finished the job."

"Yes, I'm an angel, but not the kind you mean...I'm a terrestrial angel."

As soon as he sorted out her meaning he cringed in horror once more, and he pleaded piteously, "I know what you are: you're a demon! You've come to drag me off to hell! Please don't! I did just as I was ordered. It was my first job." His mind raced back to his assignment, and he wailed, "Oh no! Not for that. It was an unconscious act, done in the confusion. It won't happen again! PUL...EEZZE! I promise to follow every instruction to the letter from now on." He clutched his hands in front of his chest and begged for understanding. "I didn't like doing it. Was I supposed to like all that slaughter? Please understand, I'm a scholar and I'm not used to the rigors of field work, but I'll learn—I promise."

It dawned on her who this Myles was. He was the Bible translator who had been Lemuel's instructor. She gave a cold laugh, and said icily, "Well, the results of your bloody pedagogy shows now, doesn't it, scholar?" She prodded him with her toe, ordered him to get up, and pointing to the Gulf, said, "Go down into the ocean and wash off that gore...scholar. I think you should meet a friend of mine, and I don't want that bloody mess near my trailer. I think you should tell him what you did in the name of the Almighty."

He waded into the water fully clothed, and he soaked and scrubbed. "Use sand!" she ordered. Finally clean, but dripping, he came out of the water and stood meekly beside her. At the trailer, Lemuel greeted Myles enthusiastically. He grabbed the scholar's slight shoulders with both hands, and then pulled him close and gave him a hearty bear hug and clapped him on the back. Lemuel's smiling heartiness faded when Myles's response was a flaccid smile that seemed filled with shame and tragedy. "Have you done something to him, Abigail?" he accused.

"Not me...ask him," she replied.

They sat on canvas chairs beneath the awning on Abigail's Turkoman courtyard. Myles hung his head and stared blankly at the six-armed Kali. He tried to start several times, but each time his story broke into sobs. Lemuel got the bourbon and glasses, and poured them a round of drinks. Myles downed the shot neat and held out his glass for another. After the third mind-dimming potion, Myles explained that he had been reduced in rank to avenging angel, and managing a twisted

HOW THE GOOD TAILOR GOT TO HEAVEN — 367

smile, said that Lemuel now outranked him. Lemuel told him that he was lucky they hadn't dropped him all the way down to guardian angel, or permanent sparrow detail. "That's the worst duty ever," he assured him.

"It couldn't be," Myles remarked, and told his story. "There's a little town near here named New Jerusalem, and I was ordered to go there and make a mark on the forehead of all the men that sigh and cry for the abominations committed by the inhabitants." Myles held out his inkhorn and the reed scriber.

"Something like another Passover?" Abigail observed

"Sort of," he agreed, "but I had only studied the incident from the objective, theological, perspective." He helped himself to another couple of fingers of bourbon, and said thickly, "Just as I'm sure this slaughter was justified." Myles's ambivalence was fear driven; now he shuddered. "The whole town turned out for the high school ball game. None of them were sighing or crying over the abominations against the Lord. So, I began to ask them, 'Have you been sighing or crying over the abominations against the Lord?'[17] Most of them just looked at me as though I were odd, some even pushed me away. Then during the third inning when they were all happy, drinking from waxed paper cups and eating hot dogs, some of the boys and girls were holding hands, and small children were running from friend to friend in front of the grandstand, six men came from the way of the higher gate. Every man had his slaughter weapon in his hand, a machine gun, and without a word they opened fire on the crowd. And then the Lord spoke to the slaughterers: 'Go through the city and smite: let not your eye spare, neither have ye pity: Slay utterly old and young, both maids and little children, and women: But come not near any man upon whom is the mark.'

"I managed to mark one man. I don't know whether he had ever sighed or cried over the abominations that were committed against the Lord, but he alone was spared." Myles covered his face with both hands and sobbed. He wailed, "Oh the blood! The screams, the panic-stricken mortals diving for cover." He groaned deeply, "Oh! Those poor people.

Then I panicked, and I flew until I got here to the ocean, but before I could get out of earshot, I heard those machine guns raking the town…glass breaking, and more screaming." He put both hands to his ears, and cried, "And I can still hear it." Then he nodded toward Abigail, and said, "That's when you found me."

"How could you possibly think that something like that was…justified?" Abigail asked.

"It's Biblically justified. It was done to fulfill Ezekiel's vision about what awaits the backsliders," Myles explained.

Abigail shed her squeamishness over the Lord's killing sprees thousands of years ago, and she always left the scene when the slaughtering started. Seldom was any of the souls hers. She noticed that the incidents of wholesale slaughter seemed to be increasing in frequency and quantity of mortals slain as the world spun toward the millennium. However, the killing of innocent babies and little children still distressed her, and she blamed the ethereal angels. "I don't see how you can stomach working for that organization. Yahweh's getting to be a real psycho."

Now full of Dutch courage, Myles said he had to return to complete the job. He was to meet cherubim on a throne, and "Go in between the wheels, even under the cherub, and rake out the coals of the fire with my hands from between the cherubim and scatter them over the city."[18]

Abigail decided to go with him to see if any of the souls belonged to her. When she and Myles got to the scene of the carnage, the flies and rats were already at work on the corpses, and just like the Biblical description, the courts, streets, and houses were filled with the slain, and dogs lapped at the pools of blood. Skulls spilled their blood-covered contents on the pavement, sticky and fly-covered intestines poured out on the ground, rats crawled into gaping holes in bloody children, and there was dead silence. Suddenly the silence was shattered by hysterical laughter. The maniacal shrieks came from a tailor shop where a man sat at a sewing machine and he had an ink mark on his forehead.

"The man I marked," Myles explained.

HOW THE GOOD TAILOR GOT TO HEAVEN

Then there appeared over them, a sapphire stone, in the likeness of a throne, and Myles reported the matter, saying, "I have done as thou hast commanded me." And while he spread the fiery coals over the city, hundreds of deliverance angels appeared and gathered up the souls two and three at a time. The scene made Abigail nauseous, and she returned to the trailer and told Lemuel what she had seen.

Lemuel raised his hands prayerfully, and praised the Lord. "O Thank you Lord, for forgiving their sins and taking them up to heaven."

He may as well have slapped her face, and as Abigail seethed at his cold insensibility, she said sharply, "Lem, I want out of the contract! I'll give you your soul back, and I want my IOU. I want you to go! Leave with Myles…just leave me alone."

The black smoke of a burning town across the Laguna Madre rose up in the clear blue sky. When Myles returned, Lemuel was on his knees pleading with Abigail. He held her hand, kissed her knees, rubbed his chin on her leg, and believe it or not, tears welled up in his eyes. Myles was surprised to see Lemuel grovel at the feet of the demon. Lemuel told him about the contract and explained that she wanted to cancel it.

He gave Lemuel a surprised glance, and uttered in astonishment, "You gave your soul to a demon?"

"Oh no! I only pledged it to her for two thousand years against her loan."

Abigail pushed him away, and said, "I'd lose my mind if I thought I was helping your vile corporation one little bit. Haven't you any sense of right and wrong?"

"God's ways are mysterious, Abby." Then realizing how genuinely angry she was, Lemuel pleaded, "Dearest Abby, one never knows when the day of the Lord will come, but we must have faith that He meant it for good. And as you saw yourself, all their souls were taken up to heaven. Isn't that why the mortals pray?"

She realized that Lemuel was right. They wanted to go to heaven when they died, and that's where they were going. She grudgingly concurred, "I guess I was being too sentimental, but I have lived with the mortals ever since creation and it is possible to become fond of some of them."

"Of course. Just as a shepherd is fond of his flock."

"No, I mean as individuals."

"Oh, I wouldn't go that far," Lemuel said.

With bourbon-induced courage, Myles bristled and reminded Lemuel that he had been a mortal. "Are you forgetting that I was a mortal? They're not like sheep. I know how they must have felt in those last terrifying moments. If it hadn't been for them torturing me, I'd have never done that job for them!" Tipsy and lachrymose, he smiled crookedly through his tears at Abigail, and said, "I don't care if she is a demon. She's nice, and I like her."

Abigail looked from Myles to Lemuel, and asked, "Torture?"

"Well…ah…he committed blasphemy when he was instructing me."

"Torture? Lemuel? Isn't that what you accused the demons of?" Her green eyes sparkled angrily.

"Order has to be maintained for the sake of the organization, and sometimes it's necessary to use condign correction. An incident of blasphemy merits much more than a demotion. Myles was teaching that Jesus might not be divine; it was a direct attack on the Holy Trinity. If he had continued, it might have led to questions about the virginity of Mary. Those doubts might cause the whole system to unravel. Without order, there'd be chaos, an even more evil torment."

Their conversation turned to a discussion of hell. Myles was surprised to find out how sparsely populated it was, and that if he wanted to he could soar over and see for himself. "Not a foul stinking pit of fiery brimstone? No vicious demons working sadistic torments? And you mean they get real mortal food to eat? And not that miserable manna day in and day out? And there are day and night, and not that blasted eternal light?" Then he added, "Lemuel, we picked the wrong side!" But of course he was drunk when he said it.

Abigail also told them that Satan lived in a castle in Scotland where he spent his time playing croquet and entertaining the more worldly

HOW THE GOOD TAILOR GOT TO HEAVEN — 371

members of the royal family. Naturally the Queen was never invited to his soirees. It is doubtful that she would accept anyway. But Abigail provided the incontrovertible and absolute proof that Satan lived in Scotland, because the Highland Regiments are called, "The ladies from hell."

Myles was curious about a plant that he'd heard about that was raised by the Indians in the new world. It was introduced to England after Myles died by Sir Walter Raleigh. "They dried the leaves and smoked it in a long pipe."

Abigail said, "You mean tobacco? Its use has been condemned by every council of public decency and defender of civic morality ever since. I don't have any pipe tobacco, but I have some fine cigars. Would you like to try one?"

The cigars were long slender panatellas, and Abigail demonstrated how to bite the end off, light it, and she handed the lit cigar to Myles.

Lemuel asked, "What about me? I'd like to try one too."

"They're bad for your health."

Lemuel said, "What about Myles? Aren't they bad for his health?" Both Abigail and Myles thought that uproariously funny, and Lemuel sulked. Then he realized that it wasn't the cigar Lemuel wanted; what he really wanted was for Abigail to stop being so attentive to Myles. A very un-angelic attitude colored his thinking; an attitude common to mortals, but never angels: jealousy. She was his demon, and he didn't want to share her attention with anyone.

It was a fine cigar and Myles enjoyed it, and he liked the bourbon. He took off his glasses and held them in front of him examining the way they distorted objects as he changed the angle. He said, smiling, "I wonder if there's any way for me to stay down here and be a demon too?"

Abigail said, "You have got a real flair for worldliness, Myles. I think it can be arranged."

Lemuel hissed warily, "Tomas warned me that you were a Satanist. Don't even joke about such things." He swivelled his head to look for secret listeners and he sternly rebuked him in hushed tones, "That's treasonous talk Myles. You know what happens to traitors."

"They get shot and go to hell," Myles smirked.

"Oh, quit the bravado. You're just trying to impress Abigail." Like a student who gets the opportunity to correct their instructor, Lemuel was filled with indignant superiority. He said, "You've had too much to drink. You don't know what you're saying. Even if they don't get you for this now, it is the sort of thing that goes into your permanent record. If they ever hear about this, they'll bring it up before the promotion board. You'll be asked to explain…"

"Are you sure it's my record you're worried about, or is it your own? There's been some rumor going around about Esther's condition when she got back from her miraculous visitation." Then the sly grin slid from his face. It was replaced with the solicitousness of a drunk, and he reassured Lemuel, "Oh you don't have to worry about Esther. She's a good sport. She won't tell and neither will I. " Then his grin reappeared, and he confided, "But I think you can expect visits from time to time from some of your old buddies." His grin widened as he looked toward Abigail, and engagingly as possible, asked, "That is, if it's all right with you?"

Abigail hadn't considered the possibility of undermining the entire corporate structure of the Ethereal Establishment. A scheme like that seemed too enormous to even consider, even if all the demons cooperated in the effort. Of course they wouldn't cooperate. That would require organization, bureaucracy, and a command structure, and none of them would stand for that. In order to defeat the Ethereal Establishment, they'd have to be like them, and what, then, would be the point? But she wondered how many other angels were dissatisfied. *They couldn't all be myrmidons: mindless automatons.* There was the accidental soul switching that brought her and Lemuel together. It seemed to be just an innocent prank at the time, but she wondered. Then she noticed the cut of the suit that Myles wore. It was well-made. Not like the shoddy, cheap suits that the angels always wore. She called Lemuel's attention to Myles's suit. "A

HOW THE GOOD TAILOR GOT TO HEAVEN

bit out of style, single-breasted, overly-wide lapels, loose-fitting pleated pants; but better cut and more carefully tailored than anything I've ever seen on angels."

Lemuel admitted that the suit was better than his.

Myles said, "Oh, yeah. I guess you haven't heard. They have a new seraph angel overseer at the clothing factory. He set up a quality control unit with inspectors and everything, and the whole operation has been tightened up. They say he was a mortal too."

"A seraph!" Lemuel exclaimed, and searched Abigail's face, but she seemed as surprised as he was. She snickered gleefully, and said, "You don't think…"

"No! I don't think… I know!"

"What do you two know about?" Myles asked.

Lemuel was slowly shaking his head with disbelief, and muttered, "A seraph…he's a seraph. I don't believe it…a seraph…right up there next to God himself."

Abigail, still chuckling said, "You might say Lemuel has friends in high places, Myles."

* * *

Myles had to leave. "Before the press gang comes to get me," he said wryly, kidding on the square. He took a handful of panatellas, and hoped he could sneak them past the gate guards. He gave Abigail a tight hug, and an enthusiastic kiss on the cheek. Too tight and too enthusiastic for Lemuel's comfort. Then he soared off, a little wobbly, toward the ninth celestial sphere. His speed was below the decreed speed-of-thought ordinance for angels within range of mortal radar and the booze he drank caused a very erratic flight pattern. He was picked up by the Corpus Christi airport tower where another UFO sighting was logged in their recorder. This tape was quickly grabbed by the special government agency that confiscates the records of such sightings, marks them, "Top Secret," and denies their existence to the public. Although why the government should want to keep angel sightings from the public is a mystery to this author when the Bible clearly reports their presence. Go figure!

Lemuel had been stunned by the tailor's promotion. He imagined how miserable Tomas must feel. Although technically Tomas and Myles were of equal rank, Tomas had seniority and was not required to take orders from the mortal made angel. But this was a new development. All the lower orders were under a former mortal, and if word ever got out about his part in bringing in an unworthy soul, he'd be scorned and ostracized by all the rest of the angels. With all of them out to get him, it was only a matter of time before he'd stumble and suffer horribly for it. He was in the position of someone selling their house in an all-white neighborhood to a black family, and then trying to live on the same block. He said, "Abigail, we must never tell anyone about us swapping souls."

"Why not? I think it's funny."

"It's not funny. It's very serious. This will have celestial ramifications as portentous as the renting of the veil. A mortal has been made a seraph."

"So, what's the big deal? What's a seraph anyway?"

"What's a seraph? That's the highest order of angel is all! They get to fly about the throne of the Lord and are privy to all his words of wisdom. They're like a board of directors, or cabinet secretaries, or even higher, nearly as important as a senior executive vice president of the Disney Corporation, or the Prudential Life Insurance Company. There is only one position higher in the entire universe. Don't you realize how important that is? And the perks, wow! They're issued six wings[19] and full-length glories, and they get penthouse apartments in Thelassar with a platoon of servants, and nine hundred and ninety-nine houris…"

"So what? If you stripped them all naked and stood them next to any other angel, or even a mortal soul, could you see any difference?"

"That's an outrageous thing to say. I've never even thought of what they'd look like without their royal robes."

"I think you may have lucked out, Lem. If the seraphim are as powerful as you say, and you are the one responsible for this one being in heaven, it sounds to me like you've got a direct line to the inside track.

It's almost as good as being the boss's nephew." An impish smile played about her lips as she added, "Of course, it will be some time before you'll be able to use your pull...your IOU, remember? You owe me two thousand years service."

That brought him out of his daze, and he shot back, "That's only if I can't repay the loan." Abigail gave one of her nasty demon sniggers. And he said, "Never mind laughing at me. Get busy conjuring the money. The sooner we start, the better my chances of paying you back."

Chapter 21

ABIGAIL CONJURED SEVERAL TEN THOUSAND DOLLAR T-BILLS into existence, examined them carefully, and then closed her eyes. Intense concentration hardened her features as she projected her powers to the distant Treasury Department to insert the bill's serial numbers into the department's computer records, and into the maturity date files, and to cause those numbers to appear on the notes themselves. The sales receipts, in triplicate, were as hard to make as the bills themselves. The government's bureaucratic check and double-check system made everything much more difficult for Abigail to conjure than ordinary currency, but fifteen million dollars cash money, even in hundred dollar bills, amounted to more bulk than she had storage space.

"Can't you make them any faster than that?" Lemuel asked impatiently.

"I'm going as fast as I can. There's a lot more to this than conjuring ordinary currency, and if I don't do it right, these notes would be worthless counterfeits." Then she added the bills to the small pile of bills already on the table and placed the Bible on top of them for a paperweight. She had made about a hundred of them, and was getting tired. "I'm quitting for the day. This is hard work."

"Aw, come on Abigail, you've only conjured a million dollars. You said we'd need at least fifteen million. It'll take you two weeks at this rate. "

"No more today. I'll do some more tomorrow." She massaged her neck and rubbed her eyes. "Would you mind getting me a cup of coffee, Lem? Creating wealth is hard work, and you know how I feel about work."

The night sky was spattered with multicolored diamond chips, all intensely glinting in the moonless arch of the universe, and out on the ocean, miles away, beyond the white-crowned breakers, the lights of a row of oil derricks reflected like luminous eyes of creatures from another planet sucking up the world's lubricant. Perhaps it will stop spinning when they suck it dry.

Lemuel and Abigail brought the TV set outside and were watching a news program. One of the segments was about a fifty-times billionaire, and Abigail said petulantly,"Do you realize that, if he gets a five percent return on his money, he makes as much in two days as it me two weeks to make? Somehow it doesn't seem fair that he can make that much without lifting a finger and I had to work so hard today just to make one million."

"He doesn't have to work Abby. His money works for him."

"When he gets to heaven, I hope they'll give him a really nasty job," she said spitefully.

"Oh, he'll probably be raking in the gold, just like he's doing now, Abby," Lemuel said, thinking of John d'Are.

Still in a foul humor, Abigail switched off the TV, and asked, "Have you given any thought as to what kind of services you're going to have? So far every bit of your soul-saving project has been on my shoulders. I'm beginning to feel used."

Naturally Lemuel, as an emissary of the forces of goodness, had accepted her contribution as though it were the ordained usufruct of the

HOW THE GOOD TAILOR GOT TO HEAVEN

Godly and never considered that Abigail, representing the forces of badness, might have the remotest interest in the process of soul-saving. He felt that only the Godly had any valid claim to righteousness. Lemuel was to discover that she felt that she had a good deal to say about the matter. He said, "Since we've decided to have a tabernacle tent constructed according to God's specifications, I think we should follow through all the way." He made a clicking sound with his tongue, winked forcefully, and punched the air with his fist. "Our liturgy should be historically accurate also, and conform to God's instructions to Moses."

"Weren't those instructions for the Israelites, and as God's chosen, aren't they automatically considered saved? Unless you plan to convert the American gentiles to Judaism, you'd better pick something else."

"Fundamentally, most of the Christian rituals are derived from these instructions. Their embroidered vestments, the bishop's miters, and preacher's homilies about what is sacred and what is profane come directly from these instructions. But we don't have to be dogmatic about it: it's cleanliness of heart, and spirit, that God requires of man.[20]"

"I think you should do something that appeals to the American taste."

"What do you suggest?"

"How about something like the bean suppers the churches in New England have. Those Yankees raise a lot of money that way, but I think we should give the food away. Of course here in Texas we should serve Texas Chili, and that big brass grill should be large enough to barbeque a couple of hogs."

"That's the altar for the burnt sacrifice."

"Yeah, we'll sacrifice the hogs," she said, completely oblivious to pork profaning the sacred brazier, and added, "And that little golden table, we could heap high with tamales."

"The show bread, Abigail. That's for the show bread."

"Uh huh. And we could alternate that with a good old-fashioned fish fry with big chunks of corn bread, and set out platters full of shrimp creole with cheese rice…you know these big Gulf shrimp are the best in the world, and we should also serve some hot spicy crawfish, and crabs, and spiny lobster tails…"

"You're putting the wrong twist on the ceremony, Abigail! We don't give them food. They're supposed to bring their offerings. Sacrifices are what the congregation offers to the Lord! They're supposed to bring in the firstlings of their flocks and so forth. There are peace offerings, and sin offerings, and meat offerings, and wave offerings, and heave offerings. Offerings are not food they come to receive. You've got it backwards."

"You said that you wanted to attract the multitude? I'll bet the multitude would be attracted by some blackened red snapper, and hush puppies, and refried beans."

"You don't understand. We're not giving a party!"

"And while they're eating you could mingle with them in your fine priestly robes, you know, reach out to them on a personal level, and then get up on your platform and deliver your homily like it was an after-diner speech."

"Abigail, you're missing a key element—sacrifice! They're supposed to sacrifice; submit their offerings as willing self-denial; acknowledge the Lord's primacy in their lives. What you're suggesting would degenerate into a milling disorderly mob. They'd be discussing politics, or how their children were doing in school, or making business deals—worldly things."

"Okay, so I don't know much about the Bible, but I do remember hearing something about fishes, and loaves, and a sermon from a mound. How would this be any different from that?" Then she ridiculed Jacob's promise to tithe: "And I don't recall the multitude giving back any ten percent either. If you want to attract a multitude…you feed them!"

Now it was Lemuel's turn to seek the subreption properties of a couple of shots of bourbon. Several minutes later, Lemuel said solicitously, "You've had a hard day, Abby. Let's sleep on it, and we'll attack the problem with fresh minds in the morning."

HOW THE GOOD TAILOR GOT TO HEAVEN

* * *

Morning found the two soul gatherers once more locked in genteel disagreement, with Abigail saying, "This stuff is for sickos!"

Lemuel, just as vehemently, responded, "It's the attitude of sacrifice that you've got to get through your thick demon skull. Understand? Submission!" He had advised her to read a few chapters of Leviticus.

She read no further than the fifth verse of the first chapter when the outburst occurred and her expression turned to disgust. Then she said, "It looks like you've swapped a nice threshing floor ritual for a slaughterhouse. I hope you don't really intend to pour all that blood around and smear it on the furniture and the draperies. And look what it says over here: 'Moses and Aaron, and his sons wash their hands and feet in the brass laver and then use the water to wash the bullock's inwards and his legs. That's disgusting! Washing the butchered parts in the same water they washed their hands and feet in?'[21] If you want to attract a sanguinary crowd, why not have cockfights, or bear-baiting with pit bulls? Just over the border they have bullfights. That might interest your flock."

Then she laid down some preliminary conditions that Lemuel was to promise to follow if he wanted her to conjure any more money. "No cannibalism and no drinking blood...either real or symbolic! No groveling on the ground, handling poisonous snakes, or drinking poison...it was dangerous and crazy. No sacrificial lambs nor any other animals were to be ritually slaughtered. No hate mongering rhetoric from the pulpit ...and positively no lying! On this last proviso Lemuel managed to wring from her the concession that he didn't have to volunteer information either.

"Well, if it's in the Bible, I guess they can read it for themselves," she conceded.

After several moments of silence, Abigail said, "How about something like this?" She conjured a large poster; boldly red, white, and blue, and spangled with stars. Across the top was a photograph of Lemuel in full regalia standing by the entrance to the tabernacle tent. The lettering was in bold, carnival, Barnum & Bailey style, and read: "The Real Soul Food," and so there would be no misunderstanding, a bill of fare listed the selections. The word "free" was liberally printed at angles many times. In small print at the bottom were the words: "All donations gratefully accepted."

"With this approach you'll have a full house every night."

"Full of vagrants, maybe. That's much too crude, Abigail. I can't imagine Saint Paul or any of the Holy fathers being involved in anything so gross."

"Okay, fishes and loaves are out..."

"You're twisting things again, aren't you? You're turning the blessed words with your little demon twists."

"I can do healing the same as the establishment angels, and then if you want evidence of the Holy Ghost, I could cause a holy fire to appear above the tabernacle, or fiery pillars; just name it and I'll make it happen. Of course we'll make it appear as though you had a direct line to the Lord himself. Or do you want to amaze them by walking on water? We can do that."

They pondered in silence. So far they had agreed only that they both liked music, and they both agreed that neither one liked the modern, discordant, unmelodious, claxon-like sounds that pass for music today, but Lemuel favored inspirational and spiritual tunes and Abigail liked classical, Gypsy folk dances, and some jazz. "The Psalms are songs and they're spiritual," Lemuel said. "Let's look there. The Psalms are the song book of the faithful."

"This may be something." He started to read: "But let the righteous be glad: let him rejoice before God: yea, let them exceedingly rejoice...The singers went before, the players on instruments followed after; among them were damsels playing with timbrels.[22] Do you think we should include something like that?" Lemuel was learning to be selective with Biblical verse when reading to Abigail. She'd have bristled angrily at the cause of the rejoicing. The preceding verse read, *That thy foot be dipped in the blood of thy enemies, and the tongue of thy dogs in the same.*[23] Then he turned several pages and read from the very last Psalm:

"Praise ye the Lord. Praise God in his sanctuary...Praise him with the sound of the trumpet: praise him with the psaltery and harp. Praise him with the timbrel and dance: praise him with stringed instruments and organs. Praise him upon the loud cymbals: praise him upon the high sounding cymbals. Let everything that hath breath praise the Lord."

"That sounds nice, full of singing and dancing." And she expanded on it imaginatively. "How about this?" Her arms moved gracefully to visually show a smooth flow as she talked. " A costumed procession leading from the courtyard and into the tabernacle, and you, wearing that fancy getup in their midst, proceeding to the dias. As the procession passed down the aisles with the pretty damsels waving their tambourines rhythmically, and swiveling with anguine enticements, have them go in among the assembly, and by using promising smiles and gentle tugs, urge them to join the procession to the altar. When you get them up there, you get them to commit their souls to God." She danced through the movements, and said, "Once they get up front, they can't back down without looking foolish."

Lemuel, captivated by her enthusiasm, said, "And all this while the chorus and the dancing girls would be singing." He suggested a couple of hymns from the *Broadman Hymnal*, *Oh Come All Ye Faithful* and *O Why Not Tonight*.

Abigail snickered, and said; "I suppose you spell it c-o-m-e and not c-u-m all ye faithful."

Her pun was over Lemuel's head, but he liked the general idea, and he sang a couple of bars from *O Why Not Tonight*. "And wilt thou thus his love requite/ Renounce at once thy stubborn will/ Be saved O tonight." This also caused a few nasty chuckles from the demon; Lord only knows what she could have been thinking.

However, there was a glaring inconsistency with the plan. They were combining the Book of Psalms with the Book of Exodus; joining Moses's time with David's time, which was a difference of about three hundred years. Furthermore, David had returned to the ancient practice of holding his religious services on a threshing floor. The customs would be different and people would dress differently. The Book of Exodus describes with great detail what the chief priest and his assistants were to wear: an ephod of gold, blue, purple and scarlet, and fine-twined linen; shoulder pieces; a curious girdle; a breastplate of cunning work; and even the gems to use to represent the twelve tribes. Sardis, topaz, carbuncle, emerald, sapphire and diamond; a lingure, agate, and amethyst; and beryl, onyx, and jasper; and the hems of the robes had pomegranates and little gold bells; and the assistants were to wear mitres and coats of fine white linen; and Moses's mitre was like a gold crown, and engraved with the words "Holiness to the Lord." And there was blue lace placed upon the mitre.[24] But nowhere in any of this detail was there any mention of musical instruments or dancing damsels with timbrels that the Psalms of David described. He mentioned this discrepancy to Abigail, and worried that now Christianity was the way to salvation, he wondered how all these contradictory directives could be reconciled. "There are nearly six centuries between David and Jesus."

"I'm a terrestrial angel, remember? We don't care about such details. But I can get them to come to the cookout and up to the altar...the rest is up to you."

"Okay! But just the clothes; three hundred years can make a big difference. Three centuries ago the men wore tricorn hats, and knee britches, and lace; and the women wore billowing skirts that reached the ground, and bonnets. We want to be as authentic as possible. What kind of clothes did the Israelites wear at the exodus and what were they wearing in David's time?"

"I suppose it all depended on whether they were rich or poor, same as today. In Egypt, in Moses's time, they wore very little; not much more than a towel wrapped around their waist, like a kilt, and ordinary people went barefooted, and bareheaded. Women of the privileged class might wear a tight sheath that covered them from the calf to just beneath their breasts, and with wide shoulder straps to hold them up. Both men and women wore colorful jewelry, but not necessarily gemstones. Usually the stones were just colorful paste beads called faience."

The idea of wearing a kilt didn't appeal to Lemuel, and he said, "I suppose that's why the Lord ordered the priests to cover their nakedness from their loins even unto their thighs with linen breeches[25]. It would be unnerving to some parishioners to have the priests' genitals and buttocks exposed during the sacred moments of supplication before the altar."

Abigail laughed at his overly serious considerations, and continued, "Those who could afford to please their vanity might have their kilts accordion-pleated, and both the men and women wore capes if it was chilly. The ladies were fashionably coiffed and sometimes they wore wigs, but in Moses's day the Egyptian dancing girls and the musicians and the acrobats usually wore nothing but a few pieces of jewelry, or they might wear a G-string." Lemuel looked puzzled, and she explained, "A G-string is what strippers wear. You've seen them; something like the thong swim suits you've seen the girls wearing today. The Egyptians were as proud of their bodies as the Spartans, and thought nothing of parading around showing them off. But the Israelites in David's time would have been more modestly clothed."

Lemuel remembered the tableau of David dancing before the Ark of the Covenant, which showed David wearing a kind of short-sleeved garment, slightly longer than a shirt, and tied with a sash. He danced without his linen breeches and allowed his secret parts to be exposed, which caused the handmaidens to blush and giggle. His exhibitionism was what caused Michal to behave shrewishly, and for which she was punished. But Lemuel decided that if he was going to do any dancing, he would definitely wear the linen breeches, and he didn't think that the dancing girls with the timbrels, and the alluring smiles, should be naked either. Although he suspected that David would have continued using the traditional costumes.

Abigail said, "But more modestly clothed doesn't mean they'd be dressed like nuns or wear something like the choir robes that they wear today. The fine twined linen was diaphanous as the sheerest batiste and clung like jersey; little would be left to the imagination. And the

Egyptians thought their navels to be really sexy. It was the fashion of the day for both men and women to drape their kilts from above their hips in the back and fasten them low in front, well below their navels."

"Solomon liked navels too. He said to the beautiful Shulamite, 'Thy navel is like a round goblet, which wanteth not liquor, thy belly is like a heap of wheat set about with lilies; Thy two breasts are like two young roes that are twins.'"[26]

Abigail was surprised that Yahweh permitted something like that to be written in his Holy Book and Lemuel told her that she had the wrong idea about the Lord. "The Bible is joyous and loving. It is true that some of the prophets can be a bit stuffy, but the Lord isn't always wrathful and vengeful, he's also a loving God. The New Testament tells us; 'He that loveth not, knoweth not God; for God is love.'[27] And Jesus's ministry is very liberal; there's much more freedom in the New Testament. Jesus bound his followers to two basic commandments: to love God and to love one another. If you'd read the Bible instead of criticizing it, you'd see that. And you liked those verses in Psalms that I read to you, that's Old Testament scripture. Christians believe that God's new covenant is revealed in the New Testament, but the New cannot be understood without the Old. The liturgy and ceremonies draw on the Hebrew rites, and their prayers make use of the Old Testament, especially the Psalms. Jesus began his ministry by quoting Psalm Two: 'The Lord hath said unto me, thou art my son, this day have I begotten thee.' So our ministry must use both books because Christianity is based on the old Hebrew religion and the God of Abraham as the Creator."

"Oh! I see...Jesus's commandments weren't added to the Ten Commandments; they replaced them."

Lemuel shook his head and sighed. She was hopeless. No matter what he said, it became perverted by her twisted demon mind. He decided to drop these finer theological points, which she would never understand anyway, and stick to rediscovering the historically authentic proper rituals. From what he could imagine, David's dance before the ark would be a combination of some of the wilder gyrations of modern rock stars, the hora, and the sensational pelvis swiveling of Elvis. He decided that his disciples should be more sedate and he asked Abigail what sort of dance she remembered from that period.

"It would be more *Seraglio* than *Swan Lake*. The Semites are eastern people. Do you remember the little Salome dance I did, and the belly dance Esther did? It would be something like that. Watch, I'll show you." She stood and did a few bumps and grinds, and softly whistled a few bars from *Scheherazade*. By vibrating her vocal cords as she whistled, she achieved an eerie sound suggestive of the ancient fertile crescent, and her movements progressed to a fairly accomplished belly dance.

Esther's motile middle had been partially covered by her miraculous visitation robe, but Abigail wore only a skimpy swim suit, and as Lemuel watched her belly undulate, he gulped, and said, "It's not possible to do that. I mean, no mortal woman could make her stomach leap about in such a fashion."

"Of course it takes practice, and the next time Esther visits us, get her to strip and dance for you. Then you'll really see some belly motion. The Gypsy style is more like a flamenco or an adagio."

* * *

Having been denied a pulpit in an established organization, Lemuel, with Abigail's help, was trying to put togther a service that would be authentic to the ancient Holy Land, the age of the prophets, the apostles, and to be Biblically accurate at the same time. With the Bible as his only guide, it was turning out to be more Eastern exotic than Western gothic; more Byzantium than Canterbury; but the influence of Rome was also in evidence. Caesar and Christ were virtual contemporaries, but the Holy Land was in the Eastern half of the Roman Empire, which was suffused with oriental mysticism and sweltering heat. One also wonders why our soul-savers did not think it strange that their instruction book was authorized and officially endorsed by an English King. There in that cold foggy island of heavy tweeds and overcoats, the ambience was as different as though on another planet.

Abigail made a few more T-bills. One million a day was her limit, so she conjured them and then picked up the Bible for a little relaxing reading. "Where's that section about the girl's navel like a cup that wanteth not liquor, and breasts like twin roes?"

"It's the Song of Solomon near the middle of the book," he answered.

She found it and read for a while, and said, "Some of these metaphors are pretty graphic. 'My beloved put in his hand by the *hole of the door*, and my bowels were moved for him. I rose up to open to my beloved...I opened to my beloved.' Lem, are you absolutely sure that temple prostitution is forbidden?"

"Yes, and that story proves it. She remains faithful to her shepherd lover, even though she has attracted the love of the king. She rejects Solomon and lets him know that her vineyard is her own. She tells him to go back to his thousand, and the two hundred he's already impregnated. The king tells her that she is more desirable than his three score queens, and four score concubines, and virgins without number. And she is so beautiful they all praise her and want her to join them. They say she is fair as the moon and clear as the sun, but the women of the king's harem derided her for being true to her shepherd boy. They say she is as formidably terrible as an army with banners defending her virtue."

"Well, it may be poetic to some, but I don't think I'd like to have my eyes compared to fish pools and my nose to the tower of Lebanon, even if it was a king saying it. Then he says her stature is like a palm tree. How's that? Tall, bent and scaly? And her breasts are like a clusters of grapes? What's that mean? Lumpy?" Then she asked, "Where's this Book of Psalms that you said showed the inspirational side of the church?" She flipped through the pages to find the book and started to read.

Lemuel became edgy and nervously offered to read to her. He reached for his Bible and she pushed his hand away. "I can read!" she snapped. Then she looked at him suspiciously, and added, "A Gypsy can smell deceit in a Gorgio at a hundred yards. You'd rather I wouldn't read this, huh? Wouldn't you?" Her eyes narrowed, and she exclaimed;

HOW THE GOOD TAILOR GOT TO HEAVEN

"Inspirational? . . .Hah! . . .Peacefully serene? . . .Hah! . . . Ennobling? . . . Hopeful? . . . Joyous? . . . Listen to this: 'Break them with a rod of iron, dash them in pieces; smite enemies on the cheek, break their teeth; Destroy them O God, let them fall by their own council. . . .'"

"That's the kind of thing lying angels do. They make the Lord's enemies believe false council," Lemuel explained.

"I know what you do. Listen to this: 'Weary with groaning, mine eye is consumed; Save me from them that persecute, prepare instruments of death, ordaineth arrows against persecutors: destructions are come to perpetual end, destroy cities'. . . "

"That's what the avenging angels do."

"Covetness, mouthful of cursing and deceit, lieth in wait, break the arm of the wicked; He shall rain snares, fire and brimstone; They speak vanity with flattering lips, and a double heart; Let mine enemies say that I have prevailed; they are all altogether become filthy, there is none that doeth good, no not one; He that back biteth, he that putteth money to usury; their sorrows shall be multiplied; Deliver my soul from *the wicked which is thy sword.*'"

"David means the mortals under the power of the evil angels there. When the Huns came out of the Asian steps and laid waste to Europe, they were rightly called the sword of God."

"'Smoke out of his nostrils, and fire out of his mouth devoured: coals were kindled by it, darkness, thick clouds, secret place, hailstones and coals of fire...'"

"You used hailstones yourself, remember?"

" . . .'overtaking enemies and consuming them, I have wounded them that they were not able to rise, Thou hast given me the necks of my enemies to destroy, they cried out but there was none to save them; they are brought down and fallen, but we are risen; The Lord shall swallow them in his wrath, and the fire shall devour them, their fruit Thou shalt destroy from the earth.' Then we get to the Twenty-second Psalm: 'My God, my God, why hast thou forsaken me?'"

She grew more and more disgusted as she read, and asked, "Where's all this love you were talking about? I won't help you preach this kind of stuff. And they let the church instruct little children in morality? How awful! No wonder the country has so much violent crime in their schools. These are the ravings of a manic-depressive, schizoid paranoiac. David sees enemies everywhere, and his verse jumps from benign to malignant, from elated to depressed, and all within the same Psalm. He needs some double-strength Prozac."

"The Twenty-third Psalm is nice, Abigail. You didn't get to the twenty-third."

"And what about the rest of them if this is what is in the first twenty-two?"

"I read the hundred and fiftieth to you, and you thought it was nice."

Abigail turned page after page, and muttered in undertones, "Iniquities, deliver from enemies, hate whisper together against me, breaketh ships, teach thee terrible things, live and not see corruption, thy tongue deviseth mischief working deceitfully. Oh here's a good one: 'The wicked are estranged from the womb: they go astray as soon as they be born, speaking lies. Their poison is like the poison of a serpent' Oh yes, I can see this Book of Psalms sure is a fount of joyfulness, and the proper manual to instruct the kiddies in righteousness." Then she asked even more sarcastically, "Is this the sort of happiness you intend to preach? Psalm 137: 'O daughter of Babylon...Happy shall he be, that taketh and dasheth thy little ones against the stones.' It's hard to find any joy there. I'm beginning to understand why your ministers preach so much hatred from their pulpits."

"No, no! I won't preach like that. I'll only use the nice things that are in the Bible."

She laughed without mirth, and asked, "Are there any?"

"Oh sure. I'll take my sermons from the New Testament. You'll see, there's a whole shift in philosophy. Jesus's message is a spiritual uplift. He told his followers to love one another and to love even their enemies."

HOW THE GOOD TAILOR GOT TO HEAVEN

"All right, but I refuse to support Yahweh's mean-spiritedness, and I cannot think of one single reason to justify killing babies, nor anyone else for that matter." She dropped the Bible heavily onto the coffee table, and added, "I don't think you should be supporting any political schemes, either. That's what causes wars, and even the most noble sounding cause is usually just another way to legalize theft. And no lying. That's just another form of theft, and that's worse than stealing money. Liars are stealing knowledge of right and wrong."

"How about using parables?"

"No, that's lying! If you're going to take their souls, you've got to do it without lying."

Her conditions were sharply opposite the lessons Tomas had taught. Tomas taught the ends justified the means. Get those souls committed no matter what you have to do or say. He hoped Abigail wouldn't examine the New Testament too closely. Paul's moral coloration was as consistent as a chameleon's skin. He adjusted his message to suit every audience.

Silence became a viable presence. The blood thirst of the ritual slaughter in the tabernacle, and the Psalms evoking the Almighty's powers to be merciless against opponents, had made her waspish. There was a heavy ambience of malaise gathering between them. Lemuel picked up the Bible looking for something that might return the smile to Abigail's face. He searched through page after page trying to find something that might please her. Dark deeds and reverse interpretations leapt out at him from every page. He could find nothing to disperse his own growing doubts about its sublime purpose. Abigail's expression reflected a strange weariness that Lemuel had not seen before. The weariness of being too long a spectator of the eternal melodrama now made Lemuel feel that his highest reward would be to return the smile to her face. He returned to the Songs of Solomon: *I am black but comely...Look not upon me because I am black, because the sun hath looked upon me.* Was Solomon writing about Abishag? The most beautiful damsel that could be found throughout Israel.[28] Hadn't she lain with old David to keep him warm? Lemuel thought that if she were half as beautiful as Abigail, he could understand how Adonijah might surrender his claim to the throne in exchange for her. [29] He could also see how Solomon would be willing to slay his brother to keep her.[30] And he wished Abigail would lay with him to keep him warm.

But Abigail was right. Solomon was overrated as a poet. His metaphors were not flattering, and his tale was woefully unconnected, but he did accurately record the Middle-Eastern culture of Biblical times. Perhaps that was why the book escaped the flames of the Sanhedrin censors, and because publishers do not lightly excise the writings of famous kings and celebrities. The council of Nicea also had problems with accepting the open sensuality expressed, but it had survived those book burners because the councilors with dexterous perspicacity regarded it as allegory, and so Lemuel was as free to use it as any other book in the Bible. Abigail's understanding of what was expressed was unimaginatively current and Lemuel counted this as a blessing.

* * *

It would be a mistake for the reader to conclude that because of some recessive personality flaw, Lemuel was conceding sacerdotal offices to the demon. Abigail was not dominating the angel as he saw it, as long as her conditions fell within the bounds of the Holy Bible, they were all right with him. It wasn't as though she were advocating burning incense to strange gods…anything like that and he would put his foot down. For the present he was glad that he had found such a useful ally in a strange and often hostile culture. It didn't matter to him that his helpful liaison to that culture had a few minor personality flaws…such as, being a demon. Lemuel was also quite aware of the old saw that: 'Love is the delusion that one woman is different from another.' He thought it quite accurately reflected his own attitude toward all the women that he had ever met. Abigail was, of course, different. She was not a mortal woman; she was an earth angel.

He decided that as a divertissement from their labors in the vineyard of the Lord that a trip to the urbanized southern tip of the island was called for. Abigail liked shopping. They could get lunch in a nice restaurant and he wanted to buy some fishing tackle. He felt that it was high time that he contributed to their table.

* * *

As it happened, a beauty contest was being held in the ballroom of the grandest hotel on the island, and contestants from all over the world were competing to see who was the most beautiful girl in the Universe. Lemuel knew he was escorting the most beautiful girl in the universe, but Abigail declined to be a contestant in anything so degrading. Besides, as she pointed out, the officials wouldn't permit an entry from hell. If she won, it would detract from the wholesome goodness the officials wanted to project. However, the Ethereal Establishment decided to enter a contestant, because so far only worldly women had competed. The heavenly hosts felt that as part of this universe their females should be given equal opportunity, and they sent heaven's most famous beauty to prove that angels were more beautiful than humans. Esther won in a close decision over a beauty from Bali. It was the talent performance that made the difference. The judges thought Esther's belly dance was superior to the Balinese temple dance.

Lemuel had never seen Esther without her robes before and the voluptuous exhibition of curvaceous ectoplasm caused him to blush, cover his eyes, and peep at her through parted fingers. He realized that he would never again imagine her as a school marm. He disagreed with Abigail's spiteful opinion that the vote was rigged to favor the emissary from the God of Abraham over a Vishnu worshipper; Yahweh over Brahma. Lemuel said that he thought Esther was the second most beautiful creature in the Universe next to Abigail, and he told Abigail so, and made her smile. Esther was kept too busy accepting awards and applause to visit with them, but she promised to stop in for a brief visit before she went back to the empyrean.

On the way back, they stopped at a huge new shopping mall. Lemuel had watched with interest the surf fishermen and wanted to try it himself. The most expensive general merchandise store in Texas had an outlet there, and while Abigail dallied in the ladies' section, Lemuel visited the well-stocked sporting goods section. An unctuous clerk sold him a ten-foot graphite rod that the salesman assured him would cast a lure a hundred and fifty yards. He also needed a sand spike to hold the rod while he baited his line, hip boots, a spinning reel, two spools of monofilament, and enough lures and sinkers to cause him to grunt when he picked up his new, fully-loaded, tackle box. The salesman also sold him, at reduced price, a booklet titled *The Art of Surf Fishing*. It contained drawings showing how to handle the long rod, diagrams of all the sure kill methods of attaching lures and rigs, and twenty step-by-step drawings of monofilament knot tying. The equipment cost him the entire thousand dollars that he had pocketed, the money which Abigail had created so he could buy himself a new suit.

As they drove back along the beach, he studied the water and imagined he saw fish in every curling wave; all stupidly waiting to be outsmarted by the lures he had bought. Some of the lures were so enticing that he felt that if he were a fish, he'd bite on them himself.

He and Abigail spent that evening loading line onto the spool of the reel and learning about snap swivels, three way swivels, spread rigs, Hopkins lures, treble hooks, fish finder rigs, leather bumpers, bucktails, pyramid sinkers, and the other esoterica of that particular denomination of sport fishing. He took the long rod outside and whipped it through several imaginary casts, and admired its response and balance. It flexed perfectly without back spring, which would slow the line feeding through the graduated ring guides funneling the speeding monofilament to the slender flexible tip. He grasped the long, thick, cork butt of the handle in his left hand and held firmly the rod and the foot of the reel in his right hand. The rod felt as though it were a natural extension of his arms. He planned to try his luck at dawn with the incoming tide. The booklet assured him that would be when the fishing was best. Before falling asleep that night he promised Abigail that they would have fresh fish for breakfast and by dint of his expectant enthusiasm, the Bible and all things ecclesiastical were forgotten.

The dawn-lightened sky found Lemuel walking alone along the

beach stalking the elusive hollows beneath the waves where, the instruction manual said, the fish came teeming in with rapacious appetites. Abigail mumbled, "good luck," rolled over, and went back to sleep. Pride swelled within Lemuel's breast. This was the natural order of things. He was the mighty hunter; the provider. Abigail was female and the weaker vessel. This morning the correct primal roles were being enacted. No longer would he have to vacillate, weakly conceding points of argument to her. He was the provider and she would do as he commanded.

The air was chilly on his bare legs and the Gulf water warm on his bare feet. The sand felt secure and solid, and sloped toward the deep, at the pitch of a cedar shingle. A hunch caused him to keen his eye toward a darker patch of water on the broad green expanse. For his first cast he selected a two-ounce Hopkins, attached a six-inch piece of soft plastic tubing to the treble hook, and, as he had practiced last night, swung the rod back and then brought it forward forcefully. The handle spun wildly, and the lure plopped into the water about twenty-five feet from where he stood. He had forgotten to open the bail. He said a few unangel-like things, retrieved the line, and cast again. This time the lure splashed a satisfying two hundred feet out, but only halfway to the dark patch he was aiming for.

Even though the lure had fallen short of its mark, he worked the rod as he had learned from the illustrations in the surf fishing booklet. He imagined the bright chrome lure with its red plastic exciter bounding up with every pull on his rod, and enticing the fish to bite. No luck, but it was only his first cast. The common belief among surf fishermen is that if you catch a fish on your first cast you'll catch no more fish for the rest of the day, and so Lemuel regarded this as an auspicious sign. For his next cast he waded out to mid-thigh depth and a soft wave rose up, chest high, pushing him off balance. He retreated to where the waves rose only to his waist. He tried another cast, and once again the line flew true, and he did exactly as the booklet said, but caught nothing. Lemuel's arms were not bulky. His muscles were long and wiry, but his wrists were thick and strong, and soon he was casting a hundred yards, all to no avail, however. He changed lures, used bucktails, plastic eels, different color lures that resembled fish, different shapes and colors of plastic tubing—and still nothing. After an hour and a half his muscles began to ache and he had a cramp in his right thigh. And worse, Abigail had finally gotten up, came out onto the beach to see how he was faring, and increased his growing disenchantment with the whole process by asking, "Where's breakfast? I'm hungry!"

Suddenly his rod tip quivered and then arced in a graceful curve. The tip wiggled madly up and down. The drag started to click rapidly as the line played out from the spool and Lemuel's face grew a smug smile. He waded backward to where she stood on the beach and wound in a writhing twisting redfish weighing about six pounds. "There you are! How's that for service?" he said, pretty pleased with himself.

Lemuel's breast filled with the hunter's pride; the hunter who provides meat for the table, the hunter who by lone might and persistence has placed the morning's food before his mate. There was the proof of his manly self-reliance flapping before him on the sand. And as he decapitated his catch and pulled the hook from its mouth, he found an unexpected bonus: there was a fifty dollar bill in the fish's mouth.[31]

* * *

Before Lemuel, Abigail's lifestyle was uncomplicated and carefree. She had found the gypsy ways, and her luxurious trailer, allowed her the maximum comfort possible with the least expenditure of effort. She owned no property other than her vehicles, she paid for all her needs with cash, and she could conjure a driver's license, vehicle registration cards, automobile insurance certification cards, or any necessary documents with a snap of her fingers. The only traffic ticket she ever received was handled similarly. Her ticket and the officer's copy disappeared, as well as the gasoline in the tank of his motorcycle. But now that she had gone into the churching business, she was a woman of moderate wealth.

The stack of notes, representing millions of dollars, was growing. In her mind the notes were only pieces of paper with fancy printing, but

HOW THE GOOD TAILOR GOT TO HEAVEN

she knew that the mortal world was not of that same opinion. The mortals jealously overlaid the possession of such bits of paper with intricate regulations, caveats, bureaucratic red tape, tariffs, investigations, and locked them away behind thick steel doors. All things abhorrent to her. For all her powers and worldly travels she actually knew very little about the world of high finance. She had never even had a bank account and her mailing address was a street in Berkeley that was not to be found on any maps. Now that she was a multi-millionairess owning a thick stack of negotiable securities, she was faced with the problem of how to turn that paper into the tabernacle.

Chapter 22

AT FIRST ESTHER LIKED THE FAWNING, PAWING, STROKING, AND pampering that celebrity brought her. But the mob of men and butch women that surrounded her grew too large, and pressed too tightly for even God's love goddess to tolerate, and she disappeared. There ensued a full twenty minutes of groping each other before the mob discovered she had slipped away. She reappeared at Abigail's trailer with her crown askew and her clothing torn. "My God! The Medes and the Philistines showed more respect…even the bloody Hittites. What possessed you to live with these savage barbarians Abigail?"

Abigail laughed at her, and still smiling with amusement said, "I manage all right, but I keep a very low profile."

"Well, authorized permission or not, I was getting ready to fill their whole fucking ballroom with a plague of locusts."

"I could have done that for you," Abigail replied, while still laughing. "We don't need permission."

Lemuel brought the ladies some lemonade and Esther wanted a couple of shots of vodka in hers. Her harem pantaloons and short embroidered bolero jacket were shredded. Souvenir strips had been torn out, sequins and beads had been torn from her bra, and she groaned, "I can't go back looking like this. What if one of my kids should see me? I'm afraid to go back to the hotel to get my robes. The official chaperones would love to sell me to the tabloids. Somehow word got around about me and the palace guards."

None of Abigail's diminutive outfits would fit Esther's amazonian proportions, but a pair of Lemuel's blue jeans, cut off and fashionably frayed, and one of his white dress shirts with the sleeves rolled up to her elbows, fit perfectly. After washing off her heavy make-up, combing her hair and tying it in a ponytail, she was transformed into just another pretty vacationer, and no one would notice that she was actually the most beautiful female in the universe. The second most beautiful, according to Lemuel, but Esther had won the official title, twice. Esther calmed a bit when Abigail suggested that they would go shopping and buy some new clothes for her.

Esther noticed the stack of T-bills that Abigail had carelessly left on the table. Her curiosity was aroused and she asked what they were. When told, she looked puzzled, and asked, "What's fifteen million dollars?"

"It's a lot of money." Abigail replied.

Esther laughed, and said, "Quit kidding, Abby...money is coin, gold, silver, bronze...those are just pieces of paper." As Queen of Persia, Esther was no stranger to wealth, but in her mind, wealth was a thing substantial and tangible; it was arable lands, manufactories, slaves[32], palaces, delicate fabrics, beautiful rugs and tapestries, rare jewels, and precious metals. She could not believe it was possible for any normal intellect to attain the degree of self-deception necessary to regard pieces of paper as valuable. When Abigail told her the worth in sanctuary weight gold shekels, she was stunned. "And you say I can learn to make those pieces of paper?" she asked greedily.

"Sure. But these pieces of paper require more skill than ordinary paper money. These are individually registered in the government computers, and you have to hack into their records and insert receipts in

HOW THE GOOD TAILOR GOT TO HEAVEN — 401

their files. It's the extra paperwork that causes the trouble. You have to hack into the computers for ordinary money too, but that's simple compared to these bills."

"Computers?"

"Yes. They're something like an abacus, but instead of using your fingers to move beads, you move bytes with a keyboard, or by using your psychokinetic powers. It's really neat. Everyone's abacus is connected to everyone else's over the telephone wires, so you can shift the beads on anyone's abacus anywhere in the world. It's pretty simple when you learn how to project your powers into the phone lines."

Esther stared at the T-bills greedily and imagined the enormous pile of shekels they represented, considered the life of luxury she could have with them, and she announced, "I'm not going back! Please teach me how to do that, Abby. Puleeeze!"

Lemuel's face darkened and he became as wrathful as Isaiah. "Esther! That's treason! And it goes against the prime directive. We're not allowed to interfere with the unseen hand. The worldly economy doesn't need another demon diluting its currency."

Esther snapped back, "Treason, huh? Just what would you call shacking up with a demon for four months?"

"Abby volunteered to help me doing the Lord's work, and she doesn't like to be called a demon. She's an earth angel!"

"Well! That's what I'll be too."

"They'll send the press gang after you. You'll be punished. They might even send you to Abaddon."

This defection wasn't expected, but Abigail was quick to press her advantage. "Lem stop intimidating her! There's an agreement, remember? According to the intergalactic treaty, worldliness belongs to us, and if Esther is determined to stay in the world, I don't think they can take her." Then the crafty little demon argued that Esther's defection was actually an act of righteousness. "She'd still be doing the Lord's work, and when the press gang comes for her, she can tell them that. Besides, you want that big tabernacle tent, don't you? We need all the help we can get. You've got to start facing facts Lem. Esther and I aren't going to be nearly enough help. You'll need at least a dozen strong roustabouts just to move your tabernacle, put it up and take it down, and set up the chairs and such. Moses had the twelve tribes to do the heavy lifting, and if Esther wants to help, you better let her do it." Without showing a trace of ulterior motive, she added, "Unless you can get a dozen angels to help; we're going to need some muscle."

The notion of doing physical labor hadn't occurred to Esther. She had something else in mind. Something like Versailles with the orangery, and the sculpted formal gardens, and mirrored walls, and groined arcades, and coffered ceilings covered with gold, and hundreds of servants to wait on her. She couldn't understand why Abigail, who could live like a queen, chose to live like a vagabond. But until Abigail taught her how to make her own money, that palace would have to wait, and a dozen hard-bodied men were some consolation.

The saying "facts are stubborn things," always befuddled Lemuel. He suspected demonic intervention. In this belief he was on solid footing. Hadn't the president who beat the evil empire of earth, and brought down the Berlin Wall, confirmed it when he stated, "Facts are stupid things."

And Abigail continued to burden his mind with more facts. "Saving souls is big business now and you're going to have to be businesslike. Those dozen men are going to have to be paid wages, and that means withholding taxes, Social Security, and since they'll travel with us, they'll need trailers to live in, and vehicles to tow the trailers. And we'll need a couple of large trucks to haul everything around, unless you plan to use camels and asses. Trucks, trailers, and tow vehicles will have to be registered, insured, and pass state inspection. On top of that you'll have to hire musicians skilled with the ancient instruments, and the dancing girls, and chorus...."

All this fact was becoming as confusing as hermeneutics, and he held up both hands to stem the flow of fact. "Wait! Wait! I thought you said churches didn't have to pay taxes?"

"They don't, but the church's employees do, and as their employer we are responsible for seeing that their taxes are paid. We'll have to get employer I.D. numbers. There's a lot of book work involved. We'll need an accountant."

Lemuel was, to explain it in worldly terms, like a civil servant, a government employee, or a corporate functionary, a mere cog in the machine of the Ethereal Establishment, accustomed to obeying all authority above him, and extracting obedience from all those beneath him in rank. It made his position simple, routine, and, as long as everyone performed their assigned duties, worry free. All the paperwork for the firm was taken care of by those souls specializing in office work. It hadn't occurred to him that the secular authorities would expect him to perform such drudgery himself as part of his missionary work.

Esther didn't think that a dozen male angels would be of much use, to herself anyway, and wanted to know why the nation's ruler couldn't donate several slave families to the temple: "Xerxes always gave generously to the church. He gave one temple five hundred families. True, he took their golden idol, but he always gave them lots of slaves." Then she suggested that if the authorities wouldn't give them slaves they could buy slaves to do the work and avoid paying wages, and all the paperwork. "All Abby would have to do is to make a few more pieces of paper money. How much could a dozen strapping men cost today?" She added with a salacious leer. "But don't buy any eunuchs...they're not as," she paused to think of the proper word, "robust."

"You can't do that anymore, Esther. They did away with slavery about a hundred and fifty years ago. They found it was impractical, economically. Now the government makes you pay wages to your slaves, but you only have to pay them for the length of time they work for you...unless, of course, they volunteer their time and labor freely."

That jogged Lemuel's memory and he turned to the Bible for guidance. He found the answer. "I know what we'll do. Instead of paying wages to a dozen servants, we'll take on a dozen unpaid volunteer assistants and we can call them apostles. And the same goes for the chorus, the dancers, and the musicians. We'll need about seventy of them[33], and we can call them disciples. Our lambs will not be subject to the bureaucratic wolves. They'll need neither purse nor scrip nor shoes. See what it says here: 'the multitude of them that believed were of one heart and one soul: neither said any of them that aught of the things which he possessed was his own; but they had all things in common. Neither was there any among them that lacked: for as many as were possessors of lands or houses sold them, and brought the prices of the things that were sold, and laid them down at the apostles' feet: and distribution was made unto every man according as he had need.[34] '" Well pleased with himself, he beamed, "You see Abigail, it's true. The Bible has the answer to every problem."

Always the consummate sceptic, Abigail replied, "That must have been Jesus's greatest miracle: finding eighty-two people willing to work for nothing. It will be interesting to see how you duplicate it."

Esther sprang up, and said joyfully, "Now that we've solved that problem, let's go on that shopping trip that you promised. Come on Abby…please…I haven't been shopping for thousands of years."

* * *

Abigail and Esther, although of origins ethereally profound, and exquisitely antique, were not so jaded as to dismiss one of the more enjoyable pursuits that comes along with their gender's estrogen infusions. Although they had unlimited access to currency, there is something about the words "sale," "up to 50% off," "designer labels," and "at discount prices," that catalyzes this particular chromosome resulting in a mesmeric attraction. That this peculiar hormonal aberration is known to both the merchandiser and those afflicted, in no way lessens its impact. There are no scientists currently working on a solution for this malady. Rumors of a payoff have been heard, but as it now stands, the ladies may as well try to not scratch a mosquito bite.

Another, more frustrating manifestation of this syndrome is that no matter how many miles of chromium pipe are bowed down with fabric

HOW THE GOOD TAILOR GOT TO HEAVEN   —m—   405

wares, offered for sale, and perused, nothing ever fits. Esther wore a size twelve tall womens', and Abigail wore a four junior miss. There were dozens and dozens of garments in those two sizes, probably hundreds, but none of them fit properly, or if they did fit, they were sure to be the wrong color. Even worse were the shoe stores. Esther wore a 10A, and Abigail wore a 6AA, and although there were heaps and heaps of shoe boxes before them in every shop they visited, all imprinted with the correct sizing code, nothing was ever suitable. Furthermore, the dearth of commodity in those places was nothing compared to the pitiful lack of lingerie in the stores purporting to specialize in such garb.

One of the great mysteries is why all females everywhere do not protest, Godiva like, this vicious plot by the clothing industry to cause intense frustration to half of the country's population. In spite of all these hardships, Abigail and Esther managed to overcome all obstacles and successfully filled nearly half the bed of the pickup with boxes and bags of quite flattering apparel. Far easier was purchasing the temple tent for the crusade.

As they started to return to the trailer, Abigail suddenly snapped her fingers. "We're forgetting something," she said as she pulled off onto the shoulder of the road.

"Something for Lem?" Esther asked helpfully.

"Yeah…this won't take but a minute." She made a quick U-turn and drove into one of the tougher neighborhoods in Brownsville. The houses were one-story, frame or cinder block. Some had the tattered remains of imitation stone, asphalt siding clinging to cracked and chipped bungalow siding. TV antennas were bent at peculiar angles and most of the roofs had shingles missing. One house had a goat tethered to the front porch, another had a fence made of alternating headboards, footboards, and coil bedsprings. Laundry, which had been left hanging for days, flapped from lines in rear yards, and chickens roosted in a rusting Hudson that had one window remaining. Several young men wearing black T-shirts and leather motorcycle caps were socializing on one of the porches. They called obscenities to the passing *"gringas,"* but the ladies ignored their amorous propositions. At the end of the oiled, sandy street stood a two-car garage.

The garage was made of cinder blocks and had a slanting shed roof. On either side of the building were disorderly piles of rusting auto parts and car and truck bodies. All were partially dismembered, dented, scarred, and rusted. The building had been painted, not less than a decade ago, with a pale green, cement-based paint. To the right of the entrance was a thermometer which bore an ad for Carta Blanca, and above the door was a crudely-painted sign on the concrete lintel: "Bezaleel & Aholiab, Camping Supplies." Under that was lettered: "Est. 1220 B.C.," and then the claim: "Filled in wisdom and in knowledge of all manner of workmanship, able to devise cunning works in gold, and in silver, and in brass, also the cutting of stones and carving of wood[35]; excelling in carburetor repairs, and minor tuneups."

As the two, now stylishly-dressed, ladies approached, an oil-smeared and dusty short-haired white cur thumped his tail lazily while lying before a truck tire. "We Fix Flats," was painted on the sidewall of the tire in aged and weather-crazed white paint. They entered the dark interior where a single fly-specked light bulb seemed to accentuate the gloom and make the interior even darker. Along one wall hung fan belts, a few tail pipes, oily rags, and on the floor were fifty-gallon drums and open cases of motor oil. Along the other wall was a row of used tires, and an air compressor that hissed periodically and then gulped into spasmodic hiccupping.

Their eyes gradually became darkness adjusted and they saw a glass display counter at the rear of the small building. This was the camping outfitter section of the establishment. Through the smudged and scratched glass they saw several clasp knives mounted on a cardboard stand, a small assortment of sheath knives, several army surplus canteens, two sheathed hatchets, a cardboard display of waterproof containers for matches with compasses in the lids, an assortment of boxes of shotgun shells; the twelve gauge number sixes had been opened and "35 cents each" was written on the lid. Atop the counter was a stack of sur-

HOW THE GOOD TAILOR GOT TO HEAVEN   407

plus ponchos beside several boxes of oil filters and air cleaners. Everything in the place was covered with a layer of fine brown dust. Tattered cobwebs hung from the open rafters and in every corner.

A heavyset man wearing greasy coveralls, an army campaign cap from the Second word War, which hadn't been cleaned since, and with a four-day stubble of black and gray whiskers, leaned against a grimy workbench off to the side. He silently sized up his customers, took a long pull from a bottle of tequila, and then put the bottle into a cardboard junk box under the bench. He crossed the greasy concrete floor toward them, walking on a slight angle with short quick steps like a tightrope walker, wiped his hands with a greasy rag, and asked them if he could be of assistance.

Abigail described the tabernacle briefly and he assured her that he knew exactly what they wanted. He and his partner, (who was out with the wrecker at the moment obtaining elephant platforms for the Raja of Rajampour's tiger hunt), had the plans for that very item. It seems that their great, great, great, etceteras, grandfathers had built just such a tabernacle, and the specifications were still in their file cabinet. In fact, the partners were having a special on them that very week: fifteen million, four hundred thousand, nine hundred and ninety-five dollars. He required the usual ten percent deposit.

He wrote the order on a three-by-five order pad: "One Moses Tabernacle—Will Call. Deposit paid: One million, five hundred thousand dollars." It took a few minutes for Abigail to endorse the one hundred and fifty, ten thousand dollar T-bills, and she had to surrender three more of her hard-conjured notes to cover the discount rate.

Mr. Bezleel apologized for having to charge a premium. He pointed out that her notes were new ninety-day notes, and that only the Lord Almighty might know what the currency exchange rates would be ninety days from now. He muttered a few choice Semitic oaths directed at the Bretton Woods conferees, and then blamed the whole unreliable exchange rate system on the Uruguay round of the G7 conference. He said, "The only currency that has maintained its value ever since the

Spanish American War was the exchange rate of Pacific Islander cowrie shells for pigs, or wives. That has remained constant through two world wars, the Depression, and the economic distortions of the cargo cults. You can't even depend on gold anymore!"

Abigail sympathized with him and decided to order the trailers for the troupe while she was there so she could lock in a favorable dollar exchange rate. She called the Airstream dealer in El Paso. These, and their tow vehicles, would be delivered within ten days, the voice on the phone assured her, after they received the certified check. She thanked Mr. Bezaleel for letting her use his phone. He grumbled that it was a long distance call to El Paso, and that he'd put it on her bill.

Abigail and Esther were pleased with the results of their shopping excursion; they had saved three hundred, and sixty-seven dollars off the list price of the clothes they had bought. "And don't forget the five dollars we saved on the tabernacle," Abigail reminded her. In fact they had saved so much money that they decided to treat themselves to a nice lunch. They stopped at Los Escudos Cantina for a fine meal of Mexican fare. Their lunch was fifty dollars, but that was a pittance compared to all they had saved by shrewd bargain hunting.

* * *

Back at the trailer that afternoon, as they carried their bags and boxes of shrewdly acquired valuables, they chattered about their adventures. Abigail said to Lemuel, "You've no idea how much trouble we had. The sales girls were rude, even Esther, angel that she is, had to tell one off; and the shoe clerk started to get fresh…"

"I thought he was cute…"

"Well, he didn't have a thing in your size. And what about the midriff on the dresses I was trying on? I don't know who they think has a waist way up there."

"Hah! What about that harness they tried to get me to buy to hold up my breasts. Those straps would have made permanent furrows in my shoulders and I don't need anything to hold them up."

Lemuel interrupted them to ask, "Did you get a chance to find a contractor to build our sacred tabernacle?"

"Oh, that'll be ready in two weeks, but honestly Esther, I think those heels really make your legs look good! So what if you tower over most men, you do in flats too."

"One place was nice. They were very polite to us in that second shoe store. I think it helped that the manager couldn't keep his eyes off of Abigail."

"Either one of us. Oh, the trailers will be ready soon too. How about fixing us some martinis, Lem. We've had a tough day and need to relax."

Later there was much happy animated talk about finally moving forward with Lemuel's mission. Lemuel was pleased to learn that the firm of Bezaleel and Aholiab would construct the temple, instead of some unreliable, quick-buck contractor who might take the deposit money and run. He was also treated to a fashion show as the ladies proudly showed off their new clothes. Over dinner there was a lot of excited feminine talk about the costumes their staff of holy celebrants should wear during the services. They were as excited as brides selecting bridesmaids costumes. Esther was in favor of the older, more traditional dress and wanted to go topless like the Egyptians, but Abigail, who had much less to exhibit, thought bras, such as the one Esther wore in the beauty contest, would be less likely to offend the more inhibited parishioners.

The hours passed and it was time for bed. There was one small problem: Abigail's trailer had only two double beds. Esther assumed, wrongly, that certain physical transactions had transpired between Lemuel and Abigail, and asked, "Which bed do you two use?" And then asked with mock innocence, "Or do you want me to bunk with Lemuel?" Abigail, although devoid of any trace of human jealousy, felt that putting Lemuel and Esther together in the same bed might be misunderstood and lead to a sleepless night for all three of them. This left her with two choices.

She decided that in order for everyone to get any sleep that Esther should sleep with her. It wasn't a bad choice altogether. Esther felt soft and warm as she snuggled against Abigail, and maternal, and Abigail felt like the little doll that Esther never had because she'd never had a childhood, nor any children. Lemuel stared blankly off into the inky night for the next several hours, disturbed by the knowledge that the two most beautiful females in the universe were asleep only twelve feet away from him.

* * *

Because of the large sums of money involved, Abigail knew that they couldn't continue operations on a cash only basis. All demons have learned that the only way to avoid the oppressive regimentation of modern society, class over class, and bosses on top of bosses, was to quietly conjure whatever funds they needed, live simply, and pay cash for everything. Most demons live ordinary simple lives in modest houses in middle-class neighborhoods. They usually move every few years, take no part in civic or neighborhood associations, and the chances are very good that you might have one for a neighbor and never realize it. Abigail had further reduced her exposure to the complications of modern life by not even owning any real estate.

With the Biblical assertion that social hierarchy and wealth were divinely ordained, and because of his long experience with the structured regulations and institutions of the heavenly firm, Lemuel was actually better adapted to the class gradations of society, and its plethora of confusing, often contradictory, laws and regulations dictating procedure for everything from sorting trash to international protocol. But Abigail knew that large sums were going to flow and if Lemuel's church was going to be legitimate, he'd need a bank account. So early the next morning, she packed the rest of her T-bills into a brown paper grocery bag, and she and Lemuel left to go to Brownsville to visit a bank. Esther mumbled sleepily that she'd look after things at the trailer and for them to have a good time. She turned her head to the wall and went back to sleep.

All normal infants, only minutes old, have an instinctive urge to grasp, and bankers have developed this instinct to the level of one of the higher arts. This Abigail knew and was depending on. She assumed that this Brownsville banker would have covert contact with a *compadre* across the river in Matamores, Mexico, and that they could run the notes through the routine money laundering process: offshore banks, Swiss accounts, back to dummy corporations, and then redeposited as a donation to their tax-free church account.

The reader will be pleased to know that there is at least one honest banker, and when Abigail made the proposal to him, he eyed the paper bag suspiciously and positively refused to have anything to do with laundering drug money. He assumed that Abigail might have had a couple hundred thousand dollars in that sack. But when Abigail plopped fifteen million dollars in T-bills on his desk he realized that this was a legitimate transaction. He understood perfectly the complications that would be evinced if the two principals of the church deposited their own money. Questions would be asked about where it came from, how it was earned, and whether taxes had been paid on it. Tax avoidance, unlike money laundering, was honorable and honest, and frequently practiced by some of the nation's finest families. Some Texans regarded tax avoidance as a sacred obligation so as to keep the money out of the hands of the secular humanists who had taken over the government and are leading us down the slippery slope to godless socialism. Tax avoidance was not at all a criminal activity like laundering drug money.

This bank was a full service bank and had a very reliable trust department. The banker was delighted to set up their account, and draw up and file the necessary forms with the county clerk to establish their church as a tax-exempt organization. He suggested that as an open-ended partnership, such as law firms use, it would avoid the problem of withholding taxes. Each subsequent partner would own an equal share of the church's assets, but none would be responsible for any other partner's personal debts. Lemuel insisted on that provision because he didn't want to be responsible for causing the damnation of his apostles should he default on his debt to Abigail. The application forms listed Lemuel Smith as the chairman and senior partner, hereafter called "God's Devoted Evangel," or simply "The Evangel." He was to have absolute power over ritual, righteousness, hortatory, salvation, sacraments, and scriptural interpretation, as well as veto power over the junior partners, hereafter called: "Apostles." The apostles would, as they entered the partnership, have equal voting rights as directors. Abigail Jones was listed in a lesser position: "Treasurer." Her minutial responsibility was purchasing and disposing of any church property, overseer of the currency, signer all the checks, and all other worldly affairs. They listed Esther Xerxes as "Chatelaine to the Apostles" whose responsibility was to review resumes for presentation to the senior partner and to assure the comfort of all the associates. They weren't sure what surname to give her. Old Uncle Mordecai was a Benjamite, but as a God-created angel, Esther was not, strictly speaking, Mordecai's offspring, so they decided to use her married name.

The purpose of the organization was "To do good works." Then the banker asked, "What denomination is your church?"

They hadn't discussed a name for their church, but Lemuel thought that as they were evangelists, and their doctrine was to be taken exclusively from the Gospels, and since they were all originally from the ethereal regions, he quickly decided to call his church: The Church of the Ethereal Evangelicals. Lemuel steepled his hands in a prayerful position, eyed the banker imploringly, and assured the banker that everyone who was needful of salvation through God's grace would certainly be welcome.

The banker sensed that Lemuel was about to ask him to do something undignified; something like kneeling right there on the floor of the bank and praying with him. If it were not for that thick stack of T-bills, Lemuel would have been asked to leave, but the banker quickly agreed the world was indeed needful of salvation and he assured Lemuel that he was a born-again Christian several years ago. He attended church with his family every Sunday and with the Lord's guidance wrote, "Evangelical Church," as the tax-exempt religious organization.

Abigail also had the banker convert some of the bills to a certified

HOW THE GOOD TAILOR GOT TO HEAVEN — 413

check which they mailed to the El Paso Airstream dealer. This act was to give them some trouble later.

* * *

While Lemuel and Abigail were taking care of business affairs, Esther finally awoke, blessed Abigail for leaving the coffee pot on, fixed herself a couple of slices of raisin toast, quickly became bored with the TV, and decided to take a stroll along the beach. Her first impulse was to wear nothing as was her custom when, as Queen of Persia, she strolled along the beaches of the Persian Gulf. She sighed and decided to dress modestly like the other ladies in this foreign country, and wear the thong swim suit that she'd bought with Abigail. It consisted of three tiny pieces of triangular cloth: two barely covered her nipples and areolas, and a larger piece covered the labial cleft at the juncture of her thighs. These were held in place by straps no wider than shoelaces, one of which was worn down the cleft of her high-rounded bottom, and rubbed uncomfortably on a very sensitive part of her anatomy: her coccyx. Unlike Abigail, Esther was clean-shaven, so unsightly pubic hair was no problem.

Down the beach, toward civilization, she noticed a couple of figures, tiny silhouettes in the distance, who were performing a strange twisting ballet in the surf, and she went toward them to see what they were doing. They were fishing with cast nets. The young men wore only ragged khakis torn off below their knees, and their strange dance was performed as they swung the weighted round nets high into the air to open over the water, and then fall in a large circle over the shallows. Then they pulled a line to close the purse over any fish caught underneath. It was several minutes before they noticed Esther and when they did, they couldn't take their eyes off the nearly naked beauty.

She said, quite simply, "Follow me, and I will make you fishers of men."[36]

They left their nets and followed her. Their names were Pete and Andy, and they were brothers. Esther said she hoped they were loving brothers and were not overcome by sibling rivalry like Jacob and Esau, arguing about which came first.

Each wore a broad grin, and Pete said, "No, we won't argue; we'll flip a coin."

And Andy asked, "Who are Jacob and Esau?"

As the threesome walked back toward the trailer they saw, anchored a couple of hundred feet offshore, a boat where three men were repairing their fishing nets. Esther called to them. They were Jimmy, Johnny, and their father, Zebedee. The two youngsters immediately left their ship and their father, and waded the short distance to the beach, and followed Esther, Pete, and Andy.[37] And Esther thought, *There's nothing to this gathering apostles, all you have to do is walk along the beach, and there they are.*

When old Zebedee saw his sons leaving and following some pretty girl down the beach, and when he realized they were going off with her, he yelled a few heated words of scorn and abuse. "Where the hell do you think you're going? Get back here, you two worthless sons of Belial and help me with these nets." And as they ignored him and continued following Esther, he became more enraged, and yelled louder; "Goddamn pussy-crazed bastards. I'll take a two-by-four to you when you get home."

Pete and Andy didn't exactly relish having to share Esther with a couple of strangers, but, as the most fair-minded of the group, Pete thought that eliminated coin flipping as a decision-maker. "I guess we'll have to cut cards, or draw straws," he said.

Andy didn't agree. "No way man! We were first. You and I can flip for it, and when we're done, they can flip."

They were walking five abreast and Esther put her arms over the shoulders of the two beside her, hugged them to her, and said, "Boys, boys! Don't squabble. Paradise awaits us all. First. Last. What difference does it make? For it is written: 'many that are first shall be last; and the last shall be first.'"[38]"

For this bit of wisdom Esther received a couple of calloused hands stroking each cheek of her bare buttocks and then a couple of hard squeezes.

However, the paradise the boys had in mind would have to wait. When they arrived at the trailer, Lemuel and Abigail had returned from their business trip and were still wearing their business suits. They had the stern demeanor of no nonsense parsons about them, and Lemuel was holding his Bible in both hands against his abdomen. The twenty-four carat, gold leaf letters, "Holy Bible," glowed in the shadow of the awning. Abigail said sharply, "I thought you were going to look after the trailer, Esther. You can't just go off and leave everything wide open in this world."

Esther just smiled, and said, "I've been trolling for apostles and I think I found four of them for you, Lem." Introductions were made all around.

Lemuel asked if she had discussed their mission with the young men, and Esther assured him that they had discussed paradise. Then she pulled Pete up close and licked his ear. He responded by tightening his arm around her waist. Quickly, before their caresses became more impassioned, Abigail asked Esther if she'd mind helping her prepare lunch. Actually, her tone was more a command than a request. She added with a sour smile, "Lemuel can talk to the boys without us."

"Well, let me give these boys the holy kiss[39] first, Abby," and she ran her hand softly over each of their bare chests and kissed each one passionately. "And the kiss of charity[40] for the parson," she said, and kissed Lemuel.

Abigail grabbed her wrist and tugged her toward the trailer, as Esther looked coyly at the young men, and said, "We'll be right back. Don't go away."

With her amorous sensuality, Esther leveled the men to their common denominator, and Lemuel awkwardly tried to regain a semblance of dignity. He invited them to have a seat, and said, "Esther is the Chatelaine for our ministry and she takes the Lord's commandment to love one another very seriously. And of course she loves the God who created her, and directs her every thought and emotion. However, she does have a tendency to be overly demonstrative. I hope her strong feelings haven't offended you."

Pete became the self-appointed spokesman for the group, and quickly assured Lemuel, "She ain't offended nobody," and the others enthusiastically agreed.

However, "nobody" didn't include Abigail, because angry sounds could be heard coming from the trailer. The words were not distinct, but it was clear that Abigail was scolding Esther for something. Esther was slightly louder, and an occasional word of her repartee could be heard, "Oh grow up!" and, "You little hypocrite! You run around naked yourself."

Abigail muttered something, and Esther responded, "The kiss of charity is too, Biblical!" And Abigail's voice could be heard saying, "I don't think that includes ramming your tongue down his throat."

Lemuel stepped over to the open door, and said, "I think the boys would like lemonade to go with those sandwiches."

The fishermen exchanged glances, and Lemuel said, "They're busy making sandwiches." He sat with his prospective apostles and explained the new-style ministry that he was founding. "Our ministry will be historically accurate, true to the Bible, and nothing like today's commonplace religious institutions. They have been corrupted by commercialization and worldliness. They're judgmental about human affairs, and the Bible teaches: 'Judgment is mine, sayeth the Lord.' They have tried to usurp God's prerogative, and with monumental hubris, proclaim themselves to be godly, and the moral leaders of the nation. They would shun one of God's angels if he appeared to them and turn away those who are truly devoted to God, and whose sole purpose in this life is to bring the Holy Ghost to the unsaved. Our church scorns the temptations of worldly custom and its misplaced faith in human institutions."

With that said, Abigail and Esther appeared with a tray of sandwiches and a large pitcher of lemonade beaded with icy dew, glasses to go around, and a fifth of gin. "In case anyone needs a lift," Abigail explained. She had also changed from her severe business suit into something more comfortable: her little yellow bikini. Although it was considerably more modest than the three little patches of cloth that Esther wore, it revealed enough to bring awed smiles to the fishermen's faces. Little Jimmy voiced the aesthetically shared opinion for the boys, "Wow! Rev, your old lady's a beaut!" And they all jumped up and offered their chairs.

"We're not married," Lemuel quickly assured them. "Abigail is the treasurer for the mission and she handles our business affairs."

"Did you explain the conditions of apostleship to the boys, Lem?" Abigail asked.

"No. We hadn't gotten around to that yet," he replied. "But I so easily overlook these worldly matters, and since you're the treasurer, the one they'll be turning all their worldly wealth over to, why don't you explain it to them?"

"It's quite simple boys. All you have to do is to sell everything you own and give the money to me. In return, anything that you need will be provided."

* * *

Fishermen are not overly-intellectual, and these lads were normal for their trade, but the burgeoning population growth of south Texas brought a human diversity that ranged from tricksters and hookers, to retired senior citizens, and vacationers with widely varied budgets. The primary occupation of the region is getting money away from those who have brought it down there from somewhere else. Exposure to this way of life gave the lads a smattering of sophistication and they thought they could recognize a scam, especially a scam so obvious. They did wonder why a pair of thousand-dollar hookers would be wasting time on them. The combined assets of the four of them wouldn't add up to a thousand. Pete asked, "What do you mean anything we need will be provided? Suppose I needed a new pickup." His old truck looked like a reject from Bezaleel & Aholiab's junk pile.

"That will be provided," Lemuel said.

Since Esther had recruited the lads, she felt responsible for their presence, almost maternal toward them, and she said, "I don't think you've fully explained what you want them for, Lem. The way Abigail put it, it sounded like a swindle of some sort. Did you explain that they had the opportunity to bring the true faith to thousands of poor misguided people. Have you even asked them what their beliefs are?"

The lads didn't go to any church and they had a few choice words for the religious community: smug; stuck-up; do-gooders; phoneys; thieves who'd steal a widow's last cent. It was the usual tirade of the unchurched. And Lemuel agreed with them, "That's because they are too filled with the world and have no real spirituality. But you must believe in something, don't you?"

Pete shot back, "Nah! We don't have to believe in nothin'. The law guarantees us freedom of religion," and the others nodded in agreement.

Lemuel reasoned, "Well, freedom *of* religion doesn't mean freedom *from* religion. You have to pick something to believe in."

Pete smirked, and said, "Okay then, we're secular humanists. How's that?"

Lemuel was shocked. "That's worse than being Satanists! You don't mean that you're atheists, do you?"

Very few atheists will ever come right out flat and admit their total and absolute non-belief in any higher power...especially to a man of the cloth. Atheists will usually hedge and admit to agnosticism, or call themselves deists. Also, there was the higher power that had brought them there in the first place, and she was shaking her head with disappointment. So to please Esther, and giving Abigail a wink, Pete said, "Well, atheist may be a bit strong. Let's say we have doubts."

Over the next hour and a half Lemuel outlined the complete program for the Church of the Ethereal Evangelicals. He explained that as apostles their duties would be to instill the true faith in the souls of the unsaved. He cited Scripture in response to their questions, and emphasized the

HOW THE GOOD TAILOR GOT TO HEAVEN   419

verse where Jesus said: 'Go and sell that thou hast, and give to the poor, and thou shalt have treasure in heaven: and come and follow me[41].' And when Jimmy and Johnny expressed guilt over leaving their father, Zebedee, he responded with more Scripture: 'Everyone that hath forsaken houses, or brethren, or sisters, or father, or mother or wife, or children, or lands, for my name's sake shall receive a hundredfold.'[42]

Then Pete had a question. "If we forsake everything and follow you, what shall we have?[43] What do you mean by a hundredfold?"

Abigail answered, "Well, to start with, you get a new trailer just like mine, and a new pickup just like mine, and some decent clothes to wear, and if you're very good, maybe Esther will come and tuck you into bed at night." Then she asked Lemuel to read that part about laying all their money from the sale of all their belongings at the apostles' feet instead of giving it to the poor. "That part about from each according to their ability, and to each according to their need. That's why you bring the money to me. I control the purse."

The lads huddled off to the side. Then Johnny asked, "Can we bring our girlfriends?" And they were told yes, but they were subject to the same deal. They had to sell everything they had and give the money to the church.

Lemuel read to them what happens to cheaters: "'Ananias with Sapphira sold a possession, and kept back part of the price, his wife also being privy to it, and brought a certain part, and laid it at the apostles' feet. But Peter said Ananias why hath Satan filled thy heart to lie to the Holy Ghost, and to keep back part of the price of the land? Why hast thou conceived this thing in thine heart? Thou hast not lied unto men, but unto God. And Ananias fell down and gave up the ghost: and great fear came upon all them that heard these things. And the young men rose up and buried Ananias; and when Sapphria came in Peter said; How is it that ye have agreed together to tempt the Spirit of the Lord? Then she fell down and gave up the ghost, and the young men found her dead, and buried her along side her husband.'[44] You see, God knew how much the land sold for and knew they were holding back from all the rest. So God must have told Peter to indict those cheaters and His punishment was swift. So, don't think you can cheat God."

The apostles went back into their huddle and discussed this new revelation. This was a fearsome test of either their belief in God's powers, or their atheism. We don't know whether God or atheism won, but Peter's head rose from the huddle, and asked, "My ole lady's mother stays with us. Ken she come too?"

Lemuel answered, "Of course. That's your main job: to spread the good tidings. We'll bruit the gospel all across the land. We mustn't hide our light under a bushel, so bring everyone you can. But if she joins our crusade, the same conditions apply to her."

They all promised to return as soon as they could put their affairs in order and agreed that anything they couldn't sell they'd bring along for everyone to use. Andy had a wonderfully loud stereo with high volume tweeters and woofers. Esther gave each one another holy kiss, and walked back up the beach with them.

* * *

She was gone a long time, and when she returned, she was carrying the bottom section of her thong swimsuit in her hand. She plopped heavily into one of the chairs and poured out a large glass of lemonade, laced it with gin, and drank thirstily. Then she announced, "That does it. I can't go back for sure now," and she winked. "But I think we can count on those fellows coming with us."

"You didn't?" Abigail's tone expressed both shock and accusation.

"Yes, I did," Esther answered with a smile.

"How? You're closed up there, just like me."

"Correction Abby, *was* closed up there. They restore our hymens, but it's wide open now. That's why I can't go back. But it was only after the second go round that I had an orgasm. Then I couldn't stop." She looked from Lemuel to Abigail with a puzzled expression on her face, and asked, "You mean you're still a virgin?"

Abigail's dark cheeks turned as plum red as a monsignor's biretta. It meant that if Esther could, then she could, and all the female souls

HOW THE GOOD TAILOR GOT TO HEAVEN 421

could, and she asked Lemuel if he knew about this. Lemuel said embarrassedly, "I suspect that's why the females are examined by the elders at the gates of the city. It's a weekly ritual for them. The elders inspect each one for their tokens of virginity. The Bible says: 'And if the tokens of virginity be not found; then the men of her city shall stone her with stones that she die; because she has played the whore in her father's house.'[45] You've heard me say it often enough: there's no sin permitted in heaven."

Esther explained, "None of the male souls or angels can get an erection without drinking the waters of life. And if they tried to drink it while they were beyond the ninth orb, they'd immediately fall to earth and a living body would never survive. Heaven won't support life and life wouldn't survive the fall.

"Before the flood, some angels took flasks of life water down to earth, drank it, became mortal, and went in unto the daughters of men, and that's when they made the waters off-limits to all the angels, but women are different. I guess they examine us to see if we've been masturbating or using the donkeys or the horses. Approaching any beast to lie down thereto is another stoning offense.[46] And we're examined after every miraculous visitation or any time we're on a mission outside the pearly gates, too.

"The Bible doesn't even mention female angels until Zechariah,[47] and that was only about fifty years before I was sent down. And when they did send us down, it was just to do some dumb thing, like lifting an ephah up and suspending it between earth and heaven. The male angels get to do all the good stuff, and they wouldn't have sent me down if the other gods hadn't crowned Ashtoreth, the goddess of the Zidonians,[48] Queen of Heaven.[49] So God got wroth; He was always wroth about something. The directorate decided they should send in a competing love goddess and they sent me down, so I was mortal for a while. They let me become mortal so they could test the power of sex appeal alone. I couldn't do anything magical like insuring bountiful harvests or granting that healthy babies be born. And I didn't have any babies either.

Anyway, I'm never going back there. I'd be stoned. When will you teach me how to make that paper money, Abby?"

"You can't be stoned to death. You can't die, and neither can any of the souls."

"No, but they can chain you to a wall for twenty years beside a big pile of rocks and everyone passing by is supposed to throw stones at you. They have different-sized stones for different offenses, and they're marked with signs. I'd be chained next to the rock pile with the sign that said: 'for whores only.' Even the blasphemers get stoned with smaller stones."

That night in bed, after she had fallen asleep, Abigail felt Esther's fingers checking to see if she was telling the truth.

Chapter 23

ESTHER DISCOVERED THAT ABIGAIL WASN'T LYING; HER HYMEN was intact. Awed, and reverentially, she softly petted Abigail's furry mons and Abigail permitted those gentle caresses for several minutes before she pushed Esther's hand away. She liked being stroked, and Lemuel had kneaded and massaged most of her body at one time or another, everywhere but there. She gave Esther a sisterly kiss, and said, "That's *marimay*. You know…unclean."

"Didn't you just get out of the shower? It feels soft and fluffy."

"Not unclean that way, silly. The Gypsies believe it's ritually unclean. You know, taboo. You're a Jewess. Doesn't your Book of Laws say you're not supposed to do that?"

"Of course not. The law doesn't prohibit women from pleasuring each other. Those laws only apply to men. You know, faggots, queers, gays. Men can't sleep with men as they would with women[50], but it's all right for the women to have sex with each other. They just can't do it with animals. With Solomon's nine hundred wives, and only one cock in the hen house, what do you think those wives were doing? And his wives were just as eager for the dark-skinned Shulamite maid as Solomon was. That's why they wanted her to join their harem[51]." Then she nuzzled Abigail's neck.

"Go to sleep, Esther."

* * *

The next morning, about dawn, someone knocked on their door and Lemuel sleepily asked who was there. The ladies merely stirred and went back to sleep.

"It's the Salvation Army," was the response.

Still wearing his angel wing pajamas, Lemuel opened the door to a strange apparition. It took several seconds for Lemuel to recognize Myles because of the strange outfit he was wearing. He had on a pork pie hat with a brim nearly as wide as a sombrero; a red and white hat band, striped like a barberpole; and enough gaudy feathers stuffed into one side of the band to make a feather duster. His baggy pants bloused out like a Zouave's pantaloons and the cuffs were pegged tight at his ankles. His single-breasted sports coat looked to be several sizes too large; the wide lapels reached to his shoulder seams, and the shoulders held enough padding for a football player's shoulder pads. The jacket was long and came nearly to his knees. His shoes were long and pointed, and of two-toned leather. He had a long key chain that looped from his waistband, down beneath his knee and back up to his pocket. He pulled it from his pocket and twirled it propeller fashion around his finger, and he said, "Greetings gates!"

Lemuel's astonishment left him speechless for several moments, then he called to the drowsy ladies, "It's Myles. Come look at this."

As a Biblical scholar, Myles knew of Esther's great beauty, but they had never met before, and when she emerged from the trailer and he saw her in full ectoplasmic glory, or in the flesh so to speak, wearing a see-through peignoir, he was dumbstruck. Even tousle-haired and sleepy-eyed, she was magnificent. Myles fell in love in one instant.

Behind her was Abigail, of at least equal beauty, but the difference was like comparing a precious piece of jewelry to a great work of architecture; the Hope diamond to the Taj Mahal, each was exquisite in their own way. When Abigail saw Myles she laughed, and said, "You're wearing a zoot suit. I haven't seen anything like that for fifty years or more."

"Heaven has become fashion conscious and this is the new Salvation Army uniform," Myles explained. "When we're on worldly detail we dress in the height of the avant-garde style during this nation's greatest moments. Something about clothing influencing the gods. Since America has become the dominant terrestrial nation, the higher orders decided its rise to power began when this was the garb of the sophisticates who launched that ascendancy." Then he opened his jacket. The gaudy lining looked like striped satin wallpaper, and he said, "Look here! Whoever heard of having the waistband of your trousers up under your armpits. The cuffs are so tight that it's a struggle to get them on over your feet." He also wore a very wide, very loud necktie, a black satin shirt, and a pair of wide, yellow knit suspenders with matching yellow socks.

Abigail said, "Whoever decided on that style is about fifty years out of date."

Myles admitted he wouldn't know anything about today's fashions. "But this is what the 'hep cats' wore in America's most magnificent times. It's supposed to be the cutting edge of modern fashion; the *sine qua non* of the ascendent culture and its mores."

When Myles was alive, clothing styles were just as absurd, and he was inured to ridiculous fashion. In his day, the men wore striped waistcoats under flounced doublets, skin tight knee britches, white silk hose, velvet toque hats, and dandies might decorate their toque with a long feather. They wore very wide, starched, and pleated collars which stood out from their necks, and there was a lot of fancy lace on their shirts. The ladies wore long billowing skirts with leg o' mutton sleeves, little lace caps, and the decolletage exposed their breasts nearly to their nipples. Some of the more daring ladies' dressmakers designed bodices that bared, lifted and openly presented their entire breasts. Tudor England was a bawdy age.

Myles shrugged and innocently startled Lemuel by adding, "But fashions change. There aren't any white robes in heaven anymore, our new robes have colorful paisley prints with plunging necklines and high collars. I suppose the holy tailor wants to bring us all back to a period of high fashion."

"The holy tailor?" Lemuel sputtered, and Abigail chuckled.

Their reaction puzzled Myles, and he nervously swung his key chain in circles. He explained, hesitantly, "Yes, the holy tailor. You know who I mean; you delivered his soul. He's been made the chief seraph, and they say he sits on a small throne in the throne room, right beside the Trinity, and designs the latest styles."

"Is that why you came? Did anyone mention me?" Then without thinking he implicated his partner in perfidy, and added, "Or Abigail?"

Myles didn't understand Lemuel's concern, but if he had discovered their treacherous act, switching the tailors' souls, he'd have to report it to the Oversight Directory (the office of the O.D.). If he didn't report their wickedness, and it was discovered, they'd all be hauled before the Sacred Rota, the highest court in the universe, and from which there is no appeal. They might reduce him and Myles to being ordinary souls for eternity, and Esther, too, if she learned their secret. But Myles didn't get the connection, and he said, "No. What would Abigail have to do with firmament business? She's a demon. They sent me down to bring Esther back."

"I'm not going back. I'm staying down here with Abigail."

Myles hadn't expected such a flat out refusal from Esther, and Lemuel's nervousness was certainly mysterious. Abigail looked too smug. Something was up. He imagined that Esther's contrary stiff-necked attitude was due to some corruption worked by Abigail, and that Lemuel must know about it, because he was obviously concealing some guilty secret. "They thought you were busy with your official duties as the most beautiful woman in the universe, but the agents from the Central Intelligence Angels discovered that you ran away. They had a hard time finding you. After you were located, they sent me down to bring you back."

"I'm leaving heaven for good, Myles. I'm not going back—ever. I'm going to stay here and be a terrestrial angel like Abigail. I'm not going back!"

"You can't do that. They sent me because we're colleagues. Teachers. Intellectuals. They said you were probably distracted, visiting or something, and just needed a reminder."

"Well you can tell the O. D., and the higher orders, to kiss my foot. I'm not leaving."

Her haughty invective caused her to look even more alluring to Myles, and he looked down at her shapely foot and thought, *Yes, thou art all fair, my love; there is no spot in thee. How beautiful are thy feet, O prince's daughter. Eeven kissing your feet would be a pleasure.*But instead of versifying he pleaded with her to change her mind, and she crossed her arms over her chest, and said, "No!"

Abigail said, "Come on, Esther, let's get dressed and have breakfast."

Lemuel was relieved that the real cause of his distress was still a secret, and cheerfully invited Myles to join them. The women wore casual beachwear, and Lemuel changed into the jeans they had cut off for Esther, and a T-shirt. Their simple fare, scrambled eggs, coffee, toast and butter, was a long past savory delight for both Esther and Myles. Esther nudged him, and said, "See, the food alone is worth defecting. Wasn't that better than manna?"

"Positively iniquitous. It has been a long time since I've tasted real food. I'm afraid we'll pay for it though."

"Not if we don't go back," Esther said, and winked at Abigail. She stroked Myles'ss cheek. "Why not stay down here with us for a while?"

"Don't include me in that. You have to come back. They'll send in a swat team, the God squad, the strong arm boys, the guys from the prisoner chase detail, and drag you back." Myles pleaded, "You'll like the new clothing styles, Esther."

"If we wanted paisley robes, we could buy them down here. Couldn't we Abby?"

Abigail objected. "They can't force her to go back. The Intergalactic Treaty says terra is neutral territory. We can't harm or interfere with ethereal angels doing their duties and you can't bother us…until Armageddon anyway."

"I'm not a lawyer and I haven't studied the agreement, but I'm sure the Sacred Rota would decide differently. The non-interference clause applies to only mortal affairs. We can't interfere with your right to corrupt the mortals and you can't interfere with our right to lead them to salvation, but I don't think it pertains to angels enforcing heaven's regulations on their own angels. We can't interfere with your right to enforce your own laws on the other demons."

"Terrestrial angels, please, and we don't have any laws to enforce. That's your bag." Naturally Abigail didn't know one jot of celestial law, but she asserted, "I guess you haven't heard: women have free choice now. It's the law! We can do anything we want and if the ethereal angels want a fight, we'll give it to 'em. We'll demonstrate."

Demons always twist facts and misinterpret laws.

* * *

The discussion about other-world legalisms was interrupted by a visitor. A gray sedan with a U.S. Government shield decal affixed to the door, and bearing U.S. Government tags, pulled into their sandy cove. A tall skinny man, clutching a briefcase to his chest, scuttled, crab-like, over the sand to their trailer. Lemuel and Abigail stepped outside to greet him. The government agent wore a seersucker suit; a natural colored straw hat with a red white and blue band; black-rimmed glasses that magnified his eyes to double their size; and black, box-toed orthopedic shoes with a built up wedge beneath one sole. He removed his hat and held it to his chest atop his briefcase. His hair was black and straight, and combed back slick against his temples. He bowed unctuously, but with a scoliotic twist. Lemuel indicated an empty chair, offered coffee, and asked Abigail to join them. The coffee was declined, but the man accepted a glass of water, "without ice." The agent sat crookedly in the camp chair sipping the tepid water, and introduced himself as Agent Matthews of the I.R.S. as he presented his card.

Without ceremony he stated his purpose: "The religious organization, which you've cited as tax exempt, does not exist in our records." He searched through the papers in his briefcase. "Ah, here we are. Furthermore, the Church of the Ethereal Evangelicals is not listed in any registry of churches, and none of the registered Evangelical churches have ever heard of you. I see that you have only two church officials listed. He squinted through his magnifiers with his best don't-trifle-with-this-fed stare, and read, "Charge of terrestrial affairs, and treasurer…Abigail Jones; and the office of the Empyreal Evangel…one…Lemuel Smith." He looked at Lemuel and said, "That would be you, I take it." A reflected sunray glared from his eyeglasses, and he expertly directed the blinding shaft of light into Lemuel's eyes. "Two people don't make a church, Mr. Smith." Then Matthews asked, "Where were you ordained? And where did you attend divinity school?"

Lemuel was flustered, and shifted uneasily in his chair to avoid the penetrating glare. Caught off-guard by the revenue agent's verbal thrusts, he only managed to point over his head, and finally he parried, "Where? Where all true religious vocation derives. It is God's will."

"I'm afraid that's not a sufficient answer for the I.R.S., Mr. Smith." Then Matthews sneered sarcastically, "Or do you prefer Reverend?" His lips curled back into a wry grimace, and he looked like a ferret hot after his prey.

Lemuel asked, "Are you religious, Mr. Matthews?"

"My beliefs are not the question, your credentials are. And I'm not questioning your sincerity…just your qualifications for tax exemption." He rustled through the papers in his briefcase and brought out a government pamphlet printed on cheap newsprint, and handed the booklet to Lemuel. "This explains the tax code regarding your claim for exemption. You must comply with all these provisions. I'm sure you understand. Without certification standards, anyone could claim to be a religious organization to avoid paying taxes."

Abigail crossed her legs at the ankles and placed her bare feet against the trailer's hubcap. She wore her swim suit bottom and an overly-large navy blue sweatshirt. Matthews turned toward her long enough to acknowledge that he appreciated a shapely leg and a high-arched foot, even on a negress. After nodding toward her, he continued, "There are certain tax advantages for married couples filing joint returns. In your tax bracket it's worth looking into." He pulled a few forms and more instruction pamphlets from his briefcase, and indicated some of the tables as he handed them to Lemuel. With avuncular solicitude, he pointed out certain sections with a well-sharpened yellow pencil.

With brazen eclat, Abigail disclosed, "We're not married. We just live together."

The tax man's eyes barely squinted at that revelation, and to himself, he thought, *What nerve. Living in sin. Miscegenation. And claiming a religious exemption.* But he continued instructing Lemuel on the code.

At this point the reader is probably blaming the Brownsville banker for betraying the church's confidences by mishandling the money launder...ah...I mean tax avoidance operation. That would be a mistake. The problem was Abigail's own fault. It was that certified check for $203,000 she had wired from the Brownsville bank to the Airstream dealer's El Paso account. It was reported by the El Paso bank to the government, and that set off the alarm bells on the treasury department's computers, which automatically relayed the information to the I.R.S. computers, which had spit out the information that a currency exchange above ten thousand had taken place. A quick check by the I.R.S. revealed that neither Abigail Jones nor Lemuel Smith had ever filed a tax return of any kind. Furthermore, it didn't help that the mailing address for the church's headquarters was just a post office box number in Berkeley, California, and for the location of their rectory, Abigail had honestly written "four miles north of the Star of Texas"—the storm-tossed and beached tugboat. Matthews had no trouble finding them.

Fortunately the tax bill was not on the entire fifteen million, but only on the two hundred and three thousand of income, making their tax bill about fifty thousand. Abigail thought of conjuring the money and being rid of this government pest, but Lemuel was opposed to that. He felt that his church was as entitled to a tax exemption as any other. He also believed that it would be wrong to dilute the economy with any more demon created currency than was absolutely necessary. Every angel knows of the anarchic evil that would occur if the United States government was forced to back, with its full faith and credit, currency created outside of the legitimate free market institutions that are authorized to create currency: the banks, the credit unions, the savings and loan, money market funds, Wall Street, the investment bankers, the international currency exchanges, the clearing houses, and so forth. That is why angels on mortality detail are only issued a parsimonious three hundred dollars. After all, money must be earned honestly and not just created out of thin air! Any problems with the precise mechanism that moves the financial world are the result of demon-created currency, and Lemuel did not want to add to the situation.

Matthews continued to press forms and instructions on Lemuel. He had no problem understanding the jargon of the I.R.S. nor the rationale behind its regulations. Much of it was similar to sections of Leviticus and Deuteronomy with clean and unclean laws, the governing of legal relationships, and prohibitions about harnessing an ox and ass together, or against muzzling the ox as he threshes out the grain, or bringing the price of a dog, or the hire of a whore into the house of the Lord. Lemuel was far more acclimated to the code than was Abigail. But Lemuel's main concern was soul-saving; in this he persisted. "The state of your soul is far more important than these forms, Matthews. I perceive that you are a man of authority, and to some you say stay, and they must stay, and to others you say go, and they must go.[52] These are issues of faith, and faith is the rock upon which our tax exemption rests; your faith Matthews. Your salvation may depend on the decision you make here today. The scriptures tell us that your power comes from on high. All power is God given[53]; and you have, this very day, reached that fork in the road where you must decide which path to take. You, Matthews, have the power to make your decision in favor of the Lord, or you may decide to blacken your soul and find in favor of worldliness." Lemuel reached over and placed his hand on Matthews' bent and bony shoulder, and added, "Make the right decision, my brother."

When Lemuel laid his hand on Matthews' shoulder, Matthews felt a shock race down his spine and his life-long affliction, scoliosis, disappeared. Lemuel was as surprised as Matthews. It was his first experience at healing by the laying on of hands. Abigail merely smiled.

Matthews was not easily deterred from doing his job and it would take more than a miraculous healing to convince him of Lemuel's righteousness. His job was to collect all the taxes due the government and this was not the first time that some tax evader had threatened him with the loss of his soul, although the thought was usually expressed as: "Goddamn Bastard!" It was frequently uttered when he failed to grant surcease. That, and worse, were common threats. He removed his thick glasses and polished them with his handkerchief. Everything appeared blurred and slightly foggy as he squinted out across the dunes, and in the shade even Abigail had no definite form.

Abigail said, "Mister Matthews seems to have gotten some sand in his eyes, Lem. Wet your thumbs in that glass of water and wipe the sand out of his eyes." Matthews protested slightly, but Lemuel did as Abigail instructed. When Matthews opened his eyes again, his vision was perfect[54], without his glasses. She asked, "Isn't that better, Mr. Matthews?"

Matthews was nearly speechless with awe and when he regained his faculties, he said, "H...H...How did that happen?" He picked up one of the forms he had been working on and said, "I can even read the small print without my glasses. It's a miracle! I've worn glasses since I was seven years old."

Abigail and Lemuel exchanged satisfied glances, and Lemuel said, "Faith can work miracles, Matthews."

"Why yes! It is a miracle. My spine has been straightened and I can see everything clearly now." He placed his glasses in his breast pocket

HOW THE GOOD TAILOR GOT TO HEAVEN — 433

and studied the forms. Then he took out his pencil and wrote some figures on the worksheet. He occasionally held the paper at arms' length, and beamed. He could actually read his own figures at arms' length. He repeated "It's a miracle!" several more times while he figured. Then he looked up and with a more serious inflection, said, "As I make it, this is only an estimate you understand, and you have the right to appeal. You owe the government $48,300."

Lemuel quickly got between Matthews and Abigail, whose eyebrows had arched evilly and had emerald lightning bolts shooting from her eyes. Lemuel said soft soothing things to calm her down and pointed out that Matthews' sense of dedication, his unswerving diligence to his profession, was exactly the sort of character trait the church needs. Any experience apart from his purpose was extraneous, an exiguous detail, and no more relevant to Matthews' mission than a housefly. Were his eyes to suddenly lose their focus, he would have merely replaced his glasses and gone on with his duties. He was exactly the sort of person that Lemuel wanted for an apostle.

Matthews did not know the dangerous game he was playing. Abigail considered turning him into a tadpole and casting him out among the gulf fishes. She also considered making both of his eyes pop out of their sockets and flop about on his cheeks like paddle-balls on short rubber bands. Next, she thought of changing all tax collectors into toads, and a wicked smile appeared as she imagined all the revenue service corridors and offices abounding in leaping, warty, croaking little beasts.

Matthews was still occupied with their tax forms, and he said, "I see that you list someone named Esther 'Ecxer-ecxess' as chatelaine to the apostles. I hope you have filed a W-2 form for her and that you are remitting her withholding taxes."

"She's a volunteer. She doesn't get paid, and her name is pronounced 'Zurk-seez,'" Abigail snapped. She contemplated causing the earth to open beneath all tax offices everywhere and swallow every last stone, brick, desk, file cabinet, record, and computer tape.

Lemuel explained, "There are no wages for Abigail or myself, nor anyone else that joins our mission. Salvation is not about wages."

Not realizing how close he was to perdition, Matthews snapped back, "Anything that has monetary value that Ms. Xerxes, or anyone else, receives: food, lodging, clothing, transportation, or services, must be counted as income. You'll have to keep a record of the fair market value of everything that you give her, or that you receive for your personal use, and if it amounts to more than $6,500 you'll have to file a 1040 form. And the same goes for every one of your so-called volunteers." Then to Lemuel he said, "We don't have a record of your income, but ministers have to pay taxes on their income even if it's just meals, lodging or services, just like everyone else."

Lemuel looked bewildered, and Abigail said sweetly, "Don't worry dear. I'm sure they'll change that rule before the second coming. I don't really think they would tax Jesus."

Matthews leaned forward and pointed his sharp pencil toward Lemuel's chest, and said, "If you were Jesus you'd have to list the value of the food you ate at the last supper, and if you were to feed the five thousand with the fishes and loaves, the way these new tax laws are written, where they include bartered income, and in-kind income, and even though you gave it all away to the multitude, you'd still have to pay tax on the value of the goods."

Lemuel was shocked. "Are you a religious man, Mr. Matthews?"

"I certainly am. I was baptized when I was twelve, but this has nothing to do with religion. We're discussing the Internal Revenue Code. Jesus couldn't deduct what he fed the multitude as a business expense since it wouldn't be necessary for his carpentry work, nor as a charitable contribution since the multitude isn't a recognized charitable organization. It isn't a church, a veterans' group, a cultural group, a university, a library, museum or anything—the multitude are just people. Furthermore; it is not recognized that Jesus himself is a charitable organization, nor is he part of any recognized church, so he would have to pay income taxes on the value of what he had created and then given away.

HOW THE GOOD TAILOR GOT TO HEAVEN   435

Abigail was beginning to enjoy this colloquy, not that she wanted to pay any of her hard-conjured money in taxes, but the absurdity of taxing in-kind exchanges struck her as lunacy. She asked, "Would that include the market value of all the healing he did? How does your back feel, Matthews? And isn't it nice not to have to wear glasses? What monetary value will you claim on your own 1040 form, Matthews?"

Then a spectacular vision appeared framed in the doorway of the trailer. Esther overheard their colloquy and surmised that a government man had arrived. "Oh good. He's come with our allotment of helots? Did you tell him we don't want any eunuchs?" Esther cooed as she descended the couple of steps.

Myles followed right behind her, and said, "Didn't Abby tell you they don't have slaves anymore? He's here to give Lemuel his share of the tithes that the government collects for the churches."

Lemuel explained, "No you're both wrong. Matthews isn't here to give us anything. He's here to collect taxes from us."

Esther was barefoot, wore a short wrap-around skirt that draped low on her hips, and a peasant blouse which showed a lot of cleavage. Her open midriff bared her belly button. Myles had removed his zoot suit jacket. Esther added with imperious disdain, like a Jewish princess, "Abby, if that's all he wants, why don't you give this tiresome little man some money, and send him on his way?"

"Absolutely not!" Lemuel asserted. "There's a principle involved here. Religious organizations are supposed to be tax exempt."

Matthews stared at the odd pair. They looked less like church folks than Lemuel and Abigail. Esther was nearly a head taller than Myles, and Matthews wondered what such a beauty could see in that little pip-squeak. He surmised there was some sort of iniquity going on with this foursome. This pair looked familiar and he tried to remember where he had seen them before. Esther's photograph was a third page news item for several days: "The Disappearing Beauty Queen," but in those photos she was shown with her crown on her head, wearing her belly dancing costume, and with a thin veil drawn across the lower half of her face.

There was also some "reliable source" commentary about her and the palace guards, but Matthews didn't make the connection.

Esther's companion was of slight build, with a prominent nose, and a sallow pockmarked complexion. His eyes were bulbous and very bloodshot with some red veins evident. He looked like some actor he'd seen in the old B movies shown on late night TV; the actor who always played the gangster. And the girl, Esther, had a face and figure so sexually idealized that no mortal woman could ever match her dimensions. She was the incarnation of all erotic fantasies. Suddenly he realized where he had seen them before. It wasn't in the old movies, they were characters out of an old comic strip. The man was dressed as Matthews remembered, right down to the key chain, but Esther was dressed wrong. In the comic strip, she was smudged with dirt and wore a tattered black polka dot dress torn off raggedly at her thighs, and she kept pigs. Esther revealed the same amount of cleavage as the comic strip character and he seemed to remember that she smoked a corncob pipe. They looked exactly like Evil Eye Fleagle, and Moonbeam McSwine. Characters out of Lil Abner.

Abigail saw Matthews' astonishment and decided to add to his confusion. First she introduced them, "This is Esther Xerxes, our chatelaine, and former Queen of Persia, and this is Myles Coverdale, confessor to Edward VI, Bible expert, and now on a mission to restore America's golden age of men's fashions."

Matthews shook their hands and mumbled the usual courtesies. What Abigail said as she introduced them hadn't registered fully, so she added: "They've just come from the ninth celestial orb and we're trying to convince Myles to join our mission. We need an expert in hermeneutics." Lemuel signaled Abigail to be quiet, and put his finger to his lips and frowned, but Abigail ignored him. "The higher authorities want Esther to come back to their firm, but she says the rewards are greater with our establishment. What do you think Mr. Matthews…would you like to see Esther leave us?"

Matthews was completely at sea. He decided they were all lunatics

HOW THE GOOD TAILOR GOT TO HEAVEN — 437

or junkies, and he sputtered, "Well, I don't know. That should be up to her."

"There, you see Myles. You've heard it from this high government official. Mr. Matthews says Esther can stay." Then she placed a sheet of paper on the coffee table, and said; "Would you mind putting that in writing for us? Everyone seems to put so much importance on written records."

Matthews sputtered, "I can't authorize that."

"Oh, I thought you represented the United States Government. Well, who in the government could give her permission to remain with us?"

Matthews was completely flustered. "I don't know. Is she a citizen? The immigration service, or the White House could, I suppose."

"Oh, I didn't know that the president was so powerful. If I had a letter from a president authorizing our religious tax exempt status, then you'd accept it?" She reached under her sweatshirt and pulled out a letter, and handed it to Matthews. "That's from the president. If you'll notice the date, it's the same as the date of Lemuel's ordination. January, 1980. Your office must have overlooked it. I'm sure you have a copy in your files."

Matthews took it and stared at it suspiciously. The envelope had been mailed from Washington, and both it and the letter bore the official seal of the Office of the President. The letter read:

> Dear Rosco:
>
> Lemuel Smith and Abigail Jones are two of the finest Americans that it has ever been my pleasure to meet. These two wonderful people have a devotion to our Lord which is so sincere that I feel it is necessary for me to take pen in hand and bypass the normal bureaucratic red tape. The church they have started is so devoted to the principals of democracy and freedom, and the American way of life, that I have decided, by executive order, to include their fine religious organization on our

list of churches entitled to tax exemption. This is a wonderful and unselfish thing that these two fine young people are doing, and I can only compare them to those other holy Americans, Brigham Young and Joseph Smith, and their followers who did so much to settle and populate our American West. Well, I expect to see the Temple of the Ethereal Evangelicals right up there preaching the holy word and the principals of Americanism, beside all those other churches who, because of our religious freedoms, can exist openly, and whose parishioners are free to worship only because of our system of freedom to worship the Lord and the American way of life.

These fine God-fearing Americans can show us what volunteerism means in America. They have a job to do and they shouldn't have the government on their back. Let them get on with their job. We know what they will do for America. It will be mouth-to-mouth—hand-to-hand—contact, and their four-square resistance to the evil empire, that makes their cause so deserving. These Christian soldiers are the kind of heros that our freedom-loving nation should be proud of, and not burden them with taxes.

When I was a cavalry officer under Generalissimo Sam Goldwin, I said "Sam, (it was while we were defending the Alamo from those sneakin' Redskins), I said Sam, why don't you just outlaw them and push this button?"

There were a couple more poignant and equally-wise anecdotes about American history, and the letter ended, "Yours truly," and was signed by the President, the Vice-President, the Secretaries of State and Treasury, the Attorney General, the Chairman of the Senate Finance

Committee, and was notarized by the Chief Justice, and four associate justices of the Supreme Court. Matthews was properly awed by this document, and it had been sent by registered and certified mail, and bore the signatures of Postmasters all along the route, including that of the Postmaster General.

"This all looks authentic and in apple pie order to me," Matthews said. Now cowed by authority he smiled insipidly, realizing that he was in the presence of greatness. Esther was royalty; the odd little guy with her was the advisor to an English king which, no doubt, explained his strange attire; and Lemuel and Abigail were friends of the president. "I'll check our records once more and if the records aren't there, I'll personally see to it that the proper forms are on file. May I make copies of this letter, and return it when I come back with your certification?"

Abigail replied, "You won't need to. I have enough copies. We wouldn't want anyone to get in trouble over a little missing red tape." Matthews never realized how near trouble he had approached.

Lemuel definitely wanted Matthews to become an apostle. He was the sort of individual whose unswerving single-minded dedication to his assigned task, combined with his respect for the complex infinity of rungs on society's hierarchical ladder, made him a perfect candidate for the First Estate. If he were not mortal, he would have made an excellent angel.

Matthews' authority had been superceded and pushed off balance by the important connections of the people he intended to dominate. Lemuel figured that a couple more jabs and a righteous hook, and he'd have a knock down. He punched with his right. "You've witnessed miracles today Matthew (he unconsciously dropped the 's' from Matthews' name), your spine has been made straight, and your vision is now unimpaired. Won't you kneel with us and give thanks to our Lord?" He dropped to his knees and placed his hand on Matthews' arm, urging him to join him in prayer. Both Myles and Esther knelt beside him, and Esther took hold of Matthews' other hand, also urging him the kneel. Abigail remained where she was.

The round went to the Lord. Overcome with this display of piety by these VIPs, Matthews dropped down, and Abigail decided to assist Lemuel's K.O. by creating an imitation of the sacred fires of the Holy Ghost to swirl about their heads. It was a very nice fire: bluish green and orange with little gold and silver sparklies.

The Holy Ghost entered Matthews' heart that day, at least that's who we think it was, and he vowed, with tears streaming down his cheeks, that from now on he'd be guided by the Lord. He was fully prepared to turn all of his cares over to the Lord. He vowed that from now on the Lord would be his pilot, and, as frequently happens when strong men surrender their will to the higher powers, he broke down and blubbered and groveled before the angels. Abigail was disgusted by the whole performance and lost what little respect she ever had for him.

The publican who came to assert his authority over Lemuel no longer existed: he had been given a new heart[55]. How swiftly and miraculously the mysterious thing we call power can be shifted by some invisible force is a marvelous work and wonder. Matthews came to impose his might over Lemuel and was now on his knees before him confessing all his sins. And having found God, Matthew would never be able to collect taxes again. No man can serve two masters, for he will love the one and hate the other. Matthew could no longer serve mammon.[56] His usefulness as a tax collector was finished. Having confessed his sins and cleansed his heart, he had reached that crossroad where he should enter either the free market where gain or loss was determined honestly by competition and the sacred unseen hand of the market, or he could cast off worldliness altogether and join the Church of the Ethereal Evangelicals.

So, as he had for Peter, Andrew, James, and John (the fishermen Esther had snagged), Lemuel laid out the strict conditions of his mission for Matthew, the publican. This time real substance was involved, not the condo he occupied, or the furniture he sat on, or the automobile he drove; they were really owned by the bank that allowed him to use those things so long as he made his payments on time. But he did own his clothes, the food that was in his refrigerator, and a fairly hefty sum in his government pension plan.

Although salvation does not exclude unlearned and ignorant men, the gospels report that Peter and John were perceived as unlearned and ignorant men[57]; on the other hand, stupidity is not a requirement, and many we believe to be highly educated have as much faith. Those worldly skills one had before accepting Christ are still remembered. Matthews was a whiz at figures, and quickly calculated the debit and credit sides of the assets. By joining the church and handing his assets over to Abigail, his net gain would be several thousand dollars, but Matthews was only figuring the assets that he knew about. Lemuel had neglected to tell him about the millions that were being launder...oops ...tax advantaged. Matthews told them that he would have to consider their proposition very carefully.

He became philosophical about his decision to leave the civil service. "The pastor of my church has been warning about the powers of Satan and his evil empire for the last twenty years. I've been ashamed to admit to people that I was a publican. For a secure position and a steady paycheck, I'm like Esau selling my birthright for a bowl of pottage. I've collected money from good decent folks, like yourselves, to be spent by those demon-possessed liberals that have taken control of our government, and used your tax money to finance and abet their godless abominations: abortions, race mixing, and denying our children the right to pray in school. They've removed the Ten Commandments from the classroom, and then handed out condoms in school to promote promiscuity. I've wondered how low this nation would sink before the Lord destroyed it, as he did Sodom and Gomorrah."

Esther smiled broadly, batted her long eyelashes at him, and said, "Oh my, yes! How right you are Matthew. We certainly don't want to be possessed by demons, but do you really think there are such things?"

"Of course demons exist. The Bible mentions demons and it tells how they can possess people and cause them to do wicked things."

"Well...I don't know. Do you think you would recognize one if you saw it?" Esther looked at Abigail and gave her a mischievous wink.

"I certainly could and I can see the results. How else do you explain the President and that slut, the ACLU, the abortion clinics, Ralph Nader, and homosexuals? Do you realize there is an admitted socialist in our House of Representatives? How do you explain those things other than demons?"

Afraid that Esther might blurt out something that could divulge Abigail's true identity, Lemuel changed the subject by suggesting that Matthews join them for lunch. He assured Matthews that: "Obviously there is much sin throughout the land, and Sister Abigail and I are going to bring salvation to as many of those poor lost souls as we can." He asked the ladies if they would mind preparing sandwiches, and then suggested that they bring an appropriate libation and a of box cigars so they might properly celebrate Matthews' deliverance from the clutches of worldliness. As Esther and Abigail left, he turned to Matthews and said, "In your position as tax collector I suppose you became more knowledgeable than the average man about mortal folly. You could be of enormous help to our mission as an advisor and partner."

When the bottle of Old Charter and the box of Cuban panatellas was set before them, Matthews blanched. He looked reproachfully at the whisky and tobacco. The tobacco was illegally smuggled across the border from Matamores, the product of Castro's evil empire, and he realized this church of the Ethereal Evangelicals cleaved to a different theology than he'd heard from his strict hard-shell Baptist preacher. The Reverend Smith was actually pouring over ice cubes and serving spiritous liquor. "I don't drink or smoke," he said, and held up his hand.

"Demon rum and the devil's weed?" Abigail teased, and set a platter of ham on rye sandwiches on the coffee table. "Go on, try it. You might like it. It is offered to celebrate your being healed. Think of it as a sacrament."

Esther put a platter of steamed shrimp, spicy Cajun crab cakes, and smoked eel beside Abigail's offering, sat opposite Matthews and crossed

HOW THE GOOD TAILOR GOT TO HEAVEN — 443

her legs. The split in her wrap-around skirt opened exposing Esther's thigh. Myles, sitting next to Esther, raised his drink and offered a toast: "May your young men see visions and your maids dream dreams, and a drink for those whose heart may grow faint in the wilderness." They all raised their glasses to honor the occasion. Matthews raised his glass, but did not drink.

"I thought the Scriptures forbade strong drink?" he said.

"Oh no," Myles contradicted him. "'For how great is His goodness, and how great is His beauty! Corn shall make the young men cheerful, and new wine for the maids.' Zechariah 9:17. And just what is bourbon? It's corn liquor to make the young men cheerful."

"I can't quote the Scriptures but it seems that there's a lot in the Bible about drunkenness."

"This is for cheerfulness lad; cheerfulness, not drunkenness."

"Well even if you're right, the verse that you quoted said, 'new wine for the maids.'"

"Who says we're maids?" Esther said, and winked lewdly while using the same skillful subtlety of leg movement that she had used on Haman and slid her left leg up a bit higher. She exposed the secret parts that the Lord threatened to discover,[58] and since Esther wasn't wearing panties, the sight caused Matthews to gasp and swallow half his drink before he realized what he had done.

"There, that wasn't so bad was it?" Myles continued. "And just where did you get the notion to reject any of God's provenance? 'The God which made the world and *all* things therein': Acts seventeen, verse twenty four."

Esther slowly moved her leg higher and Matthews gulped down the rest of his drink. She said, "That's right Matthew. All the things therein."

Myles added more scriptural evidence to his dissertation about spiritous drink. "And Timothy said: 'Drink no longer water, but use a little wine for thy stomach's sake, and thine other infirmities.' And didn't our Lord, Himself, change water into wine?"

Matthews drew his eyes away from Esther's proffering, and replied,

"Well our minister said he only made a little bit of wine, and that was only to please his mother." Then his eyes strayed back to Esther's legs and she opened them a bit wider.

Myles countered, "A little bit? It was six water pots...eighteen firkins...about a hundred and fifty gallons! And do you recall what the governor of the feast said of the wine? 'You have saved the good wine for last, unlike some who bring out the cheap stuff when all the men have well drunk.' So they had already consumed plenty of wine.[59]"

Matthews nervously helped himself to a refill, and his eyes switched back and forth from his interlocutor's face to Esther's legs. Lemuel was sitting beside Matthews and could have easily witnessed Esther's exhibitionism, but he was busily searching the Bible for a particular passage that might convince Matthews to become a partner in faith. He believed that Matthews had been corrupted by his Baptist minister's misinterpretation of the Scriptures and by the cynical worldliness of his job as a publican. Then he found what he was looking for, and he read aloud, "'There is not a prophet greater than John the Baptist, but he that is least in the kingdom of God is greater than he, and the publicans,' that would be you, Matthews, 'justified God, being baptized with the baptism of John. But the Pharisees and the lawyers rejected the counsel of God.' And Jesus scolded them for their perverse morality, and He says, 'For John the Baptist came neither eating bread nor drinking wine; and ye say he hath a devil. The Son of man is come eating and drinking; and ye say, Behold a gluttonous man, and a wine bibber, a friend of publicans and sinners!'[60] Do you see Matthews? Jesus taught that God made the world and all the things therein to be appreciated, even publicans, and sinners, and wine bibbers." He turned a few more pages, and continued, "God spoke to Peter a second time about his denial of God's gifts. He said to Peter, 'What God hath cleansed, that call not thou common!'[61] And Peter denied God, and said, 'Not so, Lord, for I have never eaten any thing that is common or unclean.' And the Lord had to tell him the third time, 'What God hath cleansed *that* call thou not common.' As Paul said to the Romans, 'I know and am persuaded by the Lord Jesus, that there is *nothing* unclean of itself.'"[62]"

HOW THE GOOD TAILOR GOT TO HEAVEN — 445

Esther turned toward Abigail, and said, "You see, Abby. It's not *marimay*."

Abigail replied, "I think the rest of that verse says; 'it is if you think it is.'"

Matthews' attention seemed to have strayed, and so Lemuel wound up with, "Your infirmities have been healed by faith Matthews. Will you make the Lord speak the second and the third time to make your commitment? Do you think you deserve God's special attention the second and the third time?"

Matthews had started on his third bourbon on the rocks. He obviously didn't think it was *marimay*. He was staring openly at one of God's creations that he would have loved to taste, and borough his nose and lips and fingers into, and if it were not for Myles noticing his intense stare and salacious expression, he might have dropped to his knees right there.

Myles glanced at Esther's lap and quickly figured it out. He calmly leaned over and whispered into her ear. She modestly closed her legs and pulled down her skirt, but as she did so she pouted and her expression clearly signaled reluctance.

As though a shade had suddenly been drawn, Matthews was momentarily disoriented and the Scriptures that Lemuel had been droning on about gradually entered his consciousness. He arose, slightly unsteadily, and assured them that he would love to join their mission if they thought him worthy. He made a courtly bow to Abigail, kissed her hand, and promised to deliver his worldly goods to her as soon as he could wind up his affairs. Esther bestowed the kiss of charity on Matthews and he departed, fanning his reddened face with his straw hat.

I feel that when the roll is called up yonder, Matthews will be among the apostles after he gets back to his office and examines the church's entire financial statement.

* * *

With Matthews gone, the four evangelists felt they could talk more openly and Abigail begins to discover how nearly impossible it was to corrupt with worldliness those whose morality is Scripturally decreed. Myles was curious to find out how much of his instruction Lemuel planned to put into practice. He was as direct as a catechist examining an acolyte. "By the way Lemuel, have you decided which liturgical dogma you plan to use for your mission: feast or fast?" Then he bit into a prawn the size of a chicken's drumstick. "Oh how I miss mortal food."

"We plan to be an itinerant mission and we thought we'd reproduce the tabernacle tent that Moses erected in the wilderness. Abigail wants to use period costumes and authentic musical instruments. For the opening procession, she thought that the Book of Psalms described a real attention-getter. The apostles and I would be in the procession down the aisles with the singers and the players on musical instruments, and the damsels playing timbrels would weave their way among us. The damsels would also spread out among the parishioners and entice those willing to join the procession to come to the altar where we'd be waiting to get them to commit to God. Abigail said that once the girls got them to come up to the altar, they'd be too embarrassed to leave without testifying for the Lord.

"She said that in order to get them to come to our services in the first place, we could use the brazen altar for cooking barbeques and the food would be like a communion. We'd have kegs of ice cold beer, too. What do you think? She said Texans can't resist a good barbeque."

"I think it smacks of popery. I might have known Tomas would corrupt you: the ceremonial pinch of salt once in a while, and then back to worldliness as usual. Where's the total abnegation of the self to the higher entity; the surrender of their ego; their plight of eternal troth to the Supreme Order?"

"Abigail said we had to get their attention first."

"Abigail said?...Abigail said?...She's a demon!...What's she got to do with this?"

Abigail snapped back, "I've heard Lemuel say many times, 'The potter hath power over the clay.' Doesn't the Bible say everything is predestined, so what difference does it make what I am?"

HOW THE GOOD TAILOR GOT TO HEAVEN

"All right! But there has to be more to it than a performance. They have to make a lasting commitment. Since you plan to feed the multitude, it doesn't sound like mortification of the flesh. I suppose you intend to abjure worldly values by indifferently squandering them. I've heard that might be the best approach to lure the Americans. They're not enured to the stiff upper lip, like the British. They're more like the flabby Frenchies. Have you considered a totem? You'll use the cross, of course."

"We thought that we'd honor all divisions of the God of Abraham and use the Cross, the Star of David, and the Crescent. Their souls all go to heaven."

A concupiscent leer spread across Myles's face, and he suggested, "How about serpents? Did you consider using serpents? Remember Moses and his fiery serpent?"

"Of course we did. I remembered your lessons. We attended one ceremony where they used serpents, but Abby thought it smacked of ignorance and superstition, and she was right. It didn't even come close to paying homage to the serpent who gave man knowledge, and she said it was very dangerous. She doesn't want to get involved in anything harmful."

"Abigail thought!…Abigail said!…Abigail wanted!…Are you losing control of your church? It sounds like you're letting a demon run your ministry."

"No, of course not. She is financing it, so she feels that she has some say, but don't think for one minute that she's running things. I really put my foot down on one of her suggestions. She thought temple prostitution would attract converts. I wouldn't stand for that."

Esther's blue eyes sparkled and she smiled broadly at Abigail, and said, "Oh my! Really! Temple prostitution? What an interesting idea, Abby…Ummmm."

"Esther! I was just fooling." Then the perverse little imp jeered, "They're already doing it. Doesn't the church advertize itself as the place to go to meet girls? And after the boys meet those girls, what do you think they do with them? I just thought we ought to be honest about it and cash in on it."

"It sounds perfectly reasonable to me," Esther said. "But suppose somebody wanted to partake of the sacraments and didn't have enough money? I think it'd be cruel to deny anyone salvation."

What Abigail had intended to be biting satire, and her opinion about the hypocrisy of the godly, was taken as a serious proposal. She wasn't surprised by Esther, but she thought the learned theologian, Myles Coverdale, would have recited some Biblical verse to counter such bold immorality. Instead, he launched on a historical dissertation:

"That, Esther, was precisely why the early Christians disavowed all property rights. Acts, two, verse forty four: 'All who believed were together, and had all things in common. There is neither Jew nor Greek, neither bond nor free, neither male nor female: for ye are all one in Jesus Christ.'[63] Prostitution might deny participation to some of the most devout believers, merely for the lack of coin. So they had all things in common. Wives and daughters could not be kept for someone's exclusive use, but must be shared among all of them that believed. For example Jesus said, 'Whosoever he be of you that forsaketh not all that he hath, he cannot be my disciple.[64]' It would be hard to consider those words as a parable, or try to derive some metaphoric meaning; they're as straightforward as sunlight. And, 'all that he hath', means 'all that he hath'... wives, children, coin, property...all that he hath. And 'all that he hath' is to be laid before the apostles for the use of all of them that believe, as they have need.'[65]"

Esther said, "It's a shame male angels are impotent. I'd service your need anytime Myles." Then she rolled her eyes at Lemuel and observed, "But Lem's mortal now, isn't he Abby?" Abigail arched one eyebrow and glowered.

Myles asserted, "My interest is purely academic, Esther. I've always wondered if a truly fundamentalist church would attract worshipers in this modern world. It has been so corrupted by worldliness and the law. I'd like to see if those professing their faith the loudest, are not merely hypocrites, 'who love to pray standing in the synagogues, and in the corners of the streets, that they may be seen of men,' Myles pointed upward to emphasize: 'Verily I say unto you, They have their reward![66]' The truly faithful would be like the sainted Nicolaus, who upon being accused by the apostles of being a jealous guardian of his beautiful wife, brought her forward and said that anyone who wished could have her. That is the proper spirit. 'For the flesh lusteth against the Spirit, and the Spirit against the flesh ...but if ye be led by the Spirit, ye are not under the law.[67] *And they that are Christ's have crucified the flesh with affections and lusts*'*. So with that simple offering, Nicolaus showed himself to be free of the law. He crucified any worldly possessiveness he felt toward his wife by sharing her with the affections and lusts of them that believed, had all things in common, and demonstrated that he was truly of the Spirit."

Lemuel shifted uneasily, darted a glance at Abigail, and decided that he could never be as good a Christian as Nicolaus, so he sought to counter Myles'ss rather unique interpretation of the Scriptures. "In Revelations, the angel is speaking to John and the angel says; 'But this thou hast, that thou hatest the deeds of the Nicolaitans, which I also hate.'[68] We shouldn't do anything that is hateful. Abigail absolutely forbids anything hateful, either in word or deed."

And Myles said, "I'll bet the angel was none other than our illustrious inquisitor general: Tomas; hero of the Spanish Inquisition. He hates everything."

Abigail pulled her chair around to face Myles, and explained the facts of life to him. "Listen here, you. I'm the banker of this enterprise and I want to see it succeed. Forget the law, custom, and middle class morality. What you propose won't work. It's been tried, and it always fails. You're not the first to find those meanings in the Bible. Shortly after the Pilgrims came, some of the colonists formed antinomian groups based on those same meanings. There were naked Adamites; peripatetic Seekers; and orgiastic Ranters, and they were all scorned, driven into the wilderness, or hanged as witches, and devil worshipers. There was a rash of them during the Victorian age; they were called bohemians, and later there were communistic settlements all over the northeast; all failed. And most recently the hippies formed all sorts of communes, most of them sexually promiscuous, and they're all gone now. One of the last attempts just came to a fiery end in Waco."

Esther had been looking forward to those rites of righteousness, and crestfallen, she muttered, "What else would you expect from a six-thousand-year-old virgin?" Then aloud she countered, "It's not hateful; it's love shared among all who believe."

"Esther, I have a lot of respect for your powers. I know the revelations of Esther, rather than the Revelation of Saint John attracted our four fishermen and beguiled Matthews. I may have healed Matthews, and did the Holy Ghost fire thing, but that won't persuade him. When he gets back to the IRS office and looks at our entire bank balance, it will spin the numbers in his little calculating mind, but the thing he'll remember most is that the most beautiful girl in the universe exposed her twat to him. And to prove my point about the problems you'll run into, for all of Myles's so-called academic objectivity, I noticed how subjective he became when he realized what you were doing."

"You've put the wrong twist on my motives. I merely whispered to her that those members of the body on which we bestow more abundant honor, Matthew may think less honorable, and those parts which we think have more abundant comeliness, he may think uncomely.[69] Besides, he hadn't made a firm commitment, and wasn't entitled to see Esther's comely parts."

"Oh, is that what 'pull your skirt down' means?" Esther snickered.

Abigail believed her plot to get the angels to defect was succeeding. She was sure of Lemuel's soul, Esther was determined to stay, and it was beginning to look as though she might be able to capture Myles also. He hadn't mentioned a word about taking Esther back with him since that morning. Nor had he mentioned leaving. The poor lovesick scholar was so infatuated with Esther that only extreme measures by the heavenly powers could force him to leave her. They'd have to drag him back in chains. She decided to give the angels plenty of liturgical leeway and, by using the church, see if she could attract a few more defectors. She didn't want to appear to be a pushover so she reluctantly agreed to allow Myles's orgies. That would keep Esther in the fold too. She said tentatively, "Well…if you're sure it shows divine infusions of love, but don't expect me to participate. If it gets out of control, I'll cut off your money." Then directly to Lemuel, she said, "Just remember our deal: absolutely no preaching hatred from the pulpit, and no condoning violence or vengeance."

"Yes dear, of course. Jesus could agree with your conditions."

Chapter 24

THAT EVENING ESTHER BECAME MORE AMUSED THAN WAS warranted by any trivial offhand remark Lemuel might make. She treated his most inane comments as precious gems of wisdom, frequently found reasons to get close to him, and occasionally brushed against his arm or back with her large firm breasts. Abigail was not insensible to Esther openly flirting with Lemuel, and she was not ignorant of her motives. Neither was Myles, and no matter how brilliant, and witty his conversation, Esther seemed to prefer the student, Lemuel, to Myles the pedant. While the tutor was perfectly willing to accept certain arousals of the Holy Spirit, academically, Abigail was right: the factual proclivities of the most beautiful woman in the universe led him to contemplate an unsavory, to his own mind, scene between Esther and Lemuel. He began to see that sexually segregated quarters might reflect some prudence, and at the same time, this would relieve him of exhibiting any taint of jealousy. He felt it showed his Nicolaitan-like liberality with Esther's body (the body his orders had given him charge of), since he was willing to accept her sleeping with a demon.

But it wasn't until bedtime that Abigail realized the situation. She assumed that Myles would sleep next to Lemuel and that Esther would return to her bed. It wasn't until Myles offered to spend the night in the club chair and Lemuel said that he would sleep there tonight, and then they would take turns. Myles could sleep in the club chair tomorrow night. She remembered Esther's Levitical remark the night before: that man could not lie with man as he does with woman, and that prohibition was evidently firmly programmed into these angels' psyche. So, to keep everyone comfortable, she decided to sleep with Lemuel and Myles would sleep with Esther. She certainly didn't decide out of jealously, nor to snub Esther for flirting with her angel, and she didn't even object to Esther's soft caresses when they slept together, but the thought of Lemuel rutting with Esther made her green eyes glint venomously. Those sleeping arrangements made Myles very happy. And, judging by the slurping sounds and female moans that came from their bed, Esther wasn't altogether disappointed by the arrangement.

Around midnight they were suddenly awakened by a tremendous noise overhead. It sounded as though a thousand shamans were swinging bull roarers. Then a brilliance lit up the beach. It was as though a million arc lights had suddenly been switched on. It bathed every blade of grass in its stark, blue-white light, and illuminated every corner of the trailer. Then a booming voice, many decibels above the general din, poured in through every opening of the trailer. It shook the glassware, the dishes in the cabinets, and seemed loud enough to compress the flesh: "ALL RIGHT YOU DIRTY ROTTEN DEMON…RELEASE THOSE HOSTAGES!!! WE KNOW YOU'VE GOT CAPTIVE ANGELS IN THERE…SO YOU HAVE!!! AND WE WANT THEM RELEASED IMMEDIATELY…IF NOT SOONER!…SO WE DO!!!"

Everyone was startled awake and Abigail set her lips in a thin angry line. Exasperated with rage, she snorted a forceful gust of air through her nostrils, grabbed her frilly, pink, short robe, and stamped past the terrified angels. She slammed open the screen door and shook the whole trailer as she stamped down the folding steps. With firmly planted, widespread legs, and arms crossed over her chest, she stood at the edge of the rug and faced the attack.

Above her head and high in the sky were two fiery wheels, ten stories tall. Coruscant showers, like Fourth of July pinwheels, spun off wildly into the inky sky. They swirled closer, as amber and purple flames belched from the hubs as intermittent shrieks, wails, and groans reverberated painfully against the eardrums. A foul stench like burning rubber tires hung in the air. A great whirlwind came from out of the north and swirled up a cloud of stinging sand missiles, and a fire infolding itself was in the cloud, with a brightness all about it. As the fearsome apparitions came closer, they appeared to expand and contract, like flaming wheels within flaming wheels. The fiery rims turned first one way, growing smaller, and then reversed and grew larger as they spun in the other direction. Then they came even closer.

Near terror, the angels tumbled from the trailer. Esther and Myles held on to each other in a trembling huddle and Lemuel stood by their side with one arm protectively reaching over them. His other hand was raised to shield his eyes from the brilliance. Abigail strode about fifty feet toward the oncoming threat, stood with her legs spread wide, her bare toes dug into the sand, her hands on her hips, and in her pink robe she was ready to hold her ground against the menace.

Gigantic man-like forms appeared behind the fiery wheels and each had four faces and four wings. Their feet were straight and long like the hooves of foundered ponies, and they sparkled like the color of burnished brass. As the wheels came closer it became clear that they weren't wheels; they were blazing keys on the end of long key chains, and they were being swung full circle around the index fingers of two angels wearing zoot suits. They towered three stories high over Abigail, who hadn't stirred one inch from her stand. She said, "Well, well! What have we here? The ethereal press gang?" Then she pointed to the sand in front of her, and said, "Get down here to normal size before some mortal sces you[70] and reports that we're being invaded by Martians or has a heart attack."

Lemuel ran forward and stood beside Abigail, albeit slightly behind her.

The booming voice of one visitor, the chunkier built one, roared down on them, "Get out of the way, Satan! You're interfering with the Lord's work, so you are." In a mean snarl it addressed Lemuel. "And you'll get yours too, Willy!...Later!...You don't stay mortal forever, so you don't."

The visions towered above Abigail, and she said, "You two are on my turf now. If you can't behave yourselves, you two gates can swing right on back to where you came from." She'd promised to protect Esther and Myles, and she stepped forward and posed like James J. Corbit, waving her tiny fists at the pair of monstrous apparitions.

Lemuel whispered to Abigail, "It's Orson, the supply angel. Remember? I told you about him."

Orson boomed down at her, "Get out of the way, toots. We come to get those two reprobates. All'a youens been under surveillance, an' we know what ya been up ta, so we do. Esther's been out whoring, an' Myles an' her been doin' sodomy. Now get outta da way an' let us do our job."

Abigail stood her ground, and ordered, "Get down here to normal size if you want to discuss this."

"Dey ain't nottin ta discuss!"

The other angel spoke to Lemuel. "We heard that you gone bad Lem: taking up with demons. I didn't want to believe it, but now I've seen it for myself. Boy are you in for it when you get back." This was Lemuel's squad mate, Winfred. Then he sneered, "But those two are going to get theirs' now."

Lemuel greeted him weakly. "Hi, Winnie. This isn't what it looks like..."

The commotion the pair of angels made stirred up all the wildlife in the area. Birds flew from their nests in all directions, small animals, wild ponies, and deer crashed their way through the tall marsh grass, and a small mongrel puppy ran from the sea oats and stood shaking between

Abigail's legs. She picked him up, and he proceeded to excitedly lick her chin and neck. She said to the pup, "No, Cerberus. Don't tear them limb from limb yet. Give them a chance to go back."

"Dat ain't Cerberus. Who do you'uns think yer foolin, Toots? Dat pup ain't got three heads, an he don't belch fire, an he ain't got teeth like sabers."

"That's because he's in disguise, but he'll change quick enough if you don't behave. He'll become the biggest, fire breathing dragon you've ever seen, and with his roc-like talons, he'll tear you limb from limb."

The pup became heartened by Abigail's fearlessness and started to yap at the two intruders, and they shrank to normal size. Orson and Winfred advanced menacingly, carrying handcuffs and leg irons. "We ain't got nut'ing personal against you two, but weuns gotta take youens in."

Abigail blocked Orson's path. He was obviously in charge of the detail and she thought that a bluff might work. The angels were fed so much propaganda about the sinister ruthlessness of their cast down brethren that she thought she might be able to finesse an upset and get the upper hand with a threat. After all, anyone who'd spend their last dollar for a used Edsel could probably be sold anything. "Okay, now you've done it. We'll have it out right here and now. We've been waiting for another shot at you angels."

"Have what out, you nutty broad?"

"Armageddon!" she spat out harshly, and her green eyes glittered from behind her angry squinting eyelids. "One step further, and I'll summon every demon, imp, and malicious spirit there are: all the mighty legions of the evil empire. Satan and the whole troop have been itching for another crack at you slime balls. This is as good a place as any for that final battle." She raised her arm and poised her fingers as though ready to snap them.

"Hold on a minute, Abby!" Lemuel's voice quavered fearfully. He believed she could do it and he grabbed her hand to prevent the fatal signal.

Lemuel's genuine show of fear spread to Orson and Winfred. Orson sized up the situation, and he thought, *Dis is a trap, so it is.*

South Padre Island is nothing like the plains of Megiddo which had been so carefully reproduced in heaven. The field of battle where the Lord's armies have been practicing their battle maneuvers ever since Saint John wrote the Book of Revelations. The chariots would bog down in the soft sand, the pikemen and lancers would mire in the marshes, and there was no room for the carefully worked-out battle plans in that narrow spit of dunes and marsh grass. And worse, there was water on every side, and the Lord didn't have a navy. True, some of Jesus's apostles had fishing boats, but they had quickly abandoned the seafaring trade when they took up the business of fishing for men. Very likely, here, a few legions of demons could turn God's mighty army into a routed shambles. Orson said, "We'uns ain't got no authorization for anythin like dat, lady."

"That's tough. What did you expect? Marquis d'Queensberry rules? Did you think the forces of evil would fight fair? Haven't you heard all's fair in love and war? Well, this is war. You two came down here…disturbed my sleep…pestered my guests…I don't care what happens now." Then she started calling out the names of demons: "Azazel!…Belial!…Beelzebub!…." Her feigned fury aroused the puppy's hunting pack instinct and he began to yap and growl with puppy-like rage.

Orson placed his finger to his lips and made shushing sounds, then he pushed both hands out in front of him and waved them downward. "Okay, lady…keep your pants on …well youens know what I mean…hold it down…pu…leeze!" And to the puppy "Nice doggie, nice…no, don't bark.…"

"Molech!…Garm!…Eblis!…All demons everywhere! Arise demons…the time has come!…Briareus—these have a hundred hands each—wait til you see what these beauties can do to you puny angels. Hecatonchires!…Aegaeon!…Cottus…Gyges…"

"Aw come on…have a heart, Miz demon." And placating the pup, he cajoled, "Nice doggie, nice…nice. Be a good doggie."

"It's too late now. You'd better call your troops. You've gotten your last soul from this planet, Buster!"

"Aw, come on…have a heart, Miz demon." Orson dropped to his knees, and clasped his hands in front of him. The very names of the fiends terrorized him. "We'uns ain't got no autorization for nuttin like dis. We's assigned to prisoner chase duty. Here, look at our orders." Orson handed the stenciled orders to Abigail.

She took the sheet of paper and by the trailer's lights could make out the crude ink blots. They were letters and numbers, but their meaning meant nothing to her: "All M 6s trans HQ Batt; Com. Div. assgn opp Skeez. Mt 1800 hrs Brief. Rm 6; 3rd Inf. Reg. Maneuv. Russ Frnt." Underlined with red pencil was: "An 1st Grd. Orson; An Prob.Winfred; Rpt Grd Hse; Unifrm. Amer." Many more meaningless letters and numbers filled the page. One item seemed less esoteric to her, and she pointed it out to Lemuel: "Ly Prob An Tamar assgn Wht Hse intern detail."

Lemuel said, "That little liar. She caused all that trouble in King Jamesburg. Now she's off to see the president."

Abigail handed the special orders back to Orson, and said, "So what. You're orders don't mean anything to demons. The world is our territory. We only let you pick up your souls, work your lies and sneaky tricks on the mortals because of the truce—but if you want to end it right here and now…after this battle the mortals of this world will be free of your meddling, and your people won't get any more of their tithes, either."

Winfred had been obediently silent, deferring to his superior, but having the end come before he'd had a chance at mortality was something he didn't want to risk. He moved away from Orson, and pleaded, "You don't understand Ma'am. We have to bring them back with us. If we don't, we have to do their penance for them until they are brought back. That's the way this prisoner chase detail works." In spite of the warm, air he shivered.

"That's easily fixed. Don't go back…defect" Abigail teased.

Winfred took her suggestion seriously, and considered facing an eternity of impotence against a few decades of being chained to the wall next to a stone pile, and he said, "I haven't had my mortality detail yet. Maybe after that." Then he nudged Orson and said, "I think she's bluffing. That little puppy isn't Cerberus. Look, he's even wagging his tail."

Orson had one of the best jobs available to an ordinary first grade angel and didn't want to risk his secure position for worldly chaos. He got up, brushed the sand from his knees, turned a baleful eye on Esther and Myles, and said less assertively, "The Suffragan Commission is gonna hear about this. You'uns better come along peacefully."

Esther saw Abigail's bluff was working and felt braver, she stood beside her, and protested, "I'm not going back, ever! And this isn't fair to Myles. He hasn't even had a proper mortality yet."

"So what! Nobody does. He ain't allowed two mortalities. He got one, same as any other mortal. An he knew what to expect better'n any other mortal of his time. He put it down in plain English, so he did. He shouldn'ta poked his nose inta church doctrine."

Slightly more emboldened, Esther argued, "Well, he's an angel now, but he's not like the rest of us angels. He was ordained without prior experience of the world before the flood. A lot of you male angels had five or six mortalities—that's why they built the wall around Thelassar and keep the waters of life under heavy guard. How many times did you come down to make out with the daughters of men?"

"Maybe a couple, but that don't make no difference. He knew what to expect. It's all written down in the Bible, ain't it? "

Then Myles edged forward and stood beside Esther. He muttered, "I sure didn't expect to be celibate for eternity."

"Wha'd ya expect? Some kinda Ishmaelites' paradise, wid seventy houris ta screw? Where does it say anythin like that in the Bible?"

"Of course it does not, and I didn't expect it to be like the tree of a mustard seed either,[71] but I expected my baser desires would be left behind with the flesh; surpassed with glorious rapture."

"How many times you prayed: 'Thy will be done on earth as it is in heaven?' What made you think you'd feel any different?"

Abigail had never felt the mortal's romantic malady, so she didn't

HOW THE GOOD TAILOR GOT TO HEAVEN — 461

understand it and was disgusted by it, but she knew the affliction had fevered Myles's mind. He was smitten with Esther. It was hard to tell how Esther felt since she exuded signals like pheromones, indiscriminately, and she seemed driven to accept every man. She had even tried to seduce Lemuel, not that it mattered to Abigail; she was above petty jealousy. She wondered if they were given another mortality, would they be any more prudent the second time?

Orson and Winfred had been easing away, and watching fearfully for the arrival of the army of fiends that Abigail had summoned. Orson's eyes flitted between Esther and Myles, and as they stared at each other, Abigail said, "You better make up your mind. Either stay or go. The troops will be here any minute. This will be the end of the world for you angels." Then she called out the names of several more demons.

"Le'me think, will ya?" He and Winfred put their heads together and the wide brims of their hats hid their faces. An occasional phrase could be understood as they reasoned together: "Tree times the regular number, hum, tirty thousan, dat's a couple of brigades." There was some barely audible mumbles, and then the words, "The line on the southern front has ruptured and they's swarming across like ants. We need more troops."

Orson rubbed his chin thoughtfully, and said, "They might go for that." Then he faced Abigail and said, "I'll tell you what, toots. I'll submit this offer to the front office. We'll lend you them two runaways, but each one has to fill the regulation recruitment quota. We'll let the higher ups decide. Now, how 'bout callin off your demons."

* * *

The crisis passed. Orson and Winfred explained to the Heavenly Review Board how they had managed to outwit a demon who nearly caused the end of the world. They managed to escape just before Cerberus attacked, and only seconds ahead of all the demonic forces of earth. They did manage to wring from the super powerful arch fiend a tremendous deal for the Empyreal Establishment. The two reprobates would serve their penance on the evil world, steeped in worldliness among the wicked mortals, and they must enlist an extra twenty thousand souls in addition to the ten thousand probationary angel Lemuel was charged with bringing to salvation. They said it was the best deal the establishment has made in that part of the world since the church financed Columbus' discovery and brought salvation to the heathen Indians.

* * *

The next morning Myles thought he should blend in with the rest of the group, so he borrowed a pair of Lemuel's jeans and a shirt. He emptied the contents of his zoot suit pockets onto the table. His billfold contained the standard issue three hundred dollars; a weekly bus pass; his draft card, he was 4F; two tickets to a Gene Krupa performance at the Starlight Ballroom; and a package of three condoms, Sheiks. His pants pockets held: a six-inch switch blade knife, several coins, and a bus token; his key chain had a house key to some unknown lock. His shirt pocket held a pack of Lucky Strikes with the statement, "Lucky Strike green has gone to war," printed on the white package. (The green never returned; it was another war casualty.) Several hand-rolled "reefers" had been substituted for the regular cigarettes, and a silver plated Ronson cigarette lighter was in his jacket pocket.

Abigail said, "You've got everything a swinging gate, an in-the-groove hep cat would carry…about fifty-five years ago. The Starlight Ballroom is gone, so are weekly bus passes that cost a buck and a quarter, draft cards are different now, but with a 4F classification you wouldn't have been drafted, and that much marijuana would have gotten you a couple of years hard time, but it's only a misdemeanor now. The Ronson Company is gone, but people are still using rubbers."

Esther removed one from the package and looked at it curiously.

Abigail said, "The man puts it over his penis to catch his sperm."

"How's this little disk going to catch any sperm? It'd come off inside me."

Abigail put it over two of Esther's fingers and unrolled it part way. Esther understood immediately and unrolled it completely, waved it

HOW THE GOOD TAILOR GOT TO HEAVEN — 463

about, blew it up and ran her forefinger over the swollen balloon. She fantasized about the delights it could hold.

Abigail considered Esther's proclivity toward multiple divertissements and warned, "They're used to prevent venereal diseases and as contraceptives. I know angels can't catch anything, but you could spread it. If you like the feel of bare flesh, you had better stick to one lover. In the forties, when the zoot suits represented the counterculture of the day, promiscuity wasn't as rampant as it is today, so VD was rare. When Columbus' sailors swapped Europe's Christianity for America's syphilis it quickly spread all over Europe, so about the seventeenth century someone invented sheaths made of lamb skin. They weren't much good, and lots of people got paresis, went insane, or died young. It was an egalitarian disease that infected all classes. Then people found out about latex rubber. That helped to control it, and also attitudes toward women changed. They were adored, glorified, idealized, protected, and put on a pedestal. They hadn't invented the Pill yet, and the condoms were mostly for birth control. In those days if you got some girl pregnant, you were supposed to marry her. But the zoot suiters were more like today's generation: irresponsible, oversexed, and wild over rock and roll. Women were whores for fucking, not marrying, and VD has bloomed once more. I guess your holy tailor is right. They were the avant garde for today's culture."

The discourse between Esther and Abigail led Myles and Lemuel to consider the theological implications of such devices. Lemuel was concerned that the use of birth control devices would thwart the intended purpose of the "Circle of Love," and the "Kiss of Peace." He said, "God is the creator of life, so the offering of the holy seed should be a completely uninhibited sacrament. These devices assign willful, and therefore sinful, responsibility for the act that is supposed to be regarded spiritually and an acknowledgment of God's life-bestowing powers."

But Myles argued, "Our Lord Lord commanded us to love one another, but nowhere in his teaching did he place any importance on conception. The truly devout women of the congregation would have no inhibiting reservations, but some of the younger women wanting to express their most impassioned love might be reluctant to participate in the sacraments if they risked becoming pregnant. I'm afraid you have been too influenced by Tomas' Roman churchyness.

"How can you be so obtuse, Myles? Don't you remember your own instructions to me about the begetting ceremony? 'I will be begotten, and I will beget!' The Acts of John...remember? The reason for having all things in common, including the women, is because at the Circle of Love sacrament, when the members become engorged with the Holy Spirit, and the communicants express their divine love for each other, is that if these unions are blessed with offspring, the babies will have come by chance."

Abigail whispered into Esther's ear, "That's what I heard Zacharias told Mary when she went to visit her cousin Elizabeth, and the Holy Spirit raised up his horn of salvation[72]." They both snickered together, and Esther said, "Do you think Mary stroked Zacharias horn for him like I did when I touched the king's golden scepter?"[73]

"I don't know, but that story she told her husband, after staying with old Zack for three months, sure was a whopper."

Their womanly tittle-tattle was quickly challenged by Lemuel. "Your wicked little demon mind is too full of worldliness. Jesus said, 'and call no man your father upon earth: for one is your father, which is in Heaven.'[74] So, even if your contention was correct, it wouldn't make any difference. The Lord is Father of us all!" Then Lemuel picked up the package of condoms from the table, shook them menacingly at Myles, and said, "But if these thing are used, they would pervert the intent of the sacrament."

"Not so!" Myles objected. "They allow the woman to unreservedly participate in her devotions without worldly concerns." He enumerated on his fingers. "There are the young maids who might be moved by the spirit and are not of such physical maturity to bear pregnancy; those mothers with still young infants, and do not want to bear another right away; the especially devout women to whom partaking of the sacrament

HOW THE GOOD TAILOR GOT TO HEAVEN

is so important, but is afraid that her swollen belly would not inspire communication..."

"You mean like Elizabeth?"[75] Esther asked, and winked at Abigail, lewdly, and commented, "Old Zacharias' balls must have been turning indigo by the time Mary stopped by for her visit."

Lemuel responded, "I don't for one second believe what these two gossiping shrews are saying. The Scriptures clearly tell us that Mary was impregnated by the Holy Spirit—but what if they are right? What if those evil things had been available to Zacharias? No! I cannot go along with your position in this matter. When mortals are filled with the Holy Spirit, and feel the urge to love one another—'God is love.'[76] If they use any unnatural device they may be preventing the emergence of another John the Baptist...or one mightier..."[77]

"Oh ye of little faith, brother Lemuel. Mightier indeed! The condom would break, or the Holy Ghost would appear, as he had to Zacharias[78], and the device would be discarded. The potter hath power over the clay. Do you really think that feeble man could thwart the will of the Almighty?" Myles clucked his tongue, shook his head sadly, and said, "I see that Tomas' instruction was not as unbiased as the catechist manual requires, and I suppose Orson made his little sales pitch for the Roman church...so he did. If that's going to be your attitude, maybe you belong with the papists."

Abigail laughed, and said, "He tried, but I saved him from that." Then, in a more serious vein, she said, "I know you want to return to the fundamentals, but the most recent example I can think of for the kind of services you're proposing weren't religious at all. They're just honest sex orgies. You'd have to go back to Rasputin, and the court of Tsar Nicholas, and Alexandra to find sexual free-for-alls with a religious intent. Of course, some of the Antinomian sects that landed with the Pilgrims got pretty lively in their devotionals; and then there were the Borgias; Pope Alexander Sixth, and his children; and Cesare and Lucrezia. They say that both her father and brother took turns worshiping with Lucrezia, as well as half the court of Ferrara."

A lascivious leer crossed Esther's face, and Abigail rebuked her sternly, "Didn't your fooling around end in disaster, Esther, with you boyfriend killing the king? Well, so did all the others. The Tsarina's sex games justified a bloody end and the whole family was killed; the Antinomians were cast out; and the Borgias were responsible for hundreds of murders. Besides, I think it's wrong for men to pass women around."

"It wouldn't be as if the women were given to strangers, Abigail." Myles explained, "Esther can tell you, in the Old Testament, where Ezekiel is admonishing the Israelites for the 'work of their imperious whoredoms,'[79] he compares God as a husband whose wife commits adultery by taking strangers to her bed. But among the community of them that believed, and had all things in common, they are not strangers. They are as Jesus said: mothers, brothers and sisters of their common Father who art in Heaven."

"That may be so," Lemuel interjected, and then asserted, "but that still doesn't make birth control devices acceptable."

"What difference does it make so long as the conjunction is by the Holy Spirit's compulsion to love."

Abigail found herself in the absurd position of defending middle class morality and wholesome family values. "No self-respecting mortal woman will participate, and no husband, boyfriend, or father would let her, if he loved her."

"That attitude is selfish, vain, and wicked worldliness, Abby." Lemuel recounted the Scripture, "He that loveth father or mother more than me is not worthy of me: and he that loveth son or daughter more than me is not worthy of me."[80] So when Jesus commanded them to love one another, I'm sure he meant to love each other equally, and to reject all worldly obligations, such as the selfish notion that some are loved more than others."

Myles, irresistibly pedantic, and showing off his superior knowledge, added, "That's from the Book of Matthew, but Luke remembered his words were even more forceful." Lemuel shook his head, and tried

HOW THE GOOD TAILOR GOT TO HEAVEN

to signal Myles to shut up, but Myles continued, "Luke remembered that Jesus said, 'If any man come unto me, and hate not his father, and mother, and wife, and children, and bretheren, and sisters, yea and his own life also, he cannot be my disciple.'"[81]

Abigail was shocked. She shook her finger at Lemuel, and said, "You better not preach anything like that! We have a deal, remember? No preaching hatred from your pulpit. If you dare preach anything like that, I'll sabotage this mission." Turning on Myles, she warned, "I don't care what your review board does, if you want my protection, you'll have to obey my rules—no lies, and no hatred!"

Esther, too, was perplexed by that statement, and supported Abigail. "Look, I may like all that fooling around stuff, but I have to agree with Abby. It's wrong to hate your mother and father. And while I'm no prophetess like Hulda, correcting anyone's interpretation of the Scriptures,[82] it seems to me that the commandment to: 'Honor thy father and mother,'[83] doesn't need any special insight to understand."

Myles didn't like to disagree with Esther, the love of his life, but he patiently explained, "That's the Old Testament, Mosaic Law, Esther. The New Testament has changed all that. Christians are not bound by the old law. 'Christ hath redeemed us from the curse of the law.'[84]"

"But that's one of the Ten Commandments," Esther insisted.

Myles corrected her. "They've been discarded, Esther. 'Having abolished in his flesh the enmity, even the law of commandments contained in ordinances.'[85] So there is no more Mosaic law. The Commandments were all abolished, except for the two Jesus mentioned: that we love God, and love each other. Your mind is blinded by the veil of the Old Testament 'which veil is done away in Christ.'[86] When Jesus died on the cross the veil was rent."[87]

Abigail looked perplexed, and said, "Now you've really got me confused. How are you supposed to love everyone: your neighbors and even your enemies, and hate your family, and even your own life. Well...hatred is out! You can make up your minds to that." She was beginning to regret having saved Myles from the press gang.

Myles smiled indulgently at Abigail and said, "Lemuel, this little spat shows just how perceptive our Lord was when he said, 'Suppose ye that I am come to give peace on earth? I tell you Nay; but rather division: for henceforth there shall be five in one house divided, three against two, and two against three. The father against the son, the mother against the daughter, and the mother-in-law against daughter-in-law.'[88] And Matthew remembers him saying, 'Think not that I am come to send peace on earth: I come not to send peace, but a sword. To set a man at variance against his father, and a daughter against her mother...'[89] You are too much of the world, Abigail, and your bias is understandable. We know that Satan is the progenitor of worldliness, otherwise,he could not have offered the world to Jesus,[90] but Jesus came to breakup the family and replace it with a commune, where all who believed were together, and had all things in common. In heaven all the mortal's souls are equal. There are no wives, or husbands,[91] and neither are there any mothers, fathers, sons, or daughters. There's no family, except the family of God."

* * *

Esther rarely engaged in a sex-neutral activity, and for twenty-five hundred years had not had the opportunity to walk a beach in the darkening twilight. On this evening the sky became a dark royal blue, like Esther's eyes, and the sea shimmered like green obsidian, like Abigail's eyes, and gentle waves washed crests of frothy white meringue up the chocolate, dark, wet sand. Little phosphorous jellyfish glowed like tiny buttons of pale moonlight. As she watched the stars appear one or two at a time, she thoroughly enjoyed it all. Within a couple hundred yards their stroll became increasingly more playful, and soon they were cavorting like two ten-year-old girls. Cerberus splashed along the beach ahead of them. "I never want to go back to that dreadful place, Abby. Never! Never! Never!"

"Do you think they'll come for you again?"

"I don't know. We can run, but we can't hide. You know, 'God's eyes are in every place beholding the good and the evil.' They've always got their secret snoops watching us. Myles doesn't want to go back either."

HOW THE GOOD TAILOR GOT TO HEAVEN   469

"You're just being paranoid, Esther. They can't be watching everything and everyone all the time. Or else, why would they put so much importance on confessing things they already know about?"

"If they do come for us again, would the rest of the demons really fight them off? They didn't show up when you called them before."

"I'll tell you a secret," and she whispered into Esther's ear. Since Abigail whispered softly we don't know what she said, but we overheard an occasional comment by Esther.

"You can do anything you want? Wow! Complete freedom! It sounds great!"

Abigail did not reply for a long moment, then she said, "Um hum. But, you'd better straighten out Myles. If he keeps on talking that hate stuff, I just might let them take him back."

"I'll work on him," she promised.

The moon was rising, full and butter yellow against the black. It cast a golden highway toward them across the rippling black mirror gulf, and they both meditated in spellbound silence at the beauty of it all. Esther said, "Oh Abigail, you've no idea how tiresome eternal light can be." Then she asked, "Would the other terrestrial angels object if we joined them?"

"On the contrary. I'm sure they'd love to have you, at least most of them. I don't think Satan would care one way or the other."

"How about if you made a report to your front office and made a formal request for assistance to help us fight off the press gang if they come back? Bring the case up before one of your tribunals. I'm sure they would be interested. Myles and I are celebrities. I'm featured in my own book in the Bible and Myles is in all the history books—we're famous. Wouldn't it be a coup for your side when the word got around that we defected?"

"We don't have tribunals or a front office. We don't even have a side, and we aren't impressed by celebrity. All we have is a post office box in Berkeley where we drop in from time to time to see if there are any messages."

The moon lighted the beach to nearly daylight, and Abigail could see the dumbstruck look on Esther's face quite clearly. Esther stumbled over her words, "Wha...Wha...that can't be! What about the evil empire? If the demons are the focus of evil, that takes coordination, structure, command procedures. What about your army of evil terrorists? Surely you have arch demons in command of your forces."

Abigail sighed, shook her head, and asked, "Is that why you want to stay here? So you can be part of an evil empire?"

"No! Of course not."

"Well, why then?"

Esther opened her arms like the curator of a gallery presenting a marvelous mural. "The night sky; the seashore; the mountains; and freedom. I want to be as free as you are Abby." She put her arm over Abigail's shoulder. She gave Abigail a hug and said sheepishly, "Aw, you know why else. I have this need. Do I have to explain it to you? We're both programed for penetration. I don't see how you've denied your nature all these years."

"Do you mean you'd be part of an evil empire...for that? Yech!"

"Don't knock it til you've tried it. But that's not the only reason. I like all the freedom you have when you're not working. You have more time for fun."

Abigail gave Esther's waist a squeeze, and explained, "I'm only free like this because I can conjure all the money I want. We had it pretty hard before paper currency. We had to work, or else charm some mortal out of their money. I told fortunes, sold charms and magic potions, and that was before they had commercial advertizing; it was tough. "

"Not as tough as life beyond the ninth celestial orb. Besides, there's another reason. Up there, where everyone worships God and competes for promotion and good jobs, there isn't any time for love. Even when you're working you don't seem to be under any pressure."

"Working?"

"You know . . . corrupting the mortals...causing their damnation . . . tormenting their lost souls. . . ."

HOW THE GOOD TAILOR GOT TO HEAVEN

"They sure have filled your head with a lot of lies. Did you think I was on vacation or something?"

Esther gave her a sly knowing smile. "No, I thought you were working."

"Huh? How do you mean?"

"Joining up with Lemuel so you could lead the mortals who joined his church astray."

"Me lead them astray? Didn't you hear the kind of orgies that Myles and Lem are planning as worship services?"

"Oh, don't be such a prude. It sounds like fun."

* * *

They were walking in a southerly direction. The new high-rise condos at the tip of the island seemed like upstanding dominoes with the occasional lighted window as dots. Then they heard the faint grind and creak of another trailer being eased along the road behind the dunes. They climbed up to the top to see who their new neighbors might be. Bright headlights pierced the night, and behind trailed a celebration of red and amber running lights on a fairly large, cream-colored trailer. The rig pulled into a hard-packed cove next to their cove. The trailer looked to be new with bright chrome wire wheels and white sidewall tires. The tow car was an old Cadillac, but immaculate with maroon paint, wire wheels, whitewall tires, and a powerful engine. The driver expertly backed into position. Esther and Abigail sat atop the dune to watch their new neighbors make camp.

The couple looked to be in their late twenties, or early thirties. He wore a pair of Bermuda shorts, knee socks, a blazer, and a turtleneck sweater; and the woman wore a cardigan sweater with the wrists pushed up to her elbows, and another very soft looking sweater underneath. Abigail noticed a small cross glittering in the bright moonlight hanging on a delicate chain about her neck. Her skirt was plain and straight, ending a couple of inches above her knees, and she wore penny loafers of highly-polished, cordovan leather. Both were blond, and in the moonlight their hair appeared silver. His hair was short and smooth with a soft wave above his forehead which gave him a boyish look, and her hair was also smooth and brushed in a long pageboy. Both had sharp nordic features, and resembled each other so much they could have been twins.

They went about the business of chocking, leveling, and disconnecting the trailer with practiced precision. Abigail remarked to Esther that since they had uncoupled their car, they evidently intended to stay for a while. Both went into the trailer and they heard the muffled hum as the generator was started, and the gulping change of pitch when they turned on their air-conditioner. They opened several windows to let the entrapped heat escape and soon reappeared outside. The blond woman remarked, "Stuffy inside," and fanned her face with her hand.

Her companion quickly replied, "Was that an invitation?"

She chuckled, and answered, "Why sure," and bounced up on the trunk lid of the Cadillac, pulled her skirt up to her hips, and spread her legs wide. The man dropped his Bermuda shorts on the sand and with practiced precision pushed between her wide open legs.

Esther said, "He has a nice stroke there. She'll have hers in a minute."

The blond woman gesticulated a pumping motion with her loafers in the air, then pulled him closer with her heels, arched her back, and threw her head back. After the women's third sequel of spastic convulsions, Esther gasped, "Oh, he's very good. I'll have to pay a neighborly visit."

Abigail clucked her tongue and pouted. She said angrily, "Don't you dare come over here and make trouble, Esther." Then she added with disgust, "So that's what Lem and Myles plan for a circle of love, huh? A sacrament, huh? It's gross!" But somewhere in a remote portion of her cerebellum, a faint signal produced a momentary query from its libidinous catechism, *I wonder what it's like?*

Although unspoken, Abigail's thoughts were sensed by Esther, and she said, "I'll show you sometime," and she hugged her.

Chapter 25

WEATHER FORECASTING IS AN EXACT SCIENCE AND IF IT WAS not for the occasional interference by demons, every prediction would be as accurate as predicting the mechanical advantage of a lever or the certitudes of the astrological charts. Abigail caused some consternation within the meteorological community when she diverted the jet stream that was to have brought a day of drizzle and cold, clammy air into the Brownsville area. She had a good reason to shift the weather front farther north to the Galveston and northern Gulf region, and on across the Florida Panhandle. First, they were more accustomed to that kind of weather and would probably never notice, and secondly, she could not stand being cooped up in the trailer with Esther and Myles for the whole day. Their alternating mood shifts from joyfully playing a game of lick, slap and tickle, to mournfully anguishing over their mutual troubles with the Ethereal Establishment, was driving Abigail nuts. No matter what diversion she proposed to snap them from their manic-depressive mood swings: Scrabble, teaching them how to conjure money, charades, how to change the weather, Tarot card reading, (she even offered to read their palms, but they didn't want to know their futures), all they wanted was to sit together and watch the television set. She even thought it might be fun to change the president's cue cards into Portugese, or make him tell the truth at his press conference, but they weren't even interested in that. She shifted the gloomy weather away so she and Lemuel could go outside and enjoy the beach. It certainly wasn't because of any hostility toward weather persons.

So with the tide incoming and the weather pleasant, she and Lemuel basked on a beach blanket. Lemuel's surf rod was held by a tubular sand spike driven in at the edge of their blanket. He hadn't had any bites, so he lay on his back and used Abigail's rump and a folded towel to raise his head so he could more comfortably watch his rod tip. Any sudden flexing of the tip would be a signal that something was interested in his offering.

While they were occupied at this sport, slightly less physically demanding than chess, but far more tranquilizing, a large automobile rolled through the crossover in the dune where the cream-colored trailer of the blond couple was encamped. It was a big Mercedes; a 560SL, black, and very shiny. Its whitewall tires were scrubbed spotlessly and even the Arizona plates had been waxed. The chromium caduceus emblem affixed to the rear plate glittered and proclaimed that the owner was a doctor. The car parked with its trunk toward the water.

A very tall man, barrel-chested and wearing Eddie Bauer sporting clothes, got out and started rooting through the trunk for his gear. He pushed aside an inflatable sea horse, and a plastic beach ball, and pulled out a new tackle box about the size of an overnight suitcase. Next came his rod, his sand spike rod holder, a peach colored terrycloth beach towel, a folding aluminum beach chair, a pair of rubberized chest-high waders, and a big Ocean City 300 reel, and all of it was brand-new. Lemuel's equipment was scanty compared to this man's outfit.

Abigail thought it odd that a wealthy doctor would take up surf casting. His type usually chartered boats in Port Isabel and fished for marlin. "He may get sea sick," Lemuel suggested. They noted that he had children because of the toys. He was therefore married, and they guessed that his family was probably back at their condo on the tip of the island. The doctor could have told them that he was an excellent sailor, but one seldom sees scantily-clad beauties on charter fishing boats. His wife probably frowned on his habitual ogling the girls on the beach at their condo—especially in front of the children.

Beneath their trailer awning Abigail noticed the same blond couple whose daring performance on the trunk of their car she and Esther witnessed the night before. They also seemed to be watching the doctor and they had their heads together as though discussing a very serious matter.

The doctor readied his equipment and pulled on his waders—they reminded them of Myles'ss zoot suit pants. Then he clumped with stiff, robotic steps over to Abigail and Lemuel. Introductions were exchanged, and he and Lemuel discussed fishing prospects, but his eyes roved appreciatively over Abigail's browning body.

Lemuel said he was using shrimp for bait about the same time three nearly-naked school girls came running up the beach, and the doctor repeated distractedly, "Oh, clams. I was thinking of using shrimp." His name was Luke and he specialized in geriatrics and arthritis. His practice was in Sun City.

Lemuel told the doctor that he was a "man of the cloth"; and that he and Abigail were, "brother and sister in Christ," and that they were about to embark on an evangelical tour of Texas.

"Oh, you're not married?"

"No. There's this difference, you see."

"Mixed marriages rarely work," Abigail agreed impishly.

Luke offered some free medical advice to Abigail concerning the hazards of sun and skin cancer.

Abigail replied that she had sufficient melanin in her epidermis to protect her and that was why she was so dark and uncomely, but as a precaution, Lem kept her slathered in screening lotions.

"Oh no, my dear, you aren't uncomely at all. You are black but comely, O ye daughter of Jerusalem, as the tents of Kedar, as the curtains of

Solomon." Luke found that quoting the Scriptures as a pick-up line often worked in the Bible belt, and he had memorized most of the flattery in the Song of Solomon. He asked, "Has your brother kept you laboring too long in the vineyard?" He understood Lemuel's introduction to mean their kinship was spiritual and not legal or genetic.

Lemuel sat up, and said, "I see that you know the Bible, and your name is Luke, like the Biblical beloved physician[92]. It's gratifying to a man of the cloth to meet someone versed in the Scriptures. So many today never open the Holy Bible, let alone be able to cite it. Have you been saved?"

"Oh my yes," and he quoted from Nephri: "As the Lamb of God needed to be baptized to fulfill all righteousness, so did this simple unholy healer: yea; even by water."

Lemuel rolled from his back and was in a kneeling position on the blanket. He said, "I seem to have gotten myself into the right position, Luke. How about joining me in a quick prayer?"

"If I may lead," Luke replied. He dropped to his knees within touching distance of Abigail and mischievously placed his hand on Abigail's hip, while he prayed softly, "How fair and how pleasant art thou O love for delights. The joints of thy thighs are like jewels; the work of the hands of a cunning workman..."

Abigail slapped his hand sharply and said in a bantering voice, "I think you may have found the right church, Doc—but you've got the wrong pew. My joints don't need any medical attention."

Lemuel's mouth fairly watered over the prospect of adding a physician named Luke to his growing assemblage of apostles. He'd enrolled, but not yet ordained, four fishermen: Peter, Andrew, James, and John; he was pretty sure of Matthews, the publican; and here on this beach, as though by divine intervention, was the beloved physician, Luke. *Hath not the potter power over the clay?* "We intend to restore the fundamental values as Calvin taught. The Scriptures are the sole source of Christian truth."

Luke seemed to be very interested in their mission; at least he was

HOW THE GOOD TAILOR GOT TO HEAVEN

attentive to Abigail. He asked what her function was in the church and while he didn't come right out and ask her how she felt about polygamy, he did allude to the dreadful misfeasance by the modern ministry regarding scriptural commandments. He said, "Ninety percent of men today aren't worthy of their wives. When a single woman wants to marry and become part of a family, worldly custom often denies her a holy union with a man of substance; a conservative man; a man of high moral values. The law and demographic realities force most women to select a mate from the unfit ninety percent: a degenerate, often drunk, impecunious, brute."

Abigail had turned on her side, propped her head up with her hand, and wore a bemused smile as she listened, but Lemuel whole-heartedly concurred with Luke. He agreed that worldly law and the customs of man were anti-Biblical, and the lukewarm believers will be spewed out in the last judgement. He said that Jesus' commandment to love one another as they loved themselves would be, first and foremost, the guiding principle of his ministry. While he was speaking, Esther and Myles decided to join the group. He raised his eyes from Abigail to the nearly-naked raven-haired beauty approaching. Luke was a profoundly sophisticated man, and was able to read a double meaning behind Lemuel's Biblical comment about the faithful loving one another. While Abigail in her bikini was a dark-skinned joy to behold, the nearly-naked Esther was an ivory-toned empress of all her gender whose aura seemed to secrete erotic delights.

Lemuel introduced Luke to Myles and Esther. "Myles is the mission's expert on Biblical matters, and Esther is the chatelaine to the apostles."

Luke began to draw some decidedly lustful images. None of these missionaries was married, they were all living together, and Luke, unable to conceal his concupiscence, took Esther's hand in both of his, and asked, "Do you attend to every need of the apostles, my dear?" Then, without removing his eyes from Esther, and thinking their use of the word apostle was something akin to vestryman or deacon, he asked

Lemuel, "How does one become an apostle of your church, Reverend?" Esther stretched out beside Abigail, and the vision of the two beauties lying beside each other was overpowering.

Lemuel was nearly speechless with delight. This was truly evidence of divine intervention: a beloved physician, named Luke, wanting to become an apostle. Then Lemuel quickly outlined what was required of his apostles. Abigail condensed this lengthy dissertation succinctly. "Sell everything you have and give the money to me. Then, if she's moved by the Holy Spirit, maybe Esther will attend to your needs."

The expression on Luke's face changed from lust to chagrin in an instant. He started to walk away in disgust. Lemuel thought that the scripturally-ordained structure of their mission was misunderstood, and he arose to stay Luke. In his eagerness, he inadvertently disclosed the fabulous capital stock that the apostles shared. Luke pushed his hand away from his arm, and said, "My share would be a million and a quarter, huh? I make that much in a year just writing prescriptions for Motrin. But I'll give you credit for being the first pimp I've run across that justified their calling with the Holy Bible!"

* * *

Normal practice on an uncrowded beach is for people to stake out territories about a hundred feet apart. Abigail noticed the blond couple with the cream-colored trailer had staked their temporary territorial claim to a section of beach very near Luke's Mercedes and about fifteen feet from his chair. Even pods of humans traveling together will maintain a respectful distance, but this couple had intruded into Luke's domain. In more savage times this could be dangerous until the dominant/recessive status of the males could be ascertained.

Their beach gear was extensive and upscale. Everything looked as though it had been bought from Hammacher Schlemmer. They set up a large umbrella, a couple of padded folding chairs, a large piece of indoor/outdoor carpet, a cooler chest, and a picnic hamper. They also had a bottle of wine chilling in an ice bucket on a trivet stand. They even had a little folding table with wine glasses and a dish full of condiments.

HOW THE GOOD TAILOR GOT TO HEAVEN   479

As Luke approached their settlement, the blond woman decided to get up, stretch, and pour her companion a glass of wine.

She wore an aqua, fuchsia, and white diagonally-striped tank style swim suit that was cut high above her hips and veed sharply down to nestle a little mound at her crotch. A white, lacy smock topper, casually open; a floppy wide-brimmed straw hat with a rounded crown and a broad hat band, striped to match her suit; a pair of open toed wooden sandals with her toenails painted to match the fuchsia stripe in her suit completed her beach ensemble. He wore a pair of white slacks, a knitted aqua shirt, and a pair of cream deck mocs.

The young blond woman acknowledged Luke's presence with a polite smile, settled back into her chair, and her lacy top opened wider to frame her figure. Her companion returned to the book he was reading, *A Personal Guide to Debentures*.

The doctor welcomed his new neighbors and incidentally regarded the blond woman in the same appreciative way that he had only minutes before regarded Esther and Abigail. While his knowledge of the Holy Book may have been adequate to charm a minister's sister or an impressionable born-again young woman, in this situation he might have been better edified had he studied the twelfth, the twentieth, and the twenty-sixth chapters of Genesis. It's called the badger game by bunko squads everywhere.

Abigail resumed her half-dozing position on her stomach, and occasionally overheard scraps of their conversation, "Just call us Abe and Sadie," they told the friendly doctor. "Plain old country folks." The recent reverses in the Texas real estate market had been disastrous for them. Daddy had to sell the tower building in Houston just to hang on to their Fort Worth properties. "At fifteen dollars a barrel, the oil was hardly worth pumping out of the ground."

Abigail began to pay closer attention when she overheard Abe say, "Oh, the book on debentures. Well, Daddy decided that Sis and I should take more responsibility over the family trust."

Whereupon Sadie gave a cute little squeak, and announced, "We've completely forgotten Mommy's and Daddy's anniversary, Abe. I know the twenty-eighth isn't anything special, but we must do something. They'll disown us."

The image of their coupling flashed through Abigail's mind, and she thought, *That was some brother and sister act you put on last night.*

"Oh my, you're right, Sis. The nearest florist is all the way into Brownsville. It will take me at least three hours. Drat, just when we're getting friendly, I have to leave. You won't mind looking after Sis while I'm gone, will you Doc?"

Abigail heard Luke croak, "Be delighted."

Abigail knew that having to drive into Brownsville was utter nonsense. There was a public phone not more than three miles away and there were plenty of florists down at the tip of the island, no more than a twenty-minute drive. Besides, anyone as rich as they purported to be would have a phone in their car, and had Luke not been up to something iniquitous, he would have offered the use of his phone. The situation was getting interesting.

Abe's car had not yet disappeared when Luke removed his waders and moved in on Sadie. After a quarter of an hour of too soft to hear banter coming from the couple beneath the umbrella, which quickly led to some kissing, stroking, and massaging, both got up and walked hand-in-hand toward the trailer.

Abigail had associated with humans ever since they were created and had sated her urge to voyeurism many eons ago, but on occasion she liked to confirm her own suspicions about their employments. Demons and, alas, I fear it is also true, we mortals like to watch the machinations of con persons. While most of us must content ourselves with theater, demons, like God's angels, can observe, unobserved. The badger game is a very old scam and variants can be found in Chaucer, *Tales of Arabian Nights, the Decameron,* and if Luke had studied the whole Bible like most of us do, he'd have known how Abram, and Sarai swindled Pharaoh out of much wealth. Then, with the Lord's advice, they took aliases, called themselves Abraham and Sarah and pulled the same

HOW THE GOOD TAILOR GOT TO HEAVEN 481

trick on Abimelech, the king of the Philistines, from whom they gathered even more wealth. This occupation proved to be so profitable they taught their son Isaac and his wife Rebekah how the swindle worked, and those clever youngsters pulled the same trick on Abimelech once again. So, as a former con person herself, Abigail wanted to watch their operation and she suddenly disappeared, letting Lemuel's head fall abruptly onto the blanket.

At their trailer Abigail found that Sadie had placed a broom diagonally across the door opening as a signal to her partner that the mark had taken the bait. But, she had also, inadvertently, put up the proper hex sign that Gypsies use to keep the evil spirits and demons out. Abigail was forced to remain outside. The maroon Cadillac rolled silently up near the trailer and Abe quietly opened the door, after taking a Polaroid camera from the rear seat and a very large pistol from the glove compartment. He eased the screen door open and stepped over the broom. Abigail saw two rapid flashes light up the inside of the trailer and then she heard Sadie scream, "For God's sake, Abe! Don't shoot!"

Then Luke's hoarse croak, "Steady there, old man. I know she's your sister, but you can't get away with this. She's a consenting adult! You'll be committing murder, and they'll hang you."

Abe shouted back, in a voice quaking with rage, "My sister? Hell no! She's my wife, and I'm gonna blast your head off."

"But you led me to believe you were brother and sister. You called her Sis, and she isn't wearing a wedding ring."

"Everybody calls her Sis. That's her nickname, you bastard!"

"Oh this is horrible. You didn't say she was your wife, and you have brought guiltiness upon me."[93]

Sadie moaned and cried, "Oh Abe, please have pity on us. It was such a terrible thing. I don't know what came over me. This man beguiled me with his smooth subtle ways. Oh! I'm so ashamed. Please have pity!"

Abe snarled, "No! I'm going to blow his brains out. It's justifiable homicide here. No God-fearing jury of Texans would convict me for defending my home."

Luke moaned, "Oh thou hast brought on me and my kingdom a great sin."

Then the decibels diminished and Abigail would have liked to have seen how good their act was, but the broomstick kept her out. A moment later the screen door slammed open, and Abe appeared outside carrying Luke's Eddie Bauer pants. Sadie was naked, and Luke nearly so, and they tumbled out behind him. There was a lot more fearful pleading as Abe removed Luke's wallet from his pants.

Abe opened the wallet, removed his driver's license, and saw a plastic foldout photograph of Luke, his wife, and their two children taken beside the swimming pool in the backyard of their palatial home. Abe spat out, "And what about these lovely people? I ought to blow your head off for what you've done to them. Such nice people. They'll have to be told, of course."

Luke dropped to his knees and pleaded, "Can't I make restitution in some way? I have silver. I'll give you a thousand pieces of silver, to reprove the harm I've done.[94]"

Abe did some rapid calculations. Silver dollars were worth about five dollars apiece, and he figured compromising Sadie's purity was worth more than that. It was finally agreed that ten thousand in cash would ameliorate Luke's perfidy, provided he got back within four hours. Otherwise, Abe would go straight to Luke's wife and show her the Polaroids.

"But as for Sadie!" Abe pulled the belt from the pants and in a fresh fit of rage began to thrash her with the belt. Luke tried to recover his pants, but Abe stood on one pant leg, and pulled the other splitting them in two parts. Luke ran off over the dune wearing only his T-shirt, jumped into his waders, got into the Mercedes, and sped off. Sadie wailed piteously as he passed by and Abe continued to strap her resoundingly.

As the Mercedes disappeared in a cloud of gritty dust, Abe and Sadie fell into each other's arms in a fit of laughter. "Want to finish what

HOW THE GOOD TAILOR GOT TO HEAVEN

he started?" she invited. He nodded and the two went back inside their trailer.

* * *

Aside from neighborly nods and polite smiles of recognition, Abe and Sadie left the angels alone. Before his shearing, Luke told Sadie about the religious scam they had tried to inveigle him into. He told her, "Those two gorgeous whores are shills for their so-called church, and the preacher is nothing but a pimp." The couple half-believed this slander, and their cool indifference was more like proprietors of competing gasoline stations on opposite corners of the same intersection. There was a respectful professional formality between the two camps.

* * *

Alas, there is no honor among thieves. This extension of professional courtesy ended when Abe overheard a few snatches of conversation by Matthews, the publican. He returned to update the missionaries on a tax matter. Abe's attention was tweaked when he overheard Matthews say, "Five thousand a day; thirty-five thousand a week interest. The IRS will exempt your principle and your collection plate offerings as charitable contributions, but they want you to pay taxes on the interest you are earning." Abe did some quick mental calculations, and touched Sadie's arm to get her attention. "Did you hear that, darling? They're worth about fifteen million. I think we may be overlooking the spiritual values. We may even be jeopardizing our immortal souls."

Sadie whispered back, "Luke must have been wrong about them. The IRS thinks they're a real church. Then he must be a real minister, a man of God, and a minister wouldn't commit adultery."

Naturally the soundness of her reasoning dimmed his ardor for the game, but the notion was tantalizing, and he said, "But what if one of them did? He'd pay any price to avoid the publicity. And they've got some really big bucks. Think about it."

"Gee, I don't know, Abe. Ministers and priests are like," she replied, and her pretty features strained as she sought a definition, "…they're like…holy. We'd be damned for all eternity."

"Nah, they're men, just like any other. Do you think God pays them any special attention?" This Abe said with a certain amount of bravado, as though he were boasting to her that he'd be willing to spend the whole night in a haunted house.

Had he witnessed the scene of the following morning, he would have seen for himself the special way God corrects those who have received the calling and then are disobedient.

* * *

The angels were having their morning coffee along with pastries and juice. Myles troweled a thick, creamy coating of sweet whipped butter onto a rum and raisin Danish, and moaned sensually as he bit into it, "Oh, how I missed the simple delights. We're awfully grateful for these moments of freedom, Abigail. But if we don't go back with them the next time they come for us, I'm afraid you and Lem will be in trouble. They might recall Lem and they might try to kidnap you."

Esther daintily lifted a juicy segment of red Texas grapefruit to her lips, and said, "I refuse to go back! You'll help us, won't you, Abby? Just like you did before."

"Oh cheer up, you two. They'll grant your stay. You've got a whole lifetime ahead of you. I thought we made a pretty good case. And they can't take Lem, because he's mortal. Mortal flesh can't exist in heaven, and they can't carry me past the pearly gates."

"But what if they don't accept our petition? What about me and Myles? We're still spirits," Esther said fearfully. "You'll be able to outsmart them again, won't you?"

"Oh, stop being so gloomy. Let me see your hand, Esther. My Gypsy vibrations feel especially harmonious today and your palm will tell us what the future holds for you."

She held her hand out to Abigail, and said, "I shouldn't do this, it's sinful. The Scriptures say, 'There shall not be found among you anyone that useth divination, or an observer of times, or an enchanter, or a witch, or a charmer, or a consulter with familiar spirits, or a wizard, or...'"[95]

"If you plan to stay, it doesn't matter, does it? Besides, I thought the law of the Old Testament had been repealed with the death and resurrection of Jesus." She traced the lines of Esther's palm with an index finger. "I see that you have a prominent heart line, and a strong Ring of Solomon. See how it extends all the way around your index finger? That means you have the ability to strongly influence others. And with that heart line I can see abundant generosity, perhaps generous to a fault."

While Abigail was reading Esther's palm, an angel materialized on the beach nearby. He muttered vile obscenities at the sanderling darting about his feet, and then he swung his blackthorn crosier at them. He tried to stamp on a few that scampered close by, and spat a gobbet of yellow phlegm at the flock as it took to the air. As he shambled up the beach, the fine-grained sand clung to his suede shoes and filled the cuffs of his pegged pants. He cursed several more times.

The angels were so intent on Abigail's chiromancy that he was able to approach unnoticed. The puppy, Cerberus, darted out of his bed under the trailer and yapped at the intruder. The visitor angel lashed out at him with his staff and cursed when he missed the agile pup. His voice was like chalk screeching across a blackboard as he ordered, "Take your hand away from that black witch!"

Startled, they looked up into a pair of rheumy, oyster colored eyes that had pinprick sized pupils.

There was fear on the faces of the angels, but Abigail grinned. She knew Esther and Myles would be given another mortality, otherwise the authorities would have sent more muscle. "Well, if it isn't Tommy Torquamada. How's it been going with you, Tom? Gosh I haven't seen you since Spain. Burnt any heretics lately?"

Tomas recognized her and he glared. A vein throbbed at his temple and his rising choler blotched his face. He pointed at her with the end of his blackthorn, and screeched, "It's you! I might have known. The most vile and sacrilegious of all the demons." He pulled open the screen door, and charged with his staff held like a lance. "Foul black Gypsy Harlot! I'll smite thee unto the raging fires; deliver thy stinking flesh unto the destroyer . . ." In the midst of this violent sally, his lance became as limp as a wet noodle and he tripped on the threshold, sprawling head first into the trailer. He sat, a weakened shambles, shook his fist at Abigail, and cried, "You're the one who profaned their most Catholic majesty's holy water."

"I improved it. They say maiden pee is good for the complexion."

"Well, it didn't improve the flavor of my soup."

"I thought it might cure your dyspepsia." Then, as sweetly as the song of courting nightingales, she offered, "Would you like me to get you a glass of ale, or how about a nice dry sherry? I keep a bottle out back for special angels."

Tomas decided the best thing to do was to ignore her. He got up and turned his attention to Lemuel. "I'm disappointed in you, lad." He had an injured look on his vulpine features, and his eyes glittered in the shadow under his pork pie hat. "You've disappointed a few higher up too. Innocent III was no ordinary pope. He was one of ours on mortality detail, and he was surely impressed with your 'final solution' to the Albigensian problem. Twenty thousand, wasn't it? Well, he's an archangel now, and sort of like my rabbi. And that's what I hoped to be to you…bring you along to the higher orders with me." He sneered at Myles, and said, "These pinko liberals with their anything goes, overly fastidious sense of justice, and their queer notions of right and wrong won't be in charge forever. We've got a lot of good dedicated conservatives in high positions on the Sacred Rota, and in the front office." He poked toward Abigail with a gnarled, broken-nailed finger, "but you've taken up with evil, boy. Openly associating with this black demon. Don't think the Board of Tenure will overlook it. We've got a few of our angels on that committee too, and you'll be lucky to ever get out of your probation."

"She's not black!" Lemuel asserted. "She's sort of ecru, with a tint of umber. She's only this dark because of her suntan," he added defensively.

Abigail smirked wickedly at Tomas, and said, "Oh, you've got connections, huh? Way up on the Sacred Rota, eh? Well maybe Lem's got higher connections. How do you like your new angel suit, Tommy?" She turned to Lemuel and said, "Ignore him Lem. If he can make you think you have to go to him for favors, you'll be under his thumb forever."

Tomas blanched at the mention of his zoot suit, and he spat out, "Smart-assed slut! Go ahead, listen to her and see where it gets you. You'll be a yard bird for eternity."

"Did those marine guards rough you up, Tommy? I see you've decided to submit to the new dress code. Your zoot suit is quite flashy. I don't think I've ever seen a peach plaid before."

Tomas glared at Esther and Myles. "You told her, didn't you? It's no wonder the mortals are iniquitous. Because of your translation we have to accept heretics, and heresiarchs and schismatics of every persuasion and every perversion…devil worshippers, queers, Satanists, feminists, witches, and all because you leak critical information to our enemies." He masticated for a few moments, his wrinkled rubbery lips pushed in and out as he chewed, and then he spoke, uncertainly, as though trying to convince himself. "Well, it turns out that I was wrong about the holy tailor. They traced his history back and found out that he was an angel after all. His departure was due to a bookkeeping mistake." His finger stabbed the air as he pointed at Myles. "He certainly wasn't a mortal soul, Mr. Bible translator—they put him right up there with the highest. You should see how Gabriel and Sarakiel make a fuss over him. 'Oh yes, Holy Tailor, what can we do for you today?' It turned out that he had some kind of business dealings with Yahweh back at the beginning."

Abigail whispered to Lemuel, "Sounds like Yahweh got his bookmaker back."

"Eh? How's that? He's a tailor, not a printer."

"I know. That isn't the kind of bookmaker he was. But Lem won't need you to be his rabbi. Now what are you here for? I doubt this is a social call."

"The higher powers have decided that these two reprobates should have a chance to redeem their good graces." Esther and Myles groped for each other's hands. "I've been authorized to offer you a choice: you may either return with me now and face immediate judgment—I got them to promise to be generous in their decision if you come voluntarily now—or else." Tomas glared at Abigail. "Or else you may be able to redeem yourselves through good works as mortals, like Lemuel. You'll lose all your angel powers, and each of you will have to enroll the requisite number of new souls for the book of life."

The two clutched each other joyfully and Esther said, "Just like you said, Abby."

Abigail was not pleased. She wanted defecting angels. This way she'd have to wait until they died. She pointed out that they wouldn't be able to conjure money, and that was an enormous concession. "Life's tough without money." So she asked Tomas what kind of deal his powerful influence managed to wring from the judges.

"Esther would be able to get into the Carthusian Sisterhood." He winked at her and said, "You like the finer things, don't you dear? You'd have the chance to wait table in the archangel's dining hall. You'd like that. They have things as nice as Ahasuerus had. Remember the white, green, and blue hangings; the pillars of marble; the gold and silver beds; drinking vessels of gold; each one hand-fashioned with different patterns. They tell me they have some high times; it's right down your alley, Esther. Some of those affairs go on for a whole week.[96] I know that keeping silent might be difficult for you at first. . . ."

"Oh my, how impressive. What did you manage to wrangle for Myles, stable hand at the Augean stables?"

Myles spoke up, "Do you have the living waters with you? I think we'll do it the hard way. I'm sure we'll each be able to save ten thousand souls."

Tomas pulled two flasks from his jacket pocket and tossed them carelessly to Esther and Myles. "It's your funeral," he cackled.

"Why didn't Orson or Winfred deliver the living waters?" Abigail asked.

"Because Tomas is the only angel they trust to deliver the living

HOW THE GOOD TAILOR GOT TO HEAVEN — 489

waters to the world; the other's might try another shot at mortality themselves."

Esther eyed the bottle and said, "If I don't drink this, they'll send Orson and Winfred and an army with them, huh? Well! Here's how!" and she quickly gulped down her potion.

Myles unscrewed the cap of his potion, but his hands were shaking so badly that he had to set the flask on the table to prevent spilling the fluid. "Come on Myles. Bottoms up. We have to make up for a lot of wasted time," Esther urged.

He picked it up again, but his hand was no steadier, and the lip of the bottle clattered against his teeth. He put it back on the table. "Are you sure this will give me my life back? I was never a real angel. Maybe I'll be a newborn infant, or maybe I'll dissolve into nothing."

"Or maybe you'll be a sperm cell swimming upstream with thousands of others, hoping to find the egg before another sperm does. Just imagine hunting around in that dark belly, looking, hoping, praying for more than a few moments of existence. Do you still think condoms are a good idea, scholar?" And Tomas cackled evilly.

"You'll be exactly as you are, except you'll be alive," Esther insisted, and added, "I think." Then she asked, "You didn't have any physical problems, did you?"

"No, I was healthy." Then he asked Abigail if he might have a large tumbler and a double shot of bourbon. Perspiration beaded his forehead.

"You wouldn't go back to being a sperm, you already exist. You won that race." Esther pointed out.

"Yes, but angels were created fully adult size, like Adam and Eve, but I had to be born."

"Maybe you'll go back to being a fertilized egg in your mother's belly. Heh! Heh! Back to the fifteenth century." Tomas rubbed his hands gleefully, and slapped his thigh. "Yeah, drink it down…you won't escape the inquisition a second time." He sniffed the air. "Oh, I can just smell your flesh burning now. Or maybe you'll go back to your last living moment, just at the moment of your last conscious thought. Oh yeah, drink up and become an ordinary soul again. No more angel perks, just day-in, day-out drudgery, for eternity. I may request your soul for my personal use…heh, heh, heh!"

Myles looked to Lemuel for an answer. Lemuel shrugged and admitted he didn't know. Abigail poured a generous double shot and put a tumbler for Myles's chaser of living water beside it. "I don't think you can travel in time Myles. You can't travel through something there isn't any of. Time is just another false belief by mortals. You'll be sitting right there, just as you are right now, except you'll be mortal," she said calmly.

"Are you going to trust the word of a black Gypsy demon…you fool!" Tomas looked at Abigail with a puzzled expression. "What do you mean time doesn't exist? It's the fourth dimension."

"She doesn't believe in any of the dimensions, Tomas. She says they're all just a figment of mortal imagination; something they just made up. She doesn't even believe in arithmetic." Then Lemuel added, "Don't go into it with her, she'll drive us nuts."

"That's…that's…that's positively the most ni…hic…ni…hic…nihilistic thing I've ever heard," Myles sputtered. His speech slurred by his third double bourbon.

"Yeah, Myles, demons are like that. They're worse than Existentialists, and you want to associate with her? Okay, go ahead, drink up and see what happens." Tomas watched with intent interest, as though he were watching a butterfly being readied for mounting.

Myles tossed off the rest of the whisky and then without taking a second to reconsider, drank the living waters for a chaser. Suddenly his eyelids drooped heavily and his eyeballs rolled up into his head showing only the veined whites. His head slumped backwards and his jaw sagged open. Esther dropped to her knees beside him, grabbed his limp hand and started to rub it. "Oh, what have we done?" she cried.

Lemuel patted Myles's cheek, and said fearfully, "Do you think his soul could have gone through a black hole in space, into another universe?"

"Naw, there isn't any such thing. It's just as I said. His soul has gone back to the fifteenth century. Some deliverance angel will be here to gather up this part of him any second." Tomas looked about expectantly.

A gurgled, strangled, snore roiled up from deep in Myles's throat and startled them. Cerberus scrambled up on Myles's chest and sniffed inquisitively in Myles's gaping maw. "That's a death rattle if I ever heard one," Tomas exclaimed gleefully, and made washing motions with his hands.

The quart of bourbon had been lowered by half. Optimists would say it was half full, and pessimists would see it as half empty, but Abigail was more pragmatic. She said, "We'll have to go to the store. We're out of Alka seltzer, and faith healing won't work on hangovers." She pushed out her lower lip thoughtfully. "Better pick up some tomato juice too." Then she said to Esther; "Want to come with me? We'll stop off at the mall and do some more shopping. We really should get a few things for Myles to wear. That zoot suit is ridiculous."

"Are you sure he'll be all right?"

"He'll have a headache and an upset stomach. Remember Xerxes after he'd tied one on?"

Tomas was nearly apoplectic. "What do you mean you're going to get some other clothes for Myles? He's supposed to exhibit in his holy attire!" Esther and Abigail ignored Tomas, walked to the pickup and drove away. Tomas shook his fist after them. "Your duty is to torment the mortal's consciences, remind them of America's golden age, and make them hate themselves for their sinful pleasures and abandoning the straight and narrow ways of their forefathers. You're supposed to make them grovel before the Lord."

* * *

Poor old Tomas' mind set was still back in a simpler age. He was just becoming comfortable with the innovative idea of a Trinity. The Trinity had only been around for two thousand years, and the nature of it was still a contention among some sects. It was so simple for the first four thousand years when he only had to answer to the higher orders of angels and to Jehovah; back when he brought the Israelites success or disaster in battle; or rained destruction and plague and famine on the Jews, and the occasional Egyptian or Philistine. Then the firm decided to admit gentiles, and he had to accommodate a whole new philosophy and a different way of viewing humanity. Pythagoras and the Greeks had discovered that the order of the universe could be understood by applying the mathematical mysteries, and they also discovered the harmony of the spheres upon which the celestial bodies circled the earth. They solved the mysteries of the triangle which was equated with the trinity and used to bring them into the fold, and behind them the Romans. He'd only become adjusted to these new-fangled ideas while on his mortality detail when he was made the grand inquisitor during the Spanish Inquisition. It was the era when monarchs ruled by divine right, and his church crowned those kings; when schismatics, heretics and witches were burned at the stake; when the Moor infidels were driven out and slaughtered; when the Indians either accepted the Lord or were exterminated; when right and wrong were clearly stated in papal bulls; and when benefices could be purchased by those whom Lord had favored with enough wealth to pay for papal indulgence.

There was no identifiable structure to this modernity where even Ishmaelites were accepted, and every church preached that every soul was equal to every other soul, and where every act of disobedience was tolerated, even sanctioned by some outlandish cult like the Wesleyans, or the Calvinists, or the Mormons, or the Anabaptists. The souls would have an eternity of equality when they got to heaven, and he thought this worldly egalitarian ecumenicalism was clear evidence of Satan's influence. Tomas was certain that Luther was the anti-Christ and that his rebellion had started this age of Satan which would last for another five hundred years, and then the Lord would resume his worldly throne in the Vatican. Evidence of the iniquity was even seeping into the true church. Mass was being said in common language and priests turned their backs on the holy of holies and faced their congregations. This was

HOW THE GOOD TAILOR GOT TO HEAVEN

clearly Satanic ritual. The holy fathers were attending ecumenical councils and they were investigating strange theories of creation like the "Big Bang" theory. They'd even let Galileo out of purgatory.

And now. a strange expression was occasionally voiced within the holy walls of Thelassar: the "Sacred Square." Its usage was exchangeable and interchangeable in theological discourse with the "Holy Trinity: the Father, the Son, and the Holy Ghost." Something was trying to change the nature of God. Now, just as Tomas was getting used to this system, there were rumors that they were changing the system again. Just when he was becoming accustomed to a Trinity, they were adding the holy tailor. Something about a square being more honest than a triangle.

Moreover, Lemuel and that black demon, Abigail, knew something about it. Myles was unconscious on the sofa, and Tomas and Lemuel were alone. Tomas suggested they sit outside where their conversation wouldn't bother Myles and where he could tell Lemuel of some of the changes that had been introduced into the empyrean. Style had come to heaven. White robes were out; high fashion was in. Tomas confessed, "When I went to the laundry to get my clean robes they handed me some chartreuse paisley gowns with upturned roseate collars, and I went berserk."

"So I've heard. Esther and Myles told us that you ran out into Hallelujah Boulevard stark naked and it took six marines to hold you down."

"Yeah, Esther likes the new fashions so she can show off her big boobs, and that's another thing: whoever heard of an angel entering a beauty contest. They thought the publicity would help recruitment. They were afraid that little brown heathen might win, and we're having enough trouble making converts in her section of the world."

"Oh, are the female angels' fashions changed too?"

"Every angel. The higher your rank, the more flamboyant the color and the more outrageous the design of the fabric. Some of the ordinary souls had to be severely punished for making lewd comments."

"Why did they send you to deliver the living waters? I thought your position as catechist was a safe post and it was just a matter of time before you got promoted?"

"Huh! Job security? Tenure? You can forget all about that. Even if you do make angel they're liable to ship you off to Borneo with a pig bone through your nose, and a bear claw necklace. Heaven's new world order is based on the fashion of that culture's historic pinnacle."

"But wouldn't that glorify mortals who worshiped false gods?"

Tomas checked to make sure Myles was still out cold. Then he flew over the dunes and searched in the hidden hollows. He looked beneath the trailer where Cerberus growled at him and scuttled away. Then he came back and said, "If you ever repeat where you got this information, I'll deny everything."

Now Lemuel was really perplexed. "You can trust me."

"You knew about that trouble on the southern border, didn't you? I think it has something to do with that."

"Trouble on the southern border? You mean Mexico?"

"No, you idiot! The Evil Empire!" He pointed off into the sky. "Over there …Nirvana!"

"That's a myth. There isn't any Nirvana, is there?"

"Where did you think the Buddhist souls went, you dummy?" Tomas could see that Lemuel didn't understand theokinetics. He explained, "Most gods kept their souls within the universe through some sort of transmigration or reincarnation scheme, but Siddhartha brought them up to the realm of the gods."

This was beginning to sound like Abigail's blasphemous fairy tale. "There are no other gods," Lemuel protested.

"Don't be an idiot. You have to figure some things out for yourself. Did you think that war in Indochina was over democracy, freedom, and economic theory? It was between us and them: the Buddhists and the Christians."

"They won that war."

"Yes, that's why we have this big recruiting drive. We had good faithful Catholics in power and then the liberals started objecting to the

HOW THE GOOD TAILOR GOT TO HEAVEN   495

quality of life. Now the Buddhists will be bringing up more souls than ever to join the forces they've already massed on our southern border."

Lemuel shrunk away from Tomas as one would a madman, and Tomas clutched his wrist with his talon-like hand. "You didn't really believe we were training our army to fight in any battle of Armageddon, did you? Good God! Think, will you? First they appropriated Vishnu's souls, and Shakti's, and Shiva's, then they made inroads into the Shintoists, and the Taoists. Now they're sending out their bagwans and maharishis here into the fortress of Christianity and corrupting the gullible into embracing apostasy. Some of this nation's leaders are doing transcendental meditation, chanting mantras, and twisting their bodies with yoga. The next thing you know they'll have their monks trying to influence elections, begging alms in public places, and making more converts."

Lemuel recalled the Hari Krishnas accosting people in public places and the Buddhist monk that immolated himself to protest the war in Vietnam, and the comment by Madam Nu about roast monk. It was true. The electoral process was being controlled by Buddhist nuns. It was a religious war. Lemuel had always assumed the heathen souls went to the demons, but Abigail had denied that hell got them, so where did their souls go?

"Ah ha! I can see you're beginning to grasp the size of the threat. That's why I warned you about associating with that black demon. She could be in league with the liberals."

"You mean the Buddhists."

"No, I mean the liberals. Those soft, yellow-bellied, pseudo-intellectuals who don't have a loyal atom of ectoplasm in their bodies. They're a more insidious threat than the Evil Empire. At least we know where they stand."

Lemuel frowned, and asked, "Where do they stand?"

"'Where do they stand?' What do you mean, 'where do they stand?' They want to conquer heaven! They want to enslave all of our souls. They'd reduce our beloved Lord (Tomas crossed himself) to a demiurge;

or a mere teraphim. Good Lord, where have you been? And the liberals would let them have it too. For five hundred years we did nothing and they kept bringing their mortal's souls into heaven; flooding the neighborhood with every sort of riffraff and heathen. Finally we were forced to take action, so we sent Jesus down, and started bringing in our own souls. Six hundred years later we sent in Mohamed to gather the Ishmaelites. The heathens were bent on taking over all the real estate beyond the ninth celestial orb until we stopped them."

Lemuel steepled his fingers in silent contemplation. He listened to the waves washing over the sand, and after several seconds, he said, "Oh." Tomas had obviously gone mad. At least Abigail's blasphemous story about the other gods was told in jest, but Tomas was dead serious.

A deep moan echoed hollowly inside the trailer and Myles's feet thumped down its length. A loud retching sound came through the open bathroom window. Tomas held his finger to his lips, and said softly, "Not a word to anyone about this. Understand?" He got up to stretch and noticed the pattern on Abigail's oriental rug. The six-armed Hindu goddess seated on a lotus blossom throne and holding the emblems of six religions in her hands. Tomas paled and staggered back. He pointed to the rug, and hissed, "See? See what that heathenish whore has on her rug? Now get away from that demon—she's dangerous!"

"Abigail? Nonsense. She thinks its chic to collect religious artifacts. I found a little golden sickle like the Druids used to cut mistletoe that she treasures, and she has a silver Gypsy cane with pagan symbols on it, and she uses King Ramses' canopic jars for a kitchen cannister set. She even has a very fancy gold and silver ciborium she keeps lemon drops in."

"A ciborium?" Tomas' eyes squinted shrewdly. "Let me see it."

"You don't expect her to be celebrating Mass do you? She thinks the Mass is barbaric." But he got the sacred vessel for holding the Eucharist and offered Tomas a lemon drop. "You see, it's just as I said. She's not desecrating it in any way, she just has a thing for religious artifacts."

"I thought so! That's mine. That's my personal property and I want it back. Now give it to me!" He tried to snatch it away from Lemuel, who quickly drew it out of his reach.

Lemuel said, "They won't let you bring it into Heaven, Tomas."

"I don't care! She stole it and I want it back." He crossed his arms over his chest and said firmly, "I'm not going to leave here without it."

* * *

Abigail's truck came up the sandy trail, and the two shoppers brought in their armload of bargains. "We got presents for everybody," Esther announced gaily.

Lemuel said, "Tomas said you stole his ciborium, Abigail."

"Ask him where he got it," she said calmly, and dumped an armload of packages on the japanned dragon table.

"It was a gift from Diego Columbus, Christopher's brother. It was made from some of the first gold mined in the New word. He gave me that ciborium and two Indian slaves."

Abigail replied, "Well, I didn't steal it; you might say that I discovered it."

* * *

Abe and Sadie were proficient at their trade, but they had never made a really big score. Their namesakes swindled pharaohs and kings, but they were still in the minor leagues. They wanted desperately to make the big sting so they could retire to a nice ranch someplace and raise children. They often talked about how nice it would be to have a little Isaac.

To be sure, the Church of the Ethereal Evangels was not wealthy enough to place it on a level with pharaohs and kings, but fifteen million is a tidy sum, and Abe's and Sadie's wants were modest. They decided to test the possibilities. Lemuel was to be their mark since he seemed to be in authority, and therefore more likely to be in a position to embezzle church funds. Lemuel's manner was always that of the true leader: quiet, and dignified, but assertive. They knew that the more highly placed have a greater distance to fall and they are more apt to exercise precautions, so they knew their act would have to be more skillful than usual.

Chapter 26

THE USUAL *MODUS OPERANDI* FOR CON PERSONS IS FOR THE perpetrators to sting their mark, fold their tents, and taking the sheep, oxen, he asses, she asses, men servants, women servants, camels, pieces of silver, pieces of gold, and whatever else they have managed to take from the pigeon, move on, and take aliases. This fine old tradition extends back in time all the way to Abram and Sarai. They gulled the Pharaoh, and afterward the Lord instructed them in the wisdom of taking aliases, and they started calling themselves Abraham and Sarah. Then, using their new identities, they pulled the same game on the King of Gerar, Abimelech. Abimelech was not an overly bright person since later on Abraham's son, Isaac and his wife Rebekah, took him to the cleaners once again, using the same badger game.[97] The result is that even today we consider the Philistines as not too smart.

Since Abe and Sadie preyed almost exclusively on vacationers, such as Luke, the beloved physician from Arizona, their embarrassed marks usually quietly left the county and the couple were not forced to move on. They soon sheared another lamb that Sadie had picked up in a bar and lured out to her trailer.

They put very little credence in Dr. Luke's wild tale that the sisters in Christ were really a couple of whores, and that Lemuel and Myles were no better than pimps. However; when they overheard Matthews's disclosure about how much interest the church funds were generating, Abe and Sadie decided to watch their neighbors more closely. No matter how these practitioners of the faith gained their money, there was obviously plenty of it. From a hidden place of surveillance in the dune grass, they noted that Abigail and Esther bought very expensive goods when they went shopping. Some of the trappings and artifacts around the trailer, which they treated so casually, were highly valued antiques. They drank expensive liquor, often to excess, and the big brunette and her male companion smoked what looked to be five dollar cigars, and she wasn't the least bashful about her choice of swimwear. Esther made an excellent case for the theory that less is more. They concluded that these church people were not straitened Bible Belt types. At first Sadie was reluctant to swindle these "Holy people of God," but Abe convinced her that although they were church folks, they behaved suspiciously and probably deserved to be conned.

Their previous cool acknowledgment of having equal rights to share the sliver of sand along the gulf soon became warm overtures toward their near neighbors. They brought table scraps to Cerberus, and praised "God's glorious Gulf, and His pristine cerulean heavens." This gained an equally warm response from the angels who were always eager to save souls. They admired Lemuel's Bible and asked if they might be allowed to examine it. They purred over the fine binding, the artfully illuminated script, and asserted that the holy word should always be so gloriously presented. Sadie asked if she and Abe could be included in Lemuel's next prayer session. "Alas; our devotionals have been neglected recently."

Then coyly batting her heavy-lidded, doe brown eyes at Lemuel, she asked if he would be willing to advise her on a religious matter that had been troubling her conscience. She felt she could trust Lemuel to listen with compassion and shrive her soul of her sins.

HOW THE GOOD TAILOR GOT TO HEAVEN   501

This is not an original plan of seduction. For centuries women have been piously unburdening their souls to confessors as a way of advertizing their availability, their bag of tricks, and attract the interest of the priest. While Sadie worked on Lemuel, Abe turned his attention to Abigail and Esther. Abe's earnest brown eyes sparkled with delight when he found out that Esther was the most beautiful woman in the universe and had run away from the honor. He gallantly took Abigail's hand and vowed that she equaled Esther in beauty and had she entered the contest, the judges would have been forced to declare a tie.

This situation was better than he had expected. The tabloids would pay handsomely to know where Esther was, and Sadie was sure to snare Lemuel. The pious reverend would be doubly ruined by a homewrecker charge when Abe caught the two of them together, and he also considered a turnabout situation where Sadie would catch him with Esther. Abe would have liked a small helping of dark meat too, but a chilly aura surrounded Abigail and led him to believe she would be hopelessly intransigent.

Myles, hoping to divert Abe's attentions from Esther, drew him into a discussion about salvation and evangelism, and how Jesus had sent the seventy disciples among the populace to spread the gospels. Money becomes irrelevant when you accept Jesus into your life. The disciples went two-by-two, and carried neither purse, nor scrip, nor shoes.[98] Then he outlined the corporate structure of their church: Esther was chatelaine, Abigail was the treasurer and comptroller, Lemuel was the evangel, and he was the Bible expert.

Learning that Abigail controlled the purse, Abe applied himself more assiduously to melting the berg surrounding her; he oozed charm.

Sadie's carefully chosen words and phrases purposely intimated they were brother and sister; Abe called Sadie, "Sis," and she said their, "Daddy is in the oil business." It was the same routine they had pulled on Luke. Since Abigail knew their plan, her innate perversity compelled her to misdirect their itinerary. Her former chill disappeared and she began to play up to Abe like an affectionate kitten. He, realizing she controlled the cash, returned the attention like a pig goes for fresh swill. Abigail took him by the hand and led him over to where Lemuel was hearing Sadie's lurid confession. Most of it was fiction intended to arouse Lemuel's interest and much too pornographic to be reproduced here. Abigail asked, "Brother Lem, dear, would you mind excusing Abe and me, so he can show me his and Sister Sadie's trailer? If I like it perhaps our father would buy us one just like it." She fluttered her long dark lashes and fixed an imploring gaze on Abe, "You wouldn't mind showing it to me, would you?"

Abe was too startled to speak and looked sheepishly at Sadie. She, equally off-balance, sputtered, "Brother? I thought you two were married."

"Married? Oh my, no! It would be a wicked sin for us to marry because we're all brothers and sisters through the Lord," Abigail replied while smiling sweetly.

Lemuel confirmed Abigail's assertion with Christ's own words: "For whosoever shall do the will of God, the same is my brother, and my sister."

Myles cited the scriptural verse, "That's Mark 3:35. You see, it would be apostasy, a form of ecclesiastical incest. Like priests and nuns marrying each other."

With a vibrant display of brown tone flesh and feminine cunning she playfully tugged Abe's hand and then danced off ahead with just enough wiggle to be vaguely erotic.

This transformation of Abigail's normally dour demeanor into a playful siren surprised everyone, and Sadie hadn't expected this reverse twist in their conspiracy. But, she quickly reasoned: why not play it out the same way with the roles reversed. Lemuel and Abigail may not be married, but she and Abe were, and adultery was as illegal for the gander as for the goose. This church would want to cover up the sins of one of its sisters. It ought to work. She knew all the lines in the act, all she had to do was play Abe's role. But could she handle the pistol? And not only the pistol, but the pistol and the camera at the same time? Also,

HOW THE GOOD TAILOR GOT TO HEAVEN

while they were spying on these evangelists she noticed that Lemuel's feelings toward Sister Abigail were not wholesomely fraternal, and a cuckolded lover is apt to feel more betrayed than a husband. They had been gone for about thirty minutes when Sadie decided to see what was keeping her husband and Sister Abigail.

Lemuel was surprised. "Your husband? We thought you were brother and sister. You look enough alike to be twins."

"I'll just run over and show Sister Abigail some of the little features that only appeal to women. Abe pays no attention to things like that."

These circumstances were not neatly preplanned; normally Abe's pigeon was lured miles away from his mate so there would be no unexpected intrusion by the one being cheated upon. The blackmail only worked because of the threat of discovery; once the scheme was really exposed, they lost their leverage. In this situation the victims were camping less than hundred yards away.

Abigail wasted little time in making intimate overtures and was now bare-breasted and in the process of removing her panties when the door flew open. Abe had stripped down to his briefs. An alternate, terrifying, denouement crossed his mind. What if Lemuel appeared in the doorway with a big pistol, instead of Sadie, and he pushed Abigail away? Any instant now he would be looking down the barrel of a pistol, but in whose hand? Then the flash bulb went off, and Abe sighed with relief. It was good old Sadie, and she was threatening Abigail with the pistol.

"Your husband? I thought you were brother and sister." Abigail feigned shock, pulled her panties back up, and covered her breasts with her hands.

After stewing for several minutes, Lemuel decided to see what Abigail was up to. As he neared the other trailer, his pace quickened when he heard the sounds of arguing. His pace became a run when the commotion became distinguishable words: "Black slut! Is that what you want? A nigger whore? Okay! It's the divorce court Buster, and I hope it hits every newspaper in Texas."

When Lemuel entered the scene, Abe was on his knees with both hands clasped before him, and pleading, "Oh Sadie, think of the family's reputation. And what about her mission? If you go through with this, you'll destroy their ministry."

Abigail sobbed, "Oh yes, please! Please, find forgiveness in your heart for our sin. It was just a moment of weakness. Think of the trauma this will cause the faithful. It isn't only Lem and I who'll be destroyed; think of the thousands who'll lose their communion with God." She hoped she sounded convincing, because she was barely able to contain her glee that Lemuel cared enough to come to her rescue.

"What's going on here?" Lemuel demanded masterfully. And seeing that huge pistol aimed at his favorite demon's midsection, he stepped gallantly between the two females and raised his hands, like Jesus blessing the multitude.

Naturally, Abigail was thrilled that Lemuel was willing to risk his life to defend her, but perhaps she was looking for better bread than can be made from wheat. Sir Galahad's nobility was about to suffer. She was about to discover that many who go for wool come back shorn, and had she spent more time studying the Bible, instead of cheap romance novels, she'd have known that her little melodrama was a dud. In her ignorance, she plunged ahead. "Honestly Lem, I didn't know they were married. They look like brother and sister; they mentioned their 'Daddy' was in oil." She reproved Abe, "You should have told me." Hiding her face in her hands, she sobbed, "I'm so ashamed. We've violated the blessed sacrament of marriage."

"There, she admits it!" Sadie exclaimed, and thought, *This dodo is playing right into our hands.* Then she threatened, "You're not half as ashamed as you will be when this photograph gets published in the tabloids...and when you get named as co-respondent in court." Then she hissed, "You adulteress!" She showed the picture to Lemuel.

Lemuel glanced at the picture. It was an excellent photo. Sadie had caught what looked like the couple in a passionate embrace, instead of Abe trying to push Abigail away. Lemuel handed the picture back to

HOW THE GOOD TAILOR GOT TO HEAVEN   505

Sadie, and said, "There's no adultery here. Abigail isn't married."

"No, but Abe is! And to me!" Sadie's tone was cold, and her performance was very good, considering that it was the first time she had played that part. She put the photo in her beach bag, and gripped the pistol with both hands. The pistol was very large and very heavy, and it was feeling heavier as the time passed, as she was just a frail buttercup.

"That doesn't matter." And Lemuel explained God's definition of fornication: "If she were a virgin in her father's household, or with no father, under the protection of her brothers, and Abe seduced her, then Abe would have to marry her, or else pay the family for taking her virginity. No coitus had taken place, but even if it had, Abe couldn't be forced to pay because Abigail had left her father's house and was an unattached free agent. Only if she were already married to another man would Abe be guilty of adultery because she was someone else's wife, and the adulterous wife would be guilty for dishonoring her husband's house. They would both have to be stoned to death." Lemuel pushed out his lower lip and considered the situation thoughtfully. Then Lemuel pronounced his judgment: "The Scriptures are quite clear, none of those conditions apply, so they were not doing anything wrong."

Sadie looked puzzled. This wasn't coming out right. Slightly confused by his pronouncement, she searched Lemuel's face for a trace of insincerity, and said, "What about my rights as a betrayed wife?" And she thought, *This is an act...he's putting me on*. Only placid integrity could be read in Lemuel's face and the confidence that comes from being just. Her own certitude wavered, as did the pistol in her hand; it was a very heavy pistol. Finally she put both of her hands on her hips, with the pistol pointing at the floor, and said, "What?"

The perverseness of demons became exposed when, instead of being caught doing something she had assumed was wicked and evil, was in fact, deemed by Lemuel to be, perfectly acceptable behavior. Sir Galahad's shiny armor began to look very tarnished. She should have been overjoyed to find herself on the side of righteousness, but instead she quickly flip-flopped, and stood against the Holy Word. She exactly mimicked Sadie's stance, except it was her halter top she held against her hip, and she said, "What?"

Abe was also perplexed. He got up, and brushed off his knees. He felt like his ace had been trumped, and by a joker that he didn't know was in the deck. He too emitted a surprised…"What?"

And for the reader who searches for nits to pick, and believes that Sarai and the Pharaoh should have been stoned to death since she was in fact married to Abram, please remember that Exodus and Leviticus come after Genesis and the ruling about stoning adulterers hadn't been handed down yet.

Finding himself as the focal point of three pairs of malevolent eyes momentarily caused Lemuel some confusion. This chorus of inquisition could easily be assuaged, he thought, by the Holy Book, and he asked if he might borrow their Bible to prove his case. Abigail had assured him that every household in America had a Holy Bible. Imagine Lemuel's surprise when they admitted they didn't have a Bible. Was this a nest of heathen idolaters? They had shown intense interest in his church and Sadie had even confessed her iniquities to him, but their reactions to this situation showed they were heavily indoctrinated with sins of worldly ordination, and obviously in need of the revealed wisdom of the Holy Scripture. They sorely needed spiritual guidance by a compassionate pastor. He decided that the way to gain these souls was to invite them to join them, at their trailer, for prayer and Bible reading.

"Are you nuts? These two are nothing but a pair of crooks." Abigail was so furious she could hardly replace her bra. "They're cheap swindlers working the oldest con game in the world. And they were planning to steal the church's money." She shook her finger at Lemuel, and said, "They're probably wanted by the cops in every county from here to the Canadian border."

Lemuel tried to calm her, "A bit of Christian charity, dear Sister Abigail. Our Lord associated with publicans, wine bibbers, and sinners. And wasn't Mary Magdalen a prostitute before the Lord led her to salvation? Jesus blessed the thieves on Calvary. Abe's and Sadie's Biblical

HOW THE GOOD TAILOR GOT TO HEAVEN — 507

namesakes had the Lord's blessing: would you have the disciple be above his master? It is enough for the disciple that he be as his master, and the servant as his lord.[99] I say unto you that all Heaven rejoiceth more over one sinner that repenteth, than over ninety nine just persons which need no repentance.[100] And here we have the chance to save two whose only sins are ignorance of Biblical teaching." Lemuel opened his arms wide and looked upward. "Think how all the angels will rejoice when Abe and Sadie accept the Lord as their personal savior."

"But! But!" Abigail sputtered, and then indited with considerable vehemence, "These two were working a badger game. They took Luke for ten thousand, and then they took another sucker she picked up in a bar for forty-five hundred, every cent he could borrow on his credit card, and they were trying to swindle us. I was trying to show you what they were by twisting their little game around."

Like evil twins, Abe and Sadie sat side-by-side on the sofa and exchanged quizzical looks. Abe whispered in Sadie's ear, "If she knew all that, why didn't she turn us in to the cops? They're not as straight as they'd have us think." They both nodded.

Abigail briefly explained the badger game to Lemuel with a lot of histrionics and dark looks at Abe and Sadie. Lemuel fairly exploded. "By the God of Abraham, and Isaac ...Abigail! If the Lord graced their cleverness with great largess...how dare you call it sinful? Woe unto they who call good, evil; and evil good. They sinned when they turned aside from their Lord!" Then he realized how this dispute must look to Abe and Sadie who sat placidly exchanging glances and softly whispered words. Ministers are not supposed to get ruffled. A charismatic appeal from the pulpit is one thing, but a family argument in a neighbor's living room was in bad taste. He could not easily explain Abigail's perversity, so he decided the best thing for them to do was to make their apologies and leave. "We don't always fight like this, and I do sincerely want you to drop by any time. You may even want to join our little group. Why don't you drop in this afternoon? About fivish, okay?"

After the missionaries left, Abe and Sadie were trying to figure out what had just happened. Abe slowly replayed the scene in his mind, and then said, "Oh, they're slick all right. That was some act. Especially that Lemuel—he's the real brains of that bunch. How did you like the way he overrode our dominant position. I mean we really had them good and then suddenly everything evaporated into thin air. There was no adultery, no offense—everything was Jake with him. Yeah, he's smooth. He's the one to watch."

* * *

Abigail was as indignant as Abe and Sadie. On the walk back to their trailer she scolded and harangued Lemuel with scathing vituperation that could have caused granite to boil. Lemuel defended himself. "Look, I don't make the rules, I'm only the messenger. If God rewards that sort of behavior, who am I to argue?" Then he stopped her midway between the trailers so their argument couldn't be heard, and asked, "And you, you little Gypsy demon! Just how far were you prepared to go to carry out your little charade? What if Sadie hadn't stopped you? Would you have gone to bed with that...that...mortal?"

She retorted, "Esther has sex with mortals, and you don't object."

"That's Esther; you're different."

Back at the trailer she told Esther what had happened with Abe, and how Sadie had charged in with the pistol and the camera. Then, in high dudgeon, she told how Lemuel had come over, but instead of defending her virtue and inviting Abe outside for a good thrashing, he acted as though nothing was wrong, and even quoted some Scripture to prove it. "It was the most embarrassing thing that has ever happened to me."

Then Lemuel told his version and how he had gallantly stepped between the two squabbling fishwives to protect Abigail. He berated her for her lack of knowledge about the Scriptures. Then he softened, took her hand, and said, "Abby dear, we can't make the rules to please demons."

"Abe and Sadie are just a pair of swindlers with no more morals than alley cats. I think they are really brother and sister. The family resemblance is too strong."

HOW THE GOOD TAILOR GOT TO HEAVEN

"Well, so were Abraham and Sarah; they both had the same father, but different mothers.[101] Abraham and Sarah didn't lie about being siblings."

Then Esther asked, "What is it you object to, Abby? Their being married or the sex part? They seem like nice, polite, young people who really enjoy each other. Remember watching them going at it the other night?"

Lemuel chuckled, and said teasingly, "It couldn't be the sex she objected to; she even suggested that we support the church with temple prostitution."

Abigail, tricked by her own perversity decided she was taking the whole thing too seriously, laughed, and said, "That's different. They're doing it already. I just thought we should cash in on it."

Myles rubbed his chin thoughtfully, and said somberly, "That might be a good idea Abby. During my last mortality, when there was so much dissent against the papists, many convents were forced to earn their operating cash that way." He searched his memory to recall the specifics. "The Abbess of the nunnery," and he motioned toward Esther, and she genuflected quickly to acknowledge her agreeableness, "could secure a *callagium* by making regular payments to the Curia; and the Holy See usually didn't object as long as the payments were made on time. All we need to do is to purchase the necessary indulgence from the local bishop."

Abigail said facetiously, "I think only the pope has the authority to grant those special dispensations now. It was changed about a hundred years ago." Then she added with mock seriousness, "I doubt this pope would oblige though; he's pretty straight-laced."

"What about my church? The Bishop of Winchester always had a very liberal attitude. He'd grant us an indulgence. Winchester Cathedral was almost entirely paid for by the earnings of the girls in the stews of Southwark. We called them Winchester geese. The baths were official regulated houses of prostitution ever since Henry II, but most were owned and operated by the church. In my day the church even wanted to collect tithes from the harlots' earnings in addition to the rents they collected from the property, and they took the girls to court." Myles knew the Bible, but his worldly knowledge ended in the sixteenth century.

Lemuel's experience with the world was limited to his probationary visits, except for these last few months while he was staying with Abigail. He didn't know much more than Myles, but he knew there had been many changes since the sixteenth century. He said, "The churches do not have the powerful temporal authority of your day, Myles. State law supercedes church law. Remember all that trouble Henry VIII had, well, it's the civil law that won't allow a man to have more than one wife at a time now, and prostitution is illegal almost everywhere."

Myles had completely misunderstood the purpose of Matthews' visit, and he said, "At least we can count on our share of the taxes. Brother Matthews will see to that."

"Don't you remember? I told you that Matthews was here to collect taxes from us, and if Abby hadn't produced some authentic looking documents he'd have attached our bank account."

Myles laughed at the joke. "Oh sure, and I suppose the parishioners are just going to come and give us money. Quit pulling my leg, Lemuel. How are you going to get them to give you ten percent if you don't have the law behind you?"

Abigail said, "Believe it or not, that's exactly they way they do it in this country. Some other nations still have a state religion and collect a church tax, but the churches here depend on donations, and of course tax exemptions. Even if there were a State church, we wouldn't be considered part of it any more than the Church of England would share collections with the Pentecostals. We were lucky to get the tax exemption."

Myles could see that Abigail wasn't joking, and he considered the serious implications of the church not being able to collect its tithes. "But who takes care of the indigent? Who operates the poor houses? And the work houses? The girls of Southwark were given a choice: the bathhouse, the workhouse, or out on the street."

HOW THE GOOD TAILOR GOT TO HEAVEN

Lemuel replied, "Alas, Myles, I hate to upset your supposition that America is a pious nation. They are firmly in the hands of the secular humanists. The poor and indigent are cared for by the secular authorities and sustenance is given without regard to their piety or whether they are truly deserving. It's shocking. They can get money from the government without even attesting to their faith in the Lord."

Myles saw serious implications to the health of the church if the power to enforce its dogmas was removed, especially the power to collect their tithes from their parishioners. It would create a plethora of competing sects and the tenets of faith would be drawn to appeal to the lowest common denominators. They would be forced to rely on, just as Tomas had instructed Lemuel: envy, greed, hatred, intolerance, ignorance, superstition, vanity, and lust. He decided that under these circumstances the mission was fortunate, indeed, to have two such alluring beauties. It didn't matter that Abigail was determined to remain *virgo intacta*, the desire for her was enticement enough. The complete fulfillment would be retrogressive. Then he thought of the brown-eyed blond, Sadie, with her sensually vulnerable face and seductively broad hips. She would also be an asset. He said, "We'd be very lucky if we could convince our neighbors to worship by the true faith, and convince them to join our mission."

Abigail snapped, "Weren't you paying attention when I told you what sort of people they are? They're crooks!"

Lemuel replied, "According to the Bible, they're not crooks, their increase is a gift of God. The Lord giveth and the Lord taketh away; just like the money you created for Pearl and Zotis. However, they may be sinners. They didn't even have a Bible and I doubt they give tithes to any church."

Abigail bristled. "I created that money out of thin air myself. God didn't have anything to do with it. But those two! Okay, forget the money they stole. How about the incest? They're brother and sister, and they're fucking each other and anyone else that comes along. In another two minutes, Abe would have tried to fuck me."

Myles sighed, and indicated the Bible lying on the coffee table. "Fortunately the Scriptures are flexible enough to accommodate even that contingency. There are many instances of brothers loving sisters besides Abraham and Sarah. The most notable is when Amnon fell in love with Tamar. Her words, 'Ask the king, he will not withhold me from thee,' makes pellucidly clear that such unions are Biblically permitted. But he took her without asking David for permission, and then, after he had her, he rejected her. That's why she left David's house and went to live with her other brother, Absalom. Furthermore, there's a school of thought among the Jewish Cabala that believe that Cain slew Abel in a jealous fit over Eve, because she had bestowed her favors unequally. No, Abigail, your notions about incest are of worldly ordination. They are of secular authority—not Biblical at all."

Abigail picked up the Bible and idly riffled the pages. Then she stroked the smooth leather cover with her palm, bent the soft flexible binding, and hefted it. "Heavy," she said, and plopped it back onto the table. "But I've yet to hear one word of moral guidance. When James and John followed after Esther and left old Zebedee in the lurch, Lem said that was okay, because Jesus said it was okay. Now you tell me that it's okay for brothers and sisters to fuck, and okay for them to swindle people. I see why preachers only read a couple of carefully selected verses to their flock."

Esther interjected, "Abby's right about one thing. The Fifth Commandment says you're supposed to honor your father and mother. No matter what Jesus said about dividing up the family, we Jews believe in family values. I felt guilty about taking those two boys off."

Myles explained patiently, "This is a fundamentalist Christian mission, Esther. We want every faith to come and participate, but we intend to promote Christian values. And if Jesus proclaimed that he came to divide up the family, then who are we to oppose Him?"

Lemuel, showing off his knowledge of The Commandments, said, "That's the Fifth Commandment for Jews and Protestants, Esther, but Catholics and Lutherans believe it to be the Fourth Commandment. These errors are mortal misapprehensions. It's hard to believe they call themselves Christians. True Christians should follow the New Testament teaching of Jesus, and He gave us just two commandments: to love God with all our hearts, and to love our neighbors as ourselves. You see, we believe what the Apostle Paul taught us, that Jesus has freed us from the curse of the law; yea even the commandments.[102] That the blessing of Abraham might come on the gentiles. Abe and Sadie are receiving the blessings of Abraham, so why shouldn't we bring them into our mission and they can receive the full measure?"

Abigail laughed at Lemuel's sincerity, and said, "The politicians are trying to pass a law to display the Commandments in school. I wonder which version they'll use?"

Then Myles tried to clear up the contradictions he sensed being raised in Abigail's mind. "It wouldn't be sinful no matter which Commandments were posted. As Paul said in the Book of Romans; 'There is nothing unclean of itself: but to him that esteemeth any thing to be unclean, to him it is unclean.[103]' So if they posted the Hebrew version, it would only be a sinful perversion of the Scriptures to Catholics and Lutherans. And in Galatians he says, 'But the scripture hath concluded all under sin, that the promise by faith of Jesus Christ might be given to them that believe.' So, no matter what they wrote on their walls, the deeds are only sinful if the doer thinks they are, and it doesn't matter because, 'all are concluded under sin,[104]' anyway."

"I don't like to teach the teacher," Lemuel said, "but most Protestant versions are different from the Hebrew version, the Lutheran version is different from the Catholic version, and the Episcopalian version is different from all the others."

Abigail was becoming more amused by the minute and as the two disputed the text, she nudged the Bible with her foot, and said, "You'd think that with such an abundance of contradictions, no sane person would ever try to base a religion on the Bible."

Myles replied, "'God hath chosen the foolish things of the world to confound the wise. Because the foolishness of God is wiser than men.[105] For the wisdom of this world is foolishness with God.[106]'"

Abigail laughed, and said; "You've convinced me Myles. You've convinced me that you can justify anything, no matter how absurd, with the Bible. But couldn't you have condensed it while you were translating it. It's an awful waste of paper."

"That is the condensed version; the King James Bible is almost a synopsis."

"Sort of an ecclesiastic *Reader's Digest*, huh?"

"More or less, plus a bit of political chicanery that James added."

"King James personally autographed Lemuel's Bible for him. Wasn't that nice?"

"With all the changes and alterations he made, I guess he has the right to claim he's the author. It sure isn't the same Bible Tyndale and I translated. Cranmer, who circulated our version, was burned at the stake."

"I always thought the Bible was the Bible. If you listen to any clergyman, or the fundamentalist preachers in their electronic pulpits, you'd think that every word was absolute truth, unchangeable, irrevokable, and chiseled in adamantine by God himself."

Lemuel defended the ministry. "That's what they're supposed to say, Abigail. How else could they convince the humans to commit anything as vital as their immortal souls to the Lord if they thought the Bible contained loopholes, contingent clauses, perjured testimony, exceptions to the rule, and was changed to suit the fancy of every publisher. That book is the rock they have built their faith upon."

"Well, that rock is sitting on some very loose sand, if you ask me."

Myles replied in his best didactic style. "The Bible has undergone many changes Abigail. One of them is even mentioned in the Bible itself. In the Book of Chronicles there's a story from the time when the Jews were restoring the temple. They found money to pay the workmen in the ruins of the old temple; money which had been collected by the 'keepers of the doors' decades earlier." Myles added suspense to his voice. "Then, Hilkiah the chief priest also found, along with the money, 'a book of the law of the Lord given by Moses.'" He acted out the scene for them.

HOW THE GOOD TAILOR GOT TO HEAVEN — 515

"'And when the king heard the words of the law, he rent his clothes.' Oh, you may imagine there was much tearing of clothes, and tearing of beards, and tearing of dread locks, and wailing, and gnashing of teeth, 'Because our fathers have not kept the word of the law to do after all that is written in this book.'"

Myles smiled upon his pupils, and said, "This ought to please you ladies. All the king's priests and all the king's men couldn't figure out the significance of this find. Not even the king himself; only a woman could interpret this mystery. So he appointed Hilkiah, the priest, to go to a woman, the wife of the son of the keeper of the wardrobe, the prophetess Huldah, to find out what it meant. She told them of all the terrible things the Lord was going to do to the Jews, 'because they have forsaken Me.' But, because the king had humbled himself, and 'didst rend his clothes, and weep before me,' it would not happen while he was king.[107] So you see, the Bible isn't wholly a patriarchal document."

Abigail saw something beyond the obvious tale of altered Scripture, and the formidable occult powers of womanhood. She asked, "Does it seem to you that the Bible has an unusual number of references to clothing?" Myles wondered at her eccentric question. "I mean like that story you just told: 'the king rent his *clothes*, and the Lord was appeased.' Huldah was the daughter-in-law of the 'keeper of the *wardrobe*.' Lemuel has to wear very specific '*vestments*' in the tabernacle; Joseph wore a *coat of many colors*; the people of Nineveh put on *sack-cloth* to appease the Lord."

"You're a strange one, Abby. I don't think I ever paid much attention to what the Bible has to say about clothes. Why do you ask?"

"Because she's a demon! Just ignore her, Myles," Lemuel sputtered, and glared at Abigail.

Myles joked, "Maybe Abby thinks we should become nudists, like the Adamites. After all, Isaiah wandered naked for three years.[108] If that's what you want, Abby, even that would be Biblically sanctioned."

"That might be fun," Esther giggled, "Like Adam and Eve before they ate the fruit of the forbidden tree."

Abigail said, "That's a very good point Esther. Since all human beings since Adam and Eve supposedly know right from wrong, why do they continue to be Bibliolaters? It's obviously filled with mendacity. It permits any sort of evil; it rewards swindlers and tyrants; and to base a religion on that book seems to me to be the worst fraud imaginable. Can't any of them actually read what it says in the book they worship? Is it written in some obscure undecipherable text? Do any of them actually read it?"

"Of course they do. John Wyclif was the first to come out with an English Bible, making it available to anyone who could read English way back in 1382, but he just translated the Roman Vulgate." Then he sniggered wickedly, and said; "Oh my, didn't the Holy See roar. Then, in 1525 Bill Tyndale and I came out with *Matthew's Bible*. They were still reeling from Luther's ninety-five articles and his German translation. I'll bet that shook the earth under the Vatican."

Abigail frowned quizzically at the sectarian discord. Esther had an indulgent patronizing smile on her face and said, "Everything beyond the Pentateuch is surplus bullshit, anyway." It was all the firmament had authorized and sanctified up to her mortality detail, and Esther didn't believe the rest.

Myles could see that neither of the ladies understood the connection. "It's nearly the same as your objections to having Abe and Sadie become members of the church. Both of you would make very good papists."

Both Esther and Abigail sputtered indignantly, and Esther said; "That's an insult!"

"Both of you want all these silly rules, and that's not what the Bible says. The core of Luther's argument is that only God can bestow grace, and acceptance of God is sufficient in the eyes of the firm. Luther said that only God has the authority to indulge sin and for certain, it is not within the authority of the church to sell it. So you can see that when Tyndale and I published the New Testament in plain English, and any literate Englishman could read it and know for certain whether their priests were telling them the truth. It made old

Clement, very in-clement." He shook his head sadly. "They caught up with Tyndale about ten years later and burned him at the stake. They tried to get Wyclif too, but the people loved Wyclif. The London mob rioted when he was arrested, so they were afraid to carry their inquisition to completion. Later on, after he had died, and was buried in consecrated soil, they dug up his body and burned it. Then they threw his ashes in the river. Wyclif's doctrine taught that anyone has the right to form their religious opinions independently, on the basis of Scripture and reason."

"Well, what makes you think those swindlers, Abe and Sadie, have accepted God? They're only interested in stealing the church's money. That's their only reason for being interested in the church."

"The Lord moves in mysterious ways, Abby. So anyway, after we translated the New Testament, I continued the work and finished translating the Old Testament."

Esther nervously lit one of her panatellas, and thought, *He knows all about me. I'll bet that's why he can't get it up. He's afraid I'd make comparisons. No, wait, it's not all in there. He'd have had to read the old Persian, and Aramaic records.*

Myles continued, "The first complete English translation, *The Great Bible*, was put together for Henry VIII, and he gave me credit for it, but *The Great Bible* was about twice the size of the King James' version, and that was not as complete as the Bible we compiled a few years later at Geneva. We worked from the ancient Greek, Hebrew, Persian, and Aramaic inscriptions."

Esther blew a few smoke rings, and thought, *I never said I was a virgin. If he wants a virgin let him chase Abigail. They deserve each other: him impotent, and she a virgin, with her high Gypsy Princess airs.* She sucked on the cigar, working it in and out between her lips.

Myles continued with his bibliography. "Later, we edited *The Great Bible*, and produced what was called *Cranmer's Bible*." He shook his head and moaned, "Poor Tom."

"Burned at the stake too, wasn't he?" Lemuel interjected.

"Yeah, he got caught up in Henry's messy divorces. Pope Clement didn't like the King or Cranmer, but he made him take the Archbishopric at Canterbury. Cranmer was the one who annulled Henry's marriage to Catherine so he could marry Anne Boleyn, and he sanctioned all of his later marriages too." He paused and flicked away a tear with his forefinger. "I feel responsible for him being burned at the stake. When Henry died the line of ascension was in dispute, and I became confessor and confidante to Edward VI. He was dying, and I advised Edward to make Lady Jane Grey queen. That only lasted for nine days, and then Mary Tudor took the throne. Bloody Mary restored papal authority; had Cranmer thrown into the dungeon, where they tortured him until he confessed to heresy; and made him repudiate everything we did, the Bible we worked on, everything. They burned Cranmer at the stake and held me in the dungeon for two years. Then they exiled me to Europe. I made my way to Geneva, and joined the other scholars there working on another Bible. That was the Bible the Pilgrims used. It was the most accurate translation. We worked from the early manuscripts: Hebrew, Greek, Persian, Aramaic, and we cross-checked everything with the Latin Bible."

"Another Bible? I had no idea there were so many different versions of the inerrant word of God. If it was so dangerous to publish Bibles, why did you keep on doing it?" Abigail couldn't believe anyone would be foolish enough to risk a horrible death to publish a volume that was mostly nonsense. *They're all madmen*, she thought.

"Other than tweaking the pope's nose, you mean? I could say that the search for truth was paramount, and that we, as the leading intellectual lights of the age, were dedicated to leading the world to the age of reason, but the truth is that there was good money in it. Most of the European royal families, the important businessmen, and financiers resented the pope's power. They thought that if the Bible was written in the language of the common people, it would cause them to leave the Roman Church. Many did, and the papists lost much of their power. I'll bet people still make good money selling Bibles."

HOW THE GOOD TAILOR GOT TO HEAVEN —⁓— 519

Esther blew another smoke ring, and thought, *So, he knows. So what?* She appraised Abigail cooly. *I wonder how high and mighty she'd be if she were part of a king's harem? One of a hundred wives. No supernatural powers to help her out, just her wits and her tight little twat. You bet I made the most of my attributes.*

Abigail was in Spain with the Gypsies in the era Myles was referring to, and that was how she knew Torquemada and some of the more horrible aspects of the Spanish Inquisition. Spain was under control of their most Catholic majesties, Ferdinand and Isabella. The Gypsies survived by publicly conforming to whatever belief was prominent in whichever land they happened to reside, but they worshiped their own gods privately, and committed nothing of their beliefs to paper. The Gypsies wisely avoid becoming literate, since they know it is the height of ignorance and sloth to rely on someone else's knowledge, especially the worthless knowledge to be found in books. So she was barely aware of the turmoil the reformation was wreaking across the rest of Europe. It's unlikely Abagail would have bought a Bible anyway: demons are not valued customers of Bible salesmen. "You said James had a political reason for rewriting the Bible. Did he change very much?"

"Yeah, it's terrible what they do to a scholar's work after he's dead. I passed over from the quick to the eternal in 1569. Forty-two years later James commissioned this bowdlerized version. When some of the newly-arrived souls told me about the new abridged version of the Holy Bible, I got one and studied it in my spare time."

"That's how he got to be an angel, Abby. With so many Bibles being published, the higher orders decided they needed a Bible expert to instruct the lower orders of angels about the changes. Since humans are lower than angels,[109] they thought it would be unseemly for angels to be instructed by a human soul, so they promoted him to angel. Tomas and the rest of the conservative right wing wanted to stick with the Latin Bible. They didn't even want the Douay Bible circulated. They thought the less anyone knew the better." Lemuel turned his attention to Myles and said, "But don't believe that story about Tomas being ignorant about the King James Bible. After they dragged you away, and they called the seneschal on the carpet, I was left alone with Tomas. He flipped through that book, pointed out passages, and recited them word-for-word without even looking at them. Tomas knows that Bible just as well as you do, Myles."

"I thought so! He set me up, the papist rat, and he got the seneschal too.." Then his glower disappeared, and he smiled. "It all turned out for the best. I got a second mortality, and the most beautiful angel in the universe for a partner."

He knows, and he doesn't care. Esther beamed happily, and then thought, *If only he didn't have that problem. Maybe Abby's right. He just needs more time and a bit of persuasive reassurance.*

Abigail was struck by the fact that the divisiveness and double-dealing could go on forever. *Oh, well. On earth, as in heaven.* She was curious about why they selected Myles for the position of tutor to the angels. "Why did they select you? I'd have thought they'd have picked King James. It's his Bible isn't it?"

"James made the church subservient to the king. He believed in a strong central government and took a few liberties with our translation to reinforce his position. They couldn't make Cranmer or Tyndale angels without causing the conservatives to bolt the organization. They may have tried to set up a rival organization, like they did at Avignon, or like the followers of Arius did when the Council of Nicaea found his dogma erroneous. Cranmer and Tyndale had both been convicted by the Holy Inquisition and were burned at the stake. That would be like rewarding rebellion, 'for rebellion is as the sin of witchcraft.'[110] That's been Old Testament biblical dogma since the prophet Samuel made Saul the King. Then James slipped in his little zinger in Galatians in the New Testament that included sedition along with idolatry, witchcraft, and heresy as evil workings of the flesh.[111] That would have condemned David's rebellion and his *coup d'etat* as heresy. And of course James overlooked the fact that the Lord's prophet, Samuel, was the king-maker. The prophet Samuel had the power to make Saul king, and also had the power to remove him, and make David king. James was made king by a cabal of noblemen and political intriguers, and he persecuted both Protestants and Catholics equally, and anyone else who disagreed with him politically or objected to his laws. James said he ruled by the divine right of kings, then he published this Bible to prove his case."

"And for a man who had literary pretensions in his eagerness to twist the words to make them come out the way he wanted, he made a few literary mistakes. He was hasty to grab power, but he never heard of noblesse oblige; he wanted none of the responsibility. Turn to first Corinthians, thirteenth chapter, Abby."

She found the verses and read, "'Though I spake with the tongues of men and angels, and have not charity, I am become as a sounding brass or a tinkling cymbal.' What's wrong with that? That sounds beautiful."

"Very poetic, indeed, but wrong. The accurate translation of that verse uses the word 'love,' not 'charity.' Read down a little further to where it says: 'Faith to move mountains without *charity* is nothing.' 'And give goods to the poor, and my body be burned, but without *charity* I am nothing.' Right there you can see quite clearly where it was changed. Giving goods to the poor is charity! Phrased like that it's repetitious nonsense. Redundant. That transcription was easy for Tyndale and me. Every ancient document uses the word *love*, not charity. It should read: 'Though I spake with the tongue of men and angels, and yet had no *love*, I were even as a sounding brass, or a tinkling bell.' Faith to move mountains without *love* is nothing. If I feed the poor, and yet have no *love* it profiteth me nothing. That way there is no contradiction, and the last verse should read; 'Now abideth faith, hope, and *love* even these three; *but the chief of these is love.*' The Catholics in Rheims changed it to charity and King James kept their version."

"The Catholics have always had trouble understanding what love means. They'd incorporated the pagan deities in their pantheon of saints to gull the peasants. For example, the Celt's pagan mother deity, Bridget, who presides over the fertility of crops, was regenerated into Saint Bridget; but they were distressed when the peasants continued to worship her with the same earthy rituals. 'Holy Mary, Mother of God' became confused with the Greco-Roman goddess Demeter/Ceres, the Harvest Queen, and Roman women still offered the same cakes and honey to her that they had offered Ceres. The fields and the threshing floors were her temples. And if saints could influence God to insure the fertility of the crops and the soil, naturally He could bestow fertility on human beings. The joyful unrestrained ring dances described in the Acts of John, with the washing and begetting rituals, were like the ring dances of the dryads as they danced around the trunk of their sacred tree. John's ring dance culminated in the begetting ceremony where the blessings of fertility were celebrated. The human libido has always given the papists headaches, so they changed the uncomfortable word *love* to charity. James's motives were more venal. He used the Catholic version to convince his noblemen and bishops that God said the responsibility for feeding the poor was up to them and was in no way incumbent on the central government."

Abigail was thoughtfully probing the razor-thin space between her incisors with a thumbnail, a wicked and disgusting habit peculiar to demons, and she said, "What you're saying then is that this book isn't the word of God, but is the word of the British government under King James."

"Oh, not at all," Myles was quick to point out. "Since the powers that be are ordained of God: Romans 13:1, whatever the powerful ordain are God's workings, and James was a very powerful king. Since he ruled by divine right, everything he did was God's work. He would have no power at all if it were not given to him by God. His Bible, and all the other versions of the Bible, are as much God's word as the *Koran*, the *Torah*, the *Book of Common Prayer*, the *Book of Mormon*, and all the other sacred writings which inspire belief in the God of Abraham."

Esther was pleased that Myles's interpretation of the Scriptures emphasized love, her domain. The firmament's love goddess had been repressed and dominated too long by male blood lust, and patriarchal possessiveness. They make bloody sacrifices on brazen altars to persuade

HOW THE GOOD TAILOR GOT TO HEAVEN — 523

God to favor them with material conquests and then deny their God-given libidos. They mortify their own flesh rather than admit the powers of the pudenda, but Myles seemed to promise the ascendancy of love. He said all the right things. His ring dances and washing and begetting ceremonies sounded voluptuously delicious, and she imagined herself at a glorious orgy. So why was he still as impotent as the angels? She knew he was attracted to her. What was wrong?

She'd like to grant Lemuel her favors too, but he had his head stuck up a theological cloud, and was so smitten with Abigail that he was hopeless. And Abigail was impossible. The two of them had lived together for four months, slept together, even bathed together, and he was a fine upstanding example of manhood, but she never used him. If she asked Abigail to lend him for a few days, she'd get angry. Abigail was a tease. Her notion for their ceremonies was to use lots of sexual attraction to lure the suckers in and then deny them fulfillment; bait them with sex and switch them to some sort of born-again nonsense. It was an unnatural use of feminine enchantments; almost obscene. Myles proposed a real sex orgy where anything and everything goes. Abby was a worse cheat than Sadie. Sadie, at least, put out like an honest whore should. But Abby was the only one of the four that still had supernatural powers. She could still change the weather, conjure money, part streams, walk on water, be invisible, travel at the speed of thought, and heal the sick, the lame and the halt. Maybe, as a last resort, Esther would ask her to fix Myles. It would be demeaning to have to go to Abigail, the virgin. It would shatter her ego to ask for help in the one area where she was the supreme goddess.

Myles was droning on about his favorite subject, hermeneutics, and translating the word of God: "Even the Old Testament is a compilation of differing viewpoints by many prophets at different times and places. That's why there are two different creation stories in the first two chapters of Genesis. The chronological order of the different books of the Bible is aperiodic. For example, Zechariah comes toward the end of the Old Testament, but in real time he lived fifty years before Esther. And

Nehemiah, who oversaw the rebuilding of walls of Jerusalem after the Babylonian diaspora, is placed before Esther's story, which was during the Babylonian captivity. And in some places, God is called Jehovah; in others, Lord; and is usually thought of as a singularity. But in Hebrew He's Yahweh or Elohim; and the 'im' ending indicates a plurality of gods; just as seraphim indicates a plurality of seraphs, and cherubim indicates a plurality of cherubs...."

Abigail tittered, "He took more aliases than some credit card thieves..."

And Lemuel countered acerbically, "Satan, the Devil, Beelzebub, Belial, Old Nick, Lucifer..."

"Satan isn't responsible for what others call him," Abigail sniffed.

Esther looked bewildered. "Do you mean the Pentateuch is adulterated too?" She took a long drag on her cigar, rearranged her pose seductively, and added, "I guess we'll just have to rely on the basics."

Myles replied, "Even that becomes perverted, Esther." She frowned quizzically, and he continued, "Topical fashion regarding sex varies from era to region to culture, just like the Scriptures. The variations that please one culture, may be anathema in another. That's why intercourse is eliminated in heaven."

She shot back, "We're in this culture, and this time and place."

Abigail explained, "I think he's referring to times like classical ancient Greece, when women were drab creatures whose function was breeding and housework, and love was homosexual. Plato's dialogue about love was addressed to his young catamite. And with the rise of homosexual assertiveness happening today, Myles may be right."

"Oh bull! Don't be such a prude, Abby. Isn't all love between all human beings *homo*sexual? And the Greeks thought the courtesan Phryne's beauty was divine. She was on trial for immorality, so she merely bared her breasts to the judges, who quickly agreed such beauties were gifts of the goddess Aphrodite, and let her off. Well, I'll put my assets against hers anytime. I like Abby's idea for a nudist colony. Why should we hide our most glorious treasures?"

HOW THE GOOD TAILOR GOT TO HEAVEN 525

"That wasn't my idea! I just asked why there were so many references in the Bible to clothes. You and Myles got carried away with the nudity idea."

* * *

Aton had passed his apogee and was now slipping down the slope of the firmament toward the Tuat, and his nightly confrontation with the evil god Am, a.k.a Apep, and a hundred other aliases. Abigail remembered that Lemuel had invited Abe, a.k.a. Abram, a.k.a. Abraham, and Sadie a.k.a. Sarai, a.k.a. Sarah, to come for tea at five. Fortunately Lemuel had landed, with Abigail's assistance, six nice pompanos that were now on ice in their refrigerator. She asked Esther to come give her a hand preparing the supper and went inside. She put the fish heads in a pot along with a couple of stalks of celery, onions and herbs to make a stock to poach fish. Myles came in, took the bourbon and several glasses, and as he was leaving, she said, "Would you remind Esther that she's supposed to help me with the supper."

After a few minutes, a throaty laugh wafted through the open window as Esther was amused by a ribald tale Myles told. A few minutes later, Lemuel came into the trailer, got a Coke from the refrigerator, and a bottle of dark rum from the liquor cabinet. "Esther has never had a rum and Coke," he explained quickly, and left. The screen door slammed behind him.

Abigail had to use the bathroom, and when she opened the folding door between the galley kitchen and her bedroom, she was stunned by the mess. Esther and Myles had left her bed unmade; their nightclothes were in a jumble on the foot of her bed; her toilet articles were left in disarray on her dressing counter; the face powder and foundation were left open; the brush of her mascara applicator was drying into an inky clot; there were long black hairs in her favorite pink comb; her face mirror was smudged with eye shadow; from an open drawer hung rejected undies; and both closet doors were left ajar. In the bathroom she found a similar confusion. The bottle of mouthwash was open atop the hamper behind the toilet; her favorite perfumed soap was a slime of drying lather; the glass had a wash of chalky toothpaste film; and her towels, the ones with the little lavender florets, had been carelessly tossed over the rim of the tub. Her voice quaked with rage when she called out through the open window, "Esther! If you don't get in here this minute ...I'll...I'll seal up your womb!" It was the worst Biblical malediction she could think of to pronounce on Esther.

Esther trod heavily on the steps, purposely shaking the whole trailer, and sulked into the living room. She leaned against the galley counter, looked down at the floor, and whined, "What's bothering you? I said I'd be in, in a minute." She rubbed her bare toes through the soft, loop twist carpet.

The heat of Abigail's outrage caused Cerberus to slink off into the dune grass with his tail between his legs. Lemuel and Myles dropped into sudden silence, and Esther whined again, "Well...gee, I've lost all my powers, and all you have to do is snap your fingers."

"It's your responsibility! And after you get this mess cleaned up, I want you to help me in the kitchen. Did you hear me? Now get busy! We have company coming over."

Abigail returned to the kitchen and Esther stumbled about, muttering oaths and straightening up. Abigail's fury was short-lived. She relented, waved her hand, and magically everything became orderly again. Esther gave her a bright smile. "I'll try to be neater from now on," she promised.

"It's for your own good. When you get your own trailer you'll have to do for yourself."

"Okay, Ma'am," Esther teased.

With a sinister smile, Abigail pronounced an ancient Gypsy curse: "May you have four adolescent daughters, Esther."

* * *

On their way across the dunes in the late afternoon, Abe and Sadie were engaged in a low but earnest dialogue. "I still say that he's the one we have to keep an eye on. You had the picture, the gun, everything, and he was cool and slick as a melon seed. He slid right out of that situation. He's a real pro; he could probably give us lessons."

"But why would she do it? If he's the real boss, she wouldn't have made a move like that without him setting it up. When she went off with you, he seemed pretty upset."

"Think, will ya? We're a couple of petty swindlers and they're into the big rackets. They knew all about us; she even knew our take. So if they know, obviously they're thinking about recruiting us." From the sandy hummock they looked down on the missionaries' encampment. The angels had already placed cressets of burning kerosene scented with attar of citronella to ward off the mosquitos. "Remember they won't show their hand right off, so we'll probably have to listen to a lot of religious palaver. Listen sharp for hints. That's the way they'll work. See if we're clever enough to pick up the clues."

"What about the other two?"

"You mean the hit man and that bimbo? Come on Sadie, wise up."

Chapter 27

MATTHEWS, A.K.A. MATTHEW, DROPPED BY UNEXPECTEDLY IN the late afternoon at the angel's encampment. The world had ensnared his flesh with its vile paper, and microchip tentacles. His reborn spirit wanted so earnestly to reside with these holy missionaries, particularly Sister Esther. Sister Abigail had qualities which attracted him also, but the pledges he made while he was corrupted with worldliness dragged his soul into its worldly clutches.

The bankers threatened foreclosure on his condo. They reminded Matthews that should their auction of his property not fully cover the mortgage, he would not be released from the remainder of his pledge. He had a chilling vision of the banker's nephew lolling in his apartment while he was still obligated for half its worth. His new Camaro was gathering dust in a used car dealer's consignment inventory. He was being threatened with court action by the furniture store that took back the articles, but was now dunning him for a sum nearly three quarters of the amount he owed before. His checking account, now closed, hadn't begun to cover what he owed on his credit cards.

Out of desperation he filed for bankruptcy, with the mistaken belief that the courts would release him from his debts. He was now discovering that the courts were more tyrannical than his creditors. Gun-toting deputy sheriffs replaced the bill collectors at his door.

"Just walk away from it. You are no longer Matthews; you have been reborn...Thou art henceforth Matthew. Walk away from the world, and 'Let the dead bury the dead,'"[112] Lemuel advised.

These simple words of Scripture lifted all the oppressive burdens from Matthew's heart. A side benefit of salvation was that he could put his troubles into the hands of the Lord. Lemuel's words lifted his spirits and the corn which gladdens the young men's hearts helped too. He was starting on his second bourbon over ice. "Right! Let the dead bury the dead. They can't put you in jail for unpaid debts anymore." He didn't ask, since it might be taken as a sign of mistrust, but he wondered if his share of stock in the Church of the Ethereal Evangelicals, which was listed in the street name of an Edinburgh, Scotland, stockbroker, could be traced by the courts or his creditors.

Esther greeted him with a cheerful smile. She had come to retrieve the rum and Coke she abandoned when Abigail ordered her to come inside. Matthew slipped an arm around her hips and gave her thigh a squeeze. She squealed, "Matthew! Your hands are like ice!" He laughed and playfully put the icy glass against her bare leg. She squealed again and twisted away from him. "Be nice," she pouted.

Abigail finished the preparations for their supper and settled into a chair with a cup of cold leftover coffee. She gave Matthew an artificial smile while she stirred the brew with her finger, and in an instant the coffee steamed. He was too absorbed with Esther to notice. Abigail sucked the hot coffee from her finger, and asked, "Having money troubles, Matthew?"

"I thought I did, but in this sanctuary, among the reborn, all my worldly cares have vanished."

Myles intoned the conventional affirmation, "Amen, brother."

Matthew's demeanor changed as he spoke with the mission's charge of terrestrial affairs and treasurer, Abigail. Reverting to his accountancy

HOW THE GOOD TAILOR GOT TO HEAVEN — 531

persona, he told her of the clever maneuvering of loopholes that he had accomplished on the church's behalf. "The department has agreed to allow the tax money that is owed on your accrued interest to be deposited in an escrow account. We'll have to pay it eventually, but we will collect the interest on the money in that account too. Clever eh?" He smiled and winked.

Lemuel was insecure with worldly affairs, and finances caused his greatest uneasiness. He turned to the solace of the Scriptures for comfort and advice. "Must we haggle over the tribute money? 'Render therefore unto Caesar the things which are Caesar's.'"[113]

"Ah yes, Reverend. But no more than Caesar is due," Matthew reminded him. "If I remember the rest of that verse, it says, 'And unto God the things which are God's.' Our church deserves to keep every red cent it is entitled to. Both the Bible and the law agree."

Abigail wore a beatific smile, and said, "As I write checks and dispense the funds, I imagine that I'm in spiritual communication with Yahweh. It is almost like Moses receiving his instructions about the proper way to spend the Israelite's wealth. So many shekels' worth of gold for these ornaments or that candlestick; so many shekels' worth of silver for taches, and sockets. The brazen altar figured in brass talents, the fine twined hangings, and the badger skins." She looked down shyly. "I'm often awed by the wealth and the responsibility of it all."

Her antiquated term for the Supreme Being passed by Matthew unnoticed, but the allusion to her powers did not. "I'm sure God will guide the hand that writes the checks, but if you ever need assistance or advice, please remember my field is accountancy."

Abigail found his offer amusingly ingenuous as she considered Matthew's problems with his personal finances. Esther raised her glass toward Abigail, and toasted her, "Sister Abby, 'Let your light shine before men that they may see the good works.'[114] You wouldn't believe how talented she is with money, Matthew."

Abigail flushed modestly. "It's nothing. I have no more talent than any simple country banker has. You might say that we are fellow miracle workers dealing in what J.P. Morgan once called: 'the miracle of compound interest.' The bankers have their methods, and I have mine. I've merely simplified the process by eliminating one step."

Matthews, having backslided into worldliness at the mention of money, asked, "And what step might that be, Sister Abigail?"

"I suppose you might say that I noticed that it was the depositors' cash, the collateral base of the currency; the capital reserve requirement, that hamstrings the other bankers. I don't bother with that. I merely deal in the pure compoundness of the world of finance. It eliminates all that bothersome paperwork."

Matthew was mystified by Abigail's explanation. He thought for a long while and the only meaning that he could fathom from her words was that she created money from thin air, and he knew that was impossible.

No collateral indeed! Lemuel fumed. *Only my soul for the span of fifty lifetimes if I don't repay that loan before I die. True, she wasn't charging him the normal prime rate usury, but how many mortals would be brave enough to make a similar deal with their banker? A mere fifteen and a half million dollars, in exchange for fifty lifetimes of servitude to a demon.*

Matthew continued to puzzle over Abigail's opaque explanation. *The pure compound-ness of interest? I suppose one might consider the tithes and offerings of the church's collection plate from that viewpoint. But churches have very heavy capital investments in real estate; the buildings and grounds, many have schools and universities, and expensive works of art.* He said, "You have to invest principal, in order to earn interest, don't you?"

"That's where the miracle part comes in, Brother Matthew," Abigail casually replied.

The parable of the talents occurred to Lemuel, and he turned to Myles for his theological opinion. Myles solemnly steepled his fingers, and pondered the matter. "Yes, I believe you're right, Brother Lemuel. If you identify bankers as the money exchangers with whom the servants of the wealthy lord had invested the talents, the usury would be considered blessed, thus making the wealthy lord joyful, but not the original talents of themselves. That is the whole point of the parable.[115]"

Lemuel voiced a mild objection. "No, I meant the entire sum. Shouldn't all the talents be thought of as: 'gathering where one has not strewn, and reaping where one has not sown.'"[116]

"Not quite. The original sum came into existence because of someone's self-willed effort. It was not inherited, it was not found, it did not come into being as the God given increase of the fields. It is, therefore, worldly."

Esther refined Myles's explanation, "Yeah, Lem; don't you see? It's like fertility—and it's not just the fields... it includes animals. It's like when the stud covers the mare, the ram the ewe, the bull the cow, and when Adam delved and Eve span, God's Holy Spirit gives you the increase."

Abigail placed two fingers on either side of her head and massaged her temples. She wondered how Esther could find a sexual meaning in almost everything. She asked, "How's that Esther? Do you think currency has sexual intercourse to create interest? To my terrestrial angel mind, I always thought that, 'Gathering what one has not strewn, and reaping where one had not sown,' was stealing." Then she asked very softly, "Oh, while we're on the subject of gathering what one has not strewn, Brother Lem, I meant to ask you something about the working on Sunday story. Did Jesus, or any of the apostles, own the field where they were gathering corn on that Sabbath day?"

Lemuel cleared his throat, slightly annoyed by the perversity of demons. No one had ever asked him that before, and he tried to think of an answer. Myles cleared up the point nicely for her. "They found it Abby. It's as though you were eating an oyster and you found a large pearl. Who gives that pearl to you? Or suppose you were walking along and found a golden nugget on the trail. Who gives that gold to you? Or suppose you were sitting on a park bench and you found a wallet under the bench with a lot of money in it, what would you do?"

"Look inside for identification so I could return it to the person who lost it, or turn it over to the police," she replied without remarking on the obvious, that the situations were entirely different. She pushed the flesh at her temples so that her eyes slanted like an Asian's.

"Can't you see how sinful that would be? You would be denying the increase that God had given you."

"I see. It's finders keepers, loosers weepers."

"No! You'd be ignoring the Lord's hand in controlling mankind's destiny. It would be more accurate to say: 'The Lord giveth, and the Lord taketh away.' Naturally, like Jacob, you should give the Lord his ten percent."

Abigail was not convinced. "Even if it was someone's entire salary for a whole month?" she asked.

"Ah! Better yet. The one who had lost the purse would have become poor, as was 'our Savior, who became poor, that ye through his poverty might be rich.'[117] By returning the money you would be denying that person the opportunity to do the same. Or, even more perfidious, corrupting his faith in the Lord by making him believe that the kindness of man is of the world. By keeping the purse you are teaching him to, 'Lay up your riches in Heaven, and not in the things of this world.'"

"I think I'm getting a headache,' she thought to herself and continued to massage her temples. "And you think that would be the right thing to do even though I have plenty of money myself?"

"Of course. The Scriptures tell us, 'to him that hath it shall be given; and to him that hath not: even that which he hath shall be taken from him and given to him that hath.'[118] It is prophesied in the parable of the talents." Myles asked Esther for a cigar, lit it, and blew an extravagant billow of smoke. He pointed toward Abigail with the glowing ash end. "Your problem is that you are too worldly, Sister Abigail. You identify with the worker who lost his billfold and his worldly wages. You know that to gain by your own efforts is worldliness; wages not given to you by the grace of God, but created of your own will."

Myles could see his explanation was being rejected by the skeptical look on Abigail's face. He wanted to get his point across, and he continued,

HOW THE GOOD TAILOR GOT TO HEAVEN   535

"Consider a man who takes a piece of leather and fashions a pair of shoes for himself. He created those shoes by his own self will and made his own reward. Now, suppose you have a factory full of cobblers, and they, by worldly means, create a barge load of shoes. When you pay them their wages they have their reward in worldly terms, but you sell those shoes for an enormous profit…that is like unto the increase of the fields. That is what the Lord gives to you."

Matthew was astonished. He said, "I have been with the IRS for years and it wasn't until this moment that I understood how our regulations were drawn. Now I see why they give all those special advantages and tax benefits to businessmen. It would be the same as taxing the Lord's blessings to tax profits as highly as wages." Matthew sounded reverential as he said, "That's why the same would apply to all other forms of unearned income: inheritor exemptions on estates…capital gains…interest payments…stock dividends; and why we tax wages so very high…they are worldliness!"

"You'd think he just discovered another continent," Abigail remarked in a low aside to Esther. Then to Matthew she quipped, "I'm surprised that you're surprised. I had always imagined the tax offices as being populated by holy people…sort of like the catacombs." She considered making her vision a reality, but at the moment her temples were throbbing. "Let's see if I have this straight. The department would tax Jesus on the value of the fishes and loaves because he willed them into being, and they tax in kind earnings. And since he would not be recognized as an officially, tax exempt, religious or charitable organization, he could not claim the gift of the fishes and loaves to the multitude as a charitable donation, because the multitude is not a recognized charitable organization. So he'd have to pay taxes on the value of the fishes and the loaves he fed to the five thousand. How about the manna that fed the children of Israel when they wandered in the desert?"

"That would be exempt. As I recall the story, it just appeared of itself."

"Like compound interest?"

"Exactly! However, there wouldn't be any compounding because that portion of the manna that wasn't consumed just disappeared."

"Yes, I'm definitely getting a headache."

* * *

Abe and Sadie were keeping their fivish invitation for tea and cakes when they noticed the car with the government tags parked behind Abigail's pickup. It was too late for them to flee, and Abe said, "Just play it cool Sadie. There's a fed here."

Sadie trembled, and whispered, "We haven't committed any federal crimes."

"I don't know. Maybe the Mann Act? Remember that guy in Shreveport?"

The couple approached the gathering of evangelists with an air of quiet aplomb. Lemuel introduced Matthew, and Sadie presented her delicate, finely-manicured hand to Matthew. He held it nervously for a moment and then shook Abe's hand vigorously. Abe's knees weakened when he learned that Matthew was with the IRS. *Oh my God! That's how they got Capone! Income tax evasion.* But Abe was a professional, and there wasn't a trace of fear visible except for a slight weak trembling of his right knee. Even that disappeared when he learned that Matthew was the first apostle to join the mission. *Of course, how foolish of me. A well-organized gang like this one would have a mole inside.*

The handsome blond couple, thinking they were being sized up for the mob, wore the sort of casual beach dress that they imagined successful mobsters wore. He wore a blue linen blazer, a paisley print silk necktie, white trousers, a pair of two-toned wingtips, and a white panama hat. Sadie was also smartly dressed in a taupe blouse, a simple short navy skirt, a pair of plain black pumps with a modest heel, a black beret that looked very chic with her pale blond hair, and a black bandanna tied around her neck like a Marseilles adagio dancer. The cigarettes she smoked had Chinese red tips which matched her lipstick and fingernails. She was very careful about her makeup, and had stippled the smallest possible beauty mark just above her lip with her eyebrow pencil.

HOW THE GOOD TAILOR GOT TO HEAVEN   537

Esther and Abigail had changed out of their swimsuits. Abigail wore a simple house dress, a pair of well-worn huaraches, and her hair was tied in a ponytail with a yellow ribbon. Esther wore a fashionable dress of natural linen and matching pumps with spike heels that made her tower over everyone except Lemuel. Neither one of them looked like gun molls as Sadie had expected. Lemuel didn't look like either a minister or a mobster. Abe had expected him to be dressed in a silk dressing gown with a satin collar, a silk ascot, and opera slippers; not bare-footed, and wearing a pair of old, frayed, cutoff jeans, and a chambray shirt with a torn pocket. As he sat cross-legged smoking a panatella, Myles looked more like the savage chief of a jungle kingdom than a hit man. Instead of a loin cloth, he wore only a pair of scanty bathing trunks and the wide-brimmed porkpie hat with the barber-pole striped band. Only Matthew looked his part: a corrupt G-man in his rumpled seersucker suit and panama hat.

Abigail served tea from her favorite Spode chinaware tea set and laid out her favorite set of twelfth century apostle spoons. Sadie was delighted with the neat line of cloudy bubbles around the lip of her cup and the edge of her saucer that a Chinese artisan made by embedding grains of rice. As she held the cup by its delicate, gold leaf decorated handle and admired it, she asked Abigail, "Is your tea service very old?"

"All things are relative, Sadie. Compared to the Bible, yes; but compared to myself, no."

"Well, even if they're not antiques, they're exquisite."

"Thank you. However, I suspect they are considerably more ancient than yourself." Sadie took Abigail's complement gracefully.

Most of the conversation was light and without much reference to salvation; the Holy Spirit; being washed in the blood of the lamb; or any of the other proclamations so often expressed by evangelical clergy. The badger game incident, while not forgotten, was treated as a neighborly prank and laughed off with varying degrees of amusement. Abigail, who had started the whole thing, was the least amused by the outcome. Myles did utter one or two Amens and Lemuel said, "Selah" once, so neither Abe nor Sadie could decide what sort of racket these mobsters were running.

The famous outfitters, Bezaleel and Aholiab, who the missionaries hired to construct the tabernacle, Abe knew, were the worst scoundrels this side of Harlingen. Anyone associating with them must be crooked too. Abe imagined he had a clue when Lemuel laid out the itinerary the missionaries planned to follow. Lemuel did not detail the mission's course other than to say they planned to travel along the Rio on Route 83, and bring the "Holy Spirit" to the "knowing" citizens of McAllen, Zapata, and Laredo.

"And if they are not knowing before we arrive, there shall be many to receive the Holy Spirit before we leave." Myles waved his cigar as though blessing the multitude with it. "As the prophet Joel, and the sainted apostle Peter, has foreseen: 'For these are not drunken as ye suppose;' their behavior is because of the Spirit, which I will pour out upon all flesh, and your sons and daughters shall prophesy, and your young men shall see visions, and your old men shall dream dreams.'[119] Let us pray that our mission be that successful Brother Lemuel."

Abe rubbed his chin thoughtfully. What enterprise could possibly cause this outfit to skirt along the Mexican border? *Were they making contacts with people from the other side? Probably. And if so, what could they bring over that would explain all those millions of dollars the church had? Hum? They are not drunken, but filled with a substance that caused them to become elated enough to see visions and dreams? Hum? A substance that is obviously very valuable.*

* * *

Esther was concerned that there might not be enough food for the extra guest. They had planned supper for six, but if Matthew stayed there wouldn't be enough fish for everyone. Then as she and Abigail prepared the fish, she counted seven pompanos. She shrugged and decided that she had miscounted before.

Abigail chatted as she filled the fillets with tiny shrimps and crabmeat. "This is an old Gypsy recipe, 'Pompano en papilotte.' We Gypsies

HOW THE GOOD TAILOR GOT TO HEAVEN 539

taught the Egyptians how to cook fish this way. First you wrap the fish in papyrus, like this. Then give them a thick coat of clay. Come on, it'll wash off. Then you bake them in a pit filled with hot coals. We'll use the grill. Later, a wandering Gypsy gave the recipe to the American Indians, and then it was picked up by a New Orleans hash house where they charge you a fortune."

* * *

Aton signaled readiness for his nightly combat with Apep by swelling to an enormous orange disk on the horizon, brilliantly fearsome to behold, and an equal match for the evil one. As he entered the first chamber of the Tuat, the battle with the lesser demons began. The clash of deities was ferocious this evening as evinced by the resulting streaks of the color spectrum blazing across the darkening sky. The dunes turned to mauve and purple, and beyond them bright flashes of light reflected from the rolling obsidian hummocks out on the Gulf. Abigail lit the string of Chinese lanterns that she had strung around the trailer awning, "To ward off the evil spirits," she said, but also because she thought they looked festive.

Into the circle of torchlight cast by the burning cresset, rolled an ancient, rust-rotted pickup missing one fender and the remaining one flapped noisily. It ground to a halt and Pete and Andy came forward. "Hi, Brothers and Sisters. We've come to a decision," Pete announced. They were warmly greeted and invited to join the diners.

Rounds of pre-dinner cocktails were served, and the group became animated and garrulous. To show that he was fully in agreement with the sharing tenets of the mission, Pete got a bottle of Tequila from beneath the seat of his truck, took a healthy swig, and offered the bottle to the others. Andy offered to take Abigail off to the dunes for a bit of sport, which she politely declined. However, so the other ladies would not feel rudely scorned, he also made the same offer to Esther and Sadie. Sadie's eyes widened with amazement at the crudeness of the proposition, and stammered, "No thanks." She assumed it was intended as a coarse joke by a waterfront derelict, but Esther was edging off with him.

Both Matthew and Myles looked distressed, and Abigail reminded her that she was sharing hostess duties and they were getting ready to serve dinner.

The party sat around the table and nine parchment-wrapped pompanos were served on white bone china plates, along with asparagus with hollandaise and a Mexican rice dish. While they ate, Abe sipped his chilled white wine and speculated about this ring of conspirators. In this part of the country the possibilities for nefarious collusion seemed unlimited: gun running; white slavery and prostitution; spying and counter spying; money laundering; and smuggling illegal aliens to name just a few. Abe speared a lemon wedge, and drizzled the juice over his fish. *What would make the children to prophesy? The young men to see visions? The old to dream, dreams?...DOPE!...They were drug smugglers!* A bit of angel dust, opium, marijuana or a hit of crack and people would imagine all sorts of things. They would speak in tongues or roll about in ecstacy. What better cover for their operation than posing as pious men of God?

Sadie was seated between Matthew and Abe, and Abe whispered his suspicions into her ear. Sadie dismissed that possibility from the first. The president's wife eliminated the market for illegal drugs years ago when she told the people to "say no to drugs." She gave Abe a patronizing look and whispered back, "Don't be silly darling. They're jewel thieves."

Esther sat between Pete and Andy, and the fishermen had been titillating her with lascivious suggestions ever since the meal began. Esther was at times coy, and at times showed she could match their coarseness. Myles ate methodically and silently and eschewed the wine in favor of bourbon. Matthew, Abigail, and Lemuel were engaged in their own colloquy concerning the tabernacle, and Matthew was astonished to learn how much gold was used. The other churches never mentioned anything about the enormous worth of the Israelite's tabernacle while they wandered in the wilderness. The mercy seat alone was worth more than he could have earned in a lifetime of government employment. Sadie overheard them talking about the gold, and silver, and the precious stones, which was why she thought they were jewel thieves.

Andy had stared at Sadie ever since he arrived, but, except for his one gallant invitation for a roll in the grass with her, he devoted most of his attentions to Esther. She let him grab a feel occasionally, while Abigail politely but firmly still resisted both fishermen's amorous overtures. Pete nudged Lemuel's arm and asked his minister in a low voice from the side of his mouth, "All things in common, huh? Is she a member of this church?" He nodded in Sadie's direction.

"We have great hopes," Lemuel replied.

"Yeah! I can see why," and he winked at Lemuel.

It was during the sherbet and champagne course that Pete arose to make an announcement. "Me and Andy have decided to join the church." He reached into the pocket of his jeans and pulled out a wad of bills. He ran a dirty thumbnail down the stack, as one might do with the pages of a book, and said, "Four hundred and sixty-seven dollars. It's everything we have." He thumbed over his shoulder to his truck, and said, "Couldn't give that away."

Lemuel rose to his feet and shouted a mighty hallelujah, and Matthew took their hands and welcomed the new brothers. "Yeah, welcome," Myles said without enthusiasm. Esther hugged them and kissed each of them lustily; while Abe and Sadie exchanged astonished looks. Abigail reached for the wad of bills, and said, "Thanks fellows. I'll give you your stock certificates later." Then to Esther, she winked, and said, "See, I win our bet."

"Gambling! That's the one thing I hadn't thought of," Abe said in a low aside to Sadie.

* * *

Abigail issued shares to Peter and Andrew, and Peter asked, "Now that me and Andy's apostles, do we get to wear polyester suits and have our hair styled and blowed dried?"

"Oh sure," Abigail reassured him. "Whatever you need. Just put it on the church's charge card."

Andrew was leading Esther toward the pickup and Peter extended an invitation to Abigail to join them. "C'mon doll, let's see wha your ole honny pot ken do?"

Abigail declined. "I can't leave our guests," she said.

Andrew, the more suave of the two seafarers, demonstrated his sophistication to Esther. "Well, Essy, I guess you get to do a manage a twat."

"A what?" Esther asked.

"You know, a manage a twat. That's French for you and me and Pete all together."

Esther ran her hands down the creamy linen of her dress caressing her hips, licked her raspberry red lips, and they glistened. She said huskily, "Yes, I think I can manage." In her spike heels she towered over the two of them as she walked away with her arms over their shoulders toward the pickup.

At the truck Peter said hurriedly, "C'mon, we'll go back to our place." He spread an oily scrap of tarp in the bed of the truck and said to Esther, "Hop in."

Subconsciously, like a trained circus pony, Esther obediently climbed into the back of the truck, and sat behind the cab. Andrew got behind the steering wheel and Peter got into the passenger side and sat on the milk crate they used for a passenger seat.

Matthew was momentarily stunned at the rapidity with which events seemed to be moving toward the sacramental begetting ceremony and he did not want to miss the services. His personal spiritual awakening for Esther did not give him the right to deny the Holy Spirit's arousal within his other spiritual brethren, but his own awakening urged him to suggest that they all go together in his car. Then Abigail called, "Hold on a minute, boys!"

She had taken a quick inventory of the facial expressions of the guests. Abe and Sadie sat staring into each other's eyes with disbelief clearly written there; Lemuel was smiling benevolently and waving a blessing to the trio; and Myles's expression bore the look of a torture chamber customer.

Peter said with a smug smile, "I thought so. Yer jist as hot to go as Essy. Hop up there with her."

The benevolent smile on Lemuel's face froze into a grimace. His eyes looked luminous and moist, and his hand stood motionless in mid-blessing.

Abigail thought, *Ah ha! That makes a difference, huh? I think you've been corrupted by worldliness, Lem. Both you and Myles.* At the truck she braced against the driver's door with both arms extended, and said, "I don't think Esther can go with you now. It's the wrong time of the month for her, you see. She has her sickness and if you discover her fountain while she is unclean, you will be cut off from the community.[120]"

Peter snarled, "Are you welching on this deal? We done our part."

"Oh no. It's in the Bible. You'll just have to wait."

Esther leaned around the truck cab, and said peckishly, "Abby, mind your own business. Myles can't get it up, and this way is better than none." She added, "And I'm not having my period."

"Oh yes you are," and it became true. Then she whispered angrily, "Can't you see what you're doing to Myles? I'll fix him for you. Now get down from there."

Esther saw the pained expression on Myles's face and felt a twinge of obligation to him. He stood by her when the press gang came for them. He wouldn't be there if it weren't for her, and although he was *Homoiousian*, of similar substance to the angels, and she was *Homoousian*, the same substance as angels, he was closer to her own kind than Peter and Andrew, and she agreed, "You're right Abby," and climbed down from the truck."

Peter jumped out and snarled, "Get back in there! You ain't got lockjaw or hemorrhoids."

Abigail snapped at them, "You got what you paid for; your shares of stock and your eternal salvation. What more did you expect?"

Then Peter did something he should have never done. He grabbed Abigail's wrist, and shouted, "You Bitch! Give us our money back."

She turned him into a piglet, and he ran violently toward the gulf.[121]

Cerberus, who had taken to shadowing Abigail like a protective familiar, playfully grabbed him by his little curly tail and dragged him under the truck. Then, relenting, Abigail changed him back again just as Cerberus began to shake him. Peter, restored to the human race and quaking with fear, pushed the puppy aside and crawled meekly out from under the truck. He was trembling hard. Cerberus jumped playfully on his legs. He turned white, sagged whimpering against the fender, and edged fearfully away from Abigail. The seat of his blue jeans were torn, as though an animal had bitten him.

Andrew only saw Peter clambering from beneath the truck. He gave a low whistle, and said, "Wow! You're some jujitsu expert, lady. I ain't never seed Pete throwed before…by anybody."

Already confused by this rapid sequence of uncommon events, Abe and Sadie's senses reeled by what they had just witnessed. What their own eyes had just seen was impossible, and the only realistic explanation had to be what Andrew said. They looked to Lemuel and then to Myles for any sign of wonderment; any indication they had been hypnotized or fascinated in some fashion; but their calm acceptance of this supernatural transformation indicated that nothing unusual had occurred. Matthew, whose unwavering faith made him much more amenable to accepting miracles, rubbed his eyes in disbelief.

Peter sidled down the side of the truck and away from Abigail, and Lemuel scolded her. "Abby! You shouldn't do things like that to an apostle. It's undignified."

"You better warn your apostles that sometimes violence begets violence. Some of us haven't quite gotten the hang of turning the other cheek."

Peter edged his way around the hood of the truck, and pushed Andrew over and got behind the wheel. He sat as though in a trance looking straight ahead. Abigail asked, "By the way, how many trailers did you say you wanted? Was it one apiece, or will you share?"

"Pete and me don't mind sharing things," Andrew replied, and winked at Esther.

HOW THE GOOD TAILOR GOT TO HEAVEN

"How about one for each day of the week," Peter muttered. "We're as likely to get them."

Esther walked to the other side of the truck where Peter had sunk sullenly down in his seat and caressed his cheek sympathetically. "Don't pout, we'll get together later. I won't disappoint you." Then she asked Abigail, "Haven't you got something to cheer the boys up?"

"Oh sure. I was going to surprise them with this, but they were so hot to take you off, they didn't give me the chance." She handed them a purchase order for an eighteen wheeler. "Instead of seven trailers that you'd have a hard time driving, how would you like to pilot this baby? A Peterbuilt with a Freuhauf trailer. It has stainless stacks, a chrome radiator, big chrome hubcaps, stainless saddle tanks, and more chrome under the hood than you can imagine. It has a twelve-cylinder, Detroit supercharged engine, and an Allison automatic transmission. It also has real leather seats, air suspension, and deep plush carpet all over the floor and the overhead. It's air conditioned and has a tape deck with stereo speakers."

Peter began to be cajoled out of his funk with this wonderful vision of the highest symbol of grandeur to which he, or anyone else for that matter, ever dreamed of. It was the sort of vehicle to which a king might aspire. Then he frowned, and asked caustically, "Oh sure...What color?"

"How does sky blue with large white wings painted down the side of the trailer sound to you?"

"Aw, stop the bullshit lady."

"I'm not kidding. Read the purchase order. The lettering on the doors, and on the side of the trailer, is real gold leaf with dark blue feature outlining."

He studied the paper and whistled at the price, and exclaimed, "Wow! White sidewall tires."

"We're a rolling show, and we'll need a truck driver. If you know how to drive that rig, you'll be in charge of moving the tabernacle."

"Sister Abby, I ken drive anythin that rolls, swims, or flies. C'mon Andy, we got to get us some new duds." He rubbed his hands together and exclaimed, "Polyester suits, here we come!" The rusty old pickup groaned, rattled around in a circle, and headed off down the beach. Peter yelled as they passed, "We'll be back to stand inspection tomorrow…about suppertime. We'll bring a couple of gals along to even things up. You'll really like Magda, Rev!" The truck rattled off expelling billows of blue smoke, its single headlight jiggling at a crazy angle along the dunes and sky.

Matthew gave Esther a weak smile when they rejoined the rest of their dinner guests, but the look he gave Abigail was fear mingled with adulation. His new perfect vision had allowed him to see the little swine gripped firmly in the dog's teeth and then instantly revert to human form under the truck. It happened so fast he would have doubted his senses if it were not for the miraculous cures of his spine and his eyesight. Mystery cloaked with the supernatural surrounded these odd missionaries. "We apostles can take anything we need?" he asked Lemuel, and reached for the bottle of bourbon. "I need to take this home with me tonight, to think." He carried the bottle by its neck and stumbled toward his car muttering, "Who has such strange powers…only gods, but which gods?"

Abe and Sadie also decided the hour was getting late, and thanked the missionaries for the wonderful evening and the delicious meal. They too left. As they disappeared into the darkness, Abigail grinned. Small, crescent-shaped dimples creased her cheeks, and she said, "Boy! Turn one dinner guest into a pig, and right away everybody has to leave."

* * *

And so the guests were filled and they did take up the fragments that remained. There was nearly a basket full, and they fed Cerberus some of the remains, and scattered the rest on the beach for the gulls. Esther asked softly and earnestly, "You promised."

Abigail replied, "There's nothing wrong, I tell you. It's all in his head." Then after more hushed urging from Esther, Abigail said, "Myles, we have to have a talk. Come sit with us."

Chapter 28

THE LORD'S POWER TO HEAL THE FAITHFUL HAS BEEN PROVEN the world over. From Lourdes in France, to Saint Anne's in Quebec, to Oral Roberts in Oklahoma, to small town miracle workers all across the nation, the testimonies to this fact hang moldering and collecting dust along the walls of holy shrines everywhere. God's gift to the faithful hang as silent brooding relics: wheelchairs of healed invalids; crutches of healed lame; canes of the healed blind; back and leg braces of the healed twisted; the rags of healed lepers; and the winding cloths of the re-quickened all provide undeniable evidence. However, it is a fact that miracles cannot help those whose ailments are merely psychosomatic or neurotic. Since their problems are purely psychological, their only hope of being cured lies with the highly skilled practitioners of the sciences of psychiatry and psychology. This often takes many years of careful, and very expensive, prying by dirty-minded doctors, called psychoanalysts to find where the ego has been injured, and eventually, in some cases, healing occurs.

Abigail had no formal training in this science, and she said, "What's the matter with you Myles? Don't you like Esther?"

He winced, and stuttered, "What kind of a question is that? I love Esther."

"She says that you haven't been able to…"

He sputtered, "Esther! What have you been telling her? Some things are private." He blushed.

"The truth," Abigail answered. "She says that you get her all hot and expectant with a lot of foreplay and then you don't follow through. Now get to bed and give her the loving she needs. Lem and I will stay outside so we won't bother you." She called, "Lem! Would you mind coming out here for a few minutes? Esther and Myles want to have a few minutes alone together." And she herded them toward the open trailer door.

Esther skipped eagerly ahead and pulled Myles's arm. Her expression was roguishly alluring as she led him up the steps. He tripped clumsily on the threshold.

"Now go on in there and get busy. Just act like we're not even here," Abigail said impatiently.

Lemuel turned up on his elbow, and bleated, "I'm already in bed. Is it important?" He was wearing his blue pajamas with the white angel wings.

"No, I guess not. Go back to sleep," she replied, pushed the couple into the bedroom, and closed the accordion-pleated door behind them. "I'll take Cerberus for a little walk. Just hurry up, and when you're finished, I'll go to bed. Don't worry about Lem, an erupting volcano wouldn't wake him."

Abigail took a stroll along the beach. She knew that the average duration for coitus among humans was seven minutes. About the same time as for a long distance phone call, or to read the average personal letter. Just as reading skills varied with intellect and education, some mortals managed to get the deed over within a few seconds and others, less virile she thought, required somewhat more time: nine to twelve minutes. She sympathized, somewhat, with the female humans who were obliged to endure the presence of the male organ within themselves and regarded the whole business as an absurd practical joke that the gods had played on their creations.

Nearly an hour passed and she returned to the trailer. She knew that no matter how long mortals had foregone conjugation, they soon caught up and were sated very quickly. *Much ado about nothing.* As she rounded the end of the trailer, she saw Myles sitting outside in one of the camp chairs. He was dressed in his robe and he stared blankly in front of him. His face looked very thin and drawn, his eyes were wide and sunken, and his hands hung limply down from the chair arms. She said, "Esther sure drained you in a hurry."

"Oh Abigail…it's horrible."

"Overrated, probably. Silly, certainly…but horrible? I've never heard that from your sex before." She sat on the table and took his hand. "Aw, was Esther too rough? Did she force you in some brutal way? She should have realized that you have a sensitive nature and been gentle with you."

"Stop teasing! This is serious."

"Don't worry, they say the first time is always uncomfortable. But you'll soon get to like it and be wallowing in the squalid act just like all the other mortals. You can even use it to get little favors from her."

"Damn it, Abigail, I'm impotent!"

"Are you sure? I'll bet it was that Tomas. He may have put something in your life water. I wouldn't put it past him, but I've never heard of saltpeter lasting for more than a few days." She took his hand and patted it.

Myles pulled his hand away from her, put his face down in both of his hands, and muffled his sobs. "I was afraid this would happen."

"Do you think Tomas substituted ordinary water for living water? Maybe you're still an angel."

"That's what Esther thought too, but that's not it. I'm mortal all right. I can't disappear, I can't soar, I can't work miracles, and I can't do what the normal mortals can do. We should have let her go with Peter and Andrew. Matthew. Anybody!…Everybody! Oh God…I think I'll kill myself."

Then quickly apprehending this scene—with Myles outside alone, it meant Esther was inside, alone, with Lemuel—and hot to go. A strange new emotion gripped her. She inadvertently blurted out, "What? You left that doxy in there alone with Lem? That jade! A match for Messalina, and you left her and Lem alone, together?" She leapt to the door, and darted inside. Lemuel was sleeping, and snoring lightly, and when she looked in on Esther. She was also asleep, wearing a serene smile.

"We worked something out, temporarily," Myles explained sheepishly when she reappeared.

Abigail felt foolish and quickly repressed her deviant reaction to a subliminal cell of her mind. Deviant behavior for a demon anyway, but about what she had no idea. Just because she had taken up with mortals was no excuse for her to behave like one. If the angels wanted to behave like humans, it was their problem. Actually Myles's predicament was ironic. During his former mortality he lived as celibate as any priest and he prayed nightly to be released from the lustful urges that plagued him. Driven mercilessly by lustful thoughts about women, in chapels, maids on the streets, milkmaids and shepherdesses, it seemed every woman aroused the concupiscence that lurked just behind his pious smile. Self-abuse was a staple ingredient of his confessions. Finally his desire abated, and then disappeared. He considered his later years blessedly freed from the desires of the flesh, and he was inspired to spend these years in holy works.

With his mortality restored, he resumed the quickened state at the height of his good works and at the point when he had finally conquered the lust in his heart. Abigail looked into his bleak and drawn face, and decided that he would not appreciate the humor of the situation. She knew that that foul Tomas would have been delighted if he knew how much he was tormenting Myles, so with demonic perversity to do the opposite of the Holy Cardinal, she decided to cure Myles's impotence. *And thoughts of Esther and Lem together, had nothing to do with it*, she told herself. She confided to Myles, "Myles, I know a sure-fire Gypsy remedy for your problem."

HOW THE GOOD TAILOR GOT TO HEAVEN — 551

"No witchcraft or false gods," he blurted out. Then his expression began to change. He looked sinister and a tight smile appeared. "Wait a minute. I don't care anymore. That's the kind of thinking that got me into this mess." He looked slightly mad, and he leered evilly, "Anything. I'll do anything—I'll kiss a goat's behind."

Abigail was disgusted by his reference to Satanic rituals. *Ugh! The lengths some mortals will go to, in the name of religion.* But she felt comity with her consanguineous counterparts, and while she would never help them in anything harmful, violent, or life threatening—if these two friends wanted to do this thing that was so degrading to their angelic natures, at least they weren't harming anyone. She knew there was nothing physically wrong with Myles, so no amount of faith healing, finger snapping, or nose twitching would work. She didn't have any experience as a lying angel, and she thought that if Lem were still an angel he could have told Myles one of his true lies, and cured him. At times, incompetence has its uses. Unaccustomed to lying, she began slowly, and made up a story. "Just across this island there's a magic sweet water pool. That's where Esther and I found Cerberus. Only the Gypsies know about it, and they are all sworn to secrecy…"

"If you and Esther found Cerberus there, Esther knows about it doesn't she? She's not a Gypsy."

Oh boy, this lying is tougher than I thought. "Of course she knows where it is, but she doesn't know about the magic." Abigail recovered nicely, then solemn as an augur studying the entrails, she fixed upon his eyes with a green glittering stare. "If I reveal its location to you, you must promise to never, never, never, divulge its location, or anything about it." He nodded eagerly, crossed his heart, and held up his right hand. She continued, "We do not know where the magic powers come from, or why, we only know that they always work. The Gypsies discovered that an invisible angel from an entirely different order of angels descends there from time to time and roils the placid water of the pool with his presence. They've never told me how they found out about the magic. Possibly one fell in accidentally, but they know that the first person, and only the first, to enter the pond immediately after the water roils is cured of all their infirmities.[122]"

Myles looked away from her steady gaze, and said, "I think I've heard of this magical pond before."

She shrugged, and said, "It's possible." But she thought, *I don't see how since I'm making up this nonsense as I go along.* Then she said in a barely audible voice, "Go due west, about a quarter of a mile from here, and then look off to your right and you'll see a place where the dunes resemble porches. There will be five of them in a cluster and that's where you will find the pool. The Gypsies have named the place after a little town in Maryland: Bethesda."

"Does this happen every night?"

"Oh no. Only in a certain season and we never know when, so you must stay by the pool until you see the angel trouble the waters."

"What does the angel look like? I may know it."

"You can't see the angel. It's invisible. And you wouldn't know it because it's from a different order. You have to watch the water and when it roils, that's when you jump in."

"Okay, but are there any magic words to repeat or mystic signs to make?"

Becoming impatient, she said, "Whatever comes to your mind. Just make sure you are the first being to go into the water after the angel troubles it. And be sure you watch very carefully, the angel may not trouble the water a great amount, just little ripples."

"Let's see if I have this right. A quarter mile west, and the pond will be on the left."

"To the right, Myles! To the right. Five dunes that look like porches, and when the angel troubles the water you get in…you got that?"

"Which way is west?" She pointed, and headed him in the right direction. "Okay, I've got it." And he left running at a brisk trot.

Myles found a well-worn trail in the dim moonlight. Once upon a time Indians and conquistadores came, but currently thousands of campers and indigenous fauna pounded a path through the marsh grass

HOW THE GOOD TAILOR GOT TO HEAVEN

the width of a narrow hallway all the way to the pond. A source of fresh water on a sea bounded spit still attracted many. Myles found the pool easily, and exactly as Abigail had described. Its surface had not a ripple and looked like a piece of glass that had been enameled black on its underside. Myles sat on a tussock of grass and stared intently at its surface. He waited.

As soon as Myles entered the tall grass and was out of sight, Abigail made herself invisible, and soared quickly to get to the spot before him. She floated above the pond, and waited until he was seated, and his gaze was fixed on the surface of the pond. She hovered invisibly above the surface, then reached down with her toe and touched the waters. An ever-widening, circular ripple spread across the surface and lapped gently at the reeds at the edge. Myles blinked, but did not move.

Hum? I told him the surface would be troubled. Maybe he was looking for something more dramatic. She removed her huaraches and held them up near her shoulders. She floated down a few inches and splashed about with her bare feet. *There, that's troubling the water, he couldn't mistake that for a bug or something.*

Myles got up and stood at the water's edge. He considered for a long time and then a frog bleated, "bee deep." Myles smiled with the expression of one who has discovered a natural cause for a ghostly noise and reseated himself on the tussock.

Doesn't that idiot realize it would take a hundred frogs to trouble the water that much? Abigail let herself descend a few more inches, and gave hard slaps to the water with her feet. The water splashed up, and got her legs soaking wet, and spattered the hem of her skirt. *There!* she thought.

Myles quickly dropped to his knees, scooped up a handful of water, and examined it.

Now what? Abigail sighed.

Myles said, "I don't see any turbidity. Abigail said the water would be roiled." He called softly, "Angel, are you there? Hum? Maybe a deer?"

By Christ's afterbirth! These churchmen are stiff-necked. She jumped in and splashed about with both arms and legs, and stirred up clouds of mud from the bottom. Finally, Myles entered the water.

The effect was nearly instantaneous. Myles scrambled from the pool with an erection parting the folds of his bathrobe, and of a size that reflected its three hundred eighty years of enforced desuetude. He took the tumescent member that was engorged with the Holy Spirit in his left hand, and roared a mighty hallelujah. By the joy he felt, he could have taken his bed upon his back and dragged it all the way to the center of Brownsville, and begot with Esther in front of the Main Street Baptist Church on a Sunday morning[123] with the whole congregation looking on from the curb. "Hallelujah!" he yelled again, and ran back to the trailer clutching his member before him.

Abigail slogged home after him, her clothes dripping wet and muddy, with her hair hanging like the strings of a wet mop.

* * *

In the morning the sun cast a broad avenue of coral red reflection across the gray-green Gulf. Abigail sat with her feet on the coffee table: disheveled, and damp, and nearly asleep in one of the camp chairs. She had stayed up all night with Cerberus curled up beneath her chair. Lemuel brought out a pot of coffee; it steamed effusively in the chilly morning air. He also brought a platter of croissants he'd heated in the microwave, and a container of whipped sweet butter. He poured her coffee for her and she gratefully nestled the steaming black drink in her cold hands. He broke open a hot roll, spread a bite-sized piece generously with sweet creamy butter, and offered it to her mouth. She ate it greedily.

"You look like Medusa," he teased gently. "What's the matter? Can't sleep?"

She said nothing, but slathered another roll with butter and wolfed it down, and sipped more coffee. Then the trailer's ground jacks started to slide rhythmically on their wooden pads. She motioned toward the trailer with her coffee cup, and said, "That!"

"Oh yeah. They woke me several times."

HOW THE GOOD TAILOR GOT TO HEAVEN   555

After six minutes of evenly measured sawing motions the whole trailer swayed violently for a minute and then it became motionless. A soft sigh came from the open window. Everything was silent for about fifteen minutes, and then the trailer began to rock once more. Abigail protested, "They've been doing that all night." She angrily said, "I'm calling the Airstream people this morning, and asking them to please put a rush order on one of our trailers."

No sound or motion came from the trailer for a while. The gulls out on the beach squawked loudly as they disputed over breakfast, the morning breeze from the Gulf had a chill to it, and then the water heater roared on which meant someone was running the hot water, probably taking a shower. About fifteen minutes later, Myles appeared wearing his robe and hat, smoking a cigar. He said, "I don't know which god you summoned, Abigail—Eros, Puck, Cupid, or some Gypsy god I've never heard of—but thanks, it was worth committing blasphemy." He poured himself a cup of coffee and sat wearing a dreamy smile.

About twenty minutes later, Esther descended the couple of steps from the trailer—Esther always descends steps, others come down them. Her raven black hair was wrapped in a towel like a turban, and she wore a silken wrap and golden sandals. She looked like a maharanee leaving her palace bath. She swayed past Myles and let her hand caress his cheek. She kissed him, pulled her chair close to his, and said huskily, "Oh my unicorn, my Lancelot. Not since Artabanus have I been conquered so soundly..."

"If you're through with the bath, I'd like to use it," Abigail broke in caustically.

As the tub filled, she poured in a double measure of bubble bath, sprinkled bath salts liberally, and stirred the billowy froth with her foot. Then she sank into the suds up to her nose, and as the bubbles burst they made crackling sounds like static from a distant radio. She was nearly asleep when she felt her foot being pulled from the water and slowly soaped and massaged. Lemuel continued to wash the rest of her. He shampooed her hair and rubbed her down briskly with a towel afterward.

"It's iniquitous. The washing ceremony, remember? You've committed sacrilege with a demon," she teased.

* * *

The Holy Spirit manifested itself a couple of more times within Esther, and Myles was finally forced to quit the field of veneration having fulfilled his three hundred and eighty years of missed worship services. Even holiness has limits. They joined Abigail and Lemuel, who had taken Cerberus and were dozing on the beach. Abe and Sadie soon joined them and Abe set up their beach umbrella to shade his fair-skinned sister/wife.

Lemuel had forgiven Abe for trying to seduce Abigail, and well-bred people do not discuss their dinner hostess's little *faux pas*. Therefore, Abigail, having turned one of her dinner guests into a piglet, was treated with silent circumspection. The whole thing was probably a momentary hallucination or, since everyone witnessed it, a kind of mass hypnosis. After all, some magicians can cause a whole bus to disappear right in front of a large audience. Their attitudes toward the missionaries had developed into a nervous awe. "We talked about leaving this morning, but some mysterious power seemed to hold us," Abe said.

Lemuel made a sweep with his arm that was meant to encompass everything, and said, "The Lord has given you much. Have you ever considered how you might repay his largess?"

The words, "shakedown," and "blackmail," entered the couple's minds respectively. "Do you want a donation?" Abe asked hesitantly.

"The tenth part of all that you have received from him, (Lemuel was still a bit confused about Jacob's promise to the Lord, and did not capitalize this 'him') is a Commandment, but I am hoping for something more. One tenth part of your soul cannot be saved, and ninety percent withheld. It is properly all of your soul that has to be surrendered."

Abe had heard that once in the mob you were committed for life, and he thought that Lemuel was toying with them by keeping up this

HOW THE GOOD TAILOR GOT TO HEAVEN —⚭— 557

missionary pose. He decided to play along. "We go to mass a lot, don't we Sadie? We were even married by a Catholic priest, and in a church."

Abigail silently appraised the pair of bunko artists. They had poise, charisma, and a polished sort of "presence." They'd make ideal advance people making bookings for the mission. Naturally they could never be trusted. They were completely amoral, were skillful liars, and if they had a spark of cruelty, they could easily be taken for Jesuits or Dominicans. While she studied the couple, Sadie took a fig from their lunch hamper, bit it in two, and poked the other half into Abe's mouth. Any eye could detect the consanguinity of the pair, and also their deep fondness for each other. She decided to rattle their composure, and said, "It's not legal, you know."

Abe blinked, and asked in surprise, "What's not legal?"

"Marriage of half-siblings. It's not legal in this country."[124]

Abe squinted shrewdly, considered the charge, and accepted the accusation with cool defiance. "The bend sinister is in my escutcheon and our moms would never tell for their own reasons. They signed for us to get married when we were fifteen. Besides it couldn't be proven without a DNA test." Abe watched for some reaction from Lemuel. He expected Lemuel to remonstrate with pious platitudes for having married his half sister, at least a show of preacherly disapproval, but Lemuel seemed just as unconcerned as when he found Abigail half-naked in his trailer.

Sadie quickly asserted her own opinion of convention. "So what! Our family wasn't like the ones you see on TV. Abe's the most loving, protective man I've ever known. And we've known each other since we were infants. Abraham, our father, is legally married to my mother, Sarah, and Abe's mother, Hagar, was the maid. Abe was born first, but as time went by, Sarah, my mother, started to believe that Abe's birthright shouldn't be valid, since his mother was just a servant; she wanted our father to get rid of Abe and his mother. So Abraham took Hagar and little Abe out into Death Valley and abandoned them with only a bottle of water, and a loaf of bread to sustain them.[125]"

Abigail's pity was palpable. "Oh, you poor kids! Parents can be monstrous. Believe me, I know just how bad they can be, and I think Sadie's mother was just as bad as your father."

Sadie continued to reveal more details of their sordid family. "Father Abraham decided that a male's firm hand was needed to manage his legacy and decided to marry me off. He married me seven times to seven men he trusted, usually friends of his, and they were all much older. But each time the groom died on our wedding night."

Abigail reappraised the delicate blond's talents. *She better learn to pace the action so that doesn't happen. It could ruin her business.*

Sadie continued, "With all these men dying on me, and my dearest beloved Abe gone…I wanted to kill myself. I was seven times a widow at the age of fifteen, but I had brought many estates into Abraham's coffers. He said I was underage and he kept all the money I inherited from my husbands."

As Sadie unfolded her story, Myles thought parts of it sounded familiar. He became interested and sat up. Then he asked, "How did you and Abe get back together?"

Abe replied, "It was a miracle. Hagar and I drank all the water, ate the bread, and were almost dead when we found a spring out in the desert. An old prospector, Mr. Azarias, was camped by the spring. So Mister Azarias became our guide and led us to Media where Sadie and I were reunited. Before he left us, he quoted some Scripture to us. I still remember his parting words. 'Beware, my son, of all immorality. First of all take a wife from among the descendants of your father, and do not marry a foreign woman who is not of your father's tribe. Remember my son, that Noah, Abraham, Isaac and Jacob, our fathers of old, all took wives from among their brethren. They were blessed in their children, and their posterity will inherit the land. So now my son, love your brethren, and in your heart do not disdain your brethren and the sons and daughters of your people by refusing to take a wife for yourself from among them.' Well! My mother and Sadie's mother decided that the old prospector was a holy man, and figured that the best way to preserve the birthright was to keep it all in the family. They took us to the priest that very afternoon, and Sadie and I have been together ever since."

Myles leapt to his feet excitedly and faced the group. "That man you met, Azarias, was the archangel Raphael! You two are like the most ideal couple; even more...you're a composite of the two most ideal couples in the Scriptures. In the original Book of Common Prayer, Thomas Cranmer developed for Henry VIII, Tobias and Sarah were cited as the most ideal married couple. Then when James published this expurgated Bible, and removed the Book of Tobit from the Holy Writ, they had to find another ideal couple in the Scriptures. And who do you think they selected? Abraham and Sarah! The verse that Raphael quoted to you is from Tobit[126], and your lives are just like your namesakes."

Lemuel observed calmly, "It's apocryphal, Myles. I don't think we should believe it."

Myles replied, "All Scripture is given by inspiration of God, and is profitable for doctrine, for reproof, for correction, for instruction in righteousness."[127]

Abigail said, "Having seven men die on top of you must have been very traumatic."

And Sadie responded, "It was terrible, but I think it made Abe and me have a realistic attitude toward sex. Our father made a pile of money off my little snatch. So when Abe and I got out on our own, I supported us by doing a little whoring. Then we found out we could make even more by taking pictures and threatening them with statutory rape, contributing to the delinquency of a minor, and child molesting. All the nice, juicy, scandalous perversions that will heap infamy and humiliation, and even real prison time, on the malefactors. And I always looked young for my age. I could pass for a budding pubescent until I was twenty-five."

Lemuel said, "There's that word again...statutory! Man's law! The iniquitous babbles of the secular humanists. wordliness! The Bible says, 'if she pass the flower of her age, and need so require, let him do what he will, he sinneth not.'[128] You obviously were not *virgo intacta*, and by fifteen, you were well past the flower of your age. And there certainly was no rape. You weren't forced."

Abe thought, *Doesn't anything shake this guy?* He cautioned Sadie, "Dearest, I don't think you should be shocking the reverend unless you mean it as a testimonial confession. Are you asking the reverend's absolution?"

Lemuel contradicted Abe. "She needs no absolution; she hasn't sinned. You should be very proud of her. Rahab was a whore, and Mary Magdalene, and Tamar played the whore when Onan rejected her. And didn't the Lord speak to the Prophet Hosea, and tell him to marry a whore? And he married Gomer. The Lord approves of whores. Most of the famous women in the Bible were whores, unless they were killers or prophetesses. You make your way in this world as Abraham and Sarah did. That's the kind of religious ideal they should be portraying on those family shows on television. It's right out of the Bible. Didn't you hear Myles say that you two personify the most exemplary ideals for couples to follow?"

Abe looked perplexed. "What Bible are you talking about? The same Bible that those preachers keep shaking at us on television? Somebody's confused."

Abigail laughed, and said, "Yes, confusion seems to be the normal characteristic of theologians. But our father has done much worse things than yours has."

"Do you mean that you two really are brother and sister?" Sadie was surprised by Abigail's frank admission. She studied Lemuel's lined face and his silvered temples. "He doesn't look like your brother. He looks old enough to be your father." But she was pleased to find another couple who flouted convention. She prodded Abe, and with unrestrained delight said, "They're just like us Abe. Wow, ain't that something? The unspeakable, the unpardonable, the silent sin…incest! And we're all digging it."

A vivid image of her first sight of the pair, with Sadie's loafers waving on either side of Abe's torso, flashed into Abigail's head, and she protested, "Well, not quite…"

HOW THE GOOD TAILOR GOT TO HEAVEN

Lemuel offered pedantically, "The church holds that spiritual incest occurs when a bishop, vicar, or other official receives two benefices; the one depending on the collation of the other. You haven't done that, have you?"

Sadie and Abe laughed together. Sadie pointed a finger at Abe, and said with mock severity, "Have you been doing that? You naughty boy."

The law had been very rewarding for Abe and Sadie. In their earlier years all Abe had to do was to threaten, "I'm gonna tell on you," to bring in the largess. But Sadie grew more mature, her narrow hips became womanly, their salad days had passed, and the sexual revolution had come. Morality had been turned upside down. There was no fault divorce, open marriages, some husbands and wives were into swapping, even bisexuality was becoming fashionable. Abe was forced to buy a gun. It was the low state of the nation's morality that forced Abe into the role of the heavy. He had to rely on the jury system to invoke the unwritten law, which says that a man has the right to defend his home. It was by the process of elimination they found themselves in Texas where corporal and capital punishment are still meaningful, and where the most reliable juries were found. But now the state was becoming corrupt by the influx of northern liberals. Corruption and rampant immorality were seeping southward, staining the pellucid virtue of these righteous Texans, and forcing Abe and Sadie out of their livelihood. America had come to know sin, and the couple now found themselves, not unlike Lemuel and Abigail, driven into this farthest corner of the nation: on the rim of the abyss.

They were thousands of dollars short of the little homestead of which they both dreamed and each year it was getting worse. The moral fabric of the nation was disintegrating. Abe said, "Remember that auto executive from Michigan?"

"The one whose wife wanted us to join their swap club?" Sadie recalled sadly.

"What are we going to do? I'm afraid the handwriting is on the wall."

Lemuel smiled benevolently. "Cheer up, the Lord will provide. Consider the sparrows and the lilies of the field."

"We can't live on rain water, sunlight and birdseed," Sadie said morosely.

"You're both attractive, intelligent people. Have you ever considered that your attractiveness may have been given to you by the Creator to do the Lord's work? Consider Esther's beauty. Her loveliness steered many thousands back onto the road of salvation. Heterodoxy, and even idolatry, are sweeping our nation, and Esther has volunteered to help us acquire thousands more. You two would be welcome additions to our ministry. The satisfaction that comes from bringing the Lord's ecstacy to the initiate can be amazingly rewarding."

Instead of eliciting visions of the soul's final reward, as Lemuel had intended, his use of the word "rewarding" caused them to think of crass lucre, and bringing "ecstacy" to "initiates" could only mean drugs. They thought they were being recruited into the drug trade. They both knew there were dangers and they had discussed them. Once in, you can't get out. Some type of initiation was required. They'd have to swear eternal loyalty to the organization and renounce the worldly establishment and all its works. But they had both heard of the billions of dollars that circulated in the drug trade. It even surpassed the sixty to seventy billion donated to the nation's churches, although both enterprises were tax-free. Abe asked, "This cover that you use, how much of this religious stuff are we expected to know?"

"Don't let it bother you. You won't have to prepare anything. As you speak the words will come: 'Take no thought of how or what ye shall speak: for it shall be given you in the same hour what ye speak. For it is not ye that speak but the Spirit of your Father which speaketh in you.'"[129] And Lemuel pointed above to indicate the source of the words.

Abe regarded Lemuel's recitation as a compliment to his glib tongue, and quick-wittedness. "Yeah, a few stock phrases ought to be good enough. I'll practice my amens and hallelujahs." The couple were becoming avid to join these missionaries of rapture, but nothing really incriminating had ever been admitted. It dawned on them that this mystery could only be revealed to them after their actual initiation into the gang.

Abigail knew that they wanted to join, and since Lemuel had a tendency to overlook the minor details, so as charge of terrestrial affairs, it fell to her to lay out the initiation requirements for them. As one voice they both said, "Everything!"

"Everything."

"We'll have to think about that. You understand, don't you?"

"Think of the rewards," Lemuel reminded them. Then he invited them to join the rest of the apostles that evening for a ceremonial supper and the commitment of body and soul services.

Abigail added, "Nothing fancy tonight, just hot dogs, beans, and potato salad."

Chapter 29

FRESH FROM HER SHOWER, ESTHER BRUSHED HER MAGNIFICENT black mane in the hot afternoon sun. First she brushed all of her hair over to one side of her head, tugging the stiff brush forcefully through the tangles, and then she swung the whole mass over to the other side of her head and brushed in the other direction. Her silky hair grew wavy and radiant under her brush. Myles watched every motion as though they were Delphic signs that he could understand if he observed very closely. She was still dressed in her silk wrap, and as she plied her brush, she revealed ample cleavage as her heavy breasts swayed under the silk. Abigail had slipped into a one piece sunsuit. She looked about the trailer, and then hollered out the door, "Esther! Get in here and clean up your mess! I warned you what I'd do."

Esther pouted and whined, and Myles quickly jumped up and ran into the trailer. "I'll get it for her, Abby. She says she must brush one hundred strokes every day." Abigail left the trailer muttering to herself.

Shortly after four in the afternoon Peter's pickup rounded the dune, rattled, squeaked, and growled to a grating halt. When he applied the brakes, the rivets of the linings screamed a shrill protest. Peter and

Andrew were in the cab of the truck, Andrew was seated on a plastic milk crate, and riding in the bed of the truck were James, John, and three women. Both doors opened on complaining rusty hinges, and remained gaping wide. Peter's salutation was cheery. "Hi, brothahs an sistahs." Andrew waved as though wiping a large plate glass window. Andrew had convinced Peter that his brief metamorphosis into a piglet was a hallucination, probably caused by a knock on the head when Abigail tossed him. Peter accepted the explanation, but circumspectly kept a good ten-foot space between them, and avoided all eye contact with Abigail. The troupe advanced and it was like an invasion by clowns.

The apostles had their hair styled, and their heads looked feathery and soft. *Indicative of what's beneath the hair*, Abigail thought. They had also bought polyester suits. Peter's was dove gray, and he wore a priest's collar with a black dicky. Andrew's suit was charcoal gray with a richly-embroidered, white Shantung vest. He wore a white shirt and a cranberry necktie. The tie had a pair of praying hands slightly below a tear-shaped carbuncle tie tack. Both James and John had selected more priestly black suits with white turtleneck sweaters, and all had bought new cowboy boots and broad-brimmed Stetson hats.

Peter introduced the ladies. "This here's my ole lady, Magda, and Andy's ole lady is Jael, but we call her Spike[130]. The ole woman here is Magda's mom, Naomi. She's sort of my mother-in-law. We brung Naomi to serve all of us, but she said she don't feel up to it. Can you fix her up, Rev?" Naomi was a Caucasian version of Pearl; not yet forty but more hardened, cynical, and worn.

Both girls were colorfully painted with cosmetic artistry, and thickly enough to grease the tracks of a marine railway. Magda, the taller of the two, had glittering black eyes, and purple hair that stood out on the top of her head somewhat like the prickles of a hedgehog, but the hair on the back of her head was uncut and hung like a plastic sheet to her shoulder blades. She wore a gold sequined blouse with buttons up the back, and a tight black miniskirt that looked like patent leather. Her hose was purple fishnet with a small tear behind her left knee, and chosen to coordinate with her hair color. She wore a pair of red, spike-heeled pumps. Spike was of a somewhat plump, diminutive stature, and her hair was yellow. Not blond, but yellow, about the same color that taxicabs are painted. It hung in spirals, like lathe cuttings, down from her round head. Her large blue eyes were heavily mascaraed and eye shadowed, and reminiscent of Betty Boop. Her dress was red and white checked with puffy sleeves, and it was very short. The neckline scooped very low across her *poule* plump bosom, and her shoes were high-heeled platforms with white leather straps and genuine cork. Nothing ersatz mind you, but real cork platforms. Both girls had trouble walking through the sand. They also had an eye for jewelry. Magda tended more to long, hanging ropes of colored paste, tear drop earrings that looked like lava lights, and rings of wire and turquoise on all her fingers. Spike, the more tasteful of the pair, liked mirrored, clear glass. She wore a two-inch-wide gem studded choker, earrings that were pendant prisms, and several large, white-stoned rings on her pudgy fingers. Magda's mother wore a faded blue polka-dot shirtwaist dress and was barefooted.

Speaking to Lemuel, Peter motioned toward the two young women and asked in a highly indignant voice, "Are we preachers, or not? Will you tell these two broads? They don't believe us."

"They can't be fishermen one day and preachers the next! Ya gotta go tah school or sumpin'," Spike rebutted sarcastically.

"It has surely happened before, my child," Lemuel replied solemnly. Obviously neither girl was knowledgeable about Scripture, or they would know that one day a person could indeed be a fisherman, a publican, a physician, or a carpenter, and be an ordained minister the next.

"Well, they haven't been able to cure Ma's grippe," Magda said.

And Myles suggested, "Scepticism like this has occurred before. Jesus faced the same problem when in his own country, and within his own family, there was disbelief. His neighbors asked, 'Is this not the carpenter's son? And is not his mother called Mary? And his brethren, James, and Joses, and Simon, and Judas. And his sisters, are they not all with us? And his people were offended in him.' And that was why they failed to cure your mother. Jesus said unto them, 'A prophet is not without honor, save in his own country, and in his own house. And Jesus did not many mighty works there because of their unbelief.'[131]"

For such a slender girl, Magda's hips were generously proportioned, and she obviously considered them her most endearing asset as her mode of perambulation showed. Spike's walk was more dainty and bird-like. She held her head down, her elbows in at her sides, and she shuttled her fists before her like a boxer training on the heavy bag.

A washtub filled with Lone Star beer on ice had been set out, and everyone helped themselves and settled in comfortably. As Magda dug her tortilla chip into the bean dip, she said, "But it all seems so phony. Like Pete's eyeglasses. He don't need no eye glasses; they're just plain window glass. He got them because he thought they made him look dignified. It's all a bunch of crap."

Myles snorted at Magda's doubts. "As apostles they all have cast off the restricting influences of their former lives. They have been reborn. What you see before you is the new Peter. Peter has cast off the worldly chains that others expected him to wear."

"That's sumpin' else I wanted to ask about." Magda tended to get to the central problem quickly. "It's about that free stuff," she indicated Peter with her long purple thumbnail. "He tried to tell me that since he's a clergyman, he don't have to pay no more. He told me that it was a sacrament and that I should regard it as his blessing?"

This was one of those occasions when a colloquium among strangers revealed a heretofore unknown practice to a close friend, and Spike looked shocked. "You shouldn't be charging friends, Magda. That's not nice. Whatever has possessed you?"

Abigail tried to keep a straight face and observed, "I'll bet it's demons. Do you think she's possessed by demons, Brother Lem?"

Lemuel did not need to feign solemnity. This was a serious matter. He studied Magda carefully and pronounced, "It's quite possible. What do you think, Myles?"

HOW THE GOOD TAILOR GOT TO HEAVEN —⚜— 569

Myles observed the girl cautiously, and said, "She could have as many as seven...they'll have to be exorcized of course."[132]

Magda became the focal point of all eyes as they looked for any visible evidence. She laughed uncertainly and drew back defensively. "Hey, wait a minute! I wouldn't charge him if all he wanted was a good screw." They continued to stare, and she became more self-conscious. "Listen, I give good head, and I even take it up the ass once in a while...but he's into this kinky stuff. Really weird stuff." Mustering some defiance, she blurted out, "He's got this thing about feet!" All eyes looked at Magda's feet, which were propped on the coffee table. "Not my feet! His feet! Do you know what he wants me to do? Wash his feet with my tears, and since nobody has that many tears...while I got my head down there...well, you can imagine. And then he wants me to wipe up his feet with my hair, and kiss his feet[133], Yuck! And he wants me to oil him up with lotions. Really kinky stuff...right? Well if you want kinky, you got to pay for kinky. Even friends."

It was an act that even Abigail, who had seen more of the world than most, had never heard of, and she thought the whole idea was repulsive. Esther was disgusted too, and using her glorious hair to wipe someone's feet would have caused her to retch. Her long glistening black hair was her glory[134], and she emitted a low, "Ugh."

Lemuel and Myles became flustered, and Spike, with a quick flare of anger, charged, "I'll bet you read about that in one of those dirty magazines you're always reading."

Even the more sophisticated Andrew, who had offered Esther a "manage a twat," added to the general disapproval. He shrank away from his brother, and said, "Hm! That just goes to show you. You never know do you? We was raised together, fished together all these years, and I never guessed...I always thought you was straight."

Myles was about to counter their abhorrence of this ritual act of devotion by citing the Scriptures, but Lemuel put a restraining hand on his arm. He cleared his throat to get his small flock's attention. This was exactly the sort of fractious schism his catechist, Tomas, foresaw. It was over trivial theological disputes just like this—arguments about the nature of Christ; or the selling of indulgences; or whether grace was obtained by faith alone, or were good works also necessary—that caused doubt among parishioners, and could decimate church membership. Lemuel made a quick assessment of the expressions of disapproval or approval. Both James and John thought it was a really neat perversion, and a good put down to the whole 'femi-nazi' movement. This indicated that there were four opposed to the unnatural practice and three were in favor. Myles was intellectually biased for the practice, but he would probably reverse his opinion if it were Esther's hair being used to wipe Peter's feet, and her tears and tongue washing them. Since Abigail was a demon, and would do exactly as she pleased, her opinion didn't matter. With the wisdom of Solomon deciding how to divide a baby, he asked Magda's mother what she thought. She said she felt "feverish" and couldn't concentrate on such weighty matters.

Since Magda's mother merely voted 'present,' this left the responsibility to cast the tie-breaker up to Lemuel. Beads of perspiration moistened his forehead. If he voted for the practice, and Myles flipped over to the opposite position, it would place the pastor of this flock at odds with the majority of his congregation. Unfortunately, Matthew had not shown up yet, and Lemuel sensed that an immediate decision was required. Abe and Sadie were nearby and they had been invited to this gathering, so Lemuel thought it wisest to get their independent counsel in this matter before making his decision. He dispatched John to their trailer to ask them to come right away.

John did as he was bidden, but Lemuel's invitation was relayed as, "The gang's having trouble and we need your help." Abe and Sadie thought this was a test of their courage and mob loyalty, and after checking the cylinders of his pistol, they both ran low, like skirmishers, along behind John. It took some minutes to straighten out the misunderstanding, and the couple were relieved that a fire fight was not eminent. Lemuel explained the delicate nature of the actual problem he faced.

Sadie pursed her lips and tapped them thoughtfully with her index

HOW THE GOOD TAILOR GOT TO HEAVEN — 571

finger. Then she asked Abe, "Remember that guy that wanted to do the Mazola party thing with me? Didn't we charge him two hundred and fifty dollars? But that business with the hair and the feet; I think that'd be worth at least five hundred bucks."

Abe caressed his sister/wife's smooth blond hair, and said, "That kind of perversion is worth at least a thousand, dearest."

Having heard all the evidence, and the opinion of the independent councilors, Lemuel made his decision. It would be acceptable for Peter and Magda to continue the practice, provided he paid for her services by performing services for her worth a thousand dollars. Now he knew how Solomon must have felt. He rendered a fair decision and hadn't lost a single soul. But Magda narrowed her eyes shrewdly, and announced to Peter, "You ain't gettin that for twenty bucks no more."

Matthew arrived, and Lemuel reveled in the assemblage of ecclesiastical princes and princesses he had assembled so far. Seated around him were five apostles, the Confessor to Edward VI, the Queen of Persia, and several disciples. He thought it unsuitable for these important dignitaries to have to serve themselves like commoners at a salad bar. They must be waited on. He drew Abigail off to one side and mentioned that Magda's mother needed to be healed. Then he touched Peter's mother-in-law's hand, 'and the fever left her: and she arose and ministered unto them.'[135]

* * *

The men stood or sat in a segregated cluster smoking cigars and drinking brandy as men are wont to do after a meal so important issues can be discussed without female distraction. Peter was telling them how he planned to get a spinner knob for the steering wheel of that big Peterbuilt. "One of them ones as got a picture of Loni Anderson on it."

Abe drifted away from the group and sat beside Abigail. "I've never really considered joining a ... (he winked) religious group before, and Lemuel said that I should discuss the, ahem, temporal matters with you." Abigail handed him the Bible, and he said, "I don't think you understand. You're asking Sadie and me to pay dearly for the privilege of becoming members of this group. What I wanted to examine was the books, not The Book."

"I do understand. You'll find our prospectus, our financial statement, our current net worth, and a copy of the bylaws in the little pamphlet tucked inside the cover."

Abe carefully examined the documents: the facsimile bank records and the assertion of accounting accuracy by the nation's largest accounting firm. There were deposits and withdrawals, an astounding balance; a double-A rating by Moody's; the corporation was properly registered; the bylaws were all in order; but the only reference to the firm's principal enterprise was: "To do good works." The money just seemed to come from nowhere. He considered it for a few moments, and then became cross with himself. *Of course. They wouldn't put drug peddling down in writing. We don't make our activities public either.* He imagined what his own set of books would look like. Sadie kept the real accounts, but she would never put in writing that their business was swindling and prostitution.

The papers did reveal one frightening fact. There were no connections to any of the principal crime families. This group was apparently going it alone. He asked Lemuel, "Don't you think this operation would be less risky if you were connected to one of the big organizations?"

"There are pros and cons either way. Myles and I have discussed it. We decided the rigorous initiation requirements of the big outfits were too harsh and restrictive. Their screening process denies the promise of ecstacy to multitudes; they constantly fight with each other over territory; and they try to corral each other's subjects. We'd be forced to share souls with them so our rewards would be less. The big organizations adulterate the pure spirituality with disputatious factions and worldliness. No, we'll keep our church small and peaceful, and all of our souls ourselves. The twelve apostles will be keepers of the pure word and under them will be the seventy disciples going two-by-two throughout the country. We think that with this type of organization we should be able to bring thirty thousand souls under our ministry within a year."

Abe did some rapid mental arithmetic. *Thirty thousand addicts with hundred dollar a day habits equals three million a day. A nice operation. And the twelve apostles, as he called them, will have control over the money.* He said, "If I understand your proposal, you are offering me a position as *caporegima*, or lieutenant, and you expect to have seventy *soldati*, or soldiers, to oversee the street workers. Sister Abigail is the *banchiere*, or banker, and Brother Miles is your *consigliere*, or the councilor, and this makes you, in essence, the Godfather!"

Abigail laughed and applauded, and said, "By gosh, I think he's got it!"

* * *

Someone turned on the stereo and the congregation began gaily celebrating the ring dance rites. Their religious enthusiasm was elevated by the efficacious internal application of spirits. The sky was darkening, the Chinese lanterns were lit, the radio blared, and Esther removed her robe. Clad in her three minuscule triangles of cloth, she stepped into the center of the circle of love and performed the divine belly dance that had won her the title of the most beautiful woman in the universe. Following Esther's example, others discarded various articles of restrictive clothing. Lemuel called the assemblage to order and announced that the time had come to confirm the faithful into the Church of the Ethereal Evangelicals. "Are you prepared to receive the Holy Sacraments and be ordained into the ministry?"

"We thought we wuz. We give Sister Abby all our money," Peter asserted, and went back to dancing with Esther. He had discarded most of his clothes during the dancing, but was still wearing his Roman collar and dicky, his Stetson and cowboy boots, and the others were in various states of dishabille.

Lemuel raised his voice above the din. "You must make a solemn confession of faith and renounce all worldliness."

"Oh yeah! Amen to that preach," Peter yelled, and the others nodded in agreement, clapped their hands in time with the music, and shouted more amens.

Lemuel switched off the radio and got their attention. "When you surrendered your worldly goods you renounced material worldliness, but all worldliness means you must also abjure worldly custom, and commit your body and soul to God the Father."

All five inductees swore they were wholly committed to the mission. Sadie, whose ultra-sensitive, professional antenna was receiving some familiar signs from the acolytes, which affirmed where their bodies were committed, wondered how much bodily commitment would be expected of her if she and Abe joined the gang. Judging by the signals that passed between the apostles and Esther when she did her belly dance, this was a pretty horny bunch. Except with Abe, Sadie hadn't engaged in non-commercial sexual intercourse since she was twelve. Even her father, Abraham, had sold her seven times to seven different men, and her price was somewhat more substantial than the hundred foreskins that Saul charged David for Michal.[136] This would be like a vacation, doing it for fun, like a bus driver's holiday. The thought caused her to blush and she looked shyly downward.

Myles said something about coming to the Lord with a pure heart and asked if they didn't feel the need to cleanse their souls before taking their vows. Abigail snickered, and Lemuel chided her, "Must you always be so cynical, Abigail? Only God knows what is in their hearts. Attitude is the essential determinant. They may be feeling the first charismatic awaking of the Holy Spirit."

"You should have a test so you would know for certain. You know, like they have for witches. Everyone knows water will reject the devil's own, so they used a dunking stool. You could ask them to recite the Lord's prayer. Anyone possessed by demons can't do that without making a mistake. Maybe there is a numb spot on their bodies. The devil's chosen are always marked." Her eyes flashed mischievously, and she said, "There should be some handy little sign so you could see their faith. Something like this would be nice." She waved her hand and halos appeared above the heads of the acolytes, and then she waved them away. The boys never noticed.

HOW THE GOOD TAILOR GOT TO HEAVEN — 575

"There are always signs. They may not be as apparent as halos, but they're always there. Sometimes the Spirit moves them to speak in tongues, not to impress them that believe but for the doubters[137] like you, Abigail. Sometimes they have revelations of visions, even up to the third heaven,[138] or sometimes they are given the power of interpreting of the speakers of tongues,[139] and then there's the evidence of the miraculous healing of the faithful.[140] There are always signs."

"Oh, you mean like the way you healed Matthew and Naomi?" She rolled her eyes upward and stuck her tongue in her cheek.

"Well no, of course not, but didn't you see the revealed knowledge illuminate their faces when during the ring dance Esther performed for them in the circle of love."

"Is that what it was? I noticed they were all praying to infuse their Holy Spirit with her...or me, or Sadie, or Magda, or Spike...is that what you mean?"

"It's one of those borderline cases."

Myles asked helpfully, "How about poisonous serpents? That's always a good test of faith.[141]"

During this conversation Esther bit the end from a panatella, and both James and John fumbled for lighters in their pockets. James lit her cigar for her and she asked which one of them was the captain of their fishing boat. John leapt up, flexed his biceps, and said, "Me, I'm the captain." Esther laughed, and said she wouldn't believe him unless he could show her a sailor's hornpipe. He winked lewdly at his brother, and said, "I got a sailor's hornpipe for you, baby." He grabbed his crotch and gyrated like a male stripper. Esther said she liked his show but doubted it was a sailor's hornpipe, so he squatted, and did something that looked like a Cossack dance.

James shoved him and sent him sprawling. "That ain't no hornpipe. Here lemme show ya, doll." James danced several clumsy steps of something that resembled a Highland fling. Esther applauded both efforts and pulled the boys down beside her. They sat cross-legged on either side of her chair and rested their chins on her thighs. John rubbed his unshaven bristles against her leg and called her his goddess, and James vowed she was the queen of the heavens.

Abigail joked, "Seamen have such honest, outgoing mannerisms. Don't you agree, Esther?"

Esther replied, "No more so than soldiers or kings."

Their well-intended compliments actually bordered on profane adoration of other gods. Both Lemuel and Myles were troubled, and Lemuel observed, "They profess faith and yet they unconsciously cling to idolatry. How do we know their feelings are not base carnality ...worldly lust." He propelled the words, "worldly lust," with undisguised distaste. "Or are they feeling the divine expression of God's love, as the Lord has commanded us? What do you think Brother Lemuel? They're your acolytes."

Abigail interjected her favorite Bible quote, "I know the answer to that one: it's only sinful if you think it is."

Myles shifted uncomfortably. Intellectually, at least theosophically, he knew he had no right to feel possessive about Esther. She didn't belong to him; she belonged to God, as did all the others seated here, and his gaze traveled over the assemblage and stopped when his eyes met Abigail's. Well, all but one belonged to God.

He admitted, "Actually, Sister Abigail is right. Only God, who searcheth all hearts, knows for certain. But we cannot judge. They must judge for themselves. If they regard her as a God-created being, and their souls are directed toward God through her as His instrument; if they see her as the transcendental unity of faith, then their emotions are of grace. But, if as I suspect, because they used the expressions goddess and queen of heaven, Esther was the end and sole object of their desires, the subjective object of their profane fantasies, and the end object of an erotic dream. If she was just that, of herself, then their attitudes are sinful worldliness."

"Naw! That wadden it," John said. Then he added, "It was that stuff you said before."

"Oh yeah," James assured Myles. "We didn' have any sinful thoughts; they was all as holy as that there Bible."

HOW THE GOOD TAILOR GOT TO HEAVEN 577

Abigail remarked, without concealing her incredulity or amusement, "Well, there, you have your answer, right from their own lips."

Lemuel said, with admonitory tones, "Cynicism comes naturally to you, Abigail, but how else would you know what they thought, except by what they tell us? They are simple men and their affections are expressed in simple direct ways. They obviously have an affinity for Esther, and as the Bible explains, 'No man hath seen God at any time. If we love one another, God dwelleth in us, and His love is perfected in us.'"142

Both boys nodded vigorously, and John said, "Yeah, that's what we meant."

While Lemuel and Myles contemplated the validity of the Holy Spirit within James and John, someone had turned the radio back on and lively sounds drowned out further discourse. Peter, Andrew, Magda, and Spike were moved by the spirit and started to dance. There were a lot of breasts bouncing, buttocks thrusting, heads flopping, arms flailing, high stepping, and jumping, as though the four of them were marionettes whose strings were being manipulated by a spastic puppeteer in the throws of a violent fit.

Lemuel took these energetic animated gyrations for spasms of ecstacy and clear evidence that they had been infused by the Holy Spirit. Peter's mother-in-law joined the dancers. Then James and John decided to join the dancers by singing along with the hip-hop music and clapping their hands rhythmically. No one could understand the gibberish, and Lemuel believed they were all speaking in tongues, and being moved by the Holy Spirit. Lemuel said to Myles that this was a sign that God approved the divine love that John and James directed to Esther.

Everyone except Lemuel knew what motivated James and John. Esther did not like the coldly pragmatic analysis by Lemuel and enjoyed being the center of attention. The boys resumed their positions seated on the ground on either side of her chair with their heads resting on her thighs. Evidence of the Holy Spirit's presence or not, Myles was distressed by the affectionate caresses the two seamen were bestowing on her. He said he doubted that the Holy Spirit moved them. He suspected that it was pagan idolatry and he believed they still regarded Esther as a goddess.

Lemuel said, "I don't see where Brother James's or Brother John's attitudes are very much different from yours, or brother Matthew's."

"Matthew doesn't paw her. Besides, he's a believer, and his intentions are worshipful. I think these two have immoral secular humanist leanings. I don't think these two are ready to take up the cross at this time. Perhaps later...much later...and in some other church." Myles nodded toward Abigail, and added, "And I don't think the Holy Spirit would come around her presence."

Lemuel dismissed Myles assertions as heresy. Myles should know better than to question the omnipotent powers of the Almighty. He bristled, "That's nonsense, Myles. Abigail is as essential to our mission as Esther. They're our strongest assets."

Esther had been quiet during this discourse, and was fondly stroking both boys' heads. She drew a long draft of panatella smoke and blew a series of smoke rings. She said, "Your points are interesting, but since your discussion concerns the three of us over here, I'll tell you what I think. Granted, the New Testament is a bit out of my field, but the Old Testament constantly warns God's chosen about casting their seed among strangers.[143] Well, I chose these boys. I promised certain benefits if they became our brothers and now you're trying to renege." She looked directly at Myles and said, "Their souls are just as pure as anyone else's around here."

Lemuel agreed with Esther, and he accused Myles of having worldly thoughts himself. He reminded him that his unseemly possessiveness regarding Esther was an attempt to restrict everyone else's desire to participate in the divine love. Myles muttered angrily, "You'd think differently if it was Abigail they were pawing. Besides, they haven't been formerly inducted as our brethren yet."

"We'll take care of that right now," Lemuel said, and asked, "Would you apostles mind coming forward for the anointing ceremony? Just

HOW THE GOOD TAILOR GOT TO HEAVEN

kneel here before me and we'll get this over as quickly as possible." He asked Abigail if she had any myrrh, or frankincense.

"Oh sure, I always keep a handy supply."

The frankincense was lit and Lemuel held a small jar of myrrh for the anointing. The fishermen and the publican knelt before him and Lemuel proceeded with the ceremony. Just as he was about to anoint their foreheads, Myles spoke up again, "Wait! They haven't confessed their sins. The essential proviso of the faith is they have to confess their sins, and make an atonement."

Both Esther and Abigail smiled at each other mischievously, and Abigail said, "Oh yeah, I want to hear them confess their sins."

John winked at Peter, and said, "Judging by what we been listening to, we ain't got none."

"Never taken the Lord's name in vain?" Myles asked.

"Oh yeah. I guess we done that a couple of times," Peter acknowledged, and said, "I'm sorry. How 'bout you fellas?"

Andrew piped up, and said, "Jesus Christ! I guess I have too. I must'a forgot. I'm real sorry."

Myles said with exasperation, "Lem! Did you hear what he just said? They're not redeemed at all."

Lemuel stroked his chin. These were his first converts and he didn't want to lose them. His voice was solemn as he pointed out, "You just sinned again, Andrew."

"Huh? What the hell you talking about?"

"Taking the Lord's name in vain."

"I did not!" Andrew protested. Matthew leaned over and whispered into his ear, and Andrew started in surprise, "Really?" Then to Lemuel, he said, "I didn't know. I'm real sorry. I'll never say that again...cross my heart and hope to die."

Lemuel said, "I think we can accept that as a sincere act of contrition. But you may have forgotten some other sins. We better inquire further. Do you acknowledge that it was the Lord who brought thee out of bondage?"

"Oh yeah, sure we do," Peter said, and looked down the line of vigorously nodding heads, and several more assertions of: "Yeah, sure," were heard.

As Lemuel continued, Abigail kept track of the questions on her fingers. Lemuel asked, "Have you put any other gods before the Lord?"

There was a row of vigorously shaking heads, and soft, "No"s.

Abigail put down a fourth finger as Lemuel asked, "Have you made any graven images?"

Once again all heads shook vigorously.

"Do you love the Lord with all your heart and mind?"

The row of heads all nodded up and down in agreement.

"Do you love your neighbor as yourself?" Lemuel asked sternly.

In unison all heads nodded up and down. Then Andrew charged, "Hold on Pete. What about the time Sukey broke your collarbone with the pool cue? You swore you hated his guts, and you was gonna use his bowels for bait when he got outta the pen."

"Oh, I got over that when he got fifteen for possession with intent to sell."

Myles said wryly, "That's not exactly turning the other cheek, Brother Lemuel."

"I'll be sure to tell him how sorry I am when he gets out," Peter said with an evil smile.

"It's apparent to me that these men have flawless souls, except for the serious infraction of blaspheming, for which they are most heartily sorry, and one thoughtless incident of not loving his neighbor, for which Peter has promised to correct as soon as Sukey gets out of jail. Lemuel beamed joyfully upon his new apostles, held out his hands toward them, and announced, "They're perfect." He walked over to them and shook each hand. "We'll have the annointings in a few minutes, fellows. Let us savor this glorious moment together. Oh Hallelujah!" Myles reluctantly shook their hands also. He patted each one on the back, and extended his congratulations.

Abigail frowned, and looked toward Esther, who also looked

HOW THE GOOD TAILOR GOT TO HEAVEN —�— 581

bewildered. Abagail said, "Hey! Hold on a sec there! Wait just a doggone minute! What about the rest of the questions? You only asked them six questions."

One might think that Esther had only one thing on her mind, but that was not the case. She agreed with Abigail, and said, "Hold it a minute. What kind of a church are you running here?"

Lemuel looked puzzled. "A Christian church, of course. What seems to be the trouble?"

"I wasn't counting, but I know Abby's right. You didn't ask them any of the hard questions."

"I didn't mean to circumvent your apostolic prerogatives, Esther. If you think a further inquisition is in order, you can examine them, but both Myles and I agree they have attained the requisite grace."

Esther and Abigail stood side-by-side and advanced toward the apostles with fierce expressions. The apostles backed away as the women strode forward, and at the trailer, when they could retreat no further, the fishermen squatted like monkeys with their backs against the wall. Matthew sat on the step, Peter cracked his knuckles, and John doodled circles in the sand with his forefinger. Esther drew herself up impressively, and asked sternly, "What about the Sabbath? Have you always kept the Sabbath Holy?"

Abigail nudged her, and said, "Yeah, that's a good one Esther. Let them answer that one." And she counted off another finger.

The fishermen exchanged guilty looks. They had all worked on Sunday. In fact, every Sunday that they were sober enough to get out of bed.

Just as they were clearing their throats and searching for an excuse, Myles said, "That's no longer relevant, Esther. We're using the New Testament. It supercedes the Old Testament in regard to the Sabbath. Jesus said, 'Wherefore it is lawful to do well on the Sabbath days[144]: the Sabbath was made for man, not man for the Sabbath[145]. He and his disciples plucked ears of corn on the Sabbath to make the point. We know that Jesus led the most exemplary life of any man, so you shouldn't expect these fishermen to be more pious than their Lord. The disciple is not above his master, nor the servant above his lord."

Esther and Abigail were unsettled by this, but Esther quickly recovered and thought of another Biblical reclamation. "Okay, how about your mothers and fathers? Have you always honored your parents?" Abigail nodded agreeably and ticked off her seventh finger once more.

This time Lemuel interrupted, "That doesn't apply anymore Esther. Jesus showed the new revelations of the New Testament when he scornfully denied admittance to his mother and his natural brothers and sisters. They had come to speak with him when he was talking with the people. He indicated that his disciples now fulfilled the function of brothers, and sisters, and mothers,[146] and I can't recall where he acknowledged, even once, the existence of Joseph who was a father to him and taught him a trade. Jesus said, 'Call no *man* your father upon the earth: for one is your Father, which is in heaven.'[147]"

Myles confirmed, "Oh yes, that's true Esther. You're using Old Testament law which is accursed.[148] It's pretty clear what Jesus thought of family ties. He said He came to divide the family: 'I came not to send peace, but a sword. For I am come to set man at variance against his father.[149] There shall be five in one house divided, three against two, the father against the son; the mother against the daughter; the mother-in-law against the daughter-in-law,[150]' And he prophesied, 'that the brother shall deliver up the brother to death, and the father the child: and the children shall rise up against their parents, and cause them to be put to death.[151]' The family ties of the Old Testament are carnal worldliness, Esther. Our true family is of the Spirit, and the kinship of faith."

Esther and Abigail exchanged uneasy glances. Their inquisition wasn't going as expected. They put their heads together for a few moments of consultation, and Esther said, "You ask something."

Abigail held up her seventh finger for the third time as she asked, "All right, How about killing?" It was the worst crime she could think of, and she squinted like a merciless prosecuting attorney. "Have any of you ever killed another person?"

Peter and Andrew became edgy; the others were vigorously shaking their heads. Peter looked down guiltily, away from Abigail's penetrating gaze, and he blurted out, "Maybe, in the war. Do slopes and niggers count?"

Myles interceded, "You don't have to answer that Peter. I'll repeat: 'I came not to send peace, but a sword.' We must presume the sword of Jesus isn't for whittling, Abigail."

Matthew also seemed uncertain. "I was in the navy and we blasted the shore with everything we had. I suppose somebody got killed."

Lemuel said sympathetically, "I'm sure that if you did kill anyone it was during the holy crusade against the heathen Buddhist idolaters in Vietnam, but John the Baptist made an interesting point. He said to the soldiers, 'Do violence to no man, accuse no one falsely, and be content with your wages.[152'] Did any of you veterans ever complain about your wages when you were in the military?"

Matthew replied, "Not me. It wasn't much, but we didn't need much, considering everything we needed was issued to us. After the war I got a free education and veteran's preference when I applied for my job with the IRS."

Lemuel threw up his arms as if to ask: What more do you want? And Abigail was aghast. "Lemuel! Are you condoning killing?"

"Not condoning, Sister Abigail...it's inconsequential. Only the fate of the soul is of consequence, and these boys have committed their souls to God."

"I fear I must disagree with you, Brother Lemuel," Myles spoke unctuously. "But these things are of consequence." Abigail's hopes were elevated. She presumed Myles was remorseful about his role as the Lord's finger man in the massacre in Jerusalem, Texas, but as he continued she was heartsick. "Although we are not privy to the end purpose of the Lord's grand design, we know that all things are predestined through his omnipotence. By and for his pleasure were they created, so, as our Lord has promised us: there shall be wars, and famines, and earthquakes. There will be betrayers, and false prophets, and nation shall rise against nation, and kingdom against kingdom.[153] As Paul has reminded us in the Book of Romans: 'The powers that be are ordained of God,' and our faith makes us understand that it's all for the good." Abigail wondered if that included Hitler. "If these things were not brought to pass, man might become satisfied with the world, which is the abode of demons, and lose sight of the higher promise."

Esther also saw the good that was brought about by killing. She knew Abigail would be sensitive about the seventy-five thousand deaths her first mortality detail had caused, so she avoided that subject, but she recalled enough Scripture to shed light on the goodness: "When David was king; it was out of the spoils of battles that they maintained the house of the Lord."[154]

Arguing for compassionate treatment of humans, or expecting God to treat them with a little dignity and respect, would be useless Abigail realized. After living for six thousand years among the mortals, she had become inured to the misanthropic predations of all the gods. She looked at the index finger of her right hand, which represented the seventh sin. The other six represented: taking the Lord's name in vain; acknowledging that the Lord had delivered them from bondage; not having any graven images before the Lord; having no other gods before the Lord; loving the Lord with all their heart and mind; and loving their neighbors as themselves. She recalled with distaste that Jesus said they were supposed to hate themselves[155]. "There's supposed to be at least ten of them," she muttered to herself while looking at her extended finger. Esther had asked about honoring your parents and that one was eliminated. Working on the Sabbath was okay. She had asked about killing, and that was all right. *How about adultery? Esther would never think of that one: I'll ask them that.* She pointed at them with the seventh finger, and asked, "Okay! How about adultery? Have any of you ever slept with another man's wife?"

Peter spoke up, "Oh come on now. It's the nineties! Everyone swings today. You can't count that." The others vigorously agreed by nodding their heads, and Lemuel once again interrupted their blatant admissions.

Lemuel said, "Hold on a minute fellows. You don't have to answer

HOW THE GOOD TAILOR GOT TO HEAVEN

that. That's not a sin." He turned toward the surprised Abigail, and let a weary sigh escape. "We've gone over this same path before, Abigail. It gets tiresome having to straighten you out. Your ways are worldliness."

"Lemuel! I asked them about adultery!" Abigail felt she was on firm ground there. She was certain that adultery could not be casually dismissed, but then her confidence wavered as she remembered Lemuel's reaction to Abe and Sadie, and how he justified their behavior by citing the parallel activities by their namesakes: Abram, a.k.a. Abraham, and Sarai, a.k.a. Sarah. Then there was that discussion about the antinomian doctrine of the Nocolaitans and how Nocolaous offered his wife to the apostles.

Then Myles brought the Bible over to her and indicated a passage with his finger. He said, "See what it says here? They ministered to Him of their substance. Along with Mary Magdalene, the courtesan, out of whom went seven devils, there is also mentioned, Joanna, the wife of Chuza, and Susanna, and many others, which ministered unto him of their substance.'[156] If we are supposed to imitate Jesus in our ways, it's obvious that adultery is no longer forbidden."

Abigail objected, "Just a minute there! That doesn't necessarily mean they gave their bodies to him. How do you figure that Myles?"

Myles patted her shoulder to soothe her ruffled sensibilities. He said, "What else could it mean? At that time women didn't own anything except their bodies. Their bodies were their only substance."

Esther complemented Abigail for her perseverance in rooting out sin, but she too agreed that Abigail's ways were too worldly. Abigail held up her seventh finger, and said, "I haven't been able to get past this finger, Esther. You know more about the Bible than me. You ask them the rest of the questions."

After a few moments of thought, Esther snapped out sharply, "Stealing! Stealing is a sin. I'll bet some of you have stolen lots of stuff."

"Yeah, that's a good one Esther. They look like horse thieves to me," Abigail said and wiggled her seventh finger at them; the finger that marked off the seventh sin.

Peter and Andrew exchanged dark looks, and the rest looked sheepishly toward Lemuel and Myles. Once more, to Abigail's chagrin, the sin was excused. Lemuel chided Esther, "You're as perverse as Abigail. Don't you understand what: 'He has freed us from the curse of the law,' means? The Scriptures tell us that Jesus sent two disciples into Bethany at the Mount of Olives to take a colt. If the owner of the colt wanted to know why they were taking his colt, they were to say that the Lord hath need of him. We also know Jesus taught by parable so we can assume that taking another's property should not be confined to horse stealing. The lesson to be learned from this is whether there is need.[157] And since we are a sharing mission, it reminds me of Paul's words to the Philippians: 'Look not every man on his own things, but every man also on the things of others.'[158]

There goes the coveting question I was going to ask, Abigail thought.

"I'm sure none of these boys would take something if there was no need. Isn't that so, fellows?" They all smirked with guilty delight, nodded, and looked at their prosecutors with smug smiles.

Abigail and Esther looked at each other, and sighed. They both shrugged, and Esther said, "Give me a second or two. I'll think up another one."

Abigail said, "What's the use? I've already counted up more than ten and everything we ask gets disqualified. I'm beginning to see why the Mafioso has such a cozy relationship with the Vatican."

"Well, I'm certain there's more." Esther tapped her temple with a finger, and then she brightened. "Lying! I'll bet they've all told some whoppers. Have you borne false witness?"

Once again Lemuel abrogated the query. Abigail had forbidden him to use parables in his homilies because she said it was lying, but Jesus used many parables, so the practice is divinely authorized, and he said, "And what else is a parable, Esther? It's surely not the exact truth. Jesus said heaven was like a mustard seed that a man cast into his garden, and it grew, and waxed a great tree, with fowls of the air lodged in its branches.[159] You know heaven isn't like that, don't you?"

Abigail backed up and sat on the edge of the coffee table, and cradled one knee with both hands. She watched Esther pace aimlessly for a few steps, and then Esther seated herself behind Abigail and rested her back against Abigail's back. "Come on Esther, think of something," Abigail said over her shoulder. "There has to be some sin other than not worshiping Yahweh."

"Do you want me to ask them if they coveted their neighbor's wife before they committed adultery with her? That would be kind of dumb, don't you think?"

"Of course there are other sins," Lemuel proclaimed. "The most important objective of the Bible is to teach moral guidance. 'All Scripture is given by inspiration of God, and is profitable for doctrine, for reproof, for correction, for instruction in righteousness.' And as far as I can tell, these fellows have withstood your mean-spirited inquisition admirably. You two are just sore because you haven't been able to trip them up with your trick questions."

Esther and Abigail knocked their heads together a couple of times to vent their mutual frustrations. Abigail said, "Ask them just one more question. You said our questions weren't valid."

"What's the point, sister? They have been proved. They have been found blameless, and they are fit for the office of deacon,[160] and we think they will make excellent apostles."

"Just one more question. Please? For me...please?"

"Oh all right. Have any of you ever brought the hire of a whore, or the price of a dog, into the house of the Lord?[161]"

Abigail spun around and faced Lemuel. "What kind of a question is that? Those four have never been inside of a church."

"They couldn't have committed that sin then could they? And Matthew hasn't done that, have you Matthew?" He shook his head. "There, are you satisfied? All of them have unblemished souls."

All five apostles exchanged gleeful looks. Peter held out his hand and gave Abigail the finger, and mouthed, "Up yours, lady."

* * *

The ordination of the apostles mystified Abe and Sadie, at first, but gradually they began to realize that they were not gangsters; they were a religious organization. They weren't drug peddlers at all unless you considered "religion" as the "opiate of the masses," and that was anathematic to our American way of life. The celebration after the ordination was not like the usual hyperdulia; it resembled more a Bacchanalia. The apostles and the women were engaged in a double ring dance, where the men formed an outer ring, and the women formed an inner ring, and they circled in opposite directions. Everyone was naked and their bodies rubbed against each other as they circled. When the music stopped, the begetting partner would be whomever happened to be opposite them at the time. It was the most indecent church service Abe and Sadie ever took part in, and they would have left immediately, if it were not for the church's impressive balance sheet. They decided the best way to get close to that money was to join the festivities, and after several cups of the vodka-laced punch, they cast off their clothes and entered the circles. As the epistles proclaim: 'If we love one another, His love is perfected in us.'

Abigail and Lemuel sat off to the side. Peter had forgiven her for asking all those embarrassing questions and invited her personally, but she declined. She hadn't seen worship services like this since Rasputin and the tsar's court. While the celebrants danced, she nudged Lemuel and asked him if this wasn't just the sort of thing Moses found the Israelites doing when he came down from the mountain. The naked festivities that made him so mad he smashed God's tablets.[162]

"Oh Abigail, you're such a prude in these matters. The world is too much with you, and you misinterpret everything. Moses was enraged because the people were worshiping the golden calf. They had sunken to idolatry and worshiping false gods. Aaron told Moses: 'For they said unto me. Make us gods, which shall go before us: for as for this Moses, the man that brought us out of the land of Egypt, we wot not what is become of him.' Don't you see? Their sin was making other gods to go before them.

"This celebration of love has the Lord's blessing. The Lord was pleased when David sported with Michal's serving maids and he punished Michal for disapproving. Absalom sported with David's concubines right on the roof of the palace where everyone could see him. Orgies are in the finest Biblical tradition. 'Conscience, I say, not thine own, but of another: for why is my liberty judged of another man's conscience? For if I by grace be a partaker of, why am I evil spoken of for that which I give thanks? Whether therefore ye eat, or drink, or *whatsoever ye do*, do all to the glory of God.'[163] And that's what our small congregation is doing."

Chapter 30

FOUR SHINY NEW TRAILERS AND TOW VEHICLES ARRIVED the next morning. The apostles and their disciples had spent the night on the beach and now cheered lustily as the caravan swung around and parked. They were positioned in the shape of an open-bottomed trapezoid with the Gulf at the open end and Abigail's trailer across the top. The plaza formed between the trailers was consecrated land and would be the site of the tabernacle, whenever Aholiab and Bazeleel finished fabricating it. For now it would serve as the site for their campfire and religious ceremonies. A nascent commune was taking shape where, since each soul is of equal worth, so, too, were the trailers and the tow trucks. All identical down to the configuration of the tumblers on the door locks and ignition locks. Significantly, all the keys were identical.

Abe and Sadie had not yet cast off their worldly encumbrances, but they had joined in the joyous revelry with the apostles the night before. Although not fully committed, they thought of themselves as prospective members of the church so the arrival of the Airstreams excited their interest. They were soon enviously inspecting and comparing the quality and quantity of the equipment that was being given to the churchmen. The Airstreams were a slight upgrade over their trailer, but all camper trailers function basically the same, and they spent the rest of the afternoon instructing the novice nomads on the proper use of their equipment.

Abigail, disgusted by the bacchanal of the night before, persuaded Lemuel to take a walk and let their congregation become acquainted with their new homes. The Gulf was millpond smooth this morning and along the bottom, in the watery shade dappled sand, tiny fish could be seen darting around their feet as they walked. Suddenly Abigail said; "Oh look!" She reached down into the water and pulled up an old Spanish doubloon. "They wash up from the old wrecked galleons," she said, and flipped the coin. "It's the ninth one I've found along this beach." Then her hand dipped into the water once more and she pulled out a common Atlantic sundial, a perfectly formed spiral intricately colored in shades of yellow and ochre. "These are much prettier, though." She returned to Lemuel's side, and handed him the doubloon and the shell for comparison.

"The gold is God's. The gold and silver is mine sayeth the Lord, and is sacred to God. That's why there's so much of it used in the holy of holies, and his mercy seat, and the rest of the tabernacle."

"It's not sacred. People only think it is, because it has a monetary value. Suppose doubloons were as common as sea shells. Then which do you think Yahweh would choose? And how much do you think people would value it? Mister Aholiab said the only currency that has retained its value was the cowrie shells the Pacific islanders used to buy their wives. Remember when Esther compared bank interest to God's increase of the fields, and I said I did the same thing when I created money?"

"You're not making sense."

She held up the shell. "This shell is real and its value lies in its beauty, but this," and she held up the coin between her two fingers, "has no dependable value. The price of gold fluctuates. It has been as high as eight hundred dollars an ounce, and now it's less than three hundred

HOW THE GOOD TAILOR GOT TO HEAVEN

dollars. What happens to the money when the price of this goes down? Where does all that lost value disappear to? I think the mortals are really lucky that there are a few earth angels around creating paper money to replace their losses. Yahweh wouldn't do it. He just wants his ten percent."

* * *

They walked about a half-mile up the lonely beach and were startled to see four girls sitting on a heavy driftwood log. This was miles from the populated southern section of the island. They had watched Abigail and Lemuel for quite a while. The girls, somber as shades, arose as if on command, and walked toward them. They were wearing denim bib overalls that were faded to the color of the sky, and frayed and worn through in many places. They each wore Mexican straw hats, ubiquitous in the farm worker community, and well-worn huaraches that were mended with twine in several places. Two girls were flaxen-haired blonds and two were curly-haired brunettes. None appeared to be older than sixteen and the youngest appeared to be about twelve. All hung their heads, as though guilty about something. The eldest, a brunette, stepped forward and said morosely, "We've been expecting you."

The youngest, a blond, said, "Oh, Leila, think of them as friends who have come for a visit."

Abigail and Lemuel exchanged puzzled looks, and Leila, the eldest, said, "You're here from the welfare department, aren't you? You've come to check up on us, haven't you?"

Abigail smiled and said, "No, nothing like that…"

"You're truant officers from the school board then?"

"No. We're not that either."

"Are you here from the parole board? You're here to check up on Philip, aren't you? Why can't you government busybodies just leave us alone?"

Lemuel quickly reassured them that he didn't have anything to do with the government. "We're evangelical missionaries and we've camped down the beach with some of our congregation."

"Oh, do gooders from the church. I knew you were some kinda butinskies."

"What makes you think that?" Lemuel asked.

Leila's dark brown eyes darted between Lemuel's and Abigail's faces, and then to Lemuel, she said, "Only time you ever see a white and a bla..." She halted in mid-word. Her eyes darted swiftly back to Abigail. She studied her face carefully, and fixed a surprised stare on Abigail's eyes. "Green! You've got green eyes. You aren't a negra and you aren't Mexican either, but you're just as dark. And you're pretty; real pretty." Then a quizzical expression crossed her face, and she exchanged glances with her sisters, and all four nodded. She reached out toward Abigail, and asked, "May I?" Abigail nodded and the girl felt the texture of Abigail's cheek and throat, as if to assure herself that the flesh was real. "Beautiful skin," she affirmed.

"Who's Philip?" Abigail asked as the girl's fingers lingered on her cheek.

"Our Dad. Want to meet him?"

The four girls' names were: Leila, just sixteen; Dagmar, a pretty blond nearly fifteen; Delores, a brunette who was just fourteen that month; and Gail, the youngest, a sweet little blond girl who was just budding into puberty. They led the way through a notch in the dune, walking single file, and waited as a kind of receiving line on the flat sandy expanse beyond.

The encampment that lay beyond the girls was not like those of holiday campers. Their tent was surplus military from the Korean War era, now shabby, and probably leaky. A rusty stovepipe stuck up through the peak of the tent. There were half a dozen, or so, plastic garbage bags lined up on a weathered plank along one side of the tent. They seemed to be stuffed with clothing and personal paraphernalia. A galvanized washtub leaned against the end of the plank, and a dozen plastic buckets of incongruously gay colors were lined up along the ground and covered with more plastic garbage bags. A dipper handle protruded from one. There were several pieces of mismatched lawn chairs placed haphazardly around beneath the fly of the tent, and there was a folding aluminum table, bent and sprung so that one leg looked as though it were poised in mid step. On one end of the table was a double burner Sterno stove. There was an old congolium rug for a ground cover beneath the fly with a printed pattern that was reminiscent of a cheery colonial kitchen. The rug was frayed and cracked with several holes punched through.

On one flattened lawn chair a naked man with a towel draped over his loins lay in the shade of the fly; his mouth hung slackly open and he snored softly. His right arm hung limply onto the rug and by his hand was an empty bottle of cheap Mexican rum.

As they walked toward their home, the girls seemed to have developed an instant affinity toward Abigail. They walked close to her and Abigail asked them about their mother. "Our mother has passed on," Gail replied, and Delores corrected, "She's dead." Abigail surmised they saw a mother substitute in her and put a sympathetic arm over the shoulders of the two nearest as they walked.

When they approached the tent, Leila said, "He's still drunk and passed out."

Dagmar saw it differently. "He's tired, and needs his rest."

Gail ran forward and shook his leg. He snorted several times, like a horse, awoke, and smiled crookedly at his daughter. She said, "We have guests, Philip."

He rolled up onto one elbow and his bleary vision cleared enough for him to discern there were two strangers present. He fumbled beside his chair, found a pair of ragged chinos and pulled them on as he stood up. He held out his hand to greet the company, and said, "Can't offer you a drink. It seems to be all gone. How about some tea? ... Leila!" The command came as from one accustomed to commanding obedient servants. He shook Lemuel's hand, and took Abigail's, bowed curtly, and kissed her fingers. "Charmed to meet you," he said with a cultured, southern gentleman's voice.

He was a man of slight stature and limb, with thinning light brown hair, a high and slightly freckled forehead, and a thin, prominent, slightly hooked nose. His smile was warm and friendly, but one front tooth was broken diagonally. He had a scattering of freckles across his shoulders and down his forearms, and a thin hairless chest. He and Lemuel exchanged meaningless pleasantries about the weather, and Lemuel mentioned the mission, but Philip's attention seemed to be directed more toward Abigail, inordinately so, although she sat quietly and said nothing.

Lemuel began to think that Philip and the girls may have spotted Abigail for a demon. Some people have this ability, but usually their talent can only discern demons after they have taken possession of some mortal. Demonic possession is what causes irrational sacrilegious behavior, and the demons must be ritually exorcized. However, it's rare when a mortal can distinguish a free form, non-inhabiting demon from a genuine mortal. The four girls also seemed to be in exceptional awe of her and he began to feel edgy. He sensed there was some magnetic attraction, a sixth sense, that he didn't understand, and he felt himself outside of the force field. Then a more horrible thought occurred.

Gail calmly dipped water from a plastic bucket into a blackened saucepan, Leila lit the Sterno stove, and Delores, and Dagmar got teacups and saucers from inside the tent. While they were busy, Lemuel's overactive imagination made him even more paranoid. They were being overly attentive to Abigail and virtually ignored his sacred office. When he told them he was a man of the cloth, Philip merely raised an eyebrow and nodded.

Maybe he was not being left out of the loop. Without the reinforcing presence of other partners of faith, his old fears returned. *Suppose these are all witches, and Abigail was about to betray him, and use his mortal body for some devilish perversity. Or worse, use him for the main sacrifice in an unholy witch's Sabbat!* He suddenly arose, and gushed an apology to Philip. "This is a bad time for a visit. You weren't expecting visitors, so we'll come back another time." He started edging away.

The girls cried out in unison, "Oh no! We were expecting her." And Leila said, "We were waiting for her for such a long time."

Philip suddenly dropped to his knees, and pleaded, "Please don't go." Then he bowed forward and groveled before Abigail's feet.

Abigail was flustered, but secretly delighted, and she asked, "What's this about? I'm not royalty. I'm a bit too dark to be taken for Princess Margaret. Now get up and tell me what's going on here?"

This obeisance to Abigail confirmed Lemuel's worst suspicions. *They're demon worshipers. She's led me into the midst of a coven of witches.*

Abigail reached down, got Philip to his feet, and said, "We're not leaving before we've had tea. That would be rude, Lem. Please explain what's this all about. Do I look like the girls' mother...your ex-wife?"

Philip said shyly, "You know who you are."

"Yes, I know who I am. I want to know who you think I am?"

Leila said, "You're Atargatis, aren't you?" Then Dagmar and Dolores took Abigail's hand and led her into the tent. Toward the back she saw what appeared to be a shrine of some sort. Resting on three plastic milk cases she saw a bronze figurine that looked very much like the little mermaid of Copenhagen Harbor. It was about three feet tall, and several candles burned in saucers at its base. The interior of the tent was dark, except for the candles and the light from the doorway.

Abigail asked them if they'd mind if they took the idol outside where she could examine it. The figurine was heavy and the girls struggled to lift it, but Abigail put a hand under it and lightened the load to no more than a feather weighs. She explained away her strength as they exchanged astonished looks. "I've been working out with weights." The entire shrine was moved outside and set up under the shade of the fly.

Lemuel cast fearful glances at the little statue and instantly noticed the resemblance to Abigail. It was uncanny: the sun had bronzed her skin to the same color as the bronze idol. Its eyes were pure white ivory inset with emerald irises and onyx pupils, and they glittered the same as Abigail's. The facial features were identical, as was the hair, and from the waist upward the torso was an exact duplicate of Abigail's figure. Except for the fish tail it was Abigail. Or, Abigail was the idol made full size and woman. This was, by far, much worse than mere Satanism. They were idolaters worshiping false gods, it would be better if they did worship the demon. At least Abigail belonged to the same species of angel.

The resemblance unnerved Abigail, and she said, "I see why you were startled. I could have modeled for it, but it's not me. Now let's have some of that rum to sweeten our tea."

"Excuse my gluttony, O mistress of the sea, but I drank it all," Philip apologized.

"Oh, I'm sure there's enough for us to have a sip or two."

In spite of Abigail's denial of her deification, Philip and the girls attended to her as though she were a goddess. Leila tilted the bottle and there was a corner, about a tablespoon, left, so she upended the bottle over Abigail's tea, and out poured a good double shot. Then Abigail told her to pour some for Philip too. When Leila looked again the amber corner seemed to have grown and when she poured it into her father's cup, out came another double shot. When she set the bottle down it was two-thirds full. "See, I told you there was some left," Abigail said, "and if you'll bring a pitcher, I'll fix some Daiquiris."

"There are no limes," Dolores said sadly.

Leila intoned, "Or ice."

"We'll pretend," Abigail replied. Gail brought a battered old camp pitcher, and Abigail prepared the mixture and poured the drinks into the teacups. They tasted exactly like iced diquiris, and the girl's drinks turned out to be pink Chablis, poured from the same pitcher. She said, "New wine is for the maids," and Gail's was pink lemonade.

"If you're not the goddess Atargatis, how did you do that?" Leila asked.

"An old Gypsy secret," she replied, while looking mysterious and laying a finger alongside her nose.

The girls were delighted that Abigail was a Gypsy, which explained her swarthy complexion. They asked if she could tell fortunes and she had four palms thrust forward for her consideration.

While Abigail solemnly studied each hand, Lemuel nursed his drink, and he also nursed his disapproval of this group of heathens.

HOW THE GOOD TAILOR GOT TO HEAVEN

When Philip toasted both Atargatis and Abigail with his cup, Lemuel made a show of placing his drink on the table and not joining in the blaspheming. On impulse he blurted out, "Have you been saved, Philip? Reborn through the Holy Spirit?"

Philip looked as though Lemuel had asked him if he were a murderer, or if he had sold his mother into slavery, or if he were in favor of littering the roadsides of Texas with trash. He shot cautious glances toward his daughters, and said, "Please, not in front of the girls."

Lemuel persisted, "Do you think that denying Christ, worshiping false gods...and idolatry...may be the cause of your present low station in life? I've seen the signs. I'm not blind. You're accustomed to better. You've come down in the world, haven't you?"

The girls were absorbed by Abigail's chiromancy, and Philip moved closer to Lemuel and spoke softly. It was obvious that he didn't want the girls to hear the story he was about to tell. "Yes, at one time I had a farm that supported many families. The worker's compound was really a small village, and my hacienda had twenty-two rooms. We had a staff of twelve house servants. I had a stable with twenty of the finest thoroughbreds in east Texas. The girls had their own riding horses and the garage held two Rolls Royces, a Mercedes limousine, three Cadillacs, and a Porsche. There were beautiful tapestries on the walls. We had several original O'Keeffe's, and some of the old masters, Rubens and Monets hanging in the foyer and throughout the house. The chandeliers were old Spanish wrought iron and crystal, and the furnishings were all valuable antiques. My wife and I slept in an empire bed that was reputed to belong to Napoleon. When my wife was alive, we often speculated about how many times Josephine had slept in our bed."

"Did the death of your wife cause you to renounce God?"

He saluted the idol with his cup, and said, "By the great goddess, Atargatis, No! I only wish I had noticed the signs sooner, but in my ignorance I turned more to the Christians than ever...."

"I wish you wouldn't blaspheme."

"We were hard shell...no...steel cased Baptists," as he pronounced the denomination his esses hissed venomously. "It was church every Sunday, no liquor, no tobacco, no dancing. Hard work, and business, was like an adjunct to our faith."

Lemuel thought, *How heavenly. They were model souls, an inspiration to all those who doubt the benefits of Godliness.*

"I was in the Masons, my wife was Eastern Star, and the girls were in Job's Daughters. That should have taught me about God's merciless hubris, but I didn't heed the message, and I thanked the Lord for his blessing at every opportunity. I always dutifully tithed of my largess. I was president of the Optimists, and a councilor at the Youth Fellowship League."

"What message? You say you received a message?"

"It seemed to be a freak accident at the time. We had donated a new altar for the church, and Jemima, my wife, and our two strapping young sons, Ezra and Samuel, went to the church to oversee its construction. Then there came a great wind, like a tornado, from out of the wilderness, and smote the four corners of the house of the Lord, and it fell upon them and killed them all. There was a second omen: A prairie fire destroyed my prize herd of Santa Gertrudis cattle and twelve of my most faithful caballeros, and I said, naked came I out of my mother's womb. There still remained enormous wealth; the ranch, no, not a ranch, it was a latifundium, and my four beautiful daughters: the fairest in all Texas. I prayed all the harder, and then I broke out in boils from the sole of my foot to the top of my head,[164] and the doctor said it was probably stress and hypertension. He lanced the boils and prescribed black salve and tranquilizers.

We clung more tenaciously than ever to the church. I gave money to every Christian cause, every patriotic American group, and supported every morality campaign. We got heavily into the mysteries and the esoteric interpretations of the Scriptures, and began a serious study group with the minister. The minister spent extra time with the girls and they spent nearly every afternoon after school, at his rectory. His special interest in them became noticeable and I caught looks from those ubiquitous church gossips, those old crones, whenever the reverend took them into his private study. You know, those smug, knowing, accusative looks."

Lemuel winced and began to fidget.

"Oh, that wasn't it." Philip waved as though discouraging a mosquito. "I wish that was all there was to it. Something that venial, that trivial." He leaned forward and spoke more softly, as though revealing the secret whereabouts of Rudolph Hess's secret diary. "He took me aside one Sunday after services and told me about the girls. He said the girls were gifted: they...prophesied."

Since they were a nest of idolaters, Lemuel drew the natural inference. "You mean they're witches? They can augur, divine from the entrails, and interpret the omens." And to himself he thought, *Poor unfortunate man. They'll have to be stoned, of course, their blood shall be upon them.*[165] He cast a baleful eye on the group of girls. Abigail was holding Dagmar's hand, tracing the lines in her palm, and explaining to her and her absorbed siblings about her cheerful aspect, her prospects for love and travel, and the hidden creative talents that the mounts, creases, the shape of her hand, and fingers disclosed.

"Oh no. Nothing as harmless as that," Philip said softly. He dropped his voice until it was barely audible. "They prophesied from the Bible. It's like a curse and I've gone through hell trying to break them of it."

Lemuel exploded, "Good Lord man! God has blessed you with four daughters who prophesied[166], and you think of it as a curse?"

Philip made shushing sounds. He put his fingers over Lemuel's lips, and said, "That's why we worship Atargatis, the sun, and the moon, the patterns of the stars in the sky, and all the spirits of the sea, and in the groves. It has been almost two months now since we cast out the false beliefs of the Bible, and returned to the faithful old gods.[167] Your God's evil has been too much to bear."

Lemuel began to pity the man. The compassion showed in his face, and he said, "Oh, that is too bad. Their prophesies were false then. As the

Scriptures say, 'When a prophet speaketh in the name of the Lord, and it not come to pass, even that prophet shall die.'[168] They'll have to be stoned to death. That's too bad."

"Who could tell if their prophesies were false. They quoted the Scriptures verbatim, but they always contradicted each other. The verses they quoted never agreed, and they were arguing and fighting with each other all the time." He smiled benevolently at the group of girls, and said, "Look at them now. They're so peaceful, so happy there with Atargatis. And the wonderful spiritous bounty she has given us is greatly appreciated." He raised his teacup and saluted Abigail.

Lemuel was stunned. Abigail's magic had trapped him between two iniquitous alternatives: either approve of the girls' idolatry, or, confess that Abigail was a demon, and then accept that worshiping demons was all right. He sputtered, "But you can't deny this gift of prophesy is from God. Every good gift, and every perfect gift is from above.[169]"

"I wish He'd poke His gift in his ear. Who asked Him for it anyway?" Then he asked Leila and Dagmar to come sit beside him. They complied shyly and he put an arm around each girl's waist. His hand slipped beneath their overall bibs, and he gave each girl's belly a playful squeeze. He said, "We don't worship your God anymore, Reverend. He has brought us nothing but pain and confusion. I'll have the girls give you a demonstration." He called the other girls over, and said, "Gail, what does Jehovah say to you?"

Gail, the youngest, stood forward and clasped her hands beneath her chin. She seemed to go into a trance and she wore a beatific smile as she recited: "It hath reached me, O auspicious Sire, that the peacemakers are to be blessed, for they shall be called the children of God."[170]

Then, without prompting or encouragement, Dolores went into a similar trance with her hands beneath her chin, and intoned; "O auspicious Sire, my sibling is truly a dolt: for then Jesus could be called neither the Son of God, nor blessed, for he said; 'Think not that I am come to send peace on earth: I come not to send peace, but a sword.[171]' So the holy word sayeth."

HOW THE GOOD TAILOR GOT TO HEAVEN

Dagmar slipped away from Philip's arm and stood beside her sisters. Her face seemed to radiate glory and she too, in a semiconscious state, prophesied: "O auspicious Sire, ignore your sorrow filled pathetic excuse for a daughter. These words doth cry from my heart; 'The fruit of the Spirit is love, joy, peace, patience, gentleness, faith, meekness, and temperance.'[172] Pay no attention to her dour vibrations."

Whereupon Leila joined the lineup of siblings, and spoke: "O auspicious Sire, and you my sweet but ingenuous sister; thinkest thou these words bespeak of love, joy, and peace: 'For our God is a consuming fire.'[173] And this from the Psalmist: 'For all our days are passed away in Thy wrath; we spend our years as a tale that is told.[174] And the tale that is told and retold is a tale of sorrow and misery; the pleasant things are noted but once, as they occur."

Throughout this recitation Philip hung his head and held his hands to his ears. When Leila finished her verses, he pleaded, "No more, my darlings. Be silent now. We worship Atargatis. Resist the confusion that the evil one sends to plague your thoughts. His voice is unholy gibberish." He sought Abigail's eyes and managed a weak smile as he asked, "Is there any more wine in the pitcher? Maybe that will calm them." The girls were drinking from small jelly glasses and Abigail filled them to the brim. And from the same pitcher Abigail poured more lemonade for Gail. Philip looked expectantly toward the pitcher and Abigail poured out another daiquiri into his teacup. He thanked her graciously. Then he addressed Lemuel, "The girl's prophesies are always, as you heard. They constantly contradict one another. It's a curse. If Dagmar predicts a sunny day with mild sea breezes, then Leila is sure to predict a dark storm with lashing wind and rain. Since neither one knows when this is to occur, or which will happen first...well...I'm sure you can see the problem.

"But this ability to recite God's Holy Scripture, without previously memorizing it, is miraculous. You shouldn't expect them to agree. As James said, 'Out of the same mouth proceedeth blessing and cursing. My brethren, these things ought not to be. Doth a fountain send forth at the same place sweet water and bitter? Can the fig tree bear olive berries, either a vine figs? So can no fountain yield both salt water and fresh.[175,] Their gifts are foretold quite clearly in the Scriptures."

Then Leila arose and said, "O auspicious Sire, it hath come to me that this fool knoweth not of what he speaks; does not the Sainted Matthew say, 'for he maketh his sun to rise on the evil and on the good, and sendeth rain on the just and on the unjust.'[176] The sun and the rain both flow from the same source, do they not O auspicious Sire?"

Philip quickly wrapped his arms around Leila to prevent any more versifying, and said, "Certainly, my darling daughter. But the source is not the evil god of the Bible. All good things come from Atargatis. Did you not just witness her pouring Daiquiris, pink Chablis, and lemonade from the same pitcher? And doesn't that tell you that the Bible tells lies and spreads confusion?"

Lemuel wanted to tell Philip that Abigail wasn't a goddess, she was a disobedient angel who had been cast down, but how could he explain his own association with her. He said, "I know you've had some setbacks, but the Lord never sends us more than we can bear. Perhaps He's testing you, as He did Job? But afterward, 'the Lord blessed the latter end of Job more than the beginning with sheep and camels and oxen, and other wives, and seven sons, and three daughters.'[177]"

Philip gave a snide snort, and said, "Listen to the rest of my story and then maybe you'll understand. As I've already told you we were rich, and we were faithful believers and churchgoers. After the deaths of my wife and sons we accepted the preacher into our home more frequently."

Tomas' words, 'Get 'em while they're down, and their resistance is low.' echoed in Lemuel's ears.

Philip continued, "He insinuated his way into our family, and he nurtured their tendencies, the poor innocent little girls." Philip had glittering gray eyes that fixed on Lemuel's soft blue ones, and his voice was low, but it sounded mean as barbed wire. "Every farmer knows who Cain was. They never mention it, but they know. He was a farmer, and

Abel was a huntsman and a herdsman. And every farmer knows God found Abel's offering more pleasing, and the Lord had respect unto Abel and his offering, but unto Cain, and his offering he had not respect.[178] Every farmer knows how Cain sweated behind his plow in the broiling hot sun while Abel walked lightly with nothing but an irresponsible presumption and a light weapon. Cain was dull, plodding, dependable, and sure. Cain fed the family while Abel took chances: Abel was a speculator. The time came when Dagmar, she was just little then, was prophesying." He raised his voice to mimic a small child's. "'O auspicious Sire; it hath reached me that The desire of all nations shall come, and I will fill this house with glory; The silver is mine, and the gold is mine, sayeth the Lord of Hosts.'[179] And dear Leila, oh, how I should have listened to Leila. She said, 'O auspicious Sire; it hath reached me that, Your gold and silver is cankered, and the rust of them shall be a witness against you.'[180]

"Opposing verse, right? Which do you follow? Consider the temper of the times. The price of gold and silver was rising; a madness suffused the land; and people were hoarding precious metals and paying any price to get them. The financial consultants were advising everyone how much of their investment portfolios should be in gold and silver. It was not whether to buy, that was unthinkable; how much to buy was the only prudent course. The economists were predicting that the country would soon return to the gold standard. Preachers lashed out from their pulpits against the evil government that had stolen the value from our currency, and imposed the cruelest tax of all on the backs of working men and women, and the poor—inflation. They preached that the nation must return to God's ways: 'gold and silver are mine sayeth the Lord.' My beautiful silver haired daughter had seen correctly." He groaned, "Or so I thought!" He sniffed back a sob. "It was made to seem that it was your patriotic duty to buy gold and silver to save this nation from bankruptcy. When the nation was awash in worthless currency, the wise will have saved it with God's ordained currency. So I started to buy silver and gold. The price of silver was rising fast, it went from five dollars an ounce to sixty; and gold went from forty-five dollars an ounce to eight hundred dollars an ounce, and they predicted it would soon go to twelve hundred dollars.

"The richest, most God-fearing man in Texas was buying silver, and since wealth and righteousness are sure signs of wisdom, who was I to disagree with his lead, and the advice of so many experts? Little Gail prophesied, 'And when the Queen of Sheba had seen the wisdom of Solomon and the house he had built, she said, "It was a true report which I heard in my own land of thine acts, and of thy wisdom."'[181] Then Gail described the precious gifts the Queen of Sheba gave to Solomon because of his great wisdom. Then Gail prophesied, 'Besides that which chapmen and merchants brought. And all the kings of Arabia, and governors of the country brought gold and silver to Solomon.'[182]

"I didn't heed Dolores's warning. She pointed out that the weight of gold that came to Solomon in one year was six hundred, three score, and six talents. She pleaded with me to be cautious because that number was the mark of the beast: 666. And she said the Book of Revelations foretold, 'And that no man might buy or sell, save he had that mark.'[183] O auspicious Sire, you do not bear Satan's mark. And as for the reputed great wisdom, O auspicious Sire, it hath come to me: 'For it is written, I will destroy the wisdom of the wise, and will bring to nothing the understanding of the prudent. And so God hath chosen the foolish things of the world to confound the wise.'[184] Please harken to my words O auspicious Sire.

"The warning was barely out of her mouth when the price of silver dropped from sixty to six dollars, overnight it seemed. I had borrowed heavily to buy precious metal and the bankers would not extend my loans. They had also taken a bloody bath. And the rich man whose wise lead we all followed? His losses were so great they threatened the banking system for the entire country and the government was forced to bail him out. But in the economic scheme of things, I was an monetary flea and not worth bothering about. The banks foreclosed, the sheriff's auction disposed of my goods, and I was forced to go on welfare. The decline was over agonizing months, drawn out painfully, and inexorably downward. Toward the end, a motorcycle gang, calling themselves the Sabeans,[185] raided my weakened estate, killed what was left of my servants, and slaughtered and roasted my one remaining milk cow. I had dreamt of the riches of Solomon and I got the plagues of Job.

"The preacher came by to console me and the girls. We all prayed together, and the preacher said: 'Gird up thy loins now like a man. Wilt thou also disannul God's judgement? Wilt thou condemn God that thou mayest be righteous? Then wilt I also confess unto thee that thine own right hand can save thee.'[186] And I used that right hand. I smashed the preacher in the face with it. And when he fell, I kicked him in the balls and drove them up into his groin. Then I started to kick in his ribs; managed to break most of them on his right side, too. I'd have killed the bastard if the girls hadn't pulled me off."

"You don't sound remorseful," Lemuel observed.

"That's what the judge said when he sentenced me. I told him the whole story. I explained to the judge that I had to do it to save my daughter's lives. It had finally gotten through to me that if I continued to worship your God that my beautiful daughters were going to die, like Job's first daughters." Frank tears streamed down Philip's face. "All I had left were my beautiful girls. Job may have been content with replacement sons and daughters and wives, but I wanted these daughters, whom I devoutly love, and I didn't want other daughters in exchange.[187]"

* * *

Lemuel reasoned with Philip. He told Philip that his apostasy was futile and explained to him that by turning against God he was still actually obeying God's will. He quoted Jeremiah: "O Lord, I know that the way of man is not in himself: it is not in man that walketh to direct his steps."[188] Then he explained how lying angels had been sent by the Lord to cause him, "'To err from His ways, (by worshiping Atargatis) and to harden your heart from thy fear.'[189] just as he had the Israelites before." And he cited Paul's speech on Mars hill: "God made the world and all the things therein…including Atargatis… and he giveth to all life, and breath, and *all things*…and the times and bounds of your habitation."[190] Then he reinforced his argument by quoting Isaiah: "I am the Lord, and there is none else, there is no god besides me: I form the light, and create darkness: I make peace, and create evil: I the Lord do all these things.'[191] So your apostasy is futile: even that is God's will."

He spoke of the girl's inheritances being…*predestined*…according to the purpose of Him who worketh all things.[192] And he spoke of God having…"*predestined* us unto the adoption of children by Jesus Christ according to the good pleasure of his will."[193] Lemuel spoke convincingly of the absolute power of the Lord and how the cosmos, and all in it, were created by Him, and for Him. "And He is before all things, and by Him all things consist.'[194]" And through it all Philip remained stoically impassive.

He began to make some headway when he asked Philip to consider his feelings toward his daughters. He explained that since God can never be understood, never seen, nor felt by human senses, that in place of the divine experience, God had given the humans love to tide them over until that glorious day…for God is love[195]."

Although Philip did not state his reason, he assumed that if he closed off all further intercourse with Lemuel that he would never see this incarnation of Atargatis again. His idol made flesh. He watched Abigail with the girls and could not bear to deprive them, and himself, of their fond companionship. "I'll consider what you've said," he replied.

Chapter 31

APART FROM THE MANIFEST BENEFITS PERMEATING THEIR SOULS by the Holy Spirit to do good works, the apostles received some additional perquisites that are hardly worth mentioning: the accommodations were top of the line, albeit a middle class line; the meals were cordon bleu quality; the flow of free spiritous liquors, wines and beers was unending; tobacco and other legal stimulants were freely available; the needs of their uncomely members were sated at will and without worldly inhibitions; there were no bills to pay, no time clocks to punch, and no heavy lifting; and their revels were regarded as sacraments.

The "Woodstock" like ambience was noised throughout the region, and it soon attracted several drop-in worshipers, but none were interested in becoming apostles and cleave to the rigorous conditions demanded of apostles. The concupiscence of many of these casual visitors was of the worldly variety and they and their lewd proposals were quickly rejected. One was found acceptable to the sacred synod, and his name was Didymous Judas Thomas. Judas's mother and father were Copts from Egypt, and the Gospel of Thomas is right beside the snoptic verses of Matthew, Mark, and Luke in their sacred writings.

Judas, James, Joses, and Simon were all brothers of Jesus, but Judas, according to the writings of the apostles, was Jesus' twin brother. Didymous means twin, and his parents named Jesus's twin brother, Judas Thomas. Twin in faith, and by blood to the Lord[196].

According to the Gospel of Judas Thomas, (and who should know our Lord's teachings better than his own twin brother) Jesus taught that in order to return to man's original sinlessness, one must separate from the world by "stripping off" the fleshly garment, and "passing by" the present corruptible existence. Then the disciple can experience the new world, the kingdom of light, peace and life.

According to the Gospel of Thomas, Jesus said, 'If you fast, you will give rise to sin for yourselves,' and in this Church of the Ethereal Evangelicals the table was always laden with succulent feasts, so there was little chance of iniquitous fasting. Neither did the appetites of their comely members lack satisfaction.

According to the Gospel of Thomas, the disciples asked Jesus, 'When will you become revealed to us?' and Jesus replied, 'When you disrobe without being ashamed, and take up your garments and place them under your feet like little children and tread on them, then you will see the Son of the Living One and you will not be afraid.'[197] The comportment of the missionaries conformed with these directives of the Lord too.

In order to avoid any associated odium attached to the name Judas, because of the treachery of Iscariot when he ordained Judas, Lemuel said that henceforth he was to be called the apostle Thomas.

This namesake of Jesus's twin abjured the ritual nakedness and adopted a distinctive mode of dress: a black slouch hat, tight black slacks, a black turtleneck sweater, a black cape with a high collar and flame red lining, and he wore a crucifix that was strangely fabricated. The cross arm was near the base and the little image of Christ was head downward. He had a thin, pencil-line moustache, parted his black hair in the middle, and slicked back tight to his head, and his sideburns were trimmed to sharp points.

Thomas usually took no part in the circle of love devotionals of the other apostles. The fishermen brushed him off rudely, the publican would tolerate his advances only after imbibing deeply of the liquid spirits, and Myles was secretly glad that Thomas had no interest in Esther and allowed occasional caresses. While watching the rest of the apostles during their devotionals, he leaned slightly backward with his left arm crossed over his chest, his left hand supported his right elbow, his right hand was held up to his chin with two fingers resting on his cheek, and his right eyebrow would rise cynically. Thomas doubted the orgies were sacred without the presence of a billy goat.

Of the women, he was only attentive to Abigail. His eyes followed her frequently and obsessively. When he occasioned to cross Abigail's path, and it was obvious that he went out of his way to do so, he would smile knowingly and bow curtly from the waist. Abigail thought his interest in her noisome, but she was always coolly polite.

He often uttered Biblical references to her: "Genesis, three, four;[198] Numbers, twenty one, nine[199]."

Since Abigail knew virtually nothing of the Bible, his message was opaque to her, so she joked with him by responding with a quarterback's call: "Hike!" Another time his message was, "Luke; eighteen, nineteen.[200]" She advised him to talk to either Lemuel or Myles if he wanted theological guidance. Her own responsibility was limited to terrestrial affairs.

Much to everyone's delight, Leila, Dagmar, Dolores, Gail, and their father Philip decided to join the group. Philip convinced the apostles that he was repentant, had been born again, and was willing to donate all his worldly possessions to the church. His only valuable worldly possession was the idol, Atargatis, but he reminded them that since God made all things, she would be acceptable as a work of art. He assured them he foreswore any superstitious beliefs about the goddess' powers to effect men's souls.

Although Lemuel was not entirely convinced of Philip's renunciation of idolatry, the other apostles convinced him that their mission needed Philip's daughters since they prophesied from the Holy Scriptures. They assured him that the Holy Spirit was speaking to them with unmistakable clarity. The apostles voted to accept Philip as an apostle and the girls as disciples. Abigail, Philip and the girls cleaned up their old camp, and Atargatis was brought back and set up in an unobtrusive corner of the courtyard.

The same spiritual stirring that arose within the apostles had not infused itself within the girls and they shied away from the laying on of strange hands. Instead, they sought out Abigail and were continually in her company.

Esther reacted to the little bronze goddess with ambivalence. Atargatis had been one of her competitors. In the ancient world Esther was forced to share the deified incarnation of eroticism and fertility with a whole pantheon of love goddesses: Ishtar, Inanna, Astarte, Aphrodite, Venus, Ashtoreth, and Isis, to name but a few. These sister goddesses of love were kinswomen of the temple prostitute sent to tame the bestial lusting Enkidu: the huge hairy monster the gods sent to menace King Gilgamesh's subjects. In the ancient Sumerian and Babylonian historical epics, the harlot made herself naked and welcomed his eagerness, and for six days and seven nights they lay together, and when Enkidu was grown weak, she led him like a mother and taught him the benefits of civilization. Esther could hold her own in that competition. She'd brought the most powerful king of the ancient world, Xerxes (Ahasuerus), under her control, hadn't she? And like Gilgamesh's beautiful harlot who tamed the beast and made the world safe for civilization, Esther had made Ahasuerus's empire safe for all the Jews from the Indus River to Ethiopia. But this little mermaid that looked so much like Abigail, had a strange attraction, virginity: mermaids have piscine genitalia and cannot conjoin in sexual intercourse. As she considered the mermaid's fish tail, she thought it was appropriate.

Esther thought her charms were being tested in some fashion and the presence of Philip's beautiful young daughters added to her quandary. She became competitively more seductive; her attire was more scanty; she frequently went topless or wore nothing at all; and Sadie, Spike, Magda, and Naomi all followed her lead. But Abigail, true to her demonic perversity, refused to compete and concealed more as the others vied in lasciviousness. Philip's girls followed Abigail's example.

Thomas showed no interest in any of the other women, but continued to shadow Abigail. During one of his contrived encounters with her, he whispered, "John 6:70."[201] But Abigail, being innocent of most scriptural knowledge, merely ignored Thomas's intuitive observation. Esther thought Thomas's interest in Abigail was a kind of demonic possession and in order to save him from the demon's clutches, invited him to move into the trailer she shared with Myles. Myles was happy for the intellectual companionship and assistance with domestic chores. Moreover, Thomas was not continually lusting for Esther's body. Except for Abigail, he was more of a man's man, and Myles occasionally indulged the variation. Thomas had been a bachelor all his life and acquired housekeeping skills for which neither Myles or Esther had much talent.

* * *

As the carefree missionaries became Adamite in their attire, and insouciantly more antinomian in religious activity, Abigail found herself cast into a weird role reversal. Normally she was indifferent to the bizarre behavior humans frequently exhibited. But she and Philip's daughters were fond of each other, and she became their companion and confidant. As though she were the headmistress of a mid-Victorian convent, and a staunch defender of conventional morality, she found herself saying, "Some inhibitions are good: they protect you from foolish mistakes."

The five of them were busily building a sand castle at the water's edge. It was nearly as tall as Gail. They chattered happily while they carved windows, dug a moat, and placed a slab of driftwood for a drawbridge. They made a circular donjon in the center courtyard, and Dagmar, as the tallest, made the crenelating around the parapet walls. They landscaped their structure with seaweed. When finished, they deemed it worthy of nobility.

Abigail was pleased that the girls were normal healthy youngsters when they were away from Scripture-spouting preachers. As the tide and waves moved in to wash their castle away, the five of them played in the surf. The girls feigned disappointment when Abigail refused to grow her fish tail for swimming. She would have complied, but there were other people on the beach and she thought it best to appear human.

The girls made a game of picking up shells to see if they could stump Abigail as to the name of the species. While they were playing this game, Leila mentioned casually that she thought it would be a good idea if she and Dagmar visited an obstetrician; they had both missed two periods. Would Abigail take them?

Naturally Abigail was surprised, and after making sure they knew what they were talking about, she asked if Philip was aware of their condition.

"Oh yes, and he's delighted," Dagmar assured her, and then added calmly, "He's the father of course."

The image of his nakedness when Lemuel and she first met Philip, and his caressing the two girl's bellies crossed Abigail's mind. He had hurriedly pulled on his pants for their benefit, not the girls', and she hoped that what she suspected at the time wasn't true, but it evidently was. Another thing she realized was that Philip was strangely indifferent to Esther's erotic exhibitionism and none of the other women excited his interest. And she saw that he was extremely protective and possessive of his daughters. No wonder. It wasn't paternal concern for the girls' virtue that caused his possessiveness; his daughters were his harem.

It certainly wasn't a unique situation. In her six thousand years of association with humans, she knew it was quite ordinary. She wasn't shocked, but she was disappointed. She had allowed herself to become fond of these humans and while this didn't change her affections, she knew that our modern culture would not be as forgiving or accepting. She said, "You girls know the Scriptures," and Philip purports to have returned to the church, and to cleave to Christian teaching. How could he have done this to you?" She didn't hide the concern in her face. In turn, Leila became distressed, and admonished, "Say, just what kind of girls did you think we were? Did you think that we might be with child by those dirty-minded boys at school? Or by some one night stand, some casual pickup? Just some dirty thing without love?" Her dark eyes flashed accusingly. "Playing the harlot in your father's house is a stoning offence, according to the Bible."

"But...but...doesn't the Bible say this is wrong too?"

"Of course not! Read any book in the Bible and you won't find any place where it's wrong. Saint Paul even recommends it where he says, 'If a man have a virgin, and she is past the flower of her age, and need so require, let him do what he will, he sinneth not. Let them marry.'[202] What we have together is love, and you're trying to make out that it's something dirty or blasphemous. Philip loves us and we love him, and for people that love each other, it's how you show your love."

The heterogenous rationalizations and regulations humans contrived regarding sexual matters had always seemed awkward and silly to Abigail. She liked little babies and children, no matter how they were conceived, but there seemed to be a practical side to this situation. She said, "Both of you are too young. You're still children yourselves."

Dagmar replied, "We're all old enough, but it was Leila and I who were the ones lucky enough to be blessed with bringing new life into the world, and saving Philip's seed.[203] Our mother is dead, and our brothers, and the Bible says to not cast your seed among strangers."

"You are not old enough! Gail isn't even thirteen."

Dolores corrected her; "The Bible says we're old enough. Gail passed the flowers of her age nearly a year ago."

"You're not married! It's against the law for fathers to marry their daughters."

"Oh yes we are. We're married in God's eyes. We prophesied to the preacher using Paul's words, and so he said the marrying words. That was before Philip turned away from the church and beat him up so badly."

Abigail's instincts were those of a nomadic Gypsy, and the law was usually the enemy. Government was a fraud; a *fashono;* a *gorgio fakement* invented by non-gypsies to restrict her freedom. It was a monolithic force to be outwitted, but she heard herself say, "There are laws...the government has laws to protect little children." But her asocial Gypsy nature would never permit her to report the incident to the authorities.

"We obey God's higher laws," Dagmar said with a bright smile.

Dolores gave her a superior look, and said, "I don't see a ring on your finger." Abigail knew they wouldn't believe that her association with Lemuel was chaste, and emitted a sharp frustrated snort. "And as for the law, Gail is old enough to marry in Massachusetts and California, so they agree with the Bible. Dagmar and I are old enough in eleven more states, and every state but three thinks Leila is old enough to marry. Do you think you are wiser that those governments?"

Abigail felt as though the sand beneath her feet were being undermined. The girls were cornering her, and like a trapped animal she snapped, "None of the states allow you to have sex with your father."

Then it was Leila's turn to contradict her. "That's not altogether true, Abigail. It depends on what you mean by having sex with your father. It's all a matter of degree. A father may hug and kiss his daughter in ways that would be unseemly if it were his son. Quite a few fathers dance with their daughters, and if a father did that with a son it would be considered wrong. The society corrupted with worldliness may frown on it, but there's nothing unlawful about a father and his family being nudists, where privacy permits. And no law prevents a nude father from dancing and hugging and kissing his nude daughter in the private. So what we are really talking about is...the degree of sexual contact permitted. It seems to us that nearly everything except penetration is permitted by the law...and the Bible permits that."

"O auspicious Abigail, we obey the higher laws of God. Not the worldly man-made laws. Dearly beloved friend, 'For why is our liberty judged by another's conscience; for if we by grace partake, why should we be evil thought of: for that which we give thanks.[204] We are made,

HOW THE GOOD TAILOR GOT TO HEAVEN 617

not after the law of carnal commandment, but after the power of an endless life.[205] We bring that to Philip, just as Lot's daughters brought to him[206]; and were sanctified by the omniscient, omnipotent God." She patted her own belly and nodded toward Dagmar. "Lot and his daughters were blessed with nations, Moab, and Amon. Without Moab there would have been no Ruth, and no house of Jessie, no David, and, 'Hath not the Scripture said, That Christ cometh of the seed of David.[207'] Who's to say who we carry for Philip? Our father, just like Lot, lost his home and his wife, and everything except his daughters."

The activities of the mission's apostles and the disciples, and the condition of Philip's daughters, ironically mocked Lemuel's solemn words about the Bible providing moral guidance for the humans, and she recalled his challenging outburst when he said, 'I'd hate to see what sort of rules you demons would create for them.' So far Lemuel had excused stealing, adultery, swindling, killing, and lying among the apostles, and Abe and Sadie's incestuous marriage. He accepted their swindling way of life as sacred to Abraham's covenant, and judging by what these girls were saying, he'd probably excuse father-daughter incest too. "The family that prays together stays together," came to mind, and she thought, *Well, at least they weren't hating their parents for Jesus*, but she kept the sarcasm to herself. Then she asked, "What kind of futures do you think you'll have?"

"We have put our faith in Jesus." Dagmar's face was aglow with conviction, and she added, "He will decide our futures for us."

Dolores, uncharacteristically enthusiastic, said, "We will devote our lives to doing good works for the Lord as missionaries with your church."

"Ouch!" The "your church" inference stung. Abigail tried to deny any responsibility by pointing out that she was not an apostle or a disciple, and that she was only in charge of terrestrial affairs. "And the world can be cruel. How would you support yourselves if you had to? Did you believe these missionaries are responsible people just because they proclaim their faith in God or because they're adults? They're not! Like all church people they're either foolish or corrupt, or even more dangerous to your fates...both. You may be out on your own some day, and how would you support yourselves...and your children?"

Little Gail spoke up, "O auspicious Abigail. It hath reached me that God hath chosen the foolish things of the world to confound the wise."

"Yes, so it seems," Abigail agreed with a shrug. Then she added, "People always get into trouble with their genitals and you're no different, my little friends. Maybe God made people that way to ensure that they remained foolish. I think God must have done it to reverse the effects of eating the fruit of the tree of knowledge of good and evil. When the libido is aroused, common sense evaporates, and all thoughts of good and evil disappear."

"Then, you don't condemn us?"

"Oh no...of course not. You're just human."

Then Leila surprised her. The reality of their condition loomed large, and she scolded her little sister, "Just because God chooses foolish, weak, despised, and base things is no reason for us to do so. Oh, Abigail, please tell us what to do."

Abigail could have reversed their condition as quickly as the undo button of a computer can cancel unintended ideas, but she said simply, "I can't."

Dagmar pleaded, "Please. Pretend you're our mother." Her cornflower blue eyes overfilled with glistening fluid and tears ran down her cheeks.

"Do you mean, pretend I was Philip's wife, and you were our daughters? If that were the case, I wouldn't be a very good person to ask because you would have made yourselves women in competition with me. My security would be undermined by my own daughters. I don't think I could decide fairly. I might even be so angry that I'd want to have Philip locked up and have your babies aborted for my own selfish reasons. No, in that case I wouldn't be a good person to ask for advice."

Abigail looked out across the water with the foaming surf washing her feet. The girls were standing behind her. Leila moved to her side, put her hand on Abigail's arm, and said, "It's not too late. We could have abortions. Please advise us Abigail."

Abigail put her arm across Leila's shoulder. She felt a strange stinging sensation in her eyes and a peculiar tight throb catch at her larynx, and she couldn't speak for a moment. She waited until she could make words with her tight vocal cords. "No, I can't," she insisted. It was all she could get out without breaking down in sobs.

Leila spun away from her, and spat out hotly, "You're a demon! You're not human."

"That may be true…but it doesn't alter anything. I still won't tell you what to do. I can't! " She knew Leila hadn't guessed how truly she spoke, but the epithet caused her to consider her own biases. As a determinedly proud virgin, could she understand? Was she upset because the girls were pregnant, because their father had made them pregnant, or was it because they were no longer virgins? Then she tried to see the situation from Esther's viewpoint. But Esther didn't have children. To her, children were the inconvenient by-products of eroticism. She said, "Consider this: no matter what I decided there would come a time when you'd hate me for it, and I don't want you to hate me. You and Philip are the ones who must live with the decision, and since he is *your* father, as well as *the* father, you must make him face this double reality, and this so-called church isn't reality."

"You'll have to decide between yourselves. There are too many out there who'll want to impose society's vengeance and call down the wrath of God, so to speak. If you ask a school councilor or your teacher, they'd be inclined toward whatever brand of social philosophy they happened to believe in or the pressures of the school board's guidelines. The law will only take the "public's interest" into consideration, plus the judge's personal prejudice. And as for the church, their concern is for souls, not lives. The minister is mostly afraid of the damnation of his own soul, and his advice would be from that viewpoint. And any of those options would probably land Philip in prison and you girls into the hands of the juvenile authorities. That wouldn't help anyone. As I see it none of you have lied, stolen, harmed anyone else, or committed murder. In fact you've done the opposite; you've created life. You've got to sit with Philip and have a serious and sober adult talk."

A solemn ambiance settled over the small group as they seated themselves in a small ring, each lost in their own thoughts. Then Lemuel appeared, walking from the direction of the encampment. He walked slowly and was reading the Bible which he held open before him. He approached the small circle, snapped the Bible shut, placed it under his arm, and greeted them warmly. He received half-hearted salutations in return. He looked around and asked, "Why is everyone looking so serious? It's a beautiful day. The sea is warm, the breeze is gentle, God's in His heaven, and all's right with the world."

"Just girl talk, Lem. Nothing you'd understand," Abigail replied.

"Of course I would. Just try me. As a minister, it's my job to guide troubled souls." He smiled, and presented the Bible with both hands. "Within this book is every answer to any and all of mankind's problems. It's all mortal men need to guide their lives. Put your faith in the Lord, be guided by His words, and you will find your answer."

Piercing glances shot back and forth between the women. There was a deep silence. A wave sighed a long angular curl upon the beach, and then another. Gail broke the grasp of angry anguish. She stood up and turned toward Lemuel. Then she took the Bible from his hand, slammed it onto the sand, and stamped it with her foot. "That's not the answer to anything! That's the problem with everything!" she cried out, her cheeks were wet with tears.

Lemuel staggered back from the outraged young girl, glared at Abigail, and accused, "This is your doing. You're corrupting them with your wicked worldliness. You've been turning them against the divine word, haven't you? I thought you were going to help with this mission."

"Lemuel! Shut up! If you don't shut up…well…do you remember Jonah?" Abigail sounded angry enough to carry out her threat. Then she said in a voice as cold as the Siberian express, "Pick up your book and come with me. These girls want to be alone to do some serious thinking right now." Then she asked them to tell her what they and Philip decided, and hinted that she might be able to help what ever they decided.

Lemuel muttered, "You're interfering with God's will again, aren't you?"

"How could I? Haven't you often said, 'The potter hath power over the clay.' If that's true, I'm just acting as an instrument of *His* will."

* * *

Abigail and Lemuel left the girls sitting in a tight little huddle, and as they walked back to the camp, she complained of the turpitude of the people she was forced to associate with since she'd taken up church work. She enumerated her many objections. "Your church members are all moral degenerates; amoral, semi-literate fishermen, one of whom has a foot fetish; their hooker girlfriends; a pair of con artists who thought they were joining a drug ring; a homosexual devil worshiper who wants to be doing Black Masses; a corrupt tax collector; a Bible scholar with satyriasis; a nymphomaniac; and several cases of incest. Not a single one comes from a normal household. The women are all whores, and the men use them like receptacles for their excrement. What next?" Then she muttered, "I hope none of the other demons ever find out about this. I'll be a laughingstock."

Chapter 32

ABIGAIL'S MOOD SOON CHANGED. OF MERCURIAL TEMPERAment, she did not dwell long on grave matters. Such things were of mortal concern and usually depressing; a macabre burlesque arranged for Yahweh's sadistic enjoyment. A divine comedy, yes, but it was black humor, and not the sort of thing to long occupy a pleasantly disposed demon. Long ago she had decided that the mortals were not to be taken seriously. First, when they persisted in obsequious adulation of the deity who confused their tongues at Babel, and again when they continued to worship Him after His genocidal flood. Then the gentiles acceded in the confusion ridden precepts of Christianity and elevated Yahweh above his station. She concluded long ago that their limited capacity to reason was eclipsed by their penchant to believe almost anything.

Furthermore, she had a nagging suspicion that the gods created humans to torment the demons, but she had to admit it was a nice touch of whimsy creating them, 'in our own image,' and 'a little lower than the angels.' If only they'd show a little bit of common sense.

And there was this nettlesome impulse she felt about the mortal's kids. In general, she liked them. When they were at play, such as building the sand castle with Philip's daughters, or playing a game of touch football or "One Knocker" baseball, or when their curious natures allowed them to examine the diversity of flora and fauna without theological assertions or drawing anthropomorphic parallels, or while they were still able to consider a straight shooting aggie to be more valuable than a baguette cut emerald of equal size, and when the things of wonderment were the balance scales in a grocery store, the magic of a magnifying glass, a box full of tools, or a basket full of sewing stuff. But when they developed past that age, someone ought to pinch their heads off. Of course if she had children of her own they would turn out perfect, and lately, she wished she were mortal just to prove the point.

Abigail laced her fingers together and pressed her flat stomach with the palms of her hands. She wondered what it was like to have another being inside her. She thought of the two pregnant girls and the problems they faced. She hoped she told them all the right things, but they were such trite things...well, sometimes the trite things are the right things. She had the power to snap her fingers and expel the reality, restore their virginity if they wanted, and even dispel their memories of the experience, but it was a puzzle. From her immortal point of view, all decisions were right decisions. It really made no difference.

Then she smiled at the irony of how Philip's celebration of the flesh, as a sacrament to an ancient fertility goddess, Atargatis, was justified by his daughters, and without having to shift deities, confirmed its propriety with the Bible. The only sin Philip was guilty of was having the wrong attitude. As they walked along, she slipped her hand beneath Lemuel's arm and he squeezed it against his side.

He looked down at her and asked what she was smiling about.

Her smile broadened into a grin, and she said, "Interesting religion you got there, Lem. Teaches people a moral code, you say? Gives them a sense of propriety, huh?"

"Oh most certainly. Without Biblical guidance, chaos would replace the rule of order."

HOW THE GOOD TAILOR GOT TO HEAVEN

Her grin became a chuckle, and she said, "I see. Chaos, like in those places where they worship false gods?"

"Exactly!"

"Or like in those places where they don't worship any gods at all?"

"What are you getting at? Are you trying to confuse me with your perverse little demon mind?"

She smiled and her green eyes flashed with merriment. Lemuel dropped her hand, hugged her, and gave her a kiss. "Stop teasing me, you little imp!"

She broke from him and darted into the water. She raised each foot exaggeratedly high, like a Tennessee walking horse, and made huge satisfying splashes in the shallow water. Lemuel had to quickly dart sideways to prevent from being soaked. Still laughing, she ran to him, grabbed his hand and pulled him toward the water. He quickly slipped his hand from hers, and she nearly fell over backwards into the waves. She returned to his side and took his arm once again, this time in both her hands, and they went on with their stroll along the beach. Each was lost in their own thoughts, and pleased to be alone together—it was their first time alone since Esther and Myles had joined them.

Then, hesitantly, as people do when presenting a delicate matter, she asked, "Lem, have you ever considered that you should find a mate for yourself? Now that you're mortal you can make love as they do, and you could have children. Wouldn't you like that?"

"Only if you were that mate." He hugged her, nuzzled her ears, nose, eyes and neck, and then gave her a long lingering kiss. "I've thought of it. It's been my constant companion ever since the forty days we spent in the mountains, ever since I saw you sunning on that rock by the swimming pond. In fact, I think I was subconsciously thinking about it when you were teasing me when we first met in that park in King Jamesburg. I think I loved you even before I became mortal. You've been in my thoughts constantly, and I love you fifty lifetimes worth." He bent to kiss her again, and she turned her head away.

"You know we can't. You must serve your God, and I have my own limits."

"Why? Because of this," and he shook the Bible angrily. Then he let it fall to the sand and drop-kicked it up the beach.

Then the clicking sound of someone snapping their tongue against the roof of their mouth carried across the beach. This was followed by an evil cackle, and a harsh voice said, "Shame, shame. That's no way to treat a King James authorized and autographed edition."

They were both startled and looked in the direction of the words. Seated on a driftwood log, no more than twenty-five paces away, a withered and sunken-mouthed angel with oystery eyes sat prodding something with a blackthorn crosier. It was Tomas, and he was probing into the gesticulating legs of a captured horseshoe crab. First he would let the crab creep a few inches away, then flip it over onto its back and poke into its soft underbelly with the tip of his crosier. Tomas cackled as the crab's long pointed tail, shaped like a triangular bayonet, waved blindly to defend itself. He allowed it to turn itself over, then he flipped it over again and repeated the prodding.

They approached the inquisitor general. He pointed at Abigail with his stick and said to Lemuel, "I see you're still cohabiting with that black slut. Why don't you take up company with something more pleasant, like a sow, so you could wallow in real slop instead of the slime she fills your head with?"

Abigail curtsied with mock deference and greeted him with honeyed tones. "Charmed to see you too, my dear old scabious pustule on the anus of a stink beetle, and how's your evil old fart[208]-breathed father?"

Lemuel picked up the Bible from the sand and looked for a verse. Then he poked it beneath Tomas'ss nose and said, "See what it says here? 'But I say unto you, Love your enemies.'[209] So doesn't that mean that we're supposed to love these demons? Aren't they supposed to be our enemies?" Then he added, "Well, I love this demon. I'm merely obeying the Good Book's instructions."

HOW THE GOOD TAILOR GOT TO HEAVEN

Tomas shoved the Bible aside, and snarled, "We'll see about that when we get your soul back in the empyrean. That should give you something to think about while you're luxuriating in mortal iniquity." He gave the horseshoe crab a vicious stab with his stick and skewered it. Then he tossed the beast with its wildly flailing legs toward the water. "We've wasted enough time on pleasantries. I'm here to give you instructions and tell you the good news." He was dressed in the new angelic fashion, but his zoot suit had a few custom details. The crown of his broad-brimmed hat was red and shaped like a cardinal's biretta, and at the end of his key chain was a key to the executive washroom. He swung the key slowly so Lemuel would notice, and said, "You'll be happy to know that your old catechist has been promoted to seneschal." He stood, brushed the sand from the seat of his trousers, and held out his scrawny pallid claw intending Lemuel to kiss his large signet ring. Lemuel ignored the honor. Tomas scowled and his eyes glittered in the shade beneath the broad brim of his hat.

Tomas was nearly a head shorter than Lemuel and he wanted his tutorial to ascend from above, so he motioned for them to be seated. Abigail sat on the sand and leaned back against the log, and Lemuel sat on the log beside her. She rested her head on his knee. Tomas snarled, "Just wait, my disobedient proselyte. Just you wait til you get back upstairs." Then he hissed, "Get away from that harlot!" Lemuel ignored the order, and brazenly placed his arm over her shoulder.

Tomas glared at the insolent couple. "You better pay more attention to your trade, Lemuel. You've been in the field for six months and I count only five souls on your account sheet."

"What? I make it to be sixteen,." Lemuel objected.

"You're splitting your account with Esther and Myles, remember?" and he cackled. A string of saliva dribbled from his chin as he drew his lips back and revealed his one yellow tooth and mottled gums in an evil smile. He cackled happily, "Of course there'll be two more when those two sows drop their piglets. You ought to give Philip all the encouragement you can. Get the other two knocked up. You might even lend a hand there if you've a mind to. We want every soul we can get. You better get cracking. Hide the birth control pills them other broody hens are using, put pin holes in their diaphragms and condoms." He wheezed with sadistic delight, "Hee, hee…you'd better get cracking. If you don't get your quota, you'll come back as an ordinary soul."

The threat no longer caused trepidation as it would have done before Lemuel realized he was in love with Abigail. He had borrowed fifteen million dollars from her and signed a promissory note obligating his soul to her for fifty lifetimes if he didn't repay the loan. His debt to Abigail made him free for the first time in his life.

The inquisitor general's mouth was working, but Lemuel heard no intelligible words. It was as though the muezzin's mouth were stopt with dust. The eternal light of the eternal city with its polish, order and discipline were nothing compared to the feel of Abigail's firm slippery flesh when they swam and played together.

Lemuel was brought to his senses, not by the moving finger of fate, but by a sharp blow to his shins from Tomas' black stick. "Pay attention!" the old angel commanded. "As I was saying, the zoot suit crusade is winning the hearts and minds of America and infiltrating the chic vanguard of the western nations. We thought it would be the brown-shirted goose steppers, but the zoot suits won. It took three generations, but we've finally brought the atheistic Bolsheviks down beneath a fusillade of jitterbugging, hip-hopping, jazz-playing, hard rock swinging, sex-crazed young people. There's hardly a commercial anywhere in the world that doesn't use rock-n-roll tempos to push their product. Every radio station blasts out the beat. It's only a step from the nostalgic to the metaphysical, and it all started with the zoot suits. As I told you back in the garden of Thelassar, 'give em what they want, *but get their souls!*' The Father, the Son, the Holy Ghost, and the Holy Tailor have ordained the sanctified ritual of rock and roll, and free love." He pulled his keychain from his pocket, and Lemuel noticed there was a square medallion at the end of Tomas' key to the executive washroom.

Tomas kissed the square and blessed Lemuel by making the sign of

HOW THE GOOD TAILOR GOT TO HEAVEN

the cross over Lemuel with the icon, and then kissed the square once again. Lemuel asked if he could examine the sacred object and Tomas permitted him to look at it. There was a small image of Christ on the cross, and beneath him, a tiny image of a tailor sitting cross-legged on the ground of Golgotha mending Christ's robe[210]. "Look at this!" he said, and showed the icon to Abigail.

"The Holy Tailor, of course!" Tomas replied.

"What Holy Tailor?"

"The one of the sacred square, of course. The one who draped obscene flesh ever since the world began, and mended the Lord's raiment. The one Jesus mentioned when he proclaimed: 'How much more will He cloth you, O ye of little faith.'[211] That He is the holy tailor."

Abigail was stunned. She finally managed to sputter, "T...ta ...tailor? Be serious, you crazy old man. You got a good tailor, only because Lem and I switched souls. I did it for a joke, and Lem wanted to get a decent suit."

"You may have thought it was a joke, but you forget—'the potter hath power over the clay.' And since we deified the tailor, you won't be getting any more souls at all. You don't get nothing, you little black beast."

Tomas withdrew a familiar flask from his pocket, and tossing it to Abigail said, "Here's your death warrant, slut!"

"What makes you think I'll drink it?" she asked, and stared hypnotically at the little bottle containing the waters of life.

"Because you can't get any more souls. What else is left for you?"

"Nothing you'd understand, you old goat. I'm free and you are bound by strict unquestioning obedience. I do as I please, and you must bend your servile old knees. You're an insignificant supernumerary in a tyrannical system where only sadists and masochists could find any joy, that is if your twisted overlords can ever find joy in tormenting. Did you really enjoy skewering that dumb brute? Have you ever found joy in fear? That's the correct term, isn't it? God-fearing? And isn't that what you sought to instill in that dumb brute—fear? As you fear Yahweh, that's how you wanted that crab to fear you. That's what your whole crock of a system is…layers upon layers of fear!"

Tomas swung his stick at her in a snarling rage. Abigail turned it into a serpent. It wrapped tightly around his arm, and it sank its fangs into his wrist. He winced in pain and fell to his knees pleading, "Get it off!"

Abigail reversed the spell and restored his stick. Tomas crouched like an angry cat, and raised his bony prehensile claw to attack the demon with all the sorcery at his command. Abigail lofted the heavy driftwood log intending to crush Tomas with it. Lemuel stepped in between the two combatants and ordered, "Put that log down, Abigail!" Then he faced Tomas, and said, "Calm down, Tomas. You'll get demerits for unauthorized hostile action in the neutral zone."

The more visible signs of rage subsided as Lemuel succeeded in convincing the antagonists to behave themselves. The two angels strode back and forth working off the adrenaline surging through their systems. Each warily eyed the other for a breach of the truce.

Lemuel asked Tomas what the other news was, besides adding another deity to the one God. "Okay, I get it. It's not a triangular trinity anymore. Now it's a quadrangle; the sacred square. So what's the good news?"

"That was the good news, you ninny! But you'll be happy to know that most of us have been promoted a level or two. I've been promoted to seneschal, replacing the angel Brigham, and I'm next in line to be made archangel. As you know, this position gives me some influence with the assignment commission. I could recommend that you get assigned to a cushy district with a lot of matured souls. Those accounts that are well-seasoned and accustomed to their obligations. You don't want to be chasing after green souls who'll try to shirk, do you?"

Lemuel said, "It may be a while before I'm free to return. I've borrowed a lot of money from Abigail to build the Tabernacle tent and if I can't repay it, she has a claim on my soul for fifty lifetimes."

"Don't be silly. You don't have to pay the devil."

"Oh yes. Yes I do. We signed papers and everything…"

HOW THE GOOD TAILOR GOT TO HEAVEN 631

"That's preposterous. That would never stand up in the Supreme Sacred Rota. Demons can forge anything. How could she prove she hadn't forged it? You weren't stupid enough to sign it in blood were you?"

Confession cleanses the soul and frees the conscience of its burden of sin, and Lemuel did feel strangely released from the grip of his inquisitor, as he confessed, "As a matter of fact we both made our bloody thumb prints over our signatures."

"Curses! How could you be so stupid? Look at the smirk on her face. Okay, everything isn't lost. A Tabernacle tent, you say? How much do you owe? A few thousand?"

"Fifteen and a half million," Lemuel said sheepishly. "I wanted an exact replica of the tent the Lord commanded Moses to make. There's a lot of gold, and silver..."

Abigail, chuckling, said, "Yahweh has some pretty expensive tastes. Don't blame Lemuel. If you're thinking of conjuring the money for him...well...I hope you're prepared to spend several months..."

Tomas was in a furious rage. He kicked the sand angrily, threw himself down and beat the sand with both fists. He sat up and roared at Abigail, "You rotten black slut! Drink your living waters. I dare you. I want your soul when you die. You'll wish you'd never been created..."

"Just as I said: fear! That's all you have going for you, you evil old curmudgeon. Don't blame Lemuel. Yahweh wanted all that expensive stuff. There was a time when he was satisfied with a rock or a mound of dirt for an altar. He was happy with a few simple sacrifices, firstlings of the flock, and that sort of thing. But after Yahweh's chosen people acquired a taste for opulence while they were in Egypt, all of a sudden he started wanting to be treated as an equal with the Egyptian gods. He had to have gold, and silver, and badger skins, and fine twined linens, and shittim wood. Did you know the shittah tree is extinct? Our contractor had to substitute acacia. Then if he didn't get his way, he'd send down famine, and plagues, and destroy the cities. If you didn't threaten these poor mortal simpletons, your cruel, petty little Yahweh would still be a minor demiurge among the gods."

Tomas shook his crosier at her, and yelled, "Liar! There are no other gods."

"I'm not the liar. Your God is the one who sends down the lying angels, remember? You forget, I've been down here the whole time, and I watched how you've manipulated and deceived the humans. You've stolen every bit of your theology from the other gods. When your Jews had multiplied enough to form tribes and populate cities, Yahweh figured out that all the other civilizations who worshiped other gods had laws. He copied their laws, most of which he stole from the Babylonian, Hammurabi."

Tomas sneered, "Our laws were much better than his laws. They were so good we picked up a few of their souls."

"No, you didn't convince them to obey; you forced them to obey. I've been talking to Esther. I know how she worked Ahasuerus over with the help of her pimp Mordecai. And I'll tell you something else: Esther feels pretty bad about the seventy-five thousand deaths she was responsible for, and she swears she won't go back. You've lost Esther."

"We'll see about that when she's on her deathbed."

"I like Esther, and I promised to help her stay on earth."

Tomas snarled, "You think you've captured two of our angels, Huh?"

"Oh, I plan to keep Myles, too," she said, and continued, "Then you stole another idea from the Babylonians. First you stole their laws, and then you stole the idea of having judges."

"Of course we had judges. If you have laws, you have to have judges. The humans always try to weasel their way around the laws."

"Listen, you old goat. Yahweh never had one single original idea. He was still copying the civilized nations when He decided the Jews should have kings…"

"Yeah, so what? If you're creating a nation, you've got to have a civil government. He had a lot of modern innovations, like the census. That was original. God ordered Moses to number Israel so He could see how many souls He owned."

HOW THE GOOD TAILOR GOT TO HEAVEN — 633

"Yahweh only did that because he wanted to brag about how important he was to the other gods. He hoped they'd invite Him to some of the better parties and spectacles. I'll bet He still didn't get invited though. He had some really nasty habits, like wearing his hat in the house, trying to discover the ladies' secret parts, and swearing in Yiddish."

Tomas snarled, "They had to pay attention to Him when David got to be king. David really lambasted the cities of the other gods. The Lord's armies slaughtered the Philistines by the thousands, obliterated the Ammonites, 'put them under saws, and harrows of iron, and under axes of iron, and made them pass through the brickkiln, and thus did he unto all the children of Ammon.'[212] This time when the tribes of Israel and Judah were numbered there were eight hundred thousand valiant men who drew the sword in Israel, and five hundred thousand fighting men in Judah. It took Joab, David's loyal general, his major-domo, and chief assassin, nearly ten months to take the census. And with a hundred and thirty thousand warriors at his command,[213] the Lord was getting to be very powerful."

Lemuel asked, "Why do those big doors on the Numbers building show David numbering Israel and not Moses? And why does one door on the building show Satan[214] commanding David to take the census, and the other door shows God[215] commanding him?"

"Because taking the census is a wicked thing. God punished David for taking the census by sending an avenging angel to spread the pestilence that killed seventy thousand men from Dan to Beersheba.[216] When you take a census it reduces a man's freedom. It forces him to acknowledge that he's a subject of the government. It makes him understand that he is property, his body is property, and even his soul is property, and they are all at the beck and call of the higher authorities. That's why we have the Numbers building. It's where we keep the records of every soul that belongs to the Lord. And it doesn't matter what they call Him: Allah, Lord, Yahweh, Jehovah, or Christ…His soul belongs to us. Those doors show the dual nature of God. He creates both the good and the evil. That's why we get the Satanists. It's all the same establishment."

Lemuel was confused. "You mean God punished David for doing what He had ordered him to do?"

And Abigail snipped, "I told you so. Yahweh's a loony; a paranoid schizophrenic. He's a liar and a cheat, and as crazy as Nero." And she added, "He punished David by killing seventy thousand Israelites. Wouldn't you call that crazy? If he wanted to punish David, all he had to do was to send Uriah back to Bathsheba."

"Think so, eh? Well we were after bigger things than soap opera theatrics. We were becoming a powerful force in that part of the world. The other nations began to merge into empires for their mutual protection. That caused a lot of confusion among the local false gods. They were losing souls to the bigger gods who weren't really gods at all. Gods like Marduk, and Baal, and Ashtoreth. The smaller gods formed a loose association: the Astral Fraternity of Lares, and the Celestial Incarnate Omnipotents—the AFL and CIO—I'm sure you've heard of it. Anyway, they had some unworkable scheme to pool all the souls, and portion them out according to need, importance of purview, and I seem to remember something about seniority. Can you imagine? Seniority! Some shamanistic animist deity from the Olduvai Gorge would be entitled to souls. They invited us to join their union. Naturally, we wouldn't have any part of it."

Most of this was new to Abigail. She, having been forced onto the world with the rest of the fallen angels long before any of this occurred, was uninformed about the politics beyond the ninth celestial orb since her departure. Abigail was entranced as Tomas unfolded the saga of Yahweh's rise to power. She poked Lemuel in the ribs, and whispered into his ear, "I didn't know about that. Did you?"

He whispered back, "Shush…Yes, of course I did. It wasn't just David that got punished. I was on avenging angel duty spreading the pestilence and they didn't know who gave the order, so they demoted me to guardian again." He put his finger up to his lips signaling her to be quiet because Tomas was still talking.

Tomas had been overtaken with pedagogic fever and he paced peripatetically while instructing. He paused and pointed his staff at his students, and said, "Silence! You're disrupting the class!"

Abigail started to speak, and Tomas barked, "Raise your hand if you want to be recognized."

"You old buzzard! I'm not your acolyte. I was going to ask why Yahweh didn't go along with the others. It sounded like a very sensible solution to me."

"Because the others are not gods, dummy! Besides, it would be contrary to the tenets of the unseen hand's laws regarding competition and free enterprise."

Abigail clapped her hands and giggled. She taunted mischievously, "Tomas! You're a genius. I do believe you've created another god, an even higher god!"

Tomas shook his blackthorn crosier at her, and attempted to persuade her with volume. "There's only one God!" he shouted, and added, "the Father—the Son—the Holy Ghost—and the Holy Tailor!" He swung his key chain in great circles, and averred solemnly, "The Sacred Square!"

"Well you could include this unseen hand of competition in your group and call it the Holy Quincunx. You could have the Father, the Son, the Holy Ghost, the Sacred Tailor, at each corner of the quincunx, and the unseen hand of the market in the center. That would really go over big in America.

Tomas became apoplectic with rage. Livid blotches mottled his face and animal sounds welled from deep in his throat. He began to hyperventilate, and Abigail became concerned that he might explode. When angels explode it could easily be mistaken by mortals for a hydrogen bomb, so she tried to calm him down. She got up and put her arm over the old angel's shoulders, patted his chest with her other hand, and said a lot of soothing words to him: "There, there, there now. Calm down." Lemuel also came to Tomas' aide. They both led him to the log and seated him, and they sat one on each side of him.

Abigail patted his hand and continued to say soft soothing things.

When his breathing became normal, she said, "I was only fooling. Why don't you tell me what happened after those other gods, which we all know are not really gods at all, formed their organization? I'd really and truly like to hear about it."

"No! You just want to poke more fun at me."

"Oh no, I wouldn't do that." She sounded like the very model of sincerity. She said sweetly, " If I could understand what happened, maybe I'd be convinced to drink the waters of life. Then I can become mortal and get into Heaven as an ordinary soul. Wouldn't you like that?" she asked.

"You might? Really?"

"Really."

Although Tomas assumed the guise of a wizened old man for theatrical purposes, underneath he was just like all the other sons of God. As seneschal he had special privileges, and he could request specific souls to attend him, and usually the request would be granted. He imagined Abigail as his personal servant; washing his feet with her tears, and drying them with her hair. He wore a twisted smile as he said, "Why sure girly. I'm sure you'll be impressed with the cleverness of our scheme."

"First of all, we had a real problem with name recognition. There were many mortals all over the world who had never heard of us. To most of them, a Jew was just another Arab with funny hair styling. The AFL and CIO was going great, so we sent a few angels down in mortal guise and they started to spread rumors among the mortals. We spread the word that there was a God who'd work cheap. We told them that they didn't need all those expensive temples and sacrifices. And we offered them something they'd never heard of before: freedom. Oh, we harped on that! 'Freedom! Freedom! Freedom!' was heard everywhere. Of course it was a lie, but we realized that no matter how big the lie was, if you repeated it often enough, the mortals would believe it."

"I think it's called propaganda, union busting, and scabbing," Abigail observed.

HOW THE GOOD TAILOR GOT TO HEAVEN — 637

"It wasn't as successful as we hoped. We had more converts when we forced them with our armies. The stupid mortals were still worshiping their false gods, and some of our people were lost to some of the more lubricious enticements of their goddesses.^{217} So we had a convention that was attended by every tenured angel and all of the higher orders. It's a shame you were a probationer Lemuel. You'd have enjoyed rubbing elbows with the mighty and the illustrious. Even the seraphim and the cherubim listened to us ordinary angels, and chatted with us as though we were just as good as they were. I still get goose pimples when I think about it."

After several moments lost in fond memories, Tomas continued, "What we decided to do was to find out just what it was that appealed most to mortals. Do you remember when we sent you down to ask all those questions? You thought it was stupid at the time, didn't you?"

"Okay, so you took a market survey. What was the result?" Abigail asked.

"We found that no matter what they had done, they would always point an accusing finger at someone else who, they said, had done worse. And they all wanted to be 'understood' and 'forgiven.' Their excuses ranged from the nearly clever to the incredulous, and no matter how scurrilous a bastard the mortal might be, every one of them wanted to be loved. We knew that the other gods always assumed an adversarial position with the threat of retribution if they weren't placated. We had always used the same technique, but we added a caveat. It was a new idea. Their iniquities could be absolved by heaping their sins on a scapegoat, and they would be loved and forgiven if they obeyed our laws. It's true we took most of the laws from the pagan code, but we added a lot of dietary prohibitions and absurdities, like circumcision, to make the Jews think they were unique. Clever, huh? Still, we had absolutely no name recognition. That's when we took our big gamble. We knew we'd lose a lot of souls to the false gods, but we had big plans. If it worked, we'd get all those souls back again and all of the infidel's souls as well.

"We caused the diaspora. 'They shall know I am the Lord, when I shall scatter them among the nations, and disperse them in the countries.'[218] First we caused the Jews to err,[219] and then to punish them for their sins. We sent a lying angel to Zedekiah, and caused him to prophesy a lie to the people. And we delivered them into the hand of Nebuchadrezzar king of Babylon.[220] We knew they were a stiff-necked people and even if most of them worshiped the heathen gods, there would remain a faithful core of souls dedicated to the Lord. It didn't matter what we did to some of them. We caused famine, and pestilence, and slaughtered them with the sword, and they worshiped us all the more. So we dispersed them throughout the Mediterranean and Persian Gulf region. It's a shame we didn't have enough to cover India and the rest of the Orient. It was a brilliant plan, and all of the other gods laughed at us, but what they had forgotten was that mortals talk with each other. Even with their slaves! That's how the divinity of the Holy Tailor was spread to America: in the holds of the slave ships. It started simply. We sent in the negress slave, lying angel Tituba, to establish witchcraft in Salem, and this raised fear in the hearts of the pious. They established the reformation here in America and segregated the blacks as unworthy. The segregation allowed them to develop their jungle music as jazz, and it became a powerful religion with the zoot suiters. But I'm getting ahead of myself."

"Enough Jews clung to their belief to convince some of the other humans that there might be something to it. As I taught Machiavelli when I was the inquisitor general, men will change their kings with the hope of bettering their circumstances. So after implanting the notion of benevolent loving god among the foreigners, we brought the whole bunch of Jews back together in their promised land."

"Wow, that was risky." Abigail sounded impressed, and that pleased Tomas. She leaned back supporting one knee with her fingers laced together beneath her kneecap. "The usual practice is to test market your product in some small but representative region. It should be a small area that's typical to the demography and the cultural tastes of your

HOW THE GOOD TAILOR GOT TO HEAVEN — 639

prospective customers. But you really went out there and blanketed the whole market? My, my."

"Well, mostly it was the Middle East, but we did send some as far off as Ethiopia."

"Yeah, that sounds more plausible. How long did you leave your product on the shelves? And if you were going to all that trouble to saturate the market, why did you reverse the scheme? Why bring them back together again?"

"That was the most beautiful part of the plan." Tomas rubbed his old gnarled hands together. "We knew the true faith would become adulterated with impure beliefs. After all, we'd only left seven thousand faithful Jews behind,[221] to mind the store, so to speak, and they were becoming discouraged. This went on for several hundred years, and even the most stiff-necked began to have doubts. So anyway, you know how a big community project, like a new football stadium, unites the public? Well, that's what we did. Our project was called the Second Temple and the idea even impressed King Cyrus. Besides, he was getting fed up with the Jews holding all the cushy jobs in his empire. That was Esther's contribution to our success. But Cyrus let the Jews return to Israel—or, to be more accurate, threw them out of Persia—and they brought with them a wide variety of ideas from these other cultures. Then we established a commission to sort through all the notions and beliefs to see which had the most usable properties."

"That's called 'eye appeal' or 'marketability,'" Abigail posited. Then she asked, "But how did you get so much diversity to coalesce?"

Tomas' vigor returned and he jumped up and danced a few jitterbug steps. Sand flew and his baggy, zoot suit trousers flapped around his spindly legs. He cackled, "That was the simplest thing of all. We had them find a scroll in the ruins of the old temple." He clapped his hands and laughed as though it was the funniest joke ever told. "Oh! You should have seen those priests scurrying about, wringing their hands, pulling at their beards, and tearing their robes. 'Oh we've been doing it wrong all these years,' they cried. Hee! Hee! Hee! They cried and wailed, and we roared with laughter. I still have to laugh about it. All those long worried faces…heh, heh."

"What about the Jews that didn't come back? There must have been a lot of them."

"Oh, you mean risk losing their souls. No way, dearie! Every time they took a leak they were reminded to whom their souls belonged."

"Okay, but how did you get from there to Christianity and Islam?"

"I'll admit that was a bit more difficult. Some of those pagan rites were very attractive to the humans. We had to suffer a lot of humiliation from the AF of L, & CIO. Their believers controlled everything from Lisbon to the Caspian Sea, and from Scotland to the Sudan, but we had our Jews scattered throughout their territory. Usually they were low key about their practices. Most of them avoided infant sacrifices and such, but their adamantine stiff-neckness made some of the heathens question a few of their own ideas. These doubts were all we needed for the time being. Besides, we were having our own problems with 'thermidor' right there in the Holy Land. It was a frothy mixture of beliefs. The contention between the Essenes, Sadducees, and the Pharisees only hint at our problems. That's when we decided to play our trump card."

"You'd be surprised how hard it was to find some angel willing to make the sacrifice. Finally we got some bumpkin with more ambition than common sense. God! He was stupid. He couldn't make one simple statement without contradicting himself ten minutes later. We had him memorize a whole lot of parables, taught him how to deliver them as though they were profound wisdom, and hoped it would handle the problem. Then we made the switch."

"Switch? What do you mean, switch? Isn't there supposed to be something about a virgin birth here?" Abigail searched Tomas' face for an indication of mendacity.

"Lemuel! Don't you require Bible reading of your disciples? That girl…what's her name…?"

"Do you mean Mary?" Lemuel answered.

"Yeah, that's the one. She got herself knocked up by her cousin's

HOW THE GOOD TAILOR GOT TO HEAVEN 641

husband, Zacharaiah. We had a hard time talking her husband, Joseph, out of having her stoned. Anyway, she had Judas Thomas and Jesus. When Jesus grew up, the Lord met him on the mountain top and gave him his instructions. It could have just as easily been Judas. Read your Bible, girly. You may have to do a little reading between the lines, but it's all there."

Tomas' wild story came very close to the gossip she and Esther had exchanged, but Abigail wanted to know why it took forty days and forty nights on the mountain. Couldn't Yahweh offer him the world?

"No! Of course not. There were all those other false gods. They might be false gods, Zeus, Odin, Ahura Mazda, and even Isis, but they were very powerful gods. It took our angel forty days and forty nights just to work up the courage to drink the waters of life and become mortal. And he had to learn all those beatitudes, and parables."

"All right, so it took your angel forty days and forty nights to learn all that stuff and work up the courage to drink his living water. What about the other one, the Prophet Mohammed?"

"Well, after they saw what happened to Jesus, no angel would volunteer for that duty again. It took us six hundred years, the promise of a luxurious mortality, a peaceful death in bed in his old age, and all the fame that goes with being a best-selling author before we could find a willing spirit."

Tomas' contempt for the humans disgusted her. Worse, was his naked ambition. Just because they were a little lower than the angels, and just because they were gullible simpletons, was no reason to bully and cozen the dim-witted creatures. As a Gypsy, Abigail had cozened many humans herself, but that was before she learned to conjure money. It was a matter of her personal survival. Tomas cheated them for the benefit of his bosses and the reward of a key to the executive washroom. Somehow she expected the Ethereal Establishment to have more compassion toward its faithful believers. Heaven had the same merciless environment as the, anything-for-a-buck, mercantile world. She thought, *Oh well, Thy will be done, on earth as in heaven. But I don't know how much of this cruelty and immorality I'll be able to take. If Lemuel doesn't see the horror of it all—I'll have to leave.*

During Tomas' dissertation, Lemuel doodled idly in the sand with a stalk of straw. From time to time he glanced up sheepishly, as though asking Abigail to not judge every angel by Tomas. He knew her well enough to know she was nearing her toleration limit. Before this confrontation with Tomas, she told him what she thought of the apostles, and that she was getting tired of associating with the low-life crowd the church attracted. Now Tomas was adding to her disgust with religion, and if she became angry enough, she might tear up his IOU and walk away from the whole mess. Would she make him choose between her and his vocation? He realized he liked the idea of being obligated to her for fifty lifetimes.

She asked, "By the way, I've always wondered why Yahweh allowed Jesus to be crucified? At the end Jesus thought Yahweh had forsaken him."

Tomas sneered, "It's very simple, dearie. We did that to prove to you liberals that humans cannot be trusted to make decisions for themselves. Jesus preached to the multitude about peace and love, fed the multitude fishes and loaves, performed miracles for them, healed them, and even managed to convince them that he was the Son of God, but when he was imprisoned and about to be crucified, and Pilate offered to free a prisoner of their choosing, they chose to free the thief and murderer: Barabbas. There you have it, toots—democracy in action!" Tomas smirked. Then he crowed, "You've been here all along. Have you ever known the people to make the right choice? Don't they always vote against themselves? That's why we rule with such an iron hand. To quote John Winthrop, one of America's Pilgrim fathers, on the subject of democracy, "It would bring the government from being a mixed aristocracy, to a mere democracy…the meanest, and worst of all forms of government.' We agree with the Puritan fathers. An American oligarchy of financiers will rise one day to relieve these mortals of their oppressive democracy. Their leader will be hailed as a great benefactor, or a great something or other. And the politically incorrect will be put away so they can't adulterate these *United* States with perverse thoughts."

Turning to Abigail, Lemuel thought she was smiling in some twisted fashion, but then he realized she was seething with rage. If Tomas was right, there would be no place in the world for Abigail's individuality; her feminine delicacy; her sense of self worth; her pride. Everyone's mind, body, and soul would belong to the establishment and the people would be like a band of myrmidons, or a savage tribe. The mission of the Ethereal Evangelicals was the future. Angry tears traced shiny streaks down her dark cheeks and she turned her back on both of them. Lemuel was at her side in an instant and held her head against his shoulder. He kissed both of her eyes and brushed away her tears. Then he put his arm around her and led her away.

Tomas yelled after them, "Come back here! I'm not finished instructing you yet, Lemuel."

Lemuel turned and glared at him, and said, "Oh, you're through instructing me, all right. In fact, you don't even exist." He raised his hand, snapped his fingers, and in that instant Tomas disappeared.

He was too concerned about Abigail's misery to be startled, and he led her back to the driftwood log where they sat and watched the scurrying sandpipers and sanderling. The small flocks flew like wind-driven leaves out over the waves, and returning, swooped back to the shore to resume feeding just ahead of the sea lambent sand.

Chapter 33

THE REGULAR CADENCE OF THE WAVES WASHING UPON THE shore beguiled A false belief in a rational universe. What was, will be, they seemed to say as the gods mocked Abigail. All mortal sins were forgiven. There were no more souls in hell; they had all gone to their reward, which was an eternity of gainful employment, or they were inducted into the armies of the Lord. The angels were free to go about their duties guiding mankind toward God's predestined grand design without demonic obstruction. When Yahweh claimed purview over both the good and the evil, the only souls left to the demons were the good tailors, and now even the tailors were taken away.

The mergers and acquisitions as the early gods incorporated their territories and markets were all hostile takeovers and required human blood to be sacrificed. When you're creating empires, sacrifices must be made. Zeus, CEO of the Greek god's Olympus Corp., conquered the Egyptian gods along with their dead souls, and then both territories and souls were taken over by the Roman gods whose CEO was Jupiter. In the ensuing down-sizing, Zeus was pensioned off with a golden parachute. Some of the lesser gods were given new names, and retained under the new management. Cleopatra managed to find a niche for Isis among the Romans. The Germanic Wotan & Company never quite succeeded with its hostile takeover of the Scandinavian Odin Inc., but their constant battles weakened both companies. When Yahweh moved in with his mighty Christian Crusade Corp., both fell in a river of blood. The souls of Valhalla and Asgard were a welcome addition to the armies of the Lord. Yahweh allowed the appropriated lesser deities to be retained to name the days of the week, and some of the months. The gods of the Midddle East were not easily conquered by a reformulated Jew, and then the Ethereal Establishment recalled that Abraham had two sons. The scimitars of the Ishmaelites soon brought the true faith to those infidels.

Although Tomas was gone, he left a memento of his visit, a reminder that he existed: the small flask of living waters. It was half-buried in the sand at Abigail's feet.

For the moment there was only the birds, the sea, the sand, and the rustle of the dune grass as they sat together on the log. Abigail thought it was evidence of the unity of their souls when Lemuel had the courage to dismiss Tomas and cleave to her. But she wanted more. She wanted him to disavow the entire Ethereal Establishment just as he had rejected Torquemada. She noticed the flask at her feet, picked it up, and studied it thoughtfully. "What do you think I should do with this?"

Lemuel knew the flask contained life, but also death. The consequences of mortality deluged his thoughts. He saw her as the personification of perfection, and he exclaimed, "Pour it out!" Fearful that she'd even consider drinking it, he reached for the flask, and said, "Don't get any weird notions. This one's irrevokable and I want you to stay just as you are...forever."

"I think I'll keep it." She opened the flask and sniffed it. "It smells just like ordinary water. Maybe Tomas was playing one of his sick jokes."

"Who?"

"Tomas, you know Torquemada, the inquisitor general, the angel you made disappear. How'd you do that? We terrestrial angels don't have the power to make ethereal angels disappear. Do you think it's possible that mortals can do something we angels can't do?"

"What are you talking about? Torquemada died in the fifteenth century."

She was surprised by his absolute denial. "Are you going senile, already? Of course he exists. Evil is real. And to tell the truth, I'm getting fed up with excusing every deviant and degenerate that comes along just to fulfill your quota of souls. Doesn't your company require some semblance of rectitude for its believers or honor by its agents? Don't you think people should learn to take responsibility for their actions instead of blaming some supernatural power for controlling their acts? It isn't the devil that gets into them, it's your god—Yahweh. Your Bible lessons have taught me that much."

Their conversation was interrupted by the sound of an engine laboring and firing irregularly. Turning in the direction of the sound they saw an old dune buggy approaching. It was a made over Volkswagen Beetle with the fenders cut out to make room for its enormous balloon tires. All the glass was removed and it was painted in psychedelic colors: irregularly meandering stripes of orange, and purple, and red, and black coursed like zebra stripes all over the body. The buggy stopped and the driver came over to them.

"Iss this the vay to Meheco?" he asked.

Their interlocutor was a man of moderate height with a fair complexion, and although well-fed, not fat. He could have been any well-preserved age above sixty-five. He exuded self-confidence like a successful stock broker. His hands were well-groomed, clean, and uncalloused, with polished nails. He wore a dark blue, serge, double-breasted suit with a thin pin stripe and a vest. His shoes were black highly-polished oxfords, and he wore a slate blue Homburg hat, which he tipped respectfully for Abigail. His salt and pepper hair was brush cut, and he wore a monocle in his right eye with the ribbon fastened to his lapel.

The Volkswagen was cluttered with cardboard boxes and suitcases that appeared to be hastily packed, then tossed in a jumble into the front and rear seats. Abigail answered his question, "Well, not exactly to Mexico. This island ends before you get to the border, but a few miles down you can cross over the new bridge onto the mainland and there is a border crossing at Brownsville. You can get Mexican insurance and everything you'll need there."

"Vell, dot's vunderful. Iss dere a fishing village about? I chust love fishing, perhaps charter boats?" he asked, smiling pleasantly.

Abigail nodded, stumbled through the name, "Port Isabel," and looked questioningly at Lemuel.

Not even Lemuel could miss what was so obvious, but he did not know why this fine looking man was trying to get out of the country. He certainly didn't look like a criminal, but this man was obviously on the run. Exuding ministerial comfort and sincerity, he said, "I'm a Christian minister and I'm used to hearing people's problems. You seem like a man burdened. Would you care to share your troubles with me? The load is lighter when the burden is shared."

The man responded with an overly cheery smile as his gestures became nervous and agitated. He said, "Broblems? I haff no broplems. Chust a vacation, an extended veekend, undt a bit of fishing."

Lemuel nodded, but his expression was skeptical and he commiserated with the stranger, "The world is filled with suspicion, fear, and envy, and even a fine person like yourself can be falsely accused. One slight deviation from the rigid worldly code of conduct and they want to put you in jail, and make you defend yourself." Then he disclosed a personal confidence. "I'm going to tell you a story about how wrong the masses can be. Actually, I'm on the run. There's a warrant out for me for a heinous crime, but I am completely innocent of the charge. They want me for child molestation. All I did was to try to save their souls…"

"That's true," Abigail said, adding, "The only thing he's guilty of is folly, and perhaps guilelessness. He has a tendency to trust everyone." She wondered if he wasn't making the same error again.

"Yess. I know vhat you mean. Ve trust, undt den because ve trust, ve trust dair inzstitutions, undt de orders of our leaders. Den, chust because ve haff been good Chermans, ve are pursued. Der Fuhrer vas right: bolitics iss evil! Untrustworthy in der hands of der beoble. Undt now, dose Chews are coming after me. Ve must haff a new vorld order."

"How true. If people would follow the Biblical guidelines they could make wise decisions. But since they do not, some leader should arise to make them follow the Christian code of morality, as prescribed in the Holy Book. The Bible is the only truly moral code. Jesus is the answer." Then Lemuel asked, "Are you a Christian, sir?"

"Lutheran."

"Yes, that would be natural, of course. But do you practice your religion?"

"I thought I did, but my religion deserted me vhen I needed it most."

"When was that?"

"Vhen ve vass being overrun by der atheistic Bolsheviks, undt ven der so-called Christian nations allied themselves mit atheistic communists. Dhey shouldt haff joined mit uns to stamp out der anti-Christ, der evil empire. As history shows: Gott iss mit uns."

Abigail instinctively identified with the world's most persecuted populations. The Gypsies were her favorite outcasts, but all forms of unjust persecution distressed her, and she wondered what appropriate torment for this Nazi would repay his crimes. She considered transporting him to Tel Aviv. Then she wondered what awaited the souls of the Nazis when they arrived in the heaven of a Jewish god.

Lemuel agreed with him. "Yes, that's true, but God is in the process of rectifying that error now. One by one the atheistic totalitarian nations are falling to the forces of the godly. The Lord works in mysterious ways. Mortal life is short so it is easy to lose sight of the broad reach of the hand of God, the great architect of the universe, as He directs mankind's fate. People thought the Nazi holocaust was evil at the time, but because of it, Israel has been reborn."

One sensed the man's brain working. He removed his monocle and polished it with his neatly folded handkerchief. Then replaced it in his eye. "I never thought ve ver evil, der Juden ver evil, but I never thought of it as Gott's vill. Dot's very interesting."

"Oh yes, these things are all predestined according to the purpose of Him who worketh all things after the counsel of His own will.[222] And we know that all things work together for good to them that love God.[223] Whatever you did it was an act of God's will and it was all for the best."

"Zomtink bodders me Reverend; Vhy vas itt dot der Christian nations attacked uns? Dey shouldt haff helped uns."

"Perhaps it was because you allied yourself with a heathen nation, the Japanese, who bombed us at Pearl Harbor. The Americans are a devout people, but the Japanese worshiped false gods. In God's eyes, worshiping false gods is much worse than not worshiping any gods. The Bible tells us, 'He hath concluded them all in unbelief, in order to have mercy upon all.'[224] So if the Russians did not believe in any god, it is by God's will and God will forgive them. But the Japanese worshiped false gods and that is an abomination and extremely offensive to the Lord. They were not qualified to receive His mercy. What did you do in the war?"

"I vas a captain in vun off der labor camps. You know, you beoble in der vest do not understand vat dey vas all about, even today. Der Chews haff brainvashed you. Doze camps ver a force for goodt. Der Chews vheedled, undt connived, vile der Christians did all der vork. Undt der Chews corrupted der young beobles. Dey vas immoral, look behindt every piece of smut undt you find der Chews. Ve vas teaching dem der value of vorking for dare bread. Ve had an iron arch mit a sign, '*ARBEIT MACHT FREI*' over the camp entrance to teach der Chews, der Bolsheviks, undt der Gypsies der value of hardt vork. Undt I am glad you understand dat ve vas doing Gott's vill."

Lemuel agreed, nodding solemnly. "It would have been sinful to disobey your superiors. 'The powers that be are ordained of God.' To disobey would be blasphemous. God does not shrink from wholesale slaughtering, His Holy word records many instances. And as for the charge that you were committing genocide, that's absurd. The Jews were

HOW THE GOOD TAILOR GOT TO HEAVEN — 651

all over the globe, and there's no way you could have killed them all, any more than the Jews could kill all the Philistines. The Lord's ways are beyond human understanding. For example, the Lord sent the angels to help Joshua destroy all the inhabitants of Jericho, save the harlot Rahab and her family[225]. The Lord commanded Joshua to enslave the Gibeonites [226], and you were only repaying the Jews with equal measure. The Lord held the sun motionless in its path so there would be daylight enough for Joshua to slaughter all the Amorites.[227] And the Lord approves of genocide. He hated Esau and even Esau's children, the Amalekites, so much that he told Moses: 'I will utterly put out the remembrance of Amalek from under the heaven.'[228] In the battle Moses watched from the hillside. If Moses held up his hand Joshua prevailed; if he put his hand down, Amalek prevailed. When Moses grew weary and his hands grew heavy, Aaron and Hur held up his hands for him until the Lord allowed the sun to set. Joshua discomfited Amalek and his people with the edge of the sword. The Lord approves of genocide and wholesale slaughter. Some Jews even talk of a 'final solution' regarding the Palestinians today. It's amazing Christian people regard it as evil, and at the same time claim to believe in the Bible. It's God's will. When David drove the Ammonites through the brickkilns of Rabbah[229], how was that any different from the Nazis putting Jews into gas chambers? Except possibly more painful for the Ammonites..."

While Lemuel justified the Holocaust with the Bible, Abigail began to fade.

Lemuel didn't notice that Abigail was becoming transparent, and he stood, embraced the German, and directed him to his mission where he assured him he would find sanctuary. "I'll be along and introduce you to the apostles," he said.

Abigail disappeared completely.

He turned to receive her consent and was astounded that she had disappeared. He looked around and there was no trace of Abigail anywhere. "Where did she go? Did you see where she went?" Lemuel asked the German.

He responded, "She vas a Gypsy, vas she not? Dey're notoriou tricksters, undt ve are all better rid of dem."

* * *

Lemuel ignored the German. Abigail had disappeared. He searched frantically for her up and down the beach. There wasn't so much as a footprint in the sand to show where she'd gone. There was no trace of her anywhere, and he began hunting through the through the tall dune grass. He called her name, but there was no reply. He shouted over and over, and panic raised his voice to a shrillness, but it seemed to be muted, and to not leave his throat. The tall grass clung to his legs. His movement was restrained as he tried to push them through the heavy growth. A cricket set up an annoying buzz. He reached out to smash the annoying insect. The weight of the grass was holding his arms, made them feel weak, and he could barely force them to move. The buzzing continued. It was as though he had put his head in a beehive. Thankfully the buzzing disappeared with a click

He felt something soft, warm and wet fluttering over his face and ears. Some small beast had planted its paws on his chest and was pulling at the covers with its teeth. Lemuel buried his head under the pillow, and then he heard Abigail calling as though from a long distance away. "Lem! It's time to get up! Didn't you hear the alarm?" She nudged his shoulder, "Come on. Today's your big day isn't it? The promotion board, remember? Get up sleepy head."

He waved his hand at her and said, "Don't worry Abby. We've escaped. I'll protect you. We'll make Arkansas before nightfall and camp beside the big muddy."

"What?"

He pushed the pillow from his head, and looked around in bewilderment. Gradually he realized where he was as familiar things drew into focus. There was the double dresser with the large framed mirror, the double hung wooden windows with the Cape Cod curtains, the green colonial print wallpaper, Abigail's rocker and footstool, and the brightly lit bathroom cast a shaft of golden light into the bedroom.

HOW THE GOOD TAILOR GOT TO HEAVEN 653

Abigail stood at the foot of the bed drying her hair with a big Turkish towel, and wearing a terrycloth bathrobe. Their little puppy, Loki, was eyeing him playfully, and he reached out and scratched the dog's ears. He realized he must have been dreaming. The whole thing had been a dream, just a bad dream.

Abigail said, "You tossed and turned all night. You talked in your sleep about the neighbors, the church, father Angus and his new curate father Didymus, and about getting promoted . . . you're not afraid to face the seraphim are you?"

Lemuel worked for the world's largest life insurance company, and it was growing larger through mergers and acquisitions. It's influence was metastasizing throughout the financial world. He was an actuary and dealt with numbers and statistical projections. Theoretically, he knew when everyone was going to die. After twenty years with the company he was being considered for a supervisory position, and he was to be interviewed by the senior vice-president of his division this morning. It was her perverse irreverent nature that caused Abigail to refer to the VP as a seraph. She also derisively called the company President; the C.E.O.; and the Chairman of the Board the Holy Trinity, and his company was the Kingdom of God. She called the lesser company officials archangels or cherubim, and Lemuel was only a disciple. After promotion he would be an apostle. She'd frequently tease Lemuel, "Did god smile down upon you today?" And in a sense it was true. The top officials of the corporation always came from some god-like segment of humanity who were created in the rarified atmosphere of the penthouse offices atop the corporate world. None of those jobs were filled from the ranks. The only time Lemuel saw their smiling faces was if he looked at their portraits in the rotunda of the home office.

Abigail urged him to get up, "Come on Lem, get up! The promotion board, remember?" In their large walk-in closet, chock-a-block with clothing, she selected a suit. "Wear your new suit. You look very dignified in it. That'll impress 'em."

Now fully awake he said, " I don't think I will, Abby."

"That's why you bought it!" She exclaimed.

"I know, but I'm not going to work today."

"What???" She came to the edge of the bed, and put her hand on his forehead, "Are you feeling alright?"

"I'm fine, but I'm not going to work anymore. I've decided to quit, and spend the rest of my life making love to you. I dreamt I lost you, and I was terrified. Oh, come here." He opened her robe, slipped his arm around her and pulled her close to him and kissed her belly, her naval, her breasts, and worked his lips down to her nether beard, and nuzzled the ample soft fur. Between the kisses he muttered, "Oh, my darling wife, my beautiful wonderful wife." He kissed the vermilion cleft, and ran his tongue inside. She swung her leg over his body to give him freer access, and looked down at him with a bemused smile. Closing her eyes, she began to purr kittenishly.

Then, she pushed his head away and said, "Not now Lem. We have to go to work."

"I want you to quit too."

She assumed he was joking, and searched his face for a clue, but he looked perfectly sincere. She sat on the edge of the bed and asked, "Are you afraid of the promotion board?" He'd always seemed completely in control of any situation, and she was puzzled.

"No, it was my dream. It made me realize that you are the most precious thing in my life, and nothing else matters. Just before I woke-up, I dreamed you had vanished, and I searched frantically for you. Oh, I was so afraid I'd lost you. I was nuzzling you to reassure myself that you're mine, and that you're real, and I'm, *oh, so grateful that you are*. I want to hold you in my arms forever. Together we make the cosmic harmony that holds my universe together, and when we're apart, I feel like a robot going through meaningless tasks in a meaningless world. The rat race keeps us apart . . . let's both quit!"

"I love you too, Lem, but we have obligations. I think you're afraid of the seraphim."

"Absolutely not! But they'll probably promote Tomas. He'd be a dangerous man to have under you, and if he got the job I wouldn't want him over me. Besides, I don't need a key to the executive washroom." He pulled her down beside himself, and told her about Tomas' role in his strange dream. "He and I were angels in the Heavenly Establishment, and he'd do anything to get promoted."

Abigail currently worked for a small investment-banking firm that also dabbled in the currency market. In a sense she did create money out of thin air, but the "ready necessary," the cash reserve belonged to someone else. She tracked the esoteric world of derivatives, and had made fifteen and a half million dollars for her bosses when a British bank went bankrupt. Someone at the bank's Hong Kong branch made the bank vulnerable by overinvesting in the yen futures. When the value of the yen collapsed, the bank's derivative assets were converted to liabilities, and it was forced into bankruptcy. Abigail had borrowed heavily in the yen market, sold the bank stock short, and made a small fortune by repaying the loans with devalued yen.

Lemuel met Abigail in the small community park during a pro-choice/pro-life confrontation. While out for a stroll one evening Lemuel noticed the small crowd where signs were being waved, an angry voice blared over a loud speaker, and there was much jeering coming from the crowd. He entered the park to find out what the to do was all about. Abigail was standing beneath a lamppost, well dressed in a simple sheath dress, and quietly observing the furor. She seemed to be detached from the turmoil, indifferent, as though it were beneath her, and an occasional smile brightened her face as the rhetoric became overly absurd. Her calm unruffled attitude gave her a poise and dignity beyond her years, and when he saw her he was instantly smitten. The demonstration gave him an excuse to approach the girl and ask what was happening. That was over ten years ago, and they had just celebrated their tenth anniversary.

Abigail was nearly a generation younger than Lemuel, and he dreamed her as Abishag, the Shunamite maiden. The dark skinned beauty who lay with David in his old age [230] and was the inspiration for *The*

Song of Solomon. Their age difference might also explain the charge of child molestation of his dream, but Abigail was not a maiden when they met. He would have liked to have been her one and only. Maybe that was why she was a virgin in his dream, but the driving lesson of his dream may have been a Freudian substitution for the reality. And there was a Bathsheba in his past, from whom he was divorced, and whom the courts obliged him to support.

He told her a little more of his dream, and how accurate her simile was about the Kingdom of Heaven, and the kingdom where he worked. "They're identical, except for the money: Heaven's profits are figured in souls." He briefly outlined the regimen of the ethereal establishment, and his place in it: an angel sent to earth to lead ten thousand souls to salvation.

She laughed, "Something like selling life insurance, huh?"

"I was an imitation Jesus, but without supernatural powers. You were a demon with magical powers, and did the miracles for me."

"Why did you dream of me as a demon? I thought you loved me."

"You were a very nice demon, but you're a free spirit; not much impressed by titles and honorifics. You love nature, the shore, the mountains, the farms and fields; you love the world, and that's worldliness. That makes you an enemy of God: therefore, a demon."

"Am not!"

"Prove it. Don't go to work. Stay here with me. When you were a demon you didn't work. We were together all the time, and we were both happy. You made money out of thin air: just enough to meet your needs though, and no more. Then I corrupted you with the church, and you made millions more than we needed just to hold on to me."

Abigail was a restless spirit, and had had five jobs in the ten years they had been married. When she got bored, or disappointed, she moved on. He'd often teased her about her gypsy nature. He told her that in his dream she masqueraded as a Gypsy princess, and lived in a travel trailer and how they went anywhere they wanted.

The simplicity of life in a trailer, and the idyllic wooded glade in the

HOW THE GOOD TAILOR GOT TO HEAVEN

mountains sounded inviting to Abigail, and she urged him to tell her more. "I suppose we could take a vacation. Esther and Myles can look after the house for us while we're gone."

"They were in my dream. They were angels too. (Abigail looked skeptically amused.) When I started gathering my flock, Esther and Myles came down from Heaven and became apostles in my church."

Abigail laughed and said, "You mean Esther from next door? Oh, she'd make a dandy nun, but I think temple prostitute would suit her better. And Myles could be the high priest of orgies."

Their neighbors were friendly, honest, helpful, and completely amoral about sexual matters. Esther was beautiful, and had no compunction about showing off her beauty in all its majestic natural splendor while sunning on their back yard patio. Theirs was an open marriage where house parties became swinging affairs, and swapping was customary. Although often invited, Lemuel and Abigail politely declined. Abigail said, "I've always had my suspicions about you and her."

"You don't have to worry. I'm completely devoted to you. And you're much prettier than she is, anyway. Besides, I'd imagine the lineup of men I'd have to share her vagina with, and I'm even repulsed by the other guys' bodies when I use the locker room. I guess that makes me homophobic." He smiled and kissed her, "Maybe I'm a lesbian in disguise. I'd be more comfortable using the ladies locker room. (She gave him a playful poke.) But in my dream Esther was God's love goddess. She had been sent down to compete with the Sumerian Ishtar, and Astarte. Then twenty five hundred years later they sent her down to enter the Miss Universe beauty contest, and she decided to stay and help with my mission. There's no sex in heaven, the Bible says so, so she was really horny. She used her sex appeal to recruit the first apostles for me, and when Myles joined us, it began to be like a commune devoted to sex. It was like one of those strange antinomian cults that you read about..."

"Huh? Antinomian? What's that?"

"That's a rather unconventional way of interpreting the Bible. Antinomians believe that when they became spiritually regenerated that

Christ had freed them from the curse of the law. (She looked puzzled) It's in the Bible. They believe that by their spiritual regeneration, Jesus freed them from all moral law. In other words, if it feels good: do it! The enlightened own all things in common, and by all things they meant all things: money, property, women, children – everything is shared. From each according to his ability, and to each according to his need. ("Wasn't that Karl Marx?") No, that's from the Bible. And since all things were created by God, that included mankind's appetites, and his libido. What God has given are blessings, to be indulged, and appreciated. So with Esther as God's love goddess, and Myles as Bible interpreter, orgies became religious rites."

She poked him again. "Demons are wicked. If I was the demon, where was I during the orgy? Leading this Black Mass? I think you'd like us to go to Esther and Myles's parties "

"Hell no! If you went over there I think I'd kill myself, but I'd strangle you first. I feel very possessive about you. In fact, in my dream you were a virgin, and the only one to maintain a sense of responsibility, and a modicum of dignity. But nothing is ever sinful for God's elect, and you were not one of God's elect. They believe: If you want to do it, do it. They believed they were being moved by the Holy Spirit. But, as a demon, you were immune to it. "

"My promotion to the next higher rank of angel depended on the success of my mission to lead souls to salvation. Fool that I was, I wanted to succeed so badly that I was excusing every sin, and accepting anyone into the church. You tolerated most of them for a while, but they kept getting worse. You started to grumble about the deviants I was anointing, and when I was on the verge of accepting a Nazi concentration camp guard, that's when you disappeared, and I woke up in such a fright. I've never felt so much panic as when I thought I'd lost you. But it made me see the futility of it all, and made me realize what was important. They'll overlook any sin to get more power. We've all become myrmidons in a senseless struggle to make our greedy establishment the king of the hill. Where did all the greed come from?"

She kissed his cheek, and observed, "It has been said many times before: Power corrupts, and absolute power corrupts absolutely . . . apparently, even in the Kingdom of God. The big lie is that there's a rational purpose to any of it."

"See, I pegged you right, Abby. You are a demon. But do you think you'd have the courage to act on what you've said? Let's drop out. Just chuck it all. The system will go on, but we don't have to be part of it."

"We can't quit work. We have to buy groceries. We have a mortgage, car payments, financial obligations. What if we had kids?" She emitted a nasty little laugh, and added, "We have to keep up appearances, our middle class status. I thought you believed in the dignity of work. Besides, if we didn't work, we'd be homeless beggars on the streets within ninety days."

He pushed out his lower lip petulantly. "I've given the company twenty years. Soldiers can retire after twenty years. Our congressman was my age, and he got a big fat pension when he lost the election. When our C.E.O. retired he got millions, and he'd only been with the company for three years."

She chuckled, and said, "You're being covetous, Lem. Doesn't your Bible say it's a sin?"

"That's what they tell you so you won't question the system," he said grumpily. "And they also tell you that God makes you rich or poor."

"I thought that was the unseen hand of the market."

"Same thing!"

Abigail slipped from his arms, got up and said, "Well I have to get dressed. One of us has to make a living, and I have a big fat commission check coming." She sought to erase his frown. "It will be enough for a new car. Let's get an SUV with four-wheel drive, and then we can take it up in the mountains, and explore the back roads. Commune with nature. And we'll buy a tent . . . ."

He was delighted by her enthusiasm and said, "Not a tent. We'll buy a trailer. I have more than enough in my retirement account. I'll take early retirement, and cash it out. I've been looking at a beauty down at

Orson's RV emporium. It has all the comforts. You'll love it. And we could stay up on the mountain for a long time."

She replied, with a wicked wink, "As long as forty days, and forty nights."

"Sure, even longer if we want. We'll sell the house. That should give us enough for a while. My pension will commence in a few years, and we can live on the equity in the house until then."

Abigail thought, *Oh, oh! mid-life crisis, he really plans to quit,* "Let's not be hasty, Lem."

"Do you love me? (She nodded.) Do you like your job? Do you like going to work every day? (She shrugged, and pushed out her lower lip.) It's all kind of meaningless, isn't it? (She nodded.) Well, I'm getting tired of contributing to the aggrandizement of a few pompous drones: the high and mighty parasites of the 'Kingdom of God,' as you so accurately called the company." He finished this interlocutory; "There's no freedom in Kingdoms — Kingdoms are dictatorships."

He got up, went to their computer, turned it on, and typed the following e-mail message to his personnel office, the payroll office, and sent copies to all the department heads:

> Dear Sirs;
> Your grand design for world domination will have to proceed without my assistance. **I QUIT!**
> Transfer all money from my retirement fund to my checking account, immediately.
> Sincerely;
> Lemuel Smith

Abigail hovered by his side. She read the message, and said fearfully, "Don't say that. It won't look good on your resume. It will go down in your permanent record."

He replied, "What I have written, I have written.[231]" and pushed the send button.

The end

Footnotes

1 Ephesians 1:11
2 James 4:15
3 2nd Thessalonians 2:11
4 Mark 16:18
5 Matthew 20:1-15
6 Matthew 22:39
7 Genesis 28:22
8 Exodus 22:16-17
9 Ruth 3:1-6
10 1st Chronicles 13:9
11 1st Chronicles 21:18, 25-26
12 1st Kings 6:2-36
13 1st Kings 4: 29 "And God gave Solomon wisdom and understanding exceeding much."
14 1st Kings 12:4
15 Exodus 35:4-38: 31
16 Exodus 12:35-36

17 Ezekiel ch. 9
18 Ezekiel 10:2
19 Isaiah 6:2
20 Isaiah 1:16; Psalm 51:10
21 Exodus 40:30-31 and Leviticus 1:9
22 Psalm 68:3 and 24-25
23 Psalm 68:23
24 Exodus 39:1-32
25 Exodus 28:42
26 Song of Solomon 7: 2-3
27 1st John 4:8
28 Song of Solomon 6:13, refer to 1st Kings 1:3
29 1st Kings 2:17-22
30 1st Kings 2:24
31 Matthew 17:27
32 Exodus 21:20-21 If a man smite his servant or his maid with a rod, and he die under his hand he shall be punished. Notwithstanding, if he continue a day or two, he shall not be punished: *for he is his money!*
33 Luke 10:1; 3-4
34 Acts 4: 32 and 34
35 Exodus 31:1-6
36 Matthew 4:19
37 Matthew 4:22
38 Matthew 19:30
39 1st Thessalonians 5:26; Romans 16:16; 1st Corinthians 16:20; 2nd Corinthians 13:12
40 1st Peter 5:14
41 Matthew 19:20
42 Matthew 19:29
43 Matthew 19:27
44 Acts 5:1-10
45 Deuteronomy 22:15, 17, 21
46 Leviticus 20:16

47 Zechariah 5:9
48 1st Kings 11:5
49 Jeremiah 7:18
50 Leviticus 20:13
51 Song of Solomon 6: 9-10
52 Matthew 8:9
53 Romans 13:1
54 Luke 18:42-43, Mark 10:52, Matthew 20:34
55 1st Samuel 10:9" God gave him another heart: and all those signs came to pass that day."
56 Matthew 6:24
57 Acts 4:13
58 Isaiah 3:17
59 John 2: 3-10
60 Luke 7:28-34
61 Acts 10:14-15 and 11:7-10
62 Romans 14:14
63 Galatians 3:28
64 Luke 14:33
65 Acts 4:32-35
66 Matthew 6:5
67 Galatians 5:17-18 and *5:24
68 Revelations 2:6
69 1st Corinthians 12:23
70 Ezekiel 1. Description of angel all of first chapter
71 Luke 13:18-19
72 Luke 1:69
73 Esther 5:2
74 Matthew 23:9
75 Luke 1:24
76 1st John 4:8
77 Luke 3:16
78 Luke 1:57

79 Ezekiel 16:30
80 Matthew 10:37
81 Luke 14:26
82 2nd Kings 22:8-14
83 Exodus 20:12
84 Galatians 3:13
85 Ephesians 2:15
86 2nd Corinthians 3:14
87 Luke 23:45, Mark 15:38, Matthew 27:51
88 Luke 12:51-53
89 Matthew 10: 34-35
90 Matthew 4: 8-9
91 Mark 12:18-25
92 Colossians 4:14
93 Genesis 26:10
94 Genesis 20:16
95 Deuteronomy 18:10-11
96 Esther 1:6-10
97 Genesis 12:16, 17:5, 20:2, 26:7
98 Luke 10:4
99 Matthew 10:25
100 Luke 15:7
101 Genesis 20:12
102 Ephesians 2:15, Galatians 2:13
103 Romans 13:14 and Galatians 3:22
104 Romans 11:32 "For God hath concluded them all in unbelief, that he might have mercy upon all."
105 1st Corinthians 1:25 and 1:27
106 1st Cor. 3:19
107 2nd Chronicles 34:14-28
108 Isaiah 20:2-3
109 Psalm 8:5
110 1st Samuel 15:23

111 Galatians 5:20
112 Matthew 8:22
113 Matthew 22:21
114 Matthew 5:16
115 Matthew 25:27
116 Matthew 25:24 and 25:26, also Mark 19:12-27
117 2nd Corinthians 8:9
118 Matthew 25:14-30
119 Acts 2:15-17, and Joel 2:28
120 Leviticus 20:18
121v Luke 8:33
122 John 5: 2-9
123 John 5: 7-9
124 Genesis 11:31 and 20:12
125 Genesis 21:12-15
126 Book of Tobit 4:12-13
127 2nd Timothy 3:16
128 1st Corinthians 7:36
129 Matthew 10:19-20
130 Judges 5:24-26
131 Matthew 13:55-58
132 Luke 8:2
133 Luke 7:44-46
134 1st Corinthians 11:15
135 Matthew 8:14-15
136 2nd Samuel 3:14
137 1st Corinthians 14:22
138 2nd Corinthians 12:1-4
139 1st Corinthians 12:10
140 James 5:15
141 Mark 16:18
142 1st John 4:12
143 Ezra 9:2 and 9:12 among many others

144 Matthew 12:1-12
145 Mark 2:27
146 Matthew 12:46-50
147 Matthew 23:9
148 Galatians 3:13
149 Matthew 10:34-35
150 Luke 12:52-53
151 Matthew 10:21
152 Luke 3:14
153 Matthew 24:5-8
154 1st Chronicles 26:27
155 Luke 14:26
156 Luke 8:2-3
157 Matthew 21:1-3, Mark 11:2-3, and Luke 19:29-35
158 Philippians 2:4
159 Luke 13:18-19
160 Timothy 2:10
161 Deuteronomy 23:18
162 Exodus 32:19-25
163 1st Corinthians 10:29-31
164 Job 1:16, 1:19, and 1:21, also Job 2:7
165 Leviticus 20:27
166 Acts 21:8 and 9
167 Job 2:9-10
168 Deuteronomy 18:20-22
169 James 1:17
170 Matthew 5:9
171 Matthew 10:34
172 Galatians 5:22-23
173 Hebrews 12:29
174 Psalms 90:9-10
175 James 3:10-12
176 Matthew 5:45

177 Job 42:12-13
178 Genesis 4:4-5
179 Haggai 2:7-8
180 James 5:3
181 2nd Chronicles 9:3 and 9:5
182 2nd Chronicles 9:13-14
183 Revelations 13:17-18
184 1st Corinthians 1:19-21
185 Job 1:15
186 Job 40:7-8 and 40:14
187 Job 42:12-15
188 Jeremiah 10:23
189 Isaiah 63:17
190 Acts 17:24-26
191 Isaiah 45:5-7
192 Ephesians 1:11
193 Ephesians 1:5
194 Colossians 1:17
195 John 4: 8 and 4:12
196 Matthew 13:55

197 Gnostic theology influences the *Gospel of Thomas,* purported to be sayings which the living Jesus spoke and which Didymos Judas Thomas wrote down.

198 The serpent told Eve, "Ye shall not surely die."

199 The Lord told Moses to make a fiery serpent and set it upon a pole.

200 Jesus said, "Why callest thou me good? None is good save one, that is God."

201 "One of you is a devil."

202 1st Corinthians 7:36

203 Genesis 19:32 and 19:36

204 1st Corinthians 10:29-30

205 Hebrews 7:16

[206] Genesis 19: 31 - 38
[207] John 7: 42
[208] Isaiah 16:11
[209] Matthew 5:44
[210] John 19:23-24, Mark 15:24, Matthew 27:25
[211] Luke 12:28
[212] 2nd Samuel 12:31
[213] 2nd Samuel 24:9
[214] 1st Chronicles 21:1. See Isaiah 45:7; "I form the light and create the darkness: I make the peace and create evil: I the Lord do all these things."
[215] 2nd Samuel 24:1
[216] 2nd Samuel 24:10-16
[217] Jeremiah 44:15-19 "When they sacrificed to the queen of heaven they had plenty, and God gave them famine and the sword when they sacrificed to Him.
[218] Ezekiel 12:15
[219] Isaiah 63:17
[220] Jeremiah 29:21
[221] 1st Kings 19:18
[222] Ephesians 1:11
[223] Romans 8:28
[224] Romans 11:32
[225] Joshua 6:21
[226] Joshua 9:16-21
[227] Joshua 10:12
[228] Exodus 17:8-14
[229] 2nd Samuel 12:31
[230] 1st Kings 1:1-4
[231] John 19:22